Ta
This Man

Three complete, captivating novels—featuring three tall, dark and *irresistible* men—from three of Silhouette's most popular and talented authors.

"Nora Roberts is the best there is—she's superb in everything she does."
—*Romantic Times Magazine*

"Her stories have fuelled the dreams of twenty-five million readers."
—*Entertainment Weekly*

"Nobody tops Diana Palmer…I love her stories."
—*New York Times* best-selling author Jayne Ann Krentz

"Ms Ferrarella finds just the right balance of love, laughter, charm and passion."
—*Romantic Times Magazine*

ABOUT THE AUTHORS

Nora Roberts is a publishing phenomenon, not only getting eleven of her titles on the *New York Times* best-seller list in a single year, but also hitting the number one spot. She has written over a hundred novels, more than eighty of them for Silhouette Books, and has over fifty million books in print. Her work has been optioned and made into films, and has been translated into over twenty-five languages and published all over the world.

Diana Palmer got her start in writing as a newspaper reporter and published her first romance for Silhouette in 1982. In 1993 she celebrated the publication of her fiftieth novel for Silhouette Books®. She is considered to be one of the top ten romance writers in America and is beloved by readers worldwide. She has over forty million copies of her books in print.

Marie Ferrarella sold her first contemporary romance to Silhouette Books fifteen years ago and her novels are loved by fans worldwide. In 1998, she celebrated the publication of her seventy-fifth book for Silhouette. Marie earned a master's degree in Shakespearean comedy and, perhaps as a result, her writing is distinguished by humour and natural dialogue. This winner of the Romance Writers of America's prestigious RITA Award, describes herself as the tired mother of two over-energetic children and the contented wife of one wonderful man.

Take This Man

Nora Roberts
Diana Palmer
Marie Ferrarella

First published in Great Britain 2000
Silhouette Books, Eton House, 18-24 Paradise Road, Richmond, Surrey TW9 1SR

ISBN 0 373 04665 0

81-0007

Printed and bound in Spain
by Litografia Rosés S.A., Barcelona

CONTENTS

Enchanted
by Nora Roberts

King's Ransom
by Diana Palmer

In the Family Way
by Marie Ferrarella

Dear Reader,

Welcome! You hold in your hand a collection of romances by the very best in the business—as indeed you can see from their biographies. These ladies are publishing phenomenons and rightly so.

Enchanted is a very special book, full of a wonderful mystic atmosphere, that stretches the boundaries of romance as only a talented writer like Nora Roberts dares. And as a bonus, those of you who are fans of her writing will be pleased to see cameo appearances by a few old friends.

King's Ransom is absolutely chock full of that special Diana Palmer magic. And it's marvellous to see what she can do with a dark and arrogant sheikh! Of course, Diana usually writes about those very popular long, tall Texan Lovers, but it's fantastic to see her ring the changes.

Last but by no means least, *In the Family Way* is a real 'slice of life' emotional drama from Marie Ferrarella, and demonstrates what a really wonderful and versatile writer she is. Marie's been published in our Desire™ series twice, our Sensation™ series three times and once in Special Edition™ in this year alone!

So, take some time for yourself and prepare to be entertained...

Enjoy!

The Editors

Enchanted

Nora Roberts

To the friends I've made in cyberspace,
with gratitude for the hours of fun

Prologue

Dark as the night and fleet of foot, the wolf raced under a hunter's moon. He ran for the love of it, and he ran alone, through the grand tower of trees, the purple shadows of the forest, the magic of the night.

The wind from across the sea spewed across the pines, sent them singing songs of the ancients and spilling their scent into the air. Small creatures with eyes that gleamed hid and watched the sleek black shape bullet through the lacy layer of mist that shimmered down the beaten path.

He knew they were there, could smell them, hear the rapid beat of their blood. But he hunted nothing that night but the night itself.

He had no pack, no mate but solitude.

A restlessness lived in him that not even speed and freedom could quell. In his quest for peace, he haunted the forest, stalked the cliffs, circled the clearings, but nothing soothed or satisfied.

As the path rose more steeply and the trees began to thin, he slowed to a trot, scenting the air. There was…something in the air, something that had lured him out to the cliffs high above the restless Pacific. With powerful strides he climbed the rocks, his golden eyes scanning, seeking.

There, at the topmost point where the waves crashed like cannon fire and the moon swam white and full, he raised his head and called. To sea, to sky, to night.

To magic.

The howl echoed, spread, filled the night with both demand and question. With power as natural as breath.

And the whispers that flickered back told him only that a change was coming. Endings, beginnings. Destiny.

His fate was waiting for him.

Again the rogue black wolf with gold eyes threw back his head and called. There was more, and he would have it. Now the earth shook, and the water swirled. Far over the sea a single spear of lightning broke the blackness with a blinding white flash. In its afterglow for an instant—a heartbeat only—was the answer.

Love waits.

And the magic trembled on the air, danced over the sea with a sound that might have been laughter. Tiny sparks of light skimmed over the surface, bobbing, twirling to spin into the star-strewn sky in a gilt cloud.

The wolf watched, and he listened. Even when he turned back to the forest and its shadows, the answer trailed after him.

Love waits.

As the restlessness in him grew, beat with his heart, he shot down the path, powerful strides tearing the fog to ribbons. Now his blood heated with the speed, and veering left, he broke through the trees toward the soft glow of lights. There the cabin stood sturdy, its windows shining with welcome. The whispers of the night fell quiet.

As he bounded up the steps, white smoke swirled, blue light shimmered. And wolf became man.

Chapter 1

When Rowan Murray got her first look at the cabin, she was filled with a sense of both relief and fear. Relief that she'd finally come to the end of the long drive from San Francisco to this sheltered spot on the coast of Oregon. And fear for the exact same reason.

She was here. She had done it.

What next?

The practical thing, of course, was to get out of the four-wheel drive, unlock the front door and give herself a tour of the place she intended to make home for the next three months. Unpack what belongings she'd brought with her. Make herself some tea. Take a hot shower.

Yes, those were all practical, reasonable things to do, she told herself. And she sat exactly where she was, in the driver's seat of the two-week-old Range

Rover, her long, slender fingers gripping white-knuckled on the wheel.

She was alone. Completely, absolutely alone.

It was what she wanted, what she needed. What she'd pushed herself to accomplish for months so that when the offer of the cabin had come, she'd snatched it as if it were a tree limb and she'd been sinking in quicksand.

Now that she had it, she couldn't even get out of the car.

"You're such a fool, Rowan." She whispered it, leaning back, closing her eyes for just a moment. "Such a coward."

She sat, gathering her energies, a small, slenderly built woman with creamy skin that had lost its sheen of rose. Her hair was straight as rain and the color of polished oak. Now, she wore it pulled back, out of the way, in a thick braid that was coming loose. Her nose was long and sharp, her mouth just slightly over wide for the triangle of her face. Her eyes, tired now from hours of driving, were a deep, dark blue, long lidded and tilted at the corners.

Elf's eyes, her father often said. And thinking of that, she felt tears welling up in them.

She'd disappointed him, and her mother. The guilt of that weighed like a stone on her heart. She hadn't been able to explain, not clearly enough, not well enough, why she'd hadn't been capable of continuing on the path they'd so carefully cleared for her. Every step she'd taken on it had been a strain, as if every step had taken her farther and farther away from where she needed to be.

What she needed to be.

So in the end she'd run. Oh, not in actuality. She was much too reasonable to have run away like a thief in the night. She'd made specific plans, followed concrete steps, but under it all she'd been fleeing from home, from career, from family. From the love that was smothering her as surely as if its hands had been clamped over her nose and mouth.

Here, she'd promised herself, she'd be able to breathe, to think, to decide. And maybe, just maybe, to understand what it was that kept her from being what everyone seemed to want her to be.

If in the end, she discovered she was wrong and everyone else was right, she was prepared to deal with it. But she would take these three months for herself.

She opened her eyes again, let herself look. And as she did, her muscles slowly relaxed. It was so beautiful, she realized. The grand majesty of trees shooting up into the sky and whistling in the wind, the two-story cabin tucked into a private glen, the silver flash of sun off the busy little steam that snaked to the west.

The cabin itself gleamed dark gold in the sunlight. Its wood was smooth, its windows sparkled. The little covered porch looked perfect for sitting on lazy mornings or quiet evenings. From where she sat, she thought she could see the brave spears of spring bulbs testing the air.

They'd find it chilly yet, she mused. Belinda had warned her to buy flannel, and to expect spring to come late to this little corner of the world.

Well, she knew how to build a fire, she told herself,

glancing at the stone chimney. One of her favorite spots in her parents' house had been in the big sprawling living room beside the hearth with a fire crackling against the damp chill of the city.

She'd build one as soon as she was settled, she promised herself. To welcome herself to her new home.

Steadier, she opened the door, stepped out. Her heavy boots snapped a thick twig with a sound like a bullet. She pressed a hand to her heart, laughing a little. New boots for the city girl, she thought. Jingling the keys just to make noise, she walked to the cabin, up the two steps to the porch. She slipped the key she'd labeled *front door* into the lock and, taking a slow breath, pushed the door open.

And fell in love.

''Oh, would you look at this!'' A smile lit her face as she stepped inside, circled. ''Belinda, God bless you.''

The walls were the color of warmly toasted bread, framed in dark wood, accented with the magical paintings her friend was renowned for. The hearth was stone, scrubbed clean and laid with kindling and logs in welcome. Colorful rugs were scattered over the polished wood floor. The furnishings were simple, clean lines, with deep cushions that picked up those wonderful tones of emerald, sapphire and ruby.

To complete the fairy-tale aspect, there were statues of dragons, wizards, bowls filled with stones or dried flowers, and sparkling geodes. Charmed, Rowan dashed up the stairs and hugged herself as she toured the two large rooms there.

One, full of light from a ring of windows, was obviously her friend's studio when she used the cabin. Canvases, paints and brushes were neatly stored, an easel stood empty, a smock hung, paint-splattered, on a brass hook.

Even here there were pretty touches—fat white candles in silver holders, glass stars, a globe of smoky crystal.

The bedroom thrilled her with its huge canopy bed draped in white linen, the little fireplace to warm the room, the carved rosewood armoire.

It felt...peaceful, Rowan realized. Settled, content, welcoming. Yes, she could breathe here. She could think here. For some inexplicable reason, she felt she could belong here.

Anxious now to begin settling in, she hurried downstairs, out the door she'd left open to her SUV. She'd grabbed the first box from the cargo area, when the skin on the back of her neck prickled. Suddenly her heart thundered in her chest, and her palms sprang with damp.

She turned quickly, managed only one strangled gasp.

The wolf was pure black with eyes like gold coins. And it stood at the edge of the trees, still as a statue carved from onyx. Watching her. She could do no more than stare while her pulse beat like fury. Why wasn't she screaming? she asked herself. Why wasn't she running?

Why was she more surprised than afraid?

Had she dreamed of him? Couldn't she just catch the edge of some misty dream where he'd run through the mist toward her? Is that why he seemed so familiar, almost…expected?

But that was ridiculous. She'd never seen a wolf outside of a zoo in her life. Surely she'd never seen one who stared so patiently at her. Into her.

"Hello." She heard herself speak with a kind of dull shock, and followed it with a nervous laugh. Then she blinked, and he was gone.

For a moment, she swayed, like a woman coming out of a trance. When she shook herself clear, she stared at the edge of the trees, searching for some movement, some shadow, some sign.

But there was only silence.

"Imagining things again," she muttered, shifting the box, turning away. "If there was anything there, it was a dog. Just a dog."

Wolves were nocturnal, weren't they? They didn't approach people in broad daylight, just stand and stare, then vanish.

She'd look it up to be sure, but it had been a dog. She was positive now. Belinda hadn't mentioned anything about neighbors or other cabins. And how odd, Rowan thought now, that she hadn't even asked about it.

Well, there was a neighbor somewhere, and he had a big, beautiful, black dog. She imagined they could all keep out of each others' way.

The wolf watched from the shadows of the trees. Who was the woman? he wondered. *Why* was the woman? She moved quickly, a little nervously, tossing glances over her shoulder as she carried things from the car to the cabin.

He'd scented her from half a mile away. Her fears, her excitement, her longings had all come to him. And had brought him to her.

His eyes narrowed with annoyance. His teeth bared in challenge. He'd be damned if he'd take her. Damned if he let her change what he was or what he wanted.

Sleek and silent, he turned away and vanished into the thick trees.

Rowan built a fire, delighted when the logs crackled and caught. She unpacked systematically. There wasn't much, really. Clothes, supplies. Most of the boxes she'd hauled in were filled with books. Books she couldn't live without, books she'd promised herself she'd make time to read. Books to study, books for pleasure. She'd grown up with a love of reading, of exploring worlds through words. And because of that great love, she often questioned her own dissatisfaction with teaching.

It should have been the right goal, just as her parents always insisted. She embraced learning and had always learned well and quickly. She'd studied, took her major and then her master's in Education. At twenty-seven, she'd already taught full-time for nearly six years.

She was good at it, she thought now as she sipped tea while standing in front of the blazing fire. She could recognize the strengths and weaknesses of her students, home in on their interests and on how to challenge them.

Yet she dragged her feet on getting her doctorate. She woke each morning vaguely discontent and came home each evening unsatisfied.

Because her heart had never been in it.

When she'd tried to explain that to the people who loved her, they'd been baffled. Her students loved and respected her, the administration at her school valued her. Why wasn't she pursuing her degree, marrying Alan, completing her nice, tidy life as she should?

Why, indeed, she thought. Because the only answer she had for them, and for herself, was in her heart.

And brooding wasn't thinking, she reminded herself. She'd go for a walk, get a sense of where she was. She wanted to see the cliffs Belinda had told her of.

She locked the door out of habit, then drew in a deep gulp of air that tasted of pine and sea. In her mind she could see the quick sketch Belinda had drawn her of the cabin, the forest, the cliffs. Ignoring her nerves, she stepped onto the path and headed due west.

She'd never lived outside of the city. Growing up in San Francisco hadn't prepared her for the vastness of the Oregon forest, its smells, its sounds. Even so, her nerves began to fade into wonder.

It was like a book, a gorgeously rich story full of color and texture. The giant Douglas firs towered over her, their bushy branches letting the sun splatter into a shifting, luminous, gilded green light nearly the color of the moss that grew so thick and soft on the ground. The trees chilled the air with their shade, scented it with their fragrance.

The forest floor was soft with shed needles and ripe with the tang of sap.

At their bases, ferns grew thick and green, some thin and sharp as swords, others lacy as fans. Like faeries, she thought in a moment's fancy, who only danced at night.

The stream bubbled along, skimming over rocks worn round and smooth, tumbling down a little rise with a sudden rush of white water that looked impossibly pure and cold. She followed the wind of it, relaxed with its music.

There was a bend up ahead, she thought idly, and around the corner there would be a stump of an old tree on the left that looked like an old man's worn face. Foxglove grew there, and in the summer it would grow tall and pale purple. It was a good place to sit, that stump, and watch the forest come to life around you.

She stopped when she came to it, staring blankly at the gnarled bark that did indeed look like an old man's face. How had she known this would be here? she wondered, rubbing the heel of her hand on her suddenly speeding heart. It wasn't on Belinda's sketch, so how had she known?

"Because she mentioned it. She told me about it, that's all. It's just the sort of fanciful thing she'd tell me, and that I'd forget about."

But Rowan didn't sit, didn't wait for the forest to come to life. It already felt alive. Enchanted, she thought and managed to smile. The enchanted woods every girl dreams of where the faeries dance and the prince waits to rescue her from the jealous hag or the evil wizard.

There was nothing to fear here. The woods were hers as long as she wanted. There was no one to shake their heads indulgently if her mind wandered toward fairy tales and the foolish. Her dreams were her own as well.

If she had a dream, or a story to tell a young girl, Rowan decided, it would be about the enchanted forest…and the prince who wandered it, searching through the green light and greener shadow for his one true love. He was under a spell, she thought, and trapped in the sleek, handsome form of a black wolf. Until the maiden came and freed him with her courage, her wit, and with her love.

She sighed once, wishing she had a talent for the details of telling stories. She wasn't bad at themes, she mused, but she could never figure out how to turn a theme into an engaging tale.

So she read instead, and admired those who could.

She heard the sea, like an echo of memory, and turned unerringly onto the left fork of the path. What began as a whisper became a roar, and she started to hurry, was nearly running by the time she burst out of the trees and saw the cliffs.

Her boots clattered as she climbed up the rocks. The wind kicked and tore what was left of her braid loose so that her hair flew wild and free. Her laughter rang out, full of delight as she came breathlessly to the top of the rise.

It was, without a doubt, the most magnificent sight

she'd ever seen. Miles of blue ocean, hemmed with fuming white waves that threw themselves in fury against the rocks below. The afternoon sun showered over it, sprinkling jewels onto that undulating mat of blue.

She could see boats in the distance, riding the waves, and a small forested island rising out of the sea like a bunched fist.

Gleaming black mussels clung to the rocks below her, and as she looked closer, she saw the thorny brown sticks of a bird's nest tucked into a crevice. On impulse she got down, bellied out and was rewarded by a glimpse of eggs.

Pillowing her chin on her hands, she watched the water until the boats sailed away, until the sea was empty, and the shadows grew long.

She pushed up, sat back on her heels and lifted her face to the sky. "And that is the first time in too long that I've done nothing at all for an afternoon." She let out a long, contented breath. "It was glorious."

She rose, stretched her arms high, turned. And nearly stumbled over the edge of the cliff.

She would have fallen if he hadn't moved quickly, so quickly she had no sense of him moving at all. But his hands closed firmly over her arms and pulled her to safe ground.

"Steady," he said, and it was more an order than a suggestion.

He might have been the prince of any woman's imaginings. Or the dark angel of her most secret dreams. His hair was black as a moonless night and flew around a face lightly gilded by the sun. A face of strong, sharp bones, of firm, unsmiling mouth, of haunting male beauty.

He was tall. She had only a sense of height as her head reeled. For he had the eyes of the wolf she'd thought she'd seen—tawny and gold, unblinking and intense—under arched brows as black as his hair. They stared directly into hers, making the blood rush hot through her veins. She felt the strength of his hands as he'd yet to release her, thought she saw both impatience and curiosity flicker over that gorgeous face.

But she might have been wrong because he continued to stare, and say nothing.

"I was—you startled me. I didn't hear you. You were just there." She nearly winced as she heard herself babble.

Which was his own fault, he supposed. He could have made her aware of him gradually. But something about the way she'd been lying on the rocks, gazing out at nothing with a half smile on her face had muddled his mind.

"You didn't hear because you were daydreaming." He arched one sweeping black eyebrow. "And talking to yourself."

"Oh. It's a bad habit of mine—talking to myself. Nervous habit."

"Why are you nervous?"

"I'm not—I wasn't." God, she'd tremble in a moment if he didn't let her go. It had been a long, long time since she'd been this close to a man other than Alan. And much too long since she'd felt any kind of response to one. She'd never experienced a reaction this strong, this violent or this disorienting, and put it down to nearly tumbling over a cliff.

"You weren't." He skimmed his hands down to her wrists, felt the jittery bump of her pulse. "Now you are."

"You startled me, as I said." It was an effort, but she glanced over her shoulder and down. "And it's a long drop."

"It is that." He tugged her away another two steps. "Better?"

"Yes, well…I'm Rowan Murray, I'm using Belinda Malone's cabin for a while." She would have offered a hand to shake, but it would have been impossible as he was still cuffing her wrists.

"Donovan. Liam Donovan." He said it quietly, while his thumbs stroked over her pulse beat and somehow steadied it.

"But you're not from around here."

"Aren't I?"

"I mean, your accent. It's beautifully Irish."

When his lips curved and his eyes smiled she very nearly sighed like a teenager faced with a rock star. "I'm from Mayo, but I've had this place as mine for nearly a year now. My cabin's less than a half-mile from Belinda's."

"You know her then?"

"Aye, well enough. We're in the way of being relations, distant ones." His smile was gone now. Her eyes were as blue as the wild bellflowers that grew in sunny patches of the forest in high summer. And in them he found no guile at all. "She didn't tell me to expect a neighbor."

“I suppose she didn’t think of it. She didn’t tell me to expect one, either.” Her hands were free now, though she could still feel the warmth of his fingers, like bracelets around her wrists. “What do you do up here?”

“As I choose. You’ll be wanting to do the same. It’ll be a good change for you.”

“Excuse me?”

“You haven’t done what you pleased often enough, have you, Rowan Murray?”

She shivered once and slipped her hands into her pockets. The sun was dipping down toward the horizon and was reason enough for the sudden chill. “I guess I’ll have to be careful what I talk to myself about with a quiet-footed neighbor around.”

“Nearly a half-mile between us should be enough. I like my solitude.” He said it firmly, and though it was ridiculous, it seemed to Rowan he wasn’t speaking to her, but to someone, something in the darkening woods beyond. Then his gaze shifted back to her face, held. “I won’t infringe on yours.”

“I didn’t mean to be unfriendly.” She tried a smile, wishing she hadn’t spoken so abruptly and irritated him. “I’ve always lived in the city—with so many neighbors I barely notice any of them.”

“It doesn’t suit you,” he said half to himself.

“What?”

“The city. It doesn’t suit you or you wouldn’t be here, would you?” And what in bloody hell did it matter to him what suited her? he asked himself. She’d be nothing to him unless he decided differently.

“I’m…just taking a little time.”

"Aye, well there's plenty of it here. Do you know your way back?"

"Back? Oh, to the cabin? Yes. I take the path to the right then follow the stream."

"Don't linger long." He turned and started down, pausing only briefly to glance up at her. "Night comes quickly here this time of year, and it's easy to be lost in the dark. In the unfamiliar."

"No, I'll start back soon. Mr. Donovan—Liam?"

He stopped again, his gaze clear enough that she caught the quick shadow of impatience in it. "Yes?"

"I was wondering…where's your dog?"

His grin was so fast, so bright and amused that she found herself beaming back at him. "I've no dog."

"But I thought—are there other cabins nearby?"

"Not for three miles and more. We're what's here, Rowan. And what lives in the forest between us." He saw her glance uneasily at the verge of trees and softened. "Nothing that's there will harm you. Enjoy your walk, and your evening. And your time."

Before she could think of another way to stop him, he'd stepped into and been swallowed up by the trees. It was then she noticed just how quickly twilight had fallen, just how chilly the air and how brisk the wind. Abandoning pride, she scrambled down the cliff path and called out to him.

"Liam? Wait a minute, would you? I'll walk back with you for a bit."

But her own voice echoed back to her, turning her throat dry. She moved quickly down the path certain she'd catch a glimpse of him in the trees. There was nothing now but deep shadow.

"Not only quiet," she mumbled, "but fast. Okay, okay." To bolster herself she paused to take three deep breaths. "There's nothing in here that wasn't here when there was more light. Just go back the way you came and stop being an idiot."

But the deeper she went, the thicker the shadows. Like a tide, a thin ground fog slid over the path, white as smoke. She would have sworn she heard music, like bells—or laughter. It harmonized with the sound of the water bubbling over rocks, whispered in counterpoint to the *whoosh* and sigh of the wind in the trees.

A radio, she thought. Or a television. Sounds carried oddly in some places. Liam had turned on music, and for some reason she could hear it playing. It only seemed as if it was just ahead of her, in the direction of her own cabin. The wind played tricks.

The sigh of relief as she came to the last bend of the stream froze in her throat as she saw the glint of gold eyes peering out of the shadows. Then with a rustle of leaves, they were gone.

Rowan increased her pace to a jog and didn't break stride until she'd reached the door. She didn't start breathing again until she was inside and the door was securely locked behind her.

She moved quickly, switching on lights until the first floor of the cabin blazed with them. Then she poured herself a glass from one of the bottles of wine she'd brought along, lifted it in a toast and swallowed deep.

"To strange beginnings, mysterious neighbors and invisible dogs."

To make herself feel more at home, she heated a can of soup and ate it standing up, dreaming, looking out the kitchen window, as she often did in her apartment in the city.

But the dreams were softer here, and yet more clear. Towering trees and bubbling water, thrashing waves and the last light of the day.

A handsome man with tawny eyes who stood on a windswept cliff and smiled at her.

She sighed, wishing she'd been clever and polished, had known a way to flirt lightly, speak casually so that he might have looked at her with interest rather than annoyance and amusement.

Which was ridiculous, she reminded herself, as Liam Donovan wasn't wasting his time thinking of her at all. So it was pointless to think of him.

Following habit, she tidied up, switching off lights as she moved upstairs. There she indulged herself by filling the wonderfully deep claw-foot tub with hot water and fragrant bubbles, settling into it with a sigh, a book and a second glass of wine.

She immediately decided this was a luxury she hadn't allowed herself nearly often enough.

''That's going to change.'' She slid back, moaning with pleasure. ''So many things are going to change. I just have to think of them all.''

When the water turned tepid, she climbed out to change into the cozy flannel pajamas she'd bought. Another indulgence was to light the bedroom fire, then crawl under the cloud-light duvet beneath the canopy and snuggle into her book.

Within ten minutes, she was asleep, with her reading glasses sliding down her nose, the lights on and the last of her wine going warm in her glass.

She dreamed of a sleek black wolf who padded silently into her room, watching her out of curious gold eyes as she slept. It seemed he spoke to her—his mind to her mind.

I wasn't looking for you. I wasn't waiting for you. I don't want what you're bringing me. Go back to your safe world, Rowan Murray. Mine isn't for you.

She couldn't answer but to think *I only want time. I'm only looking for time.*

He came close to the bed, so that her hand nearly brushed his head. *If you take it here, it may trap us both. Is that a risk you're willing to take?*

Oh, she wanted to touch, to feel, and with a sigh slid her hand over the warm fur, let her fingers dive into it. *It's time I took one.*

Under her hand wolf became man. His breath fluttered over her face as he leaned close, so close. "If I kissed you now, Rowan, what might happen?"

Her body seemed to shimmer with that sudden raw need. She moaned with it, arched, reached out.

Liam only laid a finger on her lips. "Sleep," he told her and slipped the glasses off, laid them on the table beside her. He switched off the light, closed his hand into a fist as the urge to touch her, to really touch her, lanced through him.

"Damn it. I don't want this. I don't want her."

He flung up his hand and vanished.

Later, much later, she dreamed of a wolf, black as midnight on the cliffs over the sea. With his head thrown back he called to the swimming moon.

Chapter 2

It became a habit over the next few days for Rowan to look for the wolf. She would see him, most often early in the morning or just before twilight, standing at the edge of the trees.

Watching the house, she thought. Watching her.

She realized, on those mornings when she didn't see him, that she was disappointed. So much so that she began leaving food out in hopes to lure him closer, to keep him a regular visitor in what she was starting to consider her little world.

He was on her mind quite a bit. Nearly every morning she woke with fading snippets of dreams just at the edge of her mind. Dreams where he sat by her bed while she slept, where she sometimes roused just enough to reach out and stroke that soft silky fur or feel the strong ridge of muscle along his back.

Now and then, the wolf became mixed in her

dreams with her neighbor. On those mornings, she climbed out of sleep with her system still quivering from an aching sexual frustration that baffled and embarrassed her.

When she was logical, she could remind herself that Liam Donovan was the only human being she'd seen in the best part of a week. As a sample of the species, he was spectacular and the perfect fodder for erotic dreams.

But all in all she preferred thinking of the wolf, weaving a story about him. She liked pretending he was her guardian, protecting her from any evil spirits that lived in the forest.

She spent most of her time reading or sketching, or taking long walks. And trying not to think that it was nearly time to make her promised weekly call home to her parents.

She often heard music, drifting through the woods or in through her windows. Pipes and flutes, bells and strings. Once there was harpsong so sweet and so pure that it made her throat ache with tears.

While she wallowed in the peace, the solitude, the lack of demand on her time and attention, there were also moments of loneliness so acute it hurt the heart. Even when the need for another voice, for human contact pulled at her, she couldn't quite gather the courage, or find a reasonable excuse, to seek out Liam.

To offer him a cup of coffee, she thought as twilight slipped through the trees and there was no sign of her wolf. Or maybe a hot meal. A little conversation, she mused, absently twisting the tip of her braid around her finger.

"Doesn't he ever get lonely?" she wondered. "What does he do all day, all night?"

The wind rose, and in the distance thunder mumbled. A storm brewing, she thought, moving to the door to fling it open to the fast, cool air. Looking up, she watched dark clouds roll and bump, caught the faint blink of far-off lightning.

She thought it would be lovely to sleep with the sound of rain falling on the roof. Better, to curl up in bed with a book and read half the night while the wind howled and the rain lashed.

Smiling at the idea, she shifted her gaze. And looked directly into the glinting eyes of the wolf.

She stumbled back a step, pressing a hand to her throat where her heart had leaped. He was halfway across the clearing, closer than he'd ever come. Wiping her nervous hands on her jeans, she cautiously stepped out on the porch.

"Hello." She laughed a little, but kept one hand firmly on the doorknob. Just in case. "You're so beautiful," she murmured while he stood, still as a stone carving. "I look for you every day. You never eat the food I leave out. Nothing else does, either. I'm not a very good cook. I keep wishing you'd come closer."

As her pulse began to level, she lowered slowly into a crouch. "I won't hurt you," she murmured. "I've been reading about wolves. Isn't it odd that I brought a book about you with me? I don't even remember packing it, but I brought so many books. You shouldn't be interested in me,'' she said with a sigh. ''You should be running with a pack, with your mate.''

The sadness hit so quickly, so sharply, that she closed her eyes against it. ''Wolves mate for life,'' she said quietly, then jolted when lightning slashed and the bellow of thunder answered by shaking the sky.

The clearing was empty. The black wolf was gone. Rowan walked to the porch rocker, sat and curled up her legs to watch the rain sweep in.

He was thinking about her far too much and far too often. It infuriated him. Liam was a man who prided himself on self-control. When one possessed power, control must walk with it. Power untempered could corrupt. It could destroy.

He'd been taught from birth his responsibilities as well as his advantages. His gifts as well as his curses. Solitude was his way of escaping all of it, at least for short spans of time.

He knew, too well, no one escaped destiny.

The son of princes was expected to accept destiny.

Alone in his cabin, he thought of her. The way she'd looked when he'd come into the clearing. The way fear had danced around her even as she'd stepped outside.

There was such sweetness in her, it pulled at him, even as he struggled to stay away. She thought she was putting him at ease, letting him grow accustomed to her by leaving him food. Speaking to him in that quiet voice that trembled with nerves.

He wondered how many other women, alone in what was essentially wilderness, would have the courage or the desire to talk to a wolf, much less reassure him.

She thought she was a coward—he'd touched her mind gently, but enough to scan her thoughts. She didn't have any concept of what she had inside her, hadn't explored it, or been allowed to.

Strong sense of family, great loyalty and pitifully low self-esteem.

He shook his head as he sipped coffee and watched the storm build. What in Finn's name was he supposed to do about her?

If it had just been a matter of giving her subtle little pushes to discover herself and her own powers, that would have been…interesting, he supposed. He might have enjoyed the task. But he knew it was a great deal more.

He'd been shown just enough to worry him.

If she'd been sent to him and he accepted her, took her, the decision he'd left home and family to make would be made for him.

She was not one of his kind.

Yet already there were needs stirring. She was a lovely woman after all, vulnerable, a little lost. Those needs would have been natural enough, particularly after his long, self-imposed solitude.

Male required female.

But the needs were deeper, stronger and more demanding than he'd experienced before, and that he cared to experience. When you felt too much, control slipped. Without control, there was no choice. He'd taken this year to himself to make choices.

Yet he couldn't stay away from her. He'd been wise enough, he considered, to keep his distance in this form—at least when she was awake and aware. Still he was drawn through the forest to watch her, to listen to her mind. Or to sit alone here in this room, cast the fire and study her in the flames.

Love waits.

He set his teeth, set his cup down with a snap of china on wood as the whisper floated over him. "Damn it. I'll deal with it, with her. In my own time. In my own way. Leave me be."

In the dark window glass his own reflection faded, replaced by a woman with tumbling gold hair and eyes of the same rich color, who smiled softly. "Liam," she said. "Stubborn you are, and always were."

He cocked a brow. "Mother, 'tis easy when you learn from the best."

She laughed, eyes sparkling against the night. "That's true enough—if you're speaking of your Da. The storm breaks, and she's alone. Will you leave her that way?"

"It's best for both of us if I do just that. She's not one of us."

"Liam, when you're ready, you'll look into her heart, and into your own. Trust what you find." Then she sighed, knowing her son would follow his own path as always. "I'll give your father your best."

"Do. I love you."

''I know it. Come home soon, Liam of Donovan. We're missing you.''

As her image faded, lightning slashed out of the sky, driving down like a lance to stab the ground. It left no mark, no burn, even as thunder roared behind it; Liam understood it was his father's way of echoing his wife's words.

''All right then. Bloody hell. I'll have a look and see how well she's riding out the storm.''

He turned, focused, then flicked a wrist, jabbing a finger at the cold hearth. The fire leaped, though there was no log, no kindling to burn.

''Lightning flares and thunder moans. How does the woman fare alone? Chill the fire to let me see. As I will, so mote it be.''

He dipped his hands into his pockets as the flames settled, steadied. In the cool gold light, shadows shifted, parted, then opened to him.

He saw her carrying a candle through the dark, her face pale in its flickering light, her eyes wide. She fumbled through drawers in her kitchen, talking to herself, as she was prone to. And jolted like a frightened deer when the next flash of lightning broke the night.

Well, he hadn't thought of that, Liam admitted, and in a rare show of frustration, dragged a hand through his hair. Her power was out, and she was alone in the dark, and scared half to death. Hadn't Belinda told her how to work the little generator, or where the flashlight was? The emergency lanterns?

Apparently not.

He could hardly leave her there, could he? Shivering and stumbling around. Which, he supposed with a sour smile, was exactly what his clever, meddling cousin had known.

He'd make sure she had light, and heat, but that would be the end of it. He wouldn't linger.

While he was a witch, he was also a man. And both parts of him wanted her entirely too much for comfort.

''Just a storm, it's just a storm. No big deal.'' Rowan all but chanted the words as she lighted more candles.

She wasn't afraid of the dark, not really. But it was so *damn* dark, and the lightning had struck so close to the cabin. The thunder rattled the windows until she was certain they would just explode.

And if she hadn't been sitting outside, daydreaming while the storm blew in, she'd have had a fire built. She'd have the warmth and light from that *and* the candlelight, and it would be sort of…cozy. If she really worked on believing it.

And now the power was out, the phones were out and the storm appeared to be at its peak directly over her pretty little cabin.

There were candles, she reminded herself. Dozens and dozens of candles. White ones, blue ones, red ones, green ones. She could only think that Belinda had bought out some candle store. Some were so lovely, with odd and beautiful symbols carved into them, that she held back from lighting them. And after all, she must have fifty flaring away by now, giving adequate light and offering marvelous scents to settle the nerves.

"Okay. All right." She set yet one more candle on the table in front of the sofa and rubbed her chilled hands. "I ought to be able to see enough to get a fire going. Then I'll just curl up right here on the couch and wait it out. It'll be fine."

But even as she crouched in front of the hearth and began to arrange the kindling, the wind howled. Her door banged open like a bullet out of a gun and half the cheery candles behind her blew out.

She leaped up, whirled around. And screamed.

Liam stood a few paces away, the wind swirling through his hair, the candlelight gleaming in his eyes. She dropped kindling on her stockinged feet, yelped and fell backward into a chair.

"I seem to have startled you again," he said in that mild and beautiful voice. "Sorry."

"I—you. God! The door..."

"It's open." He turned, crossed to it and closed out the wind and rain.

She'd been certain she'd locked it when she'd rushed in out of the storm. Obviously not, she thought now and did her best to swallow her heart and get it back in its proper place.

"I thought you might have been having some trouble with the storm." He stepped toward her, each movement graceful as a dancer's. Or a stalking wolf. "It seems I was right."

"Power's out," she managed.

"So I see. You're cold." He picked up the scattered kindling and crouched to build a fire with wood and match. He thought she'd had enough surprises for one night, even if it did take quite a bit longer that way.

"I wanted to get some light before I built a fire. Belinda has a lot of candles."

"Naturally." The kindling caught with a quick crackle, and flames licked obligingly at the logs he arranged. "This'll warm the room soon. There's a small generator out back. I can start it for you if you like, but this will pass before long."

He stayed where he was, with the firelight dancing over his face. And looking at him, she forgot about the storm and fears of the dark. She wondered if all that gorgeous hair that fell nearly to his shoulders was as soft as it looked, wondered why it seemed she knew exactly how it would feel under her fingers.

Why she had an image of him leaning over her, leaning close, with his mouth a breath away from hers. Only a breath away.

"You're daydreaming again, Rowan."

"Oh." She blinked, flushed, shook herself clear. "Sorry. The storm's made me jumpy. Would you like some wine?" She pushed herself up, began backing quickly toward the kitchen. "I have a very nice Italian white I tried last night. I'll just...pour some. Won't be a minute."

For Lord's sake, for Lord's sake, she berated herself as she dashed into the kitchen where a half-dozen candles glowed on the counter. Why did being around him make her so skittish and stupid! She'd been alone with attractive men before. She was a grown woman, wasn't she?

She got the bottle out of the refrigerator by the light of the candles, found glasses and filled them. When she turned, a glass in each hand, he was there just there behind her, and she jolted.

Wine sloshed over the rim and onto the back of her hand.

"*Must* you do that!" She snapped it out before she could stop herself, then watched that fast, fabulous grin flash over his face, bright and blinding as the lightning in the storm.

"I suppose not." Ah, the hell with it, he decided. He was entitled to some small pleasures. With his eyes on hers, he lifted her damp hand, bent his head and slowly licked.

The best she could manage was a small, quiet moan.

"You're right. It's very nice wine." He took the glass and when her freed hand fell limply to her side, smiled. Sipped. "You've a lovely face, Rowan Murray. I've thought of it since last I saw you."

"You have?"

"Did you think I wouldn't?"

She was so obviously befuddled it was tempting to press his advantage, to go with the urge grinding in him to take before she knew all he wanted, and what he refused to want. One step closer, he mused, the slow slide of his fingers around the base of her neck where the flesh was warm and smooth. Fragile. His mouth to hers while the taste of her was still mixed with the wine on his tongue.

And he wouldn't be in the mood to leave it at something quite so simple, or quite so innocent.

''Come in by the fire.'' He stepped back to give her room to pass. ''Where it's warmer.''

She recognized the ache spreading inside her. The same ache, she thought, as she woke with whenever she dreamed of him. She moved past him, into the living room, praying she could think of something to say that wouldn't sound idiotic.

''If you came here to relax,'' he began with just a hint of impatience in his voice, ''you're doing a preciously poor job of it. Sit down and stop fretting. The storm won't stay long, and neither will I.''

''I like the company. I'm not used to being alone for such long stretches of time.''

She sat, managing a smile. But he stood by the fire, leaned against the mantel. He watched her. Watched her in a way that reminded her of—

''Isn't that why you came here?'' He said it to interrupt her thoughts before they inched too close to what she wasn't prepared to know. ''To have time alone?''

''Yes. And I like it. But it's odd just the same. I was a teacher for a long time. I'm used to having a lot of people around.''

''Do you like them?''

''Them? Students?''

''No, people.'' He made a vague and oddly dismissive gesture with one elegant hand. ''In general.''

''Why...yes.'' She laughed a little, leaning back in her chair without being aware her shoulders had lost their knots of tension. ''Don't you?''

''Not particularly—as a rule.'' He took a sip of wine, reflecting. ''So many of them are demanding, selfish, self-absorbed. And while that's not so much of a problem, they often hurt each other quite consciously, quite carelessly. There's no point, and there should be no pride in causing harm."

"Most people don't mean to." She saw the light in his eye and shook her head. "Oh, you're cynical. I can't understand cynics."

"That's because you're a romantic, and a naive one at that. But it's charming on you."

"Now, should I be flattered or insulted?" she wondered aloud, smiling with more ease than she'd ever felt with him, even when he moved to sit at the ottoman in front of her chair.

"Truth can be accepted without either. What do you teach?"

"Literature—or I used to."

"That would explain the books." They were stacked on the coffee table and in a box beside the couch. He'd seen others piled on the kitchen table and knew there were still more in her bedroom upstairs.

"Reading's one of my greatest pleasures. I love sliding into a story."

"But this..." He leaned back, reached over and plucked up the top book on the table. "*The Study of Wolves, Their History and Habits.* That wouldn't be a story, would it?"

"No. I bought that on impulse one day, and didn't even realize I'd packed it. But I'm glad I did." In a habitual gesture she brushed at the hair that had come loose from her braid. "You must have seen him." She eased forward, the delight in her large, dark eyes nearly irresistible. ''The black wolf that comes around.''

He continued to look into her eyes, straight in as he enjoyed his wine. ''I can't say I have.''

''Oh, but I've seen him nearly every day since I came. He's gorgeous, and doesn't seem as wary of people as you'd expect. He came into the clearing right before the storm tonight. And sometimes I hear him calling, or it seems I do. Haven't you?''

''I'm closer to the sea,'' he told her. ''That's what I listen to. A wolf is a wild thing, Rowan, as I'm sure your book has told you. And a rogue, one who runs alone, the wildest of all.''

''I wouldn't want to tame him. I'd say we're just curious about each other at this point.'' She glanced toward the window, wondered if the wolf had found a warm dry place for the night. ''They don't hunt for sport,'' she added, absently tossing her braid behind her back. ''Or out of viciousness. They hunt to feed. Most often they live in packs, families. Protect their young, and—'' She broke off, jumping a little when lightning flashed bright and close.

''Nature's a violent thing. It only tolerates the rest of us. Nature can be generous or ruthless.'' He put the book aside. ''You have to have a care how you deal with it, and you'll never understand it.''

Their knees were brushing, their bodies close. She caught the scent of him, sharply male, almost animal, and absolutely dangerous. His lips curved in a smile as he nodded. ''Exactly so,'' he murmured, then set his glass aside and rose. ''I'll start the generator for you. You'll be happier with some electricity.''

"Yes, I suppose you're right." She got to her feet, wondering why her heart was pounding. It had nothing to do with the storm raging outside now, and everything to do with the one so suddenly brewing inside her. "Thank you for helping."

"It's not a problem." He wasn't going to let it be a problem. "It'll only be a moment." Briefly, lightly, his fingers danced over the back of her hand. "It was good wine," he murmured, and walked out to the kitchen.

It took her ten long seconds to get her breath back, to lower the hand she'd pressed to her cheek and follow him. Just as she stepped into the kitchen, the lights flashed on, making her yelp. Even as she laughed at herself, she wondered how the man moved so fast. The kitchen was empty, her lights were on, and it was as if he'd never been there.

She pulled open the back door and winced when the wind and rain lashed at her. Shivering a little, she leaned out. "Liam?" But there was nothing but the rain and the dark. "Don't go," she murmured, leaning on the doorjamb as the rain soaked her shirt. "Please don't leave me alone."

The next burst of lightning shot the forest into bright relief. And gleamed off the coat of the wolf that stood in the driving rain at the foot of the steps.

"God." She fumbled on the wall for the light switch, flicked it and had the floodlights pouring on. He was still there, his coat gleaming with wet, his eyes patiently watching. She moistened her lips, took a slow step back. "You should come in out of the rain."

A thrill sprinted up her spine as he leaped gracefully onto the porch. She didn't realize she was holding her breath until his damp fur brushed her leg as he walked inside, and she released it with a shiver.

"Well." Trembling a little, she turned so they watched each other. "There's a wolf in the house. An incredibly handsome wolf," she murmured and found herself not thinking twice about shutting the door and closing them inside together. "Um, I'm going to go in..." She gestured vaguely. "There. It's warm. You can—"

She broke off, charmed and baffled when he simply swung around and stalked through the doorway. She followed to see him walk to the fire, settle himself then look back at her as if waiting.

"Smart, aren't you?" she murmured. "Very smart." As she approached cautiously, his gaze never left her face. She lowered herself to the ottoman. "Do you belong to anyone?" She lifted her hand, her fingers itching to touch. She waited for a growl, a snarl, a warning, and when none came she lightly laid her hand on his head. "No, you wouldn't belong to anyone but yourself. That's how it is for the brave and the beautiful."

When her fingers stroked down to his neck, rubbing gently, his eyes narrowed. She thought she recognized pleasure in them and smiled a little. "You like that? Me, too. Touching's as good as being touched, and no one's really touched me for so long. But you don't want to hear the story of my life. It's not very interesting. Yours would be," she mused. "I bet you'd have fascinating tales to tell."

He smelled of the forest, of the rain. Of animal. And oddly, of something…familiar. She grew bolder, running her hands down his back, over his flanks, back to his head. ''You'll dry here by the fire,'' she began, then her hand paused in midstroke, her brows drew together.

''He wasn't wet,'' she said quietly. ''He came through the rain, but he wasn't wet. Was he?'' Puzzled, she stared out the dark window. Liam's hair was as black as the wolf's fur, but it hadn't gleamed with rain or damp. Had it?

''How could that be? Even if he'd driven over he had to get from a car to the door, and…''

She trailed off when the wolf moved closer, when his handsome head nuzzled her thigh. With a murmur of pleasure, she began to stroke him again, grinning when the rumble in his throat reminded her of a very human, very male sound of approval.

''Maybe you're lonely, too.''

And she sat with him while the storm shifted out to sea, the thunder quieted, and the whips of rain and wind turned to soft patters.

It didn't surprise her that he walked through the house with her. Somehow it seemed perfectly natural that he would accompany her as she blew out candles, switched off lights. He climbed the stairs with her and sat by her side as she lighted the bedroom fire.

''I love it here,'' she murmured, sitting back on her heels to watch the flames catch. ''Even when I'm lonely, like I was tonight, it feels right being here. As if I've always needed to come to this place.''

She turned her head, smiled a little. They were eye

to eye now, deep blue to dark gold. Reaching out she skimmed her hand under his powerful jaw, rubbing the silky line of his throat. ''No one would believe me. No one I know would believe me if I told them I was in a cabin in Oregon talking to a big, black, gorgeous wolf. And maybe I'm just dreaming. I do a lot of that,'' she added as she rose. ''Maybe everyone's right and I do too much dreaming.''

She crossed to the dresser and took a pair of pajamas from the drawer. ''I guess it's pretty pitiful when your dreams are the most interesting part of your life. I really want to change that. I don't mean I have to climb mountains or jump out of planes...''

He stopped listening—and he had listened all along. But now, as she spoke, she tugged the navy sweatshirt she wore over her head and began to unbutton the simple plaid shirt beneath.

He stopped hearing the words as she slipped the shirt off, stood folding the sweatshirt wearing only a lacy white bra and jeans.

She was small and slender, her skin milk pale. Her jeans bagged a bit at the waist, making the man inside the wolf nearly groan as her fingers reached for the button. His blood warmed, his pulse quickened as she let the denim slide carelessly down her legs.

The swatch of white rode low on her hips. He wanted his mouth there, just there along that lovely curve. To taste the flesh, to feel the shape of bone. And to slide his tongue under the white until she quivered.

She sat, tugging off her socks, shaking her feet free

of the jeans. And nearly drove him mad as she stood to lay them aside.

The low growl in his throat went unnoticed by both of them as she unhooked her bra in an innocent striptease. He felt his control slipping as he imagined cupping his hands there, over small white breasts, skimming his thumbs over pale pink nipples.

Lowering his head until his mouth was—

The sudden violent slash of lightning had her jumping, muffling a scream. "God! The storm must be coming back. I thought..." She stopped in midsentence as she glanced over, saw those gold eyes glinting. In an instinctive gesture, she crossed her arms over her naked breasts. Beneath them her heart bounced like a rabbit.

His eyes looked so...human, she thought with a quick panic. The expression in them hungry. "Why do I suddenly feel like Little Red Riding Hood?" She eased out a breath, drew in another. "That's just foolish." But her voice wasn't quite steady as she made the grab for her pajama top. She made a little squeak of surprise when he caught the dangling sleeve in his teeth and dragged it away.

A laugh bubbled up and out. She grabbed the collar of the flannel, pulled. The quick, unexpected tug-of-war made her laugh again. "You think it's funny?" she demanded. Damn if she didn't see amusement in those fascinating eyes. "I just bought these. They may not be pretty, but they're warm—and it's cold in here. Now, let go!"

When he did, abruptly, she stumbled back two paces before she caught her balance. Wonderfully naked but for that triangle at her hips, she narrowed her eyes at him. ''A real joker, aren't you?'' She held the top up, searching for tears or teeth marks, and found none. ''Well, at least you didn't eat it.''

He watched her slip it on, button it. There was something erotic even in that, in the way the brightly patterned flannel skimmed her thighs. But before she could pull on the bottoms he pleased himself by shifting his head, running his tongue from her ankle to the back of her knee.

She chuckled, bent down to scratch his ears as though he were the family dog. ''I like you, too.'' After pulling the bottoms on, she reached up to loosen what was left of her braid. As she reached for her brush, the wolf padded over to the bed, leaped up and stretched out at the foot.

''Oh, I don't think so.'' Amused, she turned, running the brush through her hair. ''I really don't. You'll have to get down from there.''

He watched her unblinkingly. She would have sworn he smiled. Huffing out a breath, she shook her hair back, set the brush aside, then walked to the side of the bed. In her best teacher's voice she ordered him down and pointed meaningfully at the floor.

This time she *knew* he smiled.

''You're not sleeping in the bed.'' She reached out, intended to pull him off. But when he bared his teeth, she cleared her throat. ''Well, one night. What could it hurt?''

Watching him cautiously, she climbed up, sliding under the duvet. He simply lay, his head snugged between his front paws. She picked up her glasses, her book, shrugging when the wolf lay still. Satisfied, she piled the pillows behind her and settled in to read.

Only moments later, the mattress shifted, and the wolf moved over to lie at her side, laying his head in her lap. Without a thought, Rowan stroked him and began to read aloud.

She read until her eyes grew heavy, her voice thick, and once more slipped into sleep with a book in her hand.

The air quivered as wolf became man. Liam touched a finger to her forehead. ''Dream, Rowan,'' he murmured, pausing as he felt her slide deeper. He took her book, her glasses and set them neatly on the bedside table. Then he eased her down, lifting her head so he could spread out the pillows.

''You must be waking every morning stiff as a board,'' he murmured. ''Forever falling asleep sitting up.'' He skimmed the back of his hand over her cheek, then sighed.

The scent of her, silky and female and subtle was enough to drive him mad. Each quiet breath through those full and parted lips was a kind of invitation.

''Damn it, Rowan, you lie in bed with me with the rain on the roof and read Yeats aloud in that soft, almost prim voice of yours. How should I resist that? I'll have to have you sooner or later. Later's the better for both of us. But I need something tonight.''

He took her hand, pressed palm to palm, linked fingers. And shut his eyes. ''Come with me, two minds, one dream. Sleep is not now what it seems. Give what I need, and take what you'll have from me. As I will, so mote it be.''

She moaned. And moved. Her free arm flung up over her head, her lips parting on a shuddering breath that seemed to whisper in his blood. His own pulse thickened as he made love to her with his mind. Tasted her, touched her with his thoughts. Gave himself to hers.

Lost in dreams, she arched up, her body shuddering under phantom hands.

She smelled him, that musky, half-animal scent that had already stirred her more than once in dreams. Images, sensations, desires, confused and tangled and arousing beyond belief swarmed through her. Embracing them, she murmured his name and opened to him, body and mind.

The hot wave of his thoughts lifted her up, held her trembling, aching, quivering, then stabbed her with unspeakable pleasure. She heard her name, said quietly, almost desperately. Repeated. Desire drugged the mind, swirled through it, then slid silently away into fulfillment.

He sat, his eyes still closed, his hand still joined with hers. Listened to the rain, her soft and steady breathing. Resisting the urge to lie with her, to touch her now with more than his mind, he threw his head back. And vanished.

Chapter 3

She woke early, blissfully relaxed. Her body seemed to glow. Her mind was calm, clear and content. Rowan was out of bed and in the shower before she remembered anything. Then with a muttered curse, she jumped out, dripping, grabbed a towel and dashed back into the bedroom.

The bed was empty. There was no beautiful wolf curled in front of the cold fire. Ignoring the water sliding down her legs she dashed downstairs, searching the house and leaving a trail of damp behind her.

The kitchen door hung open, letting in the chill of the morning. Still she stepped out, her cold toes curling up in protest as she scanned the line of trees.

How did he get out—and where did he go? she wondered. Since when do wolves open doors?

She hadn't imagined it. No, she refused to believe that her imagination could create such clear images, such textures, such events. That would make her crazy, wouldn't it? she thought with a half laugh as she backed inside again and closed the door.

The wolf had been in the house. He'd sat with her, stayed with her. Even slept on the bed. She could remember exactly the feel of his fur, the scent of rain and wild on it, the expressions in his eyes, and the warmth, the simple comfort, when he'd laid his head on her lap.

However...unusual the evening, it had happened. However odd her own actions, letting him in, petting him, she had done so.

And if she'd had a brain cell in her head, she'd have thought to grab her camera and take a few pictures of him.

To prove what? To show to whom? The wolf, she realized, was her personal and private joy. She didn't want to share him.

She went back upstairs, back to the shower, wondering how long it would be before he came back.

She caught herself singing and grinned. She couldn't remember ever waking up happier or with more energy. And wasn't that part of the plan? she thought as she lifted her face to the spray and let the hot water stream. To find out just what made her happy. If it happened to be spending a stormy night with a wolf, so what?

"Try to explain that one, Rowan." Laughing at herself, she toweled off. Humming, she started to wipe the steam from the bathroom mirror, then paused, staring at her own misty reflection.

Did she look different? she wondered, leaning

closer to study her face, the glow of her skin, the sleek sheen of wet hair, and most of all the light in her eyes.

What had put that there? She lifted her hand, running her fingers curiously along the ridge of her cheekbones just under her eyes.

Dreams. And her fingers trembled lightly as she dropped them. Hot and shivering dreams. Colors and shapes pulsing through her mind, through her body. So stunning, so…erotic. Hands on her breasts, but not. A mouth crushing down on hers but never really touching.

Closing her eyes, she let the towel fall, skimmed her hands over her breasts, down, up again, trying to focus on where she had journeyed in sleep.

The taste of male skin, the hot slide of it over her own. Needs rocketing through the mind to be met and met again until the beauty of it brought tears.

She'd never experienced anything like that, not even in life. How could she find it in dreams?

And why should she go to sleep with a wolf and dream of a man.

Of Liam.

She knew it had been Liam. She could all but feel the shape of his mouth on hers. But how could that be? she wondered, tracing a fingertip over her lips. How could she be so sure she knew just what it would be like to meet his mouth with hers.

"Because you want to," she murmured, opening her eyes to meet those in the mirror again. "Because you want him and you've never wanted anyone else like this. And, Rowan, you moron, you don't have the slightest idea how to make it happen, except in dreams. So that's where it happens for you. Psychology 101—real basic stuff.''

Not certain if she should be amused or appalled at herself, she dressed, went down to brew her morning coffee. Snug in her sweater, she flung open the windows to the cool, fresh air left behind by the rain.

She thought, without enthusiasm, about cereal or toast or yogurt. She had a yen for chocolate chip cookies, which was absurd at barely eight in the morning, so she told herself. Dutifully she opened the cupboard for cereal, then slammed it shut.

If she wanted cookies, she was having them. And with a grin on her face and a gleam in her eye, began to drag out ingredients. She slopped flour, scattered sugar on the counter. And mixed with abandon. There was no one to see her lick dough from her fingers. No one to gently remind her that she should tidy up between each step of the process.

She made an unholy mess.

Dancing with impatience, she waited for the first batch to bake. ''Come on, come on. I've got to have one.'' The minute the buzzer went off, she grabbed the cookie sheet out, dropped it on the top of the stove, then scooped up the first cookie with a spatula. She blew on it, slipped it off and tossed it from hand to hand. Still she burned her tongue on hot, gleaming chocolate as she bit in. And rolling her eyes dramatically, she swallowed with a hedonistic groan.

''Good job. Really good job. More.''

She ate a dozen before the second batch was baked. It felt decadent, childish. And wonderful.

When the phone rang, she popped the next batch in, and lifted the receiver with doughy fingers. ''Hello?''

''Rowan. Good morning.''

For a moment the voice meant nothing to her, then with a guilty start she realized it was Alan. ''Good morning.''

''I hope I didn't wake you?''

''No, no. I've been up quite a while. I'm...'' She grinned and chose another cookie. ''Just having breakfast.''

''Glad to hear it. You tend to skip too many meals.''

She put the whole cookie into her mouth and talked around it. ''Not this time. Maybe the mountain air...'' She managed to swallow. ''Stimulates my appetite.''

''You don't sound like yourself.''

''Really?'' I'm not myself, she wanted to say. I'm better. And I'm not nearly finished yet.

''You sound a little giddy. Are you all right?''

''I'm fine. I'm wonderful.'' How could she explain to this solid and serious man with his solid and serious voice that she'd been dancing in the kitchen eating cookies, that she'd spent the evening with a wolf, that she'd had erotic dreams about a man she barely knew?

And that she wouldn't change a moment of any of those experiences.

''I'm getting lots of reading done,'' she said instead. ''Taking long walks. I've been doing some sketching, too. I'd forgotten how much I enjoy it. It's a gorgeous morning. The sky's unbelievably blue.''

"I checked the weather for your area last night. There were reports of a severe thunderstorm. I tried to call, but your lines were out."

"Yes, we had a storm. That's probably why it's so spectacular this morning."

"I was worried, Rowan. If I hadn't been able to reach you this morning, I was going to fly to Portland and rent a car."

The thought of it, just the thought of him invading her magical little world filled her with panic. She had to fight to keep it out of her voice. "Oh, Alan, there's absolutely no need to worry. I'm fine. The storm was exciting, actually. And I have a generator, emergency lights."

"I don't like thinking of you up there alone, in some rustic little hut in the middle of nowhere. What if you hurt yourself, or fell ill, got a flat tire?"

Her mood began to deflate, degree by degree. She could actually feel the drop. He'd said the same words to her before, and so had her parents, with the exact same tone of bafflement mixed with concern.

"Alan, it's a lovely, sturdy and very spacious cabin, not a hut. I'm only about five miles outside of a very nice little town, which makes this far from the middle of nowhere. If I hurt myself or get sick, I'll go to a doctor. If I get a flat tire, I suppose I'll figure out how to change it."

"You're still alone, Rowan, and as last night proved, easily cut off."

"The phone's working just fine now," she said between clenched teeth. "And I have a cell phone in the Rover. Added to that, I believe I have a moderately intelligent mind, I'm in perfect health, I'm twenty-seven years old and the entire purpose of my coming here was to be alone."

There was a moment's silence, a moment just long enough to let her know she'd hurt his feelings. And more than long enough to bring her a swift wash of guilt. "Alan—"

"I'd hoped you'd be ready to come home, but that apparently isn't the case. I miss you, Rowan. Your family misses you. I only wanted to let you know."

"I'm sorry." How many times in her life had she said those words? she wondered as she pressed her fingers to the dull ache forming in her temple. "I didn't mean to snap at you, Alan. I suppose I feel a little defensive. No, I'm not ready to come back. If you speak to my parents, tell them I'll call them later this evening, and that I'm fine."

"I'll be seeing your father later today." His voice was stiff now, his way—she knew—of letting her know he was hurt. "I'll tell him. Please keep in touch."

"I will. Of course, I will. It was nice of you to call. I'll, ah, write you a long letter later this week."

"I'd enjoy that. Goodbye, Rowan."

Her cheerful mood totally evaporated, she hung up, turned and looked at the chaos of the kitchen. As penance, she cleaned every inch of it, then put the cookies in a plastic container, sealing them away.

"No, I am not going to brood. Absolutely not." She banged open a cupboard door, took out a smaller container and transferred half the cookies into it.

Before she could talk herself out of it, she grabbed

a light jacket from the hook by the door, and tucking the container under her arm, stepped outside.

She didn't have a clue where Liam's cabin was, but he'd said he was closer to the sea. It only made sense to hunt it out, she decided. In case of...an emergency. She'd take a walk, and if she didn't find it... Well, she thought shaking the cookies, she wouldn't starve while she was looking.

She walked into the trees, struck again at how much cooler, how much greener it was inside them. There was birdsong, the whisper of the trees and the sweet smell of pine. Where sunlight could dapple through, it danced on the forest floor, sparkled on the water of the stream.

The deeper she walked, the higher her mood rose again. She paused briefly, just to close her eyes, to let the wind ruffle her hair, play against her cheeks. How could she explain this, just this, to a man like Alan? she wondered. Alan whose every want was logical, whose every step was reasonable and solid.

How could she make him, or anyone else from the world she'd run from, understand what it was like to crave something as intangible as the sound of trees singing, the sharp taste the sea added to the air, the simple peace of standing alone in something so vast and so alive?

"I'm not going back there." The words, more than the sound of her own voice, had her eyes snapping open in surprise. She hadn't realized she'd decided anything, much less something that momentous. The half laugh that escaped was tinged with triumph. "I'm not going back,'' she repeated. ''I don't know where I'm going, but it won't be back.''

She laughed again, longer, fuller as she turned a dizzy circle. With a spring to her step, she started to take the curve of the path to the right. Out of the corner of her eye, she saw a flash of white. Turning, she stared with openmouthed wonder at the white doe.

They watched each other with the tumbling stream between them, the doe with serene gold eyes and a hide as white as clouds, and the woman with both shock and awe glowing in her face.

Captivated, Rowan stepped forward. The deer stood, elegant as a sculpture of ice. Then with a lift of her head, she turned fluidly and leaped into the trees. Without a moment's hesitation, Rowan scrambled across the stream, using polished rocks as stepping stones. She saw the path immediately, then the deer, a bounding blur of white.

She hurried after, taking each twist and turn of the path at a run. But always the deer stayed just ahead, with no more than a quick glimpse of gleaming white, and the thunder of hooves on the packed ground.

Then she was in a clearing. It seemed to open up out of nowhere, a perfect circle of soft earth ringed by majestic trees. And within the circle, another circle, made of dark gray stones, the shortest as high as her shoulder, the tallest just over her head.

Stunned, she reached out, touched her fingertips to the surface of the nearest stone. And would have sworn she felt a vibration, like harp strings being plucked. And heard in some secret part of her mind, the answering note.

A stone dance in Oregon? That was…certainly improbable, she decided. Yet here it was. It didn't strike her as being new, but surely it couldn't be otherwise. If it was ancient, someone would have written about it, tourists would come to see it, scientists to study.

Curious, she started to step through two stones, then immediately stepped back again. It seemed the air within quivered. The light was different—richer, and the sound of the sea closer than it had seemed only a moment before.

She told herself she was a rational woman, that there was no life in stone, nor any difference between the air where she stood and that one foot inside the circle. But rational or not, she skirted around rather than walking through.

It was as if the deer had waited, halfway around the dance just down a thin, shadowy path through the trees. Just as it seemed she looked at Rowan with understanding, and amusement before she bounded gracefully ahead.

This time when she followed, Rowan lost all sense of direction. She could hear the sea, but was it ahead, to the left, or to the right? The path twisted, turned and narrowed until it was no more than a track. She climbed over a fallen log, skidded down an incline and wandered through shadows deep as twilight.

When the path ended abruptly, leaving her surrounded by trees and thick brush, she cursed herself for an idiot. She turned, intending to retrace her steps, and saw that the track veered off in two directions.

For the life of her she couldn't remember which to take.

Then she saw the flash of white again, just a glimmer to the left. Heaving a breath, then holding it, Rowan pushed through the brush, fought her way out of the grasp of a thick, thorny vine. She slipped, righted herself. Cursing vividly now, she tripped and stumbled clear of the trees.

The cabin stood nearly on the cliffs, ringed by trees on three sides and backed by the rocks on the fourth. Smoke billowed from the chimney and was whisked away to nothing in the wind.

She pushed the hair out of her face, smeared a tiny drop of blood from a nick a thorn had given her. It was smaller than Belinda's cabin, and made of stone rather than wood. Sunlight had the mica glittering like diamonds. The porch was wide, but uncovered. On the second floor a small and charming stone balcony jutted out from glass doors.

When she lowered her gaze from it, Liam was standing on the porch. He had his thumbs hooked in the front pockets of his jeans, a black sweatshirt with its arms shoved up to the elbows. And he didn't look particularly happy to see her.

But he nodded. "Come in, Rowan. Have some tea."

He walked back inside without waiting for her response, and left the door open wide behind him. When she came closer, she heard the music, pipes and strings tangled in a weepy melody. She barely stopped her hands from twisting together as she stepped inside.

The living area seemed larger than she'd expected, but thought it was because the furnishings were very spare. A single wide chair, a long sofa, both in warm rust colors. A fire blazed under a mantel of dull gray slate. Gracing it was a jagged green stone as big as a man's fist and a statue of a woman carved in alabaster with her arms uplifted, her head thrown back, her naked body slender as a wand.

She wanted to move closer, to study the face, but it seemed rude. Instead she walked toward the back and found Liam in a small, tidy kitchen with a kettle already on the boil and lovely china cups of sunny yellow set out.

''I wasn't sure I'd find you,'' she began, then lost the rest of her thought as he turned from the stove, as those intense eyes locked on hers.

''Weren't you?''

''No, I hoped I would, but...I wasn't sure.'' Nerves reared up and grabbed her by the throat. ''I made some cookies. I brought you some to thank you for helping me out last night.''

He smiled a little and poured boiling water into a yellow pot. ''What kind?'' he asked. Though he knew. He'd smelled them, and her before she'd stepped out of the woods.

''Chocolate chip.'' She managed a smile of her own. ''Is there another kind?'' She busied her hands by opening the container. ''They're pretty good. I've eaten two dozen at least already.''

''Then sit. You can wash them back with tea. You'll have gotten chilled wandering about. The wind's brisk today.''

"I suppose." She sat at the little kitchen table, just big enough for two. "I don't even know how long I've been out," she began, shoving at her tangled hair as he brought the pot to the table. "I was distracted by—" She broke off as he skimmed his thumb over her cheek.

"You've scratched your face." He said it softly as the tiny drop of blood lay warm and intimate on his thumb.

"Oh, I...got tangled up. Some thorns." She was lost in his eyes, could have drown in them. Wanted to. "Liam."

He touched her face again, took away the sting she was too befuddled to notice. "You were distracted," he said, shifting back, then sitting across from her. "When you were in the forest."

"Ah...yes. By the white doe."

He lifted a brow as he poured out the tea. "A white deer? Were you on a quest, Rowan?"

She smiled self-consciously. "The white deer, or bird, or horse. The traditional symbol of quest in literature. I suppose I was on a mild sort of quest, to find you. But I did see her."

"I don't doubt it," he said mildly. His mother enjoyed traditional symbols.

"Have you?"

"Yes." He lifted his tea. "Though it's been some time."

"She's beautiful, isn't she?"

"Aye, that she is. Warm yourself, Rowan. You've bird bones and you'll take a chill."

"I grew up in San Francisco. I'm used to chills.

Anyway, I saw her, and couldn't stop myself from following her. I ended up in this clearing, with a stone circle.''

His eyes sharpened, glinted. ''She led you there?''

''I suppose you could put it that way. You know the place? I never expected to find something like it here. You think of Ireland or Britain, Wales or Cornwall—not Oregon—when you think of stone dances.''

''You find them where they're wanted. Or needed. Did you go in?''

''No. It's silly, but it spooked me a little, so I went around. And got completely lost.''

He knew he should have felt relieved, but instead there was a vague sense of disappointment. But of course, he reminded himself, he'd have known if she'd stepped inside. Instantly. ''Hardly lost since you're here.''

''It seemed like I was lost. The path disappeared and I couldn't get my sense of direction. I probably have a poor one anyway. The tea's wonderful,'' she commented. It was warm and strong and smooth, with something lovely and sweet just under it.

''An old family blend,'' he said with a hint of a smile, then sampled one of her cookies. ''They're good. So you cook, do you, Rowan?''

''I do, but the results are hit and miss.'' All of her early-morning cheer was back and bubbling in her voice. ''This morning, I hit. I like your house. It's like something out of a book, standing here with its back to the cliffs and sea and the stones glittering in the sunlight.''

"It does for me. For now."

"And the views..." She rose to go to the window over the sink, and caught her breath at the sight of the cliffs. "Spectacular. It must be spellbinding during a storm like the one we had last night."

Spellbinding, he thought, knowing his father's habit of manipulating the weather for his needs, was exactly what the storm had been. "And did you sleep well?"

She felt the heat rise up her throat. She could hardly tell him she'd dreamed he'd made love to her. "I don't remember ever sleeping better."

He laughed, rose. "It's flattering." He watched her shoulders draw in. "To know my company relaxed you."

"Hmm." Struggling to shake off the feeling that he knew exactly where her mind had wandered, she started to turn. She noticed the open door and the little room beyond where he'd left a light burning on a desk, and a sleek black computer running.

"Is that your office?"

"In a manner of speaking."

"I've interrupted your work, then."

"It's not pressing." He shook his head. "Why don't you ask if you want to see?"

"I do," she admitted. "If it's all right."

In answer he simply gestured and waited for her to step into the room ahead of him.

The room was small, but the window was wide enough to let in that stunning view of the cliffs. She wondered how anyone could concentrate on work with that to dream on. Then laughed when she saw what was on the monitor screen.

"So you were playing games? I know this one. My students were wild for it. 'The Secrets Of Myor.'"

"Don't you play games?"

"I'm terrible at them. Especially this kind because I tend to get wrapped up in them, and then every step is so vital. I can't take the pressure." Laughing again, she leaned closer, studying the screen with its lightning-stalked castle and glowing faeries. "I've only gotten to the third level where Brinda the witch queen promises to open the Door Of Enchantment if you can find the three stones. I usually find one, then fall into The Pit Of Forever."

"There are always traps on the way to enchantment. Or there wouldn't be pleasure in finding it. Do you want to try again?"

"No, my palms get damp and my fingers fumble. It's humiliating."

"Some games you take seriously, some you don't."

"They're all serious to me." She glanced at the CD jacket, admiring the illustration, then blinked at the small lettering: Copyright By The Donovan Legacy. "It's your game?" Delighted, she straightened, turned. "You create computer games? That's so clever."

"It's entertaining."

"To someone who's barely stumbled their way onto the internet, it's genius. Myor's a wonderful story. The graphics are gorgeous, but I really admire the story itself. It's just magical. A challenging fairy tale with rewards and consequences.''

Her eyes took on tiny silver flecks of light when she was happy, he noted. And the scent of her warmed with her mood. He knew how to make it warm still more, and how to cause those silver flecks to drown in deep, dark blue.

''All fairy tales have both. I like your hair this way.'' He stepped closer, skimmed his fingers through it, testing weight and texture. ''Tumbled and tangled.''

Her throat snapped closed. ''I forgot to braid it this morning.''

''The wind's had it,'' he murmured, lifting a handful to his face. ''I can smell the wind on it, and the sea.'' It was reckless, he knew, but he had dreamed as well. And he remembered every rise and fall. ''I'd taste both on your skin.''

Her knees had jellied. The blood was swimming so fast in her veins that she could hear the roar of it in her head. She couldn't move, could barely breathe. So only stood, staring into his eyes, waiting.

''Rowan Murray with the faerie eyes. Do you want me to touch you.'' He laid a hand on her heart, felt each separate hammer blow pound between the gentle curves of her breasts. ''Like this.'' Then spread his fingers, circled them over one slope, under.

Her bones dissolved, her eyes clouded, and the breath shuddered between her lips in a yielding sigh. His fingers lay lightly on her, but the heat from them seemed to scorch through to flesh. Still she moved neither toward him nor away.

"You've only to say no," he murmured. "When I ask if you want me to taste you."

But her head fell back, those clouded eyes closed when he lowered his head to graze his teeth along her jawline. "The sea and the wind, and innocence as well." His own needs thickened his voice, but there was an edge on it. "Will you give me that as well, do nothing to stop me taking it?" He eased back, waiting, willing her eyes to open and look into his. "If I kissed you now, Rowan, what might happen?"

Her lips trembled apart as memory of a question once asked in dreams and never answered struggled to surface. Then his mouth was on hers, and every thought willingly died. Lights, a wild swirl of them behind the eyes. Heat, a hot gush of it in the belly. The first sound she made was a whimper that might have been fear, but the next was a moan that was unmistakably pleasure.

He was more gentle than she'd expected, perhaps more than he'd intended. His lips skimmed, sipped, nipped and nuzzled until hers went pillow soft and warm under them. She swayed against him in surrender, and request.

Oh, yes, I want this. Just this.

A shiver coursed through her as his hand circled the back of her neck, as he urged her head back, took the kiss deeper with a tangle of tongues and tastes, a mingle of breath that grew unsteady and quick. She gripped his shoulders, first for balance, then for the sheer joy of feeling that hard, dangerous strength, the bunch of muscles.

Her hands slid over and into his hair.

She had a flash of the wolf, the rich black pelt and sinewy strength, then of the man, sitting on her bed, gripping her hand as her body shuddered.

The memory of what could be in dreams, the barrage of sensations of what was, battered each other.

And she erupted.

Her mouth went wild under his, tore at his control. Her surrender had been sweet, but her demands were staggering. As his blood leaped he dragged her closer, let the kiss fly from warm, to hungry to something almost savage.

Still she urged him on, pulling him with her until he buried his face in her throat and had to fight not to use his teeth.

"You're not ready for me." He managed to pant it out, then yanked her back, shook her lightly. "By Finn, I'm not ready for you. There might come a time when that won't matter, and we'll take our chances. But it matters now." His grip lightened, his tone gentled. "It matters today. Go home, Rowan, where you'll be safe."

Her head was still spinning, her pulse still roaring. "No one's ever made me feel like that. I never knew anyone could."

Something flashed into his eyes that made her shiver in anticipation. But then he muttered in a language she didn't understand and lowered his brow to hers. "Honesty can be dangerous. I'm not always civilized, Rowan, but I work to be fair. Have a care how much you offer, for I'm likely to take more."

"I'm terrible at lying."

It made him laugh, and his eyes were calm again

when he straightened. "Then be quiet, for God's sake. Go home now. Not the way you came. You'll see the path when you head out the front. Follow it and you'll get home right enough."

"Liam, I want—"

"I know what you want." Firmly now he took her by the arm and led her out. "If it were as simple as going upstairs and rolling around on the bed for an afternoon, we'd already be there." While she sputtered, he continued to pull her to the front door. "But you're not as simple as you've been taught to think. God knows I'm not. Go on home with you, Rowan."

He all but shoved her out the door. Her rare and occasionally awesome temper shot to the surface as the wind slapped her face. "All right, Liam, because I don't want it to be simple." Her eyes flared at him as she dragged her hair back. "I'm tired of settling for simple. So don't put your hands on me again unless you mean to complicate things."

Riding on anger, she spun around, and didn't question the fact that the path was there, wide and clear. She just marched to it and strode into the trees.

From the porch he watched; long after she was out of sight, he continued to watch her, smiling a bit when she finally reached her own home and slammed the door behind her.

"Good for you, Rowan Murray."

Chapter 4

The man had thrown her out of his house, Rowan thought as she stormed into her own. One minute he'd been kissing her brainless, holding her against that marvelously male body—and the next he'd marched her to the door. Given her the boot as if she'd been some pesky saleswoman hawking an inferior product.

Oh, it was mortifying.

With temper still ringing in her ears like bells she strode around the living room, circled it twice. He'd put his hands on her, he'd made the moves. *He'd* kissed her, damn it. She hadn't done anything.

Except stand there like a dolt, she realized as temper sagged miserably into embarrassment. She'd just stood there, she thought as she wandered into the kitchen. And let him put his hands on her, let him kiss her. She'd have let him do anything, that was how dazzled she'd been.

"Oh, you're such a fool, Rowan." She dropped into a chair, and leaning over, lightly beat her head against the kitchen table. "Such a jerk, such a wimp."

She'd gone to him, hadn't she? Stumbling around in the woods like Gretel with a bunch of cookies instead of bread crumbs. Looking for magic, she thought and rested her cheek on the smooth wood. Always looking for something wonderful, she acknowledged with a sigh. And this time, for just a moment, she'd found it.

It was worse, she realized, when you had that staggering glimpse, then had the door slammed in your face.

God, was she so needy that she'd fall at the feet of a man she'd only met twice before, knew next to nothing about? Was she so weak and wobbly that she'd built fantasies around him because he had a beautiful face?

Not just his face, she admitted. It was the…essence of him, she supposed. The mystery, the romance of him that had very simply bewitched her. There was no other word that fit what he made her feel.

Obviously, quite obviously, it showed.

And when he had touched her because he'd seen through her pitiful ploy of seeking him out to thank him, she'd climbed all over him.

No wonder he'd shown her the door.

But he hadn't had to be so cruel about it, she thought, shoving up again. He'd humiliated her.

"You're not ready for me," she muttered, remembering what he'd said. "How the hell does he know what I'm ready for when I don't know myself? He's not a damn mind reader.''

Sulking now, she ripped the top off the container of cookies and snatched one. She ate it with a scowl on her face as she replayed that last scene, and gave herself wonderful, pithy lines to put Liam Donovan in his place.

''So, he didn't want me,'' she muttered. ''Who expected him to? I'll just stay out of his way. Completely. Totally.'' She shoved another cookie into her mouth. ''I came here to figure out myself, not to try to understand some Irish recluse.''

Slightly ill from the cookies, she snapped the lid back on. The first thing she was going to do was drive into town and find a bookstore. She was going to buy some how-to books. Basic home maintenance, she decided, stalking back into the living room for her purse.

She wasn't going to go fumbling around the next time something happened. She'd figure out how to fix it herself. And, she thought darkly as she marched out of the house, if Liam came to her door offering to fix it for her, she'd coolly tell him she could take care of herself.

She slammed the door of the Rover, gunned the engine. An errant thought about flat tires made her think she'd better find a book on car repair while she was at it.

She bumped along the dirt road, clamping down on the urge to work off some of her frustration by stomping on the gas. Just where Belinda's little lane met the main road, she saw the silver bird.

He was huge, magnificent. An eagle, she thought automatically stepping on the brake to stop and study him. Though she didn't know if any type of eagle was that regal silvery-gray or if they tended to perch on road signs to stare—balefully, she decided—at passing cars.

What wonderfully odd fauna they had in Oregon, she mused and reminded herself to read the books on local wildlife she'd brought with her more carefully. Unable to resist, she rolled down the window and leaned out.

"You're so handsome." She smiled as the bird ruffled his feathers and seemed to preen. "So regal. I bet you look magnificent in the air. I wonder what it feels like to fly. To just…own the sky. You'd know."

His eyes were green, she realized. A silver-gray eagle with eyes green as a cat's. For an instant, she thought she saw a glint of gold resting in his breast feathers, as if he wore a pendant. Just a trick of the light, she decided and with some regret leaned back in the window.

"Wolves and deer and eagles. Why would anybody live in the city? Bye, your highness."

When the Rover was out of sight, the eagle spread its wings, rose majestically into the sky with a triumphant call that echoed over hill and forest and sea. He soared over the trees, circled, then dived. White smoke swirled, the light shimmered, blue as a lightning flash.

And he touched down on the forest floor softly, on two booted feet.

He stood just over six feet, with a mane of silver

hair, eyes of glass green and a face so sharply defined it might have been carved from the marble found in the dark Irish hills. A burnished gold chain hung around his neck, and dangling from it was the amulet of his rank.

"Runs like a rabbit," he muttered. "Then blames herself for the fox."

"She's young, Finn." The woman who stepped out of the green shadows was lovely, with gilded hair flowing down her back, soft tawny eyes, skin white and smooth as alabaster. "And she doesn't know what's inside her, or understand what's inside of Liam."

"A backbone's what she's needing, a bit more of that spirit she showed when she spat in his eye not long ago." His fierce face gentled with a smile. "Never was a lack of spine or spirit a problem of yours, Arianna."

She laughed and cupped her husband's face in her hands. The gold ring of their marriage gleamed on one hand, and the fire of a ruby sparked on the other. "I've needed both with the likes of you, *a stor.* They're on their path, Finn. Now we must let them follow it in their own way."

"And who was it who led the girl to the dance, then to the lad?" he asked with an arrogantly raised eyebrow.

"Well then." Lightly, she trained a fingertip down his cheek. "I never said we couldn't give them a bit of a nudge, now and then. The lass is troubled, and Liam—oh, he's a difficult man, is Liam. Like his Da."

"Takes after his mother more." Still smiling, Finn leaned down to kiss his wife. "When the girl comes into her own, the boy will have his hands full. He'll be humbled before he finds the truth of pride. She'll be hurt before she finds the full of her strength."

"Then, if it's meant, they'll find each other. You like her." Arianna linked her hands at the back of Finn's neck. "She appealed to your vanity, sighing over you, calling you handsome."

His silver brows rose again, his grin flashed bright. "I am handsome—and so you've said yourself. We'll leave them to themselves a bit." He slid his arms around her waist. "Let's be home, *a ghra.* I'm already missing Ireland."

With a swirl of white smoke, a shiver of white light, they were home.

By the time Rowan got home, heated up a can of soup and devoured a section on basic plumbing repairs, it was sunset. For the first time since her arrival she didn't stop and stare and wonder at the glorious fire of the dying day. As the light dimmed, she merely leaned closer to the page.

With her elbows propped on the kitchen table, and her tea going cold, she almost wished a pipe would spring a leak so she could test out her new knowledge.

She felt smug and prepared, and decided to tackle the section on electrical work next. But first she'd make the phone call she'd been putting off. She considered fortifying herself with a glass of wine first, but decided that would be weak.

She took off her reading glasses, set them aside. Slipped a bookmark into the pages, closed the book. And stared at the phone.

It was terrible to dread calling people you loved.

She put it off just a little longer by neatly stacking the books she'd bought. There were more than a dozen, and she was still amused at herself for picking up several on myths and legends.

They'd be entertaining, she thought, and wasted a little more time selecting the one she wanted for bedtime reading.

Then there was wood to be brought in for the evening fire, the soup bowl to wash and carefully dry. Her nightly scan of the woods for the wolf she hadn't seen all day.

When she couldn't find anything else to engage her time, she picked up the phone and dialed.

Twenty minutes later, she was sitting on the back steps, the backwash of light from the kitchen spilling over her. And she was weeping.

She'd nearly buckled under the benign pressure, nearly crumbled beneath the puzzled, injured tone of her mother's voice. Yes, yes, of course, she'd come home. She'd go back to teaching, get her doctorate, marry Alan, start a family. She'd live in a pretty house in a safe neighborhood. She'd be anything they wanted her to be as long as it made them happy.

Not saying all of those things, not doing them was so hard. And so necessary.

Her tears were hot and from the heart. She wished she understood why she was always, always pulled in a different direction, why she needed so desperately to see what was blurred at the edges of her mind.

Something was there, waiting for her. Something she was or needed to be. It was all she was sure of.

When the wolf nudged his head under her hand, she simply wrapped her arms around him and pressed her face to his throat.

''Oh, I hate hurting anyone. I can't bear it, and I can't stop it. What's wrong with me?''

Her tears dampened his neck. And touched his heart. To comfort he nuzzled her cheek, let her cling. Then he slipped a quiet thought into her mind.

Betray yourself, and you betray all they've given you. Love opens doors. It doesn't close them. When you go through it and find yourself, they'll still be there.

She let out a shuddering breath, rubbed her face against his fur. ''I can't go back, even though part of me wants to. If I did, I know something inside me would just…stop.'' She leaned back, holding his head in her hands. ''If I went back, I'd never find anything like you again. Even if it were there, I wouldn't really see it. I'd never follow a white doe or talk to an eagle.''

Sighing, she stroked his head, his powerful shoulders. ''I'd never let some gorgeous Irishman with a bad attitude kiss me, or do something as fun and foolish as eat cookies for breakfast.''

Comforted, she rested her head against his. ''I need to do those things, to be the kind of person who does them. That's what they can't understand, you know?

And it hurts and frightens them because they love me.''

She sighed again, leaned back, stroking his head absently as she studied the woods with their deep shadows, their whispering secrets. ''So I have to make this all work, so they stop being hurt and stop being frightened. Part of me is scared that I will make it work—and part of me is scared I won't.'' Her lips curved ruefully. ''I'm such a coward.''

His eyes narrowed, glinted, a low growl sounded in his throat making her blink. Their faces were close, and she could see those strong, deadly white teeth. Swallowing hard, she stroked his head with fingers that trembled.

''There now. Easy. Are you hungry? I have cookies.'' Heart hammering, she got slowly to her feet as he continued to growl. She kept her eyes on him, walking backward as he came up the steps toward her.

As she reached the door, one part of her mind screamed for her to slam it, lock it. He was a wild thing, feral, not to be trusted. But with her eyes locked on his, all she could think was how he had pressed his muzzle against her, how he had been there when she wept.

She left the door open.

Though her hand shook, she picked up a cookie, held it out. ''It's probably bad for you, but so many good things are.'' She muffled a yelp when he nipped it, with surprising delicacy, from her fingertips.

She'd have sworn his eyes laughed at her.

''Well okay, now we know sugar's as good as music for soothing savage beasts. One more, but that's it.''

When he rose onto his hind legs with surprising speed and grace, set those magnificent front paws on her shoulders, she could only manage a choked gasp. Her eyes, wide and round and shocked, met his glinting ones. Then he licked her, from collarbone to ear, one long, warm stroke, and made her laugh.

''What a pair we are,'' she murmured and pressed her lips to the ruff of his neck. ''What a pair.''

He lowered, just as gracefully, snatching the cookie from her fingers on the way.

''Clever, very clever.'' Eyeing him, she closed the lid on the cookies and set them on top of the refrigerator. ''What I need is a hot bath and a book,'' she decided. ''And that glass of wine I didn't let myself have before. I'm not going to think about what someone else wants,'' she continued as she turned to open the refrigerator. ''I'm not going to think about sexy neighbors with outrageously wonderful mouths. I'm going to think about how lovely it is to have all this time, all this space.''

She finished pouring the wine and lifted her glass in toast as he watched her. ''And to have you. Why don't you come upstairs and keep me company while I have that bath?''

The wolf ran his tongue around his teeth, let out a low sound that resembled a laugh and thought, *why don't I?*

She fascinated him. It wasn't a terribly comfortable sensation, but he couldn't shake it. It didn't matter how often he reminded himself she was an ordinary woman, and one with entirely too much baggage to become involved with.

He just couldn't stay away.

He'd been certain he'd tuned her out when she'd slammed her door behind her. Even though he'd been delighted with that flare of temper, the way it had flashed in her eyes, firmed that lovely soft mouth, he'd wanted to put her out of his mind for a few days.

Smarter, safer that way.

But he'd heard her weeping. Sitting in his little office, toying with a spin-off game for Myor, he'd heard those sounds of heartbreak, and despite the block he'd imposed, had felt her guilt and grief ripping at his heart.

He hadn't been able to ignore it. So he'd gone to her, offered a little comfort. Then she'd infuriated him, absolutely infuriated him by calling herself a coward. By believing it.

And what had the coward done, he thought, when a rogue wolf had snarled at her? Offered him a cookie.

A cookie, for Finn's sake.

She was utterly charming.

Then he had entertained, and tortured himself, by sitting and watching her lazily undress. Sweet God the woman had a way of sliding out of her clothes that made a man's head spin. Then, in a red robe she hadn't bothered to belt, she'd filled the old-fashioned tub with frothy bubbles that smelled of jasmine.

She'd lighted candles. Such a…female thing to do. She ran the water too hot, and had turned music on seductively low. As she shrugged out of the robe, she daydreamed. He resisted sliding into her mind to see what put that faraway look in her eyes, that faint smile on her lips.

Her body delighted him. It was so slender, so smooth, with a pearly sheen to the skin and slim, subtle curves. Delicate bones, tiny feet, and breasts tipped fragile blush-pink.

He wanted to taste there, to run his tongue from white to pink to white.

When she'd leaned over to turn off the taps, it had taken an enormous act of will to prevent himself from nipping at that firm, naked bottom.

It both irritated and charmed him that she seemed to have no vanity, no self-awareness. She piled her hair on top of her head in a gloriously messy mass, and didn't so much as glance at herself in the mirror.

Instead she talked to him, chattering nonsense, then hissed out a breath as she stepped into the tub. Steam billowed as she gingerly lowered herself, until the bubbles played prettily over her breasts.

Until he longed to reform and slip into the tub with her as a man.

She only laughed when he walked forward to sniff at her. Only ran a hand over his head absently while she picked up a book with the other.

Home Maintenance for the Confused and Inept.

It made him chuckle, the sound coming out as a soft *woof.* She gave his ears a quick scratch, then reached for her wine.

"It says here," she began, "that I should always have a few basic tools on hand. I think I saw all of these in the utility room, but I'd better make a list and compare. The next time the power goes out, or I blow a fuse—or is it a breaker?—I'm handling it myself. I won't be rescued by anyone, especially Liam Donovan.''

She gasped then chuckled when the wolf dipped his tongue into her glass and drank. ''Hey, hey! This is a very fine sauvignon blanc, and not for you, pal.'' She lifted the glass out of reach. ''It explains how to do simple rewiring,'' she continued. ''Not that I'm planning on doing any, but it doesn't look terribly complicated. I'm very good at following directions.''

A frown marred her brow. ''Entirely too good.'' She sipped wine, slid lower in the tub. ''That's the core of the problem. I'm *used* to following directions, so everyone's startled that I've taken a detour.''

She set the book aside, idly lifted a leg out of the water, skimmed a fingertip up her calf.

His mind moaned.

''No one's more surprised than I am that I like detours. Adventures,'' she added and grinned over at him. ''This is really my first adventure.'' She eased up again, bubbles clinging to her breasts. She scooped up a handful and idly rubbed them up and down her arm.

She only laughed when he ran his tongue slowly from her elbow to her shoulder. ''All in all, it's been a hell of an adventure so far.''

She lingered in the tub for a half hour, innocently delighting him. The scent of her as she toweled off made him yearn. He found her no less alluring when she slipped into the flannel pajamas.

When she crouched to build up the bedroom fire, he nipped and nuzzled, making her giggle. The next thing she knew she was wrestling playfully with a wolf on the hearth rug. His breath tickled her throat. She rubbed his belly and made him rumble with pleasure. His tongue was warm and wet on her cheek. Breathlessly happy she knelt to throw her arms around his neck, to hug fiercely.

"Oh, I'm so glad you're here. I'm so glad I found you." She pressed her cheek hard against his, locked her fingers in that silky fur. "Or did you find me?" she murmured. "It doesn't matter. It's so good to have a friend who doesn't expect anything but friendship."

She curled up with him to watch the fire, smiling at the pictures she found in the flames. "I've always liked doing this. When I was a little girl I was sure I saw things in the fire. Magic things," she murmured, and settled her head on his neck. "Beautiful things. Castles and clouds and cliffs." Her voice slurred as her eyes grew heavy. "Handsome princes and enchanted hills. I used to think I could go there, through the smoke and into the magic." She sighed, drifted. "Now there are only shapes and light."

And slept.

When she slept, he let himself be Liam, stroking her hair while he watched the fire she'd built. There was a way through the smoke and into the magic, he thought. What would she think if he showed her? If he took her there?

"But you'd have to come back to the other, Rowan. There's no way for me to keep you. I don't want to keep you,'' he corrected, firmly. ''But God, I want to have you.''

In sleep she sighed, shifted. Her arm came around him. He closed his eyes. ''You'd best hurry,'' he told her. ''Hurry and find out what you want and where you intend to go. Sooner or later I'll send for you.''

He rose, lifting her gently to carry her to bed. ''If you come to me,'' he whispered as he lowered her to the bed, spread the cover over her. ''If you come to me, Rowan Murray, I'll show you magic.'' Lightly he touched his lips to hers. ''Dream what you will tonight, and dream alone.''

He kissed her again, for himself this time. He left her as a man. And prowled the night mists as a wolf.

She spent the next week in the grip of tremendous energy, compelled to fill every minute of every day with something new. She explored the woods, haunted the cliffs and pleased herself by sketching whatever appealed to the eye.

As the weather gradually warmed, the bulbs she'd spotted began to bud. The night still carried a chill, but spring was ready to reign. Delighted, she left the windows open to welcome it in.

For that week she saw no one but the wolf. It was rare for him not to spend at least an hour with her. Walking with her on her hikes through the woods, waiting patiently while she examined the beginnings of a wildflower, a circle of toadstools or stopped to sketch the trees.

Her weekly call home made her heart ache, but she

told herself she felt strong. Dutifully she wrote a long letter to Alan, but said nothing about coming back.

Each morning she woke content. Each night she slipped into bed satisfied. Her only frustration was that she'd yet to discover what she needed to do. Unless, she sometimes thought, what she needed was simply to live alone with her books, her drawings and the wolf.

She hoped there was more.

Liam did not wake every morning content. Nor did he go to bed every night satisfied. He blamed her for it, though he knew it was unfair.

Still if she'd been less innocent, he would have taken what she'd once offered him. The physical need would have been met. And he assured himself this emotional pull would fade.

He refused to accept whatever fate had in store for him, for them, until he was completely in control of his own mind and body.

He stood facing the sea on a clear afternoon when the wind was warm and the air full of rioting spring. He'd come out to clear his head. His work wouldn't quite gel. And though he claimed continually that it was no more than a diversion, an amusement, he took a great deal of pride in the stories he created.

Absently he fingered the small crystal of fluorite he'd slipped into his pocket. It should have calmed him, helped to steady his mind. Instead his mind was as restless as the sea he studied.

He could feel the impatience in the air, mostly his own. But he knew the sense of waiting was from others. Whatever destination he was meant to reach, the steps to it were his own. Those who waited asked when he would take them.

"When I'm damned ready," he muttered. "My life remains mine. There's always a choice. Even with responsibility, even with fate, there is a choice. Liam, son of Finn, will make his own."

He wasn't surprised to see the white gull soar overhead. Her wing caught the sunlight, tipped gracefully as she flew down. And her eyes glinted, gold as his own, when she perched on a rock.

"Blessed be, Mother."

With only a bit more flourish than necessary, Arianna swirled from bird to woman. She smiled, opened her arms. "Blessed me, my love."

He went to her, enfolded her, pressed his face into her hair. "I've missed you. Oh, you smell of home."

"Where you, too, are missed." She eased back, but framed his face in her hands. "You look tired. You aren't sleeping well."

Now his smile was rueful. "No, not well. Do you expect me to?"

"No." And she laughed, kissed both his cheeks before turning to look out to sea. "This place you've chosen to spend some time is beautiful. You've always chosen well, Liam, and you will always have a choice." She slanted a look up at him. "The woman is lovely, and pure of heart."

"Did you send her to me?"

"The one day? Yes, or I showed her the way." Arianna shrugged and walked back to sit on the rock. "But did I send her here, no. There are powers beyond mine and yours that set events in order. You know that.'' She crossed her legs and the long white dress she wore whispered. ''You find her attractive.''

''Why wouldn't I?''

''She's not the usual type you're drawn to, at least to dally with.''

He set his teeth. ''A grown man doesn't care to have his mother discuss his sex life.''

''Oh.'' She waved a hand dismissively and set her rings flashing. ''Sex, when tempered with respect and affection, is healthy. I want my only child to be healthy, don't I? You won't dally with her because you worry it will involve more than sex, more than affection.''

''And what then?'' Anger simmered in his voice. ''Do I take her, engage her heart only to hurt her? 'An it harm none.' Does that only apply to magic?''

''No.'' She spoke gently, held out a hand to him. ''It should apply to life. Why assume you'll harm her, Liam?''

''I'm bound to.''

''No more than any man hurts any woman when their hearts bump together. You would take the same risks with her.'' She angled her head as she studied his face. ''Do you think your father and I have loved over thirty years without a scratch or bruise?''

''She's not like us.'' He squeezed the hand he held, then released it. ''If I take the steps, if I let us both feel more than we do now, I'd have to let her go or turn my back on my obligations. Obligations you know I came here to sort out.'' Furious with himself, he turned back to the sea. "I haven't even done that. I know my father wants me to take his place."

"Well not quite yet," Arianna said with a laugh. "But yes, when the time is right, it's hoped you'll stand as head of the family, as Liam of Donovan, to guide."

"It's a power I can pass to another. That's my right."

"Aye, Liam." Concerned now, she slid from the rock to go to him. "It's your right to step aside, to let another wear the amulet. Is that what you want?"

"I don't know." Frustration rang in his voice. "I'm not my father. I don't have his...way with others. His judgment. His patience or his compassion."

"No. You have your own." She laid a hand on his arm. "If you weren't fit for the responsibility, you would not be given it."

"I've thought of that, tried to come to accept it. And I know that if I commit to a woman not of elfin blood, I abdicate the right to take those responsibilities. If I let myself love her, I turn my back on my obligations to my family."

Arianna's eyes sharpened as she studied his face. "Would you?"

"If I let myself love her, I'd turn my back on anything, on everything but her."

She closed her eyes then, felt the tears welling in them. "Oh, it's proud I am to hear it, Liam." Eyes drenched she lay a hand on his heart. "There is no stronger magic, no truer power than love. This above all I want you to learn, to know, to feel."

Her hand closed into a fist so quickly, her eyes

flashed with annoyance so abruptly, he could only gape when she rapped his chest. ‘‘And for the love of Finn why haven’t you looked? Your powers are your gifts, your birthright and more acute than any I know but your father. What have you been doing?’’ she demanded, throwing up her hands and whirling with a spin of white silk. ‘‘Prowling the woods, calling to the moon, spinning your games. And brooding,’’ she added, jabbing a finger at him as she turned back. ‘‘Oh, a champion brooder you ever were, and that’s the truth of it. You’ll torture yourself with the wanting of her, go keep her company during a storm—’’

‘‘Which I know bloody well Da brewed.’’

‘‘That’s beside the point,’’ she snapped and skewered him with the sharp, daunting look he remembered from childhood. ‘‘If you don’t spend time with the girl you won’t think with anything but your glands, will you? The sex won’t answer it all, you horse’s ass. It’s just like a man to think it will.’’

‘‘Well, damn it, I *am* a man.’’

‘‘What you are is a pinhead, and don’t you raise your voice to me, Liam Donovan.’’

He threw up his hands as well, added a short, pithy curse in Gaelic. ‘‘I’m not twelve any longer.’’

‘‘I don’t care if you’re a hundred and twelve, you’ll show your mother proper respect.’’

He smoldered, seethed and sucked it in. ‘‘Yes, ma’am.’’

‘‘Aye.’’ She nodded once. ‘‘That’ll do. Now stop tormenting yourself with what may be, and look at what is. And if your lofty principles won’t let you look deep enough, ask her about her mother's family.''

Arianna let out a huff of breath, smoothed down her hair. ''And kiss me goodbye like a good lad. She'll be here any second.''

Because he was still scowling she kissed him instead, then grinned sunnily. ''There are times you look so like your Da. Now don't look so fierce, you'll frighten the girl. Blessed be, Liam,'' she added, then with a shiver of the light, spread white wings and soared into the sky.

Chapter 5

He hadn't sensed her, and that irritated him. His temper had been up, blocking his instincts. Now, even as he turned, he caught that scent—female, innocence with a light whiff of jasmine.

He watched her come out of the trees, though she didn't see him—not at first. The sun was behind him, and she looked the other way as she started up the rough path to the apex of the cliffs.

She had her hair tied back, he noted, in a careless tail of gleaming brown the wind caught and whipped. She carried a trim leather bag with its strap crosswise over her body. Her gray slacks showed some wear and her shirt was the color of daffodils.

Her mouth was unpainted, her nails short, her boots—so obviously new—showed a long, fresh scar across the left toe. The sight of her, muttering to herself as she climbed, both relaxed and annoyed him.

Then both sensations turned to pure amusement as she spotted him, jolted and scowled before she could school her expression to disinterest.

''Good morning to you, Rowan.''

She nodded, then clasped both hands on the strap of her bag as if she didn't know what else to do with them. Her eyes were cool, in direct contrast to those nervous hands, and quite deliberately skimmed past him.

''Hello. I'd have gone another way if I'd known you were here. I imagine you want to be alone.''

''Not particularly.''

Her gaze veered back to his, then away again. ''Well, I do,'' she said very definitely and began to make her way along the rocks away from him.

''Hold a grudge, do you, Rowan Murray?''

Stiffening with pride, she kept walking. ''Apparently.''

''You won't be able to for long, you know. It's not natural for you.''

She jerked a shoulder, knowing the gesture was bad-tempered and childish. She'd come to sketch the sea, the little boats that bobbed on it, the birds that soared and called above. And damn it, she'd wanted to look at the eggs in the nest to see if they'd hatched.

She hadn't wanted to see him, to be reminded of what had happened between them, what it had stirred inside her. But neither was she going to be chased away like a mouse by a cat. Setting her teeth, she sat on a ledge of rock, opened her bag. With precise movements she pulled out her bottle of water, put it beside her, then her sketchbook, then a pencil.

Ordering herself to focus, she looked out at the water, gave herself time to scan and absorb. She began to sketch, telling herself she would not look over at him. Oh, he was still there, she was sure of it. Why else would every muscle in her body be on alert, why would her heart still be tripping in her chest?

But she would not look.

Of course she looked. And he was still there, a few paces away, his hands tucked casually in his pockets, his face turned toward the water. It was just bad luck, she supposed, that he was so attractive, that he could stand there with the wind in all that glorious hair, his profile sharp and clean, and remind her of Heathcliff or Byron or some other poetic hero.

A knight before battle, a prince surveying his realm.

Oh, yes, he could be any and all of them—as romantic in jeans and a sweatshirt as any warrior glinting in polished armor.

"I don't mean to do battle with you, Rowan."

She thought she heard him say it, but that was nonsense. He was too far away for those soft words to carry. She'd just imagined that's what he *would* say in response if she'd spoken her thoughts aloud. So she sniffed, glanced back down at her book and to her disgust noted that she'd begun to sketch him without realizing it.

With an irritated flick, she turned to a blank page.

"There's no point in being angry with me—or yourself."

This time she knew he'd spoken, and looked up to see that he'd strolled over to her. She had to squint, to shade her eyes with the flat of her hand as the sun streamed behind him and shimmered its light like a nimbus around his head and shoulders.

"There's no point in discussing it."

She huffed out a breath as he sat companionably beside her. When he lapsed into silence, appeared to be settling in for a nice long visit, she tapped her pencil on her pad.

"It's a long coast. Would you mind plopping down on another part of it?"

"I like it here." When she hissed and started to rise, he simply tugged her back down. "Don't be foolish."

"Don't tell me I'm foolish. I'm really, really tired of being told I'm foolish." She jerked her arm free. "And you don't even know me."

He shifted so they were face-to-face. "That could be part of it. What are you drawing there in your book?"

"Nothing apparently." Miffed, she stuffed the book back into her bag. Once again she started to rise. Once again he tugged her easily back.

"All right," she snapped. "We'll discuss it. I admit I stumbled my way through the woods because I wanted to see you. I was attracted—I'm sure you're used to women being attracted to you. I did want to thank you for your help, but that was only part of it. I intruded, no question, but you were the one who kissed me."

"I did indeed," he murmured. He wanted to do so again, right now when her mouth was in a stubborn pout and there was both distress and temper in her eyes.

"And I overreacted to it." The memory of that still made her blood heat. "You had a perfect right to tell me to go, but you didn't have the right to be so unkind about it. No one has the right to be unkind. Now, obviously, you didn't have the same…response I did and you want to keep your distance."

She pushed at the hair that was coming loose from her ponytail to fly in her face. "So why are you here?"

"Let's take this in order," he decided. "Yes, I'm used to women being attracted to me. As I've a fondness for women I appreciate that." A smile tugged at his lips as she made a quiet sound of disgust. "You'd think more of me if I lied about that, but I find false modesty inane and deceitful. And though I most often prefer to be alone, your visit wasn't intrusive. I kissed you because I wanted to, because you have a pretty mouth."

He watched it register surprise before it thinned and she angled her face away. No one's told her that before, he realized, and shook his head over the idiocy of the male gender.

"Because you have eyes that remind me of the elves that dance in the hills of my country. Hair like oak that's aged and polished to a gleam. And skin so soft it seems my hand should pass through it as it would with water."

"Don't do that." Her voice shook as she lifted her arms, wrapped them tight to hug her elbows. "Don't. It's not fair."

Perhaps it wasn't, to use words on a woman who so obviously wasn't used to hearing them. But he shrugged. "It's just truth. And my response to you was more…acute than I'd bargained for. So I was unkind. I apologize for that, Rowan, but only for that."

She was over her head with him, and wished the terror of that wasn't quite so enjoyable. "You're sorry for being unkind, or for having a response to me?"

Clever woman, he mused, and gave her the simple truth. "For both if it comes to it. I said I wasn't ready for you, Rowan. I meant it."

It was hearing simple truth that softened her heart—and made it tremble just a little. She didn't speak for a moment, but stared down at the fingers she'd locked together in her lap while waves crashed below and gulls soared overhead.

"Maybe I understand that, a little. I'm at an odd place in my life," she said slowly. "A kind of crossroads, I suppose. I think people are most vulnerable when they come to the end of something and have to decide which beginning they're going to take. I don't know you, Liam." She made herself shift back to face him again. "And I don't know what to say to you, or what to do."

Was there a man alive who could resist that kind of unstudied honesty? he wondered. "Offer me tea."

"What?"

He smiled, took her hand. "Offer me tea. Rain's coming and we should go in."

"Rain? But the sun's—" Even as she said it, the light changed. Dark clouds slipped through the sky without a sound and the first drops, soft as a wish, fell.

His father wasn't the only one who could use the weather for his own purposes.

"Oh, it was supposed to be clear all day." She stuffed the bottle of water back into her bag, then let out a quick gasp when he pulled her to her feet with casual, effortless strength that left her limbs oddly weak.

"It's just a shower, and a warm one at that." He began to guide her through the rocks, down the path. "Soft weather, we call it at home. Do you mind the rain?"

"No, I like it. It always makes me dreamy." She lifted her face, let a few drops kiss it. "The sun's still shining."

"You'll have a rainbow," he promised and tugged her into the sheltering trees where the air was warm and wet, and shadows lay in deep green pools. "Will I have tea?"

She slanted him a look, and a smile. "I suppose."

"There, I told you." He gave her hand a little squeeze. "You don't know how to hold a grudge."

"I just need practice," she said and made him laugh.

"I'm likely to give you plenty of cause for practice before we're done."

"Do you make a habit of annoying people?"

"Oh, aye. I'm a difficult man." They strolled by the stream where damp ferns and rich moss spread, and foxglove waited to bloom. "My mother says I'm a brooder, and my father that I've a head like a rock. They should know."

"Are they in Ireland?"

"Mmm." He couldn't be sure unless he looked—and he damn well didn't want to know if they were lingering nearby watching him.

"Do you miss them?"

"I do, yes. But we…keep in touch." It was the wistfulness in her voice that had him glancing down as they walked into her clearing. "You're missing your family?"

"I'm feeling guilty because I don't miss them as much as I probably should. I've never been away alone before, and I'm—"

"Enjoying it," he finished.

"Enormously." She laughed a little and fished her keys out of her pocket.

"No shame in that." He cocked his head as she unlocked the door. "Who are you locking out?"

Her smile was a little sheepish as she stepped inside. "Habit. I'll put the tea on. I baked some cinnamon rolls earlier, but they're burned on the bottom. One of my misses."

"I'll take one off your hands." He wandered into the kitchen behind her.

She kept the room neat, he noted, and had added a few touches—the sort he recognized as a kind of nesting. Female making a home. Some pretty twigs speared out of one of Belinda's colorful bottles and stood in the center of the kitchen table beside a white bowl filled with bright green apples.

He remembered when she'd scouted out the twigs.

The wolf had walked with her—and had regally ignored her attempts to teach him to fetch.

He sat comfortably at her table, enjoying the quiet patter of rain. And thought of his mother's words. No, he wouldn't look that deeply. He didn't mind a skim through the thoughts, but that deliberate search was something he considered an abuse of power.

A man who demanded privacy had to respect that of others.

But he would pry without a qualm.

"Your family lives in San Francisco."

"Hmm. Yes." She had the kettle on and was choosing from one of Belinda's delightful collection of teapots. "They're both college professors. My father chairs the English department at the university."

"And your mother?" Idly, he slipped the sketchpad out of the bag she tossed on the table.

"She teaches history." After a mild debate, she selected a pot shaped like a faerie with wings for the handle. "They're brilliant," she continued, carefully measuring out tea. "And really marvelous instructors. My mother was made assistant dean last year and..."

She trailed off, stunned and just a little horrified when she saw Liam studying her sketch of the wolf.

"These are wonderful." He didn't bother to look up, but turned another page and narrowed his eyes in concentration at her drawing of a stand of trees and lacy ferns. Peeking through those airy shapes were the suggestion of wings, of laughing eyes.

She saw the faeries, he thought and smiled.

"They're just doodles." Her fingers itched to

snatch the book, close it away, but manners held her back. "It's just a hobby."

And when his eyes shot to hers, she nearly shivered.

"Why would you say that, and try to believe it, when you have a talent and a love for it?"

"It's only something I do in my spare time—now and again."

He turned the next page. She'd done a study of the cottage, made it look like something out of an old and charming legend with its ring of trees and welcoming porch. "And you're insulted when someone calls you foolish?" he muttered. "It's foolish you are if you don't do what you love instead of wringing your hands about it."

"That's a ridiculous thing to say. I do not wring my hands." She turned back to take the kettle off the bowl and prevent herself from doing exactly that. "It's a hobby. Most people have one."

"It's your gift," he corrected, "and you've been neglecting it."

"You can't make a living off of doodles."

"What does making a living have to do with it?"

His tone was so arrogantly royal, she had to laugh. "Oh, nothing other than food, shelter, responsibility." She came back to set the pot on the table, turned to fetch cups. "Little things like that from the real world."

"Then sell your art if you've a need to make a living."

"Nobody's going to buy pencil sketches from an English teacher."

"I'll buy this one." He rose and held the book open to one of her studies of the wolf. In it, the wolf stood, facing the onlooker with a challenging glint in his eyes exactly like the one in Liam's. "Name your price."

"I'm not selling it, and you're not buying it to make some point." Refusing to take him seriously, she waved him back. "Sit down and have your tea."

"Then give me the sketch." He angled his head as he looked at it again. "I like it. And this one." He flipped the page to the trees and fern faeries. "I could use something like this in the game I'm doing. I've no talent for drawing."

"Then who does the drawings for your graphics?" She asked hoping to change the subject, and as a last resort, got out the burned buns.

"Mmm. Different people for different moods." He sat again, absently took one of the rolls. It was hard and undeniably burned, but if you got past that, it was wonderfully sweet and generously filled with currants.

"So how do you—"

"Do either of your parents draw?" he interrupted.

"No." Even the thought of it made her chuckle. The idea of either of her smart and busy parents settling down to dream with pencil and paper. "They gave me lessons when I was a child and showed an interest. And my mother actually keeps a sketch I made of the bay when I was a teenager framed and in her office at the university."

"So she appreciates your talent."

"She loves her daughter," Rowan corrected and poured the tea.

"Then she should expect the daughter she loves to pursue her own gifts, explore her own talents," he said casually, but continued down the path of her family. "Perhaps one of your grandparents was an artist."

"No, my paternal grandfather was a teacher. It seems to come naturally through the family. My grandmother on that side was what I suppose you'd call a typical wife and mother of her time. She still keeps a lovely home."

He struggled against impatience—and against a wince as Rowan added three spoons of sugar to her cup. "And on your mother's side?"

"Oh, my grandfather's retired now. They live in San Diego. My grandmother does beautiful needlework, so I suppose that's a kind of art." Her lips pursed for a moment as she stirred her tea. "Now that I think of it, her mother—my great-grandmother painted. We have a couple of her oils. I think my grandmother and her brother have the rest. She was...eccentric," Rowan said with a grin.

"Was she now? And how was she eccentric?"

"I never knew her, but children pick up bits and pieces when adults gossip. She read palms and talked to animals—all decidedly against her husband's wishes. He was, as I recall, a very pragmatic Englishman, and she was a dreamy Irishwoman."

"So, she was Irish, was she?" Liam felt a low vibration along his spine. A warning, a frisson of power. "And her family name?"

"Ah..." Rowan searched back through her memory. "O'Meara. I'm named for her," she continued, contentedly drinking tea while everything inside Liam went on alert. "My mother named me for her in what she calls an irresistible flash of sentiment. I suppose that's why she—my great-grandmother—left me her pendant. It's a lovely old piece. An oval moonstone in a hammered silver setting."

In a slow and deliberate move, Liam set aside the tea he could no longer taste. "She was Rowan O'Meara."

"That's right. I think there was some wonderfully romantic story—or else I've made it up—about how my great-grandfather met her when he was on holiday in Ireland. She was painting on the cliffs—in Clare. That's odd, I don't know why I'm so sure it was Clare."

She puzzled over that for a moment, then shrugged it away. "Anyway, they fell in love on the spot, and she went back to England with him, left her home and her family. Then they immigrated to America, and eventually settled in San Francisco."

Rowan O'Meara from Clare. By the goddess, fate had twisted around and laid one more trap for him. He picked up his tea again to wet his throat. "My mother's family name is O'Meara." He spoke in a voice that was flat and cool. "Your great-grandmother would be a distant cousin of mine."

"You're kidding." Stunned and delighted, Rowan beamed at him.

"In matters such as family, I try not to joke."

"That would be amazing. Absolutely. Well, it's a small world." She laughed and lifted her cup. "Nice to meet you. Cousin Liam."

In the name of the goddess, he thought, and fatalistically tapped his cup to hers. The woman currently smiling at him out of those big, beautiful eyes had elfin blood, and didn't even know it.

"There's your rainbow, Rowan." He continued to look at her, but he knew the colored arch had spread in the sky outside. He hadn't conjured it—but sensed his father had.

"Oh!" She leaped up, and after one quick peek out the window, dashed to the door. "Come out and see. It's wonderful!"

She raced out, clattered down the steps and looked up.

She'd never seen one so clear, so perfectly defined. Against the watery-blue sky, each luminous layer stood out, shimmering at the edges with gold, melting into the next color, from rose to lavender to delicate yellow to candy-pink. It spread high, each tip grazing the tops of the trees.

"I've never seen one so beautiful."

When he joined her, he was both disconcerted and touched when she took his hand. But even as he looked up at the arch, he promised himself he wouldn't fall in love with her unless it was what he wanted.

He wouldn't be maneuvered, cajoled, seduced. He would make his decision with a clear mind.

But that didn't mean he couldn't take some of what he wanted in the meantime.

"This means nothing more, and nothing less than the other," he said.

"What?"

"This." He cupped her face, bent down and laid his lips on hers.

Soft as silk, gentle as the rain that was still falling through the pearly sunlight. He would keep it that way, for both of them, and lock down on the needs that were fiercer, more keen than was wise or safe.

Just a taste of that innocence, a glimpse of that tender heart she had no idea how to defend, he told himself. He would do what he could to keep that heart from falling too deeply or he might be forced to break it.

But when her hand came up to rest on his shoulder, when her mouth yielded so utterly under his, he felt those darker needs clawing for freedom.

She couldn't stop herself from giving, could hold nothing back against such tenderness. Even when the fingers on her face tightened, his mouth remained soft, easy, as if teaching hers what there was, what there could be.

Instinctively she soothed her hands over the tension of his shoulders and let herself sink into him.

He eased away before desire could outrace reason. When she only stared up at him with those exotic eyes blurred, those soft lips parted, he let her go.

"I guess it's just, ah, chemistry." Her heart was pounding in great, hammering leaps.

"Chemistry," he said, "can be dangerous."

"You can't make discoveries without some risks." It should have shocked her, a comment like that coming out of her mouth, such an obvious invitation to continue, to finish. But it seemed natural, and right.

"In this case it's best you know all the elements

you're dealing with. How much are you willing to find out, I wonder?''

''I came here to find out all sorts of things.'' She let out a quiet breath. ''I didn't expect to find you.''

''No. You're looking for Rowan first.'' He hooked his thumbs in his pockets, rocked back on his heels. ''If I took you inside, took you here for that matter, you'd find a part of her quickly enough. Is that what you want?''

''No.'' It was another surprise to hear the denial when every nerve in her body was sizzling. ''Because then it would be as you said before. Simple. I'm not looking for simple.''

''Still, I'll kiss you again, when I've a mind to.''

She angled her head, ignored the quick flutter in her belly. ''I'll let you kiss me again, when *I've* a mind to.''

He flashed a grin full of power and appreciation. ''You've some of that Irishwoman in you, Rowan of the O'Mearas.''

''Maybe I do.'' It pleased her enormously just then to think so. ''Maybe I'll have to find more.''

''That you will.'' His grin faded. ''When you do, I hope you know what to do about it. Pick a day next week and come over. Bring your sketchbook.''

''What for?''

''An idea I have brewing. We'll see if it suits both of us.''

It couldn't hurt, she mused. And it would give her some time to think about everything that had happened that morning. ''All right, but one day's the same as the next to me. My schedule's open these days.''

''You'll know which day when it comes.'' He reached out to toy with the ends of her hair. ''So will I.''

''And that, I suppose, is some kind of Irish mysticism.''

''You don't know the half of it,'' he murmured. ''A good day to you, Cousin Rowan.''

He gave her hair an absent tug, then turned and walked away.

Well, she thought, as days went, it hadn't been half-bad so far.

And when he came to her again in dreams, she welcomed him. When his mind touched hers, seduced it, aroused it, she sighed, yielded, offered.

She shivered in pleasure, breathed his name and sensed somehow that he was as vulnerable as she. For just that moment, just that misty space of time he was tangled with her, helpless not to give what she asked.

If only she knew the question.

Even when her body glowed, her mind soared, part of her fretted.

What should she ask him? What did she need to know?

In the dark, with the half-moon spilling delicate light through her open windows, she woke alone. She burrowed into the pillows and listened with her heart aching at the sound of the wolf calling to the night.

Chapter 6

Rowan watched spring burst into life. And watching, it seemed something burst into life inside her as well. Daffodils and windflowers shimmered into bloom. The little pear tree outside the kitchen window opened its delicate white blossoms and danced in the wind.

Deep in the forest, the wild azaleas began to show hints of pink and white, and the foxglove grew fat buds. There were others, so many others; she promised herself a book on local wildflowers on her next trip into town. She wanted to know them, learn their habits and their names.

All the while she felt herself begin to bloom. Was there more color in her face? she wondered, more light in her eyes? She knew she smiled more often, enjoyed the sensation of feeling her own lips curve up for no particular reason as she walked or sketched or simply sat on the porch in the warming air to read for hours.

Nights no longer seemed lonely. When the wolf came, she talked to him about whatever was on her mind. When he didn't, she was content to spend her evening alone.

She wasn't entirely sure what was different, only that something was. And that there were other, bigger changes yet to come.

Maybe it was the decision she'd made not to go back to San Francisco, or to teaching, or the practical apartment minutes from her parents' home.

She'd been cautious with money, she reminded herself. She'd never felt any particular urge to collect things or fill her closet with clothes or take elaborate vacations. Added to that was the small inheritance that had come down to her through her mother's family. One she had cautiously invested and watched grow neatly over the last few years.

There was enough to draw on for a down payment for a little house somewhere.

Somewhere quiet and beautiful, she thought now as she stood on the front porch with a cup of steaming coffee to welcome another morning. It had to be a house, she knew. No more apartment living. And somewhere in the country. She wasn't going to be happy in the bustle and rush of the city ever again. She'd have a garden she planted herself—once she learned how—and maybe a little creek or pond.

It had to be close enough to the sea that she could walk to it, hear its song at night as she drifted toward sleep.

Maybe, just maybe, on that next trip to town she'd visit a realtor. Just to see what was available.

It was such a big step—choosing a spot, buying a house—furnishing it, maintaining it. She caught herself winding the tip of her braid around her finger and deliberately dropped her hand. She was ready to make that step. She *would* make it.

And she'd find work, the kind that satisfied her. She didn't need a great deal of money. She'd be blissfully content puttering around some little cottage of her own, doing the painting, the repairs, watching her garden grow.

If she found something nearby, she wouldn't have to leave the wolf.

Or Liam.

With that thought, she shook her head. No, she couldn't add Liam into the equation, or make him part of the reason she was considering settling in the area. He was his own man, and would come and go when and where he pleased.

Just like the wolf, she realized and sighed. Neither one of them were hers, after all. They were both loners, both beautiful creatures who belonged to no one. And who'd come into her life—helped change it in some ways, she supposed. Though the biggest changes were up to her.

It seemed that after three weeks in the little cabin in the clearing, she was ready to make them. Not just drifting anymore, she thought. Not just wondering. Time to take definite steps.

The subtle tug at her mind had her eyes narrowing, her head angling as if to hear something soft whispered in the distance. It was almost as if she could hear her name, quietly called.

He'd said to come to him, she remembered. That she'd know when the time was right. Well, there was no time like the present, no better time than when she was in such a decisive mood. And after the visit, she'd drive into town and see that realtor.

He knew she was coming. He'd been careful to keep his contact with her limited over the past several days. Perhaps he hadn't been able to stay away completely. He did worry about her just a bit, thinking of her alone, and more out of her element than she knew.

But it was easy enough to check up on her, to walk to her door and have her open it for him. He could hardly deny he enjoyed the way she welcomed him, bending down to stroke his head and back or nuzzle her face against his throat.

She had no fear of the wolf, he mused. He only made her wary when he was a man.

But she was coming to the man, and would have to deal with him. He thought his plan a good one, for both of them. One that would give her the opportunity to explore her own talents—and would give each of them time to learn more about the other.

He wouldn't touch her again until they did. He'd promised himself that. It was too difficult to sample and not take fully. And on those nights he allowed himself to take her with his mind, he left her glowing and satisfied. And left himself oddly unfulfilled.

Still, it was preparing her for him, for the night when he would make those half dreams full reality.

For the night when it was his hands and not his mind on her.

The thought of it had his stomach knotting, his muscles bunching tight. Infuriated with the reaction, he ordered his mind to clear, his body to relax. And was only more infuriated when even his powers didn't calm all the tension.

"The day hasn't come when I can't handle a physical reaction to some pretty half witch," he muttered, and walked back inside his cabin.

Damned if he was going to stand on the porch like some starry-eyed lover and watch for her.

So instead he paced and uttered vile Gaelic curses until he heard the knock on his door.

Mood inexplicably foul, Liam flung open the door. And there she stood, with the sun streaming behind her, a delighted smile on her face, her hair coming loose from her braid and a clutch of tiny purple flowers in her hand.

"Good morning. I think they're wood violets, but I'm not completely sure. I need to buy a book."

She offered them, and Liam felt the heart he was so determined to defend, tremble in his breast. Innocence shined in her eyes, lovely color glowed in her cheeks. And there were wildflowers in her hand.

All he could do was stare. And want.

When he didn't respond, she lowered her hand. "Don't you like flowers?"

"I do, yes. Sorry, I was distracted." For the goddess's sake, get a hold of yourself, Donovan. But even with the order, his scowl was in direct contrast to his words. "Come in, Rowan Murray. You're welcome here, as are your flowers."

"If I've come at a bad time," she began, but he was already stepping back, widening the opening of the door in invitation. "I thought I would come by before I drove into town."

"For more books?" He left the door open, as if to give her a route of escape.

"For those, and to talk to someone about property. I'm thinking of buying some in the area."

"Are you now?" His brow winged up. "Is this the place for you?"

"It seems to be. It could be." She moved her shoulders. "Someplace must be."

"And have you decided—how did you put it—what you'll do to make your living?"

"Not exactly." The light in her eyes dimmed a little with worry. "But I will."

He was sorry to have put that doubt on her face. "I have an idea about that. Come back to the kitchen, and we'll find something to put your little flowers in."

"Have you been in the woods? Everything's starting to pop and bloom. It's wonderful. And all these marvelous flowers around Belinda's cottage. I don't recognize half of them, or the ones around yours."

"Most are simple, and useful for one thing or another." He rooted out a tiny blue vase for the violets as she craned up to peer out his kitchen window.

"Oh, you've more back here. Are they herbs?"

"Aye, herbs they are."

"For cooking."

"For that." A smile tugged at his lips as he slipped the delicate stems into the glass. "And all manner of things. Will you hunt up a book on herbs now?"

"Probably." She laughed and dropped back to the flats of her feet. "There's so much I've never paid attention to. Now I can't seem to find out enough."

"And that includes yourself."

She blinked. "I suppose it does."

"So..." He couldn't resist and pleased himself by toying with the ends of her braid. "What have you found out about Rowan?"

"That she's not as inept as she thought."

His gaze swept back up to hers, sharpened. "And why would you have thought that?"

"Oh, I don't mean about everything. I know how to learn, and how to apply what I learn. I'm organized and practical and I have a good mind. It was the little things and the really big ones I never seemed to know what to do about. Anything in between I handled just fine. But the little things I let go, and the big ones...I always felt I should do what others thought I should do about them."

"I'm about to give you a suggestion on what you'd call a big thing. I expect you to do as you like about it."

"What is it?"

"In a bit," he said with a vague wave of his hand. "Come in here and have a look at what I'm doing."

Baffled, she walked into the adjoining office with him. His computer was up and running, the screen saver swimming with moons and stars and symbols she didn't recognize. He tapped a key and had text popping up.

"What do you think?" he asked her, and she bent forward to read. A moment later she was laughing. "I think I can't read what appears to be computer signals and some foreign language."

He glanced down, let out an impatient huff of breath. He'd gotten so involved in the story line he hadn't considered. Well, that could be fixed. He nearly flicked his wrist to have the straight story line brought up, caught himself not a moment too soon, then made a show of tapping keys while the basic spell ran through his mind.

"There." The screen jiggled, then blipped and brought up new text. "Sit down and read it."

Since nothing would have delighted her more, she did as he asked. It only took a few lines for her to understand. "It's a sequel to Myor." Thrilled, she turned her face up to his. "That's wonderful. You've written another. Have you finished it?"

"If you'd read it you'd see for yourself."

"Yes, yes." This time it was she who waved him away as she settled down to be entertained. "Oh! Kidnapped. She's been kidnapped and the evil warlock's put a spell on her to strip her of her powers."

"Witch," he muttered, wincing a little. "A male witch is still a witch."

"Really? Well... He's locked all her gifts up in a magic box. It's because he's in love with her, isn't it?"

"What?"

"It has to be," Rowan insisted. "Brinda's so beautiful and strong and full of light. He'd want her, and this is his way of forcing her to belong to him."

Considering, Liam slipped his hands into his pockets. "Is it now?"

"It must be. Yes, here's the handsome warlock—I mean witch who'll do battle with the evil one to get the box of power. It's wonderful."

She all but put her nose to the screen, annoyed she hadn't thought to put on her reading glasses. "Just look at all the traps and spells he'll have to fight just to get to her. Then when he frees her, she won't have any magic to help. Just her wits," Rowan murmured, delighted with the story. "They'll face all this together, risk destruction. Wow, The Valley of Storms. Sounds ominous, passionate. This is what was missing from the first one."

More stunned than insulted, he gaped at her. "Excuse me?"

"It had such wonderful magic and adventure, but no romance. I'm so glad you've added it this time. Rilan will fall madly in love with Brinda, and she with him as they work together, face all these dangers."

Her eyes gleamed as she leaned back and refocused them on Liam. "Then when they defeat the evil witch, find the box, it should be their love that breaks the spell, opens it and gives Brinda back her powers. So they'll live happily ever after."

She smiled a bit hesitantly at the shuttered look in his eyes. "Won't they?"

"Aye, they will." With a few adjustments to the story line, he decided. But that was his task, and for later. By Finn, the woman had it right. "What do you think of the magic dragons in the Land of Mirrors."

"Magic dragons?"

"Here." He bent down, leaning close and manually scrolling to the segment. "Read this," he said and his breath feathered warm across her cheek. "And tell me your thoughts."

She had to adjust her thoughts to block out the quick jump of her pulse, but dutifully focused on the words and read. "Fabulous. Just fabulous. I can just see them flying away on the back of a dragon, over the red waters of the sea, and the mist-covered hills."

"Can you? Show me how you see it—just that. Draw it for me." He pulled her sketchbook out of her bag. "I haven't got a clear image of it."

"No? I don't know how you could write this without it." She picked up a pencil and began to draw. "The dragon should be magnificent. Fierce and beautiful, with wonderful gold wings and eyes like rubies. Long and sleek and powerful," she murmured as she sketched. "Wild and dangerous."

It was precisely what he'd wanted, Liam noted as the drawing came to life under her hand. No tame pet, no captured oddity. She had it exactly: the proud, fierce head, the long powerful body with its wide sweep of wings, the slashing tail, the feel of great movement.

"Do another now." Impatient, he tore off the first sketch, set it aside. "Of the sea and hills."

"All right." She supposed a rough drawing might help him get a more solid visual for his story. Closing her eyes a moment, she brought the image into her mind, that wide, shimmering sea with cresting waves, the jagged rocks that speared silver out of thick swirling mists, the glint of sunlight gilding the edges, and the dark shadow of mountains beyond.

When she was done with it, he ripped that page away as well, demanded she do another. This time of Yilard, the evil witch.

She had great fun with that, grinning to herself as she worked. He should be handsome, she decided. Cruelly so. No wart-faced gnome with a hunched back, but a tall, dashing man with flowing hair and hard dark eyes. She dressed him in robes, imagined they would be red, like a prince.

''Why didn't you make him ugly?'' Liam asked her.

''Because he wouldn't be. And if he were, it might seem as if Brinda refused him just because of his looks. She didn't—it was his heart she rejected. The darkness of it that you'd see in the eyes.''

''But the hero, he'd be more handsome.''

''Of course. We'd expect, even demand that. But he won't be one of those girlishly pretty men with curly gold hair.'' Lost in the story, she tore off the page herself to begin another. ''He'll be dark, dangerous, too. Brave certainly, but not without flaws. I like my heroes human. Still, he risked his life for Brinda, first for honor. And then for love.''

She laughed a little as she leaned back from the sketch. ''He looks a bit like you,'' she commented. ''But why not? It's your story. Everyone wants to be the hero of their own story after all.'' She smiled at him. ''And it's a wonderful story, Liam. Can I read the rest?''

''Not yet.'' There were changes to be made now, he thought, and switched off the screen.

''Oh.'' Disappointment rang in her voice, and fed his ego. ''I just want to see what happens after they fly out of the Land Of Mirrors.''

''If you do, you'll have to accept my proposition.''

''Proposition?''

''A business one. Do the drawings for me. All of them. It's a great deal of work as most of the levels will be complex. I'll need an exacting amount of detail for the graphics, and I'm not easily satisfied.''

She held up a hand. She wanted to stop him, to give herself time to find her voice. ''You want me to draw the story?''

''It's not a simple matter. I'll require hundreds of sketches, all manner of scenes and angles.''

''I don't have any experience.''

''No?'' He lifted her sketch of the dragon.

''I just tossed those off,'' she insisted, pushing to her feet with a sense of panic. ''I didn't think.''

''Is that the way of it?'' Interesting. ''Fine then, don't think, just draw.''

She couldn't keep up, couldn't quite catch her breath. ''You can't be serious.''

''I'm very serious,'' he corrected, and laid the sketch down again. ''Were you when you said you wanted to do what made you happy?''

''Yes.'' She was rubbing a hand over her heart, unaware of the movement.

''Then work with me on this if it pleases you.

You'll make the living you need. The Donovan Legacy will see to that part well enough. It's up to you, Rowan."

"Wait, just wait." She kept her hand up, turned away to walk to the window. The sky was still blue, she noted, the forest still green. And the wind blew with the same steady breath.

It was only her life that was changing. If she let it.

To do something she loved for a living? To use it freely and with pleasure and have it give back everything she needed? Could that be possible? Could it be real?

And it was then she realized it wasn't panic hot in her throat, pounding in her blood. It was excitement.

"Do you mean this? Do you think my sketches would suit your story?"

"I wouldn't have said so otherwise. The choice is yours."

"Mine," she said, quietly, like a breath. "Then, yes, it would please me very much." Her voice was slow, thoughtful. But when the full scope of his offer struck, she whirled around, her eyes brilliant. He saw those tiny silver lights in her eyes. "I'd love to work with you on it. When do we start?"

He took the hand she held out, clasped it firmly in his. "We just did."

Later, when Rowan was back in her kitchen celebrating with a glass of wine and a grilled cheese sandwich, she tried to remember if she'd ever been happier.

She didn't think so.

She'd never gotten into town for her books and her house hunting, but that would come. Instead, she mused, she'd found an opening to a new career. One that thrilled her.

She had a chance now, a true and tangible chance for a new direction.

Not that Liam Donovan was going to make it easy. On the contrary, she decided, licking cheese from her thumb. He was demanding, occasionally overbearing and very, very much the perfectionist.

She'd done a full dozen sketches of the gnomes of Firth before he'd approved a single one.

And his approval, as she recalled, had been a grunt and a nod.

Well, that was fine. She didn't need to be patted on the head, didn't require effusive praise. She appreciated the fact that he expected her to be good, that he already assumed they'd make a successful team.

A team. She all but hugged the word to her. That made her part of something. After all these years of quiet wishing, she was telling stories. Not with words; she never had the right words. But with her drawings. The thing she loved most and had convinced herself over the years was an acceptable hobby and no more.

Now it was hers.

Still, she was in many ways a practical woman. She'd cut through her delight to the basics and had discussed terms with him. A pity she wasn't clever enough to have masked her sheer astonishment at the amount he'd told her she'd be paid for the work.

She'd have her house now, she thought, and giggling with glee poured herself a second glass of wine. She'd buy more art supplies, more books. Plants. She'd scout out wonderful antiques to furnish her new home.

And live happily ever after, she thought, toasting herself.

Alone.

She shook off the little pang. She was getting used to alone. Enjoying alone. Maybe she still felt quick pulls and tugs of attraction for Liam, but she understood there would be no acting on them now that they were working together.

He'd certainly demonstrated no sign of wanting a more personal relationship now. If that stung the pride a bit, well, she was used to that, too.

She'd had a terrifying crush on the captain of the debate team her senior year in high school. She could clearly remember those heartbreaking flutters and thrills every time she caught sight of him. And how she'd wished, miserably, she could have been more outgoing, more brightly pretty, more confident, like the girl he'd gone steady with.

Then in college it had been an English major, a poet with soulful eyes and a dark view of life. She'd been sure she could inspire him, lift his soul. When after nearly a full semester he'd finally turned those tragic eyes her way, she'd fallen like a ripe plum from a branch.

She didn't regret it, even though after two short weeks, he'd turned those same tragic eyes to another woman. After all, she'd had two weeks of storybook romance, and had given up her virginity to a man with some sensitivity if no sense of monogamy.

It hadn't taken her long to realize that she hadn't loved him. She'd loved the idea of him. After that his careless rejection hadn't stung quite so deeply.

Men simply didn't find her…compelling, she decided. Mysterious or sexy. And unfortunately, the ones she was most attracted to always seemed to be all of that.

With Liam, he was all of that and more.

Of course, there had been Alan, she remembered. Sweet, steady, sensible Alan. Though she loved him, she'd known as soon as they'd become lovers that she'd never feel that wild thrill with him, that grinding need or that rush of longing.

She'd tried. Her parents had settled on him and it seemed logical that she would gradually fall in love, all the way in love, and make a comfortable life with him.

Hadn't it been the thought of that, a comfortable life, that had finally frightened her enough to make her run?

She could say now she'd been right to do so. It would have been wrong to settle for less than…anything, she supposed. For less than what she was finding now. Her place, her wants, her flaws and her talents.

They wouldn't understand—not yet. But in time they would. She was sure of it. After she was established in a home of her own, with a career of her own, they would see. Maybe, just maybe, they'd even be proud of her.

She glanced at the phone, considered, then shook her head. No, not yet. She wouldn't call her parents and tell them what she was doing. Not quite yet. She didn't want to hear the doubt, the concern, the carefully masked impatience in their voices, and spoil the moment.

It was such a lovely moment.

So when she heard the knock on the front door, she sprang up. It was Liam, had to be Liam. And oh, that was perfect. He'd brought more work, and they could sit in the kitchen and discuss it, toy with it.

She'd make tea, she thought as she hurried through the cabin. A glass and a half of wine was enough if she wanted her mind perfectly clear. She'd had another idea about the Land of Mirrors and how that red sea should reflect when she'd walked home.

Eager to tell him, she opened the door. Her delighted smile of welcome shifted to blank shock.

''Rowan, you shouldn't open the door without seeing who it is first. You're much too trusting for your own good.''

With the spring breeze blowing behind him, Alan stepped inside.

Chapter 7

"Alan, what are you doing here?"

She knew immediately her tone had been short and unwelcoming—and very close to accusatory. She could see it in the surprised hurt on his face.

"It's been over three weeks, Rowan. We thought you might appreciate a little face-to-face. And frankly..." He shoved at the heavy sand-colored hair that fell over his forehead. "The tenor of your last phone call worried your parents."

"The tenor?" She bristled, and struggled to fix on a pleasant smile. "I don't see why. I told them I was fine and well settled in."

"Maybe that's what concerns them."

The worry in his earnest brown eyes brought her the first trickle of guilt. Then he took off his coat, laid it neatly over the banister and made a pocket of resentment open under the guilt. "Why would that be a concern?"

"None of us really knows what you're doing up here—or what you hope to accomplish by cutting yourself off from everyone."

"I've explained all of that." Now there was weariness along with the guilt. It was her cottage, damn it, her life. They were being invaded and questioned. But manners had her gesturing to a chair. "Sit down, please. Do you want anything? Tea, coffee?"

"No, I'm fine, but thanks." He did sit, looking stiffly out of place in his trim gray suit and starched white Oxford shirt. He still wore his conservatively striped, neatly Windsor-knotted tie. It hadn't occurred to him to so much as loosen it for the trip.

He scanned the room now as he settled in a chair by the quiet fire. From his viewpoint the cabin was rustic and entirely too isolated. Where was the culture—the museums, the libraries, the theaters? How could Rowan stand burying herself in the middle of the woods for weeks on end?

All she needed, he was certain, was a subtle nudge and she'd pack up and come back with him. Her parents had assured him of it.

He smiled at her, that crooked, slightly confused smile that always touched her heart. "What in the world do you do here all day?"

"I've told you in my letters, Alan." She sat across from him, leaned forward. This time, she was certain, she could make him understand. "I'm taking some time to think, to try to figure things out. I go for long walks, read, listen to music. I've been doing a lot of sketching. In fact—''

''Rowan, that's all well and good for a few days,'' he interrupted, the patience so thick in his voice her teeth went instantly on edge. ''But this is hardly the place for you. It's easy enough to read between the lines of your letters that you've developed some sort of romantic attachment for solitude, for living in some little cottage in the middle of nowhere. But this is hardly Walden Pond.''

He shot her that smile again, but this time it failed to soften her. ''And I'm not Thoreau. Granted. But I'm happy here, Alan.''

She didn't look happy, he noted. She looked irritable and edgy. Certain he could help her, he patted her hand. ''For now, perhaps. For the moment. But what happens after a few more weeks, when you realize it's all just a...'' He gestured vaguely. ''Just an interlude,'' he decided. ''By then it'll be too late to get your position back at your school, to register for the summer courses you planned to take toward your doctorate. The lease is up for your apartment in two months.''

Her hands were locked together in her lap now, to keep them from forming fists and beating in frustration on the arms of the chair. ''It's not just an interlude. It's my life.''

''Exactly.'' He beamed at her, as she had often seen him beam at a particularly slow student who suddenly grasped a thorny concept. ''And your life is in San Francisco. Sweetheart, you and I both know you need more intellectual stimulation than you can find here. You need your studies, your students. What about your monthly book group? You have to be missing it. And the classes you planned to take? And you haven't mentioned a word about the paper you were writing."

"I haven't mentioned it because I'm not writing it. I'm not going to write it." Because it infuriated her that her fingers were beginning to tremble, she wrenched them apart and sprang up. "And I didn't plan on taking classes, other people planned that for me. The way they've planned every step I've ever taken. I don't want to study, I don't want to teach. I don't want any intellectual stimulation that I don't choose for myself. This is exactly what I've told you before, what I've told my parents before. But you simply refuse to hear."

He blinked, more than a little shocked at her sudden vehemence. "Because we care about you, Rowan. Very much." He rose as well. His voice was soothing now. She rarely lost her temper, but he understood when she did she threw up a wall no amount of logic could crack. You just had to wait her out.

"I know you care." Frustrated, she pressed her fingers to her eyes. "That's why I want you to hear, I want you to understand, or if understanding is too much, to accept. I'm doing what I need to do. And, Alan—" She dropped her hands, looked directly into his eyes. "I'm not coming back."

His face stiffened, and his eyes went cool as they did when he had outlined a logical premise and she disagreed with him. "I certainly hoped you'd had enough of this foolishness by now and would fly back with me tonight. I'm willing to find a hotel in the area for a few days, and wait."

"No, Alan, you misunderstand. I'm not coming back to San Francisco. At all. Not now, not later."

There, she thought, she'd said it. And a huge weight seemed to lift off her heart. It remained light even when she read the irritation in his eyes.

"That's just nonsense, Rowan. It's your home, of course you'll come back."

"It's your home, and it's my parents' home. That doesn't make it mine." She reached out to take his hands, so happy with her own plans she wanted him to be. "Please try to understand. I love it here. I feel so at home, so settled. I've never really felt like this before. I've even got a job sketching. It's art for a computer game. It's so much *fun,* Alan. So exciting. And I'm going to look into buying a house somewhere in the area. A place of my own, near the sea. I'm going to plant a garden and learn how to really cook and—"

"Have you lost your mind?" He turned his hands over to grip hers almost painfully. None of the sheer joy on her face registered. Only the words that were to him the next thing to madness. "Computer games? Gardens? Are you listening to yourself?"

"Yes, for the first time in my life that's just what I'm doing. You're hurting me, Alan."

"I'm hurting you?" He came as close to shouting as she'd ever heard, and transferred his grip from her hands to her shoulders. "What about what I feel, what I want? Damn it, Rowan, I've been patient with you. You're the one who suddenly and for no reason that made sense decided to change our relationship. One night we're lovers, the next day we're not. I didn't press, I didn't push. I tried to understand that you needed more time in that area.''

She'd bungled things, she realized. She'd bungled it and hurt him unnecessarily out of her inability to find the right words. Even now, she fumbled with them. ''Alan, I'm sorry. I'm so sorry. It wasn't a matter of time. It was—''

''I've circled around this incomprehensible snit of yours,'' he continued, fired up enough to give her a quick shake. ''I've given you more room than anyone could expect, believing you wanted a bit more freedom before we settled down and married. Now it's computer games? *Games?* And cabins in the woods?''

''Yes, it is. Alan—''

She was near tears, very near them, had lifted a hand to his chest, not to push him away, but to try to soothe. With a great feral howl, the wolf leaped through the open window. Fangs gleamed white in the lamplight as he sprang, a vicious snarl erupting from his throat.

His powerful forelegs caught Alan just below the shoulders, knocked him back. A table snapped as the combined weight crashed into it. And before Rowan could draw breath, Alan was lying white-faced on the floor with the black wolf snapping at his throat.

''No, no!'' Terror gave her both speed and strength. She jumped to them, dived down to wrap her arms around the wolf's neck. ''Don't, don't hurt him. He wasn't hurting me.''

She could feel the muscles vibrating beneath her, hear the growls rumble like threatening thunder. The horrible image of ripped flesh, pumping blood, screams raced through her head. Without a thought she shifted, pushed her face between them and looked into the wolf's glowing eyes.

There she saw savagery.

"He wasn't hurting me," she said calmly. "He's a friend. He's upset, but he'd never hurt me. Let him up now, please."

The wolf snarled again, and something flashed in his eyes that was almost…human, she thought. She could smell the wildness around him, in him. Very gently she laid her cheek against his. "It's all right now." Her lips grazed his fur. "Everything's all right."

Slowly he moved back. But his body shoved against hers until he stood between her and Alan. As a precaution, she kept a hand on the ruff of his neck as she got to her feet.

"I'm sorry, Alan. Are you hurt?"

"Name of God, name of God." It was all he could manage in a voice that shook. Sheer terror had his muscles weak as water. Each breath burned his lungs, and his chest was bruised where the beast had attacked him. "Get away from it, Rowan. Get back." Though he trembled all over from shock, he crawled to his feet, grabbed a lamp. "Get away, get upstairs."

"Don't you dare hit him." Indignant, she snatched the lamp out of Alan's unsteady hands. "He was only protecting me. He thought you were hurting me."

''Protecting you? For the love of God, Rowan, that's a wolf.''

She jerked back when he tried to grab her, then followed instinct and told perhaps the first outright lie of her life. ''Of course it's not. Don't be absurd. It's a dog.'' She thought she felt the wolf jolt under her hand at the claim. Out of the corner of her eye she saw him angle his head up and...well, glare at her. ''My dog,'' she insisted. ''And he did precisely what you would expect from a well-trained dog. He protected me against what he saw as a threat.''

''A dog?'' Staggered and far from convinced he wasn't about to have his throat torn out, Alan shifted his gaze to her. ''You have a dog?''

''Yes.'' The lie was starting to twist around her tongue. ''Um. And as you can see, I couldn't be safer here. With him.''

''What kind of dog is that?''

''I don't precisely know.'' Oh, she was a miserably poor liar, she thought. ''He's been wonderful company, though, and as you can see I don't have to worry about being alone. If I hadn't called him off, he'd have bitten you.''

''It looks like a damn wolf.''

''Really, Alan.'' She did her best to laugh, but it came out thin and squeaky. ''Have you ever heard of a wolf leaping through a window, or taking commands from a woman? He's marvelous.'' She leaned down to nuzzle her face against his fur. ''And as gentle with me as a Labrador.''

As if in disgust, the wolf shot her one steely look, then walked over to sit by the fire.

"See?" She didn't let her breath shudder out in relief, but she wanted to.

"You never said anything about wanting a dog. I believe I'm allergic." He dug out a handkerchief to catch the first sneeze.

"I never said a lot of things." She crossed to him again, laying her hands on his arms. "I'm sorry for that, I'm sorry I didn't know what to say or how to say it until now."

Alan's eyes kept sliding back toward the wolf. "Could you put him outside?"

Put him outside? she thought, and felt another shaky laugh tickling her throat. The wolf came and went as he pleased. "He's all right, I promise. Come sit down—you're still shaken up."

"Small wonder," he muttered. He would have asked her for a brandy, but imagined she'd have to leave the room to get it. He wasn't risking being alone with that great black hulk.

As if to show the wisdom of this decision, the wolf bared his teeth.

"Alan." Rowan sat on the couch beside him, took his hands in hers. "I am sorry. For not understanding myself soon enough or clearly enough to make you understand. For not being what you'd hoped I would be. But I can't change any of that, and I can't go back to what was."

Alan pushed his heavy hair back again. "Rowan, be reasonable."

"I'm being as reasonable as I know how. I do care for you, Alan, so much. You've been a wonderful friend to me. Now be a friend and be honest. You're not in love with me. It just seemed you should be."

"Of course I love you, Rowan."

Her smile was just a little wistful as she brushed back his hair herself. "If you were *in* love with me, you couldn't have been so reasonable about not sleeping with me anymore." Her smile warmed with affection when he fidgeted. "Alan, we've been good friends, but we were mediocre lovers. There was no passion between us, no urgency or desperation."

Discussing such a matter quite so frankly embarrassed him. He'd have risen to pace, but the wolf had growled quietly again. "Why should there be?"

"I don't know, I just know there should. There has to be." Thoughtfully she reached up to straighten his tie. "You're the son my parents always wanted. You're kind, and you're smart and so wonderfully steady. They love both of us." She lifted her gaze to his, thought—hoped—she saw the beginnings of understanding there. "So they assumed we'd cooperate and marry each other. And they convinced you that you wanted the same thing. But do you, Alan, do you really?"

He looked down at their joined hands. "I can't imagine you not being part of my life."

"I'll always be part of it." She tilted her head, leaned forward and laid her lips on his. At the gesture, the wolf rose, stalked over and snarled. She put an absent hand on his head as she drew back, and studied Alan. "Did that make your blood swim or your heart flip? Of course not," she murmured before he could answer. "You don't want me, Alan, not the way a man wildly in love wants. You can't make love and passion logical."

"If you came back, we could try." When she only shook her head, he tightened his grip on her hand. "I don't want to lose you, Rowan. You matter to me."

"Then let me be happy. Let me know that at least one person I matter to, and who matters to me, can accept what I want to do."

"I can't stop you." Resigned now, he lifted his shoulders. "You've changed, Rowan. In three short weeks, you've changed. Maybe you are happy, or maybe you're just playing at being happy. Either way, we'll all be there if you change your mind."

"I know."

"I should go. It's a long drive to the airport."

"I—I can fix you a meal. You can stay the night if you like and go back in the morning."

"It's best if I go now." Skimming a cautious glance toward the hovering wolf, he rose. "I don't know what I think, Rowan, and don't honestly know what I'll say to your parents. They were sure you'd be coming back with me."

"Tell them I love them. And I'm happy."

"I'll tell them—and try to convince them. But since I'm not sure I believe it myself…" He sneezed again, backed away. "Don't get up," he told her, certain it was safer if she kept that light hand on her dog's ferocious head. "I'll let myself out. You ought to get a collar for that thing, at least…make sure he's had his shots and—"

The sneezing fit shook his long, lanky frame so that he walked to the door with the handkerchief over his face. It looked as though the dog was grinning at him, which he knew was ridiculous.

"I'll call you," he managed to say, and rushed out into the fresh air.

"I hurt him." Rowan let out a deep sigh and laid her cheek atop the wolf's head as she listened to the sound of the rental car's engine spring to life. "I couldn't find a way not to. Just like I couldn't find the way to love him." She turned her face, comforting herself with the feel of that warm, soft fur. "You're so brave, you're so strong," she crooned. "And you scared poor Alan half to death."

She laughed a little, but the sound was perilously close to a sob. "Me, too, I guess. You looked magnificent coming through the window. So savage, so fierce. So beautiful. Teeth snapping, eyes gleaming, and that marvelous body fluid as rain."

She slid off the couch to kneel beside him, to burrow against him. "I love you," she murmured, felt him quiver as she caressed him. "It's so easy with you."

They stayed like that for a long, long time, with the wolf staring into the dying fire and listening to her quiet breathing.

Liam kept her busy and kept her close over the next three weeks. She loved the work—and that helped him justify spending so much time with her. It was true enough that most of her sketching could—even should have been done on her own. But she didn't argue when he insisted she come to him nearly every day to work.

It was only to…keep an eye on her, he told himself. To observe her, to help him decide what to do next. And when to do it. It wasn't as if he wanted her company, particularly. He preferred working alone, and certainly didn't need the distraction of her, the scent and the softness. Or the chatter, that was by turns charming and revealing. He certainly didn't need the offerings she so often brought over. Tarts and cookies and little cakes.

As often as not they were soggy or burned—and incredibly sweet.

It wasn't as if he couldn't do without her, very, very easily. That's what he told himself every day as he waited restlessly for her to arrive.

If he went to her nightly in wolf-form, it was only because he understood she was lonely, and that she looked forward to the visits. Perhaps he did enjoy lying beside her on the big canopy bed, listening to her read aloud from one of her books. Watching her fall asleep, invariably with her glasses on and the lamplight shining.

And if he often watched her in sleep, it wasn't because she was so lovely, so fragile. It was only because she was a puzzle that needed to be solved. A problem that required logical handling.

His heart, he continued to assure himself, was well-protected.

He knew the next step was approaching. A time when he would put the choice of what they became to each other in her hands.

Before he did, she would have to know who he was. And what he was.

He could have taken her as a lover without revealing himself. He had done so before, with other women. What business had it been of theirs, after all? His powers, his heritage, his life were his own.

But that might not be the case with Rowan.

She had a heritage of her own, one she knew nothing of. There would also come a time he would have to tell her of that, and convince her of what ran through her blood.

What she would do about it would be her own choice.

The choice to educate her had been his.

But he guarded his heart still. Desire was acceptable, but love was too big a risk.

On the night of the solstice, when magic was thick and the night came late, he prepared the circle. Deep in the woods, he stood in the center of the stone dance. Around him, the air sang, the sweet song of the ancients, the lively tune of the young, the shimmering strains of those who watched and waited.

And the aching harpstrings of hope.

The candles were white and slender, as were the flowers that lay between them. He wore a robe the color of moon-glow belted with the jewels of his rank.

The wind caught his unbound hair as he lifted his face to the last light of the yielding sun. Beams of it fired the trees, shot lances of glimmering gold through the branches to lie like honed swords at his feet.

"What I do here, I do freely, but I make no vow to the woman or to my blood. No duty binds me, no promises made. Hear my voice before this longest day dies. I will call her, and she will come, but I will not use what I have beyond the call. What she sees, what she remembers and believes is for her to decide.''

He watched the silver owl swoop, then perch imperiously on the king stone.

''Father,'' he said, formally and with a bow. ''Your wishes are known, but if I'm ruled by them, would I rule others wisely?''

Knowing that statement would irritate, Liam turned away before the smile could touch his lips. Once more he lifted his face. ''I call Earth.'' He opened his hand to reveal the deep rich soil he held. ''And Wind.'' The breeze rose up high and wild, tossing the earth into a spiral. ''And Fire.'' Two columns of iced blue flame speared up, shivered. ''Witness here what fate will conspire. A song in the blood, the power at hand.''

His eyes began to glow, twin flames against the glowing dark. ''To honor both I've come to this strange land. If she's mine, we both will see. As I will so mote it be.''

Then he turned, lighting each of the candles with a flick of his hand until their flames shot up clear gold and straight as arrows. The wind leaped up, howled like a thousand wolves on the hunt, but remained warm and fragrant with sea and pine and wildflowers.

It billowed the sleeves of his robe, streamed through his hair. And he tasted in it the power of the night.

''Moon rise full and Moon rise white, light her path to me tonight. Guide her here to the circle by the sea. As I will so mote it be.''

He lowered the hands he had flung up to the sky,

and peered through the night, through the trees and the dark, to where she slept restlessly in her bed.

"Rowan," he said with something like a sigh, "it's time. No harm will come to you. It's the only promise I'll make. You don't need to wake. You know the way in your dreams. I'm waiting for you."

Something...called her. She could hear it, a murmur in the mind, a question. Stirring in sleep, she searched for the answer. But there was only wonder.

She rose, stretching luxuriously, enjoying the feel of the silky new nightshirt against her thighs. It was so nice to be out of flannel. Smiling to herself, she slipped into a robe of the same deep blue as her eyes, tucked her feet into slippers.

Anticipation shivered along her skin.

In that half dream, she walked down the steps, trailing her fingertips along the banister. The light in her eyes, the smile on her lips, were those of a woman going to meet her lover.

She thought of him, of Liam, the lover of her dreams, as she walked out of the house and into the swirling white fog.

The trees were curtained behind it, the path invisible. The air, moist and warm on her skin, seemed to sigh, then to part. She moved through it without fear, into that soft white sea of mist with the full white moon riding the sky above, and the stars glimmering like points of ice.

Trees closed in, like sentinels. Ferns stirred in the damp breeze and shimmered with wet. She heard the long, deep call of an owl and turned without thought or hesitation toward the sound. Once, she saw him, huge and grand and as silver as the mist, with the glint of gold on his breast and the flash of green eyes.

Like walking through a fairy tale. A part of her mind recognized, acknowledged and embraced the magic of it, while another part slept, not yet ready to see, not yet ready to know. But her heart beat strong and steady and her steps were quick and light.

If there were eyes peeking from between the lacy branches of the ferns, if there was joyful laughter tinkling down from the high spreading branches of the firs, she could only enjoy it.

At each step, each turn of the path, the fog shimmered clear to open the way for her.

And the water sang quietly.

She saw the lights glowing, little fires in the night. She smelled sea, candle wax, sweet fragrant flowers. Her soft smile spread as she stepped into the clearing, to the dance of stones.

Fog shivered at the edges, like a foamy hem, but didn't slide between stone and candle and flowers. So he stood in the center, on clear ground, his robe white as the moonshine, the jewels belting it flashing with power and light.

If his heart jerked at the sight of her, if it trembled on the edge of where he'd vowed it would not go, he ignored it.

"Will you come in, Rowan?" he asked and held out a hand.

Something in her yearned. Something in her shuddered. But her smile remained as she took another step. "Of course I will." And walked through the stones.

Something throbbed on the air, along her skin, in her heart. She heard the stones whisper. The lights of the candles flickered, swayed, then flamed straight up again.

Their fingertips brushed. Her eyes stayed on his, trusting, when those fingers linked firm. "I dream of you, every night." She sighed it and would have moved into him but he lay a hand on her shoulder. "And long for you through the days."

"You don't understand, neither the rewards nor the consequences. And you must."

"I know I want you. You've already seduced me, Liam."

A tiny finger of guilt scraped up his spine. "I'm not without needs."

She reached up, cupped his cheek. And her voice was soft where his had been rough. "Do you need me?"

"I want you." Need was too much, too weak, too risky.

"I'm here." She lifted her face to his. "Won't you kiss me?"

"Aye." He leaned down, kept his eyes open and on hers. "Remember this," he murmured when his lips were a breath from hers. "Remember this, Rowan, if you can." And his mouth brushed over hers, once, then again. Testing. Then a gentle nip to make her shiver.

When she sighed, one long quiet breath, he covered her mouth with his, drawing out the moment, the magic, sliding into the taste and texture of her. The warm, slow tangle of tongues thickened his pulse, called to his blood.

On either side of them, the cool blue fire burned bright.

"Hold me. Liam, touch me. I've waited so long."

The sound he made in his throat was caught between growl and groan as he dragged her to him and let his hands roam.

Take her here, take her now, in the circle where we'll be bound. It would be done. That primal urge to cover her, to bury himself in her, warred viciously with his honor. What did it matter what she knew, what she wanted or believed? What did it matter what he gained or lost? There was now, only now, with her hot and eager in his arms and her mouth like a flame against his.

"Lie with me here." Her lips tore from his to race wildly over his face, down his throat. "Make love with me here." She already knew what it would be. Dreams and fantasies danced in her mind, and she knew. Urgent and elemental, fast and potent. And she wanted, wanted, wanted the mad, mindless thrill.

In one rough move, he pushed the robe from her shoulder and set his teeth on that bare flesh. The taste of her swirled through him, drugged wine to cloud the senses. "Do you know who I am?" he demanded.

"Liam." His name was already pounding in her head.

He jerked her back, stared into her dark eyes. "Do you know what I am?"

"Different." It was all she could be sure of, though more, much more hovered at the edge of her senses.

"You're still afraid to know it." And if she feared that, how much more might she fear her own blood? "When you can say it, you'll be ready to give yourself to me. And take what I give you."

Her eyes glowed, deep and blue. Her trembles weren't from fear or cold, but from desire straining for release. "Why isn't this enough?"

He stroked a hand over her hair, soothing her, struggling to soothe himself. "Magic has responsibilities. Tonight, the shortest night, it dances in the forest, sings in the hills of my home, it rides the seas and soars in the air. Tonight it celebrates. But tomorrow, always tomorrow it must remember its purpose. Feel the joy of it."

He kissed her brow, both of her cheeks. "Tonight, Rowan Murray of the O'Mearas, you'll remember what you will. And tomorrow, the choice is yours."

He stepped back, spreading his arms so that the robe whipped around him.

"The night passes, quick and bright, and dawn will break with the softest light. If blood calls to blood come then to me." He paused so that their eyes locked and held. "As you will, so mote it be."

He reached down, took a spray of moonflowers and gave it to her. "Sleep well, Rowan."

The sleeves of his robe fell back, revealing hard muscle. With one flash of power, he sent her from him.

Chapter 8

The sunlight beamed bright through the windows. With a murmur of complaint, Rowan turned from it, pressed her face into the pillow.

Sleep was what she wanted. Sleep where those wonderful and vivid dreams would come, where she could wrap herself in them. There were tatters of them still waving through her mind.

Fog and flowers. Moonbeams and candle-glow. The silver flash of an owl, the quiet roar of the sea. And Liam in a white robe that shimmered with jewels holding her in the center of a circle of stones.

She could taste that hot male flavor of him on her tongue, feel the ripple of muscle held ruthlessly in check, feel the not quite steady thud of his heart against hers.

She had only to slide back into sleep to experience it all again.

But she turned restlessly, unable to find it, or him again.

It was so real, she thought, rubbing her cheek against the pillow to watch the sunbeams shoot in through the windows. So real and so…wonderful. She'd often had very odd and textured dreams, particularly during her childhood.

Her mother had said it was imagination, and that she had a good one. But she needed to learn the difference between what was real, and what was make-believe.

Much too often, Rowan supposed, she'd preferred the make-believe. Because she'd known that had worried her parents a little, she'd buried it. She decided it was because she'd chosen to take her own road now that the dreams were coming back so often.

And it didn't take an expert to understand why her dreams were so often of Liam—and so romantic and erotic. She supposed the wisest course was to simply enjoy them—and not to forget what was real and what wasn't.

She stretched, lifting her arms high, linking her hands. And smiling to herself, replayed what she could remember.

A dream riff on the game they were working on, she thought. With Liam as hero, she as heroine. Magic and mist, romance and denial. A circle of stones that whispered, a ring of candles where the flames rose straight despite the wind. Columns of fire, blue as lake water. Fog that parted as she walked.

Lovely, she mused, then closed her eyes and tried to go back and remember what he'd said to her. She could remember very well the way he'd kissed her. Gently, then with heat and hunger. But what had he said? Something about choices and knowledge and responsibilities.

If she could put it in order she might be able to give him an idea for a story line for another game. But all that was really clear was the way his hands had moved over her—and the needs that had pumped inside her.

They were working together now, she reminded herself. Thinking of him the way she did was both inappropriate and foolish. The last thing she wanted to do was delude herself into thinking he could fall in love with her—the way she was very much aware she could fall in love with him.

So she'd think of the work instead, of the pleasure it gave her. She'd think of the house she meant to buy. It was time to do something about that. But for now, she'd get up, make her coffee, take her morning walk.

She tossed the sheets aside. And there on the bed beside her was a spray of moonflowers.

Her heart took a hard leap into her throat and snapped it shut. Her breath clogged behind it, hot and thick. Impossible, impossible, her mind insisted. But even when she squeezed her eyes tight, she could smell the delicate fragrance.

She must have picked them and forgotten. But she knew there were no such flowers around her cottage or in the woods. Flowers such as she now remembered seeing in her dream, spread like white wishes between the spears of candles.

But it couldn't be. It had been a dream, just another of the dreams that had visited her sleep since she'd come to this place. She hadn't walked through the forest in the night, through the mists. She hadn't gone to that clearing, to Liam or stepped into the stone dance.

Unless…

Sleepwalking, she thought with a quick lick of panic. Had she been sleepwalking? She scrambled out of bed, her gaze glued to the flowers as she grabbed her robe.

And the hem was damp, as if she'd walked through dew.

She clutched the robe against her, as details of the dream raced much too clearly through her mind.

"It can't be real." But the words echoed hollowly. With a sudden flurry of motion, she began to dress.

She ran all the way, not questioning when temper raced with her fear. He'd caused it, that was all she knew. Maybe there was something in that tea he brewed every day. A hallucinogenic of some kind.

It was the only rational explanation. There had to be a rational explanation.

Her breath was short, her eyes huge when she ran up the steps to pound on his door. She gripped the flowers in one white-knuckled hand.

"What did you do to me?" she demanded the moment he opened the door.

He watched her steadily as he stepped back. "Come in, Rowan."

"I want to know what you did to me. I want to know what this means." She thrust the flowers at him.

"You gave me flowers once," he said, almost brutally calm. "I know you've a fondness for them."

"Did you drug the tea?"

Now that calm snapped off into insult. "I beg your pardon?"

"It's the only explanation." She whirled away from him to pace the room. "Something in the tea to make me imagine things, to do things. I'd never walk into the woods at night in my right mind."

"I don't deal in potions of that kind." He added a dismissive shrug that had her trembling with fury.

"Oh, really." She spun back to face him. Her hair tumbling over her shoulders, her eyes snapping vivid blue. "What kind then?"

"Some that ease small hurts of body and soul. But it's not my…specialty."

"And what is your specialty then?"

He shot her a look of impatience. "If you'd open your mind you'd see you already know the answer to that."

She stared into his eyes. As the image of the wolf flashed into her mind, she shook her head and stepped back. "Who are you?"

"You know who I am. And damn it, I've given you plenty of time to deal with it."

"With what? Deal with *what?*" she repeated and stabbed a finger into his chest. "I don't understand anything about you." This time she shoved him and had his own temper peaking. "I don't understand anything about what you expect me to know. I want answers, Liam. I want them now or I want you to leave me alone. I won't be played with this way, or tricked or made a fool of. So you tell me exactly what this means.'' She ripped the flowers back out of his hand. ''Or I'm finished.''

''Finished, are you? Want answers, do you?'' Anger and insult overpowered reason and he nodded. ''Oh aye, then, here's an answer for you.''

He threw out his hands. Light, brought on by temper rather than need flashed cold blue from his fingertips. A thin white mist swirled around his body, leaving only those gold eyes bright and clear.

Then it was the eyes of the wolf, glinting at her as he bared his teeth in what might have been a sneer, his pelt gleaming midnight-black.

The blood drained out of her head, left it light and giddy as the mists faded. She could hear in some dim distance, the harsh, ragged sound of her own breath and the trembling scream that sounded only in her mind.

She stepped back, staggered. Her vision grayed at the edges. Tiny lights danced in front of her eyes.

When her knees buckled, he cursed ripely, and his hands caught her before she could fall.

''Damn if you'll faint and make me feel like a monster.'' He eased her into a chair and shoved her head between her knees. ''Catch your breath, and next time have a care with what you wish for.''

There was a hive of bees buzzing in her head, a hundred icy fingers skimming over her skin. She babbled something when he lifted her head. She would have pulled back, but he had his hands firm on her face. ''Just look,'' he murmured, gently now. ''Just look at me. Be calm.''

Awake and aware this time, she felt his mind touch her. Instinct had her struggling, had her hands lifting to push at him.

"No, don't fight me on this. I won't harm you."

"No...I know you won't." She knew that, was inexplicably certain of it. "Could I—could I have some water?"

She blinked at the glass she hadn't known was in his hand, hesitated and saw that flicker of annoyance in his eyes. "It's only water. You've my word on it."

"Your word." She sipped, let out a shaky breath. "You're a..." It was too ridiculous, but she'd seen. For Lord's sake, she'd seen. "You're a werewolf."

His eyes rounded in what could only be shock, then he shoved himself to his feet to stare at her in baffled fury. "A werewolf? For the love of Finn where do you come up with these things? A werewolf." He muttered it now as he prowled the room. "You're not stupid, you're just stubborn. It's the broad light of day, isn't it? Do you see a full moon out there? Did I come snapping at your throat?"

He muttered curses in Gaelic as he whirled back around to glare at her. "I'm Liam of Donovan," he said with pride ringing in his voice. "And I'm a witch."

"Oh, well then." Her laugh was quick and lightly hysterical. "That's all right then."

"Don't cringe from me." He snapped it out, cut to the core when she hugged her arms over her chest. "I've given you time to see, to prepare. I'd not have shown you so abruptly if you hadn't pushed me."

"Time to see? To prepare? For *this?*" She ran an

unsteady hand through her hair. "Who could? Maybe I'm dreaming again," she murmured, then bolted straight in the chair. "Dreaming. Oh, my God."

He saw her thoughts, jammed his hands into his pockets. "I took nothing you weren't willing to give."

"You made love to me—you came to my bed while I slept and—"

"My mind to your mind," he interrupted. "I kept my hands off you—for the most part."

The blood had come back into her face and flamed there now. "They weren't dreams."

"They were dreams right enough. You'd have given me more than that, Rowan. We both know the truth of it. I won't apologize for dreaming with you."

"Dreaming with me." She ordered herself to her feet, but had to brace a hand on the chair to stay on them. "Am I supposed to believe this?"

"Aye." A smile ghosted around his mouth. "That you are."

"Believe you're a witch. That you can change into a wolf and come into my dreams whenever you like."

"Whenever you like as well." A different tack, he mused, might be in order. One that would please them both. "You sighed for me, Rowan. Trembled for me." He moved forward to skim his hands up her arms. "And smiled in your sleep when I left you."

"What you're talking about happens in books, in the games you write."

"And in the world as well. You've been in that world. I've taken you there. You remember last night, I can see it in you mind."

"Don't look in my mind." She jerked back, mortified because she believed he could. "Thoughts are private things."

"And yours are often so clear on your face I don't have to look any further. I won't look further if it upsets you."

"It does." She caught her bottom lip between her teeth. "You're a psychic?"

He blew out a huff of breath. "I've the power to see, if that's your meaning. To brew a spell, to call the thunder." He shrugged negligently, elegantly. "To shift shapes at my will."

Shape-shifter. Good God. She'd read of such things, of course she had. In novels, in books on myths and legends. It couldn't be real. And yet…could she deny what she'd seen with her own eyes? What she knew in her own heart?

"You came to me as the wolf." If she was mad, she thought, she might as well have mad answers.

"You weren't afraid of me then. Others would have been, but not you. You welcomed me in, put your arms around me, wept on my neck."

"I didn't know it was you. If I'd known—" She broke off as other memories crept back. "You watched me undress! You sat there while I was in the tub."

"It's a lovely body you have. Why should you be shamed that I've seen it? Only hours ago you asked me to touch you."

"That's entirely different."

Something that might have been reluctant amusement flickered in his eyes. ''Ask me to touch you now, knowing, and it will be even more different.''

She swallowed hard. ''Why haven't you…touched me already?''

''You needed time to know me, and yourself. I've no right to take innocence, even when it's offered, when no knowledge goes with it.''

''I'm not innocent. I've been with men before.''

Now there was something dark shimmering in his eyes, something not quite tame. But his voice was even when he spoke. ''They didn't touch your innocence, didn't change it. I will. If you lie with me, Rowan, it'll be as the first time. I'll give you pleasure that will make you burn….''

His voice had lowered. When he traced a finger down her throat she shivered, but didn't step back. Whoever—whatever—he was, he moved her. He called to her. ''What will you feel?''

''Delight,'' he murmured, easing closer to brush his mouth over her cheek. ''Demand. Desire. It's the passion you wanted that you didn't find in others. Urgency, you said. And desperation. I feel that for you, whether I will or no. That much power you have over me. Is it enough for you?''

''I don't know. No one's ever felt that for me.''

''I do.'' He brought his hands over, slipped the first two buttons free on her simple cotton shirt. ''Let me see you, Rowan. Here, in the light of day.''

''Liam.'' It was insanity. How could it be real? Yet everything she felt was too intense, too immediate to be otherwise. Nothing, she realized with a dull sense of shock, had ever been more real to her. ''I believe this.'' Her breath trembled free. ''I want this.''

He looked in her eyes, saw both the fear and the acceptance. ''So do I.''

The skim of his knuckles over her skin left a hot trail down her skin as he unbuttoned her blouse, slipped it off her shoulders. Her heart tumbled in her chest as he smiled. ''You were in a hurry this morning,'' he murmured, noting she hadn't taken the time for a bra.

To please himself he traced a fingertip lightly down the subtle slope, over the tip, and watched her eyes go opaque. ''You know I can't stop you,'' she said, watching him.

''Aye, you can.'' Through sheer will he kept his touch gentle. ''With but a word. I hope you won't for it'll drive me mad not to have you now. Do you want me to touch you?''

''Yes.'' More than she wanted to breathe.

''You said once that it shouldn't be simple.'' With his eyes on hers, he unbuttoned her jeans. ''It won't be.'' Skilled fingertips skimmed under denim to tease, to awaken. ''Not for either of us.''

It was like a dream, she thought. Just one more glorious dream. ''Why do you want this?''

''Because you're in my mind, in my blood.'' That much was true, but he told himself he could block her out of his heart. Leaning forward, he caught her jaw gently between his teeth. ''I'm in yours.''

Why should she deny it? Why shouldn't she accept, even embrace these outrageous sensations, this heat in the belly and flutter in the pulse? He was what she wanted, with a giddy greed she'd felt for no other man.

So take, her mind murmured, and pay whatever price is asked.

Still her fingers shook slightly as she tugged his shirt over his head. Then, with a kind of wonder, she spread her hands over his chest.

Hard, warm. Strength just on the edge of danger held ruthlessly in check. She knew it, even as her curious fingers traced up, over broad shoulders, down the taut muscles of his arms. She heard the soft feline purr before she realized it had come from her own throat.

Her gaze shot up to his, and in her eyes was a mix of shock and delight. "I've done this before…in my dreams."

"With much the same results." He'd intended his tone to be dry, but there was an edge to it that stunned him. Gently, he ordered himself, she should be treated gently. "Will you move beyond dreams now, Rowan, and lie with me?"

For an answer she stepped to him, rising onto her toes so that her mouth met his. The beauty of that, just that, had his arms coming hard around her. "Hold tight," he murmured.

She felt the air shudder, heard a rustle of wind. There was a sensation of rising, spinning, then tumbling all in the space of a single heartbeat. Before fear could fully form, before the gasp of it could shudder from her mouth to his, she was lying beneath him, dipped deep into a bed soft as clouds.

Her eyes flew open. She could see the polished

beams of a wood ceiling, the stream of sunlight. ''But how—''

''I've magic for you, Rowan.'' His mouth moved to the vulnerable flesh of her throat. ''All manner of magic.''

They were in his bed, she realized. In the blink of an eye they'd moved from one room to another. And now his hands...oh, sweet Lord, how could the simple touch of flesh to flesh cause such *feeling?*

''Give me your thoughts.'' His voice was rough, his hands light as air. ''Let me touch them, and show you.''

She opened her mind to him, gasping when she not only felt the heat of his body, the skim of his hands, but saw, the images forming out of the mists in her mind, the two of them tangled together on a huge, yielding bed in a path of early summer sunlight.

Every sensation now, every shimmering layer was reflected back, as if a thousand silver mirrors shone out of her heart. And so with a kiss only, one long, drugging kiss, he brought her softly to peak.

She moaned out the pleasure of it, the sheer wonder of having her body slide over a velvet edge. Her thoughts scattered, dimmed, reformed in a mixed maze of colors, only to fly apart again as his teeth grazed her shoulder.

She was beyond price. An unexpected treasure in her openness, her utter surrender to him and to her own pleasures. Now, at last now his hands could take, his mouth could feast. Soft, silky flesh, pale as the moon, delicate curves and subtle scents.

The animal that beat in his blood wanted to ravage,

to grasp and plunge. She would not deny him. Knowing that, he wrapped the chain tighter around his own pounding throat and offered only tenderness.

She moved beneath him, all quiet sighs and luxurious stretches. Her hands roamed over him freely, building and banking small fires. Dark and heavy, her eyes met his when he lifted his head.

And her lips curved slowly.

"I've waited so long to feel like this." She lifted a hand to slide her fingers through his hair. "I never knew I was waiting."

Love waits.

The words came back to him like a drumbeat, a warning, a whisper. Ignoring it, he lowered again to take her breast with his mouth. She arched, gave a little cry as the movement had been sudden and just a bit rough.

Then she groaned, and the hand that had combed lazily through his hair fisted tight, pressing him urgently against her. Heat flashed, a quick bolt to the center. His tongue tormented, his teeth hinted of pain. She gave herself over to it, to him, trembling again as both mind and body steeped in pleasure.

No one had ever touched her this way, so deep it seemed he knew her needs and secrets better than she herself. Her heart quaked, then soared under his quietly ruthless mouth. And opened wide as love flooded it.

She clung to him now, murmuring mindlessly as they rolled over the bed, as flesh grew damp with desire and minds misted with delight.

She was...glory, he thought dimly while he tumbled to a depth he'd never explored with a woman. His keen senses were barraged with her. Scent like spice on the wind, taste like honeyed wine, texture like heated silk. Whatever he asked for she gave, a rose opening petal by petal.

She rose up when he reached for her, her body impossibly fluid, her lips like a flame on his shoulder, across his chest, against his greedy mouth.

Against his hand she was warm and wet, and her body arched back like a drawn bow when his fingers found her. Eyes sharp on her face, he watched that fresh rush of shock and pleasure and fear flicker over hers as he took her up, urged her over.

Her breath sobbed out, her body shook as that new arrow of sensation pinned her, left her quivering helplessly. Even as her head dropped limply on the shoulder her nails had just bit into, he sent her spinning up again.

When they tumbled back, he gripped her hands, waited for his vision to clear, waited for her eyes to open and meet his. The air dragged in and out of his lungs. ''Now.''

The word was nearly an oath as he drove into her.

Held there, held quivering to watch her eyes go wide and blind. Held there, held gasping while the thrill of filling her burned in his blood.

Then she began to move.

A lift of the hips, a falling away that drew him down. Slow, achingly slow, with a low moan for each long, deep thrust.

It was his eyes, only his eyes she saw now, brilliantly gold, stunningly intense as they took each other to a secret space where the air fluttered like velvet on the skin. Her fingers clung to his, her eyes stayed open and aware. Every pulse that beat in her body gathered into one steady throb that filled the heart to bursting.

When it burst, and her mind and body with it, she arched high and hard against him, called out his name with a kind of wonder. Saying hers, he buried his face in her hair and dived with her.

He stretched over her, his head between her breasts, his long body lax. She kept her eyes closed, the better to hold on to that sensation of flying, of falling. Never before had she been so aware, so in tune with her own desires or with a man's.

And never, she realized, had she been so willing, even eager, to surrender to both.

A small smile curved her lips as she lazily stroked his hair. In her mind she could see them together there. Wantonly sprawled, naked, damp and tangled.

She wondered how long it would be before he'd want to touch her again.

"I already do." Liam's voice was thick and low. His tongue skimmed carelessly over the side of her breast and made her shiver.

"Thoughts are private."

She was so soft and warm in the afterglow of love, and that lazy sip of her flesh so delightful. He slid a hand up, molded her gently and shifted to nibble. "I've been inside your thoughts." Her nipple hardened against a flick of his tongue and needs stirred again. "I've been inside you, *a ghra.* What's the point of secrets now?"

"Thoughts are private," she repeated, but the last word ended on a moan.

"As you wish." He slipped out of her mind even as he slipped into her.

She must have slept. Though she remembered nothing but curling around him after that second, surprising slide into heaven. She stirred in bed, and found herself alone.

Sunny morning had become rainy afternoon. The sound of its steady patter, the golden haze that seemed to linger inside her body, both urged her to simply snuggle back and sleep again.

But curiosity was stronger. This was his bed, she thought, smiling foolishly. His room. Shoving at her tangled hair, she sat up and looked.

The bed was amazing. A lake of feathers covered in smooth, silky sheets, backed by a headboard of dark polished wood carved with stars and symbols and lettering she couldn't make out. Idly she traced her fingers in the grooves.

He, too, had a fireplace facing the bed. It was fashioned of some kind of rich green stone and topped by a mantel of the same material. Gracing that were colorful crystals. She imagined their facets would catch the sun brilliantly. Fat white candles stood at one end in a triad.

There was a tall chair with its back carved in much the same way as the headboard. A deep blue throw woven with crescent moons was tossed over one of its arms.

The tables by the bed held lamps with bases of bronze mermaids. Charmed, she ran a finger along the curving tails.

He kept the furnishings spare, she noted, but he chose what he kept around him with care.

She rose, stretched, shook back her hair. The rain made her feel beautifully lazy. Instead of looking for her clothes, she walked to his closet hoping she would find a robe to bundle into.

She found a robe, and it made her fingers jerk on the door. A long white robe with wide sleeves.

He'd worn it the night before. In the stone dance. Under the moonlight. A witch's robe.

Closing the door quickly, she spun around, looked around wildly for her clothes. Downstairs, she remembered with a jolt. He'd undressed her downstairs, and then…

What was she doing? What was she thinking of? Was this real or had she gone mad?

Had she just spent hours in bed with him?

And if it was real, if what she'd always thought was fantasy was suddenly truth, had he used it to lure her here?

For lack of anything else, she snatched up the throw, wrapped it around herself. She grasped the ends tight as the door of the bedroom opened.

He lifted a brow when he saw her, draped in the cloth his mother had woven for him when he'd turned twenty-one. She looked tumbled and lovely and outrageously desirable. He took a step toward her before he caught the glint of suspicion in her eyes.

Annoyed, he moved past her to set the tea tray he'd carried up on the bedside table. "What have you thought of that I haven't explained?"

"How can you explain what should be impossible?"

"What is, is," he said simply. "I am a hereditary witch, descended from Finn of the Celts. What powers I have are my birthright."

She had to accept that. She had seen, she had felt. She kept her shoulders straight and her voice even. "Did you use those powers on me, Liam?"

"You ask me not to touch your thoughts. Since I respect your wishes, try to be more specific in your questions." Obviously irritated, he sat on the side of the bed and picked up a cup of tea.

"I was attracted to you, strongly and physically attracted to you from the first minute. I behaved with you as I've never behaved with a man. I've just gone to bed with you and felt things..." She took a long, steadying breath as he watched her, as she saw a little gleam that had to be triumph light his eyes. "Did you put a spell on me to get me into bed?"

The gleam went dark, and triumph became fury so swiftly she stumbled back a step in instinctive defense. China cracked on wood as he slammed the cup down. From somewhere not so far away, came the irritable grumble of thunder.

But he got to his feet slowly, like a wolf, she thought, stalking prey.

"Love spells, love potions?" He came toward her.

She backed away. ''I'm a witch not a charlatan. I'm a man not a cheat. Do you think I would abuse my gifts, shame my name for sex?''

He made a dismissive gesture; the window shuddered and cracked, giving her a clue just how dangerous was his temper. ''I didn't ask for you, woman. Whatever part fate played in it, you came to this place, and to me, of your own will. And you're free to go in the same manner.''

''How can you expect me not to wonder?'' she shot back. ''I'm just supposed to shrug and accept. Oh, Liam's a witch. He can turn into a wolf and read my mind and blink us from one room to the next whenever he likes. Isn't that handy?''

She whirled away from him, the throw flicking out around her bare legs. ''I'm an educated woman who's just been dropped headfirst into some kind of fairy tale. I'll ask whatever questions I damn well please.''

''You appeal to me when you're angry,'' he murmured. ''Why is that, I wonder?''

''I have no idea.'' She spun back. ''I don't *get* angry, by the way. And I never shout, but I'm shouting at you. I don't fall naked into bed with men or have arguments wearing nothing but a blanket, so if I ask if you've done something to make me behave this way, I think it's a perfectly logical question.''

''Perhaps it is. Insulting, but logical. The answer is no.'' He said it almost wearily as he went back to sit on the bed and sip his tea. ''I cast no spell, wove no magic. I'm Wiccan, Rowan. There is one law we live by, one rule that cannot be broken. 'An it harm none.' I will do nothing to harm you. And my pride alone would prevent me from influencing your response to me. What you feel, you feel.''

When she said nothing, he moved his shoulder in a careless jerk, as if there wasn't a sharp clawed fist around his heart. ''You'll want your clothes.'' With no more than those words, her jeans and shirt appeared on the chair.

She let out a short laugh, shook her head. ''And you don't think I should be dazzled by something like that. You expect a great deal, Liam.''

He looked at her again, thought of what ran in her blood. Not nearly ready to know, he decided, annoyed with his own impatience. ''Aye, I suppose I do. You have a great deal, Rowan, if you'd only trust yourself.''

''No one's ever really believed in me.'' Steady now, she walked to him. ''That's a kind of magic you offer me that means more than all the flash and wonder. I'll start with trusting this much—I'll believe that what I feel for you is real. Is that enough for now?''

He lifted a hand to lay it over the one that held the ends of the throw. The tenderness that filled him was new, unexplained and too sweet to question. ''It's enough. Sit, have some tea.''

''I don't want tea.'' It thrilled her to be so bold, to loosen her grip and let the throw fall away. ''And I don't want my clothes. But I do want you.''

Chapter 9

She was under a spell. Not one that required incantations, Rowan thought dreamily. Not one that called on mystical powers and forces. She was in love, and that, she supposed, was the oldest and the most natural of magics.

She'd never been as comfortable nor as uneasy with any other man. Never been quite so shy, nor ever so bold as she was with Liam. Looking back, gauging her actions, her reactions, her words and her wishes, she realized she'd fallen under that spell the moment she'd turned and seen him behind her on the cliffs.

The wind in his hair, annoyance in his eyes, Ireland in his voice. That graceful, muscular body with its power held ruthlessly in check.

Love at first sight, she thought. Just one more page of her own personal fairy tale.

And after love, her love, they'd found their way to

a friendship she treasured every bit as much. Companionship, an ease of being. She knew he enjoyed having her with him, for work, for talk, for sitting quietly and watching the sky change with evening.

She could tell by the way he smiled at her, or laughed, or absently brushed a hand through her hair.

At times like that she could sense that restlessness that prowled in him shifting into a kind of contentment. The way it had, she remembered, when he'd come to her as a wolf and laid down beside her to listen to her read.

Wasn't it odd, she mused, that in searching for her own peace of mind, she'd given him some?

Life, she decided as she settled down to sketch a line of foxglove on the banks of the stream, was a wonderful thing. And now, finally, she was beginning to live it.

It was lovely to do something she enjoyed, to sit in a place that made her happy and spend time exploring her own talents, to study the way the sun filtered through the treetops, the way the narrow ribbon of water curved and sparkled.

All these shades of green to explore, the shapes of things, the marvelously complicated bark of a Douglas fir, the charming fancy of a lush fern.

There was time for them now, time for herself.

No longer was she required to get up in the morning and put on a neat, conservative suit, to wade through morning traffic, drive through the rain with a briefcase full of papers and plans and projects in the seat beside her. And to stand at the front of the classroom knowing that she wasn't quite good enough, certainly not dedicated enough an instructor as each one of her students deserved.

She would never again have to come home every evening to an apartment that had never really felt like home, to eat her solitary dinner, grade her papers, go to bed. Except for every Wednesday and Sunday when she would be expected for dinner by her parents. They would discuss their respective weeks, and she would listen to their advice on the direction of her career.

Week after week, month after month, year after year. It was hardly any wonder they'd been so shocked and hurt when she'd broken that sacred routine. What would they say if she told them she'd gone way beyond the scope of any imaginings and had fallen headlong in love with a witch? A shape-shifter, a magician. A wonder.

The idea made her laugh, shake her head in delighted amusement. No, she thought, it was best to keep certain areas of her new life all to herself.

Her much-loved and decidedly earthbound parents would never believe, much less understand it.

She couldn't understand it herself. It was real, it was true, there was no way to deny it. Yet how could he be what he claimed to be? How could he do what she had seen him do?

Her pencil faltered, and she reached up to toy nervously with the end of her braid. She *had* seen it, less than a week ago. And since then there had been a dozen small, baffling moments.

She'd seen him light candles with a thought, pluck a white rose out of the air, and once—in one of his rare foolish moods—he'd whisked her clothes away with no more than a grin.

It amazed and delighted her. Thrilled her. But she could admit here, alone, in her deepest thoughts, that part of her feared it as well.

He had such powers. Over the elements, and over her.

He'll never use them to harm you.

The voice in her head made her jolt so that her sketchpad slapped facedown on the forest floor. Even as she pressed a hand to her jumping heart she saw the silver owl swoop down. He watched her from the low branch of a tree out of unblinking eyes of sharp green. Gold glinted against the silver of his breast.

Another page from the fairy tale, she thought giddily and managed to get to her feet. "Hello." It came out as a croak, forcing her to clear her throat. "I'm Rowan."

She bit back a shriek as the owl spread his regal wings, soared down from the tree and with a ripple of silver light, became a man.

"I know well enough who you are, girl." There was music and magic in his voice, and the echo of green hills and misty valleys.

Her nerves were forgotten in sheer pleasure. "You're Liam's father."

"So I am." The stern expression on his face softened into a smile. He moved toward her, footsteps silent in soft brown boots. And taking her hand, lifted it gallantly to kiss. "It is a pleasure to be meeting you, young Rowan. Why do you sit here alone, worrying?"

"I like to sit alone sometimes. And worrying's one of my best things."

He shook his head, gave a quick snap of his fingers and had her sketchpad fluttering up into his hand. "No, this is." He sat comfortably on the fallen tree, cocking his head so that his hair flowed like liquid silver to his shoulders. "You've a gift here, and a charming one." He gave the space beside him an absent pat. "Sit yourself," he said when she didn't move. "I'll not eat you."

"It's all so…dumbfounding."

His gaze shifted to hers with honest puzzlement lighting the green. "Why?"

"Why?" She was sitting on a tree in the woods beside a witch, the second she'd met so far. "You'd be used to it, but it's just a little surprising to a mere mortal."

His eyes narrowed, and if Rowan had been able to read his mind she'd have been stunned to read his quick and annoyed thoughts aimed at his son. *The stubborn whelp hasn't told her yet. What is he waiting for?*

Finn had to remind himself it was Liam's place and not his own and smiled at Rowan again.

"You've read stories, haven't you? Heard legends and songs that speak of us?"

"Yes, of course, but—"

"And where, young Rowan, do you think stories and legends and songs come from if not from grains of truth?" He gave her hand a fatherly pat. "Not that truth doesn't all too often become stretched and twisted. There you have witches tormenting innocent young children, popping them into ovens for dinner. Do you think we're after baking you up for a feast?''

The amusement in his voice was contagious. ''No, of course not.''

''Well then, stop your fretting.'' Dismissing her concerns he paged through her sketches. ''You'll do well here. You do well here.'' His grin flashed as he came to one with faerie eyes peeking through a thick flood of flowers. ''Well and fine here, girl. Why is it you don't use colors?''

''I'm no good with paints,'' she began. ''But I thought I might get some chalks. I haven't done much with pastels and thought it might be fun.''

He made a sound of approval and continued to flip pages. When he came to one of Liam standing spread-legged and arrogant on the cliffs, he grinned like a boy. And there was pride in his eyes, in his voice. ''Oh, this is like him, isn't it? You've got him.''

''Have I?'' she murmured, then flushed when that green gaze rested on her face again.

''Every woman has power, Rowan. She's only to learn to use it. Ask him for something.''

''For what?''

''What pleases you.'' Then he tapped a finger on the page. ''Will you give me this? For his mother.''

''Yes, of course.'' But when she started to tear the page out, it vanished.

''She misses him,'' Finn said simply. ''Good day to you, Rowan of the O'Mearas.''

''Oh, but won't you—'' He was gone before she could ask him to walk to Liam's with her. '''There are more things on heaven and earth, Horatio,'" she murmured, and rising, walked to Liam's alone.

He wasn't waiting for her. That's what he told himself. He had a great deal to occupy his mind and fill his time. He certainly wasn't roaming aimlessly around the house waiting for a woman. Wishing for her.

Hadn't he told her he didn't intend to work that day? Hadn't he said that specifically, so they'd each have a little time apart? They both required their little pieces of solitude, didn't they?

So where the devil was she? he wondered as he roamed aimlessly around the house.

He could have looked, but it would be too undeniable an admission that he wanted her there. And she had been very clear about her expectations of privacy. No one knew or respected the need for privacy more.

And he was giving it to her, wasn't he? He didn't follow the urge just to take a quick glance into the glass and see, or skim lightly into her thoughts.

Damn it.

He could call her. He stopped his restless pacing and considered. A quiet murmur of her name on the air. It was hardly an intrusion, and she was free to ignore it if she wished. Tempted, sorely tempted, he moved to the door, opened it to step out into the balmy air.

But she wouldn't ignore it, he thought. She was too generous, too giving. If he asked, she'd come. And if he asked, it would be like an admission of weakness for her.

It was only a physical need yet, he assured himself. Just a longing for the taste of her, the shape, the scent. If it was sharper than was comfortable it was likely due to his own restraint.

He'd been gentle with her, always. No matter how his blood burned, he'd treated her carefully. When every instinct clawed at him to take more, he'd held back.

She was tender, he reminded himself. It was his responsibility to control the tone of their lovemaking, to yank back the fury of it less he frighten her.

But he wanted more, craved it.

Why shouldn't he have it? Liam jammed his hands into his pockets and strode up and down the porch. Why the devil shouldn't he do as he pleased with her? If he decided—and it was still his decision to make—to accept her as a mate, she would have to accept him as well. All aspects of him.

He'd had enough of waiting around while she was off somewhere ignoring him. As he paced, his temper and the passion stirring to life beneath grew more fierce and more restless. And he'd had enough of minding his step with her.

It was time she knew what she was dealing with—in him and in herself.

"Rowan Murray," he muttered, and his eyes seared the air. "You'd best be ready for the likes of me."

He flung up his arms. The flash of light that snapped out, simmered to a glow as he reformed on her porch.

And knew immediately she wasn't there.

He snarled, cursed, furious with himself, not only for the act that had demonstrated his need for her, but with her for not being exactly where he expected her to be.

By the goddess, he could fix that, couldn't he?

Rowan smiled as she stepped out of the trees. She could hardly wait to tell Liam she'd met his father. She imagined they would settle down in the kitchen where he would tell her stories about his family. He had such a marvelous way of telling stories. She could listen to that musical rise and fall of his voice for hours.

And now that she'd met his father, there might be a way to ask him if she could meet other members of his family. He'd mentioned cousins from time to time, so…

She stopped, staggered with the sudden realization. Belinda. For heaven's sake, he'd told her that first day that he and Belinda were related. Didn't that mean Belinda was…

"Oh!" With a laugh Rowan turned in a circle. "Life is just astonishing."

As she said it, as her laughter rose up, the air shook. The pad fell out of her hands for the second time that day as she raised her hands to her throat. Earthquake? she thought with a dim, dizzy panic.

She felt herself spin, the wind gallop. Light, bright and blinding, flashed in front of her eyes. She tried to call out for Liam, but the words stuck in her throat.

Then she was crushed against him, lights still whirling, wind still rushing as his mouth ravaged hers.

She couldn't get her breath, couldn't find a single coherent thought. Her heart boomed in her chest, in her head as she struggled for both. Suddenly her feet were dangling in the air as he yanked her off them with a strength that was both casual and terrifying.

His mouth was brutal on hers, hard and greedy as it swallowed her gasps. He was in her mind as well, tangled in her thoughts, ruthlessly seducing it as he ruthlessly seduced her body. Unable to separate the two, she began to shake.

"Liam, wait—"

"Take what I give you." He dragged her head back by the hair so that she had one terrifying glimpse of the fire in his eyes. "Want what I am."

He savaged her throat, spurred on by each helpless whimper. And with his mind drove her violently to peak. When she cried out, he fell with her onto the bed. Her hair tumbled free as he liked it best, spread out around her head like a gleaming lake. Her eyes were wide, the passion that rode with the fear turning them midnight-dark.

"Give me what I need."

When her mind whispered yes, he took it.

Heat came in floods, sensations struck like fists. All was a confused mass of wrenching feelings as he drove her beyond the civilized. He was the wolf now, she thought, as he tore at her clothes. If not in form, in temperament. Savage and wild. She heard the growl sound in his throat as he bared her breast to his mouth.

Then she heard her own scream. And it was one of glory.

No time to float or to sigh. Only to race and to moan with every nerve inside her scraped raw and sparking. Her breath heaved out of tortured lungs, her body arched and twisted, energized by every new outrageous demand.

His hands bruised her, his teeth nipped and each separate, small pain was the darkest of pleasures.

And somewhere inside her came the answering call for more.

He yanked her up so that they knelt on the bed, torso to torso, and his hands could find more. Take more. Freed, the animal inside him devoured, and it ravaged. And still it hunted.

Hands slipped over flesh slick with sex. Mouths met like thunder. They rolled over the bed, locked and lost together. Desire had fangs, and a voice that howled like a beast.

He drove her up again, hard and fast so that she wept out his name, so that her body shuddered and her nails clawed at him. She gasped for air, felt it sear her throat and struggled to find some steady ground.

Then he found her with his mouth.

She went wild beneath him, bucking, arching. Her head whipped from side to side as she clawed at the bedclothes, his hair, his back. With tongue and teeth he drove both of them mad, shuddering himself when the orgasm ripped through her, when her body rose up with it like a flame, then melted, slow and soft as candle wax.

"You'll come with me." He panted it out as he moved up her body with hot, greedy kisses over still-quivering flesh. With one jerk, he lifted her hips, opened her to him.

Then plunged.

Hot, hard, fast, their bodies and minds climbed together. He buried himself deep, locking his teeth on her shoulder as he drove into her with savage thrusts. Mindlessly she locked around him, hungering for each dark and dangerous thrill. Energy pumped through her, wild and sweet, so her movements and demands were as fierce as his.

Blood called to blood and heart to heart. With one last violent stroke, with one low feral cry he emptied into her. And she willingly let herself come apart.

He was too appalled to speak, too stunned to move. He knew he weighed heavily on her, could feel the quick, hard trembles that shook her beneath him. Her breath sounded short and harsh in his ear and shamed him.

He'd used her without control.

Deliberately, purposefully, selfishly.

It was perfectly clear that he'd allowed himself to rationalize it for his own needs, and giving her no choice had taken her like a beast rutting in the woods.

He'd sacrificed compassion for passion, kindness for a momentarily physical release.

Now he had to face the consequences: her fear of him and his own discarding of his most sacred vow.

He rolled aside, not quite ready to look at her face. He imagined it would be pale, her eyes glazed with fright.

''Rowan…'' He cursed himself again. Every apology he could think of had less substance than air.

''Liam.'' She sighed it. When she shifted to curl against him, he pulled away abruptly, then rose to go to the window.

''Do you want water?''

''No.'' Her body continued to glow as she sat up. She didn't think to pull the sheets up as she usually did, but sat with them tangled around her legs. As she studied his stiff back, the glow began to fade. Doubts moved in.

''What did I do wrong?''

''What?'' He glanced back. Her hair was a tangled mass of rich and gleaming brown around her shoulders, her body, so smooth and white, showed the marks of his hands, of the stubble he'd neglected to shave.

''I thought—well, but obviously I wasn't…I don't have any experience with what just happened here,'' she said with a faint edge to her voice. ''If I did something wrong, or didn't do something you were expecting, the least you can do is tell me.''

He could only stare. ''Are you out of your mind?''

''I'm perfectly rational.'' So much so she wanted to bury her head in the pillow, pound her fists on the bed and weep. And scream. ''Maybe I don't know a great deal about sex in practice, but I do know that without communication and honesty, that aspect of a relationship, as any other, is bound to fail.''

''The woman's giving me a lecture,'' he murmured, dragging both hands through his hair. ''At such a time she's giving me a lecture.''

"Fine. Don't listen." Insulted, mortally wounded, she climbed out of bed. "You just stay there brooding out the window and I'll go home."

"You are home." He was nearly amused. "It's your cabin, your bedroom and your bed I just savaged you in."

"But—" Confused, and with the tattered remains of her shirt dangling from her hand, she focused. It was her bedroom, she realized. The big canopy bed stood between them, her lace curtains fluttered at the window where Liam stood, naked and irritable.

"Well then." She clutched her shirt and what was left of dignity. "You can go."

"You've a right to be angry."

"I certainly do." And she wasn't about to stand there having a crisis without any clothes on. She marched to the armoir and dragged out a robe.

"I'll apologize, Rowan, but it seems weightless after what I did to you. You had my word I wouldn't hurt you, and I broke it."

Unsure, she turned back, lifting the robe to her breasts rather than slipping it on. "Hurt me?"

"I wanted you, and I didn't think beyond that. Deliberately didn't think beyond it. I took what I pleased and I hurt you."

It wasn't annoyance in his eyes, she realized. It was guilt. And just one more wonder. "You didn't hurt me, Liam."

"There are marks on you I put there. You've tender flesh, Rowan, and I bruised it with carelessness. That I can fix easily enough, but—"

"Wait a minute, just a minute." She held up a hand

as he started forward. He stopped immediately, winced before he could prevent it.

"I don't mean to touch you but to take the bruises away."

"Just leave my bruises where they are." To give herself time to sort it out, she turned away and slipped on the robe. "You're upset because you wanted me."

"Because I wanted you enough to forget myself."

"Really?" She was smiling when she turned back and was thrilled to see his eyes narrow in what had to be confusion. "Well, I'm delighted. No one's ever wanted me enough for that. In my life no one's ever wanted me like that. I never imagined they could. My imagination isn't that...expansive," she decided.

It was she who stepped to him. "Now I don't have to imagine, because I know."

He combed his fingers through her hair before he realized he wanted to. Needed to. "I took your thoughts after you asked me not to."

"And gave me yours. Under these particular circumstances, I'm not complaining." She cupped her elbows, refused to be shy now. "What happened just now was thrilling. It was wonderful. You made me feel desired. Outrageously desired. The only thing that would hurt me is if you're sorry for it."

She was more than he'd understood, he realized. And her needs perhaps less...delicate. "Then I'm not a bit sorry." Still he took her hand, slid up the sleeve of her robe. "Let me take the bruises away. I don't want marks on you, Rowan. It matters to me."

He kissed her fingers, sending her heart into a long, slow flip. Then her lips, making it settle. As his lips rubbed gently on hers she felt the cool slide of something over her skin. The tiny aches she'd hardly noticed faded away.

"Will I get used to it, do you think?"

"To what?"

"Magic."

He wound a lock of her hair around his finger. "I don't know." *You would know,* a voice murmured in his head, *if you looked.*

"I've had a very magical day." She smiled. "I was going to see you when you...changed venues. I wanted to tell you that I met your father."

The finger in her hair stilled as his eyes whipped to hers. "My father?"

"I was sketching in the woods, and there he was. Well, the owl first, but I think I realized almost at once. I've seen him before," she added. "Once as an eagle. He wears a gold pendant always around his neck."

"Aye, he does." One that Liam had to accept or refuse.

"Then he—well, changed, and we talked. He's very handsome and very kind."

More than a little uneasy, Liam turned away to dress. "What did you speak of?"

"My sketches for the most part. He wanted one I'd done of you for your mother. I hope she likes it."

"That she will. She's partial to me."

She heard the affection in his voice and smiled. "He says she misses you—but I think he was speaking as much of himself. Actually I thought he might come to see you." Bottom lip caught between her teeth, she glanced at the tangled sheets of the bed. ''It's a good thing he didn't, ah, drop in.''

''He wouldn't be slipping into your bedroom for a visit,'' Liam said, and relieved now, grinned wickedly. ''That's for me to do.''

''But you'd like to see him, just the same.''

''We keep in touch,'' he said, and found himself both amused and charmed as she walked over to tidy the bed. Wasting your time, Rowan Murray, for I'll be having you back in it before long.

''He's proud of you, and I think he liked me. He said—I probably shouldn't tell you.''

''But you will.'' Liam tossed back his hair, moving to her as she plumped the pillows. ''You've no guile at all.''

''That's not such a bad thing.'' She nearly sulked, but felt too happy to bother. ''He said I should ask you for something.''

''Did he?'' With a laugh, Liam sat on the bed. ''And what will you, Rowan Murray? What should I conjure for you? A sapphire to go with your eyes? Diamonds to sparkle at your feet? If you want a boon from me, you've only to ask.''

He grinned, fully amused now as she caught her bottom lip between her teeth once more. Women enjoyed baubles, he thought and began to wonder what sort he would give her.

''I'd like to meet more of your family.'' She blurted it out before she could change her mind.

He blinked twice. ''My family?''

''Yes, well, I've met your father now, and Belinda—you said she was a relative, but I didn't know she was... Is she?''

''Aye.'' He said it absently, trying to realign his thoughts. ''You'd rather that than diamonds?''

''What would I do with diamonds? I suppose you think it's silly, but I'd just like to see how your family...lives.''

He considered, began to see the advantages and the path. ''It would make it easier for you to understand the magic, the life.''

''Yes, at least it seems it might. And I'm curious,'' she admitted. ''But if you'd rather not—''

He waved off her words. ''I've some cousins I haven't seen in some time.''

''In Ireland?''

''No, in California.'' He was too involved planning to note her quickly masked disappointment.

She had a craving to see Ireland.

''We'll pay them a visit,'' he decided, and rising held out a hand.

''Now?''

''Why not now?''

''Because I...'' She'd never expected him to agree or to move so quickly and could only look down helplessly at her robe and bare feet. ''Well, I need to dress for one thing.''

With a delighted laugh, he grabbed her hand. ''Don't be foolish,'' he said and vanished them both.

Chapter 10

The next thing Rowan was absolutely sure of was standing with her arms locked like iron around Liam and her face pressed into his shoulder. Her heart was sprinting, her stomach jumping and there was the echo of rushing wind in her head.

''Beam me up, Scotty,'' was the best she could manage. And it made him roar with laughter.

''This is much simpler, and more enjoyable,'' he decided as he nudged her face up and indulged himself in a long, mind-numbing kiss.

''It has its points.'' Her voice had thickened, the way it did when she was stirred. It made Liam wonder if this impulsive trip might have been put off just a little while longer. As she loosened her grip, he kept his arms snug around her waist. ''Where are we?''

''My cousin Morgana's garden. She kept one of the old family homes, raises her family here.''

She jerked back, looked down and with a mixture of shock and relief noted her robe had been replaced by simple slacks and a shirt the color of ripening peaches.

She lifted a hand to her hair, found it still tousled. "I don't suppose I could have a brush."

"I like your hair this way," was his answer, as he drew her back so he could sniff it. "It's easier to get my hands into it."

"Hmm." As her system began to level, she could smell the flowers. Wild roses, heliotrope, lilies. She shifted and scanned the beams of sunlight, the cool pockets of shade. Arbors buried under triumphant blooms, sweeps of color, spears of shape with little stone paths winding through, seemingly at will.

"It's beautiful. Wonderful. Oh, I wish I knew how to make something as magical as this." She drew away to turn, to take in the trees sculpted by wind into bent, eerie shapes. Then she beamed as a gray wolf walked majestically down the path toward them. "Oh, is that—"

"A wolf," Liam said, anticipating her. "Not a relative. He's Morgana's." A child with dark hair and eyes as blue as lapis darted over the stones, then stopped with a keen and curious look in those striking eyes. "And so is he. Blessed be, cousin."

Liam felt the tug on his mind, stronger than he'd have expected from a boy no more than five, and lifted a brow. "It's rude to look so deep, or attempt to, without permission."

"You're in my garden," the boy said simply, but

his lips curved in a sweet smile. ''You're cousin Liam.''

''And you're Donovan. Blessed be, cousin.'' Liam stepped forward and offered a hand with great formality. ''I've brought a friend. This is Rowan. And she prefers to keep her thoughts to herself.''

Young Donovan Kirkland tilted his head, but minding his manners did no more than study her face. ''She has good eyes. You can come in. Mama's in the kitchen.''

Then the intense look faded from his face and he was just a normal little boy skipping ahead of them on the path with a dog prancing beside him, rushing to tell his mother they had company.

''He's a—he's a witch?'' The full force of it struck her then. He was a child, astonishingly pretty with a missing front tooth, but he had power.

''Yes, of course. His father isn't, but blood runs strong in my family.''

''I bet.'' Rowan let out a long breath. Witches or not, she thought, this was still a home and Liam hadn't bothered to, well, call ahead. ''We shouldn't just…drop in like this on your cousin. She might be busy.''

''We'll be welcome.''

''It's just like a man to assume—'' Then every thought ran out of her head as she caught her first glimpse of the house. It was tall, rambling, glinting in the sunlight. Towers and turrets speared up to that blue bowl that was the sky over Monterey. ''Oh! It's like something out of a book. What a marvelous place to live.''

Then the back door opened and Rowan was struck dumb with a combination of awe and pure female envy.

It was obvious where the boy got his looks. She'd never seen a more beautiful woman. Black hair cascaded over slim, strong shoulders, eyes of cobalt were heavily fringed by inky lashes. Her skin was creamy and smooth, her features fine and graceful. She stood, one hand on her son's shoulder, the other on the fierce head of the wolf while a large white cat ribboned between her legs.

And she smiled.

"Blessed be, cousin. You're welcome here." She moved to them, kissed Liam on both cheeks. "It's so good to see you. And you, Rowan."

"I hope we're not disturbing you," Rowan began.

"Family is always welcome. Come in, we'll have something cool to drink. Donovan, run up and tell your father we have company." As she spoke, she turned and gave her son a narrow glance. "Don't be lazy now. Go upstairs and tell him properly."

With a weary shrug of his shoulders, the boy dashed back in, shouting for his father.

"Well, close enough," Morgana murmured.

"He has a strong gift of sight."

"And he'll learn to use it well." Her voice took on the edge of an experienced and somewhat exasperated mother. "We'll have some iced tea," she said as they went into the large, airy kitchen. "Pan, sit."

"I don't mind him," Rowan said quickly, rubbing his ears as he sniffed at her. "He's gorgeous."

"I supposed you'd be used to handsome wolves,

wouldn't you.'' Sending Liam an amused look, she took out a clear pitcher filled with golden tea. ''It's still your favorite form, isn't it, Liam?''

''It suits me.''

''That it does.'' She glanced over as Donovan rushed in, side by side with his double.

''He's coming,'' Donovan said. ''He has to kill somebody first.''

''With a really big, sharp knife,'' said the twin, with relish.

''That's nice.'' After the absent comment, Morgana caught the look of shock on Rowan's face and laughed. ''Nash writes screenplays,'' she explained. ''He often murders gruesomely on paper.''

''Oh, yes.'' She accepted the glass of tea. ''Of course.''

''Can we have cookies?'' the twins wanted to know in unison.

''Yes. But sit down and behave.'' She only sighed as a tall glass jar filled with frosted cookies soared off the counter and landed on the table with a small crash and a wild wobble. ''Allysia, you'll wait until I serve our company.''

''Yes, ma'am.'' But she grinned mischievously as her brother giggled.

''I'll just sit, too…if you don't mind.'' Her legs had gone weak and Rowan dropped into a chair. ''I'm sorry, I just can't—I'm not really used to all this.''

''You're not…'' Morgana cut herself off, re-evaluating, and offered an easy smile. ''My children definitely take some getting used to.''

She reached for plates and opened her mind to her cousin. *You haven't told her yet, you dolt?*

It's my business. She's not ready.

Omission is kin to deceit.

I know what I'm doing. Serve your tea and cookies, Morgana, and let me handle this in my own way.

Stubborn mule.

Liam smiled a little, remembering she'd threatened to turn him into one during some scrap during their childhood. She might have managed it, he mused. She had a great deal of power in that particular area.

"I'm Ally, who are you?"

"I'm Rowan." Steadier, she smiled at the girl. A girl, she realized, she'd initially taken for a boy because of the scrappy little body and scraped knees. "I'm a friend of your cousin."

"You wouldn't remember me." Liam walked over to take a seat at the table. "But I remember you, young Allysia, and your brother, and the night you were born. In a storm it was, here in this house as your mother had been born in a storm in that same room. And in the hills of home there was starlight and singing to celebrate it."

"Sometimes we go to Ireland to visit Granda and Grandmama in our castle," Donovan told him. "One day I'll have a castle of my own on a high cliff by the sea."

"I hope you manage to figure out how to clean up your room first." This came from a man who stepped in with a rosy-cheeked girl tucked into each arm.

"My husband, Nash, and our daughters, Eryn and

Moira. This is my cousin Liam, Nash, and his friend Rowan.''

''Nice to meet you. The girls woke up from their naps smelling cookies.''

He set the girls down. One toddled to the wolf who was sitting by the table hoping for crumbs. She fell adoringly on his neck. The other went directly to Rowan, crawled into her lap and kissed both of her cheeks much as her mother had kissed Liam in greeting.

Charmed, Rowan hugged her and rubbed a cheek on the soft golden hair. ''Oh, you have such beautiful children.''

Like, Liam thought as Moira settled cozily on Rowan's lap, often recognizes like.

''We've decided to keep them.'' Nash reached out to tickle the ribs of the older twins. ''Until something better comes along.''

''Daddy.'' Allysia sent him an adoring look, then nimbly snatched up her cookie before he could make the grab.

''You're quick.'' Nash tickled her again, and nipped the cookie out of her fingers. ''But I'm smarter.''

''Greedier,'' Morgana corrected. ''Mind your cookies, Rowan, he's not to be trusted around sweets.''

''What man is?'' Liam stole one from Rowan's plate and had Donovan snickering. ''How are Anastasia and Sebastian, their families?''

''You can judge for yourself,'' Morgana decided on the spot to invite her two cousins and their spouses and families over. ''We'll have a family cookout to-night to welcome you—and your friend.''

Magic could be confusing, and it could be casual, Rowan discovered. It could be stunning or as natural as rain. Surrounded by the Donovans, flooded by the scents from Morgana's garden, she began to believe there could be little in this world that was more natural or more normal.

Morgana's husband, Nash, her cousin Sebastian and Anastasia's husband, Boone, bickered over the proper way to fire the grill. Ana sat comfortably in a wicker chair nursing her infant son while her three toddlers raced around the yard with the other children and the dogs, all to the clashing sympathy of laughter, shouts and wild barks.

At ease, Morgana nibbled on canapés and talked lazily with Sebastian's wife, Mel—about children, work, men, the weather, all the usual sorts of subjects friends and family speak of on summer afternoons.

Rowan thought Liam held himself a bit aloof, and wondered why. But when Ana's little sunshine-haired daughter held up her arms to him she saw him smile, pluck her up and fit her with casual skill on his hip.

She watched with some surprise as he walked with her and apparently listened with great interest as she babbled on to him.

He likes children, she realized, and the inner flutter of longing nearly made her sigh.

This was a home, she thought. Whatever power lived here, it was a home where children laughed and squabbled, where they tumbled and whined just like children everywhere. And men argued and talked of sports, women sat and spoke of babies.

And they were all so striking, she mused. Physically stunning. Morgana with her dazzling dark beauty, Anastasia so delicate and lovely, Mel sharp and sexy, her long body made only more compelling with its belly swollen with child.

Then the men. Just look at them, she thought. Gorgeous. Nash was dashing, golden, movie star handsome; Sebastian as romantic as a storybook prince with just an edge of wicked. And Boone tall and rugged.

And Liam, of course. Always Liam, dark and brooding with those wonderful flashes of amusement that glinted in his gold eyes.

Could she have stopped herself from falling in love with him? she wondered. No, not in a million years, not with all the power in heaven and earth in her hands.

''Ladies.'' Sebastian strolled over. Though he smiled at Rowan there was an intense look in his eyes that had her nerves dancing lightly. ''The men require beer in order to accomplish such manly work.''

Mel snorted. ''Then you should be man enough to get it out of the cooler yourself.''

''It's so much more fun being served.'' He stroked a hand over the slope of her belly. ''She's restless,'' he murmured. ''Do you want to lie down?''

''We're fine.'' She patted his hand. ''Don't hover.''

But when he leaned down, murmured something soft in her ear, her smile turned into a quiet glow.

''Get your beer, Donovan, and go play with your little friends.''

''You know how excited I get when you insult me.'' He nipped her ear, making her laugh, before he plucked four bottles from the cooler and strolled off.

''The man gets mushy around babies,'' Mel commented, shifting herself so that she could reach the platter of finger food. ''When Aiden was born Sebastian walked around as if he'd accomplished the whole deal by himself.''

She watched their son wrap his arms around Sebastian's leg, then observed her elegant husband's limping, playful progress back to the men with Aiden in tow.

''He's a wonderful father.'' Ana lifted the heavy-eyed baby to her shoulder, gently rubbed his back. She smiled when her stepdaughter hurried over, glossy brown hair bouncing.

''Can I hold him now? I'll walk him until he's asleep then put him in the daybed in the shade. Please, Mama, I'll be careful.''

''I know you will, Jessie. Here, take your brother.''

Rowan watched, studying the girl of ten. Since she was Ana's stepdaughter and Boone wasn't...then neither was Jessie. Yet the girl didn't appear to feel out of place among her cousins. In fact, Rowan had seen her speak with the sharp impatience an older child often had for a younger one when Donovan had beaned her with a rubber ball.

''Would you like some wine, Rowan?'' Without waiting for an answer, Morgana poured delicate straw-colored liquid into a glass.

‘‘Thanks. It’s so nice of you to have us here, to go to all this trouble without a bit of notice.’’

‘‘It’s our pleasure. Liam so rarely visits.’’ Her eyes were warm and friendly as they met Rowan’s. ‘‘Now why don’t you tell us how you managed to get him here?’’

‘‘I just asked to meet some of his family.’’

‘‘Just asked.’’ Morgana exchanged a meaningful look with Ana. ‘‘Isn’t that…interesting?’’

‘‘I hope you’ll stay for a few days.’’ Ana gave her cousin a warning pinch under the table. ‘‘I’ve kept my old house next door to where we live for family and friends when they visit. You’re welcome to stay there.’’

‘‘Thank you, but I didn’t bring anything with me.’’ She glanced down at the trim cotton blouse and slacks, reminding herself she’d left Oregon in nothing but a robe and had popped into Monterey neatly outfitted. ‘‘I suppose that doesn’t matter, does it?’’

‘‘You’ll get used to it.’’ Mel laughed and bit into a carrot stick. ‘‘Mostly.’’

Rowan wasn’t sure about that, but she did know she was comfortable here, with these people. Sipping her wine, she glanced over to where Liam stood with Sebastian. It was so nice for him, she thought, to have family to talk with, who understood and supported him.

‘‘You’re a moron,’’ Sebastian said coolly.

‘‘It’s my business.’’

‘‘So you always say.’’ Tipping back his beer, Sebastian eyed his cousin out of amused gray eyes. ''You don't change, Liam.''

''Why should I?'' He knew it was a childish response, but Sebastian often made him feel defensive and annoyed.

''What are you trying to accomplish? What do you need to prove? She's meant for you.''

A chilly line he refused to recognize as fear snaked up Liam's spine. ''It's still my decision.''

Sebastian would have laughed, but he caught the flicker of unease in Liam's eyes, felt the shimmer of it in his mind. ''More fool you,'' he murmured, but with some sympathy. ''And if you feel that way, cousin, why haven't you told her?''

''I told her who I am.'' Liam spoke evenly, determined not to sound defensive. ''Shown her. She nearly fainted.'' He remembered that moment, and the fury, the guilt he'd felt. ''She's been raised not to believe.''

''But she does believe. What she is has always been there. Until you tell her, she has no choice. And isn't choice your most prized possession?''

Liam studied Sebastian's smug smile with the active dislike only family could feel. When they'd been boys, Liam had competed ruthlessly against his older cousin, determined to be as fast, as clever, as smart. Under that competitive streak had been a secret layer of hero worship.

Even now, as a grown man, he wanted Sebastian's respect.

''When she's ready, she'll have the choice. And she'll make it.''

"When *you're* ready," Sebastian corrected. "Is it arrogance, Liam, or fear?"

"It's sense," Liam shot back and fought not to let his teeth go on edge. "She's barely had time to absorb what I've told her already, much less to fully understand. Her own heritage is buried so deep there's hardly a glimmer of it in her mind. She's just begun to discover herself as a woman, how can I ask her to accept her gifts?"

Or me. But he didn't say that, infuriated himself that he would even think it.

He's in love with her, Sebastian realized as Liam turned to scowl down at the beach. In love and too hardheaded to admit it. For a second time a smile trembled on his lips with laughter just beneath. So the mighty fall, he mused, fighting all the way.

"It may be, Liam, you don't give the woman enough credit." He glanced back to where Rowan sat with his wife at the table. "She's lovely."

"She sees herself as plain, as simple. As ordinary. She's none of those things." Liam didn't look around. He could see her in his mind's eye clearly enough if he chose. "But she is tender. I may end up asking her for a great deal more than she's prepared to give."

Lovesick, Sebastian thought, though not without sympathy. He'd been similarly afflicted when he'd met Mel. And had very likely made similar stupid mistakes because of it.

"Living with you's more than any woman could be prepared for." He grinned when Liam turned his head and shot him a look with those hard gold eyes.

"I pity her at the thought of seeing that ugly, scowling face of yours day after day."

Liam's smile was sharp as a blade. "And how does your wife tolerate yours, cousin?"

"She's crazy about me."

"She strikes me as a smart woman."

"Her mind's like a dagger," Sebastian said, with a grinning glance at his wife.

"So how much time did it take you to weavc the spell into her mind for that?"

This time Sebastian did laugh, and in a quick move grabbed Liam in a snug headlock. "A much shorter time than it'll take you to make your pretty lady believe you're a prize to look at."

"Kiss my—" He could only curse, struggle against laughter as Sebastian kissed him full on the mouth. "I'll have to kill you for that," he began, then lifted a brow as little Aiden dashed over to throw his arms around his father's legs. "Later," Liam decided and plucked the child up himself.

It was late when Liam left Rowan sleeping in the house Ana kept by the sea. He was restless, unsettled, and baffled by the ache around his heart that refused to ease.

He thought of running along the water, or flying over it. Racing until he was settled again.

And he thought of Rowan, sweetly sleeping in the quiet house.

He walked through the shadows and scents of Ana's garden, searching for peace of mind. He stepped through the hedge of faerie roses, crossed the lawn and stepped up on the deck on the house where Ana lived with her family.

He'd known she was there.

"You should be asleep."

Ana simply held out a hand. "I thought you'd want to talk."

But taking her hand, he sat beside her and contented himself with silence. He knew of no one more comfortable to sit with, to be with than Anastasia.

Overhead the moon winked in and out of clouds, the stars glimmered. The house where Rowan slept was dark and full of dreams.

"I didn't know how much I missed you, all of you, until I saw you again."

Ana gave his hand a supportive squeeze. "You needed to be alone for a while."

"Aye. It wasn't because you didn't matter that I blocked you all out for a time." He touched her hair. "It was because you did."

"I know that, Liam." She brushed her fingers over his cheek, felt his conflict in her own heart. "Your mind's so troubled." Her quiet gray eyes looked into his, her lips curved gently. "Must you always think so hard?"

"It's the only way I know." Still he felt the strain ease as he sat with her, sliding away knot by knot. That was Ana's gift. "You've a lovely family, Ana, and have made a lovely home here. Your mate is your match. Your children your joy. I can see how happy you are."

"Just as I can see how unhappy you are. Isn't a

family and a home what you want, Liam? What would make you happy?''

He studied their linked fingers, knowing he could and would say things to her he wouldn't to another. ''I might not be good at it.''

Ah, she realized, of course. Liam's standards for himself were always higher than anyone else's could be. ''What makes you think that?''

''I'm used to thinking for and of myself. Used to doing as I please. And I like it.'' He lifted his gaze to hers, smiled. ''I'm a selfish man, and fate's asking me to take the responsibility my father's borne so well, to take a woman who'll understand only pieces of what that means.''

''You're not giving either of you credit for who you are.'' There was impatience in her voice now, all the more effective as it was so rare. ''You've been stubborn, and you've been proud, but you've never been selfish, Liam. What you are is too bloody serious about too many things. And so you too often miss the joy of them.'' She sighed, shook her head. ''And Rowan can and will understand a great deal more than you seem to think.''

''I like going my own way.''

''And your own way led you straight to her, didn't it?'' This time Ana laughed. He looked so irritated that logic had turned back and nipped him. ''Do you know one of the things I've always admired most about you? Your instinct to question and pick apart everything. It's a fascinating and annoying trait. And you do it because you care so much. You'd rather not, but you care.''

''What would you do, Ana, if you were standing where I am?''

''Oh, that's easy for me.'' Her smoky eyes were soft, her smile gentle. ''I'd listen to my heart. I always do. You'll do the same when you're ready.''

''Not everyone's heart speaks as clearly as yours.'' Restless again, he drummed his fingers against the bench. ''I've shown her who I am, but I haven't told her what that might mean to her. I've made her my lover, but I haven't given her love. I've shown her my family without telling her about her own. So yes, it troubles me.''

''You can change it. It's in your hands.''

He nodded, stared into the night. ''I'm taking her back in the morning, when she wakes. And I'll show her what's sleeping inside her. As for the rest, I don't know yet.''

''Don't only show her the obligations, Liam, the duties. Show her the joys, too.'' She rose, keeping her hand in his. ''The baby's stirring. He'll be hungry. I'll make your goodbyes in the morning if you like.''

''I'd appreciate it.'' He got to his feet, gathered her close. ''Blessed be, cousin.''

''Don't stay away so long.'' She kissed his cheeks before she drew away, and at the door paused, looked back. He stood in a shower of moonlight. Alone. ''Love waits,'' she murmured.

It waited, Liam thought when he slipped into bed beside Rowan. Here, in dreams. Would it wait in the morning when he awakened her to all she was?

Like the princess in the fairy tale, he thought,

stirred to life by a kiss. The fact that he was, in his way, a prince made him smile humorlessly into the dark.

Fate, he supposed, enjoyed its ironies.

Those thoughts, and others, kept him awake and waiting for dawn. At first light he slipped a hand over hers, linked fingers and took them back to Rowan's own bed.

She murmured, shifted, then settled again. Rising, he dressed, studying her as she slept. Then he went quietly downstairs to make very strong coffee.

He thought both of them would need it.

With his mind tuned to hers, he knew the moment she stirred. He stepped outside, carrying his coffee. She would come to him, questioning.

Upstairs, Rowan blinked in puzzlement. Had she dreamed it all? It didn't seem possible when she could remember everything so clearly. The aching blue sky of Monterey, the bright music of children's laughter. The warmth of welcome.

It had to be real.

Then she let out a weak chuckle, resting her brow on her updrawn knees. Nothing had to be real, not anymore.

She rose, and prepared to experience yet another magical day.

Chapter 11

When she saw him standing on the porch, it struck her all over again. The wild thrill, the rush of love, the wonder. That this stunning, extraordinary man should want her left her speechless with delight.

Moving on pure emotion, she rushed through the door to throw her arms around him, press her cheek against that strong back.

It staggered him, those sweet, fresh feelings that poured out of her so freely, the quick rise of his own that tangled with them. He wanted to whirl around, to sweep her up and away to someplace where there was no one and nothing to think of but her.

Instead he laid his free hand over hers lightly.

"You brought us back before I had a chance to say goodbye to your family."

"You'll see them again…if you like."

"I would. I'd love to see Morgana's shop. It sounds

wonderful. And Sebastian and Mel's horses. I loved meeting all of your cousins.'' She rubbed her cheek over his shirt. ''You're so lucky to have such a big family. I have some cousins on my father's side, but they live back east. I haven't seen them since I was a child.''

His eyes narrowed. Could there have been a more perfect opening for what he meant to tell her? ''Go inside and get your coffee, Rowan. I need to talk to you.''

Her mood teetered as she loosened her grip, stepped back. She'd been so sure he'd turn and hold her. Instead he hadn't even looked at her, and his tone was cool.

What had she done wrong? she asked herself as she went inside to stare blindly at the line of cheerfully colored mugs. Had she said something? Not said something? Had she—

She squeezed her eyes shut, disgusted with herself. Why did she do that? she demanded. Why did she always, always assume she'd done something? Or lacked something?

Well, she wasn't going to do that anymore. Not with Liam. Not with anyone. A little grim, she got a mug and poured hot, black coffee to the rim.

When she turned, he was inside watching her. Ignoring the sudden dread in her stomach, she struggled to keep her voice impassive. ''What do you want to talk to me about?''

''Sit down.''

''I'm fine standing.'' She pushed at her tumbled hair, sipped coffee hot enough to scorch her tongue.

"If you're angry with me, tell me. I don't like having to guess."

"I'm not angry with you. Why should I be?"

"I have no idea." To keep herself busy, she took out a loaf of bread to make toast she imagined would stick in her throat. "Why else would you be scowling at me?"

"I'm not scowling."

She glanced back at his face, sniffed in derision. "You certainly are, and I don't care for it."

His eyebrow shot up. Her mood had certainly shifted from soft and cuddly to cold and snappy quickly. "Well, I beg your pardon then." In an irritable move, he yanked out a chair, straddled it.

Get on with it, he ordered himself.

"I took you to meet my family, and it's family I want to speak of. I'd prefer it if you'd sit the bloody hell down instead of prowling about the room."

Her shoulders wanted to hitch up in defense at the angry tone and she forced them to stay straight. "I'm making breakfast, if you don't mind."

He muttered something, then flung out his hands. A plate of lightly browned toast appeared on the counter. "There. Though how you can call that breakfast is beyond me. Now sit down with it."

"I'm perfectly capable of making my own." But she carried the plate to the table before deliberately going to the refrigerator and taking her own sweet time choosing jam.

"Rowan, you're trying my patience. I'm only asking you to sit down and talk to me."

"Asking is exactly what you didn't do, but now

that you have, I will.'' Surprised at just how smug she felt over that small victory, she came back to the table and sat down. ''Do you want some toast?''

''No, I don't.'' And hearing the snap in his voice, sighed. ''Thank you.''

She smiled at him with such sudden, such open sweetness, his heart stumbled. ''I hardly ever win arguments,'' she told him as she spread jam on the toast. ''Especially when I don't know what the argument's about.''

''Well, you won that one, didn't you?''

Her eyes danced as she bit into the toast. ''I like winning.''

He had to laugh. ''So do I.'' He laid a hand on her wrist as she lifted her mug. ''You didn't add your cream and all that sugar. You know you don't like your coffee black.''

''Only because I make lousy coffee. Yours is good. You said you wanted to talk about your family.''

''About family.'' He moved his hand so he was no longer touching her. ''You understand what runs through mine.''

''Yes.'' He was watching her so closely, his eyes so focused on hers she had to fight the urge to squirm. ''Your gift. The Donovan Legacy.'' She smiled. ''That's what you named your company.''

''Aye, that's right. Because I'm proud of where I come from. Power has obligations, responsibilities. It's not a toy, but it's not something to fear.''

''I'm not afraid of you, Liam, if that's what worries you.''

''Maybe, in part.''

''I'm not, I couldn't be.'' She wanted to reach out to him, to tell him she loved him, but he pushed back from the table and began to prowl about the room just as he'd asked her not to.

''You're seeing it as a storybook. Magic and romance and happy-ever-after. But it's just life, Rowan, with all its messes and mistakes. Its needs and demands. Life,'' he repeated, turning back to her, ''that has to be lived.''

''You're only half right,'' she told him. ''I can't help but see it as magical, as romantic, but I understand the rest. How could I not understand after meeting your cousins, seeing their families? That's what I met yesterday, a family. Not a picture in a book.''

''And you were...comfortable with them?''

''Very much.'' Her heart began to trip in her throat. It mattered to him, she could see it. Mattered that she accepted his family, and him. Because...was it possible it was because he loved her, too? That he wanted her to be part of his life?

Joy spurted through her in one long liquid gush.

''Rowan.'' He came back to sit, so that she hid her trembling hands under the table. ''My cousins are many. Here, in Ireland. In Wales, Cornwall. Some are Donovans, some Malones, some Rileys. And some are O'Mearas.''

Her heart had bounded into her head to spin dreamily. ''Yes, you said your mother was an O'Meara. We might even be distant relatives. Wouldn't that be nice? Then in some convoluted way I might be connected to Morgana and the rest.''

He bit back a sigh, then reaching for her hands, he

took them firmly in his and leaned closer. ''Rowan, I didn't say we might be cousins, but that we *are* cousins. Distant, it's true, but we share blood. A legacy.''

Puzzled by the sudden intensity she frowned at him. ''I suppose we might be. Tenth cousins or something, however many times removed. I'm not entirely clear how that works. It's interesting, but...''

This time her heart seemed to stop. ''What do you mean?'' she said slowly. ''We share a legacy?''

''Your great-grandmother, Rowan O'Meara was a witch. As I am. As you are.''

''That's absurd.'' She started to jerk her hands free, but he held them fast. ''That's absurd, Liam. I didn't even know her, and you certainly didn't.''

''I know of her.'' He spoke calmly now. ''Of Rowan O'Meara from Clare, who fell in love and married, and left her homeland, and abjured her gifts. She did this because the man she loved asked it of her. She did this freely, as was her right. And when she birthed her children, she said nothing of their heritage until they were grown.''

''You're thinking of someone else,'' was all she could say.

''So they thought her eccentric, and perhaps a bit fey, but they didn't believe. When they birthed children of their own, they only said Rowan O'Meara was odd. Kind and loving, but odd. And when the daughter of her daughter birthed a daughter, that child was raised not knowing what ran in her blood.''

''A person would have to know. How could you not know?'' This time he released her hands so she could pull back, spring to her feet. ''You'd feel it. You'd sense it.''

''And haven't you?'' He got to his feet as well, wishing he'd found a way to tell her without frightening her. ''Haven't you felt it, from time to time? Felt that stirring, that burn in the blood, wondered at it?''

''No.'' That was a lie, she thought and backed away. ''I don't know. But you're wrong, Liam. I'm just ordinary.''

''You saw pictures in the flames, dreamed your dreams as a child. Felt the tingle of power under your skin, in your mind.''

''Imagination,'' she insisted. ''Children have wonderful ones.'' But she felt a tingle now, and part of it was fear.

''You said you weren't afraid of me.'' He said it softly, as he might to a deer startled in the woods. ''Why would you be afraid of yourself?''

''I'm not afraid. I just know it's not true.''

''Then you'd be willing to test it, to see which of us is right?''

''Test what? How?''

''The first skill learned and the last to leave is the making of fire. What's inside you already knows how it's done. I'll just remind you.'' He stepped to her, taking her hand before she could evade. ''And you have my word that I won't do it myself, just as I want your word that you won't block what comes.''

It seemed even her soul was trembling now. ''I don't have to block anything because there isn't anything.''

"Then come with me."

"Where?" she demanded as he pulled her outside. But she already knew.

"The dance," he said simply. "You won't have control just yet, and it's protected."

"Liam, this is ridiculous. I'm just a normal woman, and in order to make a fire I need kindling and a match."

He paused just long enough to glare at her. "You think I'm lying to you?"

"I think you're mistaken." She had to scramble to keep up with his ground-eating strides. "There probably was a Rowan O'Meara who was a witch. There probably was, Liam, but she wasn't my great-grandmother. My great-grandmother was a sweet, slightly dotty old woman who painted beautifully and told fairy stories."

"Dotty?" The insult of that brought him up short. "Who told you that?"

"My mother—that is—"

"So." He nodded as if she'd just confirmed everything he'd said. "Dotty," he muttered as he began to stride along again. "The woman gives up everything for love and they call her dotty. Aye, maybe she was at that. She'd have been better off staying in Ireland and mating with one of her own."

Then he wouldn't be stalking down this path with Rowan's trembling hand in his, he thought.

He wasn't entirely sure if he was pleased or annoyed with that particular twist of fate.

When he reached the stone circle, he pulled her directly to the center. She was out of breath, from the quick walk and from what she could feel swimming in the air.

"The circle's cast and so it begins. I ask that all be safe within. This woman comes that she may see. As I will, so mote it be."

As the chant ended, the wind swept through the stones, wrapped like a warm caress around Rowan's body. Startled, she crossed her arms over her breasts, gripped her own shoulders. "Liam—"

"You should be calm, but that will be hard for you. Nothing here will harm you, Rowan, I swear to you." He laid his hands over hers and kissed her, gently but deeply, until the stiffness of her body softened. "If you won't trust yourself, trust me."

"I do trust you, but this—I'm afraid of this."

He stroked a hand down her hair, and realized in many ways what he was doing was like initiating a virgin to love. It should be done sweetly, patiently, and with thoughts only on her.

"Think of it as a game." He smiled at her as he stepped back. "A more basic one than you imagine just now." He drew her down to her knees. "Breathe deep and slow until you hear your heartbeat in your head. Close your eyes if it helps, until you're steady."

"You tell me I'm going to make fire out of nothing, and then ask me to be steady." But she closed her eyes. The sooner she could prove to him he was mistaken, the sooner it would be over.

"A game," she said on the first long breath. "All right, just a game, and when you see I'm no good at it, we'll go home and finish breakfast."

Remember what you weren't told, but knew. Liam's

voice was a quiet murmur inside her mind. *Feel what you always felt but never understood. Listen to your heart. Trust your blood.*

"Open your eyes, Rowan."

She wondered if this was like being hypnotized. To be so fully, almost painfully aware, yet to be somehow outside yourself. She opened her eyes, looked into his as sunlight streamed between them. "I don't know what to do."

"Don't you?" There was the faintest lilt of amusement in his voice now. "Open yourself, Rowan. Believe in yourself, accept the gift that's been waiting for you."

A game, she thought again. Just a game. In it she was a hereditary witch, with power sleeping just under the surface. Waking it was only a matter of believing, of wanting, of accepting.

She stretched out her hands, stared at them as if they belonged to someone else who watched them tremble lightly. They were narrow hands, with long slender fingers. Ringless, strangely elegant. They cast twin shadows on the ground.

She heard her own heartbeat, just as he'd told her. And she heard the slow, deep sound of her own breathing, as if she were awake listening to herself sleep.

Fire, she thought. For light, for heat. For comfort. She could see it in her mind, pale gold flames just touched with deep red at the edges. Glowing low and simmering, rising up like torches to the sky. Smokeless and beautiful.

Fire, she thought again, for heat, for light. Fire that burns both day and night.

Dizzy, she swayed a little. Liam had to fight every instinct to keep from reaching out to her.

Then her head fell back, her eyes went violently blue. The air hushed. Waited. He watched as she lost a kind of innocence.

Power whipped through her like the wind that suddenly rose to send her hair flying. The sudden heat of it made her gasp, made her shudder. Then it streaked like a rocket down her arms, seemed to shoot from her fingers into a pool of light.

She saw with dazzled eyes, the fire she'd made.

It sizzled on the ground, tiny dancing flames of gold edged with red. The heat of it warmed her knees, then her hands as she hesitantly stretched them over it. As she drew them back, the flames shot high.

"Oh. Oh, no!"

"Ease back, Rowan. You need a bit of control yet."

He brought the thin column of fire down as she stared and stuttered.

"How did I—how could I—" She snapped her gaze to his. "You."

"You know it wasn't me. It's your heritage, Rowan, and your choice whether you accept it or not."

"It came from me." She closed her eyes, inhaling, exhaling slowly until she could do so without her breath shuddering out. "It came from me," she repeated, and looked at him. She couldn't deny it now, what some part of her knew. Perhaps had always known.

"I felt it, I saw it. There were words in my head, like a chant. I don't know what to think, or what to do."

"What do you feel?"

"Amazed." She let out a dazed laugh and stared at her own hands. "Thrilled. Terrified and delighted and wonderful. There's magic in me." It shimmered in her eyes, glowed on her face. This time her laugh was full and free as she sprang up to turn circles inside the ring of stones.

Grinning widely, Liam sat with his legs crossed and watched her embrace self-discovery. It made her beautiful, he realized. This sense of sheer joy gave her a rich and textured beauty.

"All my life I've been average. Pathetically ordinary, tediously normal." She spun another circle then collapsed on the ground beside him to throw her arms around his neck. "Now there's magic in me."

"There always was."

She felt like a child with hundreds and hundreds of brightly wrapped presents waiting to be opened and explored. "You can teach me more."

"Aye." Understanding something of what was racing through her, he flicked a finger down her cheek. "I can. I will. But not just now. We've been here more than an hour, and I want my breakfast."

"An hour." She blinked as he rose and hauled her to her feet. "It seems like just a few minutes."

"It took you a while to get down to things. It won't take you so long the next time." With a thought he put out the fire. ''We'll see if we can find where your talents lie once I've had my meal.''

''Liam.'' She turned into him for a moment, pressed her lips to his throat. ''Thank you.''

She learned fast. Liam had never considered himself a good teacher, but he supposed it had something to do with the student.

This one was open and eager and quick.

It didn't take long to determine her talents channeled into magic, as Morgana's did. Within a day or two, they determined she had no real gift for seeing. She could give him her thoughts, but could only read his clearly if he put them into her head.

And while she couldn't, even after more than an hour of sweaty concentration, transform herself, she turned a footstool into a rosebush with laughing delight.

Show her the joy, Ana had told him. But he understood she was showing *him* as she danced around the clearing, turning the early summer flowers into a maze of color and shape. Rocks became jewel-colored crystals, infant blooms exploded into huge fireworks of brilliant hues. The little stream rose into an elegant waterfall of luminous blue.

He didn't rein her in. She deserved to ride on the wonder of it. Responsibilities, choices, he knew, would come soon enough.

She was creating her own fairy tale. It was so easy all at once to see it perfectly in her mind. And in seeing it, to make it real. Here was her little cottage in the forest, with the stunning witch garden spread out, the sweep of water rising, the whip of the wind blowing free.

And the man.

She turned, unaware how devastating she looked just then with her hair streaming, glossy and wild, her arms flung out and the light of young power in her eyes.

''Just for today. I know it can't stay like this, but just for today. I used to dream of being in a place just like this, with water and wind rushing, and flowers so huge and bright they dazzled your eyes. And the scent of them…''

She trailed off, realizing she had dreamed of this, exactly this. And of him, of Liam Donovan stepping off the porch of a pretty cottage and moving to her, walking under an arbor of flowers that rained pretty pink petals onto the ground.

He would pluck a rose, white as a snowflake from a bush as tall as he. And offer it to her.

''I dreamed,'' she said again. ''When I was a little girl.''

He plucked a rose, white as a snowflake from a bush as tall as he. And offered it to her. ''What did you dream, Rowan Murray?''

''Of this.'' Of you. So often of you.

''Just for today, you can have your dream.''

She sighed as she traced the rose down her cheek. Just for today, she thought, would be enough. ''I was wearing a long blue dress. A robe, really. And yours was black, with gold edgings.'' She laughed, enchanted as she felt the thin silk caress her skin. ''Did I do that, or did you?''

"Does it matter? It's your dream, Rowan, but I'm hoping I kissed you in it."

"Yes." She sighed again as she moved into his arms. "The kind of kiss dreams are made on."

He touched his lips to hers, softly at first. Warming them, softening them, until they parted on a quiet breath. Then deeper, slowly deeper while her arms came up to circle him, while her fingers slipped lazily into his hair.

As he did something trembled in his memory as well. Something once seen or once wished for. When he gave himself to it, he began to float in dreams with her. And so drew her closer.

Together they circled, a graceful dance with hearts keeping the beat.

Her feet no longer touched the ground as they spun. The dreams of a romantic young girl shimmered and shaped into the needs of a woman. Warmth skimmed over her skin as she held him tighter, drew him into her heart. As she offered him more. Offered him everything.

There were candles in her dream. Dozens of them, fragrant and white and burning in tall silver stands with gilded leaves winding around them. And a bed, lit by them, draped in white and gold.

When he carried her to it, she was dizzy with love, washed in wonder.

"How could I have known?" She drew him down to her. "How could I have forgotten?"

He wondered the same of himself, but couldn't question it now, not now when she was so soft, so giving, when her lips were parting for his and her sigh of pleasure slipped into him like wine from a golden cup.

The sun dipped down behind the trees, edging them with fire, shooting color into the deepening sky. In the trees, the birds sang to those last lights.

"You're beautiful."

She wouldn't have believed it. But here, now, she felt beautiful. She felt powerful. She felt loved. Just for today, she thought and met his mouth with hers.

He drank from her, with thirst but without greed. Held her close but without desperation. Here, they both knew, time could spin out. Time could be taken.

Tongues met and tangled in a slow, intimate dance. Breath mixed. Murmurs melded.

She stroked her hands along the silk of his robe, then beneath to flesh. So warm. So smooth. His mouth on her throat, urging her to tip her head to give him more, and the light nip of teeth where her pulse beat. The erratic bump of it tempted him to slick his tongue over her skin, to fill himself with the flavor that was only her.

He parted her robe, lightly as air. When his hands, his mouth took possession of her, she arched gently.

Enjoy me, she seemed to say. Enchant me.

She sighed with him, moved with him, while the air swam with scent and the warm, soft wind caressed her naked skin. Sensations glimmered, tangled with delights both bright and dark. Lost in them, steeped in them, she rolled with him, rose languidly over him.

Her body was wand slim, white as marble in the delicate light. Her hair was lifted by the wind, her eyes full of secrets. Captivated, he ran his hands up her thighs, over her hips, her torso, closed them over her breasts.

And there her heart beat in the same hammer blows as his own.

"Rowan," he murmured, as those secrets, as that power glinted in her eyes. "You are all manner of witch."

Her laugh was quick and triumphant. She leaned down, took his mouth hungrily with hers. Heat, sudden and brutal slammed into him, leaped into his blood like the fire she'd made only hours before.

She felt it, too, the quick change, and that she had made it. That, she thought wildly, that was power. Riding on it she took him into her, bowing back to revel in the shock of it, watching stars wheel in the black sky overhead.

His hands gripped her hips, his breath exploded from his lungs. Instinctively he struggled for control, but his already slippery grasp broke as she took him.

She took. Her hips moved like lightning, her body soared with a wild whip of energy that pushed him, raced ahead, dragged him with her.

She rocked herself to madness, then beyond, and still she drove him on. He said her name. She heard the sound break from him as his body plunged with hers. And she saw as they flew up, how his eyes flashed, then went dark and blind.

She all but wept with triumph as she grabbed hold and fell over with him.

He'd never allowed a woman to take control. Now, as Rowan lay sprawled over him, he realized he hadn't been able to stop it. Not with her. There were a great many things he hadn't been able to stop with her.

He turned his face into her hair and wondered what would come next. Only seconds later, when she spoke, he knew.

"I love you, Liam." She said it quietly, with her lips over his heart. "I love you."

He called the panic that sprang up inside him sense, responsibility. "Rowan—"

"You don't have to love me back. I just can't stand not telling you anymore. I was afraid to tell you before." She shifted, looked at him. "I don't think I'll be afraid of anything ever again. So I love you, Liam."

He sat up beside her. "You don't know all there is to know, so you can't know what you think or what you feel. Or what you'll want," he added on a huff of breath. "I have things to explain, things to show you. We'll do better at my cabin."

"All right." She made her smile easy, even as a dread filled her heart that the magic of that day was over.

Chapter 12

What else could he tell her that would shock or surprise? Rowan asked herself. He'd told her he was a witch, then had proved it and somehow made her accept it. He'd wiped out twenty-seven years of her simple beliefs about herself by telling her she was a witch as well. Had proved it. She had not only accepted it, but had embraced it.

How much more could there be?

She wished he would speak. But he said nothing as they walked through moonlight from her cabin to his. She'd known him long enough to understand when he fell into this kind of silence he would tell her nothing until he was ready.

By the time they reached his cabin and stepped inside her nerves were strung tight.

What she didn't think about, refused to consider,

was the fact that he'd withdrawn into that silence after she'd told him she loved him.

"Is it so serious?" She tried for a light tone but the words came out uneven, and very close to a plea.

"For me, yes. You'll decide what it means to you."

He moved into the bedroom and running his fingers over the wall beside the fireplace opened a door she hadn't known was there into a room she'd have sworn didn't exist.

A soft light glowed from it, as pale and cool as the moonlight.

"A secret room?"

"Not secret," he corrected. "Private. Come in, Rowan."

It was a measure of her trust in him that she stepped forward into that light. The floor was stone, smooth as a mirror, the walls and ceiling of wood, highly polished. Light and the shadow she cast reflected back off those surfaces and shimmered like water.

There was a table, richly carved and inlaid, and on it a bowl of thick blue glass, a stemmed cup of pewter, a small mirror with a silver back ornately scrolled and a slim, smooth handle of amethyst. Another bowl held small, colorful crystals. A round globe of smoky quartz stood on the silver backs of a trio of winged dragons.

What did he see when he looked into it? she wondered. What would she see?

But she turned and watched Liam light candles, watched their flames rise into air already perfumed with fragrant smoke.

She saw another table then, a small round surface on a simple pedestal. Liam opened the box resting there, took out a silver amulet on a chain. He held it a moment, as if testing its weight, then set it down with a quiet jingle of metal on wood.

"Is this…a ceremony?"

He glanced over, those tawny eyes distracted as if he'd forgotten she was there. But he hadn't forgotten her. He'd forgotten nothing.

"No. You've had a lot to deal with, haven't you, Rowan? You've asked me not to touch your thoughts so I can't know what's in your mind, how you're thinking of all this."

He hadn't meant to touch her, but found his fingers grazing her cheek. "A lot of it I can read in your eyes."

"I've told you what I think and what I feel."

"So you have."

But you haven't told me, she thought, and because it hurt her, she turned away. "Will you explain to me what everything is for?" she asked and traced a fingertip over the scrolling on the little mirror.

"Tools. Just pretty tools," he told her. "You'll need some of your own."

"Do you see things in the glass?"

"Aye."

"Are you ever afraid to look?" She smiled a little and looked back at him. "I think I might be."

"What's seen is…possibility."

She wandered, avoiding him. There was change coming. Whether it was her woman's instincts or her newly discovered gifts that told her, she was sure of it. In a glass case were more stones, stunning clusters with spears rising, smooth towers, jewel-tone globes.

He waited her out, not with patience but because for once he didn't know how to begin. When she turned back to him, her hands linked nervously, her eyes full of doubts, he had no choice but to choose.

"I knew you were coming here."

He didn't mean here, to this room, tonight. He saw her acknowledge this. "Did you know…what would happen?"

"Possibilities. There are always choices. We each made ours, and have more to make yet. You know something of your heritage and of mine, but not all. In my country, in my family, there is a tradition. It's simplest, I suppose, to compare it to rank, though it's not precisely that. But one takes a place as head of the family. To guide, and counsel. To help in settling disputes should they arise."

Once again he picked up the silver amulet, once again he set it down.

"Your father wears one of those in gold."

"Aye, he does."

"Because he's head of the family?"

She was quick, Liam thought. Foolish of him to have forgotten that. "He is, until he chooses to pass on the duty."

"To you."

"It's traditional for the amulet to be passed down to the oldest child. But there are choices, on both sides, and there are…stipulations. To inherit, one must be worthy of it."

"Of course you are."

"One must want it."

Her smile faded into a look of puzzlement. "Don't you?"

"I haven't decided." He slipped his hands into his pockets before he could pick up the amulet again. "I came here to take time, to think and consider. It must be my choice. I won't be bullied by fate."

The regal tone of his voice made her smile again. "No, you wouldn't be. That's another reason you'd be good at it." She started to go to him, but he held up a hand.

"There are other requirements. If there is marriage, it must be to a mate with elfin blood, and the marriage must be for love, not for duty. Both must enter into it freely."

"That seems only right," she began, then stopped. As Liam had said, she was quick. "I have elfin blood, and I've just told you I'm in love with you."

"And if I take you, my choices diminish."

This time it took her a moment. It had been said so coolly it was like an iced sword to the heart. "Your choices, I see." She nodded slowly while inside she fought to save the scattered pieces of her heart, the pitiful tatters of her pride. "And your choices include accepting this aspect of your heritage or abjuring it. You'd take that very, very seriously, wouldn't you, Liam?"

"How could I not?"

"And I'm more or less like a weight for the scale. You just have to decide which bowl to set me in. How…awkward for you."

"It's not as simple as that," he shot back, off balance by her sudden sharp tones. "It's my life."

"And mine," she added. "You said you knew I was coming here, but I didn't know about you. So I had no choice there. I fell in love with you the minute I saw you, but you were prepared and you had your own agenda. You *knew* I would love you."

It was hurled at him, a bitter accusation that had him staring at her. "You're mistaken."

"Oh, really? How many times did you slip into my mind to see? Or come into my house as a wolf and listen to me babble? Without giving me the choice you're so damn fond of. You knew I met the requirements, so you studied and measured and considered."

"I didn't know!" He shouted it at her, furious to have his actions tilted toward deceit. "I didn't know until you told me about your great-grandmother."

"I see. So up to that point you were either playing with me or deciding if you could use me as your out should you decide to refuse your position."

"That's ridiculous."

"Then suddenly you've got a witch on your hands. You wanted her—I don't doubt you wanted me, and I was pathetically easy. I took whatever you chose to give me, and was grateful."

It humiliated her to think of it now, to remember how she had rushed into his arms, trusting her heart. Trusting him.

"I cared for you, Rowan. I care for you."

Her cheeks were ghost pale in the flickering light, her eyes dark and deep. "Do you know how insulting that is? Do you know how humiliating it is to understand that you knew I was in love with you while you figured the angles and made your choices? What choice did I have, what choice did you give me?"

"All I could."

She shook her head fiercely. "No, all you *would*," she tossed back. "You knew exactly how vulnerable I was when I came here, how lost."

"I did, yes. That's why I—"

"So you offer me a chance to work with you," she interrupted. "Knowing I was already dazzled by you, knowing how desperately I needed something. Then, in your own good time, you told me who you were, who I was. At your pace, Liam, always at your pace. And each time I moved exactly as you expected I would. It's all been just another game."

"That's not true." Incensed, he took her arms. "I thought of you, too damn much of you. And did what I thought was right, what was best."

The jolt shot through his fingertips, up his arms, with such heat and power, it knocked him back a full two steps. This time he could only gape at her, shocked to the core that she'd caught him so completely unaware.

"Damn it, Rowan." His hands still stung from the slap of her will.

"I won't be bullied, either." Her knees were jellied at the realization she'd had not only the ability but the fury to shove him back with her mind. "This isn't what you expected, this isn't one of your possibilities. I was supposed to come in here with you tonight, listen to you, then fold my hands, bow my head like the quiet little mouse I am, and leave it all up to you."

Her eyes were vividly blue, her face no longer pale but flushed with anger, and to his annoyance outrageously beautiful. ''Not precisely,'' he said with dignity. ''But it is up to me.''

''The hell it is. You have to decide what you want, true enough, but don't expect me to sit meekly while you choose or discard me. Always, always, people have made decisions for me, chosen the way my life should go. What have you done but the same?''

''I'm not your parents,'' he shot back. ''Or your Alan. These were different circumstances entirely.''

''Whatever the circumstances, you held the controls and guided me along. I won't tolerate that. I've been ordinary.'' The words ripped out of her, straight from the belly. ''You wouldn't understand that, you've never been ordinary. But I have, all my life. I won't be ordinary again.''

''Rowan.'' He would try calm, he told himself. He would try reason. ''All I wanted for you was what you wanted for yourself.''

''And what I wanted most, was for you to love me. Just me, Liam, whatever and however I am. I didn't let myself expect it, but I wanted it. My mistake was in still not thinking enough of myself.''

Tears shone in her eyes now, unmanning him. ''Don't weep. Rowan, I never meant to hurt you.'' He took her hand now, and she let it lay limply in his.

''No, I'm sure you didn't,'' she said quietly. The force of her fury had passed. Now she was only tired. ''That only makes it sadder. And me more pathetic. I told you I loved you.'' Tears still trembled on the edge of her voice. ''And you know I do. But you can't tell me, you can't decide if it...suits you.''

She swallowed the tears, reached deep for the pride she'd used too rarely. ''From here, I decide my own fate.'' She drew her hand from him, stood back. ''And you yours.''

She turned to the door, bringing him a fresh and baffling wave of panic. ''Where are you going?''

''Where I please.'' She glanced back. ''I was your lover, Liam, but never your partner. I won't settle for that, not even for you.'' She let out a quiet breath, studying him in the shifting light. ''You had my heart in your hands,'' she murmured. ''And you didn't know what to do with it. I can tell you, without the crystal ball, without the gift, you'll never have another like it.''

As she slipped away from him he knew it was not only prophecy, it was truth.

It took her a week to deal with the practicalities. San Francisco hadn't changed in the months she'd been gone, nor in the days she'd been back. But she had.

She could look out her window now, at the city and realize it hadn't been the place that had dissatisfied her, but her place in it. It was doubtful she'd ever live there again, but she thought she could look back and find memories—good and bad. Life was made up of both.

''Are you sure you're doing the right thing, Rowan?'' Belinda asked. She was a graceful woman, with dark hair, short as a pixie's, and eyes of misty green.

Rowan glanced up from her packing and looked into Belinda's concerned face. "No, but I'm doing it just the same."

Rowan had changed, Belinda mused. She was certainly stronger, more than a little wounded. Guilt nagged at her. "I feel some responsibility in this."

"No." Rowan said it firmly, and smoothed a sweater into her suitcase. "You're not responsible."

Restless, Belinda wandered to the window. The bedroom was nearly empty now. She knew Rowan had given many of her things away, stored others. In the morning, she would be gone. "I sent you there."

"No, I asked if I could use your cabin."

Belinda turned. "There were things I could have told you."

"You weren't meant to—I understand that, Belinda."

"If I'd known Liam would be such a jackass, I—" She broke off, scowled. "I should have, I've known him all my life. A more stubborn, thickheaded, irritating man has yet to be born." Then she sighed. "But he's kind with it, and most of his stubbornness comes from caring so much."

"You don't have to explain him to me. If he'd trusted me, believed in me, things might be different." She took the last of her clothes from the closet, laid them on the bed. "If he'd loved me, everything would be different."

"Are you so sure he doesn't?"

"I've decided the only thing I can be sure of is

myself. It was the hardest and most valuable thing I learned while I was away. Do you want this blouse? It never flattered me.''

''It's more my color than yours.'' Belinda wandered over, laid a hand on Rowan's shoulder. ''Did you speak with your parents?''

''Yes. Well, I tried.'' Thoughtfully Rowan folded trousers, packed them. ''On one level it went better than I ever expected. They were upset at first, and baffled, that I'm going away, that I'm giving up teaching. Naturally, they tried to point out the flaws, the consequences.''

''Naturally,'' Belinda repeated, just dryly enough to make Rowan smile.

''They can't help it. But we talked a long time. You know, I don't think we've actually talked like that before. I explained why I was going, what I wanted to do and why—well not all the why.''

''You didn't ask your mother about what you are?''

''In the end, I couldn't. I mentioned my grandmother, and legacies, and how being named after her had turned out to be so...appropriate. My mother waved it off. No,'' Rowan corrected with a sigh, ''closed it off. It's as if she'd blocked it off—if she ever even really knew or suspected. What runs through my blood, and even through her own, simply doesn't exist in her world.''

''So you left it at that?''

''Why should I push her on something that makes her uncomfortable or unhappy?'' Rowan lifted her hands. ''I'm content with it, so that's enough. If I'd insisted on stripping away whatever barrier she'd put up, what purpose would it serve?''

''None. You did the right thing, for yourself and your mother.''

''What matters is, in the end, my parents understood as much as they're able about the decisions I've made. Because in the end all they want is for me to be happy.''

''They love you.''

''Yes, maybe more than I ever gave them credit for.'' And she smiled. ''It helps some that Alan's been seeing someone else—a math instructor. My mother finally broke down and told me she's had them over for dinner and they're charming together.''

''We'll wish them well.''

''I wish them very well. He's a nice man and deserves to be happy.''

''So do you.''

''Yes, you're right.'' Giving it one last look, Rowan closed the last suitcase. ''I intend to be. I'm excited, Belinda, nervous, but excited. Going to Ireland like this. One way ticket.'' She pressed a hand to her uneasy stomach. ''Not knowing if I'll stay or where I'll go or what I'll do. It's thrilling.''

''You'll go first to Castle Donovan in Clare? See Morgan's and Sebastian's and Ana's parents?''

''Yes. I appreciate you contacting them, and their asking me to stay.''

''You'll enjoy them, and they you.''

''I hope so. And I want to learn more.'' Rowan stared into the middle distance. ''I very much want to learn.''

"Then you will. Oh, I'll miss you. Cousin." With this Belinda caught Rowan in a hard embrace. "I have to go, before I start blubbering. Call me," she ordered, scooping up the blouse as she hurried out of the room. "Write, whistle in the wind, but keep in touch."

"I will." Rowan walked her to the door of the empty apartment, exchanged one last fierce hug. "Wish me luck."

"That and more. Blessed be, Rowan." Already sniffling, she dashed out.

Weepy herself, Rowan closed the door, turned and looked. There was nothing left here, she thought. Nothing left to do. She'd be moving on in the morning. Moving in a way she'd never imagined. She had family in Ireland, and roots. It was time to explore them, and in doing so, to explore herself.

What she'd already learned gave her the foundation to build more.

And if she thought of Liam, if she pined for him, so be it. She could live with heartache, but she couldn't—wouldn't live with distrust.

The knock on the door surprised her, then she smiled. Belinda, she imagined, not quite ready to say goodbye.

But the woman at the door was a stranger. Beautiful, elegant in a simple dress of mossy green. "Hello, Rowan, I hope I'm not disturbing you."

The voice, that lilt of Irish hills. The eyes, warm, deep gold. "No, not at all. Please come in, Mrs. Donovan."

"I wasn't sure I'd be welcome." She stepped inside, smiled. ''Since my son's made such a fool of himself.''

''I'm glad to meet you. I'm sorry—I can't even offer you a chair.''

''You're leaving then. Well, I'll give you this as a going away present.'' She held out a box of carved apple wood. ''And as a thank-you for the drawing of Liam. They're chalks, the pastels you wanted.''

''Thank you.'' Rowan took the box, grateful to have something to do with her hands. ''I'm surprised you'd want to see me since Liam and I...since we argued.''

''Ah.'' The woman waved a hand in dismissal and wandered the room. ''I've argued with him enough myself to know it's impossible not to. He's a head like a brick. But his heart isn't hard.''

When Rowan looked away, she sighed. ''I don't mean to make you uncomfortable.''

''It's all right.'' Rowan carried the box to the narrow counter that separated the living area from the kitchen. ''He's your son and you love him.''

''I do, very much. Flaws and all.'' She laid a gentle hand on Rowan's arm. ''He's hurt you, and I'm sorry for it. Oh, I could box his ears for it,'' she snapped in a lightning change of mood that had Rowan smiling uncertainly.

''Have you ever?''

''Boxed his ears?'' This time Arianna laughed, light and free. ''Oh, with Liam what choice do you have? He was never an easy one. Girl, the stories I could tell you would curl your hair. Takes after his father, he does, and can go royal on you in a blink.

Now Finn would say it's my temper running through him, and he'd be right. But if a woman doesn't have spine and temper, men like that will march right over you."

She paused, studying Rowan's face and her own eyes filled abruptly with tears. "Oh, you love him still. I didn't want to look and offend you. But I can see it."

"It doesn't matter."

But before she could turn away, Arianna gripped her hands, gave them an impatient squeeze. "Love is all that matters, and you're smart enough to know it. I've come to you as a mother only, with no more than a mother's right, and a mother's heart. He suffers, Rowan."

"Mrs. Donovan—"

"Arianna. It's your decision to make, but you need to know. He's hurt as well, and missing you."

"He doesn't love me."

"If he didn't he wouldn't have made so many foolish mistakes. I know his heart, Rowan." She said it softly and with such simple faith, Rowan felt a flutter in her stomach. "It's yours if you'll have it. I don't say it because I want him to step into his father's place. Whoever he loved would have been welcome with joy. Don't turn your back on your own happiness just to hug your pride. One's cold without the other."

"You're asking me to go to him."

"I'm asking you to listen to your heart. Nothing more or less."

Rowan crossed her arms over her breasts, rubbed her own shoulders as she paced the bare room. "I still love him. I always will. Maybe part of me recognized him in that first instant. And my heart just fell at his feet.''

''And he didn't treasure it as he should have, because he was afraid of it.''

''He didn't trust me.''

''No, Rowan, he didn't trust himself.''

''If he loves me...'' Even the thought of it weakened her, so she shook her head, turned back with her eyes level, her hands steady. ''He'll have to say it. And he'll have to accept me on equal grounds. I'll take nothing less.''

Arianna's smile was slow, and it was sweet. ''Oh, you'll do Rowan Murray, for yourself and for him. Will you go back and see?''

''Yes.'' She let out the breath she hadn't known she was holding. ''Will you help me?''

The wolf raced through the woods, as if trying to outrun the night. The thin crescent of the moon offered little light, but his eyes were keen.

His heart was burdened.

He rarely sought sleep now, for the dreams would come no matter how he willed them away. They were always of her.

When he reached the cliffs, he threw back his head and called out for his mate. Even as the sound swept away the silence, he grieved for what he'd so carelessly lost.

He tried to blame her, and did. Often. Whatever form he took, his mind worked coolly, finding dozens of ways, small and large, to shift the burden to her.

She'd been too impulsive, too rash. She'd twisted his motives, his logic. Deliberately. She'd refused to see the clear-cut sense in everything he'd done.

But tonight that line of thinking did nothing to ease his heart. He turned away from the cliffs, outraged that he couldn't stop yearning for her. When the voice whispered, *love waits* in his head, he snarled viciously and blocked it out.

He prowled the shadows. He sniffed the air, snarled again. It was Rowan he scented, some trick of the mind, he thought, infuriated with his own weakness. She'd left him, and that was the end of it.

Then he saw the light, a gold glimmer through the trees. Tawny eyes narrowed as he moved toward the circle of stones. He stepped through them, saw her standing in the center. And went very still.

She wore a long dress the color of moondust that foamed around her ankles. Her hair was loose, flowing over her shoulders, with hints of silver shining in it from the jewels wound through. There was silver at her wrists as well, at her ears.

And on the bodice of her dress lay a pendant, an oval of moonstone in a setting of hammered silver.

She stood slim and straight behind the fire she'd made. Then she smiled at him.

"Waiting for me to scratch your ears, Liam?" She caught the quick flash of temper in his eyes, and only continued to smile.

The wolf stepped forward, became a man. "You left without a word."

"I thought we had plenty of words."

"Now you've come back."

"So it seems." She arched a brow with a studied coolness even as her stomach jumped with raw nerves. "You're wearing your amulet. So you've decided."

"Aye. I'll take my duty when it comes. And you wear yours."

"My great-grandmother's legacy to me." Rowan closed her fingers around the stone, felt it calm her nerves. "I've accepted it, and myself."

His hands burned to touch her. He kept them lightly fisted at his side. "I'll be going back to Ireland."

"Really?" She said it lightly, as if it meant nothing to her. "I'm planning on leaving for Ireland myself in the morning. That's why I thought I should come back and finish this."

"Ireland?" His brows drew together. Who was this woman? was all he could think, so cool, so self-possessed.

"I want to see where I came from. It's a small country," she said with a careless shrug, "but large enough for us to stay out of each other's way. If that's what you want."

"I want you back." The words were out before he could stop them. He hissed out a curse, jammed his fisted hands into his pockets. So he'd said it, he thought, humbled himself with the words and the needs. And the hell with it. "I want you back," he repeated.

"For what?"

"For—" She baffled him. He dragged his hands free to rake them through his hair. "For what do you think? I'll take my place in the family, and I want you with me.''

''It's hardly that simple.''

He started to speak, something ill-advised and much too heated he realized, and pulled himself back. Control might be shaky—*in the name of Finn, just look at her*—but it was still there. ''All right, I hurt you. I'm sorry for it. It was never my intention, and I apologize.''

''Well then, you're sorry. Let me just jump into your arms.''

He blinked, deeply shocked at the biting tone. ''What do you want me to say? I made a mistake—more than one. I don't like admitting it.''

''You'll have to, straight out. You took your time deciding if I'd suit you—and your purposes. Once you decided what those purposes would be. When you didn't know about my bloodline you considered if you should take me and get out of the duty you weren't sure you wanted. And when you did know, then it was a matter of deciding if I'd suit you if you did accept it.''

''It wasn't that black and white.'' He let out a breath, admitting that sometimes the gray areas didn't matter. ''But yes, more or less. It would have been a big step either way.''

''For me as well,'' she tossed back, eyes firing. ''But how much did you consider that?''

She whirled away, and had him rushing after her before he'd realized he'd moved. ''Don't go.''

She hadn't intended to, just to pace off her temper,

but the quick desperation in the two words had her turning slowly.

"For pity's sake, Rowan, don't leave me again. Do you know what it was for me to come for you that morning and see you were gone. Just gone." He turned away, scrubbing his face over his hands as he struggled with the pain. "The house empty of you, and still full of you. I was going to go after you, right then and there, drag you back where I wanted you. Where I needed you."

"But you didn't."

"No." He turned to face her. "Because you were right. All the choices had been mine. This was yours and I had to live with it. I'm asking you now not to leave me again, not to make me live with it. You matter to me."

Everything inside her cried out to go to him. Instead she lifted her brows again. "Matter to you? Those are small words for such a big request."

"I care for you."

"I care for the puppy the little girl next door has. I'm not content with that from you. So if that's all—"

"I love you. Damn it, you know very well I love you." He snatched her hand to keep her from leaving. Both the gesture and the tone were anything but loverlike.

Somehow she kept her voice steady. "We've established I don't have the gift to see, so how do I know very well what you don't tell me?"

"I am telling you. Damn it, woman, can't you hear, either?" His control slipped enough to have sparks snapping in the air around them. "It's been you, all along, right from the start of it. I told myself I didn't—that I wouldn't until I decided. I made myself believe it, but there was no one ever but you."

The thrill of it—the words, the passion behind them driven by as much anger as heart—spun through her like rainbows. Even as she started to speak, he released her hand to prowl the circle much as the wolf he favored.

"And I don't like it." He flung the words over his shoulder at her. "I'm not required to like it."

"No." She wondered why she should feel delighted rather than insulted. And it came to her that it gave her an unexpected, and desperately sweet power over him. "No, you're not. Neither am I."

He whirled back, glaring at her. "I was content in my life as it was."

"No, you weren't." The answer surprised both of them. "You were restless, dissatisfied and just a little bored. And so was I."

"You were unhappy. And the way you're thinking now it's that I should have taken advantage of that. Plucked you up straight away, told you things you couldn't have been prepared to hear and carried you off to Ireland. Well, I didn't and I won't be sorry for that much. I couldn't. You think I deceived you, and maybe I did."

He shrugged now, a regal motion that made her lips want to curve into a smile. "You needed time, and so did I. When I came to you as a wolf it was to comfort. It was as a friend. And so I saw you naked—and enjoyed it. Why shouldn't I?"

"Why indeed," she murmured.

''When I loved you in dreams, we both enjoyed it.''

Since that was issued as a challenge, she merely inclined her head. ''I don't think I ever said otherwise. But still, that choice was yours.''

''Aye, it was, and I'd make it again if only to touch you with my mind. It's not easy for me to admit that I want you as I do. To tell you that I've suffered being without you. Or to ask you to forgive me for doing what I thought was right.''

''You've yet to tell me what it is you expect from me now.''

''I've been clear enough on it.'' Frustration shimmered around him. ''Do you want me to beg?''

''Yes,'' she said after a very cool, very thoughtful moment.

His eyes went bright gold with shock, then dark with what she thought was temper. When he started toward her, her knees began to tremble. Then eyes narrowed, he was down on his.

''Then I will.'' He took her hands that had gone numb. ''I'll beg for you, Rowan, if that's what it takes to have you.''

''Liam—''

''If I'm to humble myself, at least let me get on with it,'' he snapped. ''I don't think you were ordinary ever. Weak is something I don't believe you could be. What I see in you is a woman with a tender heart—too tender at times to think of herself. You're the woman I want. I've wanted before, but I've never needed. I need you. You're who I care for. I've cared before, but never loved. I love you. I'm asking that it be enough for you, Rowan.''

She'd been struck speechless, but found her voice as she laid a hand on his shoulder. ''Why did you never ask before?''

''Asking's not easy for me. If it's arrogance, that's how I am. Damn it, I'm asking you to take me as I am. You love me. I know you do.''

So much for begging, she thought and had to fight back a smile. He managed to look arrogant and not a little fierce even on his knees. ''I never said I didn't. Are you asking me for more?''

''For everything. I'm asking you to take me on— what I am and what I'll do. To be my wife, leave your home for mine and understand that it's forever. Forever, Rowan.'' The faintest of smiles touched his mouth. ''For wolves mate for life, and so do I. I'm asking you to share that life, to let me share yours. I'm asking you here, in the heart of this sacred place, to belong to me.''

He pressed his lips to her hands, held them there until she felt his words turn to feelings and the feelings rush through her like magic.

''I'll have no other but you,'' he murmured. ''You said to me that I held your heart in my hands, and that I'd never have another like it. I'm telling you now you have mine in yours, and I swear to you, Rowan, you'll never have another like it. No one will ever love you more. The choice is yours.''

She studied him, the way his face lifted to hers, how the light from the fire he'd taught her to make danced over it. She didn't need his thoughts to see now. All she wanted was there, in his eyes.

She made her choice, and lowered to her knees so their eyes were on level. "I'll take you on, Liam, as you'll take me. And I'll take nothing less than forever. I'll share the life we make together. I'll belong to you, as you belong to me. That's my choice, and my promise."

Swamped with emotion, he lowered his brow to hers. "God, I missed you. Every hour of every day. There's no magic without you. No heart in it."

He found her mouth with his, pulling her close, swaying as the force of feeling rocked him. She wrapped her arms around him, gave him every answer to every question.

"I could drown in you." He rose to his feet, lifting her high, and her laughter rang out pure and bright as she threw her arms up.

Starlight dazzled her eyes. She watched one shoot across the sky as he spun with her. A trail of gold, a shower of silver. "Tell me again!" she demanded. "Tell me now. Right now!"

"I love you. Now..." He lowered her until their mouths met again. "And ever."

She held him close, heartbeat to heartbeat. "Liam of Donovan." Leaning back, she smiled at him. Her prince, her witch. Her mate. "Will you grant me a boon?"

"Rowan of O'Meara, you have only to ask what you will."

"Take me to Ireland. Take me home."

Pleasure swirled into his eyes. "Now, *a ghra?*" My love.

"In the morning." She drew him back to her. "It's soon enough."

And when they kissed with the firelight glowing, the stars shimmering, the faeries danced in the forest. In the hills far away, pipes played in celebration, and songs of joy were sung.

Love no longer waited, but found its mark.

* * * * *

King's Ransom

Diana Palmer

Chapter One

It had been the longest three weeks of Brianna Scott's life. She had enough trouble as it was, with her twelve-year-old brother in a coma. Tad had been in the unconscious state for three years, since the tragic death of his and Brianna's parents in an automobile wreck.

Brianna's fingers stilled on the computer keys as she fed a letter into the machine's memory. She didn't like thinking about how much longer Tad might remain in the coma. His full name was Timothy Edward, but he'd been Tad since he was born. She was ten years his senior, and she'd taken to giving bottles and changing diapers immediately after he was born.

Their mother had never been in very good health, and Tad's birth had been a major setback for her. Brianna had been handy around the house, thank goodness, or the advent of a new child into the family might have been a disaster. With Brianna's help, her mother was able to regain her health and take proper care of the little boy.

"You look thoughtful," Meg Shannon Ryker mused, pausing beside Brianna's desk with Daphne, her husband's secretary.

"I was just thinking about something," Brianna said. She smiled up at the lovely blond woman who'd married the top executive of Ryker Air only two days ago. It had been a stormy courtship, and a long-standing one, but the marriage hadn't really surprised anyone. The way Steven Ryker and Meg looked at each other was enough to set off major fireworks.

"I'm taking Daphne out for lunch," Meg said. "Can you cope?"

"As long as *he* isn't around," the younger woman said grimly.

"Steven took *him* out for lunch," Meg assured her. "He'll probably go right back to his hotel afterward. After the shoot-out he endured a while ago, it's a miracle that he's still alive. Steve and I can't even take a honeymoon until we get this mess straightened out."

"Aha," Brianna said merrily. "You hate him, too, don't you?"

"Not really." Meg chuckled. "He's very nice."

"Not to me, he isn't," Brianna said shortly. "He looks at me."

"You're very pretty, you know," Meg said, noting

Brianna's exquisite complexion and big blue eyes in their frame of short, straight black hair.

"That isn't what I meant," Brianna corrected. "He...glowers at me. Glares at me. Stares daggers at me. *That* sort of looking."

"I see. Well, you did throw a paperweight at him," Meg pointed out.

"He insulted me," the younger woman muttered. "It wasn't my fault! I love barbecue. Everybody I know loves barbecue. How was I supposed to know that all his colleagues who were also cabinet ministers from Saudi Mahara were Moslems and they can't eat pork?"

"We didn't tell you, so we get to share the blame," Daphne offered, smiling. "I'm sorry. I meant to, but we got busy."

"We've never been so busy before," Meg agreed. "This new contract for Saudi Mahara's jets has been one long headache, although I certainly don't blame Ahmed for it. I'm glad we got the job. It means a stable budget for the company for years to come."

"I know that," Brianna said silently. "But..." Her eyes bulged. "Isn't that Lang?" she asked.

"Oh, Lord, don't let Steven see him," Meg squeaked, because she'd spotted the tall, husky government agent, too. Lang was well built, in his early thirties and handsome enough to turn heads. He was a wild man, though, and Steven Ryker didn't appreciate his devil-may-care attitude.

"What is he doing here?" Daphne wondered.

Lang noticed the three women staring at him. He moved toward them with a grin on his face that was reflected in his dark eyes. He was impeccably dressed in a dark suit, white shirt and conservative tie. The conservative look was a bald-faced lie. Lang was a law unto himself.

"I know, you can't resist me," Lang said, nodding. "But you're a married woman, now, Meg. Control those urges. Your husband already offered my boss a bribe to send me to Antarctica on a fact-finding mission."

"Inside a whale, if I remember correctly," Meg mused.

"Why are you here?" Brianna asked worriedly.

He evaded her searching gaze. "You'll find out soon enough," he promised. "I'm waiting for your husband," he added to Meg.

"Steven didn't mention that you were expected," Daphne said curiously.

"I asked him not to. We're very cloak-and-dagger about this," he explained. "No leaks. No loose lips."

"It's something to do with Ahmed, isn't it?" Brianna asked coolly. "Go ahead, tell me it isn't."

"He's trying to avoid being assassinated," Lang reminded her. "He's a foreign dignitary and we're sworn to protect him. We can't let somebody take him out here in Wichita. Bad for our image," he added.

"Can't you send him home and let his own people protect him?" she asked plaintively.

"Not really. Two of the ringleaders of a terrorist

squad that we captured before they did him harm got loose on the way back to Saudi Mahara. Their colleagues have organized a second coup attempt in as many weeks. This is going to be one touchy issue until we resolve it.''

''But I thought Ahmed was being sent home, too,'' Meg began.

Lang shook his head. ''Too risky now. We've come up with a way to keep his identity secret and to protect him and his king. We're installing a man impersonating the king in the Hilton with armed guards on the whole floor. He won't leave his room, and if they make a try for anybody, he'll be first. He's one of our men, of course,'' Lang added with a grimace. ''Getting the royal treatment. Lobster tails every night. Full breakfast served in bed every morning. I volunteered, God knows I did, I'd never have minded the risk. But they thought I was too eager,'' he said with disgust.

The women tried not to laugh. He flexed his broad shoulders. ''Anyway, I'm going to have my hands full. Speaking of full hands, guess who just walked in?''

Steven Ryker and Ahmed ben Rashid were about the same height, both dark haired and dark skinned, but Steven's eyes were a light silvery color and Ahmed's face showed his Arab heritage. He had a mustache, too, unlike Steven. He smiled at Meg and Daphne, but the look he gave Brianna could have fried an egg.

She gave it back with interest.

"Daphne and I were going to lunch," Meg began.

"Go ahead, darling," Steven said gently, pulling her close to kiss her. "I can't turn loose yet. We have some business to discuss."

"You aren't leaving?" Lang asked Brianna suddenly.

She hesitated a minute, startled by the question. "Well, no, not yet...."

"Good." He turned to Steven. "We'd better get to it."

"All right. See you tonight, sweet thing," Steven told Meg, and the smile they shared made Brianna faintly envious.

She turned her attention back to her work, while Daphne and Meg called their goodbyes and Lang went with Steven on into the executive office.

"Yes?" Brianna asked Ahmed with a glare. "Did you want something?"

"You are obnoxious even before you speak," he said curtly. "In my country, you would live on bread and water forever with such an attitude."

"I'd rather live on bread and water than sit at an elegant table eating lobster with *you,*" she said with smiling malice.

"As if you would ever receive such an invitation from me," he returned with faint contempt. "I have my pick of women, you see."

"The Sheik of Araby," she said under her breath.

"I beg your pardon?"

She lifted her eyes to his. "I do hope you enjoy your trip back home when you go, and the sooner the better."

He gave her an indifferent appraisal. "A woman with a tongue such as yours should welcome even the most casual conversation from a man. I am certain that you are unmarried."

"Yes, I am," she agreed happily. "Did my happy expression give me away?"

He frowned. "Give you…away?"

"Did it betray my state of unbridled bliss?" She corrected.

He didn't seem to find her comment amusing. "Women in my country delight in marrying and producing children."

"Women in mine don't have to get married and have children if they don't want to, or wear a veil, or join a harem, or become the property of their husbands," she replied sweetly.

He glared at her. "You are insulting. Such an undisciplined tongue will one day cost you any possibility of making a good marriage."

"One can only hope," she agreed with a sigh.

He said something in his own language. It sounded musical and insulting, and Brianna glared at him.

"Uh, Ahmed, could we see you for a moment?" Lang called, trying to avert a disaster.

Ahmed glanced at him and back at Brianna. He was standing stiffly beside her desk and reluctant to leave the field. The woman made him angrier than anyone in this country ever had. The death threats, the assassination attempts were all insignificant beside making this woman treat him with the respect that was his due. Women usually fell over themselves trying to catch his eye, get his attention. This one only insulted him, making a joke of his status. He couldn't remember feeling such rage.

"Ahmed?" Lang called again, more insistently.

"Oh, very well," the Arab said irritably.

Chapter Two

Brianna didn't see Ahmed again that day. But the next morning, he walked past her desk and gave her a look so icy that it made her shiver. She returned it with cold dislike as he passed through the office where she did her secretarial duties. If she disliked him, the reverse was also patently obvious.

Brianna found the tall Arab something of a puzzle, as many of the other employees also did. He'd been introduced as Ahmed ben Rashid, a cabinet official of the Arab republic of Saudi Mahara. But he had the arrogance of an emperor and a temper to match. She wondered if Lang was somewhere close by. The CIA was much involved in his protection, and there was something going on. Ahmed had been in the office just yesterday. Why was he back today? Wasn't it a risk for him to be seen in public?

If the bodyguard he carried around with him was any indication of the esteem in which his country held him, the United States government would do well to keep him safe, Brianna thought. But for her part, they could guard him on Alcatraz. She tried to imagine his regal presence sitting in a damp cell and her blue eyes twinkled with mischief.

"Nothing to do, Brianna?" Steven Ryker asked dryly from behind her.

She turned to face the president and CEO of Ryker Air, red faced. "Oh. Certainly, Mr. Ryker," she stammered. "I was just, uh, just, uh..."

"He doesn't like you any more than you like him," Steven pointed out. "The difference is that he hides it better."

"He doesn't, you know," she returned stiffly. "He called me names, he insulted me, he had me in tears...."

"You got even," he reminded her, smiling reflectively. "Do you have any idea how close you came to causing an international incident?"

"One can only dream, sir." She sighed, and smiled, pushing back her short black hair.

"You're hopeless," he murmured, laughing. "Stop glaring at him. He's one of our best customers."

"He's buying jet fighters to kill people with," she began.

He held up his hand. Since his marriage to pretty Meg, he'd mellowed just a little. "His government is," he countered.

''Same difference.'' She glared after the Arab's retreating back. ''Why is he here again today?'' she moaned.

''It's a secret,'' he said with an odd look. ''But it has something to do with the fact that somebody blew up his jet last night.''

Her eyes widened. ''Who?''

''We don't know. Fortunately it was deserted at the time. The pilot was just on his way across the tarmac. But the government has decided to conceal him here until his people back home catch the two conspirators who escaped from custody. They think he may still be a target.''

''Oh, brother,'' she said heavily, remembering all too well that Ahmed had almost been killed, and Steven and Meg and his private secretary along with him.

''The only good thing is that they don't know exactly what Ahmed looks like. The men who could have recognized him are in tight custody in Saudi Mahara.''

''Are they going to take him to Washington to protect him?'' she asked hopefully.

''Why would they want to do that?'' a deep, amused voice asked.

Brianna and Steven turned to face the newcomer. It was dark, handsome Lang. The CIA man had saved Steven's new wife from would-be kidnappers a short while ago, but Steven was still irritated at him because of the manner in which he'd saved Meg. Steven thought Lang was reckless.

"If it isn't the secret pain-in-the-neck agent," he muttered. "Hello, Lang."

"We meet again," the other man said with a grin. "Hi, Brianna, how about lunch? Or would you rather skip all the picky stuff and just get married now?"

She laughed. "You'd run a mile if I said yes."

"Probably. You could try and see."

"No, thanks. I have work to do."

"Indeed you do," Lang said, taking her arm. "Come along, Ryker. You're in on this, too."

"I am, but I don't like it."

"We've found the perfect place to hide Ahmed," he said, hurrying them toward Steven's office. "It's great. It's safe. It's the last place in the country they'd ever look for him."

"Where? Can I ask?" Brianna queried.

Lang paused at the closed door with his hand on the knob. "Why, in the bosom of his deadliest enemy, of course. Figuratively speaking," he added, and arched his eyebrows several times at Brianna.

She felt her jaw drop. He couldn't be thinking… meaning…

"Come in, and I'll explain."

Lang opened the door. Ahmed was standing at the window, his hands neatly folded behind him, his profile sharp and aristocratic as he gazed down on the parking lot below. He turned as Steven and Brianna came in with Lang, and his liquid black eyes made threatening flashes at her.

"Ahmed," Lang said brightly, "look who I've brought with me. It's your cousin by marriage, with whom you'll be living in your guise of a poor migrant cowboy."

Brianna pinched herself, but it didn't do any good. Ahmed glared viciously at the government man. Steven Ryker had to smother laughter.

"Stay with that she-cobra?" Ahmed asked haughtily. "I have told you already, I should rather live in the zoo!"

"That would suit me, too. You can stick him in the cage with the snakes!" Brianna said. She glared at Lang. "I live alone. I'm a single woman. I don't live with men. I don't like *him.* I especially would not live with him." She pointed at Ahmed.

"Everybody knows that. Which is why nobody will look for him at your apartment. And to make it even better, we're going to give him the credentials of a Mexican itinerant laborer, a cousin of yours from Chihuahua who just lost his job in Texas and needs a place to rest up and look for more work. Where better than with his favorite cousin?"

"I don't have any cousins from Chihuahua!"

"Now you do. Lucky girl," Lang added.

Brianna's fists clenched beside her neat gray skirt. She glared hotly at Ahmed's stiff face. "I don't even have male visitors. My reputation would be shot!"

"A relative can hardly be considered a blight on

your reputation,'' Lang told her. ''You'll be under constant surveillance, and you'll be safe. More important, so will he.''

''No.'' She dared Lang to argue.

He moved closer, looking apologetic. ''You have a twelve-year-old brother in a coma,'' he said quietly. ''He's in intensive care in the local hospital and your insurance is about to run out. If the insurance stops, he'll have to be moved, and the specialized treatment he's been getting will also stop.''

Brianna's heart climbed into her throat. ''How did you find that out?''

''I'm a secret agent,'' Lang said calmly. ''No secret is safe from me.''

She drew in a rough breath, aware of Ahmed's curious stare. ''What point are you trying to make?''

''If you help us, we help you. Ahmed's government is prepared to incur the expense of your brother's treatment, hospitalization and eventual rehabilitation if and when necessary.''

It was almost too much to believe. Brianna moved to a chair and sat down heavily. All her worst fears were being brought into the light and vanquished. Tad was all she had left of her family. She adored him. It was like a miracle. Almost. Having to have Ahmed in her apartment was not going to be pleasant.

''Think about it,'' Lang advised. ''Take a day or so to deliberate. Then we'll get back in touch. But we can't waste much time, you understand. If you refuse, we'll have to take other measures. That will negate our agreement to look after your brother."

Brianna winced. She couldn't refuse. Her brother's well-being was everything.

"If he moves in with me," she began, glancing uneasily at Ahmed, whose dark face was totally without expression, "how long will he have to stay?"

"Until we catch the two escaped assassins," Lang said. "We're pretty sure that they'll come here to Wichita and make a try for him. We'll be waiting if and when they do."

"What if they don't?"

"You'll have had the opportunity to learn a lot of Arab customs and your brother's bills will have been paid."

She lowered her eyes to the floor. She was going to regret this. Living with a man like Ahmed would be terrible!

"I'll be back in touch," Lang said when she was silent.

"I don't need to think about it," she said, raising her eyes. "I can't refuse. You knew it, too."

"I like to think I've planned well," he said, nodding.

"I won't be his personal slave," she added shortly, and her eyes shifted to Ahmed.

His dark eyebrows lifted. "God forbid," he said fervently. "I have very high standards for servants."

Her eyes narrowed. "And I have high ones for

houseguests. I won't be imposed upon. You won't interrupt my routine.''

He shrugged. ''My requirements are few.''

She didn't know why, but the way he said it made her uneasy. She had a suspicion that behind that tranquil expression, he was already plotting ways to upset her.

She was right. Ahmed moved in that very day, arriving with a virtual entourage of people carrying furniture, suitcases, trunks and other items.

Lang was with Ahmed, and two men accompanied him.

''This is great,'' Brianna said, glaring at all of them as she stood aside to let them into her apartment. Down the hall, doors had opened and two curious faces peered at the excitement. ''Just great. Why didn't you hire one of those lighted signs to put outside the building and announce that you were moving him in here?''

Lang grinned. ''Because we all look like poor working cowboys, don't you think?''

She stared at them intently. Well, they did rather look like working people. None of them was wearing a suit, including Lang, who was dressed in a pair of the most disreputable-looking, faded, tattered jeans she'd ever seen, with boots and a denim shirt. He didn't look like a secret agent at all.

Lang intercepted that curious look and grinned. ''It's the latest thing in spy disguises. In this sleeve is a TV camera,'' he said, holding out a big, long arm, ''and in the other is a miniature guided missile.''

She glared at him. ''What amazes me is that you still have a job at all!''

''Oh, they can't fire me,'' he said confidently. ''I have an aunt in Congress and an uncle in the President's cabinet.''

''I'm impressed,'' she said.

''So am I,'' he assured her. ''I tell people about them all the time—especially my bosses in D.C.''

''Why does that not surprise me?'' she murmured.

He chuckled. Ahmed came in behind the rest of the load carriers and looked around disdainfully, with his lean hands palm down on his hips and a disgusted look on his mustachioed face.

''To think that I should come to this,'' he muttered haughtily. ''By Allah, a tent would suit me better!''

''Not half as well as a narrow box would,'' Brianna began.

Lang dragged her off to one side. ''Now, now,'' he soothed. ''He's just not used to American apartments. You'll have to give him time to adjust. He'll get used to it.''

''I won't,'' she assured him darkly. ''Having to spend even a week with this man is going to require every thread of patience in my entire body!''

''There will be compensations,'' Lang promised. ''Your brother's medical bills will all be paid, and you have to admit that it would be worth most any sacrifice to have that.''

''It would,'' she had to agree. ''You can't imagine how worried I've been—'' She stopped and took a deep breath. ''Tad's very special to me.''

''Is that his name, Tad?''

''You know it's Timothy Edward,'' she mused, smiling knowingly at him. There wasn't much that got past Lang. ''But I've always called him Tad for short.''

''He's twelve, right?''

She nodded, averting her eyes. ''He was so young when—'' she paused ''—when we lost our parents.''

''Never give up hope,'' he said quietly. ''I've seen miracles. Even the doctors admit that they still happen.''

''I guess so. But after three years, hope dwindles.''

He patted her on the shoulder awkwardly. ''You might enjoy having our friend here for a while,'' he said. ''He's not bad company.''

She stared at him without blinking.

''Give it a chance, anyway,'' he coaxed. He glanced up at one of the men with him, who'd gone over the place with some sort of electronic equipment. ''Anything?'' he asked the man.

His colleague grinned and shook his head. ''Clean as ice.''

It was a small electronic instrument. Brianna glanced at Lang's sleeve with real curiosity.

''I was kidding about the TV camera.'' He chuckled. ''And maybe exaggerating a little about the missile launcher.''

"I saw a movie with one of those fiber-optic camera things," she remarked. "I was impressed."

"I'll wear one the very next time I come to visit," he promised with a wicked grin.

"What do I call him?" she asked with resignation.

"Ahmed?" He pulled out a brand-new ID card and a driver's license and passport and green card, all of which were intended to grace thc pockets of her houseguest. "Pedro Rivera," he said. "Age thirty-four, native of Chihuahua, Mexico, occupation, farm laborer."

"Is he really going to work on a farm?" she asked hopefully. Her smile was evil.

"Ahmed?" Lang found that hilarious. "No, he's sort of between jobs, and he's depending on you to support him while he looks for work. He'll look very hard, we'll see to that. Applications in all major local businesses, and so forth."

"You could get him a job translating," she said.

"That would be tricky."

"Oh?" Her blue eyes were curious. "Why?"

"Well, he, uh, doesn't speak any Spanish."

Her face widened into a gleeful look of triumph. "None? None at all? How interesting! And he's supposed to be a Mexican laborer?"

"He said Spanish tastes terrible in his mouth and he refuses to learn it," Lang admitted with a grimace. "He speaks French quite well."

"Then why not let him pose as a Frenchman?"

"It would take too long to explain. Trust me," he added. "This will work. It's almost foolproof."

"Like the Titanic was almost unsinkable."

"Pessimist," he accused. "Think of the service you're doing your country!"

"By harboring a Middle Eastern cabinet official? How in the world does that help my country? I'm not Arabic," she added coldly, glaring toward Ahmed, who was still muttering about his inferior surroundings.

"His country's strategic location makes it of great value to us," Lang explained. "The Middle East is a lighted stick of dynamite right now, with all sorts of factions fighting for control. We depend on oil from that part of the world."

"We shouldn't," she pointed out.

"I realize that," he said. "But the fact remains that we depend on foreign oil and we have to have it or our technology goes down the drain. We have to keep a lot of people happy overseas to ensure our continued supply. Ahmed is one of the people we have to keep happy."

"I thought his country had a king. Why don't we have to worry about keeping *him* happy?"

"If we keep Ahmed happy, it will keep *him* happy," Lang assured her.

She shrugged. "Okay by me. But for my money," she added, "they could boil him in oil and serve him on a bed of lettuce."

''What a mind. And you look so sweet,'' Lang commented dryly.

''I was sweet, until you and the Valentino clone over there invaded my life!''

Lang had to bite back laughter. He didn't dare show amusement, especially since Ahmed had overheard her and was joining them, spoiling for trouble.

''I beg your pardon?'' he asked Brianna, and his liquid black eyes made her feel intimidated.

''I said, I hope you'll be comfortable here,'' she lied. ''I'm going to cook my specialty for supper tonight.''

''Not barbecue, please,'' Lang said out of the side of his mouth.

She gave him a speaking look. ''Actually, I thought something Spanish might be in order. Chili, for example,'' she added, smiling at Ahmed, ''with jalapeño peppers and refried beans.''

''Ah, spicy fare,'' Ahmed said, smiling back.

She hesitated. ''You...like...spicy food?''

''Indeed,'' he agreed readily. ''I have no taste for bland meat.''

She'd have to remember to cook him some unsalted spaghetti.

''Are we through?'' Lang called to his cohorts.

''You bet!'' One tall man came lumbering up. ''Everything's in place—bugs, surveillance equipment, the works.''

''You're going to spy on us?'' Brianna choked.

''They might as well,'' Ahmed said haughtily, giving her an appraisal that spoke volumes. "Or were you hoping they might have something to look at?"

She clenched her small fists at her sides and forced thoughts of paid medical bills to the front of her mind.

"I'd rather eat nails," she assured him.

"No doubt you could, with a mouth like that," he agreed politely.

Lang got between them. "He's your adored cousin," he told her. "You love him. You're going to take wonderful care of him because your country wants you to."

"Then why can't my country live with him?"

Lang shook his head. "Believe me, I'd like nothing better," he said with a diplomatic smile in Ahmed's direction. "But I have some leave coming and I thought I'd go down to Texas and visit my brother and his family."

"Why can't he—" she pointed at Ahmed "—go down there with you? There are plenty more Mexicans in Texas than you're likely to find in Wichita."

"Oh, I'd hate to deprive you two of the opportunity to get to know each other," he said, tongue-in-cheek. "Think what it will do for international relations. Besides, my plans may change."

They stared at each other coldly. Lang moved out of the line of fire, motioning to his colleagues.

"Well, here you are, then," he said. "Nice and comfy, make yourself right at home. I'm sure Brianna will take excellent care of you."

"Are you?" Ahmed asked. "And what of my bodyguards?"

"They'll be around. So will our people," Lang said somberly. "Just don't take any unnecessary risks or deliberately make yourself a target. Mostly we'd like you to stay in the apartment while Brianna's at work. If you go out, mention out loud that you're going, and where. We'll have you trailed."

"This is outrageous," Ahmed said curtly. "I see no reason why my own bodyguard could not…"

"Because you're on American soil," Lang reminded him. "In this country, we're responsible for the welfare of foreign nationals. So be kind to government workers and let us do our jobs. Okay?"

Ahmed shrugged. He moved toward the window and stood there, looking out as if he felt too confined already.

"And don't spend a lot of time in front of the window," Lang pleaded. "You make an excellent target. We can't possibly watch every window in every building in Wichita twenty-four hours a day."

Ahmed moved back into the room, nodding his consent.

Lang was the last of the group out the door. "Well, I'll leave you to it."

"One moment," Ahmed called. "Who is going to unpack for me? I have no servants here."

Lang hesitated. He glanced at Brianna, who took up a belligerent stance that no one with normal perception could mistake. "Uh, well, we'll see about that later. Good day."

"I've been stabbed in the back by my own government," Brianna muttered once he was gone, her blue eyes spitting at her houseguest. "Don't expect me to help you push the knife in farther. I am not a servant. I do not unpack for my guests. You have two perfectly good hands. You can unpack for yourself."

He linked his hands behind him and stared at her. The intensity of the look made her very nervous, and she retreated to the kitchen. "I'll start working on something to eat."

He lifted the edge of a hand-crocheted doily and examined it. "I prefer shrimp cocktail for an appetizer," he remarked absently. "And with Mexican fare, I should think an aged Bordeaux would suffice."

She came out of the kitchen and looked at him. "Now listen," she said. "I do not have a wine cellar. I drink an occasional glass of sweet sherry or white wine, but I know nothing about vintages or which color wine goes with which food."

"A minor impediment," he said with a careless wave of his hand. "You can learn."

"I have no wish to learn, much less do I want a staggering Arab to put to bed at night," she added, pleased at the shocked lift of his eyebrows. "Furthermore, my budget doesn't run to shrimp cocktail. I make a good salary, but after I pay the bills, there isn't a lot left over for fancy food. You'll have to make do with what I can provide."

He sighed wistfully. ''From caviar and Brie to this,'' he said in a long-suffering tone. ''*Mon Dieu,* how are the mighty fallen.''

She went back into the kitchen, muttering under her breath about how she'd like to fell him herself.

Chapter Three

Brianna went to the hospital to see her brother that night, leaving Ahmed complaining about the meager channels she had on her cable TV. He didn't ask where she was going and she didn't volunteer any information.

She sat by Tad's bedside, as she did most nights, watching the face that was so much like her own. His eyes were closed. But when they had been open, they were as blue as hers. It seemed so long ago now that Tad had laughed and played like a normal boy his age. She missed his mischievous personality. He'd been such a happy child. Why, oh, why had this to happen?

Sometimes she felt old when she sat with him. He hadn't wasted too badly. They fed him intravenously, and the nurses turned him and checked his vital signs to make sure he was getting what he needed to support his young life. Once the doctor had talked to her about shutting off the life support, but Brianna couldn't do it. She couldn't give up hope, not after they told her that his brain seemed to be functioning with some normalcy. She refused to quit. The last thing her mother had said to her, in the wrecked car, bleeding and gasping for air, was, "Don't let Tad die." It had been an odd thing for her to say, but Brianna hadn't forgotten. Tad was in no pain, and Brianna had hope. She couldn't give up.

She talked to him. She held his frail hand and told him all about her life, about her job, about what she was doing. She didn't tell him about Ahmed. It was the first secret she'd kept, but it would do him no good to know. She talked about the apartment instead and how she was going to redecorate the guest room for him when he could come home.

By the time she got home, tired and dispirited, Ahmed was in bed. She went into her bedroom and, on an impulse, locked the door. She was too tired to worry about having a man in her apartment and soon fell asleep.

When she got home the next afternoon, after a particularly long day, she was totally unprepared for the fierce thudding sounds coming from her bedroom. It sounded as if the whole place were coming down around her ears.

She got a bigger surprise when she made it to the

door and discovered that he was supervising four dark men in business suits, who were putting away his clothes. In the process, they had unearthed half of Brianna's possessions and had deposited them in chairs, on dressers, and in the hall.

She dropped her purse in the middle of the floor and gasped, "What are you doing?"

"Making room for my things," he said from his lounging position in her best easy chair. "These quarters are hopelessly inadequate. That closet in the guest room barely holds all my suits. The other things must go in here."

"This is my room!" she wailed. "You can't move my things out!"

"I am your tenant," he said comfortably. "You must accommodate me." He stopped and called out something in curt Arabic. The men stopped what they were doing. One spoke for the rest in what sounded like an apology. Ahmed rattled off some more Arabic and made a dismissing sign with his elegant hand. The men went back to work.

"Tell them to stop," she said. "They can't do this. I have to have clothes to wear to work. I can't wear them all rumpled...!"

"Your clothes are hardly of any concern to me," Ahmed said, surprised. "It is my own appearance which is of prime importance."

She counted a long way past ten. It didn't help. "You get those men out of my bedroom!" she shouted. ''And you follow them right out the front door!''

He ignored her. So did the men.

''You can't take over my bedroom!'' she tried again.

''The guest room is inadequate. The bed is lumpy. I have no intention of sleeping on a lumpy bed.''

''Then why don't you call the President and ask if you can stay with him at the White House?'' she raged.

He considered that for a moment. Then he shook his head. ''It is a bad time,'' he said simply.

She glared at him. She glared at the men. Everybody ignored her. She picked up her purse and went into the living room. At least he hadn't tried rearranging that yet!

The men left and he came sauntering out in a white-and-gold caftan with silver threads. He looked more foreign than she'd ever seen him look in the princely regalia. She hadn't considered before how alone the two of them were. The night before, she'd been to visit Tad and the sight of him had affected her much more deeply than before. She'd arrived late, and she hadn't seen Ahmed at breakfast. She'd gone straight in to work, thinking, silly her, that it was working out very well. Ha!

''You must do something about the television,'' he began. ''There are too few channels. I want the French stations. Another thing, there is no fax machine here.'' He gestured impatiently. ''How am I expected to attend to matters of state without a facsimile machine? I need a telephone line upon which these juvenile neighbors of yours are not always discussing—what do you call them?—arcade computer games!''

She just looked at him. He still didn't understand her budget. He made it more obvious by the day.

''And these...plants,'' he muttered, fingering the leaf of a philodendron with distaste and glaring at a trailing ivy plant, ''they make the room feel like a rain forest. I prefer desert plants. They make me feel at home.''

''I'll send right out for some stinging nettles and cactus,'' she assured him.

His black eyes narrowed. He had an arrogance of carriage that sometimes made him look dangerous. He was using it now. ''You mock me. Few have dared that over the years.''

''What will you do, cut off my head?'' she challenged.

''I believe I...*we*...outlawed beheading some years ago.'' He waved his hand. ''It was becoming politically incorrect with our allies. They found it offensive.''

She couldn't believe he wasn't kidding. She moved toward the kitchen. ''I'll fix something to eat.'' She turned. ''No shrimp,'' she said. ''And no wine. I had in mind some hot dogs.''

''Hot...dogs?'' His eyes bulged. ''Hot dogs!''

''I like hot dogs with chili,'' she said.

"You served chili last night," he began.

"And I'm using up what was left tonight, on hot dogs." She sighed, exasperated, and frowned. "Don't you understand? I don't throw away food, ever! I stretch it. If I have leftover bread, I make bread pudding. I waste nothing! I can't afford to!"

It didn't register. "You have credit cards, surely."

"I owe up to the limit right now," she explained. "I just bought a new bed, for *my* bedroom," she emphasized, "because the mattress I was sleeping on was so lumpy. Until then, there wasn't a bed in the guest bedroom. Lucky you, not to have to sleep on the floor or the sofa!" she added sarcastically.

"I would never do such a thing," he said absently. "It would be unseemly. What is this limit? I have no limit."

"Why does that not surprise me?" she asked the ceiling.

He looked up to see who she was talking to, and she walked off and left him.

"I will have vichyssoise instead of hot dogs," he said. "I prefer cream and churned butter," he added with a smile.

She took down a boiler, filled it with water and put two hot dogs in it. She turned on the burner. Then she took a whole potato from the bin, walked into the living room and handed it to Ahmed.

"There you go. Instant vichyssoise. Just peel it and add cream and churned butter and a little water and simmer it for half an hour or so. Should be just delicious,'' she added, and walked right into her bedroom and closed the door with a snap.

When she came back, he was nowhere in sight. The potato was lying on the counter in the kitchen and the guest room door was closed. Her telephone had been unplugged and removed from the table by the sofa. She frowned, wondering what he could be up to.

Minutes later, he came back, carrying the telephone. He set it on the table and sprawled on the sofa.

''You might plug it back in,'' she suggested.

''Why?'' he asked. ''I unplugged it, after all, and plugged it into the bedroom wall. I am fatigued.'' He laid his head back on the sofa. ''And very hungry. I had a hamburger from the corner diner for lunch.''

He made it sound as if she should feel guilty about that. ''With fries?'' she asked cheerfully. ''They make good fries.''

''I loathe french fries,'' he informed her.

She'd mark that down mentally and soon she'd serve him some, she decided irritably.

She dished up her hot dog and added mustard and catsup to the bun she'd placed it in. ''There's one left if you want it,'' she offered.

He glared at her.

She shrugged. ''Starve yourself, then.'' She sat down at the table. Just as she lifted the hot dog to her mouth, the door buzzer sounded.

Ahmed got up and pressed the button beside the door. ''Yes?'' he asked haughtily.

There was a spate of Arabic, which he answered in kind, and pushed the door release.

"You can't do that! What if it's the people who are after you? They'll kill us all!" she raged.

He gave her a look. "It is my men," he told her. "Do you not think I know them by now?"

She started to argue, decided against it and went back to eating her hot dog.

Her peace didn't last long. An entourage of men in suits carrying boxes marched in, displaced her from the table with intimidating looks, and spread out a feast fit for a king for Ahmed. Then they left, without receiving a word of thanks.

He rubbed his hands together. "Ah," he said, inhaling the aromas of lobster and fresh sautéed vegetables and fresh-baked breads. He went into the kitchen, got a plate and utensils and proceeded to fill the plate. "You may join me if you wish," he added carelessly.

She glared at him and deliberately took a bite of the hot dog.

He hid a smile. Proud, he thought. It was an emotion of which he was not ignorant. She was no beauty, but she had spirit and compassion. Perhaps he would buy her a car when this charade was finished.

"You didn't thank your men for bringing all that to you," she remarked when she was washing up.

His face registered surprise. "Why should I? It is my fate to be served, and theirs to be my servants."

"You sound like a prophet quoting the Koran,"

she said. ''I understood you to say that you were raised a Christian.''

''I was,'' he agreed. ''But I understand and respect the religion of my people,'' he added.

He turned his attention back to the exquisite cheese cake he was just finishing. ''A most adequate meal,'' he said finally, getting up from the table to sprawl back on the sofa. The remains of his meal were strewn all over the table and the cabinet. Brianna, already tired, eyed the mess with distaste.

''You may clear away now,'' he said offhandedly.

''*I* may clear— *You* may clear!'' she raged. ''This is my home. Nobody orders me around in my own home! I'm not a servant!''

''You are my landlady,'' he said imperturbably. ''And you can hardly say that I am not paying for my stay here.''

That brought Tad back to mind. No, she thought, she couldn't say that. He wasn't paying, but his government was. She had to adapt to him. Perhaps it wouldn't be for much longer. The thought cheered her. She packed away the trash and washed up the few remaining dishes.

''I should like a cup of cappuccino,'' he murmured as he changed the channels on the television. ''Sweet, but not too sweet.''

''I don't know how to make cappuccino.''

He turned, his expression one of amazement. ''You cannot make cappuccino?''

He made it sound like a mortal sin. She shifted. "No." She hesitated. "What is it?"

"Cappuccino?"

"Yes."

"You are joking."

She shook her head. "Is it some sort of after-dinner drink?"

His expression softened as he realized just how unworldly she was. He got up from the sofa and approached her, noticing how nervous she became when he paused very close to her. "It is a coffee with frothed cream and cinnamon, very sweet. I am fond of it." He caught her arm, ever so gently, and held her in place.

"Oh. Well, I can't make it. I'm sorry," she added. His touch bothered her. How odd that it should disturb her so. She tested his hold and found him willing to let her break it. She stepped back and then looked up to see his reaction.

He was amazingly patient, almost contemplative, as he looked down at her. His black eyes mirrored his introspective mood, sweeping slowly over her exquisite bone structure, over her straight nose and down to her soft bow of a mouth.

"Women are property in your country, aren't they?" she asked, feeling chilled at the memory of what she'd read about some Arab nations.

"Not in mine, no," he replied. "We are a modern nation. There are those of our women who are not deeply religious, who consider the veil archaic and refuse to wear it. Our women work in public jobs and hold responsible positions in government.'' He smiled ruefully. ''Needless to say, I am labeled an infidel by some disgusted neighbors.''

''I expect your king is, too,'' she replied.

He cleared his throat. ''Of course.''

''Arabic is pretty,'' she said after an uncomfortable silence. ''I have a friend who can speak a few words of it. It's musical.''

''So they say.''

''But it is,'' she argued, smiling nicely. ''When you speak English, your voice has a lilt. It sounds very...intriguing,'' she said after a careful choice of words.

He lifted one dark brow. ''Intriguing? Not sexy?''

She flushed, and he smiled again.

''Vous êtes un enfant, Brianna,'' he said quietly. *''Une très belle fleur avec les yeux comme la mer.''*

She frowned. ''I don't understand French,'' she said hesitantly, registering the depth and sensual tone of his deep voice as he stared at her much too intently for a mere acquaintance.

''It is just as well,'' he said wistfully. ''Come and watch television with me.''

''What are you going to watch?'' she asked, because she knew already that it would do no good to demand access to her own television. He was being generous right now, but it wouldn't last. He didn't have it in him to be considerate for long.

''A special program on the connection between

stress and the immune system,'' he said, surprising her. ''It is a new study, one which has been challenged by many scientists. But I find the premise an interesting one.''

She did, too. Her doctor often worried about her obsession with being at the hospital four out of every five days to sit with Tad. She never missed, even if it meant freezing or getting soaked, or waiting half an hour for a ride. He said that one day she was going to fall victim to some debilitating illness because of the strain. She never had, though. Not yet. There was a minor cold and a bout with the flu, but nothing more serious than that.

However, as she watched the program with Ahmed, she began to understand the connection they were trying to present. It was a little disturbing. Tad might be in a coma for the rest of her life. What then? She felt a surge of panic as she realized what she hadn't in three years—that she might never see the light at the end of the tunnel. It was the first time she'd considered that hope might one day be lost forever.

''This is not what I expected to see,'' he said suddenly. He changed the channel. ''Illness depresses me. I had hoped for something scientific. Ah. This is much more pleasant.'' He left it on the public-television station, where a new Sherlock Holmes adventure was just beginning.

She was taken aback by his abrupt action. She couldn't find the right words to express what she felt. Illness depressed her, too, but she had no choice at all except to deal with it. She couldn't change the channel of her life to something more pleasant.

She watched the program with him, absently rubbing the edge of her blouse between her fingers. The blouse was getting frayed. She would have to scrap it before too much longer. That was disturbing. She didn't have much money for clothes.

After a few minutes, she realized just how tired she was. She got up from the sofa. "There's a bottle of cola in the fridge, if you get thirsty," she said.

"No Perrier?" he asked without looking away from the screen.

"Dream on." She sighed.

He didn't reply. She moved toward her bedroom, glancing back as she went down the hall. He obviously hadn't realized yet that he was going to sleep on that lumpy mattress in the guest room. He'd probably get the idea very soon. She wasn't giving up her brand-new bed.

She went into the bedroom and closed the door. Then she locked it and placed a chair under the doorknob. She nodded. *There you go,* she thought. *Get through that!*

Mindful of any hidden cameras, she turned out the lights before she disrobed. She was blissfully unaware that the agency had infrared cameras and film, and also that they were discreet enough not to bug her bedroom. Well, not with a camera, anyway.

Having donned her long gown and brushed her hair, she got into bed and pulled the covers up with a sigh. She was almost asleep when she heard the soft whine of the television cut off and footfalls coming down the hall.

There was a sudden stop, an exclamation, and then several loud words in Arabic at the door to her bedroom.

"You might as well calm down," she called through it. "I've double locked the door and there's a chair under the doorknob. It will take a battering ram to get in here. This is my bed, and I'm sleeping in it. If you don't like it, you can call somebody and complain!"

"You think that I will not?" came the haughty reply. "You will be surprised!"

"No, you will," she mused aloud. "Because no red-blooded American gentleman is going to try to force a woman to give up her bed."

She lay back down with a smile and closed her eyes. She didn't even feel guilty. He had no idea how hard and long she'd worked to afford this moderately priced new bed and mattress and box spring. He seemed to have no idea at all what things cost. Presumably his government fulfilled his every whim. It must be nice, she decided, to be in the diplomatic service.

If she'd thought she was home free, she was in for a surprise the next morning. He still wasn't up when she left, and she didn't leave him any breakfast. After his threats of the night before, she didn't think he deserved any. But her conscience plagued her all the way to work.

Once she got there, Mr. Ryker called her into his office. Lang was sitting cross-legged in a chair. He smiled as she came in.

"Oh, no," she pleaded. "Not you again."

"You'll break my heart if you keep talking like that," he complained. "And here I am to compliment you on the way you're taking care of your sweet cousin."

"He isn't sweet," she muttered. "He's a barracuda in a mustache. He commandeered all the closets and all my drawer space, and he even tried to get into my bed last night!"

Lang gasped. "Why, Brianna, I'm shocked!"

"Not while I was in it," she said impatiently. "I mean he tried to take over the master bedroom!"

"Yes, I know. He telephoned my boss this morning, early. He also telephoned the Pentagon, the Joint Chiefs of Staff and the Secretary of State. Not to mention," he added, "the Secretary of Defense." He shook his head. "You have no idea how much trouble you've caused."

"He didn't call all those people. He couldn't... wouldn't!"

"He did." He smiled ruefully, pushing back a stray lock of dark hair that fell onto his broad forehead when he leaned forward. He rested his forearms over his knees. "In fact, I've been chewed out since daylight this morning. If you don't let him have the master bedroom, I'm afraid his government may declare war!''

She sat back in her chair, her face almost the color of the soft red turtleneck sweater she was wearing with her gray skirt. ''I don't believe this.''

''You'd better. I'm not even joking,'' he added solemnly. ''This is a man who's quite used to getting everything he wants. He's never been refused in his life. He's rich and powerful and he isn't used to being denied—least of all by a young lady of your age and position.''

''He's only a cabinet minister,'' she protested. ''How can he have that much influence?''

''He has relatives in power in Saudi Mahara,'' he explained.

''Oh.''

''We'll furnish you with a new bed for the guest room,'' he offered. ''And a new vanity and a chifforobe. How about that?''

She hesitated. ''Why not just let him bring a bed of his own to the apartment and sleep on that?''

''Great idea. We'll suggest it to him.''

''Could you do it before I have to go home?'' she asked. ''I'm beginning to recognize several words in Arabic, and I don't think they're very nice.''

''I can guarantee it.'' He grinned sheepishly at her start of surprise. ''The bugs...?''

''Yes. The bugs.'' She turned her head a little. ''You, uh, you don't have any cameras in the bathroom or anything?''

He chuckled, noticing that Steven Ryker had put his hand strategically over his mouth.

''No, we don't. I promise you. We don't have cameras anyplace where they'd embarrass you.''

She let out a long, audible breath. ''Oh, thank God. I've been dressing and undressing in the closet.''

''No need for that. None at all.'' He hesitated. ''There's just one little thing. How did he get you to cook him vichyssoise and lobster?''

''But I didn't,'' she said. ''I have no idea how to make those things. He had his men bring them in last night.''

Lang was suddenly, starkly serious. ''He what?''

''He had his men bring all that stuff in.''

''Well, I'll be. You take five minutes to go to the men's room and look what you miss!''

''I thought you had the telephone bugged,'' Brianna said.

''I did. But Collins tripped over the wire and broke it. We were trying to make a splice.... Oh, never mind. Calling out for lobster, was he? Well, we'll see about that!''

Lang stood up, and he looked very angry. Brianna brightened. She wished she could go home and watch him give Ahmed hell.

She couldn't. But just the thought of it got her through the whole day, smiling.

Chapter Four

But when Brianna got to the apartment that night there was absolutely nothing out of the ordinary. Nothing very visible, at least.

Ahmed was sitting on her sofa glaring at the television, where a soap opera was playing. Two people were in bed, making passionate love. The sounds of it were embarrassing to Brianna, who sideskirted the sofa and went straight down the hall to her bedroom.

She took off her jacket and stretched, stiff from hours of sitting. As she turned, she noticed Ahmed in the doorway, watching her with eyes whose expression she couldn't define. She didn't know that the stretching motion had outlined her young body in the most sensuous, arousing kind of way. Or that Ahmed, a connoisseur of women, had stopped dead just to look at her.

"What is it?" she asked.

"They have removed the telephone directory and the information service does not function," he muttered. "This is your doing."

She grinned. "Yes, it is. Didn't I do good? Furthermore, I am sleeping in this very bed tonight and you are going to have a nice, new bed in the guest room. I did that, too."

"You did no such thing," he denied. "I have spoken to your friend Lang. He is sending over a bed. But it is you who will sleep on it. I am occupying this room as of tonight."

"You are not! This is my apartment, buster, and nobody kicks me out of my own bedroom!"

"If you do not vacate it, there will be an international incident of proportions which you cannot imagine," he countered smugly.

"You spoiled old brat!"

He gaped at her. "I beg your pardon!"

"Lang told me that nobody ever said no to you in your life. Well, it's time somebody did! You can't just walk in and take over. You have no right!"

"I have more rights than you," he countered. He folded his arms across his chest. The blue silk shirt he was wearing made his eyes look even darker. "Call Lang. Lodge a protest. He will not take your side against me. He will not dare."

"I don't give a frog hair who you are or what you do, this is where I live and I'm not budging!" she raged, her Southern drawl emphasized in anger.

He was frowning. "Frog hair?" He shook his head and muttered something in Arabic. "These frogs, they have no hair. Are you demented?"

"Yes," she answered him, "I am demented. That's why I allowed them to talk me into letting you stay here!"

His dark eyes sketched her angry face and lowered to the smooth, sleek lines of her body before they returned to capture her startled eyes. "How old are you?" he asked.

"That is none of your business," she said uncomfortably.

"I can find out."

"Go right ahead." She felt a little shaky. "Now, if you don't mind, I'd like to change before I have to start cooking again."

"Had you not complained, we could both be served with lobster thermidor," he reminded her.

"I don't like lobster," she muttered. "At least, I don't think I do. I could never afford any, even to taste."

He scowled. "You are paid a good salary."

"Of course I am," she agreed. "But it doesn't stretch to foods like lobster. I have a little brother in a coma, don't you understand?" she asked softly. "Every spare penny has gone toward his comfort, until now."

He seemed surprised. He moved a little awkwardly. "Yes, yes, I have heard about the boy."

"Well, he's more than gossip to me," she replied.

"I took care of him after he was born, played with him, fed him, diapered him.... I had to, because Mother wasn't well for a long time. But he was a joy, not a burden. He's a smart boy," she added, hanging on to the good times for all she was worth, fighting the hopelessness and fear. "He'll get up out of that bed one day, and play baseball again...."

Ahmed was touched by her reluctant show of emotion. He found himself wondering about the boy, about her. He hadn't been curious before, but now he was.

"What do the doctors say of his chances for recovery?"

"They say as little as possible," she replied, having regained her almost-lost composure. "Medical science can't do any more than it already has. The brain is still very much an unexplored territory, you know. Comas are unpredictable."

"His has lasted long?"

"Three years." She moved toward the door and held the doorknob impatiently. "If you don't mind?"

He moved back into the hall and she closed the door. It hurt to think how long Tad had lain in the hospital bed, knowing no one. She was going to see him tonight, but like all the other nights, it would be an exercise in futility, in loss of hope. She was growing more depressed as time passed.

She changed into jeans and a loose, long-sleeved white knit shirt and socks. She didn't bother with her hair or her face. After all, Ahmed was not an invited guest whom she wanted to impress. He was, at best, a positive irritant.

When she reached the living room, he had the television blaring on the news channel. She ignored him and went into the kitchen to cook. It was going to be meat loaf tonight, she thought heavily. She was so tired of meat loaf, but it would stretch to two days. She glanced at Ahmed and wondered how he was going to like something that unglamorous.

"What culinary delight are you planning for this evening?" he asked with resignation.

"Meat loaf, mashed potatoes and green beans."

He made a terrible face.

"There's always soup," she continued.

He made a worse face and turned away from her to glare at the television screen.

"Why don't you call the CIA and tell them you're starving here? Maybe they'll find you a nice new place to live."

He didn't reply. He looked even more unapproachable than he usually did.

She went on with her chores, humming softly to herself. If he wanted to starve himself rather than eat what normal people did, that was just too bad.

"Think of it as an exploration of ethnic fare," she told him when she'd put everything on to cook and she was sitting in the big armchair by the sofa. "This is what Americans eat every week."

"No wonder your country is so uncultured."

"Uncultured?" she asked, affronted. "And what are you, Mr. Camels-in-the-desert-under-a-tent?"

He gaped at her. "I have no camels in a desert tent!"

"You know very well what I mean," she returned. "You live in a country full of camels and tents and deserts."

"We have cities," he said. "Opera, symphony orchestras, theaters. We have libraries and great universities."

"And sand and desert and camels."

He glared at her. "You know nothing of my country."

"You know nothing of mine," she returned. "Most of us have never experienced that rarified air you breathe when you're over here. Steak and lobster, five-star hotels, chauffeured limousines.... Do you think the majority of the people in this country know what any of that is?"

He scowled at her. "You do not understand. These things are my right."

"You have it too easy," she said curtly. "You should have to work for minimum wage and live on leftovers and drive a car that always sounds like it's got half a potato shoved up its tail pipe! Then you'd know how the rest of the world lives."

"All that concerns me is how I live," he said simply. "The rest of the world must cope as it can."

"What a selfish attitude!"

"There will always be people who are poor," he

said philosophically. "Why should I deny myself because there are people less fortunate in the world?"

"You might consider doing something to help the less fortunate, like taking a cut in your salary and giving up some of the trappings of your luxurious life-style."

He drew up one long leg. He was wearing jeans, very tight ones, and she found the sight of him lounging on the sofa very disturbing. "My life-style, as you call it, is my heritage. I intend giving up nothing. However, I have done what I can for my own people," he said, ignoring her glare. "And your definition of poverty might find some resistance in my country. Our native nomadic tribesmen find their life-style satisfying and superior to the spiritual poverty which exists in our cities. They do not consider themselves poor, despite the fact that industrialized Westerners look down on them."

She frowned. "I don't understand."

"That is obvious." His dark eyes smiled faintly. "You think that because you have great machines and factories that you are superior to less developed peoples."

She hadn't considered the question before. "Well...we are. Aren't we?"

"Have you been to college, Brianna?"

She felt something flower inside her at the way he spoke her name. He made it sound musical, somehow. She had to stop and think to remember the question.

''No,'' she replied. ''I took some business courses to improve my typing and shorthand.''

''When you have the time, and your circumstances are improved, you might benefit by a few courses in sociology and racial diversity.''

''I suppose you have a college degree,'' she said.

''Indeed. I am an Oxford graduate.''

''In…?''

He smiled. ''Science, with a major in chemistry and physics. My father greatly approved my choice. Our people were the founders of science.''

''In that case, with such a background,'' she said impishly, ''perhaps you could chemically create a lobster for yourself in the kitchen.''

He frowned. Then the words made sense and he chuckled. The sound was very pleasant to Brianna's ears, deep and rich.

''Perhaps I could, given the right ingredients,'' he mused.

An item on the news caught his attention. He turned back to listen and Brianna escaped back into the kitchen.

After a few muttered comments about the lack of proper silverware and china and linen napkins, which made her glower at him, he settled down to the meal with surprised pleasure.

''I have not tasted such food before,'' he said. ''It is good.''

''You needn't sound so surprised. I'm not exactly hopeless in the kitchen. My mother was a wonderful cook. She taught me how.'' She lifted her eyes. ''Does your mother cook?''

He laughed uproariously. ''No. Her hands were never allowed to do anything so menial.''

She felt reprimanded and flushed a little. ''Yes, well, in America it isn't considered menial.''

''I beg your pardon, I did not mean to insult you,'' he said surprisingly. ''You are a good cook.''

''Thank you.''

He took a last bite of the meat loaf and sipped sweetened, creamed coffee with obvious pleasure.

''You said her hands *were* never allowed,'' she asked. ''Is your mother no longer alive?''

''What a soft way you have with words, Brianna,'' he said with a curious smile. ''Always the passive, not the active voice, when you ask something that might be hurtful.'' He put down his fork. ''Yes, she is dead. So is my father. They were murdered.''

She dropped her fork. It clattered against the inexpensive ceramic plate, the noise loud in the sudden silence. ''Oh, I am sorry,'' she stammered.

''It was a long time ago,'' he said. ''The sting is still there, but their murderers were caught and executed.''

All that reminded her that Ahmed was himself a target of would-be executioners. She grimaced as she looked at his impassive face. ''Aren't you afraid?''

''Why waste energy in such futility?'' he asked. ''I will die when my time comes.'' He shrugged. ''It is our destiny to die, is it not, one day?''

"Well, if assassins were gunning for me, I wouldn't be quite so casual about it!"

He smiled. "You are a curious girl."

"Woman," she corrected.

He lifted an eyebrow, and his eyes were old and wise. "Girl," he replied softly.

She got up a little jerkily and collected the plates. "I made a cherry pie for dessert," she said.

"Ah. My favorite."

"Is it?" She was sheepish. "Mine, too."

"A thing we have in common. Shall we find more, I wonder?"

She didn't answer him. He was getting under her skin, and he frightened her in emotional ways. She wasn't eager to let him turn her life upside down.

They finished the pie in silence. He went back to the television while she cleared the table, washed up the few dishes and went to get her coat and purse.

"Where are you going?" he asked, looking at her over his shoulder.

"To see Tad."

He got up and turned off the television. "I shall accompany you."

"Now, wait a minute," she said. "They said you shouldn't leave the apartment."

He was putting on his coat, ignoring her. "They will know that I am accompanying you. They will be watching."

She threw up her hands. "I never saw a man so enchanted with his own demise!"

He joined her at the door, ignoring her cry. "Shall we go?"

She gave up. She could hardly restrain him. He was very tall, close up, and she imagined he was very fit, too, if those muscles she'd seen in his legs and arms were any indication.

"Do you work out?" she asked suddenly.

"In a gym, you mean? Not really. I ride my horses and work with them."

"You have horses?" She was impressed. "I love horses. What sort are they?"

"Lippizaner stallions," he said.

"Those huge Austrian ones? But aren't they terribly expensive?"

"Astronomical." He noticed her suspicion and chuckled. "They are the king's," he explained. "But he allows me to train them for him, during my spare hours."

"Oh, I see. How nice of him."

He looked very smug, and lights danced in his black eyes. "Indeed."

It wasn't going to be such a bad evening, she thought. He was in a good mood.

And it lasted just until they reached her little car. He stopped and gaped at its bruised front fender, its rust spots covered with Bondo in preparation for the paint job she was having done on the installment plan. It was going to be red one day. Right now it was orange and rust and gray. Its tires were good, though, and its seats were hardly ragged at all. There was the small crack in the dash....

"You expect me to ride in that!" he exclaimed, bug-eyed.

"It's the only car I own," she informed him.

"It is...pitiful."

She put her hands on her hips and glared up at him. "It is not! It's a diamond in the rough. Just because it isn't cosmetically perfect...!"

"It is a piece of junk!" he said harshly. "Why do you not buy something new, instead of riding around in this death trap?"

"Because it's all I can afford!" she countered proudly. "Do you think everybody can just walk into a car dealership and buy a new one whenever they feel like it? This is the best I can do, and you have no right to make me feel ashamed of my car!"

He started to speak just as a car pulled slowly up to the curb, a sinister-looking black one, and stopped in front of Brianna's car. She saw it and without even thinking, she suddenly pushed Ahmed against her car and tugged his head down, so that he was between the car and her body.

"What are you doing?" he exclaimed, fighting her hold.

"Will you be still?" she squeaked. "What if it's *them?*"

"The CIA?"

"The assassins!"

"Oh. Oh, I see." He chuckled. "How very flattering, Brianna."

"Will you keep your head down?"

His lean hands found her waist and gently pushed her away from him. "Brianna, look, *chérie.*"

He turned her face toward the black car, where Lang was lounging by the back fender. He seemed lazily amused.

Brianna flushed. She quickly stepped back from Ahmed and pushed at her disheveled hair.

Lang walked toward them. "Hello, little lady," he drawled. "I was just passing and saw you and your cousin here and figured you might like a lift. Having car trouble?"

"Yes, indeed," Ahmed agreed.

"Then I'll be glad to drive you two wherever you want to go."

Ahmed put Brianna in back and himself in the passenger seat beside Lang. She was still seething about Ahmed's insults. She loved her little car, dents and all. Arrogant jerk, she thought, glaring at the back of his head.

"Would you mind telling me how it is that I have a Mexican cousin when I'm very obviously of Irish ancestry?" she asked Lang irritably.

"By marriage, of course," he said, chuckling. He glanced at her in the rearview mirror. She looked flushed and Ahmed was unusually silent. "Did you think I was going to shoot him?" he asked, gesturing toward his companion.

''I didn't know it was you,'' she protested. ''I just saw a big black limousine. Next time, I'll push him out in the street,'' she muttered under her breath. ''He insulted my car.''

''That is not a car!'' Ahmed joined in the conversation. ''It is a piece of tin with spots.''

''How dare you!''

''Excuse me,'' Lang interrupted. ''But where are we going?''

''To the hospital,'' Brianna said.

''I should have remembered. You go almost every night.'' Lang's eyes met hers in the rearview mirror. ''How long do you think you can keep it up before you collapse?''

''I've managed for almost three years,'' she said tautly. ''I'll manage for as long as it takes.''

He didn't say another word, but his expression was stark. Ahmed sat quietly pondering what he'd learned of Brianna all the way to the hospital. It surprised him to discover that she intrigued him. It must not be. They were worlds apart. She was an innocent, as well. He must marry one day for the sake of heirs, but they would of necessity have to be by an Arab woman. These flights of fancy must be suppressed. They were unrealistic.

Brianna left Lang and Ahmed in the waiting room. She was allowed into the intensive care unit alone, where she sat holding Tad's frail hand and talking to him about the weather and her day, as she always did. His dark lashes lay on his pale cheek, his unruly dark hair falling onto his forehead as he slept in his oblivion.

"Oh, Tad, I'd give anything if you'd wake up," she whispered huskily. "I'd give anything I owned!"

But he didn't, couldn't, answer her.

Lang leaned back against the wall, watching her through the glass, with an uncommunicative Ahmed at his side.

"Torture," Lang said heavily. "That's what it must be for her to go through this every day."

"Is there no other family, someone who might share her burden and lighten it?" Ahmed asked.

"There's no one…just her and the boy."

He let out a long breath. "Nurses could be arranged, you know," he said. "Around the clock. The best in the country."

"Ahmed, nurses can't cure a coma," Lang said. "You know that."

"They might spare her," he returned, nodding toward Brianna.

"Do you really think she'd stop going to see him, even if you could put round-the-clock doctors in there with the boy?" Lang mused.

"No. You are right, of course, I was not thinking." His eyes lingered on the young woman. "She is fragile to look at. But underneath, there is great strength." He turned his attention to Lang. "Do you know something of how that came about?" he added, indicating Tad.

"There was a wreck," Lang said. "They were going on vacation. A speeding car took a curve too fast and hit them head-on. The car rolled. Brianna's father and the driver of the other car were killed instantly. Brianna's brother was knocked unconscious. Her mother was…'' He hesitated. ''Her mother was fatally injured,'' he said, sparing the other man the details. ''She lived until the next morning. She died just before help came. If anyone had spotted the car even an hour sooner, she might have lived, but it went down an embankment and was hidden from the highway.''

Ahmed moved closer. ''Brianna was in the car all night?''

''Yes. Trapped. She had two cracked ribs and a broken hip. You may have noticed that at times she moves a little awkwardly.''

''No. I had not.''

''She was in terrible pain, and she'd lost some blood. But Tad was the worst. It took Brianna over a year, and therapy, to get past the nightmares.''

Ahmed studied her in silence. ''She has great courage.''

''Yes. She's an extraordinary young lady.''

''How old?'' He stared at Lang. ''How old is she?''

''She's twenty-two, I think.'' His eyes narrowed. ''If you seduce her,'' he warned quietly, ''I'll come after you. I don't give a damn about your status or company orders, I'll make you pay if you hurt her in any way.''

Ahmed's eyebrows lifted. "You are smitten with her?"

"I am protective of her," Lang corrected. "She's my friend."

Ahmed smiled quietly. "She is a rosebud, waiting for the sun. I would be a frost to deny her the hope of blossoming," he said. "I am much more aware than you think of the consequences. I have no evil intentions toward her. In between battles, I find her charming company." He glowered at Lang. "You will not tell her this, of course. One cannot afford to parade one's weaknesses before an enemy."

Lang's rigid stance relaxed. He even smiled. "No, one can't."

Ahmed clapped Lang on the back. "Despite her enmity toward me, did you see how quickly she jumped to my aid when she thought you were an assassin?" he mused. "She delights me."

"As if that tin can would have stopped a bullet from even a small-caliber weapon." Lang chuckled.

"She knows nothing of guns or wars or assassinations," Ahmed said. "Nor shall she. I must make certain that she takes no chances on my behalf again. There could have been tragic consequences had it been a true attempt on my life."

The other man sounded resigned and somehow sad. Lang found his response to Brianna curious. Ahmed was a rake, in his own fashion, although he was curiously protective of Brianna.

''We're keeping a close eye on both of you,'' Lang assured him. ''She'll come to no harm.''

''She had better not,'' Ahmed returned grimly, and his dark eyes made a threat of their own as they sought Lang's. ''I consider her welfare no less important than my own. You understand?''

''I do,'' Lang said with a slow smile. ''But I wonder if you do?''

Ahmed scowled with curiosity, but before he could take Lang up on the odd statement, Brianna came out of the ICU, had a brief word with the nurse and joined the men at the door.

''Any change?'' Lang asked.

She only shook her head, her eyes lowered. ''Can we go?'' she asked dully. ''I'm very tired.''

Chapter Five

Brianna didn't sleep well that night. The black limo, the hopelessness of Tad's condition, the arguments with Ahmed were all combining to make her emotions a wreck.

At least the nightmares hadn't come back. She got up the next morning feeling drained. For once, Ahmed was awake. She found him in the kitchen in that long, foreign-looking caftan he lounged in, trying to discover how her coffeepot worked.

"I'll do that," she said, and moved uncomfortably when his dark eyes slid over her slender figure in her nightgown and pink robe. She was perfectly decent, except for her bare feet. She wondered why he should be staring at her so.

"You should dress first," he told her quietly. "It

is unseemly for a maiden to appear before a man in her night clothing.''

''Oh, I can't do it, but it's all right for you?'' she challenged, indicating his caftan.

He smiled slowly. ''Yes.''

''I can wear my nightclothes in my own apartment if I want to,'' she informed him.

He moved closer. It was a sort of movement that Brianna had never experienced before, sensual and predatory and faintly threatening. His eyes didn't move from her face, didn't blink, and all the expression left his features. The only thing alive there was the growing dark glitter of his eyes.

''I'll, uh, just get dressed, why don't I?'' she stammered, and ran for it.

When she came back, he was dressed, too. She made breakfast and he ate it without complaint. He gave no indication that anything out of the ordinary had happened. But Brianna tingled all day remembering the look in his eyes.

When she came home that afternoon, it was to find Ahmed sitting on the top step in her apartment house. He was playing with a Slinky, a small, dark-haired little boy sitting beside him.

''Again,'' the child pleaded.

''Oh, my aching back,'' Ahmed groaned comically. ''You mean I must do it still again and chase this coil of wire down the steps?''

''Yes!'' The child laughed.

Ahmed chuckled. "Very well, then. But this is the last time.'"

"Okay."

The Slinky came slowly down the steps, picked up speed and toppled right at Brianna's feet.

Ahmed came down behind it, spotted her and smiled as he retrieved it. "We were having a bit of fun," he explained.

"So I see. Lang won't like it."

"What he doesn't know won't bother him," Ahmed informed her. He handed her the Slinky. "My friend Nick will let you play, if you like. Won't you, Nick?" he asked the little boy.

"Sure!"

Brianna smiled at the child. "And you know I'd love to. But I have to feed my cousin."

"Aww, Pedro isn't hungry, are you, Pedro?"

"Pedro" grimaced. "Well, my boy, actually I am, a bit. Do you mind? We can do this again sometime."

"No, we can't," Nick wailed. "I have to go stay with my grandma for a week. We're leaving as soon as my dad gets home."

"I am truly sorry," Ahmed told him. "I have enjoyed our games."

"Me, too. Will you come back and see me again sometime?" Nick asked, his big eyes pleading.

Ahmed smiled, smoothing over the dark hair. "Sometime," he agreed.

"Okay, then." He ran back up the stairs, making plenty of noise.

Ahmed led the way up the stairs to Brianna's apartment and held the door open for her.

"You like children," he observed.

"Very much."

"You should marry, and have some of your own," he told her.

"I have Tad to look after," she said evasively. "I need to change."

He stopped her, without touching her at all, just standing in front of her so that she couldn't get past him. "There is something more, something deep," he said, searching her evasive eyes. "You have no desire to marry. I can see it in your face."

"We're not all cut out for marriage." Her face was flushed. "Please. I have to change."

His lean hands gently closed on her thin shoulders. "Tell me."

She closed her eyes. He was impossible this way, so tender and compassionate that he seemed almost another man entirely. "I can't," she whispered. Her big blue eyes opened straight up into his. "Please let me go!"

He accommodated her, standing back. "As you wish," he said quietly.

She went quickly into the bedroom and closed the door. She leaned back against it, her face twisted in anguish, her lip very nearly bitten through. Why did he have to ask questions that hurt her? she wondered. Why couldn't he just mind his own business!

She started to go into the kitchen, as she did every day, when he stopped her.

"Lang has reconnected the telephone," he murmured dryly. "And I have taken advantage of the situation. Wait."

"You haven't ordered out again?" she said nervously. "It's taking too big a chance, even I can see that!"

"My own men are attending to my needs," he said simply. "There is no risk of infiltrators."

"The neighbors here are not blind," she said, exasperated. "How is a poor Mexican laborer affording all that expensive food? People will wonder!"

He scowled. "Poor Mexican laborer?" He echoed her words.

"You!"

He shifted, as if he found the description distasteful. "I cannot live on hot dogs," he said curtly. "I did enjoy the meat loaf and vegetables, but I am accustomed to richer fare."

"You'll die of high cholesterol and gout," she accused.

His eyebrows arched. "This from a woman who is contemplating a meal of hot dogs, which ooze cholesterol?"

"I like hot dogs!"

"And I like quenelles of sole and sautéed asparagus with crepes flambé for dessert," he replied.

"Your poor starving people," she muttered. "Do

they know that you're eating like a king while they chew on cold mutton in their desert tents?''

He pursed his lips. ''Most of them eat couscous and lamb curry,'' he replied. ''And semolina. Cold mutton is hardly appealing.''

''I was making a point.''

The knock at the door spared him an answer. He let his men enter the apartment, laden as they were with cardboard boxes of uncertain origin.

None of that looked like expensive food. It looked like the contents of a yard sale.

Ahmed grinned at her. ''Disguised cuisine,'' he said. ''Don't you approve?'' He threw orders at the Arabs, who dispersed the contents of the boxes onto the table and left the apartment minutes later.

''Lobster tails,'' Ahmed indicated. He obtained a fork, speared a morsel and held it to Brianna's startled lips. ''Taste,'' he said gently.

She took the bit of lobster into her mouth, disconcerted by the way Ahmed's attention suddenly fell on her lips as she savored it.

''It's...very nice,'' she said uncertainly.

''You have a flake of it on your chin. Be still.'' He took it on the tip of his finger and offered it at her lips. Holding her eyes, he eased it onto her bottom lip, but the movement of his fingertip was suddenly very sensual. He nudged it past her teeth and into her mouth and watched with pleasure the way her cheeks flushed and her breathing changed.

The tip of her tongue encountered his finger. She

jerked back, and she saw the expression in his eyes darken and threaten. With her last instinct for self-preservation, she stepped away from him, shaken.

"Thank you for the taste," she whispered. "But I think I still prefer hot dogs."

"As you wish."

He was finding it hard to breathe and act normally. He should not have touched her. It would make things worse.

She fixed herself a hot dog and opened a small bag of potato chips.

"Even more cholesterol," he said, pointing at the potato chips with a forkful of chive-and-butter-and-sour-cream-choked potato.

"Look who's talking," she returned.

He chuckled. "You have spirit."

"Around you, I need to have it," she muttered.

He finished the potato and pushed the plate containing it and the remains of his lobster away. He retrieved the crepe with its exquisite fruit filling and nibbled at it. "Would you care to sample this?" he asked.

She flushed, remembering her earlier weakness. "I don't like sweets, thanks," she lied.

He didn't reply. She was suddenly very transparent and he felt a weakening in himself that he didn't like. Lang was right. Involvement with Brianna would be tragic.

The nightmare she'd staved off for two days came that night. She hadn't gone to see Tad, because there was such a terrible rainstorm. The thunder and lightning frightened her, but she pulled the covers over her head and tried not to notice them. Clad in her silky green gown, because it was an unusually warm night for autumn, she lay stiffly until the worst of the lightning abated and she fell into an uneasy sleep.

But the nightmare came to replace the storm. She was trapped in the car. Her father was dead. She could see his face. Her mother's pain was vocal, almost visible. She begged Tad to wake up and talk to her. She begged Brianna not to let him die, not to let them kill him. Her voice went on and on, while Brianna struggled with pain that racked her in agony. She had to get out, to save her mother. She had to get out, but her mother cried out and the light went out of her eyes....

"No!" she screamed, fighting the hands that were trying to lift her, to save her. "No, no, no! I won't let her die...!"

"Brianna!"

She felt the whiplike movement of steely hands on her upper arms and her eyes opened by reflex. Ahmed was sitting on her bed, his face solemn in the light of the lamp by the bed. He was wearing some sort of silky dark pajama bottoms, but his broad, hair-covered chest was bare. He looked out of place in her frilly bedroom.

"Brianna, talk to me," he said, unconvinced that she was completely awake even now.

"I'm...all right. It was the nightmare," she whispered, shivering.

"You screamed. I thought the nightmares were a thing of the past," he added.

She didn't know that Lang had told him about the wreck. She sought his dark eyes. "They were," she said dully.

His gaze drifted over her face and down to the deep cleft of her breasts under the opaque lacy bodice of her gown. She hadn't realized before that the lace left her dark nipples quite visible. But then, nobody had ever seen her in the gown before.

Her hands began to lift, because his rapt gaze was disturbing. Her nipples went suddenly hard, tingling with unknown sensations, and she blushed at the blatant evidence that would tell him how much he affected her.

"Beautiful," he said gently, watching them change. "They are as the blush of dusk on the rose."

Her hands paused in midair. She watched him, puzzled, curious.

He looked into her soft, puzzled eyes. "Has no man ever described your body to you before?" he asked quietly.

"No one...has seen it," she began huskily.

His brows jerked. His eyes went over her again, appreciating the creamy satin of her skin above the gown, at the pulse in her throat, at the soft swell of her lips. He hadn't touched her. He only looked.

That was enough. He made her afraid. She didn't

understand the feelings he engendered. She wasn't sure that she liked them.

"You must go," she whispered shakily.

"In a moment," he agreed. "First, though, *chérie,* I want to be certain that the nightmares are gone."

"They are...."

"Let us make sure of it." He looked somber, very adult and mature. "The best way to stem a nightmare is to create an experience to supplant it. Do you not agree?"

"That depends...on the experience...you have in mind," she managed breathlessly.

"Something very innocent. Like you, *ma chérie,*" he added with a tender smile. "There is nothing to be afraid of, only a contact which will prove to you that innocence can be as arid as my desert."

As he spoke, he lifted her from the pillow and smoothed the spaghetti straps of her gown down her arms.

"You mustn't!" she protested when she realized what he meant to do.

But he pulled her face into his throat and continued, pushing the gown to her waist. Then he slid his lean, warm hands around her bare back and began to move her bare, hard-tipped breasts against his hair-roughened chest. She gasped. The sensation was beyond her understanding. It made her breasts swell, her body swell. There was a sudden uncomfortable tautness in her lower body, a rush of heat. Her hands stiffened where they rested on his bare shoulders, feeling his strength.

"Relax," he whispered at her ear, his voice lazily sensual, amused. She was like a tightly coiled spring, but her breasts were exquisite. He liked their softness, their hard little points digging into his muscles as he teased her body with his. "Do you like it?" he breathed, letting his hands slide under her arms now, to brush her from side to side with damning sensuality.

Her nails were biting into him unconsciously. "You must…stop," she stammered, shivering as his thumbs worked onto the soft swell of her breasts and began to caress them.

"Only this, I promise," he whispered. His teeth nibbled gently at her earlobe. "Nothing to compromise you, nothing to shame you. Let me touch you, Brianna."

Her voice broke. His touch was maddening. He made her want shameful things. She shivered, and despite her reluctant mind, her body drew away to give him complete access to her breasts, while her face burrowed, ashamed, closer against his warm throat.

"No, no," he coaxed, lowering his mouth to her tightly closed eyes. "Do not be ashamed to enjoy what I can give you. I mean you no harm." His mouth pressed hungrily at her temple while his fingers trespassed onto the fullness of her breasts and traced patterns that made her writhe before they came to rest over the hard tips of her breasts.

She clung to him, biting her lower lip almost through, letting his hands caress her while his thumbs and forefingers molded her nipples until her whole body ached.

"You delight me," he whispered roughly. He moved, sliding his exploring hands up and down her silky back in lazy sweeps while he held her nakedness against him once more. She could feel the thunder of his heartbeat shaking them both, and she hadn't the will to ask him to stop. She wanted it to go on and on, to never end. She hadn't known that there could be such joy in a man's touch.

She didn't know that her hands were in his hair until she felt him gently remove them. He lifted her away from him and laid her down against the pillow firmly, his hands on her wrists while his glittering eyes dropped to her bare breasts. The next step, she knew, would be to let him peel the rest of the gown away. She would feel his eyes on her, and then his hands, and...

"No!" she gasped. If he did that, he would see her hip. She couldn't bear for him to see it!

He was incredibly perceptive. He knew that she wasn't protesting the thought of his eyes on her body. He had a good idea, from what Lang had said, why she was so reluctant.

"Which hip is it, *chérie?*" he asked softly.

She stopped moving and stared up at him, red-faced.

"Which hip?"

She hesitated. "The...the left."

He smiled apologetically, and with slow, gentle hands, moved the fabric of her gown down over her hips and discarded it.

She lay frozen while he moved the elastic of her briefs to give him a full view of the damage that had been done in the wreck. There were scars against the smooth flesh, from the injury as well as the surgery that was needed to repair it. She held her breath, almost afraid to look at him.

But when she did, his eyes were gentle, patient. "Ah," he said softly. "Is that all?"

She shivered, in relief mingled with uncertainty.

"Brianna, such a body is a gift of the gods," he said very quietly. "A few small scars are of no consequence, except as marks of bravery and sacrifice. You are exquisite."

She felt odd. Embarrassment should have overcome her, but she didn't feel it. She searched his eyes with curiosity, wonder.

"And now there will be no more nightmares, yes?" he asked softly, smiling. "You will sleep and dream of my eyes upon you."

Heat burned into her cheeks. He smiled. "This is shyness," he said, tracing the redness across her cheekbones. "It delights me."

Without awkwardness, he pulled her gown back up

and replaced the small straps on her shoulders. He bent and brushed his lips gently across her closed eyelids. "You have given me a gift of which you are truly ignorant, are you not?" he whispered. "You have invited me to be your first lover."

"I...didn't mean to," she replied uncertainly.

He lifted his head, and his eyes were tender. "Nothing would give me greater pleasure," he said with sincerity. "But we are fated for different roles in life than to be together. I would take your innocence only if I could offer you the future. I cannot."

He was closing a door. She felt sad, but it was nothing she hadn't known already. She had Tad, and Ahmed was from another country, another culture.

Her hand lifted to his face, hesitant, until he carried it the rest of the way. She traced his wide, firm mouth, his mustache, his high cheekbones and the thick ridge where his dark eyebrows lay. His hair was thick and black and cool to the touch. She found him devastating, as dozens of women before her must have.

He took her palm to his lips and savored it. His heartbeat was still visible. *"Bonne nuit, ma chère,"* he whispered.

"I don't understand," she began shyly.

"You don't understand what?" he teased. "French, or why you permitted me such a liberty?"

"Both, perhaps."

"You are very young," he said. "Curious and shy. I find it a disturbing combination. One day, a man will carry you to bed in his arms and you will learn that a scar means nothing to a man in love."

He put her hand back down and pulled the covers over her. "Sleep well."

"You, too."

He turned out the lamp and rose from the bed, tall and suddenly dear. He paused before he closed the door to look back at her with an inscrutable expression.

Brianna slept. And there were no more nightmares.

There was a new familiarity and an equally new tension between Brianna and Ahmed after that night. He made certain that he never touched her, nor did he refer to what had happened. Brianna could have believed from his behavior that it had never happened at all. For her own peace of mind, she supposed that she should try.

But he was tense and he became more so as the days passed. Lang discovered that he was still having food imported, and a confrontation rapidly ensued.

"I cannot live on oblong orange containers of meat of mysterious origin wrapped in buns!" Ahmed raged, waving his hands expressively. "I have a palate, which is unaccustomed to common fare!"

"Hot dogs are no worse for you than that high-priced cream-covered slop you eat!" Brianna shot back.

Lang looked heavenward for guidance. "Look," he

said, stepping between them to face Ahmed, "you have to cooperate with us or we can't protect you."

"It is my own men who have been importing food for me," Ahmed informed him. He was as tall as Lang, although not quite as husky. He was formidable looking, just the same. "They have brought it in plain brown boxes, and not in their suits or native dress."

"Yes, but the restaurant where they're getting the food is a public place," Lang argued. "They've been seen coming around to the back laden with cardboard boxes. The police are watching them. They think they've stumbled onto a smuggling operation!"

Brianna hid her face in her hands and choked on laughter.

Ahmed was unamused. "You might enlighten them," he advised Lang.

"I have," he said irritably. "At considerable expense to my skin. They didn't take kindly to being left in the dark about the circumstances of your stay with Brianna."

"That is hardly my concern," the Arab said with cold hauteur.

"It should be," Lang countered. He paused, rubbing his hand over his chin, the other hand jammed into his pocket. "You're one major headache."

"If I were in charge," he informed Lang, "I should draw the assassins into the open and deal with them myself."

"We'd love to," Lang returned curtly. "But we have no idea where they are right now. We've searched the city, but we can't unearth them. We're fairly certain that they haven't made it into the country yet, although they were spotted on the Yucatán coast earlier this week. Meanwhile, it would be of great benefit to you, and to us, if you could be a little more discreet!''

Ahmed shrugged. ''I have been discreet.''

''Stop importing exotic food!''

''Tell her—'' he pointed at Brianna ''—to stop shoving oblong orange containers of suspicious meat wrapped in buns at me!''

''Hot dogs,'' Brianna corrected. ''They're hot dogs!''

''Brianna, if we bring you some groceries, can you cook him something else?'' Lang asked, trying to compromise.

''Bring me some mushrooms,'' she said with a venomous smile, ''and hemlock and beef steak. I'll fix him a meal he'll never forget!''

''You can't poison foreign dignitaries,'' Lang explained patiently. ''They have to be carefully handled.''

''Spoilsport!''

''We'll get something right over,'' Lang promised Ahmed. ''Now, will you please leave the catering bit alone?''

Ahmed was reluctant. ''I suppose that I could. She is a passable cook,'' he added without looking at Brianna.

''I'm a good cook,'' she retorted.

"Make an apple pie with whipped cream, and I'll join you for supper," Lang said.

She smiled at him. "Would you, really? Bring me some apples and whipping cream, then."

He chuckled. "I'd be delighted."

Ahmed moved between them. "A bad idea, I'm afraid," he told Lang. "You have been seen by most of the terrorist group. It would hardly be politic for you to be seen here."

Lang grimaced. "He's right," he told Brianna sadly.

"I can save you a piece of apple pie," she said with a defiant look at Ahmed.

"That's a deal. Well, I'll say so long."

She walked him to the door, aware that Ahmed was watching every move she made. She felt a new tension and wondered why.

"Watch out for him," Lang said, nodding toward the man in the distance. "He's a ladies' man, and you'd be a whole new experience for him."

She smiled at him. "Thanks, Lang. But I'm not totally stupid. I'll be fine."

"Okay. Take care."

"You, too."

She closed the door behind him, grateful that she was able to keep her expression blank. It wouldn't do to let Lang see that Ahmed had already discovered her for himself. She felt shaky inside remembering the feel of him against her. She couldn't afford to feel like that, either. This was just a passing experience. She had to remember.

She went back into the apartment and forced a smile. "How about a cup of coffee?" she offered brightly.

"Lang is attracted to you," he said shortly. "He leads a dangerous life, and he will not easily give it up."

"I know that." She was shocked. "I have no interest in Lang, except that he's very sweet and I like him."

He stared at her for a moment. Then he relaxed and turned back to drop onto the sofa. "I would enjoy a cup of coffee."

"Thank you," she prompted.

He frowned.

"Thank you," she repeated. "It's courteous to thank people when they offer to do things for you."

Ahmed continued to frown.

"A little courtesy makes people feel of value," she continued. "You might try it."

He hesitated until she went into the kitchen and started the coffee. But when she put it on the table, he looked up.

"Thank you," he said stiffly.

Brianna smiled. "You're welcome!"

Chapter Six

Lang didn't show up that night when Brianna went to see Tad, and Ahmed insisted on accompanying her. That meant he had to be crammed into the passenger seat of her tiny vehicle, and he complained all the way to the hospital parking lot.

"If you hate my poor little car so much, why insist on coming with me?" she asked angrily.

"Because it is dangerous for a woman to be outside after dark alone," he said, "in any city."

He was concerned for her. The realization made her feel warm inside, protected. She stared at him, entranced.

He touched her face lightly, aware that she was creating a sort of weakness in him. She pleasured him.

He withdrew his hand with reluctance, noticing that

she had leaned closer involuntarily, trying to maintain the light touch.

"You disturb me, Brianna," he said huskily. "It is a weakness which I can ill afford. Come."

He unwound himself from the seat and waited for her to get out. He escorted her to the hospital with a firm hand under her elbow. But before they got to the front door, his hand had begun to slide down until his long fingers could intertwine sensuously with hers.

She stopped, aware of explosive sensations caused by his touch. He looked down at her, his jaw taut as the same feelings worked on him. His fingers contracted around hers, pressing his palm hard against hers, and for long minutes they stood on the sidewalk under a streetlight and simply stared at each other.

"This is unwise," he said, his voice deep and husky. But he moved closer, so that his body was right up against hers.

"Yes." She laid her cheek slowly on his chest, over the trench coat, and listened to the hard, heavy beat of his heart.

His hand freed hers. His arms came up, slowly, and around her. He drew her close and bent his dark head over hers. He rocked her gently against him in the damp darkness and wondered at the peace he felt.

When he let her go, she was hard-pressed not to wobble on her feet. She clung to his hand as they went up in the elevator. She left him reluctantly to go see Tad.

He waited, his eyes unseeing as he stared at the

carpeted floor. Brianna was becoming too important in his life. He wasn't sure he could let her go when it became necessary. How odd that she'd managed to instill feelings in him that all the experienced women of his acquaintance couldn't. He felt tenderness with her. It was a new feeling entirely, for him to feel tender toward a woman.

When she came back, he was more disturbed than ever. He took her hand and led her back to the car, gently helping her into the driver's side before he got in beside her.

"How is he?" he asked.

She shook her head. "There's no change."

She started the car and drove back to her apartment. This time when they got out, he kept a distance between them. When they entered her apartment, he excused himself with a plea of fatigue and closeted himself in the guest bedroom.

Brianna was surprised by his sudden change of attitude. She hadn't known what to expect from him, but this certainly wasn't it. He seemed suddenly distant and unwilling to let her near him.

The next morning, when she dressed and went to fix breakfast, she overheard him speaking to Lang on the telephone. What he was saying stopped her in her tracks, out of sight in the hall.

"I tell you, I cannot stay here!" he raged. "The situation is becoming unbearable. You must make other arrangements." There was a short pause while he listened. "Talk to them, then, but I expect solutions, not excuses!"

He slammed the telephone down and Brianna retreated to her room, almost in tears. So it was like that, was it? He couldn't bear to be around her anymore. Was he afraid that she was going to embarrass him by falling to her knees and confessing undying love or something? She flushed. She must have given away something of her tumultuous feelings the night before, when she'd laid her head so trustingly against his chest at the hospital. How could she have been so weak? He attracted her, made her aware of longings she'd never experienced. She wanted him. But there was more to it than even that. She...cared for him.

She stared at her white face in the mirror. This wouldn't do. She had to get a grip on herself. She must fix breakfast and go to work and not let this upset her. She had Tad to think of, and no hope of a normal life as long as he was comatose. She had to think about Tad, not herself.

With that firmly in mind, she pinched some color into her cheeks and went back down the hall again. Ahmed was sitting on the sofa.

"I'll fix something for you to eat before I leave," she began.

"That is not necessary. I am not hungry."

She picked up her coat and purse. "Suit yourself. Goodbye."

"Are you not going to have your toast and coffee?" he asked suddenly.

''I'm not hungry, either,'' she said without looking at him.

She opened the door and went out. She felt sick all over. It had been bad enough before, when they argued. Now it was worse. He couldn't bear even to be in the apartment with her.

She'd only just made it to the steps when he opened the apartment door and called to her.

''What?'' she asked stiffly.

''It is not healthy to go without breakfast when you are accustomed to it,'' he replied formally.

She looked back at him with glaring blue eyes. ''I can take care of myself, thank you.''

His face closed up. ''Eat something at work, then,'' he said shortly. ''Presumably you have a coffee shop nearby.''

''I'll eat when I feel like it!''

His dark eyes slid over her like seeking hands. She flushed and he made an annoyed sound. He went back into the apartment and closed the door with an audible snap.

Lang came by her office at lunchtime. He perched himself on the desk and studied her with too much interest for a casual observer.

''You've been crying,'' he remarked. ''And I don't need three guesses.''

''He wants to get rid of me,'' she said furiously. ''And I want to get rid of him, too! I hate having my cooking insulted!''

He smiled wistfully. "He's protecting you," he said.

She scowled. "What?"

"He's protecting you," he repeated. "I don't think he realizes it, but he's trying to get you out of the line of fire. He thinks you're in danger as long as he's around. You are, but we're Johnny-on-the-spot. You're both as safe as you can get. And moving him out of the apartment won't solve any problems, it will only create more. I told him that."

"What did he say?" she asked, trying to sound disinterested.

"That you mustn't be hurt, whatever the cost," he said, smiling.

She flushed. "How very nice of him. That wasn't how he sounded on the phone this morning."

"He's got a lot on his mind."

"I suppose he does," she agreed reluctantly, "with spies and assassins following him around everywhere."

"And his own bodyguard," he reminded her.

"That, too."

"You don't believe me, do you?" he mused. "You think I'm making up excuses for Ahmed, to keep you in our good graces."

"You spies are all alike," she said. "You do the job, whatever it takes."

"Well, I might have exaggerated a little," he confessed, "but not much. I still think Ahmed's main concern is that you might get hurt."

"That's not what he said."

He studied the fabric of his slacks. "Not exactly."

"What did he say, exactly?"

"That he'd be climbing the walls in another two days if I didn't get him out of there," he confessed.

"He won't be the only one," she shot back, infuriated. "He's driving me batty!"

He studied her flushed face, seeing far more than she wanted him to. He pursed his lips and smiled a little and she went scarlet.

"I'll see what I can do," he promised, rising from the desk.

"Thanks, Lang."

"Meanwhile, wear pajamas at night, will you?"

She gasped, horrified.

"He only said that you had a nightmare. And you were wearing a gown designed to undermine all a man's good resolutions and moral character."

"It was not!" she exclaimed. "It's just a common, ordinary, run-of-the-mill gown, and I never asked him to take it off me!"

Lang whistled and averted his eyes. She looked even more horrified. Her face went from scarlet to stark white and her hands covered her mouth.

"No wonder he's climbing walls," Lang said wickedly.

"You get him out of my apartment!" she snapped.

"With all haste, I promise," he said comfortingly. "Meanwhile—" he leaned closer "—wear pajamas!"

"I'll wear armor," she muttered.

He chuckled and left her sitting there, dreaming up ways and means of strangling her apartment dweller. How could he! How dared he!

She fumed all day long. When she got back to the apartment that night, she'd reached flash point.

"How dare you!" She exploded the minute she closed the door behind her.

Ahmed raised both eyebrows and pushed the Off button on the television remote control. "How dare I what?" he challenged.

"How dare you tell that Peeping Tom that I had on a gown!"

He looked stunned. "I said no such thing to him," he began slowly. "Nor would I have. The memory of it is a deeply personal thing, for the two of us alone to share. It would offend my sense of honor to divulge it to anyone else."

She stopped, touched by the way he expressed the memory. "But he said…"

"Yes?"

He looked dangerous. She hesitated. "Well, he said you wanted to leave here because I was driving you up the walls."

He smiled. "You are."

She was confused, and looked it.

He got up from the sofa and took away her purse and coat, depositing them on a chair. "Sit down and have some coffee. I made it. It is surprisingly good, for a first attempt."

She couldn't have imagined Ahmed making coffee. But he was right. It was good.

He sat near her and leaned forward, his dark eyes intent. "I told Lang nothing except that I dislike the risk of remaining here."

"Because of all that catered food?" she prompted.

"Because I find you much too desirable," he said solemnly. "You have no knowledge of men, or of the deceit even an honorable man can employ when desire rides him hard. It was dangerous, the way we were together last night at the hospital. You are vulnerable to me, and I to you. I have explained already how I feel about the situation."

"Yes, I know." She sipped her coffee. "Then if you didn't tell Lang, how did he know?" The coffee cup hung in midair. "Cameras...!"

"No," he assured her. "There are no cameras in the bedroom. I had my own men sweep it, to make certain. It disturbed me that you might be spied upon as you slept."

"Thank you."

"Where is the gown you wore?"

"I washed it and hung it in the window to dry." She caught her breath. "So that's how...!"

"A telescope, no doubt," he mused. "And there are microphones which can pick up a heartbeat from a great distance."

"Oh, dear," she groaned.

"Lang would not permit such a blatant violation of

your privacy,'' he said, ''and my men would not dare eavesdrop on me.''

''I hope you're right. It nauseates me to think that someone might have watched, listened....''

His dark brows drew together slightly. ''You know very little of the world,'' he said gently. ''There are men who think nothing of...'' He laughed. ''Never mind. It is not fit talk for your ears. Drink your coffee.''

''I suppose you have your pick of women,'' she murmured without looking at him. ''In your position, I mean. Diplomats travel in high social circles, and you're not bad looking.''

''You flatter me.''

Her eyes lifted, searching his impassive face. ''I've never had much time for dating. I went out a time or two, but Mama was unwell a lot after Tad was born, and I had to help her look after the house, and after him. Most boys weren't interested in me anyway. I was always thin.'' She fingered the coffee cup. ''After the wreck, I thought my hip looked horrible.''

He laughed gently, without malice. ''And now?'' he teased. ''What do you think of it now?''

She smiled back. ''I think that you were very kind.''

''I had a great deal more than 'kindness' in mind, Brianna,'' he said softly. ''You are very desirable. I find myself lusting after you, and that is why I wish to leave here. An affair between us would be a tragic thing.''

''There must be many women in your life who would gladly give you what you want,'' she said demurely.

He looked very introspective. ''Perhaps. But it will be best if Lang can find other accommodations for me. This enforced togetherness will lead to disaster eventually.''

''I haven't any plans to drape myself nude across your bed,'' she remarked.

He looked at her with lazy appreciation. ''Even the prospect makes my head swim,'' he murmured. ''You realize that I would find it impossible to resist you?''

''I would find it impossible to behave in such a way,'' she confessed. ''I want to explain...''

The ringing of the telephone, an unusual event, stopped her in midsentence. She dived for it, listened for a minute and went deathly pale. She hung up.

''Brianna, what is it?'' he asked softly.

''It's Tad,'' she said numbly, her eyes tragic and shocked. ''He's gotten worse. I have to go to him....''

''You are in no condition to drive. Get your coat.''

He phoned for a cab, certain that the agency had bugged the telephone.

Sure enough, when they got to the curb, there was Lang with the limo. He packed them inside grimly and sped toward City General without a word.

Tad's frail body convulsed over and over again. Brianna watched until she began to cry. Ahmed drew her into his arms and comforted her all through it. He refused to leave her, even when the doctor came and gave her a sedative.

"How is she?" Lang asked when Ahmed reappeared from the room they'd given her.

"She is not well," he replied. "She has spirit, but even so much will eventually give way. The boy's condition is dangerous. He may very well die."

"And if he doesn't?" Lang asked.

Ahmed pursed his lips. "Then he may come out of it," he said with a smile. "This is what the doctor hopes. It is evidence of frenetic brain activity, which can go either way. For Brianna's sake, I hope the boy recovers."

"When will they know?" Lang asked.

"Soon, I hope."

And it was. Minutes later, Ahmed was called in by Dr. Brown, who was laughing with tears running down his cheeks. "Come and look," he said. "Then I'll let you wake Brianna and tell her."

He drew the tall Arab to the ICU, where a young boy's eyes were open and he was being examined by another doctor. He looked at Ahmed with fuzzy curiosity.

"He will recover?" Ahmed asked.

"With treatment and time, of course!"

Ahmed paused long enough to tell Lang before he burst into the room where Brianna was sleeping restlessly.

"Wake up, darling," he whispered, unaware that he'd even used the word. "Wake up, let me tell you."

She opened her eyes heavily, peering at him through a fog of tranquilizers. "What is it? He's gone?" she asked suddenly, choking on the word.

"No! He's awake. He's come out of the coma, Brianna. He's going to be all right!"

She sat up, clinging to Ahmed's strength while she fought to be lucid. "Tad's all right," she echoed. "Oh, thank God!"

He held her while she cried, then helped her as she struggled to get to her feet.

"Steady, darling," he said gently. "You'll keel over." He helped her into her shoes, unaware of the endearments he was whispering to her.

She leaned on his arm and walked into the ICU, dazed and stunned and deliriously happy when she saw Tad's blue eyes sparkle with sudden recognition.

"Sis...ter?" he whispered.

His voice sounded strange. It was the long period of disuse, Dr. Brown assured her.

"Tad," Brianna whispered back, smoothing his dark hair. "I love you, Tad."

"Love you," he managed to say. "Mom? Dad?"

She looked, anguished, at the doctor. He nodded solemnly. She looked back at Tad, forming words she didn't want to speak. "We lost them both. I'm so sorry."

He began to cry. The sound was haunting. Brianna had had three years to cope with the loss, but to Tad, they were only minutes beyond the terrible wreck. He sobbed, shaking all over, and Brianna gathered him up as best she could with all the tubes and wires, and held him, murmuring comforting words.

When he was calm again, she laid him back down and dried his tears.

"We still have each other," she told him. "You can come home and live with me. We'll be fine, Tad. Really we will."

"Head hurts," he murmured.

"We can give you something for that," Dr. Brown said.

"No!" Tad grabbed the doctor's hand. "Mustn't!"

"Don't worry," Dr. Brown said gently. "You won't go under again. You have to trust me."

He looked at Brianna, terrified. She nodded. "It's all right. None of us wants to lose you now. It's been such a long time, Tad. I've come every other day to see you. I've hardly missed a day at all."

"I know." He frowned. "Remember...your voice."

She laughed, delighted. "I told you," she said to Dr. Brown.

"Who is he?" Tad asked, looking at Ahmed. "Saw him...through the glass."

"This is, uh, Pedro," she stammered. "He's a cousin of ours. From Chihuahua," she added helpfully.

"No cousins...in Chihuahua," he murmured.

"Oh, now, Tad, you remember Uncle Gonzales, don't you, who married Aunt Margie?" She bit her lower lip.

''Don't remember…much,'' he confessed.

She relaxed. ''You will,'' she promised. ''For now, you need to get some rest. Tad, it's so good to have you back!''

''Good…to be back.'' He smiled and closed his eyes.

She looked quickly at Dr. Brown.

''He'll be all right,'' he assured her. ''Don't look like that. He'll be fine!''

''You're sure?''

''I'm sure.'' He looked at Ahmed. ''Take her home, young man, and give her two of these. She'll sleep. She needs to,'' He handed Ahmed the tablets.

''I shall see that she does,'' Ahmed assured him. He drew Brianna to his side and along the wall to the elevator.

She let him take her down to the car, where Lang was waiting, beaming. He'd already talked to the doctor. Brianna listened to the conversation, but she was too muzzy and exhausted to register much of it.

When they got to the apartment, Lang left them at the door. Ahmed herded her inside and gave her the tablets, making sure she swallowed them down with a glass of water.

''Thank you,'' she whispered.

He smiled at her. ''For what?''

''For all you did.''

''I did nothing.''

''That's what you think.'' She knew the tablets

would take several minutes to take effect, but she was already drowsy. "I'll see you tomorrow."

"Certainly. Sleep well."

She nodded, wandering down the hall to her room. She closed the door and walked to the bed, and passed out on it.

Ahmed found her sprawled there minutes later when he looked in on her.

He chuckled. It seemed to be his role in life to play valet to her. He removed her clothes and put her into her gown. He almost removed her briefs as well, but that would probably send her into hysterics, he decided, when she woke. He slid her under the covers and pulled them up over her.

Her sleeping face was very vulnerable. He studied her in silence, watching her lips part as she breathed. She looked so fragile like this, and he felt guilty for being a burden to her during his occupancy. He'd have to be more patient.

There was, of course, no hope of leaving the apartment now. She would need someone with her, and Tad would be coming home soon. He would be needed.

That was a new, and strange feeling. No one had ever really needed him before on a personal level. He found himself feeling protective of not only Brianna, but of her young brother, as well. Odd feelings for a man in his position.

Well, he could sort them out tomorrow. He started

to rise, but Brianna caught his arm and pulled it to her breasts, murmuring something in her sleep.

"What is it?" he whispered.

"Don't...go," she said drowsily, her eyes closed. "Stay."

He chuckled softly. She was in for more than a few shocks when she woke, it seemed. He pulled loose long enough to divest himself of everything except his own briefs. Then he climbed in beside Brianna and curled her into his body. She flinched a little at first, at the unfamiliar contact with a man's nearly nude body. But after a minute, she relaxed and curled trustingly back against him.

It wasn't going to be the most comfortable night of his life, he mused dryly, but he couldn't remember a time when he'd felt more at peace. He closed his eyes. Tomorrow was soon enough to face the implications of what he'd just done.

Chapter Seven

Brianna felt a weight on her arm. She moved and fell even closer to a warm, muscular sort of pillow. She must be dreaming. Her hand moved over what felt like a furry animal. It paused and moved again.

"Careful, *chérie,*" a voice whispered drowsily near her ear. "Such caresses are much too dangerous early in the morning."

She opened her eyes. A pair of liquid black ones smiled into them. She jerked up, shocked to find herself in bed with Ahmed. The sheet covered his waist, and his chest was bare.

So was hers, she discovered as the cover fell and she realized that she was nude.

She jerked the cover closer, flushing violently.

"It was your idea," he pointed out. "You felt that the gown was too hot, so you removed it. And, uh, apparently everything else. Then you curled into my body and went immediately back to sleep. I confess, I was unable to. I feel like a man who has been through the rigors of hell."

"The tranquilizers," she stammered apologetically. "I'm not used to drugs. They...sometimes make me behave...strangely."

"I did notice. You made a rather blatant request."

She groaned and pulled the cover over her head.

"There, there. I understand."

"I'm ruined!"

"Not yet," he mused. "However, if you are still of the same mind you were in last night, I find myself more than capable of accommodating you."

She groaned again. "Oh, don't!"

He chuckled, stretching. "It was a revelation, to feel you like that against all of me." He groaned softly. "I confess that I removed the rest of my own clothing, so that I could enjoy the silky warmth of you even more. It took all my willpower not to carry through. You were deliciously soft and sensuous."

She was staring at his face. "You mean...you have nothing on?" she gasped.

He rolled over onto his side and propped himself upon an elbow. "Not a stitch."

She chewed her lower lip almost through. "I have to get up."

He swept his arm toward the side of the bed invitingly.

"I can't...with you looking."

"How could I not look at something so captivatingly beautiful?" he asked simply. "You are a work of art."

She flushed. "Well...you mustn't look at me, all the same."

"Then you wish to have me get out of bed first, *n'est-ce pas?*"

"Please."

He searched her eyes with a deep laugh. "Delightful little wretch. Will you hide your eyes in your hands, I wonder, and then peek through them to see what a man looks like when he is aroused and needful of a woman?"

She flushed. "You stop that! I won't look!"

"As you wish." He threw back the covers and got up, stretching so that his body was taut and the muscles rippled all the way up and down. And Brianna, with her hands over her eyes, parted her fingers just enough to get a shocking, blatant view of him. Surprisingly, she couldn't manage to cover her face back up. She took her hands away, her heart pounding, her throat dry, and he turned completely toward her, letting her look.

"It is not something of which you need be ashamed," he said softly.

"Oh, my," she said on a shaky breath.

He smiled. "You flatter me with those big eyes, *chérie,* but they make it all the more difficult for me to practice restraint." He turned away from her and found his silk briefs and pajama bottoms. He slid them up over his slim hips and snapped them in place before he turned to look at her. The cover had dipped, so that only the tips of her breasts remained covered.

"Still so shy," he accused. "You slept with me."

She flushed. "Not...like that."

"We slept nude, in each other's arms," he said. "Like lovers."

"But we aren't!"

He smiled gently. "We will be," he said softly. "The prospect of it makes me dizzy with pleasure. You're silk and satin. Innocent and sweet and brave. What more could a man ask of life than such a woman?"

"I won't be your mistress," she managed.

"Oh, Brianna," he said tenderly, "never could I ask you to be so small a part of my life as that."

She was puzzled. Her eyes sought his and found only dancing mischief in them. "Well, then, what do you want?"

"What you whispered in my ear last night as you slept," he said.

"But I don't remember."

"You will, at the appropriate time. Get dressed while I make coffee. Tad will be awake and impatient to see you!"

"Tad!" She laughed. "It wasn't a dream, then!"

"No. Not at all. Get up."

He went out, closing the door behind him. She jumped out of bed and rushed toward the bathroom just as the door suddenly opened again and Ahmed stared at her with rapt delight.

"Stop that," she said.

He shook his head and smiled apologetically. "I couldn't resist. Hurry, now." He closed the door again.

She darted into the bathroom, embarrassed and excited. She had a new lease on life, it seemed, and Ahmed was part of it.

Tad's eyes lit up when Brianna walked into the new private room he'd been given. He looked much better, with some color in his cheeks, and his speech had improved, too.

"I feel like Rip Van Winkle." He chuckled, his voice a little rusty but much more animated than it had been the day before. "Hi, cousin!" he added, smiling at Ahmed.

"Good morning, young cousin," Ahmed said indulgently. "I trust you feel more yourself?"

"I feel much better. I was worried about Bri, though," he confessed, falling naturally back into his old familiar way of addressing her. "They told me she had to be sedated."

"I'm fine now," she assured him. "I had a good night's sleep and I'm all right."

"I'm sorry I gave you a fright," he said, wondering at her faint color.

"You can give me all the frights you want," she told him warmly. "It's so wonderful to have you awake and alert and talking to me. Tad, you're all I've got in the whole world,'' she added huskily.

''Not quite, *chérie,*'' Ahmed said from behind her, his hand gently smoothing her hair.

She flushed, looking up into dark, possessive eyes.

''When can I get out of here and come home?'' Tad asked eagerly, changing the subject.

''I'll ask your doctor. I'll pester him five times a day until he's desperate to let you leave,'' she promised dryly.

''Thanks, sis!''

But it wasn't that easy to persuade Dr. Brown to dismiss the boy. He insisted that Tad stay long enough for more tests to be conducted, and until they were certain that his body could manage on its own. However, he added with a grin, if Tad's appetite was any indication, keeping him fed was going to be the biggest headache Brianna would have.

Since the night Brianna had spent in his arms, Ahmed was convinced that marriage to her would solve some of his most pressing problems. The major one would be his hunger for her, which grew by the day. He wanted not only her perfect body but her warm heart and brave spirit. The minor problem would be his country's relations with the United States. Surely it would pave the way for better ones in future if he had an American wife. The more he thought about it, the more convinced he became that it would be a wise move. The details could come later. Now it was enough that the decision had been made.

He drew Lang to one side while Brianna was with her brother.

"You must make haste to solve this thing," he told Lang. "I can waste no more time waiting for assassins to do their deadly business."

Lang's eyebrows rose. "Are you and Brianna at each other's throat again?"

"It is not that at all," he said. "I wish to go home and be married."

Lang was shocked and trying not to show it. "Isn't this a bit sudden?" he asked.

Ahmed waved his hand expressively. "I have waited most of my life. Now this assassination plot has made me aware of my own vulnerability, of the risk to my people if I die without issue. I tell you, I believe my brother-in-law is mixed up in this," he added solemnly, his dark eyes unblinking on the other man's face. "He is the only one who could move against me with such ease and with cooperation from bribed officials. No doubt he has made many promises."

"You mentioned that once before. We've acted on it. We have operatives making every effort to wrap it up quickly."

Ahmed nodded. "I hope that it will not take much longer. Now that I have made the decision, I wish to implement it as soon as possible."

"I suppose congratulations are in order, then,"

Lang said, thinking how hard this was going to hit poor Brianna, who was so obviously infatuated with Ahmed. The man didn't even seem to notice that!

"Yes. Another thing, we must have a larger apartment for the duration of this charade," he said. "If Tad comes home with us, and I assume that he will, the apartment she now occupies will not be large enough for the three of us."

"We have a safe house nearby...."

"Unwise," Ahmed said at once. "Even if Brianna did not find it suspicious, the boy might."

"You're right. An apartment, then, in a building where we have a floor under surveillance. Will that do?"

Ahmed smiled. "Yes. Thank you."

"Where do you plan to be married, in Saudi Mahara?" Lang asked.

"It must be there, obviously," the other replied impatiently. "The duties of state," he added sadly. "I myself would prefer something quiet and simple, but it would be unthinkable not to have all the trappings."

"I understand. Well, I'll get the ball rolling," Lang replied.

Ahmed's dark eyes twinkled. "You look sad. You are a bachelor, too. One day, perhaps you will find a woman who can make you happy."

"I already did," Lang said ruefully. "But being the brilliant fellow I am, I kicked her out of my life and sent her running.'' He laughed curtly at the joke he made and went in search of a telephone.

Brianna was so excited about Tad that she hardly noticed the passing of time. But Ahmed's curiously tense attitude disturbed her and when she could manage it, she maneuvered Lang into an alcove to question him.

''Ahmed is very quiet,'' she told him. ''Has something happened that I should know about?''

He ground his teeth together. ''Sure you want to hear it?'' he asked.

''I've got Tad back,'' she replied simply. ''I think I can take anything now.''

''I hope so. He—'' he nodded toward Ahmed, who was reading a magazine in the waiting room beyond the hall ''—is impatient to go home and get married.''

Get married. *Get married.* Brianna heard the words with every heartbeat. She hadn't realized until that moment how much Ahmed meant to her. Now it dawned on her that he would certainly need to marry a woman from his own country. He was a high cabinet official. Of course! How would it look if he married a foreigner? How could she have been so stupidly blind!

''I see,'' she managed to say through a tight throat. She even smiled at a concerned Lang. ''I've been living in dreams, haven't I, Lang?''

He grimaced. ''Brianna, I wish…''

''It's all right,'' she assured him numbly. ''I've

been expecting it. Good heavens—'' she laughed ''—he couldn't very well get involved with an American woman, could he?''

Lang's eyes were sympathetic. ''I didn't want to tell you.''

She took another steadying breath. *Fate has given me a trade,* she thought. *It's traded me Tad for what I might have had with Ahmed.* She wanted to laugh hysterically, but it would not change the situation. She'd been a minor amusement for Ahmed. She'd been falling in love, but he'd been teasing, playing, while he planned all along to marry some woman back home. She felt like a fool.

''I need to go and see about Tad.''

''Time does heal things, somewhat,'' he remarked, his hands deep in his pockets and a sudden, pained look in his eyes.

''I know.'' She touched his arm gently and then walked back toward the intensive care unit. She didn't look in Ahmed's direction at all.

She didn't change her attitude toward Ahmed noticeably. She was polite and courteous. But the distance between them grew, and he noticed her reticence without understanding what was wrong.

Lang hadn't told him that he'd mentioned Ahmed's upcoming marriage. But Lang had told him that they had an agent pretending to be Ahmed installed in a classy downtown hotel being very obviously guarded in his hotel suite. And there had just been an attempt on the man's life. Ahmed was concerned now for Brianna's safety, and Tad's. If he was discovered, all the red herrings in the world weren't going to stop the terrorists from striking at him; nor would they care if they happened to kill some innocent person who simply got in the way.

Ahmed, and Lang, went with Brianna every time she went to the hospital now. But Ahmed, sensing her withdrawal, didn't come any closer. He was protective and tender, but not amorous. Not at all. She wasn't sure if she should be hurt or grateful. After all, he had somebody else, and he hadn't even been honest enough to tell her.

Tad's animated presence almost made up for Ahmed's reticence. She delighted in his company, spent every available minute with him. And when the doctor said she could, finally, take him back to the apartment, she all but danced around the room with joy.

"I have already told Lang that we must have a larger apartment so that we each have a bedroom."

That wasn't all he'd told Lang, but she didn't say any more. "It might be wise" was the only comment she made.

He scowled. "You are withdrawn," he said quietly. "Since the night I slept with you in my arms, you have hardly had three words to say to me."

"I've decided that it was a mistake," she said without looking at him. "I don't want to get involved in a relationship that has no future."

His brows jerked together. "What do you mean, no future?"

She turned her head. "I think you understand me. I'm not going to be your plaything. Not when you've got a woman back home already."

He averted his eyes. "I am a man, full grown. I feel the occasional need for a woman in my bed. I will not apologize for being human."

"I didn't ask you for an apology," she returned. "I simply said that I'm not standing in for another woman."

"There would be no question of that."

"Good. I'm glad we understand each other." She put the car into gear and drove home, with Ahmed quiet and contemplative beside her. He'd already started planning a state wedding, and here was Brianna all upset about his mistress and refusing him. He'd already telephoned to tell the woman back home that he was marrying. He'd given her a handsome compensation and provided for her old age, and they parted friends. But apparently Brianna couldn't accept that he had a past. It made him sad. He'd thought her more forgiving than that.

And she still didn't know it all. Inwardly he was remembering just how great a deception he and Lang had worked on Brianna. There was a truth she hadn't yet discovered, one that would certainly have changed their relationship or even killed it once she knew. He hadn't wanted to tell her. He'd planned to wait, to find the right words, the right time. But she seemed unwilling to even speak of a future with him now. He'd waited too long.

He looked at her sadly. She was very young, of course. Perhaps he expected too much, too soon. He would have to bide his time and hope that she wasn't as unaffected as she seemed.

By the next day, Lang had found them a new apartment. It took all of a day to have everything moved into it by Ahmed's friends. Brianna was shocked at the way he did things, literally snapping his fingers to get people to do what he wanted. She'd never been exposed to anyone with such a sense of power and confidence. She stood in awe of him, but she was determined not to let it show. The woman back home was welcome to him, she told herself. She didn't want him!

While she unpacked, Ahmed spoke privately with Lang. "The boy will be safe here with us?" he asked worriedly. "I would not have him hurt now for all the world."

"He won't be," Lang said. "You'll all be as safe here as you would be in a bomb shelter twenty stories down. You're completely surrounded. There are bugs and cameras everywhere," he added meaningfully. "For your own protection. Remember them."

"Do you think I might need to remember them?" Ahmed laughed heavily. "She has no interest in me now that her brother is conscious. I have become the forgotten man."

Lang couldn't help but feel that it was the best thing to happen, since Ahmed was making marriage plans.

"I'm sorry. I know how you feel," Lang replied, and his eyes were distant. "I've had years of being the forgotten man."

Ahmed scowled, curious. Lang looked very different when he spoke that way.

"There was a girl back home," he told the Arab wryly. "I made a mistake. I tried to apologize, but it was too late. Now I can't get near her. She hates me."

"I am truly sorry."

"Me, too," Lang replied. He got to his feet. "Life goes on. I'll leave you to it. We'll be somewhere close when you bring the boy here. No more catered meals," he added.

Ahmed raised both hands. "Very well. I suppose that in an emergency I can learn to eat cursed hot dogs." He glowered at Lang. "My counterpart enjoys filet mignon and cherry crepes jubilee nightly, I suppose?"

Lang chuckled. "One of the perks of his 'position.'"

"Yes. Well, tell him not to enjoy it too much," came the haughty reply. "His position is very temporary indeed."

"He certainly hopes so," Lang informed him. "We're very close to a solution. I can't tell you any more than that. And I'm sorry to add that you were right to suspect your brother-in-law."

"And what of my sister?" he asked solemnly.

"I don't know yet."

Ahmed was preoccupied as he rode with Brianna to the hospital to get an exhilarated Tad that very afternoon. Brianna was apparently in high spirits. Her boss had given her the day off, and the women in the office had gone in together to get a special present for Tad. They hadn't told her what it was. They'd wrapped it up, and it was very big. She was as curious as Tad about the contents.

"I would have brought it with me," she told Tad, "but the box wouldn't fit in here with the three of us."

"Unsurprising," Ahmed said with disgust, looking around him. "I do not fit in here."

"You'll have to ask your boss for a raise, Bri, so we can get a better car," Tad said.

"I like this one, thank you," she returned. "Once it's painted, it's going to be beautiful."

Tad made a sound in his throat and she smiled, but the smile never reached her eyes. Ahmed thought that he'd never seen her look so helpless. It infuriated him that she was willing to throw away what they felt for each other out of misplaced jealousy.

They unloaded Tad and his things and got him upstairs to the tenth-floor apartment. This one had three bedrooms and a living room, with a spacious kitchen.

Brianna hummed as she worked, putting together a special meal.

Meanwhile, Tad had opened the suspicious box and let out a whoop.

Brianna stuck her head around the doorway to see what he had. She burst out laughing.

It was a collection of everything from a football helmet to a baseball and bat, all that a young man needed to join the human race again, including a Walkman tape player and several tapes to play in it.

''I've never heard of any of these people,'' he murmured as he looked at the tapes.

''You'll probably love them,'' Brianna said. ''Marjorie bought the tapes, I'm sure. She has a son your age. She'll know what's popular.'' She frowned. ''My goodness, Tad, we'll have to see about getting a tutor for you, so that you can catch up to your age level in school.''

''That is easily arranged,'' Ahmed said gently. ''Later, though. Not today.''

She didn't look at him. ''Of course not today,'' she replied. She went back into the kitchen and fixed a balanced meal worthy of Tad's first night home, with all his old favorites.

''This is great.'' He sighed when he'd cleaned up the very last of the chicken-and-rice casserole and the canned apricots and homemade rolls. ''Bri, that was the best food I've ever had.''

''You flatterer,'' she said, smiling at him warmly.

"I'm glad you liked it. Your appetite is certainly going to please Dr. Brown."

He leaned back in his chair, studying Ahmed. "How did you wind up here, Cousin Pedro?" he asked curiously. "Did our aunt and uncle send you up here from Chihuahua?"

"Why, yes," Ahmed lied easily, and his eyes smiled. "To look for work. And I have," he continued. Lang had placed all sorts of applications from "Pedro" in strategic locations. But no one had called him about work.

"Sure." Tad smiled with some puzzlement. "But that Spanish accent of yours is the oddest I've ever heard."

"It's been years since you've heard one," Brianna reminded him.

"Well, yes, I guess so." He flexed his legs. "It's so good to be able to get up and walk. I don't guess any of my old friends are still around?" he added.

"Todd Brock is," she said, smiling at his surprise. "He calls every month or so to check on you. He has ever since the wreck."

"Wow! Do you have his telephone number? Can I call him?"

"Of course, I'll get it for you." She hesitated. This was going to present many complications. She couldn't let him tell Todd where he was, or who was living with them. She grimaced.

"You're worried," Tad said, suddenly curious. "You don't want me to call him. Why? What's going on?"

Chapter Eight

Brianna stood in the middle of the floor with a mind that refused to work. She couldn't think up a good reason to satisfy that suspicious look in her young brother's eyes.

"She has only just managed to reacquire you from the hospital after three long years," Ahmed said softly, smiling at the boy. "Is it not natural that she should jealously guard your company for at least the first few days you are back at her side?"

Tad colored and laughed roughly. "My gosh, yes. I'm sorry, sis. That was thoughtless of me, really!"

She walked over and hugged him warmly, her eyes mirroring her gratitude to Ahmed over Tad's shoulder. "I'm sorry," she said. "It's just that we've only just become reacquainted and I don't want to share you for a few days. So, do you mind?"

"I don't mind at all." His blue eyes twinkled. "Todd can wait."

"Thanks, Tad."

He shrugged. "What are brothers for?" he mused, and then laughed.

One disaster was averted. Brianna found it difficult to avoid the questions that kept coming, though. Inevitably Tad noticed how careful Brianna and Ahmed were about what they said, about going out, about letting anyone in. He was a sharp boy. He didn't voice any of his curiosity, but it was there in his eyes just the same. He had his own television in his room, and he was quickly and eagerly catching up on three years of news and new developments in his favorite subject, science. But he was giving his two companions looks that became more perceptive by the day.

"Tad is suspicious of us," Ahmed told Brianna one evening when they were alone in the kitchen after Tad had gone to bed.

"Yes, I know. It's a strain for all of us," she replied. "But it won't be for much longer, will it?"

"I hope not," he replied quietly. His dark eyes narrowed in impatience. "I long to be free of the necessity for this stealth and deception."

"So do I."

"You do not look at me anymore, Brianna," he said suddenly, lounging in the doorway with eyes she found difficult to meet. "You look beyond me or you talk to my chin. You avoid eye contact. Why?"

She deliberately dried a dish. There was a nice

dishwasher in the apartment, but there were too few dishes for a load. She liked the feel of the warm soapy water on her hands.

"I hadn't noticed doing any such thing," she said defensively.

"Talk to me!" he said curtly. "Explain this violent change of attitude. Is it because you learned that I once had a mistress?"

She dropped the plate in the soapy water and fished it back out quickly, with trembling hands. "Your private life is no concern of mine," she said through numb lips. "You'll be going home soon, won't you?"

He shifted irritably. "Yes, I must, once this situation is resolved. I have responsibilities which I cannot shirk."

"We all have those, I guess," she said sadly. She washed the last of the dishes and let the water out of both sinks.

He jerked away from the door facing and came to stand directly behind her, so close that she could feel the heat and strength of his tall body.

"Have you traveled at all?" he asked. His warm breath stirred her hair.

She really should move away, she told herself. And she would, in just a minute. "Not really," she replied. "I've been to Mexico, but that was just a quick trip over the border from El Paso while on vacation with my parents and Tad, when I was in my early teens."

"Have you never longed to see other places, other countries?" he continued.

She could hear the soft whisper of his breath. Her body tingled at his nearness. She had to concentrate. What had he asked?

"Yes, I'd love to travel," she said huskily. "It's a big world, and I know very little about it. Tad would like it, too. But it will be a long time before that can happen. He isn't fit for long vacations just yet."

"He is young. He will recover swiftly now."

"He likes you," she remarked.

"And I like him, Brianna. He has character, that one. Like his sister."

His hands had gone to her waist, strong hands that tugged her back into the curve of his body. His cheek was against her hair, and he was breathing more heavily now. She couldn't move. She closed her eyes and savored the sweetness of the contact.

"What has gone wrong between us, *chérie?*" he asked quietly. "Why have you turned away from me?"

She bit through the skin on her lower lip and winced at the self-inflicted pain. "We're very different," she began.

"Different." His hands contracted roughly. "And yet, so alike in many ways. I am a Christian, did you know? I never accepted the Moslem faith."

"Yes, I remember." Her fingers rested lightly over his strong hands, feeling the roughness of skin and hair and the steely strength of them as they held her.

"I enjoy classical music, as you do," he continued quietly. "I would live a simple life if I could."

Odd phrasing, she thought curiously. ''Why can't you?''

''Because of those duties and responsibilities I told you about,'' he replied. ''Many people depend on me.''

Her fingers had become involuntarily caressing over his. Her body throbbed with insistent pulses. She moved back toward him, a little stir of motion that aroused him viciously.

His lean fingers dug in at her waist and his mouth dropped to press hotly into the side of her neck. He nipped her with his teeth and, feeling her jump, slid his mouth to her ear.

''They have cameras and microphones in every room, even in this one,'' he said harshly. ''Whether you realize it or not, that small movement which you have just made was a blatant invitation, one which I madly wish I could accept. But do you really fancy making love for the amusement of our hosts?''

She gasped and tore out of his grasp, facing him from several feet away with wide, shocked eyes. ''You started it!'' she accused.

He was rigid with desire and temper, his black eyes flashing, his fists clenched by his sides. ''And you were an innocent bystander, led into sin?'' he chided icily.

''You could lead a stone boulder into sin with a voice like that!'' she snapped back. ''I'll bet you didn't stop with one mistress, I'll bet you had twenty-five!''

His eyebrows arched. ''Why should that matter to you? You have already stated, emphatically, that you have no interest whatsoever in my personal life.''

''And I don't!'' she assured him. Her blue eyes sparkled like sapphires in a face gone white with pain and hurt.

He said something she didn't understand. ''What do you want of me?''

''I want you to go home,'' she said through her teeth, ''and get out of my life!''

''Gladly,'' he agreed. ''As soon as they catch the men who are trying to kill me!''

''Someone's trying to kill you, Cousin Pedro?'' came a shocked voice from behind him.

He turned, and there was Tad, clad in pajamas and looking as if he'd been struck.

''Why are you awake?'' he asked gently. ''Could you not sleep?''

''Not with all the noise,'' he murmured dryly, glancing at his sister. ''She never used to raise her voice at all, you know.''

''Truly?'' He looked at her, and there was something very speculative in his bold stare. ''She raises it to me constantly.''

''You should try to get along,'' Tad told him. ''She's a nice girl, really.''

''I know that, to my cost,'' Ahmed said with a speaking look in Brianna's direction that made her turn scarlet.

''Who's trying to kill you?'' Tad persisted.

Ahmed grimaced. ''It was a figure of speech,'' he began.

''No, it wasn't, really,'' Tad said, grinning. ''We've got men watching the apartment from across the way with high-powered telescopes, and I've spotted two video camera fiber-optic connections. And the telephone's bugged, because I opened up the mouthpiece and looked.''

The two adults wore equally shocked looks. ''How do you know what a bug looks like?'' Ahmed asked him.

''There's these old spy movies I've been watching on television,'' Tad explained. ''And there's been an ongoing documentary on the CIA that showed about bugs and stuff. Gosh, it's so exciting! I hope you don't get shot, of course. But if you do, I know what to do for a gunshot wound,'' he continued, while Ahmed buried his face in his hand and chuckled helplessly. ''I watched a show about the medical corps, and they showed real gory pictures of how they treat wounds. It was great!''

''Oh, Tad!'' Brianna groaned. ''You shouldn't be watching that sort of thing!''

''I'm not squeamish,'' he muttered. ''I want to be in law enforcement when I grow up. Forensics, maybe. Did you know how much you can learn about a body from examining the skull?'' he continued excitedly.

''I think you should go back to bed,'' Brianna said gently.

"I guess I should," he said with a sigh of resignation. He glanced from one of them to the other. "Are you going to start yelling at each other again the minute I leave the room?" he asked politely.

"Not really," Brianna assured him. "I'm tired, too. I plan to go to bed very shortly."

"Okay." Tad stood in front of Ahmed, who towered over him again. "You don't have a Spanish accent," he said bluntly. "You speak English like Omar Sharif did in *Lawrence of Arabia.*"

Ahmed's chin rose proudly. "You are intelligent," he told the boy. "And not easily fooled."

Tad smiled. "Thanks. Does that mean I get to hear what's really going on here?"

Ahmed smiled back. "No."

Tad shrugged. "You win some, you lose some. Good night."

He went away without another argument. Ahmed watched his retreat thoughtfully.

"He would make a fine diplomat," he remarked. "He is both intuitive and observant."

"What a delightful occupation to wish on him," she said curtly. "Look at what it's done for you!"

He cocked an eyebrow, turning to stare at her. "You have a very sharp tongue," he remarked. "It has been many years since anyone, much less a woman, dared speak to me as you have."

"They were probably afraid you'd chop their heads off," she muttered.

"In the distant past, that might have been a possibility,'' he told her. His eyes grew intent on her flushed face. ''You have no idea what my culture is like, even today, have you?''

''You've got lots of oil in your country and everybody wants it,'' she replied.

He smiled. ''True.''

''You have a king and a parliament, your country was created out of Arabia just after World War I, you import high-tech items from the United States and Western Germany, your universities are some of the oldest in the Middle East, and the majority of your people are Moslem.''

He nodded. ''Very good.''

''We have a new set of encyclopedia that I'm still paying off. Why isn't there a photograph of your king in it?'' she asked suddenly.

''Because of the increased risk such publicity would afford him,'' he said simply. ''Our king has been the target of assassins before this.''

The slip didn't get past her. ''You mean they're after your king as well as you?''

He hesitated. ''Well, yes.''

''Oh, my. I hope he's well guarded.''

''He is,'' Ahmed returned dryly. ''*Too* well guarded,'' he added loudly.

In a nearby room, several dark-suited men with earphones almost rolled on the floor laughing.

''What do you mean?'' Brianna asked with a frown.

''They have him in a hotel surrounded by bodyguards and security people, being fed very well. I expect when they let him out, he will be like your Old King Cole of fantasy."

She laughed. It was the first time she had, in several days. "Roly-poly? Is he short and stocky?"

"The man in the hotel is, yes," he returned truthfully.

"I don't suppose there are many handsome kings around." She nodded and turned away.

He quickly composed himself. "I have a chessboard, if you play."

"I'm sorry," she replied. "I never learned."

"I could teach you."

She shook her head. "I'm very tired. This has been a difficult week. For all of us," she added, lifting her eyes to his. "You look very tired."

"I am. Tired and a little disappointed."

"Why?"

He searched her face with eyes that adored it. "I had certain hopes, Brianna. They have come to nothing."

She stared back at him with curiosity. "This woman back home..."

"She is my *ex*-mistress," he said curtly. "There is nothing between us now."

"I didn't mean that one. The other one," she prompted.

He was very quiet. "Which...other one?"

"The one you're going to marry!" she said, exasperated.

His lips parted on a spent breath. He searched for words, but he couldn't find any appropriate ones. "Am I getting married, then?"

"You told Lang you were," she said quietly. She lowered her eyes. "He told me."

Ahmed's expression was briefly murderous. He looked around the room. "I hope he has no plans to visit the Middle East when this situation is over. I think he might look very interesting at the end of a scimitar!"

"Why are you angry with him? He only mentioned it."

"Only!" His eyes came back to her and calmed a little. She'd been jealous. Hurt, too, perhaps. Her recent behavior began to make sense. It would be all right. She wanted him. His heart felt suddenly light and carefree. He would have some very difficult arrangements to make. And then a quick trip to the altar was certainly in store, before anyone else could throw more spikes into his wheel.

He didn't stop to think if his plotting was fair to Brianna. He'd always done things to suit himself. He was doing it now. She would be well provided for, and so would her brother. She would adjust to life in another country if he could make her care for him enough. He was certain that he could.

"My marriage plans are hardly finalized yet," he said. "And the lady in question is unaware of my intentions."

"Does she love you?" she asked involuntarily, her sad eyes searching over his beloved dark face.

He saw for the first time what she couldn't hide, that she adored him. He smiled slowly. "Do you know, *petite,* I think she does."

She made a faint smile. "I wish you happiness, then."

He couldn't drag his eyes away from her. She was so pretty. He moved toward her, lifting her chin with his fingertips to study her sad blue eyes.

"Will you miss me when I go back to my own country?"

"Tad and I both will," she said hesitatingly.

"And I shall miss you." He searched her face with faint misgivings. She cared for him. But could she love him? He bent slowly toward her mouth. Incredibly, as intimate as they'd been together, he'd never kissed her. He wanted to.

But she pulled back. "The, uh, the cameras," she said discreetly.

He muttered something in Arabic and took her by the hand, pulling her with him down the hall.

"Where are we going...not in here!"

"It is the only place Lang is unlikely to put a camera," he returned, closing them up in the bathroom. He propped his hands on either side of her, where she stood with her back against the door, breathless and excited.

"I don't want this," she said unconvincingly.

"Yes, you do," he replied easily. "You think I am

being unfaithful to the woman I intend to marry. It gives you a guilty conscience to consider allowing my embraces.''

She didn't have to answer him. Her answer was plain on her face.

''As I thought,'' he said with a gentle smile. ''You are so very young, *chérie,*'' he added solemnly. He searched her eyes and then let his gaze drop to her parted mouth. ''So young...so very, very young....''

The words went into her mouth as he brushed his lightly against it. She felt the warm hardness of his lips, the velvet tickle of the thick moustache. Then, slowly, his tongue probed her lips, parting them, darting past her teeth into the silky darkness of her mouth.

He felt her stiffen. He withdrew at once, and his mouth lightly brushed hers, teasing it back into submission. When she relaxed, he started again. She was totally innocent of such loveplay. He had to remember that, and be patient with her.

It was exciting to make love to such an obvious virgin. He smiled as he made her mouth lift to seek the deepening pressure of his. He felt her shy movements, the hesitant reach of her hands around him, against his silk shirt, warm through it as they sought contact with his shoulders. She came closer and he levered his body down into hers, using the door to hold her there while he maneuvered them into greater intimacy.

She wasn't protesting anymore. Her mouth opened to the darting sensual movements of his tongue. Her body submitted to the slow, blatant drag of his hips that let her feel the strength and power of his arousal. She tasted him, experienced him, as she'd never known another man. She gave him everything he asked for.

Even when she felt his long leg push between hers, when she felt him lowering against her even more, so that his hips were squarely over hers and they were as intimate as lovers except for the layers of fabric that separated them.

She made a husky, passionate little sound in his mouth, and shifted quickly to accommodate him. He pushed against her rhythmically, letting her feel how it would be.

It was almost too late to stop. He shuddered and she clung when he tried to draw away.

His lips moved against hers when he spoke. "For a thousand reasons, this cannot continue," he whispered unsteadily. "The pleasure is becoming too urgent, too sweet to deny. All I must do is loosen two fastenings, and you will know me completely, standing here against the door. Let me stop while I can. I am too aroused to give you tenderness. It will hurt."

She felt his mouth touching her face, gentling her, as he forcibly withdrew from temptation. He held her while he covered her eyelids with kisses to calm her.

She was shivering with reaction. But there was no shame in what she felt. Finally her eyes slid open and looked up into his, curious and shy and uncertain.

"You know very little of men, *n'est-ce pas?*" he

asked huskily, searching her face with quick, sharp eyes. "Do you really think that I have experienced such violent, sweet desire with a host of other women? Do you think this is such a routine experience for me that I am completely unmoved by it when I release you?"

"I don't know," she said shakily.

"Brianna, once in a lifetime a man may experience something so earth-shattering and passionate, if he is fortunate," he explained slowly. "I have no wish whatsoever to turn our magic into a sordid tangle of arms and legs in a bed."

She flushed. "Oh."

"It is not sex. That is what you thought?"

"You seemed not to want to be close to me, after the night we spent together," she said demurely. "I thought you'd decided it was all a mistake and you only wanted to forget it."

"I went up in flames and all I thought about afterward was how quickly I could strip you and relieve the ache you leave me with," he whispered wickedly. "But afterward, it made me ashamed to want something so physical, when I knew how fragile and vulnerable you were in other ways."

"So you ignored me completely," she agreed.

"It was the only protection I could manage," he told her with a long-suffering look. "Now that Tad is here with us at night, and Lang has cameras in most of the rooms, it would be quite difficult to find enough privacy to satisfy ourselves."

"You did maneuver us into a bathroom," she stated.

"Where I came to my senses in time," he reminded her. "I care too much for you to use you, no matter how much you inflame me," he added. "I meant what I told you. A man must not allow himself to reach such a frenzy of desire when he pleasures a virgin." He traced her flaming cheeks. "He must become as the wind across the desert, slow and tender and caressing until she is prepared to receive him."

She felt hot all over as he spoke. Her eyes fell to his throat, where a pulse throbbed visibly.

"You still avoid my eyes. Why?"

"It embarrasses me, a little."

"When we have been naked together in bed?" he teased softly.

"We weren't lovers."

He drew her head to his chest and caressed her hair. "Oh, we will love," he whispered. "But not as conspirators hiding in corners."

"I don't understand."

"Did you think me such a rake, Brianna, that I could make love to you while I had a woman waiting at home, expecting to become my bride?"

She hadn't thought about that aspect of his behavior. She lifted her head and looked up into his eyes with quiet curiosity.

"Well, no," she confessed. "It did seem rather out of character. But Lang said—"

He put his lean forefinger over her mouth. "Yes.

Lang said that I was impatient for this charade to be over because I wanted to marry. Indeed I do, with all possible haste, and there are more obstacles and difficulties than you can possibly imagine because of my choice of brides.''

She scowled. Her finger idly traced a button on his white shirt. Under it, his heartbeat was quick and hard. He caught her hand and she held his eyes while she worked underneath it to unfasten two buttons, then three, then four. His lips parted as she reached inside the shirt and began to slowly caress the hair-roughened muscles of his chest.

''I love to touch you,'' she said unsteadily.

''Wait.''

She lifted her eyes again. ''Is it so uncomfortable for you?''

''Yes.'' He put her hand to one side, smiling ruefully. ''I have no plans to marry a woman from my own country. Although it is of a certainty that the woman I marry must agree that the ceremony be performed there. I am a high public official. I cannot marry in this country in secret. Do you understand?''

''Yes. No. You said you were going to get married,'' she began.

''And I am. Oh, yes, I am,'' he whispered fervently and bent to kiss her hungrily.

''Then who…?''

''You, of course. Who else occupies my mind waking and sleeping…? Brianna, marry me!'' he breathed into her mouth.

Chapter Nine

While Brianna tried to cope with what she thought she'd just heard, Ahmed made a much more thorough frontal assault on her soft mouth. She couldn't think at all. She answered his lips and her hands slid with waves of pleasure over his broad, hair-roughened chest, savoring the feel of his body under her sensitive fingers.

He groaned and lifted his head, stilling her exploring fingers. "You are killing me," he whispered.

"You asked me to marry you," she moaned, reaching up to try to capture his mouth again. "I'm saying yes...."

She kissed him. He half lifted her and deepened the kiss, making her knees go watery weak as the heat between them reached an explosive force.

"I feel I should tell you," a deep voice came from

the wall beside them, "that we had to put microphones even in the rooms where we didn't put cameras."

Ahmed's head jerked up. His blazing eyes searched the walls while fierce and probably obscene words rattled off his tongue like nails out of an air gun.

"I won't have our translator work on that." Lang chuckled. "Congratulations on your engagement. Now would you mind getting out of the bathroom and breaking this up? Some of us are turning to strong drink...."

Ahmed caught Brianna's hand and pulled her out the door into the hall. He was raging mad, and she had to muffle laughter at the expression on his face. She was glad her name wasn't Lang.

"He did warn us before we embarrassed ourselves," she reminded him.

He was breathing roughly and his cheekbones were ruddy with bad temper. His narrow dark eyes looked down into hers. He said something terse.

"Will you teach me Arabic when we're married?" she asked with a loving smile.

"Only when Lang is in another country," he promised, glaring at the walls.

"I heard that" came plainly from another part of the wall.

"Go away, Lang," Brianna said. "I'm trying to accept a proposal of marriage in here."

"Yes, ma'am," Lang said, and there was a clicking sound.

She looked back at Ahmed. "Are you sure?" she

asked. "There will be so many problems. Americans aren't well liked in your country, are they?"

"My people will like you," he said with certainty.

"What if your king refuses you permission to marry me?" she asked worriedly. "He could, couldn't he?"

"He could make it difficult, if he wished," he replied dryly. "But I can assure you that he will not. He will find you ravishing."

She knew he was exaggerating, but the flattery made her feel warm inside. "I hope so." She touched the loose buttons on his shirt. "We'll have to live in Saudi Mahara, won't we?"

He nodded.

"All the time?"

"Most of it," he said. "I travel in the performance of my duties, but our capital city of Mozambara is my home. I hope that you will learn to love it as I do."

"What about Tad?" she asked suddenly.

"He will come with us, of course," he said, as if he wondered why she should even have asked such a silly question.

"It will mean uprooting him. And myself. We'll have to learn other customs, another language...."

"You brood about things which will fall naturally into place, *chérie,*" he said, "if you love me enough."

She stared into his black eyes with building hunger. He seemed to be waiting for something. Perhaps he was as uncertain as she was about the future. "I love you enough,'' she said huskily. ''I love you more than my own life.''

He drew her close and bent his dark head over hers, his arms bruising for a moment as he realized how much she belonged to him, and he to her. There had never been a time when he had considered the need to have someone of his own permanently to cherish. But he was growing older, and Mahara would need an heir.

''Do you like children, Brianna?''

''Oh, yes,'' she murmured happily.

He drew in a long breath. ''There must be heirs. It is my duty to provide them.''

''It used to be kings who had to do that,'' she said drowsily. ''Now it's cabinet ministers, too. I won't mind at all. I love little babies.''

He winced over her head. She didn't know his identity. He was tempted to tell her, but she might panic. It would be better to wait until he could settle the resistance there would surely be among his high officials and even among some American officials to this match. She would only worry and perhaps try to back out.

He drew away and looked at her rapt face. He smiled. ''We will overcome the obstacles, together,'' he told her, reassuring himself in the process.

She pressed close and inhaled the faintly foreign scent of his cologne, secure with the heavy beat of his heart under her ear. ''I'm twenty-two,'' she said absently.

''Yes, I know.''

She lifted her head, curiously.

"Never mind how I know." He bent, smiling, to touch her mouth softly with his. "Go to bed. It is late."

"I'm tired. But I don't think I can sleep," she said.

"Lie down, at least," he said.

"Okay. But I'm undressing in the closet!" she told the walls.

There were good-natured long sighs among the men in the room next door.

Lang was repentant when he came to the apartment the next morning. Brianna had a tight hold on Ahmed's hand so that he couldn't do to Lang what his eyes threatened.

"Sorry about last night," Lang said. "Really, I am, but we thought it would be wise to warn you while there was still time. We can't afford to leave even one room unprotected."

"The sooner this is over, the better!" Ahmed said harshly.

"All of us feel the same way, believe it or not," Lang said, and Brianna noticed then how tired and drawn he looked. "We haven't slept."

"Don't you take turns?" she asked.

He shrugged. "It's still twelve-hour shifts. Manpower is scarce for constant surveillance. We're a government agency, you know. We have to beg for funding just like everybody else, and sometimes the politicians get it in for us."

"Ah, democracy at work," Ahmed taunted.

Lang glowered at him. "Well, at least if we don't

do a good job, nobody herds us into the marketplace to be decapitated."

Ahmed was affronted. "I have not decapitated anyone for a decade. We are a progressive nation. We even have protest rallies, just like the West."

"I remember your last protest rally," Lang commented.

Ahmed shifted. "It was unavoidable. They stormed the gates of the palace."

"What are you two talking about?" Brianna asked.

"Your new home," Lang replied. He fixed Ahmed with a steady look. "When are you going to tell her?"

"When I have overcome the diplomatic obstacles," Ahmed said quietly. "And ascertained that she will not be assassinated along with me on the way back to Saudi Mahara."

"Good point." Lang stretched, big muscles bulging in his arms. "Well, I'm going out for a cup of coffee and then a quick nap."

"Are there any new developments?" Ahmed asked.

"Several. You'll have company inside as well as outside tonight," he commented. He stared at Brianna, who was looking uncomfortable. "You and Tad are pretty nervy people. Think you can survive a stakeout?"

"Sure," she said. "As long as I don't have to shoot anybody."

He smiled. "We'll do the shooting. But it won't come to that. I won't put any of you in danger."

"How about yourself?" she replied.

Lang shrugged. "I'm used to it. It's what I get paid for."

"Despite your eavesdropping propensities, I should hate to see you hurt," Ahmed added.

Lang grinned at them. "None of us likes taking chances. We're pretty sure they're going to make an attempt on you tonight. We'll be ready. With any luck at all, this will wrap it all up. If we're successful," he told Ahmed, "you could be on your way home by the end of the week."

Ahmed glanced at Brianna. "Yes," he said slowly. "So I could."

She didn't understand that look. It contained worry and apprehension, and she didn't think it was just because some enemy agents might make a grab for them.

The day passed slowly. Ahmed and Tad sat together in the living room, going over some new science magazines that Lang had provided, while Brianna reluctantly went to work. Her mind wasn't on her duties, though. It was on the danger they were all in, and especially on Ahmed's proposal of marriage. She wanted to marry him. She loved him. But until now she hadn't had to deal with the complications of marriage to a foreign national.

On her lunch hour, she went to the local public library and checked out every book she could find that dealt with Saudi Mahara. It was such a small nation that she had to choose general subjects to find out anything. Then she got a book on Arab customs and copied a magazine article on women's roles in the

Middle East. This would give her some idea of the new life she was going to enjoy, she thought. It would be better for Ahmed if his new wife had foreknowledge of what would be expected of her. Not that she expected to wear a veil and walk three steps behind him, of course.

Ahmed and Tad were deep in a discussion of nuclear physics when she got home from work with her load of library books, and there were four government intelligence agents sticking out of her refrigerator.

She stopped dead at the sight of them.

Ahmed smiled complacently. "They have had nothing to eat since lunch yesterday," he explained.

"Oh, you poor guys!" Brianna exclaimed.

They turned and stared at her. One was holding a carton of yogurt. Another had a carton of milk. The other two were having a minor tug-of-war over a wrapped cheese slice. They all lifted their eyebrows hopefully.

"I'll cook you up a big pot of spaghetti and some garlic bread," she promised, dumping the books on the sofa and making a beeline into the kitchen.

"God bless you!" one of the bigger agents said fervently.

The others marched him out of the kitchen to let Brianna work. It was quick work, too. She had spaghetti down to a fine art. The sauce should have simmered for at least half an hour, she supposed, but those men would all pass out sooner than that. She handed them plates and forks and started dishing it up the minute she could combine the cooked pasta with the meat sauce. Ahmed and Tad managed to get a few bites, too, and while everyone was occupied, Brianna made a bread pudding for dessert. Even the crumbs were gone five minutes after it was taken out of the oven.

Lang arrived just in time for the dishwashing. He had a toothpick in his mouth, and the other agents all gave him accusing looks.

"What?" he challenged. "I had a fast-food hamburger. A little one, okay?"

They surrounded him. "We," the biggest one said, "had spaghetti and garlic bread, homemade and delicious," he added, addressing a beaming Brianna. "And for dessert she made us bread pudding."

"And you didn't save any for me?" Lang asked, horrified.

"You had a hamburger," the big agent reminded him with a grin.

"I'll never do it again," Lang promised. "Can't I have just a crumb of bread pudding? It's my favorite."

"Sorry. We ate it all," the big agent said. He didn't look sorry. He was smiling.

"Just wait until I have to write up this surveillance," Lang began.

"Oh, yeah?" one of the other agents said, with his hands in his pockets. "And what are you gonna say, huh?"

They all adopted the same pose. Lang sighed. "That you're a great bunch of guys to work with, and next time I'll bring four extra hamburgers back with me."

The big agent patted him on the back. "Good

man,'' he said. ''I'll recommend you for promotion when I get to be President.''

''I wouldn't hold my breath if I were you,'' Lang advised. ''You'd break the budget in a week, the way you eat.''

''What did you find out?'' another agent asked, and they were suddenly all government agents again, all business.

They went into a huddle. In a minute they began to disperse, setting up equipment and checking it.

Lang was very somber as he drew the three occupants of the apartment to one side. ''We want you to act naturally. Do what you've been doing in the evenings since Tad came here. We've swept the place for bugs and cameras, and it's clean. Just try not to be surprised at anything that goes down, okay? One of us will be with you all the time.''

It became real life then. Brianna had seen films of terrorists. They had automatic weapons and no compassion. They killed quickly, efficiently, and without mercy. She looked at Ahmed and Tad and realized that she could lose either or both of them in less than two seconds. Her face went white.

Ahmed pulled her close against his side. ''This is no time to become fainthearted,'' he said quietly. ''You must have the bearing and dignity of high office, even when under fire. It will be expected of you.''

Because he was a high official of his country, she realized. She searched his dark eyes. ''I'm not worried for myself, you know,'' she said gently.

''I realize that. Nor I, for myself.''

She smiled at him. "I won't let you down."

He brought her palm to his mouth. "Cowardice is the last thing I would ever expect from you."

She beamed. "Same here."

"Could you stop exchanging praises and just go about your business?" Lang asked amusedly.

"Of course." Ahmed let go of her and went back to the science magazines he was looking over with Tad.

The boy was wearing a new pair of jeans and a white T-shirt. He looked healthier, but he was still pale and weak. Ahmed studied him, noticing that he was as game as Brianna.

"You make me proud that I shall become part of such a family as yours," he told Tad.

The boy smiled. "That goes double for me. Will we live in your country, then?" he asked, because he knew already that he wasn't going to be left behind when Bri married. They'd made a point of telling him so.

"Most certainly."

"I'd love to learn to ride a horse. They say there are no horses in the world like the Arabians."

"This is true," Ahmed agreed. "However, the horses I own are magnificent in their own right. They are bred in Austria, and I..."

The attack was so sudden that Brianna wondered for a space of seconds if she was asleep and having another nightmare. The front door burst in with explosive force and men in masks carrying automatic weapons were spraying everything in sight with bullets.

Ahmed pulled Tad to the floor in a spectacular tackle while Brianna dropped behind the counter as soon as she heard the explosion.

The exchange of weapon fire sounded more like firecrackers popping than like real guns. It was surreal. Brianna knew better than to dare lift her head. She curled up on the floor to make as small a target as possible and hoped that the government agents were accurate with those nasty-looking weapons she'd seen under their suit coats. She didn't dare think about Ahmed or Tad, or she'd go mad.

There was a cessation of noise. A clink of glass falling. There were quick, hard footsteps and then Ahmed and Tad were bending over her.

"Are you all right?" Ahmed asked quickly, rolling her over and gathering her up close. His eyes were wild, his face pale under its natural darkness.

"Yes. Are both of you?" she asked, her eyes going frantically from Tad to Ahmed.

"We're fine," Tad assured her, but he was pale and his voice was shaking. "Gosh, that was some… something, wasn't it?"

Brianna clung to Ahmed, shivering with aftershock. Those men had come to kill him. The bullets had been meant for him. She gasped.

"All clear," Lang said, repocketing his automatic under his jacket. He looked down at Brianna, his face still showing traces of ferocity from the ordeal. He glanced over his shoulder. "Don't let her get up yet," he told Ahmed.

"Haven't you caught them?" she asked fearfully.

"Oh, yes," Lang said, and there was something in

his eyes that she didn't want to see. She looked quickly down again.

Ahmed cradled her in his arms and sat with his back against the cabinet. Tad started to peek around the corner but Ahmed jerked him back.

"No," he told the boy, and his face was unusually stern.

"Okay. I was just curious."

"Curiosity sometimes carries a high price," he was told. Ahmed looked down at Brianna's white face. "It is over," he told her softly. "All over. Lang told me earlier that he was in contact with my government. The perpetrators will be caught now. The coup attempt has failed."

"Your king will be relieved," Tad remarked. "Is he okay, do you think?"

"Oh, yes," Ahmed said absently, stroking Brianna's dark, damp hair back from her face. "The king has never been better, I am sure."

Later, when the devastation was cleared away and the enemy agents removed, Ahmed and Brianna and Tad were moved out of the wrecked apartment and into another.

Brianna had noticed stains on the carpet, but when she tried to ask about them, she was ignored.

"I'm not a baby, you know," she told Ahmed.

His smile was a little strained. "No. But I am older than you, and I have seen more. Believe me when I tell you that you need not know all of what has happened today. Trust me. Will you trust me, *chérie?*"

"Yes."

He brushed his mouth over her eyelids and left her with Tad while he moved out into the hall to talk to Lang.

"Well?" he asked the agent.

Lang was still high-strung from the experience. He leaned back against the wall, squeezing a hand exerciser to relax himself.

"I hate to be the one to tell you this," he told Ahmed. "But they've taken your sister into custody." He held up a hand when Ahmed tried to speak. "They haven't connected her to the takeover coup. They've only connected her husband. It was a preventive measure only. But you're going to have to go back with all haste and set things right. You knew that already."

"I knew. Brianna has not been told," he added. "She must not be. I need time to settle my affairs before I attempt to involve her in them. This, today, has been a salutary experience."

"It isn't the first time you've been shot at," Lang reminded him.

He nodded, looking darkly arrogant. "But it is the first time that she and Tad have," he replied. "For that alone, I have no regrets about the outcome."

Lang stared at the hand exerciser. "Assassination attempts are few and far between, you know. Your father had one. This is your second."

"This is connected to the same people, however," he said, "and they are now in custody. I must see what I can do for Yasmin. She would not try to kill me. I know this."

"Get a good lawyer," he was advised.

"I must," he said heavily. "Our court system is

even harsher than yours, and we do not play dice with the death penalty. The ringleaders of this plot will be executed if they are convicted, and there will be no stays or appeals.''

Lang whistled. ''Harsh justice, indeed.''

''The old ways are cruel,'' Ahmed agreed. ''Brianna may not be able to accept marriage when she knows my true identity. It is regrettable that I could not tell her the truth from the beginning.''

''That was our decision, not yours,'' Lang said.

He smiled ruefully. ''Will it matter, in the end, who decided?'' He moved away from the wall. ''I will be ready to leave first thing in the morning.'' He paused, and turned back to face Lang. ''Thank you for what you have done. And the others. Whatever they pay you, it is not enough for the risks you must take.''

''We get paid enough,'' Lang mused. ''The occasional pot of spaghetti and a bread pudding are icing on the cake.''

''You are brave people,'' he said sincerely. ''If your government ever fires you, you will always have a job in mine. I could use such a minister of justice.''

''Ouch,'' Lang said, wincing. ''A desk job, for a street man like me? Bite your tongue!''

''Commander-in-chief of the secret service, then.'' Ahmed chuckled.

''That's more like it, and thank you for the offer. One day I may need a job.''

Ahmed leaned closer. ''If you continue to put bugs in the bathrooms of unsuspecting people, I can almost guarantee it.''

Lang chuckled. ''I see your point.''

* * *

Tad had trouble settling down for the night after all the excitement. He still didn't know what was going on, and he wouldn't rest until somebody gave him an explanation.

Ahmed took Brianna's hand in his while they sat on the sofa drinking coffee from the new pot Lang had scrounged for them. The apartment was furnished, but a coffeepot and coffee hadn't been part of the furnishings.

"Since you were forced to endure the unpleasantness with us," Ahmed told Tad, "it is proper that you know why. There was a coup attempt back home in my country."

"Not Mexico," Tad said with dry humor.

"Not Mexico," Ahmed agreed. "My home is in Saudi Mahara, a country in the Middle East. I have been in this country to represent my people in a contract for several jets from Ryker Air, the company for which your sister works."

"They needed a place to hide him until they could find the assassins who were trying to kill him," Brianna added, still a little shaky from the ordeal. "They thought that having him masquerade as a poor Mexican laborer, our cousin, was a good disguise, since everyone in the office knew that we hated each other. The last place any enemy agent would look for him would be in my apartment."

"You hated each other?" Tad asked, smiling. "Really?"

Ahmed looked at her with tenderness. "I was immediately attracted to her when she heaved a paperweight at my head. It was the first time in my life anyone had dared to attack my person.''

''I find that hard to believe,'' Brianna murmured dryly. ''You have a way of making people bristle, you know.''

He smiled indulgently. ''At times,'' he admitted. ''But when I am at home, it is a crime to attack me.''

''Your king must think very highly of you,'' Tad remarked.

Ahmed sighed. ''At times he does. At others, he is rather disappointed in me, I fear.'' He looked at Brianna. ''You have not changed your mind about marrying me?'' he asked bluntly. ''I saw the books that you brought home to study. There may be things in them that disturb you.''

''They won't disturb me enough to take back my acceptance,'' she said firmly.

''You bet they won't,'' Tad affirmed, ''because I want to learn to ride!''

She glanced at her brother, delighted to see the animation in his face. It made her feel wonderful to see him alert and alive and happy. It was like a miracle.

''Not just yet, however,'' Ahmed said somberly. ''There is something I must tell both of you.''

''Oh?'' Brianna asked. ''What?''

He studied their linked fingers. ''I have to go home tomorrow. Alone.''

Chapter Ten

There was a flattering look of misery from Brianna and Tad. It didn't really make Ahmed feel a lot better, however. He had no idea how Brianna would react when she knew what would really be expected of her. Marrying a foreign cabinet official might not be so difficult. But he was not that. His life was one of rigorous protocol and duty. Would she be content with such a rigid life? Would she be able to accept it for Tad?

He didn't want to think about it now. "It is only a temporary absence," he assured them. "There are some things I must deal with."

"They've caught the people involved in the assassination plot, haven't they?" Brianna asked perceptively.

He nodded. He stared at his hands. "One of them is my only sister."

She put her hand over his and moved closer to lean her head against his broad shoulder. "I'm sorry," she said sincerely.

"Me, too," Tad offered. "Gee, that would be tough. Why would she want to kill you?"

"I am not certain that she did," Ahmed confessed. "I think that it was her husband's idea and not her own. But I must find out."

"You didn't really answer me," Tad persisted, his blue eyes, so much like Brianna's, unblinking.

Ahmed's broad shoulders rose and fell. "The hunger for power creates madness at times."

"But you're a cabinet minister," Brianna began.

"I must make some telephone calls," he said abruptly, glancing at the clock on the wall. "You will excuse me?" he asked formally.

She let go of his hand reluctantly. He was keeping something from her. It disturbed her.

"Of course," she said automatically.

He smiled briefly and left them, going into the middle bedroom to make his calls. He closed the door firmly behind him.

"That isn't all," Tad said. "He's hiding something."

"Yes, I know." Brianna was worried. She didn't want it to show, but it did. "Oh, Tad, I hope this really is the end of the assassination attempts."

They had a quiet supper later that night, one that Lang and the guys provided—huge pizzas.

"This is our favorite food," Lang remarked, passing Brianna another slice. "We live on it when we're on stakeout. We know all the best places."

"You could have offered to bring us a pizza instead of a little hamburger yesterday," the big agent remarked to Lang.

Lang chuckled. "I fell asleep in the booth with half the hamburger in my hand," he confessed. "I guess I went without a nap too long."

"Poor guy," one of the other agents said. "You ought to get a decent job, you know."

"I tried, but only the CIA would hire me," Lang retorted.

Listening to their banter relaxed Brianna, but Ahmed was quiet and subdued. All of them, except Brianna, knew why he was upset. Even his standing would not save his sister's life if she was found guilty of treason. He hadn't told Brianna.

When the agents left, Tad went to bed, leaving Brianna and Ahmed discreetly alone.

But there was a new distance between them. He sat in the armchair across from her place on the sofa, looking terribly remote and sad. There was an aura about him that she remembered from their earliest acquaintance, when he and his entourage first arrived at Ryker Air. She'd thought then that he had a rather regal air, as if his position gave him great importance and he expected everyone to be aware of it.

"Are you sorry that you asked me to marry you?" she asked bluntly, her blue eyes worried.

His fingers idly caressed the soft fabric over the arms of the chair. "No. Of all my recent actions, that is the one which I regret the least. You delight me."

She smiled. "Will you have to be away long?"

He shrugged. "I do not know." He wouldn't meet her eyes. "The leaders of the coup have to be dealt with."

"Yes, of course, but why do you have to be there?" she asked, frowning. "Do the cabinet ministers act as judges in your country?"

He got up from the chair and paced restlessly. "You should study those books," he said, nodding toward them. "They will help you understand the way of my culture."

"I'll do that," she said. She smoothed her hands over her jeans-clad thighs. "It should be very exciting, living near the desert."

"It disturbs you, though," he said quietly, glancing at her. "It will mean many sacrifices. Perhaps you will not want to make them."

Her expression was unguarded, and looking at it made him feel wounded. He missed her already. He moved toward her and scooped her up against his chest, holding her cradled to him with his mouth hungry against her neck. "Do not look like that!" he whispered roughly. "I cannot bear to see you so! I am only thinking of your happiness!"

"Then stop trying to push me away," she whispered miserably. "You do it all the time lately."

"Not from choice," he said fervently. His mouth became sensuous as it moved up to her face. "I adore you. I desire you. You are my life...."

His mouth found hers and he kissed her very slowly, with a tenderness that was almost painfully sweet. Her hands traced his hard face, learning its lines, while she fed on the warm expertness of his mouth.

His hands went to her hips and lifted her gently into the changing contours of his body while he kissed her. She began to moan, moving closer of her own accord.

His fingers contracted, pulling, molding, and she shuddered.

He lifted his head. His eyes were glazed with desire, blackly glittering with longings that he could only just control.

"Would you, if I asked?" he whispered huskily.

"Yes," she said simply.

He stared at her swollen lips, her misty eyes. "I want nothing in the world more," he told her. "But I cannot risk the premature birth of our child. There must be no hint of scandal, no question of his legitimacy."

Her head was swimming, but the curious wording caught her attention. "You mean I mustn't get pregnant until we're married?"

He groaned. "That is exactly what I mean."

She cleared her throat. "Oh. I forgot. I mean, your country is much more rigid than ours about a woman's chastity, isn't it?"

"I fear so."

She moved away from him a little and managed a smile. "Okay."

He was trying to breathe normally, and failing miserably. He laughed despite his hunger for her. "Just like that? Okay?"

She colored. "I didn't mean it was easy."

"Nor is it for me," he confessed. "I want you very badly. But we will wait until the rings are in place and the vows spoken."

He bent and kissed her softly one last time. "Go to bed now. It has been a long and fraught day for all of us."

"Tomorrow will be worse," she said quietly. "You'll be gone."

"Not for long, I swear it!" he said huskily. "It will be the most terrible torment, to have to be parted from you even for a few days."

"How flattering," she said with a coy smile. "I'll plan a special evening for your return."

"Not too special, if you please," he returned. "We have our reputations to consider."

She reached up to his ear. "I'll have Lang come and bug the apartment." He made a threatening sound, and she burst out laughing, hugging him close. It was heaven, to be loved and in love. She hoped, she prayed, that it would last. If only there were not this feeling of foreboding.

Ahmed left the next morning, with his entourage surrounding him and Lang bringing up the rear. He and Brianna had said a quick and uncomplicated farewell before they left the apartment. He'd taken time to hug Tad, as well. But in his expensive suit, surrounded by his own people, he looked foreign and unfamiliar.

"He's elegant, isn't he?" Tad asked as they watched out the window. Ahmed climbed into a big white stretch limo with two of his henchmen, and

Lang got into the front seat with the driver. They drew a lot of attention from people on the streets. It didn't matter now, the danger was over. Brianna hoped it was, at least. She was still worried about Ahmed going back to his own country safely.

"Yes, he's very elegant," she agreed.

"I think we're going to like living in Saudi Mahara," he said. "Is there anything in those books about it?"

She shook her head. "It's very small. They mention that it has a king, and they give some impossibly long Arabic name for the royal family, but little detailed information. It isn't what I expected," she added. "They're a pretty modern country, with industry and a structured society, and women are fairly liberated there. They're very European, in fact."

"All that oil money, I'll bet," Tad said. He sat down. He was weak, still, and tired easily. Brianna had telephoned his doctor the day before to make an appointment for today. The experience they'd been through had been upsetting, and Tad wasn't his old self yet.

"You have to see Dr. Brown at one," she reminded him.

"Do I have to?" he moaned.

"It's just a precaution. You aren't long out of the hospital. And yesterday was pretty shattering."

"Ahmed saved my life," Tad told her. "The bullets hit where I'd been sitting. Gosh, I hope nobody tries to do him in when we go to live with him."

"So do I, Tad," she said sincerely.

* * *

They kept his appointment with the doctor, who pronounced him well on the way to recovery.

Monday, Brianna went back to work, leaving Tad with an off-duty nurse—Ahmed's suggestion—and she spent her free time worrying about Ahmed. He'd telephoned twice over the weekend, but the conversation had been stilted and brief, and she felt inhibited trying to carry it on. He seemed to feel the same. His speech was more formal than she'd ever heard it.

The distance between them had grown so quickly, she thought. And Monday, he hadn't telephoned at all by the time Brianna had cooked supper and cleaned up the dishes.

Tad was skipping over channels looking for something to watch, while Brianna worked halfheartedly at crocheting a doily for the coffee table.

"Wow, look at this!" he exclaimed, pausing on one of the news channels.

Brianna looked up. There were uniformed men on horseback and some sort of procession in a Middle Eastern nation. At the center of the pomp and circumstance was a man in a military dress uniform with a blue sash of office across his chest, sitting on a throne while foreign dignitaries were presented to him.

"Why, that's Ahmed," Brianna exclaimed. "Turn it up!"

Tad did, very quickly.

"...looking very fit following an assassination attempt. His sister, the princess Yasmin, has been detained for questioning for some time. There is doubt that she was involved with the plot. Her husband's trial was brief and he was executed this morning.

Questioned about the fate of the other conspirators, a spokesman for the royal house of Rashid said only that they were being dealt with.''

The picture flashed off the screen. Royal house. Rashid. Ahmed, sitting on a throne.

Tad saw the expressions chase across Brianna's face. His own had gone pale.

''He's not a cabinet minister,'' Tad said slowly. ''He's the king of Saudi Mahara.''

Brianna's hands trembled and the crochet thread dropped in a tangle to the floor. *King.* He was the king. No wonder he'd been so well guarded. No wonder he expected people to jump when he asked for anything. *He was a king.*

''Do you think he really meant it, when he asked you to marry him?'' Tad asked, putting her worst fear into words.

''How could he have?'' she declared. ''He's a king! He wouldn't ever be allowed to marry a woman from another country…!''

''The king of Jordan did.''

''Many years ago—'' she faltered ''—and under much different circumstances. This…this changes everything!''

She got up and ran into her bedroom, closing the door. She collapsed onto the bed, tears running hot and copiously down her cheeks as she acknowledged the truth. Ahmed had been amusing himself. There was no other excuse for it. She had been a diversion while he was forced into hiding to escape being assassinated.

The telephone rang when she was a little more

composed. She went into the living room, shaking her head when Tad answered it. He got the message at once, punctuated as it was by her red-rimmed, swollen eyes.

"Yes, she's...she's fine, thanks. Yes, so am I." Tad sounded nervous. It must be Ahmed. There was a long pause. "Of course. I'll tell her. Sure. You, too." He put down the telephone.

"He said to tell you hello. He wanted to know how we were. That's about it." He grimaced. "Oh, sis, I'm sorry!"

She bit her lower lip, hoping that the pain would help stem the tears. "Me, too." She got control of herself again. "Is that all he said?"

"Yes. I don't think he knew we'd seen the broadcast. He didn't mention it."

"That was a BBC feed," she said. "He probably thought it was being shown in England instead of here, if he saw the cameras." She went to pour herself a cup of coffee. It was cold. She grimaced and put it in the microwave to heat up.

"He didn't tell us," he said.

"I know." She glanced at him. "Maybe he didn't know how," she added. "It must have been very hard for him, trying to live like a normal person when he was used to servants and luxury."

"I've never seen a king before," Tad said, trying to lessen the sad atmosphere. "It will be something to tell my friends when I start back to school, won't it?"

"Yes."

"You didn't take it seriously, did you?" he asked worriedly.

"Me?" She forced a laugh. "Don't be silly. I liked him a lot, but then, I didn't really want to have to live in some foreign country and learn another whole way of life, did you?"

"No." He shrugged. "Well, I would have liked the horses," he had to admit. "And Ahmed was a neat guy to have around. He liked talking to me about science. He knows a lot."

"He has degrees in chemistry and physics."

"Well, that explains it. I'd like to go to college one day," he said wistfully.

She heard the microwave buzz and went to take out her heated coffee. "You will," she promised. Her eyes swept over his pale face. "You're a walking miracle, did you know? I'm so glad that I still have you."

He looked embarrassed. "Yeah. Me, too." He searched her face warily. "You feeling better?"

She nodded. She sipped the hot coffee. "If Ahmed calls tomorrow, I, uh, I'd rather not talk to him. Okay?"

"Okay."

But he didn't call the next day, or even the next. Affairs of state, Brianna decided, must have claimed his full attention since his return. She tried not to listen to the news channels, but the temptation was too great. She suffered through political news and medical news and disasters just for an occasional glimpse of the king of Saudi Mahara. Once they showed him in his robes of state with a falcon on his arm. There was a very pretty young Arab woman in a designer suit with him. Brianna saw her take his arm, and she felt sick all over when the newscaster added that the woman was the widow of Ahmed's eldest brother, who had died many years ago in a yachting accident. Her name was Lillah, not Yasmin, so Brianna knew that it wasn't his sister. He was smiling at the woman, and she seemed very possessive of him. That was the last newscast she watched. She knew then that she was being an idiot. Ahmed had made it quite clear that he wanted nothing else to do with her. She might as well start living her life again.

The first step in that direction was to get her old apartment back. Now, with just herself and Tad to share it, there was no need for elaborate living quarters. Fortunately it still hadn't been rerented, and she was able to obtain it at the old rent.

Tad liked it better, mainly because there was a young man who lived on the same floor who became his shadow and idolized him—Nick, the boy whom Ahmed had befriended.

Brianna was still sad, but as the days passed, she began to enjoy life again, although not in the same way as before. She couldn't complain, she told herself. She'd had an adventure with a king, and she had her beloved young brother back. She really couldn't ask much more of life.

At work, she was promoted to assistant status and given a job working for one of the vice presidents. She'd hoped she might get to work with David Shannon, Meg Shannon Ryker's brother, who was a live wire and a delightful person. But instead, she was shifted to the office of the vice president of finance, Tarrant Blair, a rather crusty older man with a wife and four kids and a mind like a math calculator.

She didn't enjoy the job very much. Even less did she care for the way Mr. Blair treated her. He had no consideration for her time. He would think nothing of asking her to work overtime, despite the fact that he knew her young brother was home by himself, and when it wasn't really necessary. He had plenty of time to get his work done during the day, but he came in late quite frequently and spent an unbelievable amount of time on the telephone with his stockbroker.

"How are things going, Brianna?" Meg Ryker asked her one day when she'd stopped by the office to meet her husband Steve for lunch.

"Oh, fine, just fine," she lied. "I'm very happy about my raise in salary."

"How's Tad?"

"He's doing very well."

"I suppose the two of you are having a lot of fun catching up on the time you've missed together?"

Brianna grimaced. "We were. This new job requires so much overtime that I'm pretty well worn-out when I get home. It's challenging, though, and the extra money is wonderful." She smiled.

She didn't fool Meg, who continued to converse merrily until Steve showed up. Once she got her husband out of the building, she pulled him to one side.

"Why does Blair have to keep Brianna after work so much?" she asked bluntly. "Doesn't he understand that she's only just gotten her brother back from the dead, not to mention what she went through when

Ahmed was being guarded so closely? And she still has not recovered from the aftermath of that situation,'' she added meaningfully.

He scowled. ''Blair shouldn't require any overtime at all. He isn't the busiest man on staff.''

''Couldn't you check?'' Meg coaxed, tracing a button on his suit coat.

He smiled, bending to kiss her softly. ''Yes,'' he said. ''I can check.''

She smiled back, her eyes adoring his face. ''That's why I married you.''

''Because I kiss so well,'' he agreed, bending again.

''Because you're so concerned for the welfare of your employees,'' she corrected, the words muffled against his mouth.

''Exactly.'' He forgot what they were talking about for the rest of the lunch hour.

But when he returned, he had a private conversation with Mr. Blair, one which he challenged the other man to repeat on pain of firing. After that, Mr. Blair no longer required Brianna to stay after work, and his telephone calls with his broker became a thing of the past.

Three weeks after Ahmed had left town, Brianna was almost her old self again. She'd put the whole situation behind her and was ready to face the future. There was a man in her department who seemed to like her. She wished that she could encourage him. But there was no sense of excitement in her chest when he looked at her. Wherever she looked, in fact, she seemed to see liquid black eyes looking back at her.

She felt particularly remorseful one Friday afternoon when she dragged herself into the apartment, looking as if she'd just lost her last friend.

"You're positively mournful," Tad muttered. "Honestly, sis, you just can't go on like this."

"I'm only tired, Tad," she said evasively. She smiled, moving into her bedroom to change into jeans and a loose, floppy, colored shirt. "How are the lessons going?" she asked when she rejoined her blue-jeaned brother in the living room.

"My tutor says I'm bright and eager to learn," he said mischievously. "And that if I work very hard through the rest of the school year, and probably the summer," he added ruefully, "I'll be able to rejoin my age grade next fall. They've done lots of tests. He'd like you to give him a ring and go by and see him one afternoon at the board of education office." He pursed his lips. "He's thirty-eight, single and pretty passable to look at. I told him you were a ravishing model-type girl with no bad habits at all."

"Tad!"

"I didn't," he confessed, grinning at her. "But you might like him."

"It's early days yet," she said, averting her eyes. "What would you like for supper?"

"Macaroni and cheese," he said immediately. He followed her into the kitchen. "I'm sorry about how it worked out," he told her. "I know you're having a hard time getting over Ahmed."

She stiffened at just the mention of his name. "No,

I'm not,'' she assured him. ''I'm doing very well indeed since Mr. Blair suddenly decided to do his work instead of talking on the telephone all day.''

''I noticed. It's nice to have you home. But...''

She turned and ruffled his dark hair. ''I like having you at home. I'm perfectly happy and well adjusted. Now get out of here and let me work, okay?''

''Okay.''

He went reluctantly back into the living room and started to turn up the television. But the buzzer rang and he went to answer it. Brianna knew that it was probably Nick. She was banging pots and pans and didn't hear Tad's excited voice. She did hear the opening of the door a few minutes later.

''Is that Nick?'' she called over her shoulder as she took a pan of rolls out of the oven and sat them on the stove, reaching to turn off the oven.

''No,'' a familiar deep voice replied quietly. ''It is not.''

Chapter Eleven

Brianna felt her heart race madly into her throat. She froze where she stood, afraid to believe what she heard. "Ahmed?" she whispered.

"Yes."

She turned, her big blue eyes wide and unbelieving. He looked drawn, as if the weeks had been a strain. There were three men with him, big, tough-looking Arabs who took up positions in the living room where Tad was staring at them in fascination. Ahmed was wearing an elegant three-piece navy pin-striped suit with a white silk shirt. He was impeccably groomed. But then, she remembered, he was a king.

"Hello," she said hesitantly, uncertain about how to address him. Did she call him "Your Majesty" or curtsy?

Her uncertainty showed plainly on her face, and he winced.

''I...would you like to sit down?'' she asked. ''In the living room...?''

''Brianna,'' he groaned.

She moved back a step, struggling for composure. She plastered a smile on her face. ''Tad and I saw you on the news,'' she stammered. ''I'm glad they caught everyone. And your sister, I... They said that she wasn't involved. You must be very glad.''

''Yes.'' His voice was suddenly dull, lackluster. ''Very glad.''

She glanced toward the living room. Tad was talking animatedly to one of Ahmed's men, who was smiling and answering him very pleasantly.

''Tad's doing fine,'' she remarked. ''He's catching up quickly with his schoolwork.''

''And you, Brianna?''

''Oh, I'm fine, too, as you see,'' she said. The smile was beginning to hurt her face. ''Would you like coffee?''

''That would be nice.''

''Your men...?''

''They are content.''

She fumbled down a cup with a crack in it and quickly replaced it, rummaging through the cabinet and her meager store of dishes to find something that would do for a king to drink out of.

He came up behind her, catching her cold hands in his. ''Don't,'' he pleaded huskily. ''For the love of God, don't treat me like some stranger!''

''But you are.'' Hot tears stung her eyes. She closed them, but it wouldn't stem the sudden flow. ''You're a king...!''

He whirled her into his arms and bent, taking her mouth hungrily under his, oblivious to the shocked stares from the living room or Tad's voice intervening, diverting.

Tears drained down into her mouth and he tasted them. His lean hands came up to cup her face, to cherish it while he kissed away the tears and his tongue savored the sable softness of her thick eyelashes.

"So many tears," he whispered, his lips tender. "Salty and hot and sweet. They tell me, oh, so potently, that you love me, *chérie.*"

She felt his mouth covering hers, and for a few seconds, she gave in to the hunger for him, the long ache of waiting. But she couldn't forget who and what he was. She drew demurely away from him and lowered her face.

He claimed her hand, holding it to his chest, where his heartbeat was strong and quick.

"They showed her on the television," she said quietly.

"Yasmin?"

She shook her head.

"Ah. Lillah."

She nodded.

He tilted her eyes up to his indulgent ones. "And you thought... Yes, I see what you thought, this sudden color tells me."

"She's very lovely."

"She is not you," he said simply. He touched her face as if he'd forgotten what she looked like, as if he was hungry to look at her. "I did not telephone you because it is too difficult to make conversation over the coldness of an ocean. I had to have you close to me, like this, so that I could see your eyes, feel your breath as you spoke to me."

"I thought that once you were back home again, all this might seem like a bad memory to you," she said.

"I have not slept," he said quietly. "I have worked for the release of my sister. There have been charges and countercharges, and many members of the military had to be dealt with to prevent there ever being a recurrence of this coup attempt. I have been busy, Brianna. But not so busy that I could ever forget the taste and touch of you in my arms."

"That's nice."

He tilted her chin up, searching her sad eyes. "You said that you loved me enough to risk marrying me. Do you still?"

She hesitated. "Ahmed, you're a king," she said. "I could...I could be your mistress," she whispered, lowering her shamed eyes. "I could be a part of your life that way, and you wouldn't be risking anything. There are so many people in your country who don't like Americans."

"I do not have a mistress," he said gently. "I do not want one. I want you for my wife. I want you to bear the heirs to my name, my family, my kingdom."

"They would be half-American," she pointed out, worriedly.

He smiled. "So they would. How politically expedient. Not to mention the benefit of having an American wife in the complicated thread of international affairs.'' He traced a line down her cheek. ''I have made the necessary announcements, calmed fears, outtalked adversaries and placated doomsayers. All that I have accomplished since I left here. And I have arranged our wedding.'' He kissed her shocked mouth. ''Even the vice president of your own country has promised to attend. So has Lang,'' he added dryly.

''It won't be just a small church wedding,'' she murmured fearfully, gnawing on her lower lip.

''Stop doing that,'' he coaxed, his thumb freeing the soft flesh. ''You will make it sore and I cannot kiss you. No, it cannot be a small wedding. It will be a wedding of state. Televised around the world.'' He kissed her horrified eyes closed. ''You will have a gown from Paris. I will have them send a couturiere to the palace to fit you.''

''A couturiere,'' she echoed. ''To the palace. The palace?''

He brushed his mouth tenderly over hers. ''I am a king,'' he reminded her. ''Most kings live in palaces, unless they are very poor kings. I am not. My country is rich. My people are cosmopolitan and our economy is excellent. We have only the occasional student protest. Once we had to deport some foreign students, but we later learned that they were deliberate troublemakers.''

''I'm just ordinary,'' she protested.

He smiled. ''So am I. Just ordinary.''

''I'd be a queen,'' she said, just realizing it. Her eyes were like saucers. ''Oh, dear.''

''And Tad a prince,'' he reminded her. He glanced

toward the living room. "Can you really not picture him in a crown?" he teased. "He would have the finest tutors in the world, and the best education we can afford for him. Oxford, if he likes."

She wondered if she was dreaming. Her eyes slid over his beloved face. So much misery, so many tears, and now here he was and he wanted her.

"There's, uh, there's just one thing," she said jerkily.

"Yes?" His smile was tender, indulgent.

She looked up. "Do you…can you…love me?"

The backs of his fingers drew slowly down her cheek to her mouth, under her chin, her throat. "These words should be spoken only in the privacy of a bedroom," he said solemnly. His dark eyes held hers. "Be patient. I have never said them."

Her lips parted, because what was in his eyes made her feel humble.

"Say that you will marry me," he coaxed. "Say the words."

"I…will marry you," she answered.

He smiled. He kissed her forehead with exquisite tenderness. "Now," he whispered, "it begins."

She had no idea what it would involve to marry a head of state. She and Tad were whisked away to Mozambara, the capital city of Saudi Mahara, like birds on the wind, leaving everything behind and all the details of closing up the apartment and shipping furniture to Ahmed's men.

Tad was given his own suite of rooms and a personal servant to look after him. He was dressed in the finest clothing, had access to the court physician if he so much as sniffled, and a tutor was immediately engaged for him. His head spun at the sudden luxury that surrounded him. His every whim was immediately satisfied.

That worried Brianna, who managed an audience with the king to complain about it. They were never alone now. They were constantly chaperoned and protocol was strict and unrelenting.

"He's going to be spoiled," she moaned when Ahmed dismissed her fears.

"He should be spoiled," he informed her with a smile. "He has had a savage time for a boy his age. Let him enjoy it while he can. And please stop worrying."

She glanced around the throne room. It always seemed to be full of advisers and visiting potentates and politicians. "Can't we even have dinner alone together?"

He pursed his lips and his eyes were sensuous as they searched hers. "Another week," he promised, "and we can be alone together all we like." His gaze dropped to her mouth and lingered there. "I dream of it every night, Brianna," he added breathlessly. "I dream of you."

"And I of you," she said huskily.

He drew in a long breath. "Could you leave now?" he asked pleasantly. "You are quite soon going to have a visible reaction on my composure."

She cleared her throat. "Sorry."

She turned and left, nodding politely to several curious men near the door who smiled at her.

The days were long. She was fitted for the wedding gown, which was so expensive with its imported lace and specially made fabric from Paris that she thought privately she could probably buy a yacht for less. It was a marriage of state, though, and this was necessary. Everyone said so. The queen Brianna must be properly dressed. Queen Brianna. She shook her head. That was going to take some time to get used to.

She spent some of her time with Tad, and the rest daydreaming about her forthcoming marriage in the lush garden with its fish pond and flowers. Just looking at Ahmed from a distance made her heart race. Soon, there would be the two of them together, with no prying eyes. She grew breathless at just the thought.

The great day finally arrived. She was dressed and a bouquet of orchids placed in her cold, trembling hands. Tad smiled at her reassuringly, as richly dressed as the handsome bridegroom waiting at the huge altar in the church.

There were newsmen and cameras everywhere. And the crowds were huge. The people of Saudi Mahara seemed not at all unhappy to welcome their new American queen. She hoped that their welcome was sincere, and not forced by the many armed guards who surrounded the area.

She kept her eyes on Ahmed as she entered the church. It was the longest walk of her entire life, and she was terrified. The terror grew as she began to recognize some of the people in the front pews, people she'd only ever seen on television newscasts. But she made it, her nerves in disarray but her head held high and her carriage perfect.

Ahmed's pride shone out of his black eyes as she joined him at the altar. He took her hand in his and they knelt before the high clergyman who was to perform the ceremony.

Later, she remembered very little except that the beauty of it made her cry. When they exchanged rings, and then were pronounced man and wife, she began to cry. Ahmed cupped her face in his hands and looked at her with an expression she knew that she would carry to her grave, held in her heart forever. He bent and kissed away every single tear, while their audience watched in rapt approval.

It was a fairy-tale wedding. Brianna entertained congratulations from visiting dignitaries until her hand hurt and her voice began to give way.

Ahmed stood at her side, tall and proud. The festivities went on long into the night and Brianna thought that she'd never been so tired. It disappointed her to feel herself wilting, because she'd lived for this night, for her wedding night, for so long.

When he led her to the royal suite, which they would share, she was almost in tears when he closed the door behind them.

"Ah, what is this?" he whispered, brushing away the tears as he smiled gently down at her.

"I'm so tired," she wailed, her eyes seeking his. "It's been such a long day, and I want to feel excited and strong and..."

He stopped the words with his lips. "You are telling me that you are too tired to make love," he whispered, "and I know this already. *Pauvre petite,* the demands of state are sometimes a great nuisance to bear. But this is only the beginning of our time together."

"But I want you," she whispered shyly. "And I've waited so long!"

"As I have waited." He kissed her eyes closed. "I shall undress you, and myself, and we shall lie naked in each other's arms all night long. Then in the morning, when you are rested, I shall make love to you as long as your body is capable of receiving mine."

She blossomed under his warm, tender mouth, allowing him to remove the exquisite dress and the even more exquisite silk and lace things under it. He lifted her in his arms, his dark eyes adoring her silky skin, and carried her to bed.

"Oh, how magnificent!" she exclaimed as he put her down on the canopied bed. It was gold and silver, with geometrical motifs that added to the allure. The curtains were black with silver and gold threads.

"The colors of office," he informed her, moving to the dresser to empty his pockets and unfasten his cuff links and tie clasp. He glanced toward her, noticing her nervous fingers reaching for the cover.

"No, Brianna," he said softly. "Let me enjoy you."

She blushed, but she subsided back onto the bed. After a minute, the shyness began to drain away and she found pleasure in the slow boldness of his gaze.

He divested himself of everything except his briefs. Then he turned, facing her, and let her watch him remove them. He was aroused, and her body shivered as she stared at him.

"A nuisance only," he said amusedly. "I require nothing of you tonight except for your closeness."

She could never remember being less tired in her life as desire suddenly overwhelmed her. She couldn't drag her eyes away from him and as he saw her expression, his chin lifted and his eyes narrowed.

He moved to thc bed and balanced beside her with one knee. Her hand went to it involuntarily and shyly, hesitantly, traced up it. She paused, her eyes seeking his.

He nodded. She continued, her breath catching when she touched him.

He moved down beside her and his mouth eased over hers while he taught her hands to explore him gently, sensuously. The lights were all blazing, and if she'd ever thought of making love like this, she would have been horrified. But the sensuality of his hands and mouth, the lazy movements of his body, made her uninhibited and wanton.

By the time he shifted her onto her back and his body moved over her, she was mindless and totally receptive to anything he asked.

He kissed her while he made himself master of her body, feeling her shocked gasp as he began to take her. Her hands gripped his upper arms fearfully, her nails biting into him as the stinging pain briefly overcame her desire.

He lifted his head and his body stilled. "In the old days," he whispered to her, his voice a little unsteady in the heat of passion, "the old women would hang the bridal sheet out of the window the next morning to show the traces of virgin blood that clung to it. I am not supposed to know, nor are you, but they will take this one away and hide it tomorrow, so that for all our lives together they can prove that you had no lover before me, and that our children are legitimate."

She swallowed. "It hurt a little," she whispered tightly.

He smiled gently. "That is natural. But what I can give you now will make up for it. Shall I show you?" he whispered, bending.

She felt him move, shift, and his eyes held hers while he did it, until the right movement made her body jerk and her breath catch.

He whispered something in French, and his mouth began to cherish hers. She had nothing to compare the experience with, nothing to prepare her for the sudden fierce bite of passion into her body. She fought him because it frightened her more than the brief pain had. He laughed and lifted his head to watch her as he forced her body into an explosive culmination that arched her back and tore from her open mouth in a husky little scream. Only when he felt her begin to shiver in the aftermath did he allow himself the exquisite pleasure of joining her in that hot delight of ecstasy. It was, he thought as it racked him, almost too sweet to bear.

He felt as if he lost consciousness for a second or two. He became slowly aware of Brianna's whispery movement under the weight of his body. He lifted his head and looked into her wide, curious eyes.

He didn't speak. Neither did she. Her eyes went

down to where his chest lay on her breasts and back up to his mouth and then his eyes with something like wonder. She took a soft breath and then moved her hips deliberately, so that she could experience again the pressure that it exerted in the secret places of her body. She flushed.

He touched her face, raising himself slightly on his elbows, and he moved his own hips, his knee nudging her legs farther apart. She gasped.

His hand slid down her thigh and curved around it. Holding her eyes, he shifted onto his side and gently brought her into the cradle of his hips so that they lay still joined together in intimacy. He smiled and pulled at her thigh, easing her into the rhythm. In this position, she was open to his eyes and he to hers. They looked at each other in wonder, and then their eyes locked and he caught his breath at the pleasure he saw in her face.

''Here,'' he whispered huskily. ''Like this, my love.''

He pulled her hips into his and pushed slowly until she accepted him completely. She blushed at the incredible intimacy of hanging there, between heaven and earth, while she seemed to see into his soul.

''Ahmed,'' she whispered, drowning in him. ''Ahmed, I love you…so much!''

''And I you,'' he said unsteadily. ''With all my heart.''

He shivered, rolling slowly onto his back with her body still joined to his. His hands smoothed down her back, gently pulling. His body tautened under hers with each slow, delicate motion.

"Sit up and take me," he whispered.

"I don't think I can...." she began nervously.

"You are my love. My life."

"And you are mine. But I...can't!" She hid her face against his chest, and he laughed with delight at her shyness. She was a rarity in his life. A woman with inhibitions.

"So shy," he whispered. "You delight me. Brianna, you...delight...me!"

As he spoke, his hands moved her hips, making her gasp, making her shiver with pleasure.

She felt his body pull and tauten. His jaw clenched and he arched in a sinuous movement that she found incredibly arousing. Her lips touched over his chest in shaky little kisses while his hands brought them both to the most incredibly tender climax of his life.

She bit him in her oblivious pleasure, and his short laugh was as much a groan of ecstasy as he gripped her bruisingly hard and held her to the rigid clench of his body.

She felt him relax suddenly with a rough shudder, and her cheek lay heavily against his damp chest. The hairs tickled her nose and she smiled wearily.

"Is it so good, always?" she whispered.

"I think, only when two people love," he whispered back. His hands made a warm, sensuous sweep of her back and he arched up to enjoy the silky feel of her against him. "*Dieu!* You exhaust me with exquisite pleasure and then, so suddenly, I want you all over again."

She smiled against his chest, lifting up so that she could look into his dark, possessive eyes. "We're married,'' she said with quiet wonder. ''We can sleep together every night.''

He smiled. ''There will most likely be very little sleep obtained by either of us,'' he mused.

She traced the line of his jaw. ''I like making love.''

''I like it most of all with you,'' he said, sensing her quiet fears. ''I never loved before. It is the most profound experience of my life to lie with you so intimately.''

She relaxed. Her mouth brushed his and she lay against him, sated and weary. ''Can we sleep like this?''

His arms enclosed her. ''Just like this,'' he assured her. His own eyes closed in drowsy pleasure. And finally they slept.

Brianna found that there were difficulties despite her love for her husband, but none that she couldn't overcome with some patient tutoring and understanding. She got used to palace protocol and meeting visiting dignitaries' wives. She got used to the things that were expected of a queen, just as Tad rapidly adjusted to life at court. He grew and blossomed, and soon Brianna relaxed. He was going to be all right, just as Dr. Brown had predicted.

There was a grand ball a few months after their marriage. Brianna had a gown by Dior, reflecting the silver-and-gold-on-black motif of Ahmed's court. Her hair had grown long, and she had it pinned into an exquisite coiffure—one that, she knew from experience, would be quickly disposed with when she and

Ahmed were alone. She wore diamonds and pearls, and the tiara of her rank, and she met with approving glances from even the most stern ministers of Ahmed's cabinet when she joined her guests.

She was dancing with her husband when she noticed an odd expression in his eyes. His hand on her waist was curiously exploring.

"What is it?" she asked softly.

He smiled quizzically. "Is there something which you wish to tell me?" he asked gently. "Something which you have perhaps thought to save until you visited our court physician?"

"Yasmin," she said, glowering toward a gleeful sister-in-law who was wearing a guilty but very happy expression.

"Do not blame her too much. She dreams of dynasties, even as I sometimes do." He pulled her closer, his eyes loving and warm. "Tell me."

"I'm not sure," she confessed. "I've been unwell at breakfast twice this week. And there were a few other things." She searched his eyes. "I didn't want to tell you just yet."

"Why?" he asked softly.

"I was afraid you might not want to make love to me anymore if we were sure," she said hesitantly, searching his dark eyes as her hand caressed his jacket. "I thought they might take me away from you...."

"Chérie!" He stopped dancing and bent to kiss her worried eyes shut. "They would have to kill me to separate us," he whispered fervently. "And as for the

other...Brianna, I would want to make love to you if I were on my deathbed!''

Reassured, she smiled shyly. ''Would you, really?''

''I find you a delightful pupil,'' he whispered. ''Adventurous and mischievous and totally captivating.''

''I love you!''

''I love you,'' he returned. His hand pressed slowly onto her flat belly and they stood staring at each other while around them, suddenly curious and then knowing eyes began to gleam with confirmed suspicions. Without saying a word, or making an announcement, everyone at court knew that Brianna carried the heir to the throne. And it was a credit to them, and protocol, that not one suspicion was voiced until the actual announcement was made some weeks later.

Brianna's little prince was born on a bright autumn day, and bells rang from the churches to signal the event. Ahmed stood beside her bed holding the crown prince Tarin in his arms, with a beaming Tad beside him. Brianna, tired but gloriously happy, looked up at the three most important people in her life with eyes that reflected her joy.

Sensing her appraisal, Ahmed turned his head and looked down at her. His eyes were full of wonder.

''He is perfect,'' he told her, while nurses fidgeted in the background and smiled at his expression.

''A king's ransom,'' she agreed, loving him with her whole heart.

''Ah, that is not quite so,'' he whispered, bending to lay the tiny child in her waiting arms. ''For, while

I love my son with a father's great pride, *you* are the real king's ransom, my darling,'' he whispered, and he smiled at her radiant expression as he bent to kiss her.

* * * * *

In the Family Way

Marie Ferrarella

To
my family,
for making me crazy
and
for making me feel needed and loved

Chapter 1

"I'm what?"

Dana Morrow gripped the armrests of the chair she was sitting in, as if that would somehow negate what her doctor, her friend, was telling her. Her voice, suddenly thin and high, vibrated in the small office.

Shock was something Dr. Sheila Pollack had never expected to see on Dana's face. It took a little getting used to. As did, she supposed, her news.

"Pregnant," Sheila repeated. "With child. In the family way." A fond smile curved her lips, an unconscious response to the news she'd just delivered. To Sheila, there was nothing more sacred, more wonderful, than the creation of life between two people in love. But then, she was one of the lucky ones. She had Slade, and that tended to color her view of things. "There's a little human being forming and growing within you even as we speak."

For a moment, Dana felt as if she'd just received the salvo that would finally sink the ship she'd been trying so desperately to keep afloat. Sheila had to be wrong.

"That's impossible. There has to be some mistake." Dana passed her hand along her belly. There was no change to be felt there. Nothing was different than it had been from last week, last month, last year. Except that, for the last few days, her morning ritual included communing with the toilet bowl while poised before it on her knees. But that didn't mean she was pregnant. She was just coming down with the flu. People with the flu threw up all the time.

The look in her eyes willed Sheila to retract her words. "I can't be pregnant."

Dana *was* in shock, Sheila realized. Sympathy nudged its way forward. "I'm afraid that you are. All the signs are positive."

Sheila had started out her professional morning two hours earlier than usual, delivering a healthy baby boy who'd decided to make his debut three weeks before his due date. It was while she'd been rushing to get ready to leave that she'd heard her houseguest trying to muffle the sounds of retching. She'd ordered Dana to the office for an exam, fitting her in before her first appointment. As a result, there was now a roomful of women waiting for her.

She rounded the desk, took the chair beside Dana and placed her arm around the younger woman's shoulders. For a brief moment, the clock turned back twenty-three years. She was in the Morrow home, baby-sitting Dana and her younger sister, Megan, while Mr. Morrow was off to some new place in the limelight, enmeshed in yet another high profile murder case, and Mrs. Morrow was quietly looking for validation at the bottom of a bottle she thought no one knew she kept.

Five years separated her from Dana. Twenty-three years ago, the gap had felt like a wide chasm. Now there was no difference between them. Except that Sheila was happy, and Dana, it was apparent from the moment the younger woman had turned up on her doorstep yesterday morning, Mollie in tow, was not.

Why was it that some people were never allowed their share of happiness? Sheila wondered. God knew Dana had both earned and deserved it. "I take it this isn't a welcome turn of events."

A welcome turn of events? Dana thought. It might have been, once, when she and Steven had first gotten together. Then she'd believed in the possibility of love. Now she knew better. It had taken her a while, but she had finally learned.

Numb, she could only shake her head in response.

"No chance of this bringing about a reconciliation?" Sheila looked at her hopefully. Dana had been pretty vague about what had brought her back to Bedford, only that she'd left the man she was living with.

Dana could feel her mind scrambling around, like a tiny mouse looking for a way out of the maze before it died there. A baby. Oh God, this was terrible, really terrible. The timing couldn't have been worse than if it had been wished on her as a curse.

Struggling for composure even as she felt herself sinking, Dana shook her head. "More chance of Megan walking in through that door, telling me she's here for Mollie."

Just one damn thing on top of another and another, Dana thought, her anger rising. Anger had always been her edge. It kept her from slipping under, from being shredded by the talons of despair. The way her mother eventually had been. No one needed to know that beneath the anger, the bravado, was the small child from long ago who still hurt.

Sheila hugged Dana to her, wishing there was something she could do. But there wasn't, other than to be there for her friend. "Have I told you how very sorry I was to hear about Megan and her husband?"

Dana drew back to look at Sheila. "You don't have to say anything, Sheila. I saw it in your eyes when Mollie and I descended on you yesterday like the plague."

Sheila frowned at the description. They were friends. More than friends. Almost sisters. Sisters were not beholden to one another. They were just there, to act as buffers whenever necessary.

"You didn't descend," she corrected, then added pointedly, "locusts descend."

The faint outline of a smile lifted a corner of Dana's mouth. She'd gone to Sheila rather than to the place school records had once cited as her home because she'd needed to see the sight of an understanding face almost more than she'd needed to breathe. And because Sheila would accept her without asking for any explanations, any excuses. Unlike her father.

"Like I said—"

Sheila didn't want Dana's gratitude, just her well-being. "You're welcome at my house, Dana, you and Mollie," she said in the no-nonsense tone that her husband teased her about. "For as long as you want to stay."

"I want to stay forever." The tired smile widened just a little. "However, Slade might have different ideas."

"Slade and I think very much alike." His kindness was one of the qualities that endeared him to her so much. "Besides, being around Mollie is good practice for him. Rebecca isn't going to be a toddler forever. He might as well see what he's in for a few years down the line."

Dana was tempted, just for a second, to take Sheila up on her hospitality. But that would be hiding from the world, and Dana had never allowed herself to be a coward. Once begun, it would be a hard habit to break.

"Thanks, but I really can't hide out at your place forever." Dana looked at her abdomen. How could she be pregnant? Why now, of all times? Now, when she'd left her position at the law firm, her apartment, and abandoned her things? Everything except for a few of Mollie's belongings and the box of photographs she treasured. The box of photographs she'd always meant to place into an album someday.

The box that held visual evidence of the very best pieces of her life.

Frustration welled inside her. It just wasn't fair.

Damn it, anyway. Damn Steven for making me believe. Damn me for believing.

She pressed the heel of her hand hard against her stomach,

as if to rub the tiny seed out, erasing it. Silly thought, she upbraided herself.

"Seems like I can't hide at all." Dana caught her lower lip between her teeth, afraid that her voice would break.

"It's okay to cry," Sheila whispered soothingly.

"I'm not going to cry," Dana answered quietly as the numbness continued to pour through her, anesthetizing everything in its path. "I'm just not sure I can breathe very well at the moment."

Been there, done that, Sheila thought. "If it helps any, I felt the same way you did when I found out I was pregnant."

Dana looked at Sheila. She couldn't remotely picture Sheila being as devastated as she felt right at this moment. If anyone had ever been born to be a mother, it was Sheila. Sheila adored babies.

So did she. She just didn't want to have one right now, Dana thought miserably.

Sheila saw the look of disbelief in Dana's eyes. "Don't forget, Slade wasn't in my life anymore by the time I realized I was carrying his child. He was overseas, dodging bullets and writing headlines. I thought having a baby, *raising* a baby, was going to be something I was going to go through alone." She remembered how much she'd resisted loving him when he returned—and how futile that had been. "Until he showed up, like the cavalry."

That might have been true for Sheila, but Dana didn't live in a fairy-tale world.

"Steven isn't the cavalry." Her voice was flat, stripped of feelings. "He'd be something the cavalry would be saving me from." That, too, she had learned the hard way. Steven had changed the way he seemed to be—kind, funny, thoughtful—to the man he really was. Self-centered and egotistical, and impossible to live with. It had taken Mollie's coming to live with her to realize the truth.

She saw the look on Sheila's face. Ever the optimist, Sheila was going to try to find something good to say about a man she'd never met. That was just Sheila's way. To forage for the positive. But there was nothing positive to say about Steven. Not anymore.

Once she'd thought otherwise. Steven had entered her life like a song. No, like a poem, Dana amended.

She'd almost forgotten about that. Steven used to write the loveliest poems to her. He'd create them while she sat and listened. His words had vibrated with such feeling. Such love.

It was the poems that had convinced her. Convinced her she'd finally found someone to love. Someone who really loved her in return, the way George had loved her sister.

Not everyone was destined to have love in their lives, she thought cynically. She was living proof of that.

Sorrow yawned before her, its jaws wide and sharp, threatening to swallow her up. Just for a moment, Dana felt completely helpless.

"Oh, Sheila, if there was ever a time not to be pregnant, this is it."

Concern overwhelmed Sheila. She'd never seen Dana like this. Yesterday, when Dana had come to her, she'd seemed no different than the girl she'd always known. A little older, to be sure, but there was still an air of strength about her, still a hint of laughter in her eyes. Today, she was the portrait of a troubled woman.

"What are you going to do?" The offer of support was silent but understood.

"You mean besides throw up?" Dana mustered a ghost of a smile. "I don't know. Be numb, I guess, at least for a while."

Pregnant.

The word echoed in Dana's brain, mocking her. She still couldn't bring herself to believe it. She'd been so careful. "Sheila, how could this have happened?"

"My guess is the usual way." Sympathy and humor filled her eyes. "Didn't anyone ever tell you about the birds and the bees?"

Dana laughed shortly. "Yes, but in my case, the bird was practicing birth control."

Rising, Sheila pushed her hands deep into the pockets of her lab coat. A baby's arrival should be something to look forward to, not despair of. She couldn't think of anything sadder than not to want the child you were blessed with. "Nothing's foolproof."

"Emphasis on the word fool."

Sheila studied Dana's face. "Are you talking about him or you?"

"Me." She raised her chin, a sliver of defiance wedging its way in. "For ever having gotten mixed up with him."

That was more like it, Sheila thought. For a moment there, she'd been afraid that Dana was going to break down. "From what you wrote me, he was quite charming."

"Yes, he was." But in Steven's case, charming was merely camouflage for shallow. "In the beginning," Dana qualified. "He actually wrote poetry to me. We started out like poetry and wound up like a limerick, the kind that leaves a bad taste in your mouth."

She should have left earlier, Dana thought, annoyed with herself. Left when the first signs had begun to show. When the romance had begun to unravel. Cut her losses and go. If she had, at least she wouldn't be in this predicament.

Dana needed something to get her mind off this, off everything, Sheila thought. There was so much that was resting on her slim shoulders these days. Custody of her orphaned niece, a failed relationship, uprooting her life and an as-yet-untried reconciliation with a father who, in Sheila's estimation, most saints would have had trouble with. With the pregnancy on top of that, a weaker person would be coming unglued.

"Listen, why don't the three of us go out tonight? Pilar can stay with the kids." Her housekeeper was excellent with children. "Slade just wrapped up an investigative series he was working on, and if the stork's willing to cooperate, I don't have anyone due to deliver for another few weeks. I could use the break."

But it wasn't Sheila who needed the break, and they both knew it. Dana appreciated the gesture but shook her head.

''I don't like leaving Mollie alone for more than an hour or so at the moment. She hasn't been well.'' Mollie was all that was making life worthwhile for her these days. It had been Mollie she was thinking of when she finally made the break from Steven. Mollie, so young to already have been touched by the darker side of life, needed the opportunity to laugh, to play, to be a normal little girl. To grow up into a happy young woman. Mollie wouldn't have gotten her chance if Dana had remained with Steven.

Sheila frowned, trying to remember. Had she missed something? The little girl had seemed pale but otherwise all right to her. ''I didn't notice—''

''She's run-down, listless, coughing. It may just be a run-of-the-mill cold, but I don't think so. Maybe it's even psychological.'' All she knew was that she'd watched Mollie's spirit and her health decline a little with each week that passed. ''Losing her parents like that, and then coming to live with me—with us,'' she amended, thinking of Steven, ''it's unsettling for someone her age. And Steven didn't make it very easy on her.'' She left it at that. There was no need to go into detail.

But that had been the last straw, what had finally sent her on her way. The way Steven had behaved toward Mollie. As if she was an intrusion into his life, something to be pushed out of the way and then ignored like a piece of offending furniture. Dana had seen herself and her father all over again. Except that her father had never been that direct. For the most part, when he was around at all, her father had ignored her and Megan completely.

When he did acknowledge their existence, it was to criticize. Nothing they did was ever good enough for him. He'd wanted more from them. Always more. Meggie had gone out of her way to give it to him. Dana had simply gone.

Sheila wondered how much of Mollie's problem was real and how much Dana might be imagining, transferring her grief to the child. ''I forget, how long has she been with you?''

It seemed like forever. And only yesterday. "Straight out of the hospital." Dana didn't need to pause to calculate the length of time. It was engraved in her brain. Mollie had come to live with her after the fatal accident that had taken Megan and George. "Six months." Mollie had been like a broken sparrow in need of so much attention, so much love, just to heal. And Steven had become jealous of the time she'd devoted to the little girl. Time, he claimed, that was stolen from him.

That was when Dana had finally wiped the cobwebs from her eycs. She'd taken off with Mollie while he was at work, sparing herself the grief of yet another nasty, drawn-out argument. By the time he'd realized she wasn't at work, she and Mollie had been on the road for eight hours.

Sheila began to edge to the door, acutely aware of just how far behind schedule she'd fallen. She paused for one last word of assurance.

"I can take a look at Mollie when I get home tonight, if you like. But if you're really worried, I can recommend an excellent pediatrician. His patients love him, and his patients' parents think the man walks on water."

The analogy succeeded in bringing a smile to Dana's lips. "Does he?"

Sheila gave Rafael Saldana her unqualified seal of approval. "Pretty much. He's really terrific. I did my residency with him, and there's no one I'd rather entrust my baby to than Rafe."

"Rebecca has a pediatrician?"

"Yes." Sheila rested her hand on the doorknob. "Why is that so surprising?"

Dana shrugged. "I just thought a doctor wouldn't need to send members of her family to another doctor unless there was something drastically wrong and she needed a specialist."

"No, but she does need to admit she's human and not all-knowing," Sheila pointed out. "Rafe's idea of recreational reading is to immerse himself in the latest AMA findings in pediatric care. He's really dedicated. Like I said, he's the best.'' She opened the door. The soft murmur of voices from the reception area floated to her. Time to get rolling or she would be here straight through the evening. ''I'll have Lisa arrange an appointment. Do you want to take Mollie to him this afternoon?''

The sooner the better. The coughing episodes were getting worse. Dana smiled her appreciation.

''I'd feel better knowing there's nothing wrong with Mollie. Then all I'll have to come to grips with is the news you just laid on me.'' She blew out a breath. ''That, and making peace with my father.''

Sheila knew why Dana had chosen to return to Bedford after all this time rather than settle somewhere else. She'd been the one to write to her friend, telling Dana of her father's recent stroke. Sheila didn't envy the road Dana had before her. ''Remember, you're welcome to stay with us for as long as you'd like.''

Dana knew the invitation was tendered in earnest, and part of her wanted to accept, to pull the covers over her head and hide from the world. For just a little while.

But she really didn't have that luxury. Time, for all she knew, might be running out for her father.

''I came back to mend fences, Sheila. Before...before there's no one to mend fences with.'' Meggie's sudden death had made Dana acutely aware of just how tenuous life was. And how much more so for a man past middle age and in deteriorating health.

Sheila squeezed her hand. ''That's not an easy row to hoe, Dana.''

There was no reason to pretend with Sheila. Sheila had pretty much been privy to it all. Their parents had been friends since before either one of them was born, and the two had grown up together.

''No, all rocks and hard ground,'' Dana agreed. But that wasn't a cause for pity—it was just the way things were. ''But he is my father and, except for Mollie, all the family I have.

It's not right to let things stay the way they are.'' She glanced at her stomach and the offending resident there. ''Of course, this isn't going to make things any easier.''

Sheila didn't hesitate. ''Don't tell him yet.''

Dana laughed for the first time that day. She had no intention of mentioning her pregnancy to Paul Morrow until other things were resolved between them. And perhaps not even then. She knew that finding the words to tell him would be next to impossible. An unwed pregnancy was far from unusual these days, but it wouldn't fly with her father and his particular code of morals.

''I might not even tell him until after the baby goes to college.''

''If anyone can pull that off, you can.'' Sheila laid a hand on her shoulder. She really had to get to work, but she hated to see her friend in such distress. ''You going to be all right?'' She felt Dana's shoulders stiffen beneath her hand.

''Yeah. You know me, Sheila, I thrive on challenges and rough times.'' But it would be nice, just once, to have things go smoothly, at least for a little while.

She supposed maybe she was asking for too much.

Sheila saw Lisa motioning to her from the hall. ''I'll have Lisa make that appointment,'' she promised.

Dana nodded. Well, one thing down, four million to go, she thought, leaving Sheila's office. None of which she was looking forward to.

It was five o'clock when Dana walked into Dr. Rafael Saldana's office. The appointment had been almost impossible to get. Dr. Saldana was every bit as popular as Sheila claimed. Dana had stood beside Lisa as the nurse argued with the woman on the other end of the line that, while this was not an emergency, Dr. Pollack would regard it as a personal favor as well as a professional courtesy if Dr. Saldana could somehow squeeze Mollie Aliprantis into his busy schedule. Today. The woman had finally—reluctantly—agreed to the end of the day, but not without putting Lisa on hold and consulting with the doctor.

The waiting room was empty. It looked like the aftermath of a war. An army of toys was scattered throughout the room, covering the floor and the table that was usually reserved for magazines in other offices. Dana was surprised at how many toys, most in fairly good condition, there were. How many and how varied. The doctor she and Meggie used to go to had had exactly five children's books to occupy his patients' attention. She knew, because she'd read them all until she could recite them from memory.

Dana supposed this was a good sign. At least Dr. Saldana knew children liked to play more than they like to sit still and read.

As the door closed behind them, she could feel Mollie's hand tighten on hers. The little girl was almost clinging to her. Wide, deep blue eyes looked around the room slowly. Apprehensively. Mollie didn't like anything new. Even leaving Dallas had been difficult for her.

"Why are we here, Aunt Dana?" If she could have managed it, Mollie would have melted into Dana's body. She clearly didn't want to be here.

Dana ran her hand over the silky blond curls. Hair so fine, it felt like a light mist against her fingertips. "To see the doctor, pet."

Mollie's chin trembled. "I don't like doctors."

"I know you don't, sweetie."

She had little reason to, Dana thought. Doctors meant hospitals, and hospitals were synonymous with death to the girl.

"But he's going to make you feel better, Mol." Ignoring the reception desk for the moment, Dana steered Mollie toward a huge Barbie playhouse, its accessories spread out on the floor.

Here was one doll who knew how to live, Dana mused. At least here, in the world of make-believe, opulence was synonymous with happiness.

"Will I have to go to the hospital?" Fear framed each word.

"No, honey. No hospital. I promise." She fervently hoped it was a promise she could keep. But Mollie didn't need to hear a debate about necessity or circumstance. She needed someone to make the monsters go away. "He's just going to make you feel better." *I hope,* she added silently. "Sit here for a second, baby. I'm going to announce you."

"Like a princess?" Mollie asked brightly.

Cinderella was one of Mollie's favorite stories. Dana must have read the ballroom scene to her several hundred times. Mollie liked to pretend she was Cinderella, who in turn was pretending to be a princess. Dana could readily identify with that.

"Like a princess." Dana turned toward the reception desk, her face growing somber. She hoped Dr. Saldana was half as good as Sheila thought. "Dana Morrow here, with Mollie Aliprantis," she told the young nurse at the window crisply. "Dr. Pollack's office called earlier today to make the appointment," she added when the woman looked at her blankly.

The woman came to life and reached for a clipboard. She attached several sheets to it, passing them to Dana over the counter. "Of course. If you'd just fill out these forms..."

Dana loathed paperwork, and a quick glance told her that most of the required information she didn't know or thought irrelevant. Dana waved the clipboard at the woman.

"I'm not sure I *can* fill these out." Surprise registered on the nurse's face. "We've just moved here from Dallas, and her medical records haven't caught up with us yet," Dana explained. "I don't have a permanent address or a job yet."

I do, however, have a baby on the way, she thought with a touch of bitterness she couldn't suppress. The receptionist was staring at her, dumbfounded. Obviously no one had ever objected to filling out the forms before.

"And there's no health insurance. I'll be paying by charge card."

The nurse worked her lower lip, continuing to look uncertain. "Alice—" she turned in her chair to face the back "—this lady doesn't want to fill out the forms."

An older woman with a kindly face came up behind the nurse. Dana reiterated what she had just said, emphasizing that she was paying for the visit. That was all the paperwork was for, to ensure payment, she thought.

The woman named Alice moved the clipboard toward Dana, a sympathetic smile on her lips and in her eyes. "Why don't you just fill in what you can? Patient's history, that sort of thing."

She was talking to her as if she was mentally impaired, Dana thought with a frustrated sigh. She glanced at the form, scanning it. She didn't have the answers to most of the questions. But she would, she promised herself. In time. However, that time wasn't now.

"I don't know her history." She heard the edge in her voice and was unable to stop it. "I'm her aunt. Her legal guardian," she added when she saw the two women exchange looks. Out of the corner of her eye, she saw Mollie solemnly watching her. For her sake, Dana softened her tone. "Look, I haven't gotten everything sorted out yet." She indicated the questionnaire, struggling with a temper that had already been pushed too far today. "She's not feeling well. If the doctor could just take a look at her for five minutes, that's all I need."

Not true, a small voice within her said. *I need a lot more than that. I need a miracle or two.*

"Is there a problem?" a deep voice asked from inside the office.

Ah, the doctor who walked on water, Dana thought. Maybe he was given to listening to reason. At least, since she was here, it was worth a try.

Hands splayed against the counter, Dana leaned over as far as she could, her head turned toward the sound of the voice.

"None," she informed him, "if I can just dispense with the paperwork."

Drawn by the suppressed anger he heard in the woman's

voice, Rafe Saldana walked into the reception area. "Doesn't seem like such a difficult request to me."

Looking up, Dana took a step back, startled. The gentle voice belonged to a giant of a man.

Chapter 2

Accustomed to making quick assessments, Dana scrutinized the man in the white tunic before her. With hands like that, he looked as if he would be right at home as a lumberjack, felling trees the old-fashioned way. And given his large, broad frame, he would have been considered a godsend on moving day. Everything about him pointed to a man who would be more comfortable handling large, bulky things. Definitely a physical man.

This was Sheila's pediatrician?

It took an effort to picture those hands holding a tiny baby, much less handling one gently.

Suddenly, Mollie was at her side, grabbing her hand. Dana's hand tightened on Mollie's, concerned that the man might frighten the little girl by his very stature.

Mollie moved closer to her, pressing her face against her leg. As if being close could somehow magically protect her from everything that threatened to harm her in this scary new place.

Rafe was accustomed to these first meetings. He knew all

about the fears that went along with them. He vividly remembered his first visit to Dr. Saunders. He'd been so terrified, he'd hidden under one of the chairs in the waiting room and refused to come out until the doctor had coaxed him with a candy bar and a promise that he could examine all the instruments. If he didn't miss his guess, he'd been around the same age this new patient was.

Smiling, Rafe squatted to the little girl's level and addressed the side of woman's leg where Mollie was hiding. "You must be Mollie."

Ever so slowly, Mollie peered around Dana's leg to look at him. Her eyes solemnly fixed on his face, she nodded in response. With her heart fluttering hard in her chest, she popped her thumb into her mouth. Her daddy had told her that big girls didn't do that, but right now, it made her feel better.

Rafe put out his hand to her as if she were the exact same age he was. "How do you do, Mollie? I'm Dr. Rafe." He waited, his hand extended.

After a beat, Mollie hesitantly drew her thumb out of her mouth and slipped her small, slightly damp hand into his. She watched with wavering anxiety as it was swallowed up, covered by his large, tanned fingers. His hand felt strong as he shook hers. Strong, but nice.

Rafe glanced toward the woman behind the child and saw the quizzical look on her face. "Rafe is a lot easier for a small tongue to manage than Saldana." His eyes returned to Mollie. "Isn't it, Mollie?"

She liked being talked to as if she was a grown-up. Aunt Dana talked to her like that. And so did the nice lady and man they were staying with. Not like Steven. He didn't talk to her at all. He just mumbled and grunted at her, like he didn't want to say anything. She knew he didn't like her.

"Uh-huh."

Rafe rose slowly, in order not to startle her. When he gained his feet, he was still holding her hand. "Why don't we go into the examining room?'' He glanced behind him. ''Your mom can come along, too, if she'd like.''

Mollie shook her head. Her voice was barely audible when she said, ''My mom can't come. She's gone to heaven.''

''I'm sorry to hear that, Mollie.'' Rafe looked at Dana for an explanation.

Rather than go into detail and distress Mollie further, Dana told him, ''I'm her aunt. And her legal guardian,'' she added, to forestall any concerns he might have about her right to bring Mollie in to see him. After all, this was the day and age of malpractice suits. Dana had few illusions left, and fewer about doctors. Most were more concerned about covering their tails than they were about treating their patients. Sheila was in a class by herself, but this person holding Mollie's hand wasn't Sheila. This was someone she didn't know.

Sheila's recommendation carried weight, but Dana still reserved the right to form her own opinion of the man. Right now, he was guilty until proven innocent. She'd learned that it was the safest approach to take. There was usually a lot less grief that way.

Too bad she hadn't learned that lesson earlier.

Dr. Saldana nodded, apparently taking her explanation in stride.

Leading the way, he took them into the first examining room. It was small, but its orientation allowed the afternoon sun to bounce playfully along the walls, making the room appear breezy and bright. Three of the walls were light yellow, but it was the fourth that caught her attention. There was a mural covering it, depicting a scene where children and baby animals freely mingled, playing with joyful abandon.

Mollie was staring at it, her attention temporarily drawn away from the nervous anticipation the visit to the doctor had created. Dana wondered if that was just an accident, or intentional on the doctor's part. Looking at him again, she had a feeling he wasn't the type who allowed things to happen by accident.

''Nice wall,'' Dana commented.

Rafe glanced at it. At times, he forgot that it was there. He'd put in over three weeks creating this one and the ones in the other two exam rooms, working nights and whenever he had a free bit of time.

"Thanks. But I don't think I got the colt's hooves quite right." He'd tried six times before he'd finally given up. Most of his patients would never notice, anyway. It was the total effect that he'd been after. Only the perfectionist in him had egged him on to try to improve on what he'd done.

Dana's brows came together as she studied the mural more closely. Was he serious or just seeing how gullible she was?

Glancing over her shoulder, she pinned him with a look that forbade him to lie. "You did this?"

He nodded. To him, it was no big deal. The ability to put brush to canvas had always been with him. Something he'd inherited from his mother.

"Painting relaxes me. I don't get much of a chance to do it anymore."

Or at all, if he was being truthful. Life had become one hell of a toboggan ride this last year. He hadn't taken more than a day off at a time in eighteen months. There was too much to do, and his practice continued to grow. He had trouble saying no when it involved children.

Like now. He smiled at his newest patient and was rewarded with a timid half-smile in return. Nothing better, he thought. The smile of a child was priceless and innocent. Unlike its adult counterpart.

Hands on either side of Mollie's waist, Rafe lifted her onto the examining table. It vaguely registered that he had textbooks that felt heavier than she did.

"Now then," he began in his kindest voice, looking straight into her eyes, "how old are you, Mollie?" Mollie held up five fingers. "I see." He nodded solemnly, taking in the information. "And what seems to be the problem?"

Mollie wiggled a little, blossoming in response to his tone. "I cough."

"I see." He looked properly serious. "Is it a big cough or

a little cough?'' He let the question sink in before continuing. ''Is it a cough that comes a lot?''

Mollie paused, thinking. ''A lot.''

Forcing a cough, she gave him her best demonstration. It sounded suspiciously as if she was having trouble clearing her throat.

But Rafe nodded as if impressed by what he'd heard. He took his stethoscope from around his neck and placed the ends to his ears. ''Well, let's just see what it sounds like inside you.''

Her eyes on the instrument, Mollie scrambled back on the table, moving so quickly she nearly tumbled off. Rafe grabbed the side of her overalls, catching her just in time. Dana's hands were right on top of his, less than half a heartbeat behind.

She dropped her hands to her side. ''Mollie, be careful.''

But Mollie's attention was riveted on Rafe. The fear was back, stronger than before. She'd lain in a hospital bed, her arms held down, funny long tubes running through them. She was afraid he would take her back there.

''Are you going to open me up?'' Her voice trembled. So did she.

He resisted the impulse to hug her to him until the fear had been blotted out. Instead, one hand on her shoulder to hold her still, Rafe calmly explained what he was about to do.

''We don't have to open you up, Mollie. I just listen with this.'' He tapped the stethoscope, then took it off for her to examine. He suspected that, like him, she appreciated knowing the enemy. It made things less frightening and mysterious. ''Ever see one of these?''

''She's been in the hospital,'' Dana cut in, wishing he would hurry up.

She was feeling incredibly tired all of a sudden. Fatigue had come like a huge, smothering blanket, dropping out of nowhere and oppressing her. All she could think of doing was going to Sheila's and crawling into bed once Mollie was taken care of. She vaguely recalled hearing that pregnancy did that to you in the early stages. Wiped you out without notice. Another reason to resent her condition.

Having momentarily allayed Mollie's fears, Rafe laid the stethoscope to her chest and prompted her to breathe. "When was she in the hospital?" he wanted to know.

"Six months ago," Dana answered tersely.

Was that anger in her voice? Why? He hadn't asked her anything particularly difficult or private. If he was going to treat Mollie, these were things he had to know.

Rafe turned Mollie around, pressing the stethoscope to her back, telling her to breathe again. "Why? What was she in for?"

Dana watched Mollie's face. The little girl was too involved with what the doctor was doing to pay attention to the conversation. Good.

"She was in a car accident," Dana said softly. "She had cuts, internal bruising and a broken wrist."

The same accident, Rafe surmised from the woman's tone, that had robbed the little girl of her mother. He wondered where the child's father was, and whether he took an active part in his daughter's life.

"Sound like quite an ordeal. I guess that makes you an expert," he said to Mollie. "You know, this little thing can pick up your heartbeat." Taking the stethoscope off, he angled the earpiece so that Mollie could listen to her own heart. The wonder that spread over her face tickled him. "How does that sound?"

Mollie wrinkled her nose. "Funny." She wasn't sure if she was being teased or not. Aunt Dana's friend Slade teased her, but he laughed when he did it. "Is that really me?"

"That's really you," he assured her. He coaxed the stethoscope from her fingers and hung it carefully in its place on a rack. "And that funny little noise you just heard is a very comforting sound for everyone who loves you."

"There's just Aunt Dana," Mollie solemnly told him, as if it was a secret. "And my grandpa," she remembered. Mollie leaned forward, lowering her voice. "Except that he doesn't really love me."

Rafe studied her face, trying to discern whether the little girl was being fanciful or telling the truth. And just what that might mean to Mollie's general well-being. He was always on the alert for cases of abuse. To him, there was no more heinous crime than the willful abuse of a child.

"Are you sure? I can't see anyone not loving a pretty little girl like you." Since she didn't launch into an immediate litany of what she took to be her grandfather's offense, or pull back into her shell, both indications of trouble, he decided that perhaps he was just overreacting. "Maybe you should give him another chance."

Mollie willingly agreed. "Okay." She looked at Dana for backup.

Dana had no intention of getting into a personal conversation with Mollie in front of a stranger, even if he was a pediatrician who was thought to walk on water. Since Mollie had never met her grandfather, Dana assumed that Mollie's statement could be traced to something the little girl had overheard her parents discussing. It went without saying that neither Megan nor George would ever have said anything remotely as harsh to Mollie directly.

In any case, none of this was any of the doctor's business.

"So, can you tell what's wrong with her?" Dana pressed, redirecting the conversation.

"When did this cough start?" As he spoke, Rafe continued with his examination. Mollie watched in fascination as her knee jerked in response to the little rubber hammer.

Dana paused, trying to think. Her mind felt as if it was sinking into a fog. "Two weeks ago."

He set the hammer down, picked up another instrument and examined Mollie's eyes. "Describe it."

"It's a cough," she answered shortly.

He glanced at her, apparently unfazed by her tone. "Hacking? Dry? Wet? Intermittent or continuous? Adjectives are very usefully when I play doctor."

She blew out a breath, knowing she had no right to be impatient. He was doing her a favor. It was just that this sudden wave of exhaustion was making her irritable.

"Dry, intermittent. For the past few days it's sounded as if it's getting worse." Dana edged closer to him, as if she could somehow see what he saw if only she stood close enough. "What does she have?" she asked again.

"The good news is that she doesn't seem to have the flu that's making the rounds." About every fourth child he'd seen in the last few days had a case of it, and half of those were severe. The beds at the hospital were filling up quickly.

Having carefully examined each nostril, he shut off the light and laid the instrument on a metal tray. "From what I can see, Mollie has URI—an upper respiratory infection. Don't worry, that sounds a lot worse than it is." He skimmed the tip of his finger down Mollie's small nose. "I'll write you a prescription, and she'll be fine in no time."

Dana was sure he was wrong. There had to be more to it than that. "And that's it?"

Rafe nodded. He heard the outer door closing. That meant the others had gone home for the day. Time for him to wrap this up, too. "Is she allergic to any medications?"

"Not that I know of."

He picked up his pad and wrote out a prescription for Amoxicillin. There wasn't a child born who didn't like the bubble-gum taste of the pink liquid. He tore the sheet off and handed it to Mollie's aunt.

"This should take care of any lingering infection. One teaspoon, three times a day. Keep it in the refrigerator, and make sure she finishes the bottle. If there's any problem, call me. I'll be happy to see her." Then, because he couldn't resist, he tousled Mollie's hair. "But more than likely, there won't be any need to. This dazzling young lady's going to be just fine."

Which was more, he thought, than he could say about her aunt. The woman's face was definitely pale, and her eyes looked glassy. "Are you all right?"

She probably looked like hell. God knew she felt like it. Embarrassed, impatient and exhausted, Dana waved away his question and gathered Mollie in her arms, taking her off the table. This was all the medicine she needed, she thought, right here in her arms.

"I'm fine," Dana murmured. "Just adjusting to a different time zone, that's all."

Walking her into the hall, he shut off the light behind him. "You're not from around here?"

She'd been born not ten miles from the medical building they were standing in. At the very hospital Dr. Saldana was affiliated with. The one where Sheila worked. "I am, but not recently."

He'd thought he'd detected a tiny trace of an accent, but it wasn't strong enough for him to pinpoint. "Where *are* you from? Recently."

She answered before the thought there was no reason for him to ask or to know occurred to her. "Dallas." And if she never went back, that was fine with her. Because Dallas meant Steven.

Setting Mollie on the floor, Dana took her hand and went to the receptionist's desk.

But there was no one sitting there. There was no one in the office at all. Surprised, she turned to look at the doctor. "Do I pay you?"

It was late, and he would be damned if he was going to start messing with Alice's system at this hour. The woman had everything coded and locked up. She was a jewel when it came to running the office, but she did have her idiosyncrasies. Being deemed indispensable was one of them, and the way she accomplished that was having a system that would have taken the CIA five days to crack.

Rafe raised a shoulder and let it drop carelessly. "It's on the house." It was a lot simpler that way. He knew there was no file set up on Mollie, so there was nowhere to make an initial payment notation. Besides, he'd only spent a few minutes with her.

Maybe she was being unduly sensitive, Dana thought, but she had her pride. She wasn't about to accept charity from a stranger. "I can pay."

Obviously he'd struck a nerve. "I'm sure you can." Rafe indicated the computer. "But Alice has a program running on that thing that defies logic, and after a long day, I don't feel like fooling around with it." It was off, and there was no way he was going to turn it on. He'd learned the hard way that it responded only to her password. Technology was wonderful, as long as someone else's fingers were on the keyboard. "I owe Sheila a favor. Tell her this makes us square."

It didn't square anything, Dana thought. It was Sheila he owed the favor to, not her. She took out her wallet and extracted a plastic card. She offered it to him. "Can't you just take a charge card?"

Stubborn, he thought. It wasn't a quality he normally admired unless coupled with gaining a lifelong goal or beating the odds and getting well. For the most part, it was irritating.

Very gingerly, he pushed the card toward her with the tips of his fingers.

"I can *take* it, but there isn't much I can *do* with it. Her desk's locked." He jiggled the drawer to show her. It remained shut. "If my writing off this visit somehow offends your sense of dignity or self-esteem, you can pay Alice the next time you come."

She wasn't sure if she liked his attitude. He was a little too flippant for her taste. Doctors were supposed to be somber, capable and not opinionated.

"The next time?" she repeated. Her eyes narrowed as she read more into the remark than he'd intended. "Does Mollie need a more thorough workup?"

"No, but she does need a regular pediatrician." He assumed she didn't have one or Sheila would have mentioned it. "I take it that you and Mollie are staying in the area?"

There were no options open to her right now, and even if there were, there was a responsibility to face. That precluded leaving anytime soon.

"Yes, we are."

He placed his hand on the small of her back to usher her toward the door. She jumped as if he'd touched her with a hot poker. Wondering what that was about, he silently indicated the door, then walked beside her when she finally moved.

"Good, then I'll look forward to seeing you again." The words were addressed to Mollie, whose shy smile had broadened. "Here, let me get that for you," he offered just as Dana reached for the doorknob. The door tended to stick.

"That's all right, we can see ourselves out." Turning the knob, she felt resistance. Dana braced herself and pulled, refusing to ask for help after she had just turned it down. "Thank you," she told him formally before she walked out.

Mollie waved, then grasped her aunt's hand.

"Stubborn." The door closed with the firm snap of a lock slipping into place. Rafe shook his head. "Definitely got a burr under her saddle."

Well, that was her problem. He had other things that needed his attention. Specifically, seven patients under the age of eleven with the flu, waiting for him to make his rounds at the hospital. And Timmie.

He thought of the small boy. Timmie didn't have the flu. Rafe only wished he did. He didn't know what was wrong with the six-year-old, and he was growing progressively worse. The boy was far too young to spend his days in a hospital bed. But he needed more help than Rafe could give him. Timmie needed a specialist.

And maybe a miracle or two along the way.

Too bad he wasn't in the business of making them.

He was never going to get used to it, Rafe thought. He would never truly make peace with the fact that he couldn't cure every patient who came to him. Despite the fact that he had lost his wife, Debra, during his second year of residency, he still believed deep down that he could keep all his patients well if he tried hard enough. It was his mother's optimism and his father's silent but nonetheless strong reinforcement of it that had forged the way he thought, the way he approached his life and his work.

It didn't matter who took the credit or the blame, Rafe mused. He was what he was. A man who refused to give up even in the face of defeat. Timmie was going to get well. He'd promised the boy.

Rafe went to the telephone. Maybe he would give Jim Reilly a call. His former medical school roommate was associated with the pediatric wing of the Mayo Clinic these days. No harm in approaching him for some unofficial help. What mattered was curing Timmie and licking this thing that was slowly weakening him.

He did a quick calculation on the time difference. It was late back east. Jim undoubtedly wasn't in his office now, but Rafe had several numbers he could try. Jim had to be at one of them.

Rafe sat down, stretching his legs out beneath the desk his parents had had custom-built for him. It was a gift delivered the week before he'd opened his doors for the first time.

As if they hadn't already given him more than any son could hope for.

Sighing, Rafe pulled the phone over and began tapping out the first number. It looked like it was going to be another long evening.

Sheila arrived at her house fifteen minutes after Dana and Mollie returned from their visit to the doctor. Throwing her jacket in the general direction of an antique coatrack, she announced that she had only come home to check on Slade and Rebecca before dashing to the hospital. En route home, she'd answered her cell phone, only to hear that Mrs. Masterson's twins had decided to put in an early appearance.

Mr. Masterson was on his way to the hospital with his wife. He'd sounded as if he was about to come apart when he called. She sincerely hoped he would get a grip on himself long enough to arrive at Harris Memorial in one piece.

After kissing Slade and peeking in on Rebecca, who was

sound asleep in her crib, Sheila quickly turned her attention to Dana.

She stopped to pick up one of her housekeeper's sandwiches. Pilar threw in everything but the kitchen sink. It was just what Sheila needed right now, energy on rye.

"So..." She eyed Dana as she threw the thick sandwich into a paper sack. "What did you think of him?"

Dana shrugged. She didn't want to be too critical. After all, the man was a friend of Sheila's. "He was nice to Mollie. He put her at ease." And that was the most important thing.

There was something in Dana's tone that indicated she was less than thrilled with Rafe. Sheila had expected a more positive response. Everyone else she'd sent to Rafe raved about him. "Didn't I tell you he was terrific?"

Dana's exhaustion had passed. Restless now, she felt like going for a long walk. Instead, she accompanied Sheila to the living room. She saw no point in lying. They were too close for that. But she did try to play up the positive, though there was something about him that rubbed her the wrong way.

"I wouldn't go that far. I wasn't there long enough to label him terrific. But the fact that he didn't terrify Mollie is a definite point in his favor. He has a nice manner when it comes to children."

And women, Sheila thought. Although Dana seemed to be immune to it. Her friend had lost some of her sparkle, some of her energy. It wasn't all due to the pregnancy or even the news that she was pregnant. This was not the same person she'd known. Dana seemed to have been born with a streetwise edge to her, but it had always been tempered, balanced out by her positive approach to life. Somewhere along the line, Steven or someone else had snuffed out the light that was Dana.

For now, Sheila kept her thoughts to herself. "What did he say was wrong with her?"

"An upper respiratory infection."

Sheila nodded. "Very common. Probably prescribed Amoxicillin, right?"

"Right." Dana looked at Mollie, dubious. "I don't know...."

Sheila knew that look, had seen it reflected at her in the mirror despite all the training she'd had. "Know," she echoed. "I'm sure he's right." She slipped an arm around Dana's shoulders, pulling her close. "Welcome to motherhood, Dana," Sheila teased. "If it's not one worry, it's another."

Dana was quickly learning that. Learning, too, that maybe she wasn't equipped for this. There was no way she would give up Mollie, but the baby who was growing within her...well, she didn't know that child yet. Maybe she should start thinking about giving it up for adoption. It would be the simpler thing to do.

"How do women stand it?" she wanted to know.

Ah, Sheila thought, the eternal question. Luckily, the answer was just as eternal.

"Because, my dear, squeezed in between the emergencies, the tantrums and the sleepless nights are the little slices of heaven that are absolutely priceless. Judging from your expression, you already know what I mean."

Dana laughed softly. "Yeah, I know what you mean."

Caring for Mollie these past few months had made her feel more fulfilled than she had in years. It centered her and gave her a purpose. She couldn't think just of herself anymore. There was someone else who was directly affected by everything she did, everything she said.

It was a very sobering experience.

And one, she knew, she wouldn't have traded for the world. Because having Mollie depend on her made her feel that she was equal to anything, including beginning a new life.

And trying to make amends with an old one, she suddenly thought, an image of her father in her mind.

Before it was too late.

Chapter 3

Rafe ran his hand along the back of his neck, slowly kneading the muscles beneath his mop of damp, black hair. It didn't do any good. The muscles were hours past being stiff and were in all probability on their way to becoming permanently fused into a rigid state.

It felt as if he'd spent every minute of the past three days when he wasn't at his office leaning over the railings of hospital beds and cribs, assuring his small patients—those who could understand him—and their worried parents that all would be well in a few days.

Was it his imagination, or had the annual flu season shifted its timetable to appear earlier and stay longer the past few years? It felt as if he'd been through this endless whirlwind of patients and hospital beds only a couple of months ago. As of late this afternoon, the pediatric wing at Harris Memorial was almost filled to capacity. The latest outbreak went under the whimsical identifying marker of the Singapore flu, although as far as he knew its origins were far less exotic.

Closing his eyes, Rafe took a deep breath and then exhaled

slowly. Maybe, if he stood very still, no one would notice him for five minutes. That was all he asked, just five minutes. It seemed to be his quota of rest time these days.

"Buy you a soda, sailor?"

Rafe opened his eyes and smiled before he saw her, recognizing the voice. He eyed the can of pop in her hand. "I could use more than a soda, Sheila."

"Sorry, I'm a married woman. You'll have to see someone else about that. Maybe Kate." Exhausted, Sheila leaned against the wall beside Rafe, her trim figure all but hidden beneath the green surgical livery. The mask she'd worn only ten minutes ago was dangling about her neck like a limp badge of courage. It had been a tough delivery, but it was over, and she could finally relax.

Until the next frantic call.

She peered at the tall man beside her. Rafe looked tired. Bone tired. Because they were friends, she asked, "*Have* you seen Kate lately?"

It had been more than four years since his wife had died. She'd hoped that when he started seeing one of the hospital's research biologists, Kate Mulligan, just before Christmas last year, that meant he was taking his heart out of the deep freeze. But Kate's willingness notwithstanding, the relationship didn't seem to be destined for the altar. There was something missing in Rafe's eyes whenever Kate's name came up. Something she'd seen when he had been married to Debra.

A bemused smile lifted his mouth as he gave her question due consideration.

"Actually, I don't think I've even seen the sun lately." Or, at least, he hadn't paid attention to it. Between the flu, stray patients and Timmie's mysterious ailment, he was too preoccupied to pay attention to anything.

Sheila popped the top of her can. A gentle fizz emerged, then retreated.

"It hasn't changed," she assured him, taking a long, deep drink. She offered the can to Rafe, but he passed. "Still round, still yellow. Except at sunset." She sighed, remembering the first time she had been with her husband. It had been at sunset. On the beach. He hadn't been her husband then. "I really need to see a sunset again. With Slade."

Rafe heard the longing in her voice and understood. The kind of hours they kept could be brutal. It was the price they paid for making a difference. When he wasn't falling on his face with exhaustion, like now, he figured it was worth it.

"Then you should have become a dermatologist. No one calls a dermatologist in the middle of the night to deliver an eight-pound boil." It was well past midnight. Never enough time, he thought. Rafe looked at the woman he'd interned with. It had pleased him beyond words when he had discovered that the same hospital had accepted them both once residency had become nothing more than an ugly, grueling memory. "So, what brings you to my neck of the woods? The nursery window is in the other direction."

She had heard him paged over the loudspeaker earlier in the evening and come looking for him straight out of the delivery room, hoping he was still on the premises. "I came to get you."

"Me?" Rafe straightened, the doctor in him taking over. "Why?"

"I thought you might want to examine your newest patient."

He thought of the small child with the wide eyes who'd come to see him after hours. And the pale-looking woman who had hovered protectively over her. Had he missed something during his examination?

"Mollie's here?"

Completely absorbed by the last delivery, she'd forgotten about sending Mollie to him. Chagrined, Sheila shook her head. "No, even newer than that. By the way, thanks for seeing Mollie on such short notice. Dana's an old friend, and she seemed pretty worried. I thought a pediatrician would set her mind at ease better than I could, and we all know you're the best."

Rafe ignored her last comment. Compliments only tended

to embarrass him. Instead, he recalled the woman who had been in his office earlier and the air of edgy distrust she'd exuded.

"She didn't seem all that friendly to me," he observed.

"That would make her the first." Though he seemed oblivious to it, he'd been the object of lustful comments since the day he'd arrived at the hospital. "Frankly, I don't know how you manage to keep from being yanked into the linen closet with a fair amount of regularity."

They shared the kind of relationship that was reminiscent of siblings, he and Sheila. There were times when he found talking to her immensely comforting. Other times, it was just entertaining. This was both. "Maybe I'm too large to fit."

She grinned. "Ah, you underestimate how resourceful a determined woman can be. I think you manage to avoid women having their way with you because you're oblivious to their very blatant attentions."

Rafe shrugged carelessly. He'd had his one all-consuming relationship. As far as he was concerned, that was enough for him. What he shared with Kate was a mutual interest in a variety of areas—and the luxury of being thought off the market by everyone else. It spared him embarrassing entanglements he had no time or desire for. And he did enjoy Kate's company—when their schedules permitted getting together.

Right now, he was having trouble mustering the strength to put one foot in front of the other.

Rafe turned to Sheila. "This newer patient you want me to see, does he or she have a name?"

The question made her laugh. Rafe raised a brow, waiting. If there was a joke, he could certainly stand to be let in on it. His conversation with Jim Reilly about Timmie had done little to help clear up the mystery surrounding the boy's progressively deteriorating condition.

"Only a last one," Sheila told him. "The parents were still arguing about what name to put down—or, actually, names, they had twins—when I left the delivery room. They were hoping for girls."

"And they got two boys." Murphy's Law.

Rafe smiled. He had to admit he would have been rooting for a girl if he was the one awaiting an arrival. Girls were less trouble than boys. At least, that was what his mother had always sworn. But then, he mused, she'd only had him and Gabe to go by. There were times when they were growing up that Lizzie Borden would have been less trouble than they were.

The smile turned into a grin. That, too, had come from his mother.

Sheila nodded. "Six pounds three ounces, and six, one."

"Ouch." Wincing, he let out a low whistle of appreciation. "Doesn't sound like Mama had an easy time of it."

That was definitely putting it mildly. Mrs. Arthur Masterson had not been reticent in her expression of anguish and pain, nor in her thoughts about her husband's future chances of ever laying a hand on her again, in or out of their bedroom. The nurses were going to be talking about this delivery for weeks.

"She certainly didn't. My ears are going to be ringing for a month. I'm surprised you didn't hear her." She took another sip. The bubbles were fading. "I would have laid odds that all of Newport Beach heard her sometime during the past six hours."

Rafe had spent the past half hour with a sick little girl and her worried parents. Nothing had occupied his mind at the time but making them feel at ease. Allison Adray's mother was a hypochondriac who saw the handwriting of God on the wall when only smudge marks were evident to the eye. It had taken a great deal of patience to explain that Allison only had the flu and not something far more fatal, despite what it seemed like to her mother.

He wished he could say the same thing to Timmie's parents.

For a moment, he debated sharing his burden with Sheila. When they had interned together, they'd acted as each other's buffer. Sheila had been there for him, as much as anyone could be, when his wife had died. But Sheila had her own concerns. She didn't need to hear about his. Somehow, he would find a way to work things out.

Rafe shrugged casually. "Sometimes I get lucky."

Sheila thought of the way the nurses talked about Rafe. As if he was a Greek god who regularly walked amid the mortals. Every one of them wanted her chance to touch immortality, she thought with a smile.

"I'm sure you could if you wanted to." She laughed softly when he gave her a bewildered look. "Come on, I'll introduce you to Baby Boy Masterson—One and Two. Maybe, if they get desperate enough, his parents will name one of them after you."

With the ease of a longtime friend, Rafe let himself be led off. "I could live with that."

"You're sure you want to do this so soon?"

Concern etched itself on Sheila's face as she stood regarding Dana. She'd come into Dana's room this morning to find that her friend was getting ready to see her father. Though she had been the one who had written to Dana about her father's stroke and failing condition, she was having second thoughts. Dana had had so much grief in her life these last few months, and Sheila wanted to spare her the confrontation she feared lay ahead for as long as possible.

Sheila laid a hand on Dana's arm. "You know you're welcome to stay here."

Because Mollie was still asleep, despite the fact that it was close to nine in the morning, Dana drew Sheila into the hall before answering.

"If you say that one more time, I'm going to have it embroidered on a pillow and plopped on your sofa in front of the fireplace."

She saw the protest rising to Sheila's lips. In a way, Dana thought, she was very lucky. Some people went their whole lives without finding a friend like Sheila. She knew Sheila meant what she said. Sheila and Slade would let her remain here for as long as she needed to. But she'd always prided herself on being able to stand on her own two feet. It was time she found them again.

Dana took both of her friend's hands in hers. "Sheila, you're a wonderful friend, and I appreciate everything you've done for me—"

Sheila didn't want her gratitude. She wanted Dana's peace of mind. She'd talked it all out with Slade the night after Dana and Mollie had arrived, and it was all right with him if the invitation was open-ended. His generosity of spirit was onc of thc rcasons she loved him so much. With all her heart, she wished Dana could find someone like Slade.

"What everything?" Sheila wanted to know. "It's not as if I built the bed single-handedly." A hint of a smile played on her lips. "I had help. Seriously, the bedroom was just standing there, empty. No reason it shouldn't have someone in it." She touched Dana's cheek. Sheila knew stubbornness when she saw it, and she was seeing it now. "A very special someone."

Special. When had she ever heard that word applied to her? Only once. But Steven was known for his short attention span. And it had been a lie, anyway. "Thanks, I needed that."

Sheila looked into her eyes, searching for the bravado, the steel underpinnings, she knew had to be there somewhere. They needed to be coaxed into evidence again. "You don't need me to tell you that you're special, Dana. You already know that."

It was what Dana had believed once, but that had been hubris. Like her father, she supposed. And if that was the case, she deserved to have been shot down.

"Okay," Dana said, "maybe I just needed to hear it." Sheila meant well, and she wasn't about to pay back her hospitality by arguing with her. "It doesn't make facing my father after all these years any easier, but it does help knowing that everyone doesn't see me the way he does, as completely lacking in every area." Her father hadn't attended Megan and George's funeral. To Dana, that had been the ultimate insult.

Yet here she was, trying to ignore it. Trying to ignore years of bad feelings.

Sheila thought of Paul Morrow. She'd grown up with misconceptions about her own parents because of a communication gap. Could the same be true of Dana and her father?

"Dana, I know it's hard to accept." Very slowly, Sheila tested the ground she was crossing before continuing. Dana's face remained impassive. "But maybe your father just has trouble expressing how he feels. Some men do, you know, even in our generation. And he's from the last generation, the one that dictates a man can't cry, can't let his feelings show."

That all sounded very nice, and Dana had no doubt that in some cases, for some men, it was true. But not her father. She knew better. The only thing that meant anything to her father was found within the arena of the courtroom.

"He never had any trouble expressing his displeasure." She heard a noise coming from the bedroom and peeked in. Mollie was still asleep. Probably having a dream. She hoped it wouldn't turn into one of her nightmares. "No, I think the only thing my father had—and *has*—trouble with is that God didn't give him children he felt were worth his while. I suspect he wanted sons who were exact replicas of him. Clones."

Dana pressed her lips together before she said anything more. If she wasn't careful, she was going to talk herself right out of doing what she felt she had to do. She'd returned to Bedford, rather than going somewhere else, for a reason, and she couldn't allow old wounds to get in the way.

Resigned, determined, Dana turned toward the stairs and headed down. Standing here talking about the past wasn't going to help her with the present.

Sheila was right behind her.

"Even so, I've got to go see him." Dana directed the words over her shoulder. "When he's gone, I don't want some kernel of guilt suddenly popping open inside me years down the line, telling me I should have tried to mend the break that's between us. It'll be too late then. I want to know that at least I did my part. If he doesn't want to do his—and he won't,'' she interjected before Sheila could offer her any platitudes to the contrary, ''well, then that will be that, won't it? But at least my conscience will be clear.''

''Parents have a way of surprising you,'' Sheila observed.

Hers had. She sincerely hoped that Paul Morrow would, too. Time had a way of mellowing people, making them see their mistakes. She doubted that anything in the world could have made Dana agree to be in the same room with her father five years ago, much less initiate the encounter. If Dana could mellow, why couldn't her father?

Dana shook her head. She held no such hope. ''Not mine. If there were any surprises, they came out of the box years ago.'' She looked up the stairs and wondered if she should take Mollie with her after all. She didn't like leaving the little girl, although the idea of exposing her to what might go on between her and her father appealed to Dana even less. She bit her lip, debating. ''Pilar's okay with watching Mollie until I get back?''

At least here Sheila could set Dana's mind at ease. ''Are you kidding? Pilar's the original earth mother. I don't know what I'd do without her.'' The woman's cooking abilities left a little to be desired, but the way she cared for Rebecca more than made up for that. Sheila had no reservations about leaving her child or anyone else's with Pilar.

A high-pitched noise suddenly wedged its way into the conversation, throbbing rhythmically as it demanded immediate attention. Angling the pager she wore on her belt, Sheila looked at it with resignation. It took her a moment to associate a name with the number she saw.

''Mrs. Gaetano.'' She silenced the pager. According to her records, Faye Gaetano wasn't due for another two weeks, but the woman had looked ripe enough to pop on her visit last Monday. ''This is going to play havoc with my office hours again.''

''Another early baby?'' Even as she asked, Dana was conscious of the child she was carrying. The one who had no place in her life but was there anyway.

Sheila went to the nearest telephone and picked up the receiver as she sighed. "My third this month. Must be something in the air."

Ambivalent feelings tugged at Dana, adding to the stress she was trying to manage. "Just how cold was it here last winter?"

"Obviously too cold. Business is booming, you should only pardon the expression." Sheila began dialing, then stopped when Dana opened the front door. "Will I see you when I get back?" she asked hopefully. If things went as badly between Dana and her father as Dana anticipated, Sheila was afraid she might pick Mollie up and leave without a word to anyone. That was the way it had happened last time—after a row with her father, Dana had disappeared.

"Count on it."

Sheila replaced the receiver. Mrs. Gaetano had waited this long, she could wait another minute. She surprised Dana by crossing to her and kissing her cheek. Then, moving back, Sheila used her thumb to rub away the slight trace of pink she'd branded Dana with. "Good luck."

Dana managed a smile. "Thanks. I have a feeling I'll need it."

She almost turned back twice, once halfway to her father's estate and once as she pulled up the massive driveway where she and Megan had played when they were children.

Before life had caught up to them.

But she didn't turn back. She forced herself on. In the driveway, she shut off the engine, then pocketed the key. She supposed her determination to see this through gave her something in common with her father. To her recollection, he had never backed away from a fight. On the contrary, he relished fights and the attention they garnered. He was never more alive than when he was defending a client. It seemed to her that for the price of a retainer, her father felt he owed his client far more than he owed his family.

Maybe her mother would have done better retaining him instead of marrying him.

Dana neither relished confrontations nor craved the attention, but she refused to back away. At least, she refused to back away anymore. She'd run from this house once, when life had gotten so intolerable she couldn't endure it any longer.

That had obviously been a mistake.

She was through running. Through running from her past, from her father. From everything. She was making her stand. Forging a present so that there could be a future.

This was for Mollie as much as for herself. And, she thought with a sigh, for her father. She supposed that she owed him something in return for the creature comforts she'd enjoyed while growing up. God knew she'd never lacked for anything material.

A bitter smile twisted her lips. She would have traded it all if, just for the space of one hour, she had felt as if her father loved her. Loved her not as an extension of his shadow, a bearer of the Morrow name, but as herself. As Dana.

But love was the one thing Paul Morrow couldn't dispense, because he couldn't buy it, and he had none of his own to give.

It had started raining when she'd left Sheila's, and rain followed her to her father's house. Somehow, that seemed appropriate.

Leaving her car in the center of the driveway, Dana got out and shut the door firmly. It amused her that her battered little white car looked so incongruous standing here, where only expensive cars had always been parked. The clients and associates who passed through the doors of Paul Morrow's estate were all upper crust or, barring that, at least well-moneyed. Chieftains of the corporate world, movie stars, celebrities from all walks of life, her father had rubbed elbows with them all, waiting for his next splashy trial, his next encounter with the media and fame.

As a child, she'd been awed by the parade of people. But,

relegated to the sidelines, deprived of the attention she sought from her father, watching her mother grow more and more remote as she sank deeper into anesthetizing alcohol, she'd soon tired of the circus, eventually growing to resent it.

But she hadn't come here to dwell on that or rehash past offenses. She'd come to see a father who was ailing. A father whose time left on earth might very well be finite. He'd had a stroke and been diagnosed with Parkinson's. While neither had defeated him, they certainly had limited him.

There was a time, she remembered, a very long time ago, when she'd thought Paul Morrow was invincible. She had no doubt that he'd thought the same thing.

Surprise.

Squaring her shoulders and turning up her collar against the fine mist, she went to meet the man she hadn't seen in eight years.

The queasiness that rippled from her stomach as she approached the towering double doors caught her off guard and nearly stopped her in her tracks.

"How about that—your unborn grandchild is afraid of you and he doesn't even know you," she murmured cynically under her breath. "It won't be any different when he does."

To know him is to fear him, wasn't that something one of his opponents had said? At the time it hadn't been applicable only to his adversaries in court, but to his family, as well. Her father had moods when they cowered and ran for cover.

And through it all, her mother had gone on loving him until the day she died. Dana couldn't understand it.

Had to be something there, she decided. Her mother, once a promising nurse practitioner who had given it all up to be Mrs. Paul S. Morrow, hadn't been a fool. Except for loving the wrong man.

Taking a deep breath, Dana rang the bell. The chimes sounded like hushed cathedral bells. She supposed her father had thought that appropriate. *You are now entering sacred ground.*

There was no answer. Dana counted to ten as slowly as

she could, then moved to ring the doorbell again. Before she could, the door swung open.

Esther.

The face of the tall, thin woman standing on the other side of the threshold transformed from politely reserved to joyous in the space of a breath as she recognized the visitor.

The housekeeper took a step forward, blocking the doorway with her body even though her employer was nowhere near this part of the house. She vividly remembered their parting.

"Miss Dana, is that you?"

God, but it was good to see her, good to see a familiar face and feel welcomed. She could feel herself smiling with relief.

"Yes, it's me. How've you been, Esther?"

Very little fazed Esther Cooper. It was one of the reasons she'd remained employed so long in the Morrow household, while others had come and gone. Paul Morrow valued people who knew how to control their emotions and hold their tongues.

But there were tears on Esther's lashes.

"Come in out of the rain, child." Dispensing with decorum, Esther threw her arms around the woman she had raised from a small child. The hug was warm and intense, as if she was convincing herself that Dana was actually there. She'd worried about her over the years, wondering where she was and what she was doing. And if she was well.

Standing back, she took full measure of the younger woman. Some of the wild rebellion was gone from her eyes, and she looked weary. This was no longer the go-to-hell teenager who had stormed out the door so many years ago.

"You look so thin, I hardly recognized you."

Dana laughed quietly, struggling with emotion she wasn't prepared for. "You should talk. If you didn't have rocks in your pockets, you would have blown away during one of the Santanas long ago. Those winds from the desert can get pretty mean."

Esther sniffed. "Tame stuff after what I've been through

over all these years.'' The hushed whisper was all she could manage at the moment. She pressed her lips together, drinking in the sight of Dana. ''I thought I'd never see you again.''

''That goes double for me. I know that's what my father hoped.'' Dana felt her courage flagging and clutched at it. She'd come this far—she had to see it through. ''Is he here, Esther?''

She couldn't help it. Part of Dana hoped that he wasn't here but at the office, the place she'd always thought of as his real home. Despite his failing health, or maybe because of it, she knew he would continue going to the office, continue taking cases, damning people if they cut him any slack because he was ill. Even so, on another plane, she knew he would use his illness, just as he used everything else, as a tool to help him win. It cast unconscious sympathy on his side.

Esther nodded. ''He's getting a late start today. It's been a bad week for him.''

Dana didn't want to think about what that meant. It was easier to seek refuge in cynicism. She'd learned the art of doing that at the knee of a master. ''Time away from the courtroom and the TV cameras always was.''

She looked around. It surprised her how little everything had changed. But then, had she really expected it to? The house had been decorated for the sole purpose of impressing whoever stepped through these doors. Why should anything change? The criteria hadn't.

Dana waited for a wave of nostalgia, of something, to hit her. She waited in vain. There were no warm feelings waiting for her here. This had ceased to be a home a long time ago, becoming instead an ornate mausoleum where she and her sister had felt more like prisoners than daughters. Wealthy, pampered prisoners, but prisoners nonetheless. Prisoners of her father's fame, of his expectations, of his moods.

''I've come to see him, Esther.''

If she was surprised, Esther gave no indication. Instead,

she inclined her head, ever the accommodating servant. "Shall I announce you?"

And give him time to prepare? No, she didn't think so. "I think I'd rather do that myself. For once, I'd like to catch him off guard. Which room?"

"He's in the downstairs den."

"How appropriate."

Telling herself he couldn't hurt her anymore, Dana went to face the man the newspapers had once dubbed "the lion of the courtroom."

Chapter 4

His back was to her as she entered the room. Even so, she could feel the old reaction coming over her. A pinching sensation in the pit of her stomach that threatened to slice it in half. It was too late in the day for morning sickness. This was Paul Morrow sickness. She had certainly lived through enough bouts to recognize it.

For a moment, because it was so artfully constructed, she didn't realize he was sitting in a wheelchair. Amid the jumble of nerves that had accompanied her in the drive over here, she'd somehow managed to forget that her father had lost the use of his legs. The stroke, not the disease, had done that to him, robbed him of the ability to stride across the courtroom. Spending his days in a wheelchair was a blow to his pride and to the self-image he'd so carefully constructed.

She wondered who he'd taken that out on. Probably everyone. And, just as probably, it was an ongoing thing. Her father didn't suffer what he took to be indignities and insults in silence.

He might have lost the use of his legs, but not his mind

and not his caustic tongue. Sheila had passed that along in her letter, too, but she needn't have bothered. Dana would have made book on it. As long as there was a breath left in him, her father wouldn't surrender, not to an opponent and not to a disease. She had no doubt that he practiced law harder than ever because he had something to prove to the world.

And maybe, she thought, to himself, though she knew her father would have scathingly chastised anyone who even remotely suggested that might be the case. Because that would point to a character flaw, and everyone knew he didn't have any.

Dana dragged a hand through her damp hair. For a second, she toyed with the idea of leaving before he turned around. But then she realized it was already too late.

He was sitting by a window, a book open on his lap. She could see her reflection in the glass. If she could see it, so could he.

Why hadn't he acknowledged her presence?

Why? she mocked herself. Because he was waiting for her to say the first word, to humbly genuflect before him and pay the great man homage. If he'd been prone to wearing jewelry, he would have wanted her to kiss his ring.

Dana wondered what he would say if he knew that she would gladly have done all of that once if he would only have paid the least bit of attention to his role as her father. If he had only tried to make them a family instead of occupants of a battlefield.

She hadn't wanted a great man, she'd only wanted her father. She'd gotten neither.

Slowly she drew a deep breath, bracing herself. No use lamenting over things that weren't and things that couldn't be.

She stared at the back of his head. He'd gotten gray since she'd seen him. His hair was the color of forged steel. Still thick and lush, it went with the image.

Tired of the waiting game, she met his eyes in the reflection. "Hello, Father."

Only then did he slowly turn the chair. Dana was stunned at how gaunt his face had become. She hadn't realized that, seeing only his reflection. All the more apt to frighten the opposition, she thought.

That would be his response to it. Everything was always aimed toward his goal—wiping out the opposition. Being the most famous defense lawyer of his time.

The sharp blue eyes took slow, full measure of her. There wasn't even so much as a hint of surprise or pleasure. No emotion at all. It was what she'd expected, wasn't it?

"What are you doing here?"

His voice still brought a chill to her. But she could withstand it. She'd gone to hell and back and knew that he was only a minor player in the game. Dana looked at the drops of rain gathered around her shoes.

"Dripping on your carpet, it would appear."

He nodded almost imperceptibly. "You always did make a mess no matter where you went."

He still knew how to aim straight for the heart. Dana thought she'd learned how to control her temper, but confronted with the supreme test, she failed.

Her anger swept over her, cold and galvanizing. "That's it? After eight years, that's all you have to say to me?"

The painfully thin shoulders rustled beneath the jacket of his hand-tailored suit. "I don't know. I haven't had long enough to prepare. Why don't you come back in another eight and I'll see if I can do better?"

Well, she'd certainly left herself open for that, hadn't she? She must have been crazy, having charitable feelings toward her father.

"I don't know what I was thinking of, coming here." Dana turned on her heel, determined to make it out the door in minimum time. "Goodbye."

She was almost there when she heard him ask, "You have a place to stay?"

The question froze her in her tracks. Concern about her welfare? Her comfort? Where had that come from? She turned to see if he was joking. His expression gave nothing away. As usual.

She chose not to tell him that she was staying with Sheila. She wouldn't be, soon enough. "I'll find someplace."

His eyes narrowed, twin lasers meant to cut through to the truth. "That wasn't the question."

He didn't frighten her anymore, she realized. Whether it was the wheelchair or the fact that she was older, she wasn't sure, but it didn't matter. She wasn't afraid of him anymore. She could hear that tone of voice and not cringe.

Dana took a step toward him. "Stop badgering the witness, Counselor."

If he was a storm cloud, there would be lightning and thunder right about now, she guessed. He wasn't pleased with her answer.

"You're not a witness, Dana. You are the worst thing that could possibly exist." His eyes pinned her. "Potential gone awry."

He still thought in terms of himself, of what he had wanted her to do, not what she wanted. He'd made that very clear from the moment she and Megan began attending school. They were to become lawyers, like him. Successful, like him. But never quite as successful. That, too, had gone unsaid, but it was just as important. For no one was allowed to challenge his position as supreme leader.

She stood her ground, refusing to shout, refusing to apologize. Both, she had a feeling, would have given him satisfaction. "No, Father, I was a daughter. A person, not a thing."

He sat looking at her without saying a word. Dana decided she was being dismissed and turned to leave a second time, only to be stopped again.

"Your room is still there."

Was he asking her to stay? She couldn't bring herself to believe that.

"Barring an earthquake—" she turned to face him "—I imagine it would be." Dana tried to read his reaction, but more astute people than she had failed at that. "Was that an invitation?"

Too much had happened between them for Morrow to welcome her back with open arms. He wasn't going to act like some pathetic, sentimental old fool. It was enough that he'd kept tabs on her all these years.

"That's a statement." Even as he said it, he waved it away with his hand. "Do with it what you will."

Dana stared at him, trying to understand. Was he extending a peacemaking gesture, however feeble? It didn't seem possible. It certainly wasn't like him.

And yet…

She studied his face as she spoke. "If I make use of it without your specific invitation, that's breaking and entering, isn't it?" she asked wryly.

She'd always been infuriatingly obstinate, he thought, from the moment she took her first breath during an earthquake that had shaken the foundations of the hospital. It had served as an auspicious announcement of her birth. "Not if the police aren't notified."

Dana watched his eyes as he spoke. There wasn't a flicker of emotion there. He had an ulterior motive. He had to. All her old emotions came flooding back to her, rebellion, anger, hurt. It had taken, what? All of five minutes in his presence? The man was truly in a class by himself.

He wasn't going to get away with it. Ill or not, he was going to be responsible for his actions, for his words. And if, for some strange reason, he'd changed his spots and meant to be kind, in whatever minor fashion, he had to own up to that, too.

"Why would you do that, Father? Why would you allow me to remain?"

He glared at her for questioning him. It was a look that would have frozen the blood in a man's veins. But Dana had gained an immunity over the years. And her own blood ran too hot.

"Your mother would have wanted me to," Morrow finally said.

Oh, no, he wasn't going to hide behind her mother. "You never did anything Mother wanted you to when she was alive. Why start now?"

If she was going to question his actions, then she could damn well take herself out of here. "You want to go, go, you want to stay, stay. It makes no difference to me." He turned the chair so his back was to her.

As if by magic, the anger was siphoned out of her. Maybe it was the sight of his shoulders, once so broad, so arrogant, now the slightest bit bowed. She didn't know. She had no idea why she wanted to throw her arms around him, to comfort him and be comforted. It was a stupid, weak feeling, given the man it was directed toward. But it was there just the same.

"I want Mollie to meet you."

She saw his back stiffen. She knew that Megan making her Mollie's guardian instead of him had angered her father. She would even have said wounded, except that his skin was far too thick for that. The fact that he had thrown Megan out of the house and disowned her when she married George didn't seem to enter into it for him. He saw life only from his point of view.

When he said nothing, she added, "I thought she should know her grandfather."

The chair was turned sharply. He'd been practicing, she thought. Paul Morrow wouldn't allow something like a wheelchair to interfere with the way he conducted himself.

"Why?" he demanded. "Megan didn't think she should."

Something snapped within her when she heard him utter her sister's name so contemptuously. If not for him, Megan and George would still have been in the area. And alive.

Anger gathered, hot and pulsating. "You don't know anything about Megan!"

His tone matched hers. "I know she married beneath her! I know she threw her life away!"

Shouting wasn't going to accomplish anything. Neither were the tears that gathered, a result of the tension she felt. She battled to restrain both. "George was a good man."

Morrow's eyes narrowed beneath brows that were still dark. "He was a *common* man. He didn't have a college education."

She knew it was futile to try to convince him that education was not the measure of a man. Megan had tried in her gentle way and failed. Of the two of them, it had been Megan who had been the favored one. Because Megan had listened, had tried so very hard to please. But he'd never softened to her, either.

"Don't you understand?" Dana demanded. "George made her *happy.*"

The dark look dissolved into a sneer. "There are more important things than being happy." There were responsibility and honor. He'd worked too hard to arrive where he was to watch it threatened by some simple, grinning idiot who could only work with his hands and not his mind. That wasn't part of the image. The carefully crafted image that had cost him so much to maintain.

Her eyes held his, and she didn't flinch. "I don't think so."

"So where is he? The scum you ran off with. The one who made *you* so happy?" He knew exactly where the worthless bastard was, in Texas, bedding some exotic dancer he'd picked up two weeks before Dana had left him. It was all there, every last sordid detail, in the report the detective his firm retained had given him. A coda to the ongoing eight-year assignment of keeping tabs on her.

She didn't want to tell him, but if she wasn't prepared to be honest, then returning was meaningless. She gave him the briefest answer she could. "Steven and I went our separate ways."

Morrow snorted, obviously pleased at being proven right. "About time you came to your senses."

She hated that tone, that smugness. "I didn't come back to talk about Steven."

He leaned forward in his chair, the tough attorney intent on making the witness break down on the stand. ''Why *did* you come back?''

She kept it simple. She'd learned a long time ago that the less she said, the less could be used against her. ''Sheila Pollack told me that you weren't well.''

''Sheila Pollack can mind her own damn business and go to hell. I'm doing fine,'' he insisted with haughty malice. It would have made her explode in the old days. ''So, if you came back to see if you were going to get your inheritance, you're in for a disappointment.''

He'd pushed her over the edge. ''Damn it, is it always about money with you?''

''No, it's always about money with *everyone.*'' He saw the world for what it was. He always had. That was his gift. From the time he'd run away at the age of fourteen from an abusive father and a mother who was too frightened of her own shadow, too drunk to care what was happening to her son, he'd learned what truly mattered in this world. Money and power. If you had those, no one would touch you. If you didn't, you were plowed under. ''There are the haves and the have-nots. The have-nots want what the haves have, and they'll do anything to get it.'' A mirthless smile twisted his lips. ''Like that character you were shacked up with.''

Even though when her father said *black* she had an uncontrollable urge to say *white,* it wasn't in her to come to Steven's defense. ''Shacked up? Thousand-dollar suits, and that's the best word you can come up with?''

''Low words for low life.''

She'd been wrong—she wasn't impervious to his words. At least, not all of them. ''Are you talking about Steven—or me?''

He was tired of this. He was tired of a great many things these days. ''As I said, the room's there. Do with it as you will. I've got to get to the office.''

He moved his chair to his desk and pressed a button on a

console. Within moments, a tall, fair-haired man wearing a chauffeur's uniform appeared in the doorway.

Someone new, she thought. Her father went through employees the way women went through panty hose. They were serviceable only for a short time before a defect crept up.

"Bring the car around, Dickinson, and then come for me," he ordered the man.

"Very good, sir." The chauffeur retreated quickly.

Maybe she should do the same, Dana thought.

"So, are you back?" Morrow demanded sharply.

Startled, Dana looked up. His eyes held hers, dark, demanding. She made a decision and hoped she wouldn't regret it.

"I'm back."

"Are you sure you know what you're doing?" Slade studied Dana's face. He didn't need any of the skills he'd honed as an investigative reporter to tell him that his wife's friend was not at ease with her decision to move into her father's house, however temporarily.

Dana paced the length of the patio. Inside, Pilar was playing a game with Mollie. Dana was grateful for the diversion. It gave her time to calm down. All the way home, she had felt like a person on a high-wire trying to work her way to the other side without falling.

Had she done something tremendously stupid by coming here? By trying to find a way to bridge the gap between her father and herself one last time? She couldn't settle on an answer.

"No, I'm not." Dana dragged a hand through her hair restlessly. "I don't know if I know what I'm doing." She turned to face Slade, voicing her thoughts, using him as a sounding board. "All I know is that this is where it all started going bad. This is the beginning. Maybe, if I retrace my steps, I can set things on the right course and go from there." She shrugged, wondering if that sounded naive. "I just know that, right now, my life feels like a hopeless mess, and I need to sort things out. I have to start somewhere. This seemed as likely a place as any.''

Slade took the hand that feathered restlessly through her hair. ''We're here for you if you need us.''

She smiled her thanks. ''That means a lot. Really.'' Why couldn't she meet someone like this? Someone who said he cared and meant it? She felt happy for her friend's fortune but wistful at the same time. ''Tell Sheila she's got a great guy.''

He laughed, sinking down on a chaise longue. Having wrapped up a seven-part series, he'd elected to take a few days off and was determined to enjoy his family in something other than snatches. ''Every chance I get. I think she's even starting to believe it.''

Sheila walked out to join them. The office closed at noon on Wednesdays. If she got out by two, she felt like a kid being sprung early from school. ''Believe what?'' She bent over and greeted Slade with a kiss.

He hooked his arm around her waist and pulled her onto his lap. ''What a great guy I am.''

Making herself comfortable, Sheila laced her arms around his neck. ''Ha, I just took pity on you because you're Rebecca's father and you looked like you needed a home.''

This was what she wanted, Dana thought, watching them. What Sheila had. If she hadn't witnessed this with her own eyes, she would have sworn that happy marriages, happy unions, didn't exist except in the minds of filmmakers and novelists.

No, that wasn't true, she corrected herself. There had been Megan and George. They had been happy together. It was only her father's disapproval that had cast a shadow on their happiness.

Her father. It always came back to him. Her father was the root of all the discord, all the turmoil that haunted her and tainted everything.

Could peace be made with someone like that? It was something she intended to find out.

And then there would be only nine hundred ninety-nine problems to face, instead of a thousand.

"So, how are you doing today, Mollie girl?" Rafe asked as he walked into the examining room.

Dana swung toward the door at the sound of his voice. She'd intended to take Mollie to meet her grandfather, but Mollie had been particularly wan this morning. So much so that she'd called up for an appointment. The only opening had been at four, and she'd jumped at it.

"I think she's getting worse, not better," Dana told him.

And her aunt was getting edgier, he thought. He wouldn't have pegged Sheila and this woman as friends. As far as he could see, they were complete opposites in temperament. Sheila was laid-back, calm. Dana reminded him of a firecracker about to go off.

He looked at Mollie. "Have you been taking your medicine?"

Mollie nodded solemnly, then smiled at him. "It tastes like pink gum."

"It does?" He pretended to be surprised at the comparison. "Gee, maybe I'll give it a try sometime." He scooped her up and set her on the examining table, then took out a fresh tongue depressor. "Okay, you know the drill. Open wide for me." He placed the depressor lightly against her tongue. "Oh, wow."

Dana's heart lunged. "What? What do you see?" She was beside him, attempting to peer down Mollie's throat, but it was impossible with him in the way. "Is it her tonsils? Are they enlarged?"

"You've got dinosaurs in there," he told Mollie, then spared a smile for Dana.

Dana could have hit him for the scare he'd given her. She didn't need added stress.

Mollie looked at him, her eyes huge. "I do?"

"Yup, but it's okay." He tossed out the tongue depressor

and proceeded to examine her ears and nose. ''They're the friendly kind. They're going to make sure you get better.''

''Will they protect me from mean people?''

He glanced toward Dana, wondering if that was a childish question or if there was something behind it. ''You bet. Is someone being mean to you, Mollie?'' he asked casually, checking the sides of her throat for enlarged glands.

''No.'' Mollie fidgeted on the table, picking at the paper covering. ''But Aunt Dana said she's going to take me to meet Grandpa, and he's mean.''

So she'd never actually met the man. Things fell into place. He figured what Mollie was experiencing was a case of nerves.

''Remember what we talked about,'' he reminded her. ''You're supposed to give him a chance first.''

She smiled at him brightly, clearly enamored. ''Okay.''

Stepping toward the doorway, Rafe called out, ''Sara, I'd like you to take a throat culture.'' Mollie immediately clamped both hands around her throat, clutching it as if she'd swallowed a giant chicken bone. Very gently, Rafe removed her hands one at a time. ''She's just going to tickle your throat with a long magic wand, Mollie. It'll be over before you know it.'' As Sara entered, Rafe looked at Dana. ''Can I see you outside for a second?''

Mollie was frightened at the prospect of being left alone. ''Aunt Dana?''

''We'll be right by the door,'' Rafe assured her. ''Sara has pointy elbows and she needs a lot of room when she moves around. If we stay, we'll just get in her way.''

To Dana's surprise, Mollie settled down. The little girl didn't ordinarily trust people so quickly. She supposed Sheila was right about the doctor. He was good.

She looked at him anxiously as soon as they stepped out of the room. ''What did you want to see me about?'' Dana asked, her voice low. ''Is it about Mollie?''

''Yes. I think you should lighten up.''

Dana stared. This wasn't what she'd expected him to say. "Excuse me?"

He turned his back to the doorway so his voice wouldn't carry. "You're scaring her. Kids have got fantastic radar, and she knows you're worried, so she's worried. Stop worrying. She'll be fine in a week, and this'll be all in the past. Kids get sick. It's a fact of life. You don't want a junior hypochondriac on your hands, do you?"

His tone was calm and soothing and irritated the hell out of her. Sheila had told her that he wasn't married. Well, he might treat children all day, but he had no idea what it felt like to be solely responsible for one. "Of course not, but—"

"Then do as I say and take it light. You'll both feel a lot better."

She caught his arm before he had a chance to walk into the room, surprising him. "Is that your considered medical opinion?"

Was she deliberately trying to get on his nerves? "Yes, it is. And if you don't agree with it, you're completely free to get a second opinion." With that, he entered the room.

Annoyed, she followed him as Sara walked out of the room with the culture. Dana wondered if Sheila would take offense if she asked her for the name of a different pediatrician. This one rankled her, and he had too high an opinion of himself. She didn't need two men like that in her life at the same time. Dealing with her father was going to be rough enough.

She heard Mollie giggling.

Mollie definitely responded to him, though, she thought, walking into the examining room. She hadn't heard her laugh like that in a long time. Not since Christmas, when she'd gone to Megan's for a visit. Steven had conveniently picked an argument with her before they were to leave, and she had gone alone. Megan and George had gone out of their way to make it up to her. They'd all had a wonderful time.

That had been just before the accident, she remembered with a pang that threatened to reopen the wound that had only now begun to heal.

Forcing the sadness back, Dana concentrated on the sound of Mollie's laugh.

''Okay, you're free to go.'' Mollie leaned her head against his shoulder as he picked her up off the table. Smiling, Rafe placed Mollie on the floor. ''I'll see you, okay?''

Mollie nodded with enthusiasm.

Rafe turned to Dana. ''Just keep up with her medicine. I'll have someone from the office call you if the culture comes back positive. In the meantime—'' Rafe opened Mollie's folder and extracted several forms ''—I'd like you to fill these out and bring them back the next time you come.'' He handed them to her.

Dana flipped through them. Even if her degree was in law, it didn't affect how she felt about paperwork. She hated it. ''What's this?''

''Health history forms,'' he said needlessly, then flashed a grin at Mollie, who appeared to be hanging on his every word. ''I like knowing all about my patients.''

The same forms she'd passed on filling out the first time she was here, Dana thought. But she folded them and slipped them into her purse.

''All right,'' she promised. ''The next time.''

With luck, that wouldn't be for a while. Her funds were all but depleted by now. Most of them had been eaten up by Mollie's hospital bills. Megan and George hadn't had insurance. And there was no way she would ask her father for so much as a dime, not even as a loan.

That meant she had to find a job, and soon.

Chapter 5

"Dr. Rafe is nice, isn't he, Aunt Dana?"

Dana changed lanes, easing over to the left in order to make a turn at the light.

"He's okay."

She supposed maybe she was being a little too hard on the pediatrician, taking feelings out on the man that really had nothing to do with him.

Glancing at Mollie, she smiled. "Sounds like someone's got a crush."

Mollie squirmed beneath the seat belt that restrained her, trying to turn toward her aunt. Her face was puckered the way it always was when she was trying to understand something. She was forever asking questions. It was her endless questions that had made Steven label her an annoying pest. And *that* had made Dana finally see the kind of man he really was.

"What's a crush?"

She looked so small, Dana thought, so fragile beneath that seat belt. Mollie was a little past the mandatory weight requirement for car seats. The current pale cast to her skin only contributed to that impression of fragility. She usually looked so pink, so rosy. Dana wished the medicine would do its thing already.

"A crush is when you like someone a whole bunch, sweetie."

Dana had no doubt that Dr. Rafe had a great many groupies of all sizes, shapes and ages. His looks put him in the same category as Steven. He was the kind of man who made women's heads turn, their hearts skip a couple of beats and their minds indulge in fleeting fantasies. It was a category she had little use for. Men that good-looking traded on their appearances. And the trade was never an equal one.

Mollie cocked her head. "Oh." A small smile fluttered over her lips. "I guess that means I've got a crush on you, huh?"

Dana laughed. She'd forgotten how literal an age five could be. "No, honey, the person you like has to be someone of the opposite sex."

This was even harder for Mollie to figure out. She blinked. "What's sex?"

Dana slammed on her brakes as a blue van cut directly in front of her, then sailed through the light that was already turning red. She let out a slow, measured breath, glad she had swallowed the name she was about to christen the other driver with before Mollie could hear it.

"A whole lot of trouble, sometimes," Dana finally answered. Was it her, or had traffic gotten heavier since she'd last lived in the area? Settling back, she tried again. "Okay, how about this? Girls can only have crushes on boys, and boys can only have crushes on girls." She peered at Mollie's face to see if that explanation generated any problems. "Better?"

Mollie's head bobbed up and down. "Uh-huh." Hesitantly, she asked, "Aunt Dana, did you have a crush on Steven?"

Dana couldn't think of Steven without a mixed collection of memories playing tag with one another as they raced through her head. Some good, some bad. Maybe that summed up most relationships except that, in the end, in her case, there had been a lot more bad than good.

"Yeah, I had a crush on Steven." And it had been wonderful to be in love, to feel loved. If only that hadn't turned out to be an illusion, no, a lie. She kept her eyes on the road, determined not to allow the bitterness to creep in. "But I'm all over that now."

"I'm glad."

The smile was weak, but definitely there. Mollie's lower lip protruded a little as she stole a glance at her aunt and told her what she had been afraid to say before. Afraid because, if she said it, then maybe her aunt wouldn't love her anymore or let her stay with her. And then there would be nobody to hold her when she was afraid.

"I didn't like him." Mollie wiggled in her seat, tired and impatient to get to the end of the ride. She wanted to lie down. She was so very tired. Her eyes began to drift shut. "But it's okay if you have a crush on Dr. Rafe."

Dana choked back a laugh. She would probably have to take a number, like at a bakery. But, for simplicity's sake, when Mollie looked at her quizzically, she said, "I think Dr. Rafe might have something to say about that."

Sighing deeply, Mollie settled into her seat. She was beginning to fall asleep. "Why?" she murmured.

Glad to leave the flow of traffic behind her, Dana made a right turn into Sheila's development. "Because men like to think they decide these kinds of things for themselves."

Mollie's eyes were little more than blue slits as she shifted them toward Dana. "But they don't?"

Mollie was too young to be told that men didn't like making decisions about anything, least of all commitment. Dana had learned firsthand that urges dictated their actions and any thinking that was done was generated from below their belts. Or cerebrally, like her father. But never from the heart.

No, she couldn't say that to a five-year-old, even though

her illusions would disappear soon enough. For now, they had to be preserved for as long as possible.

"We help, honey, we help." Before turning the corner onto a street that fed into the block where Sheila and Slade lived, Dana eased her foot onto the brake and brushed a kiss over her niece's head.

Rafe Saldana might think she needed to lighten up, but she swore that Mollie felt warm to her, despite her pale color. She was going to take her temperature as soon as they reached the house. Maybe she was being unnecessarily worried, but aside from her father, Mollic was all the family she had. And *she* was all the family Mollie had. Mollie's welfare was entirely in her hands.

"Looks like Sheila is going to have to put up with us a little longer. You're going to bed as soon as we get home, young lady." Any plans to move into her father's house would have to be put on hold. And she certainly had no problem with that.

"Okay," Mollie agreed.

The fact that she didn't protest going to bed so early *really* worried Dana. She pushed down on the accelerator, anxious to get Mollie to Sheila's.

She saw the long black limousine from a distance. It was parked directly in front of Sheila and Slade's house. Dana felt something twist inside her even as annoyance gelled. Without seeing the license plate, she knew the limousine belonged to her father.

"Oh, God, what's he doing here?" This was all she needed, a confrontation with her father in front of Sheila and Slade.

The sharp note in her aunt's voice roused Mollie. She peered out the window, looking around. "Who, Aunt Dana? Who's here?"

For a moment Dana felt like turning the car around and going back. But there was nowhere to go, and Mollie was sick.

She was in no mood for this. He had no right to hound her. ‘‘Your grandfather. That’s his car up ahead.’’

Mollie stared out the window, searching for someone matching the description of her grandfather she had conjured up for herself.

‘‘Is he a giant?’’ The question was a hushed whisper.

‘‘He likes to think so.’’

A giant among men, that was the sort of legacy he had always tried to carve out for himself. And no success he attained was ever great enough.

Dana realized that Mollie was shrinking in her seat as if she was trying to vanish into it. ‘‘Mollie, what’s the matter?’’

When she was really little, Mollie used to shut her eyes and think no one could see her. She wished she could do that now. ‘‘I’m afraid, Aunt Dana. I don’t want to meet him.’’

Dana couldn’t have faulted her niece for feeling that way, if she’d ever met the man before, but she hadn’t. Dana pulled the car over. She had to find out why Mollie was so afraid before she allowed her to meet her grandfather.

‘‘Mollie, did someone say something to you about your grandfather?’’

Mollie shivered, huddling into herself. ‘‘No. I heard Mommy and Daddy talking once. They thought I was sleeping. Mommy was crying, and Daddy was mad. He said Grandpa was an o—’’ Frustrated, she tried to remember the word.

Bastard started with *b,* Dana thought. Besides, George had never used profanity, even the mildest kind. What started with *o?* Mollie had asked if he was a giant.

‘‘Ogre?’’ Dana guessed.

‘‘Yeah.’’ Mollie nodded hard. ‘‘Like the one in my book that eats kids.’’

Well, that explained that. She leaned over and slipped her arm around her niece. Dana hadn’t thought she could laugh about anything connected to her father, but Mollie had proven her wrong.

"Oh, honey, he's not an ogre, he's just an old man in a wheelchair. He won't eat you, and he can't hurt you."

Mollie bit her lower lip hesitantly. *Just like Meggie,* Dana thought. "Promise?"

"Oh, yes, I promise." *He's a bastard, capable of a lot of things,* she added silently. *But he'd never physically hurt you.* "Okay?"

Mollie gave her a brave smile. "Okay."

Dana saw the trust in Mollie's eyes. It was at once humbling and a huge responsibility. One she swore she would never neglect. Not the way her father had neglected her.

And what about the baby? a small voice whispered in her head. *The one you don't want. Are you going to shirk your responsibility to it?*

Annoyed, guilty, Dana shut the voice away. With a sigh, she took the car out of Park and drove the remaining few yards to Sheila's driveway. Taking her time, she got out of the car and then rounded the hood to open Mollie's door.

"C'mon, honey, let's go inside." Because Mollie looked so unsteady on her feet, Dana scooped her up in her arms. "You *do* seem a little warm," she commented, as if Mollie had asked her for confirmation.

Dana's first inclination was to ignore the limousine parked at the sidewalk like a loitering, silent shark, but that wouldn't get rid it. So, holding Mollie to her, she approached the vehicle.

As she did, the chauffeur stepped out. The windows were rolled up in the back, darkening her view of the sunset. She wondered if her father was behind them, watching.

"Dickinson, isn't it?" she asked the chauffeur.

The man politely touched the brim of his hat. "Yes, miss, it is. Tom Dickinson."

She nodded toward the limousine. "Is my father inside, Tom?"

Dickinson looked surprised at the question, as if she should know better than to think Paul Morrow would be content to wait for anyone. "No, he's at home, miss. He sent me to bring you and his granddaughter to the house."

Dana shifted Mollie to her other side, instinctively protective. "A command performance?"

The chauffeur looked as if he wasn't sure whether he should or could safely comment. He didn't. "Mr. Morrow said that you should bring your things with you."

So, the invitation had turned into something with a little more teeth to it. She wasn't surprised. For as long as she could remember, her father had liked being in control of every situation. This was no different.

"How did he know I was here?" Dana was sure she hadn't mentioned it. Every syllable uttered during her visit with him this morning was still fresh in her mind. She had deliberately *not* told her father where she was staying, to give herself time if she needed it.

Dickinson was as devoid of curiosity as humanly possible. Morrow paid well, and that was all the information he needed. "I don't know that, miss. I was just instructed to wait until you were ready."

Nothing had changed. Her father thought that because he snapped his fingers, she would obey. She'd returned to mend fences, not to place her hand beneath his boot.

Dana raised her chin. "Tell him I have my own car, and I'll drive over when I'm ready." She paused, then added, "In the morning." No use fanning the flames too high. She didn't want another argument. She just wanted the respect he would accord one of his judicial adversaries.

"Trouble, Dana?"

She turned to see that Slade was standing in the doorway of the house.

She smiled. The cavalry. A cavalry on loan, but a cavalry nonetheless, just as she remembered Sheila saying once. Mollie murmured something unintelligible against her shoulder, and Dana feathered a hand gently along her head, soothing her.

"No, but thanks for the backup. My father sent his chauffeur to pick me up."

Slade stepped off the porch to join her. "Yes, I know. We told him you weren't here. Two hours ago."

"Well, Tom doesn't have to wait any longer." Dana saw a look of uncertainty cross the chauffeur's face. He was probably nervous about being the bearer of bad news. She didn't blame him. Her father's moods were probably worse than ever. "Please tell my father that I can't come tonight. With any luck—" she kissed the side of Mollie's head "—Mollie and I will be there in the morning."

Dickinson looked at her doubtfully. Those weren't his instructions. "Mr. Morrow was very specific about your coming tonight."

Dana laughed shortly. "I'm sure he was." She paused, choosing her words carefully. It wasn't the chauffeur's fault that her father was the way he was. And she didn't want to say anything that would generate a further tear in the already weak fabric between her and her father. Reconciliations weren't built on angry feelings. "Tell my father that I appreciate his thoughtfulness, but Mollie isn't feeling well, and I'd like her to be fresh when she meets her grandfather for the first time."

With that, she turned and walked into the house. Slade followed, closing the door behind them.

He took Mollie from her. Dana dropped her purse on the hall table and led the way upstairs to the room she and Mollie were sharing.

"What was that all about?" Slade asked.

She went into the bedroom and drew back the covers. "I'm not sure. I think my father is having me followed."

"Followed?" He laid Mollie on the bed. He knew Dana's history, but still, that didn't sound like the way a father would treat his daughter. Maybe his paternal feelings were coloring his perception, he thought.

Dana nodded, taking Mollie's running shoes off. "I never told him I was staying here." She dropped the shoes on the floor, trying to control her temper. She didn't like the idea of being followed. Of having to look over her shoulder.

"Maybe he just took an educated guess," Slade suggested for the sake of argument.

That was highly unlikely. Dana thought of her father sitting in his chair, playing God with those around him. Arranging their lives to suit his purposes. Why had she thought he'd mellowed? Not everything mellowed with age. Cheese just turned sharper.

"My father never guesses. He likes knowing."

With a dinner plate carefully held in each hand, Kate Mulligan moved cautiously into the tiny dining room that was little more than an alcove. A fastidious person, she would normally have set the table long before now. But after three broken dinner engagements in a row, she'd learned to play it by ear. It didn't matter. Rafe was worth it.

Placing one plate on either side of the two tapering candles she had lit only minutes ago, Kate smiled at Rafe. He looked so pensive. And tired, she thought. She longed to hold him, to help him find peace. She would have given anything if he could find it with her.

"I was beginning to think we were never going to get a chance to get together," she told him.

He watched her hands flutter, smoothing napkins, straightening silverware that was already straight. The candlelight brought out red highlights in her auburn hair. She was wearing it down to please him. Rafe felt a stirring of affection. But nothing more.

He shrugged noncommittally, knowing she wasn't trying to pin him down with the comment. Kate wasn't like that. "It's been pretty rough lately. Every time I turn around, someone else is coming down with the flu."

She nodded, understanding. They were backlogged at the lab. "Well, you can relax now." She glanced at the small, dark rectangle at his belt. Hardly bigger than a tie clip. She hated it. "Why don't you turn your pager off?"

He took the bottle of wine he'd brought and uncorked it. After filling her glass, he poured some into his own. But, though he'd selected it, he found himself uninterested in sampling the wine. He felt restless, as if there was a storm coming. As if there was something he'd left undone.

Probably a combination of the weather and fatigue.

He smiled tolerantly at her suggestion. "You know I can't do that, Kate."

At times, she thought, he was too damn dedicated. "But you could get someone to take your calls for you once in a while. Trade-off," she pressed. "Like every other sane doctor does."

What other doctors did didn't interest him, unless it directly affected his patients. He sat and waited for her to join him. "When my patients' parents call with a problem, they want to talk to me, not to some doctor they don't know."

Kate frowned as she moved the salad bowl toward him. "You need to have a life, Rafe."

Her comment made him smile. "Being a doctor *is* my life, remember?"

That wasn't what she'd meant, but she knew better than to argue with him about it. Kate knew about Debra, and how being a doctor was what had kept him going after she died. "If you're not careful, you're going to burn out."

In order to burn out, there had to be something left within him to burn, and there wasn't. Not the way it would have mattered to Kate, he thought.

He looked at the meal she had prepared. Eggplant parmesan. She'd called his mother for the recipe. He knew, because his brother had kidded him about it. It made him feel guilty.

"You didn't have to go to all this trouble. Take-out would have been fine."

She took a sip of wine, hoping it would quell her nerves. "But then I couldn't impress you with what a good cook I am."

His eyes rose to meet hers. "You don't have to impress me, Kate."

Kate pressed her lips together. She should have downed the entire glass for courage. She was running pitifully low right now. "Oh, yes, I do. I have to do something to nudge you along to the next level."

He pretended to be interested in his meal. "I don't nudge very well, Kate."

"Sorry." She flushed. They had an agreement, she knew that. It was just that sometimes she wanted to go beyond the confines of the agreement. She wanted him to look at her with love in his eyes. Love like she felt. "You'd think a research biologist would learn to be patient."

He set down his fork. This was his fault, not hers. Rafe reached for her hand and covered it. "No, I'm the one who's sorry, Kate. Sorry if I'm being testy. Like I said, I'm tired."

Relieved that he wasn't leaving, she placed her hand on top of his, confirming the friendship, placing everything else on hold a little longer. Again.

"You can sleep here if you'd like," she offered. "After dinner. You can stretch out on the couch or my bed. I promise I won't jump your bones unless you want me to."

He heard so many things in her voice, and for her sake he wished he could return them in kind. But it just wasn't in him. "Kate..."

She raised her hand, knowing what was coming. "Hey, no promises asked, no commitment required. I know the rules." Her smile was patient, resigned. "You were very clear, and I accepted the terms."

He shook his head. This wasn't fair, not to her, and maybe in the long run not even to him. "Kate, you need to get a nice guy."

"I did get a nice guy," she insisted. The smile curled into her brown eyes. "I just need to have him want to get me." Leaning over the tiny table, she kissed his mouth, her lips warm, willing.

As she deepened the kiss, his pager beeped. A moan of defeat escaped her as she reached to turn it off. Rafe placed his hand over hers, then drew his head back. ‘‘It’s my service.’’

She knew that. She damn well knew that. With a small sigh, Kate dragged her hand through her hair, backing away, surrendering. She knew what was coming. One by one, she removed the dishes from the table. He was going to leave. No one called a doctor at this hour just to ask a question.

Rafe frowned as he hung up the telephone. ‘‘It wasn’t my service.’’

Kate stopped midway between the kitchen and the dining room. She looked at him hopefully. ‘‘Does that mean you’re staying?’’

Preoccupied, he looked up. It took a second for her question to register, though he failed to pick up on the hope in her voice. ‘‘No, the call was from the hospital. One of my patients came into the emergency room.’’

She crossed to him, taking his hands in hers. As if that could make him stay. ‘‘Good, then they’ll be well taken care of.’’

Very gently, he extracted his hands from hers. ‘‘The patient’s aunt requested that I be called in. I’ve got to go.’’

‘‘An aunt now?’’ Kate sighed. Next it would be neighbors and total strangers. With a shake of her head, she went to the kitchen. ‘‘You know, you can’t keep running off every time someone calls.’’ She reached for the cellophane wrap, then looked at him as he entered behind her. ‘‘Someday, Rafe, you’re going to have to stop running.’’

‘‘You’re right,’’ he agreed vaguely. Quickly, he brushed his lips against hers. ‘‘Thanks for the meal. Sorry I couldn’t stay to finish it.’’

She was right. Someday he would have to stop running. Maybe. But someday, Rafe thought as he closed the door behind him, wasn’t now.

‘‘Not coming?’’ Morrow demanded, his face turning pale then red. ‘‘What do you mean she’s not coming?’’

Dickinson was twice his employer’s size. There was no

earthly reason he should feel the inclination to cringe. And yet, held by the glacier gleam in Morrow's eye, he did.

''She said that your granddaughter wasn't feeling well, and that she wanted her to be fresh when she met you for the first time.''

''That's a lie. Don't you know a lie when someone tells you one?'' he demanded. ''When I send you to bring someone, I damn well expect you to bring them to me. Do I make myself clear?''

''Yes, sir. She said to thank you for your thoughtfulness.''

That gave him pause. ''She did?''

''Yes, sir.'' Dickinson worked the brim of his hat through his hands, turning it as he waited to be dismissed. Hoped to be dismissed. From the room, not his position.

''But she still didn't come.''

Dickinson's throat felt dry. ''No, sir.''

Uttering a well-turned oath, Morrow sent the man from the room. He waited until the door was closed and he was alone before he slumped in his wheelchair. Anger exhausted him.

Kate's penthouse apartment was located across from the hospital. The easy access was what had brought Rafe and Kate together. Seeing how exhausted he was after rounds one day, she had offered him a place to crash when he needed it. Eventually, purely through her perseverance, they had drifted from friends into a comfortable relationship that included the physical and was pleasant, but devoid of passion. At least on Rafe's part.

But he liked her company. He enjoyed talking to Kate. They shared a great many interests, and while he bore affection for her, he wasn't in love with her, and she knew it. He knew she knew it, too. He'd been very careful not to lead her on, and she had been just as careful in making him understand that she was willing to settle for whatever was available. She made no demands on him.

Rafe slipped through a yellow light, then drove into the hospital compound. Kate was a good woman, and he supposed that if he ever was to marry again, it would be to her. A comfortable relationship where he was in sync with the person he was married to was the best he figured he could hope for.

But that, too, wasn't today.

After leaving his car in the doctors' parking lot, Rafe hurried through the automatic emergency room doors. A quick scan to his left took in the crowded waiting area. It looked as though it was going to be a busy night.

Rafe bypassed the registration desk and looked for the head nurse. She was walking out of the patients' area. He made his way to her before she could call the next patient.

''Hi, Nancy, I got a call that one of my patients was here.''

The nurse, a tall, sleek woman with skin like lightly brewed coffee, flashed a smile at him. Though it was worn around the edges, there was still a tiny dash of flirtation in it.

''She's in the back, Dr. Saldana. We've got her on oxygen. Looks like the croup to me. Come on.'' Nancy pushed open the door she had just walked through. ''I'll take you to her.''

He knew exactly what he would see when he pulled back the curtain. Even so, the sight of the small figure on the gurney wrenched at his heart. He was never, never going to become immune to the sight of a suffering child.

Mollie had an oxygen mask covering half her face. Her eyes were huge with fear, the sheen of perspiration on her brow.

''I suppose you still think I should lighten up.'' Dana couldn't help the bitterness in her voice when she saw the doctor walk in.

''Yes, I do,'' he answered without looking at her. ''You're still scaring the hell out of her.'' With Nancy at his elbow, Rafe picked up the chart, quickly making an assessment of the information. He added several tests to be done in addition to the ones already listed. Nancy left to set things in motion. ''She's going to be fine.''

Dana placed a hand over the chart, forcing him to look at

her. ''You said that this afternoon.'' She waved a hand at Mollie. ''Is this your definition of fine?''

''No, this is my definition of the croup.'' He moved the chart from Dana's hand so that he could return it to its place at the foot of the bed. ''I think it's best for her if she remain here overnight.''

He heard Mollie whimper beneath the mask.

Dana glared at Rafe before she hurried over to Mollie.

Chapter 6

With soft, soothing strokes, Dana brushed the damp hair from Mollie's forehead. The ends were dark with perspiration.

"It's okay, baby, it's okay. If you have to stay overnight, I'll be right here with you." She threaded her fingers through Mollie's. The small hand felt so cold, so damp, as it grasped hers. Dana squeezed it, wishing she could transfer some of her strength to Mollie. She hated seeing her frightened. "I won't leave you, I promise." She looked at Rafe, her eyes daring him to tell her she couldn't remain with Mollie.

He nodded. "We can have a cot brought in for you."

Dana sincerely doubted she would get any sleep. "I don't need a cot. All I need is a chair."

Amusement highlighted his features. "We have chairs."

"Good." A tired, relieved smile rose to her lips as Dana looked at Mollie. "See, baby? It's all settled. We'll be roommates."

Debating, Dana raised her eyes toward Rafe. She didn't like leaving herself open to pity but she had to be up-front with him. She didn't believe in playing games. That was for people like Steven. Very gently, she began to draw her hand from Mollie's. The girl hung on tightly, as if her very life depended on it.

"Mollie, I have to talk to Dr. Rafe for a second." With reluctance, Mollie let go of her hand. It had to be awful, Dana thought, to be so young and so afraid. She kissed the damp forehead. "I'll be right back."

Like two blue homing devices, Mollie's eyes followed as Dana moved to the other side of the curtain.

Rafe waited until she said the first word. He couldn't even begin to guess what this was going to be about.

Dana lowered her voice. This was hard enough to say to him. There was no need for anyone else to overhear.

"Is this going to be for just one night? Her hospital stay," she clarified, when he looked at her.

"That depends on Mollie, but I think there's a good chance she'll be able to go home sometime tomorrow." There was no telling with children. Her fever was low grade, and she'd stopped choking. All things considered, it looked promising, but he knew it was safer to remain guarded, just in case.

He studied the woman before him. Did she plan to contest his decision if he wanted Mollie to remain an extra night to be on the safe side? Rafe couldn't tell. She wasn't an easy woman to read—just an exasperating one, but that could be because she seemed so wound up.

"Good." Dana weighed her next words, not quite sure how to proceed. Being in financial difficulties was not something she was accustomed to. It felt awkward, uncomfortable. She hated it, hated admitting to anyone she was in this position, however temporarily—and she intended for it to be very temporary. As soon as she could, she was going to find a position at a law firm, even if she had to trade on her father's name to do it. But right now, she needed to get this straightened out.

"I left my last job rather suddenly." It wasn't easy to withstand the scrutiny she saw in his eyes, but she refused to look away. "Consequently, we don't have any health insurance at the moment. But I can make arrangements to pay—"

He waved the remainder of her explanation away. This was obviously very awkward for her, and he had no desire to watch her discomfort. There was nothing here that couldn't be worked out. The hospital budgeted a certain amount to be written off each year as charity. As a last resort, Mollie's bill could be referred to that department, though he had a feeling Dana wouldn't particularly appreciate hearing herself referred to as a recipient of charity.

"Why don't we worry about that later?" he suggested tactfully.

Later had a habit of catching up to you when you least wanted it to. "I'm only saying this because your bookkeeper is worried about payment *now.* I thought if you told her it was going to be made—maybe not as quickly as she'd like, but it *will* be made—she might feel better about it." Dana looked at him pointedly. "I always pay my debts, Dr. Saldana, no matter how big they might be at the outset."

"It never crossed my mind to doubt that." His eyes held hers. Pride was important to everyone, especially to stubborn, headstrong women. He allowed her hers. "I'll talk to her."

It was past eleven by the time everything had been arranged and Mollie was settled in her room. Pulling a few strings, Rafe had managed to get her one where the other two beds were empty. A minor miracle, after the way things had been the other day.

Rafe knew he should go home like, as Kate had pointed out earlier that evening, any sane doctor would have done hours ago. Even so, he found himself returning to Mollie's room to look in on the little girl one last time.

And maybe, though he didn't really know why, to look in on her aunt, as well.

If it hadn't been for the time he spent with his parents and his brother, Gabe, Rafe would have said his entire world was enclosed within the relatively small circle formed by his office and the hospital. Diagnosing and caring for children was what took up most of his time and his energy. In return, it gave him a sense of satisfaction and worth the way nothing else could. He found he needed very little else to define him as a person.

Almost all the lights were off in Mollie's room. The one above her bed was on the dimmest setting. Soft shadows hovered beyond the bed. Everything seemed peaceful, in contrast to the way things had been a short while ago.

Good, Rafe thought.

He saw Dana sitting beside Mollie's bed, her body tense, like a bow about to release an arrow. What sort of an arrow would she release if she was freed of the tension that outlined her body?

It might be interesting to speculate about, if he had the time for things like that.

He entered quietly and kept his voice low. ''How's she doing?''

Startled, Dana swung her head around to look at him. She'd been holding Mollie's hand for the past hour or so. Somewhere along the line, Mollie had fallen asleep, but Dana didn't want to risk waking her by moving. She'd lost most of the feeling in her arm, and her fingers were almost numb.

She let out a shaken breath, waiting for her heart to stop pounding.

''Sorry,'' he whispered.

She nodded, accepting the apology. It was so quiet, she wondered why she hadn't heard him approach. Gingerly, she drew her hand slowly from Mollie's, then got up. Indicating that he should retreat to the doorway, she joined him there.

''She calmed down a little,'' Dana told him in answer to his question. It had taken a while, though. She could only guess what kind of terrors Mollie was trying to deal with, being in a hospital again. ''I think placing her in the oxygen tent was a good idea. We pretended that we were camping out and that she was in this magic see-through pup tent. After that, it became a game to her.''

He smiled. "I've got to remember that the next time I need to put one of my patients in an oxygen tent." He wouldn't have pegged Dana as someone with an imagination. But then, he'd only seen her when she was coming on like gangbusters.

Dana dragged a hand through her hair, trying to smooth it. She had to look like hell. God knew she felt like it. She knew it didn't matter to him, but it did to her. She hated being at her worst.

"And how are you doing?" He couldn't help it. The doctor in him had taken over. It was something Gabe kidded him about. He approached everything as if it was a triage situation.

The question surprised her. After all, if she was being honest, she'd hadn't exactly been the model of politeness to him.

Massaging the stiff muscles of her neck, Dana answered, "I've been better." Then she shrugged as a small smile emerged. "But then, I've been worse, too, so I guess you could say I'm breaking even." She looked over her shoulder to check if Mollie was still asleep. The gentle rise and fall of the small chest reassured her. "Maybe I'm even on the plus side of the ledger."

Dana paused. Apologies never came easily to her, but she did owe him one. And she'd always hated owing anything.

The only way to do it was to do it. She pushed the words out, trying not to sound as uncomfortable as she felt.

"Listen, if I sounded as if I was going to bite your head off earlier, I'm sorry. I had no right being angry with you. It's just that Mollie means a great deal to me, and I worry about her."

It wasn't exactly news. A smile twitched his lips. He understood where she was coming from. Maybe he'd been a little hard on her. "I can't fault you for that, but you do know that you can't insulate her in bubble wrap, don't you?"

Yes, she knew that, but it didn't stop her from trying. "Maybe not, but a little padding until she's older won't hurt." Her smile was sincere. A peace offering. "Thanks for coming so quickly."

"It's my job." He thought of what Kate had said. Poor

Kate, she really had to find someone else. He wasn't any good for her. "If I didn't want to be on call, I wouldn't be. Anyway, I was in the area." He knew he should be going. He had to be at the hospital again within a matter of hours, making rounds before going to the office.

But he lingered a little longer in the darkened hallway talking to a woman he'd thought he disliked. They'd both made mistakes. "Listen, are you going to be all right here? Can I get you anything?"

A nurse had already been by to ask her that. At the time, she'd said no, far too concerned with Mollie to think of anything else. But Mollie was asleep. And getting better.

Her mouth curved. Maybe he wasn't so bad, after all. "A fairy godmother would be nice, but I'd settle for some—" She wanted coffee, but knew that wasn't wise, not in her condition. "Hot chocolate," Dana amended with reluctance. Encouraged by his offer, she risked imposing. "If you could stay with her for a couple of minutes and point me toward the vending machines, I'd really appreciate it. I never got a chance to eat dinner tonight—Mollie's attack came on very suddenly." She'd never felt so helpless, watching Mollie gasping for air, terror in her eyes, and not being able to do anything about it. "I'm afraid that if my stomach rumbles any louder, it's going to wake her up."

She looked way too exhausted to be wandering around the halls. "I've a better idea. You stay here, and I'll go get the hot chocolate."

Dana began to protest, but the words never surfaced. With a nod of thanks, she accepted his offer. "I'd give you an argument if I had more energy."

He grinned. "I know."

Rafe was back in ten minutes, carrying several containers on a tray he'd borrowed from the nurses' station. He set everything on the shelf beside the sink.

She'd almost fallen asleep waiting for him. Rousing herself, Dana crossed to where Rafe was standing and peered around his arm. Unless she was seeing things, he'd brought three containers. She'd only asked for one.

"What's this?" She looked at the containers without taking one. "Did the hot chocolate become fruitful and multiply on the way back from the vending machine?"

So she did have a sense of humor. That, too, surprised him.

"I decided that if you were going to camp out here with Mollie, you needed to be running on something other than empty. But the cafeteria's closed for the night. All I could come up with is chicken soup." He pressed a container into her hand. "It's not bad, really."

She looked at the container dubiously. Food that emerged from vending machines was notoriously long on salt, short on taste. "Are you trying to convince me—or yourself?"

"You. I've had this before. Lots of times." Taking a second cup of soup from the tray, he raised it to his lips and sampled, then nodded his approval. He saw the question in her eyes. "I didn't have a chance to eat, either."

And that was her fault, she thought. She'd called him away from the table.

"Sorry," she murmured. She smiled at the cup in her hands. "The eternal magic cure-all, chicken soup." She took a sip and was surprised to find it was pretty decent. And hot.

"Careful," he urged as she winced. "You don't want to burn your tongue."

"Too late." Eyes tearing, Dana sucked air in, trying to relieve the burning sensation dancing along her tongue.

"Sorry." He flashed her an apologetic look. "I should have warned you."

Dana let out a breath slowly. The tears retreated. "That's okay." She could feel bumps forming on the edge of her tongue. It would be days before she was rid of them. "I can still talk."

He laughed softly. The sound washed over her, uniquely comforting. For a split second, she had the oddest sensation of being warm and contented. She figured that was probably due to the soup.

"Somehow, I thought you might be able to."

She took no offense, because he meant none. Dana indicated the cup in her hand and the one still on the tray. "What do I owe you for this?"

He could certainly afford to spring for hot chocolate and soup. Especially since the latter was his idea. "Consider it atonement."

Her eyes narrowed as she tried to make sense of that. "Excuse me?"

She was going to make him spell it out, wasn't she? Well, if she could apologize, he supposed he could, too. "Maybe my bedside manner was a little abrupt when you brought Mollie in," he allowed, then added, "Sheila tells me I need to work on it sometimes."

The admission, personal in nature, took them out of the realm of strangers. "You *were* a little sharp," she agreed. "I figured it was because of me."

"It was." She looked at him, ready to square off again. It didn't take much with her, did it? he thought. "You and a lot of other things." His eyes met hers. He tried to decide if they were a royal blue, or if that was because of the dim lighting. "That's still no excuse for being tactless, though."

She agreed with him, but it was enough to hear it. She wasn't her father, to keep a man twisting in the wind for her pleasure, yanking a little on his rope whenever it threatened to go slack until such time as she saw fit to let him go.

Dana changed the subject. "Mollie's crazy about you." Deep-seated affection crept into her voice. "I think she's planning on a wedding."

He laughed. He thought he'd detected the makings of a crush earlier this afternoon.

"I guess it'll be a long engagement." And then he smiled at Dana. She was, after all, in some way responsible for the way the little girl behaved. "She's a great girl."

"No argument." The soup was cool enough to drink. It was gone in a few gulps.

He waited until she put the container down. ''What happened to her parents?''

It was on the tip of her tongue to change the subject, but that wouldn't change what had happened. Besides, as he'd pointed out, he needed the information for his files. And for any intelligent work-up on Mollie.

So she recited the words that, when she had first heard them, had ripped open her heart.

''They were killed in a car accident a little more than six months ago. Her mother was my sister. Megan. Megan died on the way to the hospital. Her husband, George, died instantly. Mollie was in the car, too.'' With all her heart, she wished she could have changed at least that much of the tragedy, that Mollie could at least have been somewhere else when it happened, not right there, to see it, to feel the crash that killed her parents.

Dana didn't realize that she shivered. ''Mollie still has nightmares, but not as often as before.'' Progress was made by inches, not giant leaps. ''That's why she was so afraid of staying here.''

He looked at the chair. It couldn't be comfortable, not for the whole night. ''Is that why you stayed?''

She nodded. ''Mollie's had enough upheaval in her life. She needs to know there's something she can count on.''

''And that would be you.'' It wasn't a question, it was a softly voiced statement.

''That would be me.'' She didn't know why, but she couldn't turn her eyes away from his. A very strange sensation rippled through her. No, rippled was the wrong word. Drifted was more like it. Drifted like a lazy, slow-moving river making its way to the sea with an eternity to get there. Mentally, she shook herself free of the feeling.

''How about her grandfather?''

Dana stiffened. She'd almost forgotten about him. Her father wouldn't take kindly to knowing he could so easily be put out of someone's mind, especially his daughter's. ''That's something that has to be worked out.''

Her tone told him that this was a private area, one where trespassers weren't welcome, and he was a trespasser.

If he was going to be of any use to anyone, Rafe thought, he had to get going.

"Well, I wish you luck." He crushed the empty soup container in his hand. "I'd better be going. If you need anything, ask one of the nurses. You'll find they're a friendly bunch." He moved closer for one last look at Mollie. "I think everything's going to be all right. Some of her color's coming back."

Her panic had settled to something manageable. She knew he was right. "Thanks for the soup."

He tossed his container into a wastepaper basket near the door. "Don't mention it."

But she had, she thought as he left. She always made it a point to mention a kindness. Accustomed to doing without them, acts of kindness always surprised her when they happened.

Just as, she mused, settling into the chair, Rafe Saldana had surprised her.

Rafe struggled to keep the grin from his lips the next afternoon.

"I never saw a little girl get well so fast before." He looked properly amazed for Mollie's benefit.

In a complete reversal from the previous evening, Mollie looked as if she was ready and able to convert the hospital bed into a trampoline and bounce right out of the room.

"That's 'cause you and Aunt Dana took good care of me," Mollie told him gleefully. Her eyes shining with happiness, she seemed light-years away from the terrified little girl who had been brought in the night before.

Concerned, Dana drew Rafe to one side. "Is this normal?" she asked doubtfully, keeping her voice low. "To be so sick one day and so full of energy the next?"

He could see why she was skeptical. It was a drastic change.

"It is when you're five. I've known kids to be sick in the morning, great in the afternoon, feverish again by five and then perfectly fine by bedtime." Rafe smiled. It never failed, that deep feeling of satisfaction that came over him whenever one of his patients pulled through. Never mind how often it happened, it was still a high. "They're exceedingly resilient at this age." He winked at Mollie, and she giggled, ready to bounce higher to impress him. With a practiced arm, he caught her and settled her down. "I don't want to be forced to put stitches in that pretty little head of yours." He glanced toward Dana. "They don't spend a lot of time lingering over things."

Unlike adults, Dana thought. She said, "Except their shoes and socks, when you want them to get ready to go somewhere." A smile lifted the corners of Dana's mouth as she exchanged looks with Mollie. The struggle over getting dressed was one they went through every day. Mollie preferred the freedom of bare feet to the confinement of shoes and socks.

Dana had a nice smile, he thought. Too bad she didn't use it more often. "I wouldn't know about that aspect of it."

Mollie looked at him, surprised. "Don't you have any kids of your own?"

"No," he told her solemnly. "I don't."

Pity filled her eyes. At five, she had a tremendous capacity for sympathy. "I could stay with you sometimes. Aunt Dana could come, too."

Sympathetic or not, Mollie was getting far too carried away here, Dana thought. She was about to change the subject when Rafe said, "That sounds like an intriguing offer, but I'm hardly ever home. We wouldn't see very much of each other."

He really was nice, Dana thought. Not everyone had the patience to listen to children. It was an admirable quality. Her thoughts drifted to Steven and the way he'd acted toward Mollie. Too bad that quality was in such short supply.

Mollie saw no problem with Rafe's revelation. "Then you'll just have to come home more."

He laughed and gave Mollie a hug. "I know someone who would agree with you."

He had someone, Dana thought suddenly, then wondered why that should surprise her. Men like Dr. Rafe Saldana were born with someone in their lives. Not having anyone would have been the surprise, not the reverse.

Rafe paused to write something on Mollie's chart. Setting it down, he looked at Mollie, then smiled. "You're free to go, Mollie."

Dana looked at her watch. It was approaching one. They'd been here a little more than twelve hours. "Then you *are* discharging her?"

"Looks that way." He lifted Mollie and set her on the floor. "C'mon, off with you. Someone else can make use of this bed."

Mollie's spirits soared at the prospect of leaving the hospital. "Are you going to make him all well, like you did me?"

"It's a her, and she's someone else's patient." Actually, the child was assigned to the bed by the window. He'd overheard the admitting doctor discussing the little girl with the head nurse. Another case of the flu. Mollie was leaving the room just in time.

Mollie looked at Rafe with pure worship in her eyes. "But you'll help, right?"

There was no point in contradicting her. Instead, he smiled at the confident little face. "Absolutely. Now, I don't want you to overdo it for a couple of days. And come by and see me at the end of the week." He looked at Dana. "If Alice gives you any flak, tell her I told you to come."

Mollie, eager to please, nodded vigorously. "Right, no flak."

Rafe exchanged glances with Dana. When he grinned at her, suppressing a laugh, it felt as if his smile went straight to her core.

* * *

''How long did you say you'd known Dr. Saldana?''

Sheila sat on the bed, watching Dana toss the few possessions she'd come with into a suitcase. Sheila still felt incredibly guilty for not being home last night when Mollie had gotten so ill. She and Slade had gone to see a play at the Performing Arts Center. Slade had gotten the tickets five months in advance to secure good seats. While the Sharks had confronted the Jets on stage, Dana had been confronted with a gasping, choking child. The thought squeezed her heart.

''Since we interned together. Four, no, five years ago. Why?'' She peered at Dana's face. Her friend's expression gave nothing away. Her father's daughter, Sheila thought. ''What's up?''

''Nothing.'' Dana folded another one of Mollie's shirts, then tucked it into the suitcase. She'd called and spoken to Esther when she arrived at Sheila's a little while ago. It was a great deal easier talking to the housekeeper than to her father. Dana asked her to relay the message that they would be arriving early that evening. ''I was just wondering how long he's been practicing.''

''Long enough to be good.'' Sheila couldn't help wondering if that was all that was on Dana's mind. There wasn't a woman alive who hadn't expressed interest in Rafe on some level. ''Actually, he was good right from the start. He's got a natural knack for it, for understanding children.'' Sheila thought of it as a gift. Not all pediatricians had it. ''It's the parents he occasionally has trouble with.'' She smiled. ''He can get a little terse with them, but that's only because he cares so much.''

Dana closed the suitcase, snapped the locks. Done. ''He said you thought he needed to improve his bedside manner.''

That didn't sound like something Rafe would casually volunteer. He usually remained pretty close-mouthed. ''Seems he did a lot of talking with you.''

''Not that much,'' Dana countered. She set the suitcase on the floor. The box of photographs was already in the car, along with Mollie's toys. It seemed like so little to represent the sum of two lives. "Besides, it was quiet. There wasn't much going on, so he looked in on Mollie around midnight," she explained when Sheila raised one eyebrow. "We talked a little over chicken soup."

"Chicken soup?" Sheila repeated. She couldn't picture Rafe sharing chicken soup with someone at midnight.

"He brought me some from a vending machine." Why was Sheila looking at her like that? They had only exchanged a handful of sentences. "I mentioned that I'd skipped dinner."

"Chicken soup and conversation." Sheila laughed. Maybe she would make it her business to run into Rafe and have a few words with him. This was beginning to sound interesting. "In some countries, you would be betrothed by now."

Dana rolled her eyes. "Something tells me you need more than an occasional evening out with your husband. You, Dr. Pollack, need a genuine vacation."

"As a matter of fact, we're going on one." In all the excitement over Mollie, she'd forgotten. "Just Slade and me. He thinks it's about time we had that honeymoon we keep postponing. He says he wants to go before he's too old to remember why he's there."

Dana had seen the looks, the touches exchanged between them. Easy, without thought, just part of their everyday lives. It gladdened her heart even as it filled it with envy. "I don't think Slade will ever be too old."

Sheila grinned. "That's exactly what I said." She thought of his reaction to that, and her skin warmed, just as it had then. "While we're gone, you're welcome to stay on. Pilar will be here, taking care of Rebecca, but you can have the run of the place."

Dana couldn't allow herself to be swayed. Otherwise, she would never leave. "Tempting, but I've put this off long enough. The longer I wait, the more ominous her grandfather becomes for Mollie."

Sheila nodded. Dana was making sense, but she still wished her friend didn't have to go. "Okay, but if you change your mind, or if you need a place to retreat for any reason, my house is yours.''

Dana smiled. Just like the old days. ''Thanks. I'll keep that in mind.''

Chapter 7

The fact that her grandfather was in a wheelchair made no difference whatsoever to Mollie. Or to Dana. Standing or sitting, Paul Morrow had always been, and continued to be, a formidable man.

It was his manner that induced and inflicted fear.

Dana and Mollie had arrived a few minutes earlier. Dickinson, who she assumed lived somewhere on the premises, opened the door to them, instead of Esther, as she'd expected. He assured Dana that their things would be immediately attended to.

There had been nothing left but to get on with Mollie's introduction to her grandfather.

He was in the den, reviewing some obscure point of law to see how he could use it to skewer his opposition. He laid the tome on the desk as soon as they entered the room.

For once, Dana noted with a sense of satisfaction, he didn't pretend to be so taken with what he was reading that he didn't hear her come in. If she hadn't known better, she would have said he'd been waiting for this. It went beyond the power of imagination to think he was actually looking forward to it.

"So, we finally meet."

Hands folded before him, Morrow looked down a nose that was a little too short to be termed hawklike, assessing his granddaughter the way he might have a client who had entered his office for the first time. Having had little time for his own children, he had no idea of the kind of care or conversation children required, only that it was annoyingly different from what he was accustomed to.

Dana placed a soothing hand on Mollie's shoulder. She could see agitation flickering across the small face. Ushering her only as far as she was willing to go, Dana softly said, "Mollie, this is your grandfather, Paul Morrow."

"No need to tell her," Morrow snapped. He hated stupidity. To him, it was the worst of all possible sins. The child wasn't slow—why did Dana have to explain who he was? "She knows who I am, don't you, Mollie?" Working the controls on the armrest, he moved his chair forward and reached out to her. Afraid, Mollie shifted so that she was partially hidden behind Dana. His blue eyes glinted. "What's the matter with her?"

"Offhand, I'd say you're frightening her." Taking her hand, Dana coaxed Mollie forward. "It's okay, Mollie, there's nothing to be afraid of." *He's just a grumpy, disgruntled old man, nothing more.*

As if he read her thoughts—she'd believed he could when she was Mollie's age—her father demanded, "What did you tell her about me?"

The silent accusation annoyed her, since she'd done the exact opposite of what he implied in an attempt to calm Mollie. And he was ruining her carefully laid groundwork by behaving the way he always did. Demanding, insensitive and overbearing. Nothing had changed.

"That you didn't eat children for breakfast," Dana answered coldly. She draped one hand around Mollie's thin shoulders, silently trying to reassure her. But the scowl across her grandfather's face did little to assuage Mollie's fears.

"What?"

This wasn't going to work, Dana thought. At least, not right away. It was going to take time, the one thing she wasn't sure she had. But there was no one to ask about that. God wasn't answering his phone today.

Dana squared off with her father, shifting so she was between him and the little girl. "She has this impression that you're an ogre because you made Megan cry."

He took umbrage. "I never made Megan cry."

There was no feeling in her smile. It was as cold as those she had seen grace his face. "You underestimate yourself, Father. At one time or other, I'm willing to speculate that you made everyone cry."

Incensed, Morrow bristled at the image she was fabricating before the child. It was a blatant lie. And he could easily prove it. "I never made you cry."

Dana raised her chin, pride forbidding her from making the admission. She wouldn't give him the satisfaction of knowing that he had twisted her young soul. A great many tears had been shed in secret before she knew better than to let him get to her.

"No, you never made me cry."

His eyes shifted once more to Mollie, to take measure. She looked well enough. "Esther said she was sick."

He was old and ill and probably afraid of contracting something. "Don't worry, she's better." As Dana spoke, she stroked Mollie's hair. Though silent, she knew Mollie was absorbing everything, every word, every nuance, just like Megan used to do before her. "She won't contaminate you."

True or not, the fear made him sound weak, and he refused to acknowledge even a hint of weakness. "That wasn't what I asked."

She knew him, and that annoyed the hell out of him, Dana thought. For a moment it almost made her feel smug. "No, but that was *why* you asked."

He damned her for her impertinence, for knowing. "I want her checked out by my doctor."

Amusement curved her mouth further. "You have a pediatrician?"

Was she laughing at him? There was a time when he wouldn't even have stopped to wonder. He would simply have had her removed. But that time was gone. Other things had moved forward to prey on his mind. He hadn't become more patient, just realized that there was a need to act as if he had in order to win. "I have the best," he countered.

The last thing Mollie needed was to be subjected to more doctors. After last night, Dana was satisfied that what Sheila said about Rafe Saldana was true. He was at the top of his profession. There was no need for a second opinion.

"So do we. Dr. Rafe Saldana." She exchanged looks with Mollie. The little girl nodded vigorously, the first sign of animation since she'd entered the house. "He signed her out of Harris Memorial and said she was fine. I believe him." Dana took Mollie's hand, ready to lead her out of the room. "I'd like to get her settled in, if you don't mind."

Though tiring, he was surprised at their withdrawal. He gestured toward Mollie. "We haven't had a chance to talk yet." They'd barely said hello.

Dana was firm, though her voice was amiable for Mollie's sake. "I thought maybe the two of you could take this in slow doses." To convince him, she knew she needed something more than her own judgment, since he'd never thought much of it before. "Dr. Saldana said not to tire her out too much."

Morrow accepted that. With a stipulation. "I still want her examined by my doctor."

There was no negotiating on this point. "Sorry, Father, I'd like to keep the poking and prodding to a minimum." She saw his face cloud. There was a time when she would have taken that as a sign to run, but that time had passed. She had nothing to lose now, and perhaps, she thought, even respect to gain. At the very least, she could protect Mollie. "Mollie is afraid of doctors. After what she's been through, I'd say she has good reason to be.''

She turned and saw the housekeeper in the doorway. ''My old room?''

Esther smiled. ''Yes, miss. I had Dickinson put your things there.'' Looking at Mollie, Esther felt as if something was squeezing her heart. The little girl was the image of Megan at that age. ''Have you ever met Logan?'' she asked Mollie.

Mollie shook her head solemnly, trying not to seem as eager to leave the room as she felt. Her mother had always said not to be rude. She didn't want to do anything to get her grandfather mad at her. ''No.''

Esther's smile was mysterious. ''Well, he's waiting to meet you.''

Mollie raised her eyes to Dana, hoping for an explanation.

She'd saved it, Dana thought, a bittersweet sensation wafting through her. Esther had saved the toy all these years. Why?

''Logan was my old teddy bear,'' she told Mollie.

''Oh.'' Mollie brightened immediately. ''Okay.'' She took the hand Esther extended to her. Before leaving the room, Mollie looked over her shoulder at her grandfather. ''Good night,'' she said politely, her expression once again subdued.

The subdued look disappeared the moment she turned toward Esther and hurried off.

This, Dana thought as she followed behind them, had the makings of a lovely friendship. Esther had been the haven she'd sought again and again during her stormy younger years.

''You kept my teddy bear?'' she had to ask. She'd thought it had been thrown out years ago, when she had outgrown it. Now she realized childhood things were not really outgrown, merely put to one side.

Esther's reply was matter-of-fact and practical, giving not even the remotest hint of the sentimentality that governed her. ''I thought you might like it for your own children someday.''

Though Dana gave no indication, the words hit far too close to home.

Morrow watched them leave. His own granddaughter and she lit up like a damn Christmas tree because a housekeeper waved a bribe in front of her like some damn carrot before a rabbit. A bribe that wasn't even hers to wave.

She was *his* granddaughter, damn it. He'd allowed her to come here. He'd allowed Dana to come here, and she didn't even have the decency to behave as if she was grateful.

Neither of them did. He knew what kind of situation his daughter found herself in, knew how low her funds were almost to the penny. And yet she behaved as if she was doing him a favor by being here.

He was the one doing the favors, damn it, not her. Not—

Morrow pressed his lips together in frustrated anger as he felt his hand begin to tremble. Glaring at the offending limb, he willed it to stop. But the palsy continued as he cursed it.

Hating what was happening to him, to the body he had always taken for granted, he placed his other hand over the one that was moving independent of his wishes. He pressed down hard, hard enough to cause tears to spring to his eyes, trying to make it stop.

It refused.

Dana couldn't sleep. Though she felt exhausted beyond words, for some reason sleep refused to come.

It had taken her the better part of the evening to get Mollie settled. Time had crawled by before she finally fell asleep. Dana had been sure that all she would have to do was lay her head on the pillow and she would be asleep within seconds.

The seconds came and went, and she was still awake.

She'd lain there with her eyes shut, waiting to be overtaken by sleep. Instead, she'd remained wide awake as the minutes, then the hours, ticked away.

Maybe it was her surroundings keeping her awake. There

was no denying they were a factor. It was hard for her to believe she was here after all this time. Back in a place she had sworn never to return to as she fled, watching the house disappear in her rearview mirror.

She'd meant it at the time.

But at the time her father had been healthy, at the top of his game. And Megan had been alive, pandering to his every whim. When she'd left home, her sister hadn't begun to develop a backbone.

That hadn't happened until George entered her life.

Dana didn't want to think about that. She really didn't want to think about anything.

Restless, she sat up and threw off the covers. Moonlight seeped through the window, a campfire lantern whose batteries were waning. It made everything look eerie, distant.

It had felt that way even when she was a child, she thought. This had never been her sanctuary. It was another room in her father's house when he was here. And even when he was gone, away in another state, defending another affluent or influential client, his presence was still felt. Felt so strongly it left a pall over the house that no amount of sunshine could lift.

Damn, what had she been thinking of, coming here? And with Mollie, too. She must have been crazy.

At two in the morning, returning felt like a colossal mistake.

Why had she been optimistic enough to think she could somehow accomplish something that had eluded her for so many years? Did she really think she had a chance of being able to coexist with her father in something other than a battlefield? She'd come to the table without any bargaining chips, without the cards stacked in her favor. How could she hope to win?

But she had come to play, and she did have one thing in her favor. He couldn't intimidate her anymore. She was an adult now. A bar-certified lawyer, just like he was.

Well, not just like he was.

No one would pay her the kind of money he could demand to defend them, but then, she wasn't ruthlessly bent on annihilating the opposition, either. And her record wasn't perfect, like his.

Dana smiled. What kind of a lawyer did that make her?

A pregnant one.

The thought reared from nowhere, attacking her unannounced as it had a dozen or so times since Sheila had dropped the devastating bombshell on her in her office.

Pregnant.

With Steven's baby.

Dana scrubbed her hands over her face. She couldn't get used to the idea. Still prayed Sheila was mistaken, although in her heart Dana knew that wasn't possible. Pregnancy was the mainstay of Sheila's profession. She should know a pregnant woman when she examined one.

Sighing deeply, Dana wrestled with her conscience. That, too, was a by-product of the hour. It was incredible, the thoughts that crawled out of the woodwork at one in the morning. Like guilt. Guilt that in the light of day would have seemed laughable.

Guilt because she hadn't told Steven he had fathered a child.

As if he really wanted to know that.

But what if he did? Bastard or not, he deserved to know. Deserved the right to hang up on her, she thought cynically.

The idea of talking to him left her cold. Given a choice, she never wanted to see him or hear from him again. She didn't have that luxury. It had to be done. Sooner or later, he had to be told.

Damn, why was life filled with so many have-tos? Why couldn't she drift through it, being taken care of by someone? Someone kind, caring. Someone like Rafe Saldana, who loved children and was dedicated to making them feel better.

Startled by the path her mind had veered onto, she abandoned the entire line of thought.

No use in wallowing in self-pity. That accomplished nothing except for wasting time. She was who she was. She was the one who took care, not the one taken care of. That was the way things were.

Muttering, she dragged the telephone from the nightstand and dialed the number that had so recently been hers. It was late, but she didn't care. She wanted to get this over with.

Her heart felt like a heavy stone in her chest as she listened to the phone ring.

Two, three, four.

And then there was a noise. Sharp needles jabbed at her nerves until she realized it was his machine that had picked up, not him.

Where the hell was he at this hour?

With that bimbo, that was where. The one he'd been sneaking around with while telling her he loved her. While verbally abusing Mollie.

"Hi, this is Steven. I can't come to the phone right now—"

Dana let the receiver drop into the cradle. He'd changed the message, she thought, irritated. *I* can't come to the phone instead of *we.*

Well, what had she expected, to have him build a shrine to her memory? If he'd been into shrine building, he wouldn't have gone tomcatting around while she was living with him. And he would have been kind to Mollie instead of treating her as if she was some subhuman irritant.

Dana glared at the telephone, cursing her stupidity. There was no reason to tell him he was going to become a father, other than the moral rightness of it. He didn't want children. He'd made that perfectly clear by the way he treated Mollie. She would have given anything if, just once, he had behaved the way Rafe Saldana did.

Her thoughts shifted to Rafe as she lay down again. She had no idea what the man would be like as a husband, but as a father, there was no question in her mind. He would be wonderful. You could tell.

And maybe, just maybe, that meant he wouldn't be so bad as a husband, either. A man who was good with kids had potential. And Rafe Saldana definitely had potential, she thought, beginning to drift off. Potential for a lot of things…

Daylight crept in, slipping between her lashes, prying apart her lids. She had half a second or so of peace before morning slammed into her with the force of a sledgehammer applied to her midsection.

She jackknifed up, stunned, confused and utterly nauseated.

Taking in her surroundings with unfocused eyes, she was unnerved. She was in her old room, amid the highly polished dark wood furniture and oppressive drapes. In the living tomb with vaulted ceilings.

If she hadn't felt so sick, that reality might have preyed even more heavily on her mind.

Her feet hit the floor, and she had just enough time to make it into the bathroom before her stomach rose up to meet her throat, determined to purge itself. She had absolutely no say in the matter.

Mercifully, this morning's episode was briefer than usual. Maybe her body was finally getting accustomed to the invader that had entered it, she thought, rising from her knees.

There had to be a better way.

Bending over the sink, Dana rinsed her mouth and splashed water on her face. She looked at her reflection, her eyes bleary from lack of sleep. Trust Steven to find a way to make her feel sick to her stomach even when he wasn't around.

It took her a while before she could summon the strength to get dressed, and even longer to find enough to face her father over breakfast.

She was grateful for the diversion of having to fetch Mollie.

Her father was at the table when she came down, Mollie's hand in hers. Dana had known he would be. Just as she'd known the look in his eyes would be critical as he observed them. It was a given.

He nodded a curt greeting as his daughter and granddaughter walked into the wide dining room. The table, too formal for a family to converge around, was intended for entertaining his peers and his clients. He favored it, foregoing the one in the kitchen. Kitchens were for working in, not for dining in, he staunchly maintained. He'd forbidden his daughters from eating there as children. Common people ate in the kitchen, he'd told them. People with no education, no future, huddled about an uneven table that wobbled each time they sat down or rose from it. Or tried to eat.

Dana and Mollie sat at the far end of the dining table, accentuating the distance between them. Annoyed, he waved his granddaughter closer.

"Sit here," he ordered Mollie, indicating the chair to his left. "Where I can see you better." Instead of obeying, Mollie looked hesitantly at Dana. He could feel his temper fraying. Why couldn't she just do as he asked? "You don't have to get your aunt's approval for everything I say. This is my house, girl."

"Mollie," Dana corrected tersely. They moved closer and reseated themselves. "Her name is Mollie."

His eyes narrowed. He didn't like being corrected. "I called *you* 'girl.'"

That was just the point. "And I hated it."

She wasn't making any sense. "Why?" he demanded.

His habit of calling her that, especially while lecturing, had irritated her for years. "Because I figured it meant you couldn't remember my name. You called Megan 'girl,' too."

Mollie looked from her grandfather to her aunt. "Did that make you girl one?"

It took a second for the words to register. When they did, Dana experienced an uncontrollable urge to laugh. And then, because tension was so close to the surface, so close to exploding, she did. It was a hell of a lot better than screaming.

"No, honey. Too as in also, not as in the number." Her eyes slid toward her father. "Your grandfather didn't give out numbers.'' Everyone was the same to him. Beings beneath him.

''So, Mollie—'' Morrow emphasized her name pointedly, momentarily raising his eyes to Dana ''—do you go to school yet?''

''I went to preschool for a while.''

He knew she'd dropped out of class after the accident, unable to attend. And then Dana had come for her and moved the girl out of state. Dana had been called, not him. That had been per instructions—his late daughter's instructions. Megan hadn't trusted him with her child. That, more than anything, rankled him. As if he, and not they, had not lived up to the faith placed in him.

''Well,'' he informed Mollie as he poured a dollop of syrup on his French toast, ''you have to go again now. To kindergarten this time.''

''It's summer, Father.'' Had he forgotten? Of course he had. The seasons were all one and the same to him, just as she and Megan had been. ''School's out in the summer. I'll have her registered by fall.''

''In your old school?'' The private school's rates were prohibitive to the average person. It was one of the reasons he'd chosen it. He liked being associated with things other men could not afford to even think about. It had been a long, hard climb to this pinnacle, and he meant to savor everything, however small. ''Just how do you intend to pay for that?''

Did he think she was going to ask him for money? ''She's going to public school.''

''Public school?'' He spat the words out as if they left a horrid taste in his mouth. ''Are you out of your mind? My granddaughter is—''

''—going to public school,'' Dana said firmly.

''If it's a matter of money, I could—''

''No,'' Dana contradicted quietly, ''you couldn't, and you won't.'' She said the next sentence slowly, so that each syllable would sink in. ''Mollie is my responsibility.''

"Responsibility is next to impossible without money to back it up."

No, Father, responsibility is a feeling, a pledge, not a check. "I have money."

He knew better. The insurance policy was almost gone, eaten up by Mollie's medical bills, as was her bank account. "Not enough."

That tore it. Dana dropped her knife on her plate with a clang. Mollie's eyes darted toward her. She hadn't meant to scare Mollie, but she was angry.

"Oh, I forgot, you would know that. Just as you knew where I was staying. And probably how many vitamins I take in the morning. Just what don't you know?" She leaned over the table. "Tell you what, why don't you tell me exactly what your detective failed to report to you, and I'll see if I can fill in the gaps!"

He threw down his napkin. A corner fell into his coffee cup, absorbing the drops that were left. "I don't know what you're talking about."

"Yes, you do. You had me investigated, tailed and God only knows what else." She drew herself up. "How dare you? How dare you invade my life like that?"

"How dare I?" he echoed. Fury entered his eyes at the challenge to his authority. No one talked to him like that. Ever. "How else was I supposed to know about you?"

It wasn't like him to miss the obvious. Except when it came to her. "There's such a thing as the telephone, Father. In eight years, you could have found time to pick it up just once. Besides, explain this to me. Why would you want to know?"

How could she even ask that? "Because you're mine."

Like a possession. Her anger rose to meet his. "Only if I want to be."

She was wrong, he thought. "Blood isn't a matter of choice, Dana. It just *is.*" He looked at Mollie, who shrank from his glare. "Remember that."

"Yes, sir," she mumbled, afraid to look away.

He pushed his chair back from the table. ''I have to get to the office.''

Dana looked at his plate. He'd hardly touched anything. ''You haven't finished your breakfast.''

He missed the veiled concern and heard only the accusation. ''I've lost my appetite.''

She rose, as if to restrain him. ''You're not well. You can't afford to skip meals.''

He wouldn't be dictated to by someone he'd brought into the world. ''Don't tell me what I can and can't do.''

She wasn't about to back away, though she wanted to. ''Somebody should.''

He fixed her with a cold look. ''Well, it won't be you.'' With that, he directed the motorized wheelchair out of the room.

''Does he hate you, Aunt Dana?'' Mollie was whispering, even though he was gone.

Dana took a deep breath before answering, trying to calm her nerves. No one could irritate her the way he could.

''No, sugar, I think it's himself he hates.'' She gave her a heartening smile. ''C'mon, don't let him spoil your appetite. Esther makes the best French toast around.'' She urged some on the girl.

Chapter 8

''I see you have a new address.''

Rafe looked up from the patient folder he was reading as he walked into the examination room. He placed Mollie's folder on the small counter against the wall. Mollie had regained her color. No loss of energy here, he thought, pleased.

''Did you move?'' He directed the question to the little girl.

She nodded. Though she would have liked to stay with Slade and Sheila, she didn't say anything to Aunt Dana. She didn't want to make her feel sad. ''We're at my grandfather's house now.''

The statement, so seriously uttered, made him smile. He had an image of Shirley Temple, playing Heidi, saying the very same thing.

''So you did finally meet him.'' His hands on either side of her waist, Rafe gently lifted her and placed her on the end of the examining table. ''Up you go. Say, have you been working out?''

She giggled, covering her mouth. There was pure adoration in her eyes. ''No.''

''Well, you certainly feel like it to me.'' He reached for his otoscope. ''So, you're living with your grandfather, huh? Is he as scary as you thought?''

She tilted her head, patiently enduring the exam even though she wanted to wiggle. ''Kinda.''

''Eyes clear,'' he pronounced for Dana's benefit. ''Ditto ears.'' He took a tongue depressor from the breast pocket of his lab coat. ''But you're giving him a chance, right?''

Mollie eyed the wooden stick with resignation. She didn't like this part. ''Uh-huh.''

''Say ah.'' He waited until she did as he asked. ''Must be a pretty nice guy to let you come live with him. Throat normal.'' He jettisoned the depressor into the basket in the corner, making the shot. Mollie clapped. Playing along, Rafe modestly bowed his head in thanks.

''It's a large house.''

Dana had no idea why she felt compelled to say that. Maybe she didn't want him thinking she'd moved back with her father because she had no options, or that she was someone who had to have other people take care of her. Not that it mattered what he thought, just that he did seem to be a pretty decent guy, and there was no point in him getting the wrong idea about her.

She'd spent part of the past hour sitting in the waiting room, listening to one testimonial after another about the fine young doctor. Sheila hadn't been kidding when she said Rafe Saldana's patients' parents sang his praises. Dana could almost hear the accompanying music as first one, then another mother volunteered stories of how good Rafe was with his young patients, how he could always be reached day or night, not like some doctors they'd had. And how he was never too busy to explain things to them. Never too busy to care.

Thirty-five minutes of that and she'd half expected to see him coming into the examining room wearing wings and a halo.

The image seemed slightly incongruent with the look in his eyes when he glanced in her direction. He had green eyes. Beautiful, soulful, light green eyes that seemed incredibly sensual when he looked directly at her. She wondered if he realized how sensual. If he did, he hadn't capitalized on it, at least not according to Sheila or his groupies.

"Any complaints?" Rafe retired his stethoscope. Her lungs were pure music. When Mollie shook her head, he raised his eyes to Dana for confirmation.

"She's been fine," Dana said. "Full of energy, as if she'd never been sick."

Nice not to see her brow furrowed with worry for a change, he thought.

"I told you, kids are wonderfully resilient." Rummaging in the coat's deep pockets, he found what he was looking for. Rafe took out a lollipop and looked at Dana before offering it to Mollie. "Is it all right?"

His thoughtfulness impressed her. She wouldn't have thought he would bother asking but just hand the treat out. Feeling oddly touched, she nodded.

He presented the cherry-flavored treat to Mollie. "This is for you, kiddo, for being such a good patient."

"Thank you." The wrapper was off before she said *you.*

Because the atmosphere was relaxed, Dana found herself thinking of Rafe as someone other than a stranger whose services she required. "Do you realize you have a fan club out there?"

He arched an eyebrow, then took the information in stride. "My nurses are required to sing my praises or I don't give them their paychecks on Friday." He made a few notes on Mollie's chart.

"No, I meant the women in the waiting room. This one women in particular—she had twins with her..."

Rafe reviewed his appointments. "That would be Nicole Lincoln. I've been taking care of Ethan and Erika since they were two months old." He'd seen them through a harrowing bout of pneumonia before their first birthday, he recalled.

''Her husband's with the Justice Department. I mess up, I'm history.'' He winked at Mollie.

In the line of fire, Dana found the wink extremely sexy, though she knew he hadn't meant it to be. If she wasn't careful, she was going to start to sound like those women she'd been talking to.

She found his modesty an incredible change of pace after Steven, and especially her father. ''She thinks you're the best thing since rain on a dry crop.''

That was a new one, he mused. ''She's also friends with Sheila.'' It was Sheila who had delivered Nicole's twins. And Sheila who had recommended him to Nicole when she sought a second opinion about a minor problem with Ethan. After the first visit, Nicole had wound up bringing both twins to him. ''That makes her prejudiced.''

That wasn't an obvious connection. ''*I'm* friends with Sheila, and I was prepared to dislike you.''

Adding a line to the file, he raised his eyes to hers. ''I think you're prepared to dislike everyone.'' Finished, Rafe flipped the file closed. ''Why is that?''

He'd delved further than she wanted him to. But because she was feeling less defensive around him, she answered, ''It's safer that way.''

He could see her argument. He saw something else, too. ''Also colder.''

Colder. The word hit her with the jarring force of a two-by-four. That was, she realized, what she'd often accused her father of being. Colder than snow. That the term was being applied to her was something she didn't care for. She cared even less for the fact that it was true. At least, looking in from the outside.

Seeing he'd struck a nerve, Rafe directed his attention to his patient. ''You, young lady, are in perfect health.'' Laying his finger on the tip of her nose, he pressed it lightly, as if to impress his next words upon her mind. ''See that you stay that way.''

Mollie shifted the lollipop to one side in her mouth in order to answer. It pouched out her cheek, making her look like a chipmunk storing nuts.

"Yes, Dr. Rafe."

He set her on the floor. And then, because he didn't want to leave the air between them cluttered with awkward discomfort, he asked Dana, "So, eaten any good chicken soup lately?"

"No, not since the hospital." She smiled, remembering how kind he'd been, then roused herself. Though she appreciated the care he gave Mollie, she didn't want him thinking she was becoming a card-carrying member of his fan club. "Right now, I'm more interested in finding some decent Tex-Mex food."

The declaration interested him. "Haven't you been to La Reina Simpatica yet?"

She was unfamiliar with the name. But then, so much had changed since she'd lived here. There were shopping malls where she had left fields ripe with corn and strawberries.

"No."

He laughed softly. Dana found the sound almost hypnotically engaging. "You don't know what you're missing. It's in Newport Beach on Pacific Coast Highway, just before you hit Laguna Beach. The food's out of this world, if you like that sort of thing."

That was the whole point, wasn't it? "I do," she maintained. Then, because he sounded so sure of his assessment, she sniffed. "But I doubt it can compare with this little hole in the wall I know in Dallas." Squeezed between what had once been a storefront church, now vacated, and a discount shoe store that was perpetually going out of business, it wasn't even remotely familiar with the term *ambience,* something that was written into the leases of the restaurants here. She paused, thinking. "I don't think it even had a name. Just a rude owner who knew the value of an excellently prepared meal." Once she'd found it, the restaurant had quickly become one of her favorite places. She'd frequented it so often, the owner had upscaled his attitude toward her to only slightly patronizing.

Steven's comment on that, she recalled, had been to ask her if she'd been sleeping with the old man.

Rafe grinned, as if tolerant of her naïveté. "Oh, I'm sure La Reina could not only compare to but surpass your little hole in the wall."

She should have let it go at that, but she couldn't. Dana had no idea what possessed her, but she heard herself asking, "You wouldn't like to make a bet on that, would you?"

His laugh, rich and deep, made her think of a streetwise con artist about to separate her from her money. "You're on. Five bucks too rich for your blood?"

She almost jeered. "No, but it shows me that you're made of the same stuff you brought me in the hospital." When he looked uncertain, she pursed her lips and said, "Chicken."

He couldn't put his finger on why her cockiness amused him. Or why the way she pursed her lips aroused him. He dismissed both. "Okay. Loser pays for the dinner."

Dana inclined her head. "Sounds fair."

Fair, the key word. He held up a finger. "One hitch. This all hinges on you." His eyes held hers. "How will I know if you're telling the truth?"

The smile on her face remained, but it grew serious around the edges. With eyes like his, she caught herself thinking, he could see right into her soul if it was necessary. But it wouldn't be.

"Because I don't lie."

No, he thought, she didn't. No matter what. Here, too, he had no idea why he believed her. He just did.

"All right. So how does tomorrow night sound? Six-thirty all right with you?"

Dana hesitated. Maybe she had gotten carried away, here.

Almost finished with her lollipop, Mollie tugged on Dana's sleeve. When Dana looked down, she asked, "Are you going out on a date with Dr. Rafe?"

For a moment, caught up in the exchange, she had forgotten Mollie was in the room. How had that happened? Dana wondered. Mollie was the only reason she was here.

Self-conscious and trying hard not to show it, Dana cleared her throat. ''Not a date, honey, dinner.''

Mollie didn't see the difference. ''But dinner can be a date.''

Was that a flush she felt creeping up her neck? God, she hoped not. ''Yes, but—''

''Yes!'' Mollie shouted, making a fist and bringing her elbow to her waist with a triumphant jerk, the way she'd seen people do on television. Aunt Dana was going on a date with Dr. Rafe. Maybe she would get to like him a lot, more than that mean old Steven. Everything was going to be perfect.

Embarrassed, Dana was at a loss. Rafe looked too amused for her to apologize, so in the end she said nothing.

He opened the door for them. ''I'll pick you up at the new address?'' Dana nodded, feeling the slightest bit numb. ''Don't forget to bring your wallet,'' he told her. Was that mischief in his eyes? ''You'll be paying for the evening.''

As she walked toward the reception desk with Mollie, Dana had the uneasy feeling he might be right—and in more ways than one.

Over the next twenty-seven hours, Dana carried on half a dozen arguments with herself. Depending on her state of mind, the final verdict regarding her going out to dinner with Rafe was sometimes yes and sometimes no.

She was leaning toward no, but yes kept cropping up like a cork that couldn't be sunk.

A woman carrying another man's child had no business going out with someone. The thought, the protest, echoed in her brain more than once, louder each time.

But as she had taken great pains to point out in front of both Mollie and Rafe, this wasn't a date. It was a meal. People had meals with one another all the time, and it didn't mean anything. Right?

Dana flounced on her bed, frustrated and not sure why. If

going out to La Reina Simpatica didn't mean anything, why was she having this damn debate with herself?

Because it had been so long since she had gone out with anyone except Steven that the prospect of doing it with anyone else felt unsettlingly new to her.

It was just because her escape from Steven had left her stressed and on edge, she silently pointed out.

Dana pulled her knees to her chest, warding off the shiver that threatened to ripple through her body. Escape. The word hummed in her brain. That was what it had been, an escape, pure and simple. An escape from a life that was swallowing her up.

A life she didn't want.

There was absolutely no doubt in her mind about that. She didn't want to spend her life emotionally tied to a man who didn't care. She'd spent her youth that way, and that was more than enough.

But she'd come back to her youth, hadn't she? The thought mocked her.

It wasn't the same.

She'd returned because her father was ill, and because there were things that needed to be fixed, loose ends that needed to be tied. Fences that needed to be mended. And then she had to close the gates.

For good.

That still didn't help her decide whether she should go through with this tonight.

Disgusted with herself, with this Ping-Pong game taking place in her brain, Dana decided it was best not to think at all.

Or would it be best not to *go* at all?

No, that would be the coward's way out, and she refused to be a coward. Besides, she was making too much of this. This wasn't a date. If it had been, he wouldn't have asked her in front of Mollie, wouldn't have worded it the way he had. This was nothing more than two people settling a bet.

She buried her head against her knees.

Excitement in her eyes, Mollie skipped into the room. Not waiting for an invitation, she scrambled onto the bed, wiggling into position beside her aunt. She deliberately mimicked her aunt's pose, scooting her knees up and wrapping her arms around them. It didn't seem all that comfortable to Mollie, but she desperately wanted to be just like Aunt Dana.

"Whatcha gonna wear tonight?" she wanted to know. "Something pretty?"

She didn't own anything pretty, Dana thought. She hadn't packed very much when she'd left Steven. Only her photographs and some of Mollie's things. Her own clothes had been a very low priority. She had just wanted to leave before she weakened and lost her resolve. Sheila had lent her a few things, but she didn't feel right about keeping them.

Dana feathered her fingers through Mollie's baby-fine hair. "I don't have much to choose from, sweetie."

"Don't these closets have things in them?" Rather than wait to be told, Mollie climbed off the bed and went to see for herself.

Dana hadn't bothered opening the walk-in closet behind the mirrored, sliding glass doors. There was no point, since she expected it to be empty. She'd used the bureau to house her things.

But when Mollie struggled and pushed one long sliding door to the side, Dana saw the closet was full.

There were clothes hanging there.

Her clothes.

Stunned, she got off the bed and crossed to the closet, a child in a fairy tale. Or, more to the point, a woman who didn't know whether she was dreaming or not.

It wasn't a dream. Or a hallucination. The clothes were there. They were real. Amazed, excited, confused, Dana slid one dress after another along the pole.

He hadn't thrown them out.

She was sure he'd had them all destroyed when she left home against his wishes. Or, at the very least, had given them away to charity.

Why had he kept them? Had he expected her to return someday? He would have known better than that.

But she had, hadn't she? she thought. She *had* returned home.

Her hands flew over the familiar items, nudging forth memories as she looked at a favorite dress or blouse. Dana pressed her lips together, rivers of happiness and sadness running together, pouring through her veins. She blew out a shaky breath as she tucked away an oversize sweatshirt the boy she'd had a crush on her junior year in high school had given her. What was his name? Jim? No, Joe. Joe Taylor.

She smiled, sentimentality tugging at her. Well, at least this solved the problem of having nothing to wear.

Mollie entertained herself by moving in and out between the long line of dresses against the back wall. "You've got lots of pretty things to pick from, Aunt Dana." She turned to look at her, awed. "Whose clothes are they?"

"Mine," Dana answered quietly, looking at a burgundy suit.

This was the suit she'd worn on her sixteenth birthday. She'd sat on the window seat, looking out. Waiting for her father to come home to take her out to celebrate, just the two of them. The way he'd promised. She slid her fingers along the sleeve. He'd called two days later to wish her a belated happy birthday. He'd been in Washington, D.C., at the time. Detained. She no longer remembered who he'd been defending. Only that she'd sworn that day never to be stupid enough to believe anything he said to her again.

Never to let him hurt her again.

Mollie burrowed into another line of clothes, reveling in the new playground she had discovered for herself.

"Are they *all* yours?"

"Yes, they're all mine. Or they *were* all mine," Dana amended. "Before I left home. I guess your grandfather kept them."

Mollie popped her head from between a mauve sundress

and a white sheath to look at her. "That was nice of him, huh?"

Nice was stretching it. But it was definitely *some*thing. She wasn't sure what. "Yes, it was," she murmured.

"How about this one?" Eager to help, to make her as pretty as possible to Dr. Rafe, Mollie held out a light blue chiffon skirt. She'd unearthed the dress Dana had worn to her senior prom. "It's very soft. Dr. Rafe'll like it."

Oh, God, she had a junior matchmaker on her hands. "I think it's a bit too formal," Dana told her tactfully.

Nodding, Mollie let the fabric go. The skirt retreated amid the rest of the garments. "Okay. You can wear that the next time."

Dana opened her mouth to correct Mollie, then shut it. It might be too daunting for Mollie to hear that there wasn't going to be a next time. This was a one-time thing. And she had accepted not because of her craving for Tex-Mex food but, she admitted to herself, because of her underlying craving to talk to a decent man for the space of an evening. It would be a nice change.

Her head filled with testimonials to Rafe Saldana's "wonderfulness," as one preschooler had said, she'd gotten carried away by the moment.

And, she supposed, by her need to be able to spend an hour or so with a man she knew she wouldn't have to fight off. Or fight with. Rafe didn't look like a pushover, and she knew he spoke his mind, but he seemed like a fair man, and that was all she required, the company of a decent, fair man. A man she didn't have to watch her back with. Or any other part of her anatomy, either.

On their first date, Steven had barely been able to keep his hands off her in the restaurant. At the time she'd found it thrilling. But she was a hundred years older now, and maybe six months wiser.

It counted for something.

She heard the front door open and then close rather loudly, then the sound of an angry voice raised in a tirade. Her father's words reverberated up the stairs. He had a voice that could carry to the back row of an opera house. He was proud of that, even boasted of it.

Glancing at her watch, she saw it was only a little past five. It was too early for her father to be home. When he wasn't in court, his usual pattern was to remain late at the office and to have dinner out. Rarely did he come home before eight, and usually sometime after ten.

But that was before, she reminded herself. Now the shell was wearing out and, she supposed, taking what passed as his soul with it.

Dana crossed to the door. She heard Mollie behind her. Turning, she motioned her back.

''Stay here, Mollie. See if you can find me something to wear,'' she added, hoping to keep her busy. Hoping, too, that she wouldn't regret it.

Mollie retreated willingly. ''Can I play dress up?''

''Be my guest.'' Looking over her shoulder, Dana grinned. ''Knock your socks off.''

Dana went to the landing and peered at the foyer below. Her father was no longer in view, and she didn't hear his voice. Wondering what was going on, she hurried down the long, curved stairway, only to encounter Esther at the bottom.

Dana looked around, but they were alone. ''Where's my father?''

Esther nodded toward the rear of the house. When he had first become confined to a wheelchair, Paul Morrow had had a master bedroom added on the ground floor and a connecting door put in the den. The two rooms, as spacious as some houses, comprised his lair. He hadn't been upstairs in over a year.

''I think he's gone into his den.'' When Dana stepped past her, Esther added, ''He doesn't want to see anyone, Miss Dana.''

No, she didn't imagine he would. But that didn't change her mind. ''I didn't come back to hide in the shadows when he was home.''

As she turned, Esther placed a hand on her arm. "I think it might be better if you let him have some time to himself. He doesn't like people seeing him when he's...indisposed."

Dana ignored the delicate euphemism. "I know what he has, Esther. I know the whole story. Sheila Pollack wrote to me in great detail. A lot of time's been wasted. Some of it my fault, a lot of it his. I don't want to waste what's left."

Concern for her rose in the housekeeper's brown eyes. "What are you going to say to him?"

Dana straightened, bracing herself. "I'll start with hello."

Chapter 9

Dana knocked on the door to the den. There was no answer. Knowing she was going to be met with extreme displeasure, she went in anyway.

There was an open decanter on his desk. The sun was filtering through it, casting an amber shadow on the opposite wall. Scotch. Her father favored brandy for socializing and Scotch for darker moments. She saw his hand shake ever so slightly as he raised the bottle and poured.

''Get out, Dickinson,'' he roared, never raising his eyes from the glass he was trying to fill. Why did something so simple require so much damn effort?

She nearly backed away. His tone unearthed memories she'd taken great pains to bury. But if those memories were to be eradicated, they had to be faced, not buried. She knew that. And that could only be accomplished one way.

Sheer grit made her hold her position. ''I came in to see what's wrong.''

The decanter slipped from his fingers and made it the last

two inches to the desk with a thud. A trickle of Scotch splashed over the thick cut-glass rim.

The look of surprise melted into one of malevolence, and his eyes narrowed. "Why? So you could bask in my mortality?"

How could he sit there and accuse her of something so heartless, so vindictively cruel? Didn't he know that no matter what had happened between them, she could never be capable of something that heinous?

The simple answer was no, he didn't know.

She stared at him in wonder that bordered on fascination.

"You really think I would do that, don't you? Be just like you." She watched as his eyes grew dangerous, but she didn't flinch. "You have no idea who your daughter is, Father. Who Megan was." Even as she said it, even though she'd been there during all his absences, it seemed incredible that he'd lived with them all those years and had still remained a stranger. "You haven't got a clue."

"I don't need clues." He gripped the armrests, his fingers channeling his fury. "I *know*."

Dana shook her head, more sad than angry. "You don't know anything."

She refused to allow him to cow her. Instead, she forced herself to move closer, until she was standing in front of him. Close enough to smell the alcohol. Close enough to smell the fear the alcohol was meant to veil. Something was very wrong.

"Why did you come home so early?" She searched his face for an answer, knowing he wouldn't volunteer one. "I can remember you staying out so late, Megan and I were convinced you never came home at all. That you were just a figment of our imaginations."

He threw back the contents of the glass the way he'd seen his father do countless times when he was a boy, then waited for the numbness to come. It didn't. He needed more. An ocean more, and then maybe the pain would go away. Or not matter.

"None of your damn business." He reached for the decanter.

Dana claimed it. "You're wrong." With an easy movement, she poured two fingers into his glass, though he had downed more than that. "It *is* my damn business." She set the intricate cut-glass bottle down. "You would have learned that, Counselor, if you had come home early once in a while when it counted. What goes on in a family is every member's business."

Her eyes met his. She searched in vain for his soul, for some small indication that she was getting through to him. A self-mocking smile curved her mouth.

"But I suppose that's really stretching it, isn't it? We were never a family. Just four people trying to survive with each other." Even that didn't ring quite true. "Or maybe three people trying to survive with you would be more accurate," she amended. The smile on her face wasn't bitter. It was the shadow of things that could have been. And hadn't.

He hated her in that moment. Hated her for what she was saying. Hated her for being young and healthy. And for having the years before her that he wouldn't. Hated her for being right.

"Get out."

Funny, once his look would have sent her running. Now it made her dig in. Did that mean she'd grown up, or that he had lost his touch?

"I didn't come home to get out, Father. I came home to take down this damn wall between us, one brick at a time if I have to." Right now, that felt like a completely impossible goal. "But maybe I flattered myself too much. I don't seem to have the tools."

She focused on why she had returned, why she had come here instead of half a dozen other places that would have done just as well. She'd returned because she realized his time was no longer endless. And she was the last of his family. She'd returned not just for herself, or for him, she'd returned for

Mollie and, in a way, for Meggie and for her mother. There had to be peace in the family.

Did he understand what she was attempting to do? She doubted it.

"You know what happens when there are walls, Father? People on either side of them don't get to see a thing that's going on on the other side. They miss a lot." She wasn't getting through. Stymied, resigned, she crossed to the door. "Good night." Dana turned the doorknob.

"I stuttered."

Not even daring to breathe, Dana slowly turned to look at him. Had her imagination conjured up his response? "What?" she whispered.

Damn it, was she going to make him say it again? "I stuttered." He spat the words, a cobra spitting venom. "Oh, it wasn't in court, it was during the briefing." For some, that might have mitigated the occurrence. Not for him. "But I stuttered."

Dana stepped away from the door, knowing what he was saying. Knowing that even the act of sharing the event was a significant step.

"So? Everyone stutters sometimes." Because it was her nature, because that much concern had survived despite everything, she tried to bury the incident for him. "The excitement of the moment, your thoughts racing faster than you tongue, even—"

Didn't she get it? This was his reputation they were talking about. "I'm not everyone. I don't stumble, and I don't stutter."

She looked at him pointedly. "Except that you did." He couldn't dwell on this. There would be other setbacks, and if he dwelled on them, they would eventually undo him. "Accept it and move on."

"Don't preach at me."

He was like a wounded animal, Dana thought, snapping at the hand that was extended only to aid him. "I wasn't aware I was preaching. I thought I was comforting."

His anger prevented him from seeing the difference. The look in his eyes was meant to make her back away. "I don't want your comfort or your pity."

She struggled to keep from lashing out at him. He made her so angry that she wanted to pummel him with both fists.

Now there was a pretty headline, she thought, restraining herself. *Renowned wheelchair-bound lawyer pummeled to death by irate estranged daughter.* The tabloid reporters would be lined up six deep for that one. A miserable coda to what had been, after all was said and done, a brilliant career.

"You don't have my pity because you stuttered or you faltered, Father. That's only human. You had my pity a long time ago because you're alone. You always were. And you know the worst part of it?" She studied his face, waiting for a spark of understanding or recognition. There was none. "It was of your own choosing."

Fury colored the sunken cheeks. "You don't know what you're talking about."

She sighed. What was the use? He only heard what he wanted to hear. She was just so much noise in the background.

"Have it your way."

Dana left the room and closed the door behind her, wishing she could do the same to this chapter of her life. Wishing she could walk away as she had the first time.

But she couldn't. Her stubborn determination forbade her.

Even when she heard the resounding crash of glass meeting wood, she kept on walking. It wasn't the first time.

Rafe arrived at her door an hour later. She'd almost called his service to cancel, then decided she needed to get out to clear her head. It was simpler just going along with the arrangements she'd made.

The first thing Rafe thought when he saw her at the door was that she cleaned up nicely. It was the first time he'd seen her in something other than jeans and a T-shirt, and he had to admit the difference was striking, even if the jeans were flattering to her curves.

Jeans didn't tell him that she had gorgeous legs. And denim did not create the same effect that formfitting fabric could. The lemon sheath definitely made her look like a sunny California girl.

The second thing that struck him was that she seemed in a hurry to leave. He found himself trailing after her to his car.

Rafe closed the passenger door for her, then rounded the rear of the car and got in himself. "I had no idea that Paul S. Morrow was your father."

It had suddenly come to him as he was going up the long, winding driveway to the house. He'd seen this shot in the Sunday *Times Magazine* section two or three years ago. Intrigued by the kind of person who would want to live in a house large enough to merit its own zip code, he'd read the article. And come away with mixed feelings about the man revealed in the pages of the article.

"Yes, Paul S. Morrow is my father." She blew out a breath. If she didn't watch her step, she was going to be as rude as her father. She slanted a glance at him.

"What does the *s* stand for?"

"Shark." And then she shook her head. "Sorry if that sounded snippy. There was a time when I thought everyone knew my father was Paul S. Morrow, that I had it stamped on my forehead, kind of like the mark of Cain."

She sounded, he thought, threading his way to MacArthur Boulevard, defensive. And hurt. "That bad?"

She was usually good about keeping her feelings in check, but this thing with her father was wearing on her. "I didn't say it was bad."

He kept his eyes on the road. "You didn't have to." A casual observer would have picked up on it.

She brushed it off. "A lot of people don't like lawyers." She left it to him to infer that she'd endured childish teasing rather than so much more.

"So why did you become one?" Feeling the way she did, he would have thought she would have picked any other career but that one.

He caught her off guard. "How did you know—Sheila?" she guessed.

"No, the form you filled out in the office. You put down lawyer under occupation."

She'd forgotten that. She had to be careful about the conclusions she jumped to. There was no reason to think he asked Sheila about her. Why would he? They were only having dinner to settle a bet. Living with Steven had left its mark, she realized. It had made her look for hidden meanings in simple statements, hidden agendas where there weren't any.

"Are you a practicing lawyer?" he asked, when she made no response to his earlier question.

She thought of the letter of resignation she'd posted from Sheila's house the day after she arrived. She'd enjoyed working for Greene and Jefferson. The firm was small enough to fit into her father's coat pocket, but it had a heart. Something she hadn't thought law firms were allowed to have.

"I practice," she acknowledged. "But at the moment I'm temporarily between positions." Temporarily between lifestyles, too, she added silently. Currently residing in limbo.

The logical solution occurred to him. "Will you be joining your father's firm?"

"As a doormat, maybe." The comment had just come out. It shouldn't have. Dana sighed. She didn't know what was wrong with her lately. She felt so edgy, so completely at odds with herself. With her world. It was as if she was revisiting the years of her teenage rebellion. "Sorry. My father and I had words before I left."

He glanced at her before looking back at the road. Her jaw was rigid enough to pass for stone. "I take it they weren't very good words."

Dana laughed shortly. "With my father, they never are."

Rafe rolled the comment over in his mind. "I felt that way

about my father.'' Coming to a red light, he eased his foot onto the brake, stealing a look at her. ''Fifteen years ago.''

''You're lucky. Your father grew up.'' She looked for a way to direct the conversation away from her. She was always uncomfortable discussing herself, her life as Paul Morrow's daughter. ''So what made you want to become a doctor?'' She went with the obvious. ''Your father's example?''

The light changed. Rafe sped up. Sunset was still more than an hour away, but he was in a hurry to get to the restaurant. Tonight, he was hungry. ''He's a cop. So's my younger brother. Me, I liked fixing things.''

She thought of George, who had been nothing short of a magician with his hands. ''Why didn't you become a mechanic?''

Rafe grinned. She liked the easy way his face softened.

''Living things,'' he clarified. ''I was ten years old when this baby sparrow fell out of his nest, right at my feet. Ugly little thing. I kind of related to it—'' He caught her dubious look out of the corner of his eye. ''I was a hell of a homely kid. My hands and feet were way too big for the rest of me. Anyway, I took the sparrow's unexpected appearance in my life as an omen. So I brought the bird home, tried to keep it warm, nurtured it. I was consumed with getting this tiny, helpless thing well. By the time it was, I was hooked on the process.''

It was hard to imagine those large hands handling something so small. ''What happened to the bird?''

Something that bordered on sentimentality tugged at the corners of his mouth.

''I set it free. My dad said it wasn't right to keep something like that as a pet. It was meant to be free.'' The grin widened. ''It bit me just as I let it go. It was either giving me a peck goodbye or letting me know I was taking too long in releasing it. It wasn't easy for me to let go until he did that.''

The road opened up, and so did he, pressing on the accelerator. There was no traffic in either direction. With houses visible on the hillside to their left and the ocean quietly flowing on their right, a sense of peace settled around him. Only Dana beside him sent ripples through it with her restless presence.

"How about you?" he prodded again. "Why did you become a lawyer?"

She remembered the moment of her decision as if it had happened only a few hours ago. Remembered, too, the way she'd felt when she made it. Not unlike Scarlett O'Hara when she'd taken her oath never to go hungry again.

"To spite my father," she said simply. "To show him I could do it. He didn't think much of my abilities."

Rafe realized that there had never been anything but supportive words for him and for Gabe for as long as he could remember. He tried to envision how it would have felt if it had been otherwise. "Why's that?"

"Because I didn't agree with him. And he was always right." Dana crossed her ankles, shifted in her seat. "I'd really rather not talk about my father, if you don't mind."

"No problem," he said obligingly. It had only been idle curiosity that had prompted him to ask. A teasing smile appeared. "Did you remember to bring your wallet?"

The expression on his face lightened her mood. She grasped the opportunity. "You really are convinced that this meal is to die for, aren't you?"

"No," he corrected. "To live for. If it weren't for the fact that being a pediatrician keeps me so busy, I'd be over at La Reina all the time. Tex-Mex is my Achilles' heel." He laughed, picturing the result. "I'd be a blimp in no time." He shrugged. There were worse things, he supposed. "But a happy one."

"Despite the snow job, I'll reserve judgment until I sample this fabulous cuisine for myself."

He nodded. He'd expected nothing less. It was what made her interesting. "You struck me as a stubborn woman the first time I saw you."

At least he had worded it politely, she thought. She'd heard the observation put in far less pleasant terms. "What gave me away?"

"Maybe it was the way you wouldn't let Alice plow you under." He thought of the older woman. Alice had been with him from the day he had opened his practice. "She's very protective of my time."

What else was she protective of? Dana wondered. Was there something going on between them?

She stopped abruptly. The direction of her thoughts annoyed her. Just because Steven liked keeping reserve entertainment around didn't mean every man was like that.

No, just the good-looking ones, she thought.

"What would she say if she knew you were frivolously using some of that time to take me to a restaurant?"

His answer wasn't the one Dana had anticipated. "She'd say it was a good thing. She's of the opinion that I don't get out enough."

It had to be a line, and not a very good one at that. Somehow, she couldn't see him as a cloistered monk. "Do you?"

He shrugged. After Debra died, he'd felt no desire to see other women. What was the point? He was never going to get married again. Most women didn't want a relationship that led nowhere. That Kate accepted those terms made her unique. But it didn't change how he felt.

"Enough to suit me. I love my work. There isn't anything I'd rather be than a pediatrician."

She believed him. And, in a way, envied him. "You're lucky. I never felt that kind of satisfaction."

Her voice was oddly empty. He looked at her. "With anything?"

How had the conversation veered from small talk into areas she'd had no intention of touching again? This was supposed to be a careless evening out, not a baring of souls.

Dana was spared the awkwardness of making an inane comment as she changed the subject, because when she opened her mouth, the sound of squealing tires and metal crashing against something large, solid and immovable interrupted her.

Dana jumped. "Oh, my God, what was that?" Eyes wide, she scanned the road.

Her breath caught in her throat, almost choking her. Less that a hundred yards ahead was a car, or what was left of it. From where they were, it gave the appearance of being a mangled toy that had been foiled in the act of attempting to climb a tree. Battered and crumpled, its hood was at a forty-five-degree angle to the ground. The crash had caused the antitheft alarm to go off, its pealing adding a surreal quality to the scene.

The driver was slumped against the steering wheel, but the other occupants had been thrown clear. Even at a distance, she could see that there was blood everywhere.

And smoke was beginning to curl from beneath the car.

Rafe jammed on his brakes. The car careened to the right, fishtailing before it finally stopped. Alert, his adrenaline running on high, Rafe was out of the vehicle even as it rocked in response to the emergency brake he had jerked into position.

Of like mind and separated by less than a heartbeat, Dana was right behind him, running toward the smoldering wreck. Her ears throbbed from the piercing noise made by the alarm.

He sensed rather than heard her. "Get back!" he shouted over his shoulder. It wasn't safe to be in the vicinity of the vehicle.

She had no intention of listening. "You're going to need help!" she insisted, raising her voice to be heard above the din. And because he had shouted at her. She didn't take that tone well, even if it was meant in her best interests.

Rafe would have argued with her, but there wasn't time to pause or push her aside. Resigned, he nodded. "Let's get the driver out."

He was wedged behind the steering wheel. Rafe tried to move the steering column, but it wasn't going anywhere. For a split second a chill passed over Rafe when he thought he wouldn't be able to rescue the man.

Dana had tried to pull the man out as Rafe pulled on the wheel, but there was no budging either one of them. ''You're going to need a crowbar,'' Dana said.

It was worth a try. He didn't want to leave her, but he had no choice. Swallowing an oath about her damn heroics, Rafe sprinted to his car and got the crowbar out of his trunk. He was back in less time than it took to think the matter through.

Moving as quickly as possible, he worked the bar between the spokes of the steering wheel. He felt his muscles fairly screaming in protest as he managed to work the steering wheel back just a fraction. It was up to Dana to pull the man free.

There was no way she could manage it, Rafe thought in frustration, but there was nothing else he could do. He couldn't be in two places at once.

''Pull, Dana, pull,'' he coached. Every fiber in his body tensed as he tried to move the wheel a little more.

Sucking in air, working on panic and adrenaline, Dana wrapped her arms around the driver's rib cage as best she could. Braced, she tugged with all her might. Her face was streaked with blood and turning a bright shade of red beneath the grime when she managed to pull the man to the side. It was all that was needed.

Rafe took it from there. He released the wheel, then dragged the man upright and slung him over his shoulder fireman style. With one hand hooked beneath Dana's arm, he hurried the three of them away from the vehicle. A moment later, the flames came, quickly eating their way up the car.

Breathless, her lungs feeling as if they were going to explode, Dana struggled to steady herself. She looked around, trying to take in the scene.

She zeroed in on the other people. There were two of them, one male and one female, both teenagers like the driver. Both conscious and crying for help.

''I've got my medical bag in the trunk.'' He set the unconscious teen on the ground as gently as he could. ''Why don't you stay here and catch your breath?''

She didn't need to be pampered. It was the others who needed his attention. ''My breath is fine. What do you want me to do to help?''

He wasted no more time. ''C'mon, then.'' Hurrying, Rafe led the way back to his car.

Along with his medical bag, he took out the fire extinguisher his father had talked him into carrying out of his trunk. God bless the old man, Rafe thought.

''Here.'' He handed it to her quickly. ''See if you can put out the fire before some breeze spreads it any farther. We can't take a chance on having the hillsides catch.''

They were well into fire season in Southern California. Whole acres of land had already been destroyed by fires.

''Leave it to me,'' she promised.

He had no other choice. He had injured people to help.

Chapter 10

If he had thought, for one moment, that Dana would get in his way with her efforts to help, Rafe quickly realized how wrong he'd been.

She was right there alongside of him, eager to do what she could to help.

It amazed him that instead of being squeamish, as most people were when exposed to the bloodied, mangled bodies involved in an accident, Dana seemed to be oblivious to the horror, focusing only on the fact that these were people who needed help and needed it in a hurry.

When he saw her toss away the empty canister, the flames mercifully extinguished, he breathed a sigh of relief. At least there wouldn't be an out-of-control fire storm to contend with.

"Dana, call the paramedics," he called out to her. "Use my cell phone in the car."

She merely nodded, doing as she was told. It took only a minute to make the connection, another two to give all the pertinent information.

"They're coming," she announced, hurrying to his side.

He was trying to immobilize the driver's broken arm. ''See anything we can use for a splint?'' Rafe asked her.

Dana looked around, but there was nothing. ''No. Why don't you tape it to his side until the paramedics arrive?''

It was what he was about to do, but he was surprised at the suggestion coming from her. ''Good thinking.'' He wanted to ask her where she had learned that, but there was no time.

They worked well together, quickly, competently, two halves of a team with an identical goal. With luck, the paramedics would be on the scene shortly. But they both knew that there were too many seconds within ''shortly'' that could prove fatal.

Not wanting to move any of the victims more than was absolutely necessary, Rafe and Dana found themselves spread out. Rafe remained with the two teenage boys while Dana tended to the girl.

''What's your name?'' Dana asked.

Her voice was as calm as if she was carrying on a conversation with someone she'd encountered in the checkout line at the supermarket. While she spoke, she was ripping the edge of the girl's T-shirt in order to make a bandage for her head wound.

''Carol.'' Her face a mask of twisted pain, the girl watched her every move. ''Am I going to die?''

Dana pressed the material against the gash in an attempt to stem the bleeding. It was far from sanitary, but it was the best she could do under the circumstances.

''No, you're not going to die,'' she said firmly. ''No one's going to die tonight.''

Dana prayed for the ambulance to come.

Was this the way it had been for Meggie? The doctor said she died on the way to the hospital. Had she lain in the car, crying, begging for help, calling for her husband, for her child? Calling without anyone hearing?

It froze her heart to think about it.

Carol clawed at her hand, desperate to hold on to something, to someone.

"It hurts so bad," Carol gasped, sobbing. "I'm afraid." Huge brown eyes, filled with shock and fear, begged Dana for something, anything, to make the pain and fear go away.

Dana held Carol's hand tightly, saying what she knew the girl wanted to hear. Saying what she would have said to Megan if she'd had the chance.

"I know. But it's going to be fine. *You're* going to be fine. Don't you give in, you hear me?" Dana raised her voice, determined to keep the teenager awake. "It can't conquer you if you don't give in."

Carol's lashes were beginning to flutter as consciousness fought injury for possession of her. "What can't?" she asked hoarsely.

Dana had to keep her talking, had to keep her awake. She said whatever came into her head. This wasn't some teenager who was a stranger to her, it was Megan. And it was for Megan she fought. "Fear, pain, you name it. All you have to do is hang on long enough."

All the color, all the strength, seemed to be draining from the young girl. It wasn't the onset of evening dusting everything around it. Carol was retreating. Fading.

"But I just want to go to sleep." She was silently begging Dana to let her go.

Dana clamped her hand on the thin shoulder. She knew she couldn't shake Carol, but she did what she could to rouse her attention.

"No, don't close your eyes," Dana ordered, struggling against the onslaught of panic. She couldn't call Rafe over to help her. He had his hands full with the other two. Who knew, maybe he was up against the same thing. Where was that damn ambulance? Why hadn't they gotten here yet? "Pain is on your side, Carol. It's trying to keep you awake. Do you hear me, Carol?"

"Yes, I...I hear you," Carol murmured distantly. The next

moment, she began to shiver. Her whole body was enveloped in one huge tremor she couldn't control.

Out of the corner of her eye, Dana saw Rafe approaching them. ''Rafe, do you have anything in the car I can put around her? A blanket? A sweater? Something?''

Squatting beside Dana, he looked at Carol and shook his head. ''Nothing, why?'' And then he saw the reason before she said another word. ''She's going into shock.'' Quickly he stripped off his jacket.

Between the two of them, they managed to wrap it around the girl without moving her.

''Keep her as warm as you can,'' he instructed, though he knew it was unnecessary to tell. Rafe couldn't help being in awe, not only of her cool competence, but also of the compassion he saw in her face. The lady was special.

Dana tucked a corner of the jacket closer to the girl. ''Okay, now stay awake,'' she ordered. But Carol's eyes were drifting shut again. Dana caught the girl's face in her hands. ''Do you hear me? Stay awake, Meggie. They'll be here soon. I swear they will.''

Her words were swallowed by the distant wail of a siren. Dana had never heard anything so wonderful, so sweet in her life. She could have cried.

''Hear that? They're already here. Don't let go, don't let go,'' she coached, wrapping her hands tightly around Carol's again. ''Hang on just a little while longer, honey. Please.''

The two ambulances arrived within a heartbeat of each other. Two gurneys were unloaded from one vehicle, one from the other. Drawing Dana to her feet, Rafe moved out of the paramedics' way. Questions and answers mingled with cries of pain.

In short, concise sentences, Rafe told the first set of paramedics what he could about the accident and the condition of the two boys, then moved on to help Dana explain what they knew of Carol's injuries.

''Anything else, Doctor?'' the first driver asked him.

Rafe shook his head. ''No, that's it.'' He watched the second gurney being lifted into the ambulance. "Where are you taking them?"

The driver checked his sheet. "Dispatch said South Community's backed up tonight. We thought maybe we'd take them to—"

"Are you independent drivers?" Rafe cut in. When the driver nodded, Rafe said, "Then take them to Harris Memorial."

The distance to the other available hospital, St. Anne's, or to Harris Memorial was almost identical. Rafe wanted to be able to keep tabs on the teenagers.

"I'm a doctor there." He reached into his back pocket for his wallet, opened it and took out two business cards, then handed one to each of the drivers. "We'll follow you in my car." It occurred to him that he was taking a lot for granted. He looked at Dana. "That is—"

That he was checking to see if she was willing to go along surprised her. It had never crossed her mind not to. They'd come this far with the victims. How could she not know if they pulled through?

"Of course we'll follow. We can't walk away now. Hey, don't forget your jacket," she said to Rafe as he began to walk away from the ambulance.

Retrieving the jacket as the second paramedic team eased Carol's gurney into their vehicle, Dana sighed, watching the rear doors being slammed shut, then turned and offered the jacket to Rafe. They had to be all right. They just had to be.

The jacket was far too bloody to put on. Fingers hooked in the collar, he slung it over his shoulder. He took her arm with his other hand. As he escorted her to his car, it felt as if a hundred years had passed since they'd gotten out of it, instead of half an hour.

Rafe opened the door for her. Dana slid in. She looked tired, he thought. After shutting the door, he walked around to his side and got in. He looked at her for a long moment before he started the car, wondering what was going on in her head, what she was thinking.

"You're sure you don't mind?"

What did it take to convince him? She would have asked to follow if he hadn't volunteered.

"We're not exactly dressed to waltz into a restaurant anymore." She glanced down. There was grease from the wreck mixed with dirt and blood across the front of her dress. "I don't think they welcome blood in the dining room unless it's coming from a rare steak."

He laughed under his breath as he followed the ambulances. He had the second one in his sights. "You're one unusual lady, Dana Morrow."

She wasn't sure just how he meant that. *Unusual* might have been synonymous with *freak* to him. It had been to some. "That's me, a square peg in a round hole."

"Not the same thing," he countered. But all the same, it was a telling remark, Rafe thought. "I'm going to call ahead to the emergency room to let them know what to be prepared for."

How could anyone be prepared for that? Dana thought, as he pressed a button on his cell phone. The musical tones she heard in response told her the number was being dialed automatically. "This happen to you often?"

"What? Oh. No, I'm not calling the emergency room directly. I'm calling the hospital switchboard." And then he was talking to a woman there, asking to be put through to the emergency room.

Dana slumped in her seat, trying to gain control of the emotions that had been rubbed raw by what she'd just lived through.

Oh, God, Meggie, I wish someone had been there for you. If not me, then someone. Someone who could have saved you.

"Who's Meggie?"

The question, coming on the heels of her thoughts, made her jump. "What?"

He tucked the telephone into his pocket with his left hand. "You called that girl Meggie. The boy who wasn't driving told me her name was Carol."

He glanced at Dana, waiting. There was dirt smeared across the front of her dress, most of her makeup was gone, and her hair was a mess. And he'd never seen any woman look more compelling.

"Meggie was my sister." She shrugged, staring straight ahead. "I guess I got a little confused in the heat of the moment."

He understood now, at least part of it. Her need to help, the fierce way she'd talked to the teenager, trying to keep her awake. She was reliving the past.

"Were you there? When the accident happened?" he clarified.

Her lips felt very dry, as did her throat. "No." Her face was immobile, her voice devoid of emotion as she added, "But I wish I had been."

He told her something his mother had said to him after Debra died. Something very basic that needed saying. "We can't control everything, no matter how much we want to."

She blew out a long breath. It didn't help. Her nerves still felt as brittle as matchsticks. "No, we can't."

He strove to lighten the air. They both needed it. There had been enough heaviness for one evening. "All right, I'll bite. Where did you learn all that?"

She blinked. It took her a moment to focus on his question. "What?"

Rafe switched on the headlights. Twilight seemed to have tiptoed in earlier than usual. "You came through like a complete trouper, and you really seemed to know what you were doing when I gave you instructions. You're not like any lawyer I know."

"I'm not like any *anything* you know," she corrected him with a glib smile. It was the cocky tone she used with her father, but she softened it enough so there was no mistaking there was no attitude behind it.

She wasn't trying to prove anything to Rafe. And right now, she was beginning to feel pretty good about herself. About the lives they had saved. Together. There was no question in her mind that if they hadn't been there just after the accident occurred, the driver would have burned to death, and the others might have bled to death before another car came along.

Dana savored the whiff of euphoria that passed over her. Taking a deep breath, she rotated her shoulders, stretching muscles that felt taut. When she turned her head in his direction, she saw that Rafe was watching her with a bemused expression on his face. He was still waiting for her answer.

"Eyes on the road, Doctor," she teased. "Or the paramedics are going to have to double back for us."

Maybe it was the moment, or the fact that they had aided in cheating death, at least for a little while. Whatever it was, she felt comfortable enough with him to share a piece of herself.

"My mother was a nurse practitioner who thought it was important that her daughters be up on first aid." That was before she'd descended into a far-reaching, black depression that ate away at her soul far more rapidly than the alcohol she used to anesthetize herself ate away at her liver. "And for a while, when I was studying for the bar, I drove an ambulance to support myself."

Rafe tried to picture that. A would-be lawyer who drove an ambulance. It boggled the mind. "Hell of a combination."

She could guess what he was thinking. "Hey, at least I drove the ambulance instead of chasing it." And then she grinned as she shook her head. "Besides, I'm not that kind of a lawyer."

The road began to snake its way to Newport Boulevard. He had to remain alert so he wouldn't miss the turnoff. "What kind of lawyer *are* you? Besides good, I mean."

She wasn't accustomed to compliments and considered them suspect or, at the very least without substance. "How would you know whether or not I'm good?"

Was that distrust he heard in her voice? Why? It didn't make sense.

"I think you'd be good at anything you put your mind to.

It's that stubbornness factor coming in again.'' He made the turn and wove his way onto the boulevard. He waited until traffic was clear enough for him to cross three lanes. ''I don't think you'd allow yourself to be average. That wouldn't satisfy you.'' He eased the car into the left turn lane. ''I heard you talking to that girl about not giving in. It didn't sound like something you picked up by reading a book.''

''I *am* good,'' Dana confirmed. There was no ego, no false modesty. There was just fact. ''A good criminal lawyer.''

The choice surprised him. ''Like your father?''

''No, not like my father.'' She'd made that a goal, not to be anything like him. ''He only goes after the high-profile cases, the ones with big headlines and big money. I figure poor people can be innocent, too.''

''A public defender?'' He could picture that. It seemed more in keeping with the woman who was beginning to emerge.

''Something like that.'' She didn't particularly feel like going into details. She'd talked more than enough about herself for one night. ''We're here,'' she pointed out to forestall any other questions.

He took the hint. ''So we are.''

Driving onto the hospital grounds, he made a choice. Rather than go all the way to the doctors' lot, he decided to park in the emergency room lot. When he got out, Dana was right beside him.

The emergency room teams he'd asked Nancy to assemble were working on the victims when he and Dana entered the ER. Rafe saw the flash of a blue uniform in the background beyond the electronic doors. That would be the police. He'd asked Nancy to notify them, as well. This had the makings of a very long evening.

He wondered if he should call a cab to take Dana home. His next thought was that he was being presumptuous. She wouldn't take kindly to his making any decisions on her behalf. She would call a cab if she wanted to leave. She'd proven she wasn't a hothouse flower.

Nancy's dark eyes shifted from the doctor to the woman beside him. They both looked worn. Seeing them together triggered recognition. The woman had been here before, with her niece. She'd asked for Dr. Saldana.

"You're back?" she asked Dana in mild surprise.

"Can't seem to get enough of this place," Dana quipped. "But this time I'm here strictly as an observer."

Nancy raised a quizzical brow toward Rafe.

"Don't let her fool you—she's an emergency room groupie." He grinned at the head nurse.

Nancy had a feeling she wasn't going to get the straight story for a while, if ever. But this was definitely food for the hospital gossip mill.

"Whatever." She moved so her body blocked Rafe's access to the examining rooms. "We can take care of things, Doctor. You both look like hell." She waved them away. "Why don't you talk to the policeman, get cleaned up and go back to what you were doing?"

Dana, he noticed, wasn't about to remain behind. Or be dismissed. Certain kinds of stubbornness, he decided, could be appealing.

"Can't," Rafe replied. "The restaurant has a very strict no-blood code."

Dr. Weinstein, the orthopedic specialist Rafe had told Nancy to call, came by, nodding to Rafe in recognition. "I'll take it from here, Nurse," he informed her.

As Dana watched, he disappeared behind the swinging glass doors where the rest of the team was assembled, leaving her outside to wonder over the fate of the three victims.

"I could have Harry get you a couple of burgers and fries from the cafeteria," Nancy volunteered, nodding toward the tall, distinguished-looking man at the reception desk. "They're about to close, but the short-order cook has a thing for Harry."

Now that she thought of it, she could stand to eat something, Dana realized. Hunger pangs were working their way through the knots that had formed in her stomach. ''She'll open the grill for him?'' Dana asked.

''It's a he,'' Nancy corrected her, a smile playing over her lips. ''And yes, he will. He's trying to win Harry over.''

Rafe exchanged looks with Dana. She nodded. Rafe took the nurse's hands in his. ''Nancy, you're an angel. Right now, burgers and fries sound like heaven.''

''Good. I'll tell Harry to get charming.'' She placed her arm around Dana's shoulders. ''While you're waiting for him to get back, why don't you come with me and get cleaned up?'' Taking charge, she led Dana off.

Dana looked over her shoulder at Rafe, but he merely shrugged his shoulders in an exaggerated motion, then went to talk to the policeman.

''This isn't exactly the way I planned for this evening to go.''

It had taken Harry longer than anticipated to return with their impromptu take-out dinner. In the interim, they'd given statements to the police and been told that, so far, all three victims were in stable condition.

When Harry returned with their dinner, Rafe had taken it and Dana to the beach across from the hospital. There was a private little stretch where he thought they could be alone and eat in peace. They'd had enough excitement for one night.

Sitting on the fence that ran along the perimeter, Dana finished the last of her hamburger. She couldn't remember when she'd had anything better.

''Can't say I was bored,'' she told him in response to his comment. She gestured toward the sky. ''And the floor show's lovely.'' Every single star ever created had come out tonight, blanketing the sky with myriad tiny, winking lights.

Sitting beside her, Rafe looked up. ''Yes, it is, isn't it?'' He smiled to himself.

She watched a dimple wink in and out of his cheek. ''What?''

She would probably think it was silly, but right now, image

didn't seem so important to him. "When I was a boy, I used to think angels had cut holes in the sky so they could look down on us. I thought the stars were heavenly lights shining from their eyes." He shrugged, a self-deprecating smile on his lips. "I was six. What did I know?"

She was charmed by the concept. "I've got to remember to tell Mollie that. Maybe we can start some sort of legend."

Dana knew Mollie would take to the concept immediately. She was convinced her parents were angels, watching over her. There were times, when she was bone weary, that Dana felt like embracing the idea herself. It made her feel less alone.

Rafe balled up his burger wrapper in his hand, then eyed hers. "Finished?"

She nodded, regretting that there wasn't more. "You sure this is hospital food?"

He took the wrapper from her and threw it into the paper bag. He offered her the last of his soda. She'd finished hers halfway through the meal. "I only work for the best. Care to go for a walk?"

Dana drained the soda, then surrendered the container. He threw the lot into the cylindrical waste basket. "Here?"

Rafe gestured. The moonlight was skimming along the water, leaving wavy yellow ribbons to mark its path. "We seem to have the beach to ourselves."

Going with impulse, Dana took off her shoes and slipped them into her oversize purse before rising from the fence. "All right."

Rafe took off his shoes and socks. He tucked the latter into the former, then picked them up with his left hand. He took her hand in his right.

It was the first time, she realized, that they'd touched all evening. The first time they'd touched at all. Oh, he'd slipped his hand along her back or her elbow, but that was to guide her or usher her along. This was different.

Right from the start.

A tingling sensation worked its way through her with the

speed of a minor electrical jolt. Not enough to shock her, just enough to make her aware that it was there. She wasn't sure if she wanted it to be.

He felt her stiffen, then force herself to relax. "What's the matter?"

"Nothing." The lie made her mouth feel dry. Words stuck to the roof of her mouth like peanut butter. "Must be the hamburger repeating itself."

That wasn't it, he thought, but he pretended to believe her. "That wouldn't have happened if we'd gotten to La Reina."

She laughed, grateful to shift attention from herself. "Yeah, yeah, I'll believe it when I taste it."

"All right, are you free tomorrow?"

"Yes," she answered before she thought. Before she could stop herself.

"Care to try again?" he proposed. "This time, I hope, without any daring rescues?"

She tried to make light of the invitation. They would merely be completing what they'd set out to do, to see which was the best restaurant. That he'd asked her out twice in two days didn't mean a thing. "You really are determined to be parted from your money, aren't you?"

His smile was slow, even sexy. "No, determined to prove I'm right."

"All right, tomorrow night," she agreed. Dana stared straight ahead, watching the moonlight shimmer and trying very hard not to think about anything. Least of all how good his hand felt around hers.

The tide was coming in closer than he'd anticipated. It lapped at the sand inches from their feet. Looking over his shoulder, he saw that behind them the tide had erased their footprints in some places. In others, it seemed to have deepened them.

The silence was not uncomfortable. But it did feel oddly pregnant, as if there were things waiting to be said, though he had no idea what.

"You were pretty terrific tonight."

Pleasure, warm and comforting, crept through her like ivy working its way up a trellis. Still, she tried to dismiss his words. She hadn't done anything out of the ordinary, just what she had been trained to do. If she'd gone about it a little more zealously, it was only because she'd been thinking of Megan.

She shrugged off his compliment, paring it down to size. "I'm at my best during an emergency. Doesn't leave much time to think, just act."

Rafe stopped walking and turned toward her. "There's something to be said for that." As he spoke, his eyes skimmed over her lips. Just as his hands skimmed along her arms to her shoulders.

Dana's heart took the elevator up and stopped at the top floor, settling in her throat. She knew what he was going to do. Knew just as surely as she knew that the sun was going to rise tomorrow.

Knew, too, that there was no place for this in her life. No place for a complication of this nature no matter how she packaged it and tried to make it acceptable.

But no matter how she argued, she couldn't force herself to do the logical thing. She couldn't turn her head away. With the wind playing with the ends of her hair, the breeze caressing her body with transparent fingers, she stood perfectly still, waiting for his lips to find hers.

And staunchly told herself that no matter what, it wasn't going to mean anything beyond a single pleasurable moment.

A moment she found herself desperately wanting.

Chapter 11

His lips touched hers slowly, gently. Smooth as silk, sweet as honey, the kiss enveloped Dana until, one by one, all her senses were drawn in. Captured. Willing prisoners in a cell with no bars.

Wonder, vast and endless, filled him. Pushed him forward. Urged him to seek more. Rafe deepened the kiss until he lost his way. And didn't care.

She could feel her heart fluttering like an agitated falcon trying vainly to navigate against a strong wind. Instincts ingrained since the moment of her conception rose up, refusing to allow her to be passively taken anywhere, even into pleasure. If her head was going to go spinning, her pulse racing, well, then, so were Rafe's.

Rising on her toes, Dana encircled his neck with her arms, bringing her body closer to his.

Bringing her soul into her kiss. And losing it.

If his socks hadn't already been off, she would have metaphorically knocked them off right then. What had begun as an impulse had turned into something he couldn't define, couldn't put a name to. In that single moment, Rafe felt freer than he had in a very long time. Free to feel, to react. Free to soar above the clouds that surrounded him.

He felt his body heating and knew he had to stop while pleasure was hot but not yet sizzling. It took effort to listen to reason while his body begged for things that lay beyond reason.

His pulse wouldn't slow down even though he drew his lips away.

Dana took a deep breath, her lips pressed tightly together. Absorbing the taste of him. Without realizing it, she ran the tip of her tongue along the outline of her mouth. She looked at him, fighting her way out of the haze around her brain.

"Why did you do that?"

He was asking himself the same thing. This wasn't something he'd ever done before with any of his patients' parents. But he didn't think she would appreciate hearing that. It sounded too much like a protest. And this, whatever this was, wasn't something to protest.

Rafe took the wisp of hair that insisted on dancing about her brow to a tune only the wind heard and tucked it behind her ear. He saw the quickening in her eyes, felt it mirrored in his body.

"I didn't think kisses needed to be explained."

"Some do." This one did. Then maybe she would understand the diametrically opposed feelings that were dueling so madly within her.

He shrugged, looking away. He wasn't sure if he should run like hell or not. All he knew was that he wanted to kiss her again.

Maybe that was why he should run like hell.

"French fries mixed with starlight raise my sugar level. I lost my head." Turning, he looked at her. "Why did you kiss back?"

Served her right for asking. A smile, more nervous around the edges than she would have liked, played over her lips. "I guess echoing the Twinkie defense would be out of order here.''

His laughter was in his eyes, not on his lips. ''Completely.''

''Then it's the hamburger.'' She nodded, then elaborated on the ridiculous answer. ''Hamburger and sea breezes.''

''Hamburger and sea breezes,'' he echoed, amusement framing his mouth.

It was just as good as French fries and starlight. Or Twinkies. Damn, why wouldn't her heart settle down? ''Does it every time.''

He liked her sense of humor. And he liked the taste of her mouth. Liked it very, very much.

''I'll have to remember that.'' Did that sound as if he meant to kiss her again? He didn't want to frighten her away, and there was something in her eyes that told him she could be frightened. ''Strictly for research purposes, of course. The AMA would be interested in hearing about this.''

Dana turned to face the hospital. From here, it looked like such a small building, perched far above them. A small, pristine white building, stretching itself to reach the sky.

She'd stayed too long. She should have gone home before he kissed her and messed with her head. Too late.

Dana nodded toward the hospital. ''Maybe we'd better get back.''

''Maybe,'' he agreed. It was getting late, and he had an early day tomorrow. Besides, if he stayed here in the moonlight with her any longer, he was going to kiss her again.

And he had a feeling that it might not be good for either one of them if he did. At least, not now.

Dana let herself into the house quietly. In the distance, she heard Rafe's car pulling away. She'd shaken his hand in the car, refused his offer to walk her to her door and gotten out as quickly as possible. A deer bolting into the forest before the hunter could get off a second shot.

Maybe that was cowardly, but in the long run, she knew it was better this way.

A feeling of déjà vu filled her as she eased the door shut.

How many times had she come sneaking in like this when she was a teenager? Even younger, she thought, than the girl who'd held her hand so tightly tonight. Her father had labeled her a bad seed and once even said he was glad her mother hadn't lived to see what she had become. She'd cursed him for having the audacity to make any reference to her mother when he was the one responsible for her death. He was the one who had driven her into her depression.

She'd thought he was going to kill her. But he never raised a hand. He didn't have to. His tongue had been his weapon of choice, doing more damage than a hundred beatings. Shredding self-esteem. Except that he hadn't managed to shred hers. Not completely.

Maybe that was what goaded him now.

Dana drew her hand from the door, satisfied that her entrance had been silent.

''You haven't changed at all, have you? Still coming in at all hours of the night.''

Dana jumped, barely managing to stifle a scream as her pulse pumped hard. Swinging around, she saw her father in the living room doorway. His eyes seemed to burn holes into her flesh. Slowly, he moved forward, an eerie figure, half man, half machine, emerging from the shadows.

''What the hell happened to you?'' He gestured at her dress. Despite Nancy's help, she still looked disheveled, as if she'd played hide-and-seek with a dirty barbecue grill and raw meat. ''Were you in an accident?''

She couldn't tell if that was concern or accusation in his voice. Probably the latter. He didn't waste his time with petty things like concern.

''No.'' Dana's response was terse. ''But I was at one.''

His eyes narrowed, sharp blue scalpels making incisions in her statement. ''What is that supposed to mean?''

Why did he always think she was trying to put something

over on him? ''It means that there was an accident on the road ahead of us, and we stopped to help.'' She began to walk toward the stairs.

He blocked her path with the wheelchair. ''Who's *we?*''

Had he displayed the slightest bit of interest in her life, as if she was an actual person rather than an extension of himself, at any time during the years she lived here, she wouldn't have found his question so offensive. But she knew from experience that her father's only concern when it came to her was how her actions reflected on him.

Nothing, apparently, had changed for him, either.

Stubbornly, she refused to answer his question directly. ''The man I went out with.''

His mouth twisted in a smirk. ''Didn't take you long, did it?''

A scathing retort hovered on the tip of her tongue, aching for release. Struggling, she held it back. Telling him what she thought of him wasn't going to help anything. Or change him. It was what he expected. So she didn't give it to him.

Instead, she shook her head. ''I'm not underage anymore, Father. That means I'm not accountable to you.''

He moved his chair again, refusing to let her pass. ''What about Mollie?''

She glared at him, her eyes just as deadly, as challenging, as his. ''What *about* Mollie?''

He leaned forward, wishing for the thousandth time that he wasn't imprisoned in this fancy piece of polished technology. That he could stand when he spoke. ''Aren't you accountable to her? What kind of an example do you think your lifestyle is setting?''

Suddenly, Dana felt bone weary. ''I don't have a lifestyle, Father.'' She resented the implications in his tone. ''I'm just settling in.''

Who did she think she was fooling? She'd lived the wild life once, thumbing her nose at him, at his reputation. And given half a chance, she would still do it. ''That'll be your excuse when you're fifty.''

"It's not an excuse, it's a fact." She wanted to run to her room, to slam the door in his face, even if he couldn't follow her. But because he couldn't follow her, because he was bound to this chair by a disease that threatened to take away what he held most dear, his dignity, she forced herself to calm down. To be civil. "Tomorrow—today," she corrected, glancing at her watch, "I'm taking Mollie with me to check out a summer program so she can be prepared to enter kindergarten in the fall. Once that's settled, I'll take the next step."

His eyes held hers. She couldn't tell whether he believed her or not. "Which is?"

"A step above the one I've taken." She pressed her lips together, sighing.

What was it about him that always made her ready to go ten rounds? One of them had to make the first move. The first ten moves, if necessary. And it looked as if that was going to fall to her. No moves were going to be made if she continued sparring like this.

"I'll be looking for work."

Her father sneered, his laugh disparaging. "I'll believe that when I see it."

"Fine, have it your way. Now, if you'll excuse me, I have to get to bed." Determined to get away before she said something vitriolic, she deliberately moved past him. "I'm very tired."

He swung his chair around, facing her back. "Living in the fast lane will do that."

Stiffening, Dana turned, suppressed fury in her eyes. "Are you accusing me of something?"

With his family, he'd always believed it was a matter of guilty until proven otherwise. "I don't have to. The evidence is all there."

She wanted to scream at him, to demand to know why he had opened his house to her only to revert to the behavior that had driven her away in the first place. What was he trying to prove, to gain? Was this all some twisted game?

"Then I suggest you get yourself another pair of glasses, Counselor, because your eyes are deceiving you. There *is* no evidence." Too tired and too angry to think clearly, Dana hurried up the stairs, knowing that if she remained, she wouldn't be able to keep her temper in check.

Detouring to Mollie's bedroom, she was gratified to see that their raised voices hadn't woken her. Dana retreated to her room. Wanting to slam her door, she eased it shut instead. Barely harnessed anger shook her body. Why did he do that to her? Why did he deliberately bait her that way?

And what the hell had made her think that if she returned, things would be different between them? If anything, they were worse.

Dana collapsed on her bed, too exhausted to undress.

Paul Morrow stared after his daughter as she fled up the stairs. Fled his accusations. Fled the truth. It wouldn't be long, he thought, before he had enough evidence against Dana to take Mollie from her. Anyone could see she was unfit to raise the child.

And if they couldn't, he meant to make them see.

Feeling suddenly exhausted, he turned the wheelchair and went to his room. With any luck, tonight he would sleep.

It had gone well.

Despite everything that had happened the night before between her father and her to color Dana's mood, the interview with the preschool staff and administrator had gone exceptionally well. For once, everything had gone beautifully from start to finish.

Mollie had chattered in the car, asking Dana all sorts of questions about her "date with Dr. Rafe." Dana gave her only the highlights, mentioning the burgers and fries and the walk on the beach. Mollie seemed enthralled, absorbing every detail like a miniature matchmaker in training.

Consequently, when they arrived at the preschool, Mollie

was relaxed, forgetting to be afraid. Defenses down, her bright, sunny nature came through loud and clear. The teachers loved her, and she ate it up. By the time they left, Mollie had made one new ''best'' friend, with the prospect of half a dozen more. Best of all, she was eager to return.

This was what Mollie needed, Dana thought, children her age to socialize with. She made a mental note to call Nicole Lincoln to thank the woman for the referral. Nicole's twins were enrolled in the school and attended three half days a week, just to get them in the swim of things. Twins, Nicole had pointed out, tended to depend too much on one another, creating their own world and shutting everyone else out.

Not unlike she and Meggie had been, Dana thought, as Mollie went on about the preschool. Oh, they hadn't been twins, but they'd behaved that way, being each other's buffer when it came to their father. Trying to make one another feel better.

And then Megan had changed. Always the gentler, quieter one, she began to do anything to please their father, feeding his ego with her compliance.

Dana became unacceptable and lacking. Megan was the good one, while Dana was the wild one.

Dana pressed her lips together. She was allowing last night's encounter with her father to get to her. Why couldn't she dwell on the good things? Like Mollie's enthusiasm about preschool? Like saving a life? Like Rafe's kiss?

Startled, she reined in her thoughts. The first two events were valid reasons for satisfaction. The last didn't belong in the same category. Dwelling on it was borrowing trouble, and God knew she had enough of that as it was.

''Aunt Dana, we're here. Aren't you going to stop the car?''

Mollie's voice penetrated Dana's thoughts. She was almost at the end of the driveway. How had that happened? ''Yes, baby, I'm going to stop the car. Thanks for watching out for me.''

Her response made Mollie puff up her chest. A moment later she practically skipped out of the car.

Esther opened the door for them, looking at Mollie. "So, how did it go?"

Mollie beamed at her. "They like me," she announced proudly.

Esther laughed, hugging the little girl quickly before she could restrain herself. Warm hugs were against type for her. "Why wouldn't they like you? You're the most likable little girl in the whole world."

Pleased by the compliment, Mollie cocked her head. "Better than Aunt Dana was?"

The housekeeper shook her head as she looked at Dana. The older Dana had become, the more difficult she'd been to deal with. "Your aunt Dana was a handful."

Mollie's eyes grew huge, darting toward Dana and then back again. "She fit in your hand?"

Esther's laughter mingled with Dana's at the literal interpretation. "No, but there was many a time I wanted to fit my hand to her bottom."

The admission surprised Dana. "I never knew that, Esther."

Esther drew herself up to her full five-foot stature. "I was very good at hiding my feelings."

Dana caught her tongue between her teeth. "Especially when your face turned purple."

Esther remained undaunted. Living here had made her ready for almost anything. "I was busy counting to a hundred and holding my breath."

Dana looked at her dubiously, wondering if the woman was putting her on. "And that helped?"

Esther nodded. "Made me too light-headed to think about wanting to throttle you. By the way, you had a phone call."

She thought of Rafe immediately, then silently called herself an idiot. "From who?"

Esther had seen the sudden light in Dana's eyes and interpreted it correctly. She hadn't been around the Morrow girls all those years without gaining some insight. She hadn't been available last night to admit Miss Dana's escort, but she'd watched them leave from a second-story window. Whoever he was, he was a handsome one, she thought. "Not a man. From Dr. Pollack."

Dana made no comment about Esther's glib comment. Instead, she focused on the information. "Sheila? Sheila called here?" She hadn't heard from her in a few days. Why had she called in the middle of the day? "Did she say what it was about?"

"No, only that you should call her back when you had the chance."

Dana started for the stairs. "Esther, do you think you can see about getting a certain young lady some cookies?"

Dana loved seeing the way Mollie's face lit up over such little things. She looked so like Megan then. Would she see the same sort of light in her own child's face? she wondered suddenly. Or would she see Steven each time she looked into the small face?

Would she be able to stand it if that was the case?

The answer was yes. Dana realized that, with no conscious debate, she had made her peace with what was happening to her. This was her child's heart beating beneath her heart. *Her* child.

And she loved it.

It helped, knowing that.

"There might be one or two cookies lying around," Esther said. She laced her fingers through Mollie's. "Want to help me find them?"

Mollie nodded and tried to contain her eagerness. Grown-ups didn't like it if you were too bouncy all the time. "Yes, please."

Esther smiled as she looked at Dana. She thought the younger woman looked a little preoccupied. But her color seemed to be improving. That was something. "Stunning manners on this child. Easy to see she was Miss Megan's."

Dana pretended to take offense. "*I* didn't have manners?"

Esther sniffed as she ushered Mollie toward the kitchen. ''None that I recall.''

The claim brought a smile to Dana's lips. Except for a few more gray hairs, Esther was still the same. Pretending not to care, to be aloof and distant. But it was an act. She knew Esther cared. The woman had been there for her and would have been there even more had Dana allowed it.

She went to her room to make her call.

She spent several minutes on hold before she was finally put through to Sheila. ''You know, you really have to put on some more up-to-date music for people to listen to while they wait for you to get to them.''

Sheila laughed as she recognized Dana's voice. ''I like oldies, and they're staying on.''

Dana shifted on the bed, trying to get comfortable. Her back was aching. Was that normal this early on? ''To each his own. Anyway, Esther said you called while I was out.''

''Right.'' Sheila edged into her reason for calling slowly. ''I just wanted to call and check how you were feeling.''

Dana thought of the confrontation last night, deliberately letting it overshadow what had come before. It was easier than exploring it. ''As well as can be expected, under the circumstances.''

''Circumstances?''

Dana sighed. She leaned forward on the bed, pressing a hand to the small of her back. Maybe soaking in the tub would help. It certainly couldn't hurt.

''My father is not exactly making this reconciliation easy.'' Maybe the blame wasn't totally his. ''And I guess he still rubs me the wrong way.'' She paused, then added, ''A lot.''

''Oh, I see.'' That wasn't what Sheila was after. She plowed ahead. ''I ran into Rafe this morning at the hospital.''

It was stupid to feel her stomach tighten, Dana upbraided herself. Too stupid for words. ''And?''

Sheila thought of Rafe's expression. She hadn't seen him look like that in a long time. ''He seemed rather buoyant.''

It didn't mean anything. She didn't want it to mean anything. Right? ''You saw him floating? Was he going out to sea?''

Sheila knew that tone. Dana was slipping behind her protective shield. ''Stop being flippant. He told me the two of you went out last night.'' When Dana made no comment, she said, ''Simon added a little color to the event.''

''Simon?''

''One of the attending physicians in the ER. He said Rafe and you came in with some victims of a car wreck.'' The rumor mill had picked up the tidbit that Rafe had come in with a young woman and run with it. Someone had made a point of mentioning it to Kate at the lab. The reaction, Sheila had heard, was not good. ''Interesting way to conduct a first date.''

''It wasn't a date,'' Dana protested quickly. ''It was a bet.''

Her friend was definitely in denial, Sheila thought. ''You're going to have to clarify that one for me.''

Dana moved restlessly from the bed, and the telephone clattered to the floor. She stooped to pick it up. ''Sorry about that. Rafe wanted to prove that some restaurant he likes serves better food than the one I used to go to in Dallas.'' She heard Sheila's soft laugh in her ear.

''A rose by any other name—''

''Still has thorns,'' Dana cut in. Her mounting frustration about her situation, about everything, stripped the situation of any humor. ''You know I can't date anyone right now.''

''You're pregnant, Dana. You don't have the bubonic plague.'' Maybe Dana and Rafe would be good for one another. God knew they'd both been through a lot.

Dana refused to capitulate. ''In either case, I'm not exactly in a position to socialize widely.''

Sheila decided to let the matter drop. Maybe she was jumping to conclusions. Maybe they *had* gone out to eat just to settle a bet. Being so happy with Slade made her want to pair everyone off so they could find the same sort of joy she had. ''About the baby, Dana.''

Dana tensed. ''Yes?''

There was no easy way to broach this, but she was Dana's doctor as well as her friend. If Dana was planning to sweep her dilemma from her life, it had to be done soon. "What are you going to do about it?"

"Do about it?" She repeated the words as if she was barely aware of what they meant. "I'm going to have it."

Sheila exhaled the breath she'd been holding. She should have known Dana wouldn't choose an abortion. Dana had always loved children. But people did change, and their priorities changed with them. "And then?"

Since she'd learned she was pregnant, the baby hadn't been out of her mind. It had lingered, hiding behind every thought she had, every response she made. It wasn't just physically a part of her. It was *part* of her, emotionally. Part of every breath she took. She knew that. Inconvenient or not, there was no denying this child. Dana placed her hand over her taut, flat belly, wondering how it would feel to have it swollen out of all proportion. "And then I'm going to love it the way every baby has a right to be loved."

Sheila hesitated, then forced herself to ask, "Even though it's Steven's?"

"Hey, the baby can't help that." Still unborn, and she was already taking its side. That had to be a good sign, right? "Just like I couldn't help being Paul Morrow's daughter."

Sheila rose to the last hurdle. "When are you planning to tell Steven that he's a father?"

"I've already tried. I can't reach him. Whenever I call, all I get is his damn answering machine. It's not the kind of brief message that belongs on a tape. If and when I get *him* rather than his annoying recording, then I'll tell him."

That brought up other problems. Problems Dana was going to have to face. Better now than down the line. "And if he wants custody?"

Dana's laugh was harsh. Steven's inability to tolerate not being the center of attention, his attempt to seize that spot from a child, was why she'd left.

"That, dear Dr. Pollack, will be the day you should sink

all your available money into winter clothing, because it will mean that hell has frozen over."

Sheila laughed, and a few minutes later she rang off.

Dana hung up and stared at the telephone, her thoughts waffling from one emotional extreme to another.

Her next call was to Rafe's office. Speaking quickly before she could change her mind, she left a message with the nurse. She asked Alice to extend her regrets to the doctor, but she wasn't going to be able to go to the restaurant with him after all.

Dana stared at the phone after she'd hung up. She'd done the right thing. She knew that. So why did doing the right thing have to feel so bad?

Chapter 12

Rafe let himself into the one-bedroom apartment he'd sublet several years ago from a friend. At the time, he'd leased it because it suited his budget.

His practice was thriving now, but he saw no reason to move. Nothing else had changed for him. He hadn't acquired any expensive hobbies that threatened to crowd the apartment with possessions, and he harbored no desire for extra space. For him, the apartment was a place to sleep and shower and, once in a while, to eat. If he wanted a good meal, there were restaurants around.

Or, better yet, there was always his parents' home. His mother loved to cook for him, and he found her meals infinitely preferable to restaurant food. The company was better, as well. Aside from a little teenage rebellion, he'd always gotten along well with both parents. That feeling extended to his brother, too. Once he and Gabe had both gotten past the age of ten, their fierce competitive streak had mellowed into something that was manageable and only reared its head occasionally when they played a little one-on-one basketball.

He knew that, day or night, the door of his parents' home was always open to him. It was a comforting thing to fall back on, but tonight, he wanted to be alone.

That being the case, he supposed that things had worked out for the best, with Dana canceling at the last minute.

Rafe stretched out on the sofa, a can of soda in his hand. Briefly, he flirted with the idea of calling for take-out, then decided to make do with whatever he found in the refrigerator.

He reached for the remote and clicked on the television set. He ignored it the minute it came on, needing only the soft blur of colors, the indistinguishable buzz of noise in the background, as company. He popped the top of the can, then brought the drink to his mouth and drank deeply, trying to quench an even deeper thirst.

It made no difference to him, Rafe thought. If Dana Morrow had decided she didn't want to go out with him, he wasn't about to push the matter. It just wasn't meant to be, that was all.

He wasn't aware of the sigh that escaped him. A lot of things weren't meant to be.

On the other hand, some things were. Sometimes, things just came together and turned out well.

The way they had with Timmie.

Toasting himself with the half-empty can, Rafe smiled. Timmie was even now undergoing treatment to purge his blood of the toxins that had come perilously close to killing him.

Who would have thought that what amounted to a few bites of contaminated ground beef could nearly destroy a boy as vibrant, as energetic, as Timmie? The boy had been afraid to confess to his mother that, curious, he had sampled the raw meat. He'd almost taken the secret with him to his grave.

And he would have, Rafe thought, if he hadn't badgered him, making the boy go over everything he'd done, everything he'd touched, in the days before he'd gotten sick. In forcing Timmie to recite the events over and over again, Rafe had almost reduced them both to tears, but he'd gotten his answer.

And now Timmie was getting his life back.

Rafe drained the rest of the soda, then placed the empty can on the coffee table, still feeling thirsty. A man couldn't feel down when he'd managed to cheat death of such a young trophy. And he did feel good, very good.

So why was there this small, nagging feeling echoing in the back of his mind, humming of dissatisfaction? The message from Dana, tendered secondhand through Alice, had taken the edge off his victory. It shouldn't have, he knew, and yet it had.

Women.

He blew out a breath and then got off the sofa. He needed another drink. Something stronger than soda.

Dana stared at the man who had been her father's partner for the past fifteen years. Jefferson Wallace had called her earlier today and mysteriously requested a meeting. A fussy, precise man who could never be accused of being larger than life the way her father was, Wallace had been very specific in selecting both the time and locale for their meeting. He wanted to see her at one o'clock in her living room. A time when he knew her father was going to be safely in court.

Dana had had absolutely no idea why Wallace wanted to see her, even after Esther had shown him in and she had taken her seat across from him.

Once he'd told her what was on his mind, Dana felt she was being set up for some sort of macabre joke. It couldn't be anything else. She waited in vain for the punch line that didn't come.

Finally she asked, "You're kidding, right?"

A mouth created for frowning pursed as eyes the color and shape of ebony marbles scrutinized her every move. With narrow, thin shoulders that hunched forward and hands that were too large for the rest of him, he was like a small, ugly statue that was so off-putting it bordered on fascinating.

"Dana, I don't have time to waste with ill-conceived pranks or poorly constructed jokes. I am very serious about this. Will you come to work for the firm?" Wallace repeated.

If her father had wanted her to join the firm, she thought, he would have said so.

Or would he?

Was this some kind of test? And if it was, which way was she to answer in order to pass? It wasn't easy, being Paul Morrow's daughter. At the very least, it bred a strain of paranoia that was hard to shake.

Cautiously, she entered the waters. "This is my father's firm. I don't really think he'd like having me there."

The marbles never shifted. They continued to bore straight into her. "It's a firm your father began," Wallace replied, correcting her. "But I'm a senior partner, and we would very much like to have a Morrow on our staff."

"You *have* a Morrow on the staff. My father."

Wallace watched her reaction to his next words. "We've been thinking of asking him to step down. Retire. For reasons of health," he added expansively.

He wasn't concerned with her father's health, Dana thought. He was concerned with the fact that her father might do something to embarrass the firm.

"And you think having me at the firm will somehow soften the blow of his knowing he'd been eased out?" She laughed harshly. She would have thought that someone at the firm would have done his homework. Paul Morrow wasn't the kind to bust his buttons with pride at his offspring's accomplishments. Especially not if it came to that offspring supplanting him. "Boy, do you have the wrong number." Her laugh faded. Wallace continued looking at her, his eyes unfathomable. She felt something twist in her stomach. Revulsion? Or fading morning sickness?

Dana leaned forward in her chair. If she hadn't thought it would give Wallace heart failure, she would have caught his hand between hers to underscore her entreaty.

"You can't do this to him." Neither she nor the family

physician she had called the other day for a prognosis knew how long her father had—six months or six years—but one thing she did know for certain. ''If you force him to retire, it will kill him. He'll have nothing to live for.'' Her voice became impassioned. ''Being a lawyer is his *life,* Mr. Wallace. His *whole* life. It's who and what he is.''

Wallace appeared uncomfortable but unmoved. ''He has you, his granddaughter and more money than Monaco.'' Every reason in the world to retire, in his book.

Dana shook her head. ''Unimportant. All unimportant. He *needs* to bc Paul S. Morrow, criminal lawyer. Take that away from him and you're guilty of putting a gun to his head.''

Her eyes could be just as cold as her father's. It was a look she had practiced and perfected in the mirror when she was very young. It never worked on her father, but it did on others. She aimed the look at Wallace, nearly succeeding in making him squirm.

''Do you want that on your conscience?''

''No, of course not.'' He tried again, a little less pompously. ''But there is a danger of his becoming an embarrassment.''

She didn't have to summon a practiced expression. The look in her eyes cut him dead. ''To whom?''

Wallace faltered a little. And as he faltered, he thought that Dana Morrow might indeed be the perfect heir apparent to her father. ''To himself.''

''Then he'll be the one who knows when to leave.'' She knew her father well enough for that. If he felt he was a liability, if he felt that others were laughing at him, he would leave immediately. She rose and looked down at Wallace. ''It *is* his firm, Mr. Wallace.'' Clamping a lid on her anger at the other man's presumption, she thought the situation over. Wallace's concern did have some validity. Her father *was* slipping. Something had to be done to pick up the slack. *That* she could do.

''If it will be of any help,'' she said, measuring her words. She'd never thought about working for her father, never wanted to work for him, but it wasn't a matter now of her values or her desires. Her father, completely unknown to him, needed her. Needed her to be his buffer. Maybe somewhere along the line, if she joined, she could even manage to have the "S" in his name stand for something other than shark. "I'll come to work for the firm. I'll do what needs to be done to smooth over any rough edges you feel are showing. I can help prepare the briefs, that sort of thing." She could hear the explosion when her father was told. "I need the work, anyway."

Because he knew in his gut that he had no choice, the compromise appeased Wallace. For the time being.

His stomach settling, he allowed himself to sample one of the pastries that Esther had put out. The amaretto-laced tart coaxed a ghost of a smile from him. "Don't know why he didn't bring you in before. You could argue the ears off a brass monkey."

That wasn't always a compliment, but she took it as her due. "If I have to."

Wallace carefully wiped his mouth with his handkerchief. "Your sister was a great deal quieter."

Until her falling out with her father over George, Megan had clerked for the firm, hoping to someday become at least a junior partner. It was a carrot her father had dangled before her but never actually offered.

"That was my fault." Her fond tone was for the memory, not the man. "I never let her get a word in edgewise."

It occurred to Wallace that condolences might still be in order. It was something he'd never been any good at. "I'm sorry about...well, about..."

She nodded, putting him out of his misery. His words meant nothing to her, nor did the social code he adhered to, which necessitated offering them. "Thanks. So, do we have a deal?"

Relieved, even entertaining a dollop of hope, Wallace extended his hand to her, sealing the bargain. "Deal."

* * *

As everyone else slept that night, sleeplessness once again haunted Paul Morrow, as it had more and more each year. He sat in his den and reviewed the surveillance tapes Dickinson had brought to him. The tapes from cameras no one else knew existed.

They were hidden strategically in several rooms in the house. Originally intended as part of a security system, of late they enabled Morrow to feel as if he was still in control of things by allowing him to eavesdrop on what was going on.

The tape from the living room camera had him leaning forward in his wheelchair. His eyes narrowed as he watched and listened to his partner, a man he trusted as much as he trusted anyone, plot to push him out of the firm he had established.

The spineless bastard was going behind his back, trying to ally himself with Dana.

If asked, his guess would have been that his daughter would have jumped at the chance to be a party to that. It amazed him to learn otherwise.

He heard his daughter, a woman he hardly knew and liked less, come to his defense. Reading people was second nature to him, a craft he'd honed over the years to help him win his cases and survive. As he watched, a side of Dana emerged he'd never been privy to. A side she'd kept hidden as they went head-to-head over everything. There was passion in her face, feeling in her voice, as she came to his defense.

Why?

Why would she come to his aid? Why would she care if his career ended? She'd never tried to reap any rewards from it. She'd made it plain that she hated the limelight, hated the notoriety of being Paul Morrow's daughter.

The question lingered in his mind. Morrow stared at the monitor long after the tape had ended, no longer seeing the screen.

Why?

* * *

Sweat poured into Rafe's eyes, stinging them. He blinked it away. Every fiber of his being was intent on making this shot.

It was a simple game of basketball. Two teams comprised of a potpourri of medical personnel, doctors, nurses, orderlies, whoever didn't mind getting sweaty and fancied himself or herself as the next Michael Jordan—or at least capable of dribbling a basketball. At stake were a couple of rounds of drinks at McGinty's, a local hangout. Losers footed the tab. The fate of the world was not riding on this shot.

Just his pride.

Which was why it would have cost him dearly had he missed. And he almost did. Because as he was lining it up, as he was about to release the ball, out of the corner of his eye, he saw Dana. Dana, with her hand holding Mollie's, came into his line of vision. Looking his way.

If it hadn't been a free shot, if he'd been in motion on the court, someone would have knocked the ball out of his hands.

"Hey, Saldana, you going to take the shot or pose for a statue?" Moore, the new plastic surgeon, hooted impatiently.

Gaining his concentration, Rafe made his shot. The basketball sailed toward the hoop and made it through cleanly. As his teammates and somewhere around half the people scattered in the bleachers in the local high school gym cheered, Rafe watched Dana usher Mollie into a seat, then sit next to her.

What were they doing here? And why should the sight of a woman he had put out of his mind make him lose his concentration?

Annoyed with himself for his lack of a satisfactory answer, he ran to the other end of the court with his team.

Mollie's eyes were glued to him from the moment she'd spotted her beloved doctor. "Dr. Rafe looks all sweaty, Aunt Dana."

Yes, he did, didn't he? She could see it from here. Sweat gleamed on his body, making it almost glow. Dana shifted restlessly in her seat.

"He's playing basketball. It's sweaty work." She found it difficult to look at anyone else.

"How come Dr. Rafe's not wearing any pants?"

Dana bit back a laugh. "He's wearing shorts, honey. It makes it easier for him to play." Dana watched Rafe's muscular legs tense and pump as he ran from one end of the court to the other. You wouldn't think a man that tall could move so fast. "Man's got a pretty nice pair of legs on him," Dana murmured to herself.

She had to admit he was in possession of a magnificent form. Dressed, there was only a hint of the body beneath. Wearing only shorts and a T-shirt and gleaming with sweat, he looked as if someone had carved him out of golden rock.

The man appeared to be solid muscle, she realized in awed fascination.

Glancing around at the female spectators, she saw she wasn't alone in her assessment.

Dana bit her bottom lip. She still didn't know what she was doing here—other than having thoughts she shouldn't about her niece's pediatrician's body.

Dana looked around, but Sheila was nowhere to be seen. Leave it to Sheila to all but strong-arm her into coming to watch her play basketball and then not have the decency to show up.

Signaling for a time-out, Rafe dropped into the stands and grabbed the water bottle he had stashed under his seat. He took a long pull and let the warm liquid trickle down his throat before turning to look at Dana. She was sitting several rows behind him. He raised a quizzical eyebrow in her direction.

She felt awkward as she lifted her shoulders in a shrug. The next thing she knew, Mollie was working her way down to where he was sitting. Muttering under her breath, Dana had no choice but to follow.

Well, this was a dumb idea, she thought. There was no question that she should have her head examined for going along with it.

"Come to the game," Sheila had said. "I need someone to cheer me on, and you need to get out. It'll be perfect. Bring Mollie."

That she needed to get out was right on the money. But she didn't need to be here, looking at Rafe when he was all sweaty and sexy as hell, suddenly reliving a kiss that had had no business happening.

Why hadn't she thought to ask Sheila if Rafe was going to be there? Because that would have made it sound as if she wanted him to be there, that was why. So she hadn't, and now look.

Irritation born of embarrassment flooded her. Damned if you do, damned if you don't.

Mollie was a one-woman fan club. She'd made herself comfortable on the bench beside Rafe. "You play good."

He took another pull of the water bottle, then laughed as he tousled her hair. "Just what I like, an unbiased opinion. How're you doing, kiddo?"

"Very well, thank you," she answered primly, her eyes sparkling like dew on tender green buds.

"Still got your manners, I see." He raised his eyes to Dana's face as she joined them. She looked flushed. And pretty. "And your aunt. What brings you here?" he asked Dana.

She told him the truth and thought it sounded like an excuse. "Sheila asked me to come and cheer her on. She said Slade couldn't make it."

Frustrated, Dana looked around, willing Sheila to materialize and save her from this awkward moment. Being face to face with Rafe served to remind her she hadn't even had the courage to break their date last week in person. It galled her that she'd behaved badly, impulsively urged on by a fear she'd momentarily been unable to manage.

It galled her more that he probably knew it, too.

"Neither could she," Rafe told her. Confused, Dana looked at him. "Sheila had an emergency delivery." His attention shifted to Mollie. ''Since *you're* here, want to act as *my* cheering section?''

''Yes!'' Mollie shouted. She clapped her hands to demonstrate.

''That's all the encouragement I need,'' he pronounced. He left the almost empty water bottle under his seat and got back into the game.

By the time the game was officially over, both sides were ready to drop. Rafe's team won by one basket, the winning shot made by an anesthesiologist who barely came up to Rafe's shoulder.

Detaching himself from his high-fiving teammates, Rafe came over to join Mollie and Dana. Mollie was standing on the bleacher, applauding wildly.

''We're going to McGinty's to celebrate.'' Rafe raised his voice above the din of crowing winners and grousing losers. ''Want to join us?''

''I don't think so. Mollie's too young to hoist a few,'' Dana pointed out. She was grateful she'd brought Mollie. Otherwise she would have been tempted to say yes, and that probably wouldn't have been a good thing.

Victory and the sight of her cheering for him had made Rafe forget they were going to a bar. A sheepish grin curved his lips.

''Sorry, what was I thinking? How about Chocolate Heaven?'' He presented his case to Mollie. ''They make the best ice cream sodas.''

Mollie looked as if she was ready to take off with him like a shot. Only ingrained training had her looking at Dana. ''Aunt Dana?''

She'd never heard her name said so hopefully. Dana couldn't find it in her heart to say no. She supposed that, with Mollie between them, she was safe from making any foolish mistakes. Like kissing Rafe again.

Unable to quite shake the feeling that she had stepped into quicksand, Dana nodded. ''All right.''

He couldn't explain the electrifying zip that went through

him at her words. He didn't even try. He began to move away, then stepped back.

"I've got to change." His eyes pinned her down. "Be here when I get back?"

"Yes."

It wasn't good enough. Dana had said yes before, then changed her mind. Rafe directed his appeal to Mollie. "Keep her here, okay?"

Mollie grinned broadly as she laced her fingers through her aunt's. "Okay."

"I'm counting on you." Leaning forward, he slid his finger down the pert nose. "She's slippery." With that, he hurried off.

Mollie's brow was puckered as she turned to her aunt. "What did he mean, Aunt Dana?"

Dana shrugged broadly. "I don't know," she lied. "He must have gotten hit on the head with the basketball before we got here." Leaning over, she whispered confidentially, "It makes him say silly things."

Mollie accepted the explanation. After all, Aunt Dana knew everything.

Rafe hurried through his shower and into his clothing. He had a feeling that, if he didn't, Dana was likely to take a powder, pint-size bodyguard or not.

"Hey." Kim Lee stopped toweling his hair dry to look bewilderedly at his friend. Rafe was dressed and stuffing his sweaty clothing into his gym bag while the rest of them were still dripping from the shower. "They timing us or something?"

Rafe didn't bother zipping the bag closed. Grabbing the handles, he was off. "No, only me." He tossed the words over his shoulder as he left the locker room.

Watching him go, Kim grinned. It had to be a woman. No man moved that fast if he didn't have someone to go to. He wondered if it was the blonde in the stands he'd seen Rafe talking to. All he could think was that it was about time.

* * *

Half of Rafe didn't expect to find Dana and Mollie there when he got to the gym, but there they were in the bleachers, right where he'd left them. Rafe exhaled slowly. He couldn't remember ever getting ready so fast, even when he was in medical school. Not even the morning he'd overslept after pulling a thirty-six-hour shift.

Seeing him coming their way, Mollie ran to greet him. "Aunt Dana thinks you have nice legs."

If there had been a hole in the gym floor to crawl into, she would have done it. Mortified, Dana made a mental note to give Mollie a lesson about the need to keep secrets.

"Oh, she does, does she?" Rafe grinned, looking at Dana, who was slowly coming toward them. "Tell Aunt Dana thank you."

"She's right here." Grabbing his hand, Mollie tugged on it, pulling him toward her aunt. "You can do it yourself."

Instead of following, he dropped to one knee beside Mollie. "I'm afraid I'll spook her, like I did the other night."

If it qualified as a whisper, it was of the stage variety. Dana met his eyes, her embarrassment dropping away. "What I said to Mollie was that your legs didn't look as bad in shorts as some of the other players' did. And for the record, you didn't spook me."

He rose to his feet, his eyes on hers. "Then why did you cancel?"

She shrugged vaguely. "Something came up."

"Something?" he repeated, waiting for her to be a little more specific.

He had a long wait ahead of him, then, she thought. "Yes, something." She took a breath. "Now, just exactly where is this Heavenly Chocolate?"

"Chocolate Heaven," he corrected.

Dana waved away the correction. "Whatever. Is it far?"

He paused, thinking. "About a mile. C'mon, I'll take you there." Reaching for Mollie's hand, he was ready to leave the gym.

Dana held out. She wanted a clean getaway available if she needed it. "You lead the way. We'll follow in my car."

Turning, he regarded her for a moment. "Can you be trusted?"

She supposed she had that coming. "Yes, I can be trusted." Biting back a comment, she raised her hand as if she was in court. "I promise."

Rafe looked at Mollie solemnly. "You're a witness, Mollie. She promised. You know what happens to people who break their promises, don't you?"

Mollie hung on his every word. "No, what?"

"They can never eat chocolate again." He deliberately made his voice sound stern.

After wavering for a second, Mollie giggled, deciding that he was teasing. "We'll follow you," she promised. "Aunt Dana loves chocolate."

This was promising. "Then she's going to love their amaretto sundae." He took Mollie's hand again. "So, did you like the game?"

Mollie thrust her other hand into her aunt's. She liked the way it felt, walking between them. Almost like when she used to walk with Mommy and Daddy. "Uh-huh. It was cool."

"Cool, huh?" he repeated. "Who taught you that word?"

"My new best friend, Becky. She goes to my preschool. Aunt Dana signed me up. I get to go three times a week. My teacher's name is..."

Mollie was off and running. And much to Dana's eternal relief, she kept up a steady stream of chatter all the way to the parking lot.

Chapter 13

Chocolate Heaven was a small shop devoted to the axiom that all good things involved chocolate in some way. The owner, who could be found on the premises at any given time, knew how to reel people in from the streets if they were passing by on foot rather than by car. Even the latter were immune only if the windows were firmly rolled up. Otherwise, the aroma of chocolate, decadent and tempting, floated out, beckoning to one and all like the crooked finger of a mischievous enchantress. Very few could resist the call.

Dana didn't even try.

Her senses were aroused and her mouth watering long before she and Mollie crossed the threshold. She took a deep breath, drawing in the scent.

"They know how to get you, don't they?" Rafe asked her, amusement in his eyes.

She laughed, looking around the shop. Several booths and small, white-topped circular tables surrounded by chairs, the kind found in old-fashioned soda shops, were scattered throughout the room. To one side was a long soda fountain, complete with stools. The back of the room was devoted to chocolate. Chocolate bars, gold-foil-covered chocolate coins, chocolate in boxes, chocolate figures and any combination of food covered with chocolate the mind could conjure up.

Wow, was all she could think. "I think I gained three pounds just by breathing."

Mollie scrunched up her face, trying to understand. "How can you do that?"

"When you're older, you'll find out," Dana assured her. She found herself wishing she could burn off excess calories as easily as Mollie could.

Rafe selected a booth, then looked at Dana for approval. She smiled, letting Mollie slip in first, then sitting beside her.

And that put her right across from Rafe, she realized. Right across from eyes the color of leaves budding in the spring. Dana decided that close scrutiny of the menu Rafe had picked up on their way in was in order.

Mollie frowned at the menu in front of her. She knew how to recognize all her letters and a few words, but this had curly stuff written all over it. She couldn't pick out a single thing she knew.

Frustrated, she looked at Rafe. "What's it say?"

He began reading the different selections to Mollie, along with their flowery descriptions. He did it with such feeling that by the time he was finished, Dana had no idea what to order.

Mollie was in the same boat. "I don't know what to get," she confessed. Her appeal for aid, Dana noted, was to Rafe, not to her.

"How about the banana split?" Rafe suggested. "At least then you can pretend it's healthy." When he winked at her, Mollie giggled.

It amazed Dana that Rafe seemed content to let Mollie chatter endlessly as they sat, waiting for their orders to be brought. He even responded in the few places where she paused for air. He wasn't just allowing Mollie to talk, Dana realized, he was listening to her.

She had to admit that the man was a rarity.

Rafe's grin widened as he looked at the expression on Dana's face. "What?"

Faced with a direct question, Dana roused herself. "Excuse me?"

She probably wasn't aware she was staring at him, he thought. "You have this look on your face like you're trying to figure me out."

Caught, she had no choice. She raised a shoulder, then let it drop. "I am."

"Not much to figure," he said simply. "I'm a doctor, I like kids. Especially bright ones." He winked at Mollie, then raised his eyes to Dana's. "If there's anything else you want to know, ask."

She did have questions, she realized. Questions about him, about his life. But answers would only lead to an intimacy she didn't want right now. An intimacy she wouldn't know what to do with.

Dana toyed with her silverware. "I don't believe in prying."

That would put her in a class by herself, he thought. "It's only prying if the other person doesn't want to answer." But even though he paused, she made no effort to ask anything. "You might be interested in knowing that the three people you helped save on our auspicious non-date have been discharged and gone home."

"You helped save people, Aunt Dana?" Mollie asked, her voice bubbling with curiosity.

Dana didn't think it was a good idea to discuss a car accident in front of Mollie. Her eyes met Rafe's, and she subtly shook her head, hoping he understood her meaning.

He did, but he couldn't ignore Mollie's question. "Your aunt's a brave lady. At least," he added significantly, "where some things are concerned."

Dana bit back a retort. Any discussion of the subject was tabled as the waiter returned with their order. Mollie's looked almost larger than she was. She beamed in anticipation.

''Looks like our fall from grace has arrived.'' Rafe raised a spoon to something described as ''fudge decadence à la mode.''

''No, it hasn't,'' Mollie corrected, confused. ''This is ice cream.''

Rafe laughed. He enjoyed the gusto with which she dug in. There was an innocence to children that faded and then disappeared completely when they got older. An innocence that gave him hope for future generations.

''For you it's ice cream,'' he pointed out. ''For me, it's three hours at the gym.''

Dana had begun to believe that, except for rare aberrations, Rafe was always at his office or the hospital. ''You work out?''

He noted her incredulous tone. ''Obviously not enough, if you have to ask.''

She took a sip of her drink, something that combined vanilla ice cream, chocolate syrup, whipped cream and Kahlúa, mint and amaretto flavorings, and let it seduce her taste buds before continuing.

''No, I just meant I thought maybe it was natural. The muscles and everything.'' She was putting this very badly. The amusement in his eyes wasn't making it any easier for her, either.

''No, just a natural by-product of working out.'' He thought back to the photographs in his mother's album. The ones he couldn't convince her to throw away. ''My natural look is early Pillsbury doughboy.'' Mollie's delighted laugh urged him to elaborate. ''No, seriously, my mother can cook like nobody else in this world. The only thing she likes more than cooking is watching Gabe and me eating.'' Only a rapid growth spurt in his late teens and a good metabolism had prevented him from being wider than he was tall. ''I started exercising in self-defense. It was either that,'' he confided to Mollie, ''or look for a job as Humpty Dumpty's stand-in.''

Now that Dana didn't believe. She let her eyes roam over his upper torso. It could have been chiseled out of rock. The blue jersey he wore accented biceps and pectorals that were usually only found in the pages of a physical fitness magazine.

She shook her head. "I can't picture you heavy."

And she was really trying. He could see it in her eyes. "Remind me to show you a few pictures sometime."

Sometime. That meant he intended to see them, her, again. Or was it a throwaway line? She didn't know. More than that, she didn't know whether or not she wanted it to be.

Common sense was weighing in on one side, but other factors were beginning to gather on the other. A side that could definitely complicate things for her.

Dana lowered her eyes and concentrated on the tall glass in front of her.

Throwing herself into eating her dessert with abandonment, Mollie still found time to eye the one before Rafe. "Boy, that looks good, too."

He could read what was on her mind as if it was printed on her forehead in big block letters. "Want a taste?"

Mollie practically glowed. "Yes, please."

Enthusiastic, but still polite. He got a tremendous kick out of Mollie. He and Gabe had never been remotely this polite when they were kids. Scooping up two layers of brownie decked out in three kinds of chocolate sauce, he offered the prize to Mollie. She leaned forward and cleaned the spoon with one bite.

"Good?"

Her mouth full, she could only respond with a pleased noise. "Uh-huh." Mollie swallowed, her eyes gleaming. Then she pushed her plate toward him. "Would you like some of mine?"

She seemed so eager to share, he couldn't refuse. "Sure."

Mimicking him, Mollie fed Rafe some of her banana split. A little ice cream was lost to the table, but Rafe pretended not to notice.

Her father would have ordered her from the table, Dana thought. And Steven would have hit the ceiling because of the mess. She felt herself smiling as she watched. Rafe Saldana was going to make a hell of a father to some lucky kid someday.

''Now you, Aunt Dana. You feed Dr. Rafe, too.''

The wide grin on Rafe's face made Dana's stomach flip over. She found herself looking at her glass instead of at him. ''No, I don't think he wants any of this.''

''Sure I do.''

''Sure he does,'' Mollie echoed.

She might have known he would do this. It was either give Rafe a taste or subject herself to an onslaught of Mollie logic.

Something warm and unnamed washed over her as she dipped her spoon into the tall glass and then held it out to Rafe. Her breath hovered in her lungs, not going in, not going out.

Waiting.

Rafe saw the slight tremor of her hand. Did he make her nervous? And why was that so appealing to him?

Holding her hand steady with his, his eyes on hers, Rafe guided the spoon slowly to his mouth. He closed his lips over it, then slid the spoon out even more slowly. The arousal he experienced was nothing new. But the intensity was.

Her breath finally materialized, evacuating her lungs rapidly. But not nearly as rapidly as her pulse was pounding. Dana dropped the long spoon into the glass, her fingers feeling oddly boneless.

''If you want any more, you can have it.'' She pushed the tall glass toward him.

He shook his head, smiling. ''No, that's all right, you finish it.'' His eyes lingered on her face, caressing it. ''Want any of mine?''

''No!'' She reddened as she realized that she'd declined a little more loudly and forcefully than she'd intended. The amused, knowing smile on his face only served to irritate her, although she couldn't have said exactly why.

He nodded, lifting his spoon to his mouth. ''Well, let me know if you do.''

For a second her eyes were drawn to his mouth, It was a strong mouth, a firm mouth. A…

Rallying, annoyed with herself, with the way she felt herself slipping, Dana squared her shoulders. "Believe me, you'll be the first to know."

Was it his imagination, or had he just been privy to a battle cry?

The evening and the company charmed her far more than she'd thought possible. And she wasn't the only one who felt the effects of spending some time with Dr. Rafe Saldana, first-rate physician and star of the basketball court as well as chocolate advocate par excellence. It was clear that Mollie was completely enamored with him.

If she'd had any lingering doubts of that, they were dispelled once she and Rafe had pulled up in her driveway. He had insisted on seeing them home, even if that meant he had to follow them in his car. Apparently chivalry was not dead.

As soon as the two cars stopped, Mollie scrambled out of theirs and ran to his, waiting impatiently for him to get out.

Hands tucked behind her back, rocking on the balls of her feet, Mollie looked at him adoringly. "Dr. Rafe?"

She sounded so serious, he suppressed the smile the mere sight of her evoked. "Yes, Mollie?"

"Will you marry me?"

The proposal caught him completely off guard. She was so earnest, so sincere, he knew it would crush her if he laughed. Banking down his initial reaction, Rafe crouched beside Mollie, taking her small hands in his. He kissed them one at a time.

"Mollie, I am very, very honored that you want to marry me."

Mollie's expression was the picture of eagerness. "Then you will?"

Regret was evident in every fiber of his countenance. How did he manage to do that? Dana wondered. Was it kindness or practice that he drew on?

"I can't, kiddo. Not right now. You're too young."

With the deadly accurate logic of the young, Mollie pointed out, "But I'll get older."

He inclined his head, conceding the point. "So will I."

Stymied, Mollie shook her head. "I don't care about that. I love you."

She touched his heart. Lightly, he feathered his hand through her hair. "And I love you, Mollie. Tell you what, I'll wait for you, and if you still want to marry me in, oh, say thirteen years—"

Her eyes widened as her voice fillcd with despair. That seemed like an eternity. "Thirteen years?" she wailed.

He nodded. "Thirteen years. You'll be eighteen then and can do whatever you want. If you still want to marry me, I'm all yours."

"Oh." The clouds lifted from her face. Hope existed, waiting for her at the end of eternity. "Okay."

Mollie was adorable. Rafe had a sudden image of Dana at that age and decided she'd probably been more in the spice category than sugar.

"So, it's decided," he said. "If you still want to get married in thirteen years, I'm your man."

"It's a deal!" Mollie stuck out her hand like a grown-up.

Rafe shook it solemnly before rising. He made eye contact with Dana and saw that the look in her eyes had softened considerably.

"That was very nice of you," she whispered.

As she spoke, her breath touched his cheek. Warming him. Reminding him. Funny how some things lingered in your mind, he mused. Just enough to haunt you.

He smiled at her. "Just covering my bets. I figure by the time she's eighteen, I might be ready to settle down, and they'll be lining up six deep for her." The look in his eyes was soft as they slid over her. "The way they probably did for you."

Thirteen years, huh? She wondered if he was putting her on notice that he wasn't available. As if that were necessary.

"No lines." She kept her voice low. "My father wouldn't have stood for it. When he was here."

And from her tone, that hadn't happened very often. "And when he wasn't?"

"Hasn't Sheila filled you in yet?" She was surprised, but maybe he just hadn't been curious enough about her to ask. "I was the original wild child."

Wild. That was the word for her. Not in the way she conducted herself, but there was a certain look that came into her eyes, a certain way she lifted her chin. A vitality that she exuded, even when she was being subdued.

He should be going, he thought. For lots of reasons. He lingered for one that remained unacknowledged. "I'd like to do this again sometime."

Nervousness danced through her. "Have ice cream, go out with the two of us or stand in my driveway and talk?"

His laugh was quiet. She couldn't be accused of making this easy. "All of the above." He paused, almost at ease with his discomfort. It kept him on his toes. "This is very awkward for me. I'm not really up on my dating skills—not that this is exactly a date." To him, a date was dinner, dancing, moonlight, the whole nine yards. But this was close.

Because he seemed momentarily uncomfortable, she wasn't. "Whatever this is, you're doing very nicely."

"Good." He looked into her eyes. "Does that mean I can call you sometime?"

"Yes." She was leaving herself open to disappointment, she upbraided herself. But somehow, the word no just didn't want to materialize on her tongue.

"Good," Rafe repeated. "I'll see you." He smiled at Mollie, then bent and kissed her cheek. "Stay healthy." Rafe surprised Dana by kissing her cheek, as well. "You, too."

Not if he kept making her heart flutter as if it was going to take off, she thought, watching him drive away.

Dana waved in unison with Mollie only because Mollie urged her to.

"I really am going to marry him, Aunt Dana," Mollie declared, taking Dana's hand. "He's the nicest man I ever met—except for Daddy. But I think he's as nice as Daddy." She paused, her small face suddenly troubled. "Is that wrong?"

Dana pushed her jumbled thoughts to the side. "No, baby, there's nothing wrong in liking someone else." *Maybe you should listen to yourself sometime. You've got feelings for the man you won't let come out and you're running for the hills.* "Let's go inside."

All she wanted when she walked into the house was some time to herself to sort out feelings that were ricocheting through her with the energy of handballs in play. But all personal desires had to be put on hold until Mollie went to sleep.

Chattering ceaselessly about Dr. Rafe and her wedding plans thirteen years in the future, Mollie gave every indication of being able to go on all night. But eventually the little girl wore herself out and fell asleep.

Relieved to finally have some time to herself, Dana slipped out of Mollie's room. Dickinson was waiting for her in the hall. Dana started, her hand flying to her chest. She looked at him accusingly.

"Sorry, didn't mean to frighten you," he murmured.

She drew in a long breath, then let it out, getting herself under control. "How long have you been standing there, Tom?"

The thin lips curved. "She was planning her wedding. I didn't want to interrupt."

Dana smiled, her annoyance vanishing. "Thanks."

And then Dickinson was all polite business again. "Your father would like to see you."

Now what? Dana turned toward the stairs, resigned. "All right."

Paul Morrow's eyes met hers when she entered the den. She had the impression he'd been staring at the door the entire time, willing her to come. Waiting. "Took you long enough."

"Mollie was too excited to sleep." That was enough of an

explanation. "Tom said you wanted to see me. What's this about?" She had a feeling she knew. Somehow, her father must have found out about Wallace hiring her. He was undoubtedly going to forbid her from setting foot in the office.

Prepared for the clash, she was surprised to hear her father ask, "How is Mollie adjusting?"

Dana watched his face warily. Where was this leading? "Fine. She seems to be a lot more resilient than I thought she'd be."

His shrug was careless, vague. "They say children are."

"But you wouldn't have any firsthand knowledge about things like that, would you?" The look in his eyes was sharp, alert. "Sorry. I can't remember you ever asking after anyone's well-being before."

Though he stared at her intently, what he was seeing was the girl she'd once been. Even at Mollie's age, she'd stood before him defiantly. He remembered being torn between annoyance and a certain amount of pride at the backbone she'd displayed, even then. "Maybe I've learned a few things."

Dana studied his expression. There was more here than what she was hearing. "Such as?" she asked slowly.

"Such as perhaps I might have conducted some business the wrong way. Such as perhaps I've placed my trust in the wrong people." His eyes narrowed. "And distrusted the wrong ones."

The calm before the storm. Dana braced herself for the onslaught of temper she knew was to come. "What wrong people?"

For the second time in the space of five minutes, her father surprised her. "The former? People I work with. The latter? You."

Her head felt as if it had been punted straight into a thick fog. "You're going to have to get more specific than that, Counselor."

"I know that," he snapped, then struggled with his temper, something he'd never bothered trying to contain before. Not here, in his own home, where pretenses weren't necessary.

Where he could throw off the harnesses of frustration and image and act upon their effects. ‘‘You think this is easy?’’

She refused to be intimidated. Instead, she met his look and matched it. ‘‘If I knew what you were doing, I could answer that.’’

He blew out a breath. Words, they were only words. He'd used endless words before. He was a master. Why was this so difficult for him?

Because these words mattered, really mattered.

Every one of them stung as they left his tongue. ‘‘I'm trying to apologize.’’

She stared at him, the fog worsening. ‘‘About what and to whom?’’

‘‘Don't play dumb, gir—Dana,’’ he corrected himself, gritting his teeth.

He couldn't be doing what she thought he was doing. Could he?

‘‘In this case, I don't have to play, I am.’’ A ghost of a smile flirted with her lips. ‘‘And thanks for remembering my name.’’

He looked at her in annoyed surprise. ‘‘Of course I remember your name. I gave it to you.’’

Dana stared at him. ‘‘You gave— I didn't know that.’’

She'd assumed her mother had named her, just as she'd named Megan. Megan was named after their maternal grandmother. Dana had never asked who she was named after. That way she could make up stories in her head when she was very young. Stories that made her feel special. As special as she desperately wanted to be.

For a second her father savored the minor triumph. ‘‘There are a great many things you don't know. A great many.’’ His eyes grew distant, looking into the past. His past. ‘‘Dana was my sister's name.’’

Dana sank on the love seat facing him. ‘‘You have a sister?’’

Her question jerked him to the present. ‘‘Had. She died when she was little more than Mollie's age.’’

Sadness. Was that sadness she heard in his voice? Her father? Dana studied him more closely. "How..."

"Parental neglect." It had been more than that. It had been parental abuse, but he had no desire to go into that. His agitation grew. "I wasn't there." He looked at her sharply, helpless frustration in his eyes. Just as there had been in his soul when it had happened. "What does it matter? Dead is dead."

It mattered, she thought. Mattered a great deal. Dana realized that this was the closest she'd ever felt to her father. "If you named me after her, you must have loved her."

He was about to deny it, to clamp the lid on his personal feelings, but that would have been like denying his sister's existence, and he couldn't bring himself to do it.

"Yes, I did. Mollie reminds me a little of her." And then suddenly, because this had cost him too much, his expression changed completely. Darkened so quickly it startled her. "I know that Wallace came here, offering you a job. Trying to get you to side with him."

"And just how do you know that?"

He waved her question away. "That's unimportant."

But Dana stood her ground. "Not to me."

His energy was limited, and he wasn't about to spend it on trivial details. "Will you just listen?" he demanded. "I also know what you said to him. Verbatim. Why?" His eyes pinned her. If she lied to him, he would know.

She tried to recall her exact words to Wallace. Just what was it her father was after? "Why did I say that to him?" she asked, guessing.

"Yes." He spat the word out.

She didn't understand why he was so angry with her. Did he resent her being on his side? Was that it? "Because it was true."

He both hated and admired the fact that she read him so well. "Why should you care?"

She looked at him for a long moment, trying to fathom what he was thinking, what he was after. It was impossible.

''If you have to ask, then the answer won't mean anything to you.''

He nodded slowly, as if to himself. He had his answer, his confirmation. Hearing it seemed suddenly superfluous. ''I do the hiring and firing at the firm.''

Dana rose. ''That's what I thought. I accepted Wallace's offer because—'' When he caught her by the hand, she could only stare uncomprehendingly at him.

''I know why you accepted. And I appreciate it.''

''You do?'' She almost stuttered.

As if realizing he'd taken her hand to keep her from leaving, he dropped it. ''Stop interrupting. You're making me tired.'' He drew a deep breath. ''Perhaps, for once, Wallace had a good idea.'' The man's name left a bad taste in his mouth. He and Wallace were going to have it out when the time was ripe. Right now, he was gearing up for Senator Johnson's trial. ''At least, half a good idea. I want you to come work for the firm.''

Dana felt as if she was hallucinating. ''You do?''

''Didn't I just say that?'' he snapped, growing exhausted.

That was more like it. ''Yes.'' Dana smiled. ''You did.''

He nodded, terminating the meeting. ''All right then, I expect to see you there in the morning. Don't mess up. Being my daughter doesn't entitle you to any privileges.''

She couldn't stop smiling. ''I already know that.''

''Good. Now get out.''

Her smile, bemused and still somewhat confused, didn't fade this time, not even as she left the room.

Chapter 14

The telephone beside her bed was ringing when Dana walked into her room. She picked it up automatically. Only when she'd lifted the receiver from the cradle did it occur to her that the call was most likely for her father.

But it wasn't. The familiar masculine voice on the other end of the line was asking to speak to her.

"Rafe?"

The pleased laugh, unintentionally seductive and sexy, curled through her belly. "I'm flattered that you recognized my voice."

It was so distinctive, there was no way she could mistake his voice for anyone else's. Why was he calling her? "Is something wrong?"

Why would something have to be wrong for him to call her? Couldn't she conceive of him calling just to hear her voice? Or wanting to prolong what had been a very nice evening, dropped in his lap like an unexpected gift?

"No, it's just sometime."

''Sometime?'' she repeated when he didn't say anything further. ''Sometime what?''

She'd forgotten. It wasn't in her to act coy, he thought. ''I asked if I could call you sometime, and you said yes. I decided that this was as good a sometime as any.''

No one could ever have accused her of being the nervous type. Yet with Rafe that was exactly what she became. A woman whose nervousness kept surfacing, full blown, with the thought of each encounter. She felt like someone stuck in a dream, doomed to repeat it until someone woke her up.

''But I just saw you,'' she pointed out.

''Which is what makes this a good time,'' he countered. The soft chuckle made her feel itchy. Itchy in places that couldn't be scratched. ''You know, we never did get to go to La Reina Simpatica.''

''No,'' she agreed slowly, ''we didn't.'' She wrapped both hands around the receiver, waiting. Calling herself an idiot for acting so adolescent. So confused. She was hoping he'd spell it out and ask her for a date. Yet if he did…

She looked at her still-flat belly. If he did, where could this go? Nowhere.

''I'm free Friday night. Would that be all right with you?'' The soft-spoken question seduced her senses and secured the answer before she realized she'd formed it.

''Friday would be fine with me.''

He gave her the particulars. She heard herself murmuring, agreeing. And her fate was sealed.

Dana hung up feeling better than she knew she should. But no self-inflicted lecture to the contrary could wipe the smile from her face.

T.G.I.F.

Dana turned the letters and the phrase they stood for over in her mind as she let herself into the house. Thank God It's Friday. It was a good phrase. She acknowledged it down to the very bottom of her being. She didn't think she could have borne it if it was only Thursday.

On an absolute scale, working for her father was turning out to be far more difficult than rescuing the victims of that car accident had been.

She dropped her purse on the hall table, missed and left it where it fell on the floor, too tired to pick it up. She stepped out of her shoes while rotating her stiff neck. Her mind was on the last encounter she and her father had had. Last battle was more like it. He wanted his answers almost as quickly as he thought of the questions, and he expected her to produce them, not excuses. She was in a position to have to anticipate his tartly worded requests, none of which was ever easy.

Dana dropped onto the sofa, every bone in her body aching. Just the way her head was. Paul S. Morrow was a demanding son of a bitch, she thought with a silent nod. He kept her on her toes constantly, dancing to his tune, in what had all the makings of a never-ending nightmare.

But she had to admit that there was a fair amount of satisfaction in continuing the dance, in—so far—not faltering. In showing him she could survive whatever he dished out. For the first time in her life, she was meeting her father on his home turf. And she was keeping up.

It felt good.

She would have sung if she wasn't too damn exhausted to carry a tune. This past week had seemed endless. She would no sooner drop her head on her pillow at night than it was time to get up again and begin the cycle all over. Work and Mollie, Mollie and work. She felt as if she was juggling, and so far, the balls were staying in the air.

With luck, they would continue that way. With more luck, she would get better at it.

One could only hope.

Hope.

She smiled. She liked the sound of that word. It was nice to feel it was in her life again.

She heard the doorbell ring. Odd. Her father was still at the office. Why would someone be calling for him here? She hoped Esther would get rid of whoever it was. She didn't feel like having to put her shoes on again to greet someone.

Out of the corner of her eye, she saw Mollie come flying into the room. The next second, she was being tackled enthusiastically.

"You're home!" Mollie exclaimed.

"Looks like it, pumpkin. Been a good girl?"

"Uh-huh. Irene invited me for a sleep over tonight. Can I go? Can I? Can I?" The words tumbled out faster than the speed of light.

Irene, Irene. Which one was she again? Oh, yes, the one with the heart-shaped face and straight, jet black hair. "Well, I don't know. Did Irene's mother say it's okay?"

"Yes, and she gave me this." From the pocket of her pink and yellow overalls, Mollie pulled out a crumpled envelope.

Dana scanned the contents quickly. It was an invitation to a birthday party sleep over. "Looks in order. But we're going to have to give Irene something. You can't go to a birthday party without a present." And where was she going to get one on such short notice?

"I've *got* a present for her," Mollie told her importantly. "Esther got it for me."

She might have known. God bless Esther—the woman was a saint.

"Then you can go." Mollie's energy was infectious, but only up to a point. "Give me a minute to catch my breath and I'll take you."

"Have you been running?" Mollie peered at her closely.

"It feels that way, baby. It sure feels that way." As she was mustering her strength to rise to her feet and face the prospect of putting her shoes on, Esther entered.

"There's a Dr. Saldana at the door, Miss Dana," she announced politely. It was the voice she used around company.

Mollie looked pleased enough to burst. "Here?" she squealed.

Dana shut her eyes. "Oh, no, I forgot."

The next moment, Rafe was in the room behind Esther, catching Mollie as she hurled herself at him. ''Forgot what?''

Dana was on her feet instantly, struggling for the balance she almost lost as she shoved her feet into her shoes. At the last minute, she braced herself on the edge of the sofa. How could shoes that fit so perfectly in the morning pinch so damn much now?

Dana swung to face him. ''Our—our bet. I'm not dressed.''

Still holding Mollie, who had wrapped her legs partially around him like an agile little monkey, Rafe scrutinized Dana. She was wearing a teal suit with a pencil-slim skirt and a hot pink blouse. The hot pink reminded him of a strawberry sundae and conjured up the words *good enough to eat* in his mind like a reflex.

''Those look like clothes to me,'' he noted mildly, his tone betraying neither what he was thinking nor what he was fantasizing about.

Dana looked at the single-breasted suit she'd unbuttoned long ago. This wasn't what she would have chosen to wear on a date. Unless it was a date with an accountant. ''Well, yes, but—''

''La Reina doesn't have a dress code, and neither do I. Clothes are clothes.'' He set Mollie down.

''Are you taking Aunt Dana out?'' Mollie wanted to know.

With the crush she had on him, Mollie might feel left out, Dana thought. Why not take her along? There was safety in numbers.

''I'm trying to, Mollie,'' he admitted. ''Give me a hand?''

She gave him two and placed both on Dana's posterior, then shoved as hard as she could. ''Go,'' Mollie ordered.

''You heard her.'' Rafe laughed, hooking his arm through Dana's. ''C'mon, Miss Morrow, you're not talking your way out of this one. I've actually got another doctor covering my calls for the rest of the night. Don't tell me I've done all this juggling for nothing.''

Esther slipped out, then rematerialized, silently holding

Dana's purse aloft. There seemed to be no fighting city hall tonight.

Dana sighed, giving up. "See that Mollie gets to her slumber party," she told Esther as she took the purse from her.

Esther nodded. "Already done, miss."

"No, it's not," Mollie protested. "I'm still here."

"A slumber party, huh?" Rafe asked. "Why don't we drop Mollie off on the way? That way you get to see her off yourself and check things out. You'll feel better."

"Yes," she agreed. "I will."

He was thoughtful without being prodded. That said a lot about a man. There seemed to be no antidote for the warm, pleased feeling tucking itself around her. Nor was she looking for one. For now.

Dana discovered that Mollie was already ready. Her overnight case had been packed within half an hour of her return from preschool. The present, a large picture puzzle, was wrapped in paper decorated with teddy bears leapfrogging over birthday cakes. Rafe carried both to his car while Mollie danced beside him, telling him all about Irene and what they planned to do tonight.

Watching, Dana thought Rafe looked incredibly domesticated. The scene suited him. She wished with all her heart that someone like Rafe had been the father of her child. Then she would have someone to share this with. Someone to love her child along with her.

"Don't get left behind," Esther told her. She waved Dana on her way. "When shall I tell Mr. Morrow you'll be back?"

"Before Christmas," Dana called, then closed the door firmly behind her.

Rafe looked amused when she approached the car. He placed Mollie in the back, then helped her with her seat belt. "I had no idea you took that long to eat a meal."

"Old habit." Dana checked the security of Mollie's seat belt before getting into the front seat. "I don't like being held accountable for my time." The metal tab of the seat belt clicked as it slid into the slot, punctuating her statement. And terminating it.

Rafe turned the key, and the car rumbled to life. "Esther's probably only asking because she knows your father might worry if he doesn't know when to expect you."

When had he gotten Esther's name? She didn't remember introducing them or mentioning it. He must have asked her, she surmised. As for why Esther had asked, she knew the answer to that. And she also knew why her father would want to be informed. Because knowing her whereabouts, her timetable, kept him in control, and he always had to be in control. Obsessively so. Now more than ever, to prove that he was still the man he once was.

"My father doesn't worry," she told Rafe simply. "He just likes being in charge."

"I take it working for your father isn't turning out."

"Oh, it's turning out," she informed him. "But it doesn't put blinders on me, either."

He sincerely doubted, as he glanced at the address on the invitation Dana handed him, that anything could blind Dana to what she perceived as the truth.

"So?"

His gaze, penetrating, unwavering and amused, made her want to wiggle her toes. And, just maybe, other parts of her body, as well.

"So?" she repeated innocently. She hid the smile she felt forming behind her glass of cider. The soft murmur of voices in the restaurant faded into soothing background noise as she looked into his eyes. For a nonalcoholic drink, the cider certainly packed a punch. Or was it his eyes that did that?

"What's the verdict, Counselor?" Rafe prodded. "About the food?"

The term, the one she used with her father, caught her by surprise. It took her a moment to collect herself.

"All things considered..." Dana paused long enough to keep him dangling, then smiled. "I guess I'll be picking up the tab for dinner. You win. This is better—although it is pretty close.'' She looked at her empty plate. It had been so good that even when she was full, she had continued eating.

The waitress arrived with the check. When she placed it on the table, Dana reached for it, but Rafe covered the small tray with his hand. She looked at him in surprise. ''What are you doing?''

He raised a brow. ''Taking the check.''

That wasn't their agreement. ''I thought I was supposed to pay.''

He'd never meant to collect. That wasn't the way he'd been raised, current mores notwithstanding. ''I only said that to appeal to your sense of competition.'' He glanced at the total to calculate the tip. ''I thought it was the best way to get you to come.''

She didn't know whether to be flattered or uneasy that he seemed to have her number. ''How would you know if I had a sense of competition?''

Rafe rolled his eyes. ''Oh, please. I've never met a more competitive woman in my life.'' He took out his wallet. ''You live for it. It's in your body language.''

She stiffened. ''I wasn't aware that my body had a language.''

His smile unfurled slowly as his eyes slid over her. Dana felt as if her suit just vanished, leaving her in a teddy that would all too soon be snug.

''Trust me, it does.'' Instead of his charge card, Rafe took out several bills and placed them on the tray to cover the bill, along with a healthy tip.

Dana looked at the tray. ''Money. How quaint. I didn't think people used money anymore.'' Good with numbers, Dana knew exactly what their dinner had cost. The size of the tip wasn't lost on her. Thoughtful *and* generous. The man was almost too good to be true. Where was the flaw? There was always a flaw.

''Old-fashioned, I guess. I only keep plastic for emergencies.'' He pocketed his wallet as the waitress came to claim the tray. He smiled his thanks at her, then turned toward Dana. "So, what would you like to do next? Go dancing?"

Her feet miraculously no longer hurt, but she didn't think that being in his arms, even in a crowd, would be the wisest move for her to make at the moment. She was seeing too much in his favor to remain on the safe side of her feelings right now.

"Truthfully?"

"Always."

She almost believed he meant that. But in her experience, people didn't always want the truth. Not when a lie could do better.

Dana sighed. "I'd like to walk off this meal. I feel like I've gained a ton. I think seeing you is definitely bad for my waistline." It was intended as a joke, but the words stuck in her throat. It wasn't seeing Rafe that was going to erase her waist.

Rafe leaned back as if studying her. He didn't need to. Her trim figure had become etched in his mind, though it had happened unintentionally. "Your waistline looks fine from where I'm sitting."

She laughed, dismissing the compliment. Right now, she wanted him to be nasty, to say one wrong thing, even half wrong, so she could pick a fight and go home. So she could squelch this desire to linger with him. "That's because from where you're sitting, you can't see it."

He laid his napkin on the table. "Then by all means, let's go for a walk, so I can make a better assessment of the subject under discussion."

Rafe rose and managed to pull back her chair for her before she could do it herself. Once again she thought he moved fast for a man his size. Almost too fast to suit her.

When Dana got to her feet, he slipped his hand around her waist to guide her out.

"Feels fine to me," he commented, as if he was taking her measure. "Maybe even on the thin side."

Color flooded her cheeks. That would change, she thought.

And soon. But as quickly as the thought surfaced, she banked it down. It had no place here, tonight, with him.

She had no place here tonight with him, she insisted silently. What had she been thinking, accepting his invitation?

She'd been thinking it would be nice, just for the space of an evening, to enjoy the company of a man she was beginning to think a great deal of—just as a friend, she insisted to herself.

"Are you warm?" he asked inside the entrance.

"What?"

"Your facc, it's flushcd." He pushed open the door, and a rush of night air swirled in.

"Yes, it's warm in here," she agreed, taking the handy excuse he'd unwittingly tendered. Standing outside, she took a deep breath, hoping that the color and the warmth that had generated it would leave her.

It was a beautiful night. Soft, serene, with the sky above them like freshly spun velvet. "Would you care to go for a walk on the boardwalk?"

Dana didn't answer. Not out loud. Instead, she laced her fingers through his, unwilling to let words spoil the mood.

There was something almost magical about the boardwalk in Laguna Beach in the early evening. She'd always believed that. During her teens, she'd come here a lot. Sometimes with friends, sometimes hitching a ride, knowing the act was stupid but taking comfort in the fact that it would have turned her father's hair gray if he'd known.

She'd done a lot of stupid things in her time. Maybe this was stupid, too, but she couldn't help herself. Didn't want to. She needed the paradoxically exciting serenity she felt being here with Rafe.

Dana smiled. She felt very close to being at peace for one of the few times in her life. The ocean softly sighed on her right, while on the left small arts-and-crafts shops and homes were interspersed with trees as old as the California coastline. The soft late spring breeze that accompanied them on their stroll completed the scene, making it almost too perfect.

Could something be too perfect?

Yes, she thought, when it wasn't real. Perfect was never real.

"So, you didn't tell me. How does it feel, working for your father?" Rafe asked.

The question, following on the heels of a comfortable, mutual silence, roused her. But she didn't have to think to answer.

"Scary. Exhilarating. One minute I think he's waiting for me to fall flat on my face, the next I almost feel he's hoping to see me succeed." Even as she said it, it seemed hard to believe. "I think being sick has mellowed him. I never thought anything would."

He knew better than she did about that. "Mortality has a way of kicking you right in the gut, making you see what a fool you've been about taking things for granted."

There was something in his voice that caught her attention. When she looked at him, his face was turned from hers. He was looking up. At someone he saw in his mind's eye?

"You sound as if you have firsthand experience."

He looked at her, a little embarrassed at drifting away. "I do. My wife died a few years ago."

"Your wife? I didn't know you were married." Somehow, she'd assumed he hadn't been. The information created a crack in the intimacy that had been building. And maybe that was for the best, she thought. If there were things in the way, obstacles, she couldn't, wouldn't be drawn to him.

He nodded, concentrating on fighting back the pain. Like an adversary relentlessly searching for a weak spot, it always found him if he let his guard down.

"Two years. It should have been longer. But Debra wanted to wait until I was through with medical school." His smile was distant, wistful, shrouded with memories. And suddenly Dana ached to have someone feel that way about her. "Thought she'd distract me otherwise."

Her response was automatic. She squeezed his hand, wanting to hug him, to tell him that, in a way, she understood.

That though their paths were different, that the events they'd gone through were different, she'd lost love, too, at the hand of someone she'd mistakenly loved.

"I'm very sorry, Rafe."

He heard the feeling in her voice, and it warmed him. "Yeah, me, too. She was a wonderful person. Supportive, always thinking of others, always willing to put other people ahead of herself." He glanced at Dana. "You know, she wasn't a thing like you."

He was smiling, and his eyes were kind, but his words… His words weren't. Dana stopped walking. "Excuse me? I'm a little confused here. Was that just an insult?"

It had come out wrong. "No, I didn't mean it that way. You're independent, Debra wasn't—" He tried again. "What I'm trying to say is that the two of you are very different from one another. Your personalities are like night and day. And yet…and yet I find myself very attracted to you."

"Attracted?" she whispered.

There was a noise in her ears, a thumping sound. Her heart? The air going in and out of her lungs? Or her pulse, which was suddenly competing in the hundred-meter dash?

"Completely." Unable to hold himself in check any longer, Rafe wove his fingers into her hair, tilting her head slightly as he brought his mouth close to hers. "I haven't felt anything for another woman since Debra died. But I feel something for you. I think I did the first moment I noticed you."

The noise stopped only long enough for her to hear him, then started again. Louder. Oh, God, was he going to kiss her?

Oh, please, let him kiss her.

"I guess I made it difficult not to notice me."

"Very."

He brought his mouth to hers. This time there was no hesitancy on her part. No list of reasons she shouldn't. Only one reason she should.

Because she desperately wanted to.

Her mouth met his with the urgency of a woman who needed to feel like one. With contact, with just the promise of contact, her blood heated instantly.

Stretching to the maximum, Dana wound her arms around his neck, letting herself go. Free-falling into the kiss, into the haven he had to offer, her body pressed close against his.

Rafe felt around the wall until his fingers came in contact with the light switch. He flipped it into the up position, and his apartment became instantly visible.

He couldn't help wondering if she was comparing it to what she was accustomed to. It probably didn't hold a candle to anything she'd ever seen. Still, he couldn't bring himself to feel embarrassed by it. This was home, such as it was, and it suited his purposes.

But none of those purposes had ever included bringing a woman like her here.

She liked it, Dana thought. There was the feel of home to it. Oh, not like hers, but then, hers had never felt like home, only a neatly cleaned display case.

Dana surveyed the room. There was just enough clutter to make it look pleasantly lived in. Her father couldn't abide clutter. As a child, she was never allowed to spread her things on the floor even for a little while. Everything always had to be put neatly away. After a while, she ceased bothering to take anything out. It was easier that way.

His apartment made her feel safe. Which was absurd, because she wasn't. Not here, alone with him, the one person she realized she could so easily let herself make a mistake with.

Dana glanced toward the door he closed behind him. "Rafe, maybe I should go."

Her bravery was gone. She was someone else now. Someone who attracted him even more. "Are you afraid of me?"

"No, of course not." She shot the words back too quickly. It was herself she was afraid of. Her weakness. Her needs. "It's just that—"

He didn't wait for her to finish. His mouth skimmed over

her lower lip, barely tasting it. Barely branding her. "Just that…what?"

Her head was spinning. "I forget," she breathed as his lips slowly worked their way down her throat. Her eyes began to flutter shut even as her body tingled with razor-edged anticipation.

With the feel of his hands along her skin.

From out of nowhere, a frenzy took hold of her. A frenzy, powerful and overwhelming, that urged her to take what he offered, to lose herself in the solace of his mouth, his touch, his body, before her mind gained control.

Before she could stop herself.

Because she didn't want to. More than anything, she wanted this, wanted to feel again, to glory in a man's desire again. *This* man's desire. She began to tug urgently at his shirt, pulling it from his waistband, fumbling at his buttons, even as he responded in kind. They undressed each other in a flurry of garments, questing hands and warm, promising kisses that raced faster than their fingers did.

Rafe wasn't sure how it happened or who took the first step. All he knew was that suddenly he was playing with fire.

And if he got singed, if he got burned to a crisp, it was one hell of a way to go.

He'd had that feeling, even if he hadn't acknowledged it, the first time she'd walked into his life, breathing fire, demanding the best for Mollie.

He'd brought her here to be alone with her. In his heart, he hadn't really known he was going to make love with her until it began happening. And then there was no question but that, somehow, it was meant to happen.

The time-honored tradition of lovemaking became something new to him that night. New because, even at the height of what he'd had with Debra, he'd never encountered such passion, such need, before. Debra had been pliable in his arms, loving and giving, but she'd never been quicksilver, first one thing and then another. Never fire and passion. Never raw need and sex.

As soon as it began, Rafe felt his desire ignited and brought to new highs, new levels. It took all he could do to harness it, to keep from taking her then and there. Somehow he maintained a shred of control. Control so he could show her what he felt before it consumed him.

He was putting her needs above his own. The thought startled her. Dana could feel him holding himself back while his hands evoked symphonies from her body. Finding secret places to make her vibrate with feeling, with sensations that rocked her and left her exhausted, yet wanting more, he stroked, caressed and conquered.

He took her breath away, not with his technique, not with his magnificent body, hard, primed, but with the gentleness that was at the heart of him. He seemed determined to bring her to the heights ahead of him, to keep her on that edge, drawing her back and taking her there again, until he was finally ready to meet her there himself.

This was something new, something entirely different. Entirely wondrous. She didn't want it to end, didn't want the coldness of thought and logic to find her here, hiding in the shelter of his arms, of his body as it cleaved to hers.

But more than that, she wanted him. Wanted him to feel this echoing crescendo of climaxes he'd created within her. With her last ounce of strength, she arched against him, tempting him. Opening for him.

There was nothing left in him with which to resist. Holding back was no longer possible. Murmuring her name like a prayer, he entered her. And burned all the bridges that ever existed behind him.

Chapter 15

Horror and guilt, sharpened, hurtful, pushed through the layers of euphoria, peeling them apart from within like so much ugliness, swelling, emerging and destroying a thing of beauty.

And then there was only a glaring awareness of what had happened. What she had allowed to happen.

How could she have done such a thing?

It was bad enough making love with one man while carrying another man's child, but how could she have put herself at risk like this again, baring her emotions, her soul, to a man? All but handing herself over to him, to do with what he would, after she had sworn never again to give any man that kind of power over her.

Dana didn't know what had come over her. Never, even in her so-called wild period, had she gone to bed with a man after knowing him such a short time. No matter what her father thought, she had values.

That was just the trouble. Somehow Rafe seemed to fit in with her values.

And that scared her most of all. Because it felt right,

seemed right. But it couldn't *be* right. Dana knew all about being lulled into a false sense of security. Believing herself to be at a wonderful place in her life, only to have it blow apart on her. Just like her mother before her.

Just like her relationship with Steven.

Wow.

All Rafe could think of was *Wow,* with a capital *W.* Whatever had just happened here, sex, lovemaking, passion, whatever name it chose to go under, he'd never experienced anything like it before. He felt as if every fiber of his being was carrying on its own celebration of the Fourth of July.

Rafe wasn't sure he could even move. But when he felt Dana stirring beside him, he knew he had to. Wanted to. Turning, he moved to put his arm around her, to hold her close and soak in this feeling that was blanketing him.

But Dana was already sitting up.

The sheets were too tangled to be of any use, and her clothes were out of reach, so Dana gathered Rafe's jacket around her to cover herself as best she could. Shame, embarrassment and anger all tugged relentlessly at her, fighting for the larger share.

How could she have let this happen?

Dana felt tears gathering in her eyes, and she cursed herself for this inopportune overflow of emotions. It had to be the pregnancy playing havoc with her hormones. She never cried, yet right now, she felt like she was comprised completely of tears.

He saw them immediately, the tears shimmering in her eyes. Bewildered, confused, Rafe sat up beside her.

''What's the matter? Did I hurt you?'' He brushed one tear away as it emerged on her cheek. It felt as if it burned his fingertip. He felt instantly guilty. ''Oh, God, Dana, I'm sorry. I meant to be gentle, to go slower, but you were so incredible, so passionate, all I could do was just hold on.'' Talking about it gave him a rush, the depth of which still rocked him. ''Anyone ever tell you how extraordinary you are?''

She struggled hard not to shake, not to let any more tears free.

"All the time," she retorted hoarsely. "Men take out full-page ads in the *Times* telling the world how extraordinary I am in bed."

He heard pain beneath the words and didn't understand why, even though he was trying. "I'm sorry, that was insensitive. You're going to have to wait until my brain catches up to my body."

She was on her feet instantly, agilely executing a maneuver that kept her modesty intact. A little late for that, don't you think? a small voice asked inside her brain.

"I can't wait." Quickly, she swept her clothes into her arms and propelled herself toward his bathroom. "I've got to go."

"Go?" He jumped off the bed, naked and unembarrassed by it. "Dana, don't go. Not yet. Dana, what's wrong?"

He found himself talking to his bathroom door as she closed it in his face. He heard the lock click. Stunned, stumped, he hurried into his pants, wanting to be ready for anything.

"Dana, if it's something I did, something I said, I'm sorry. Dana, please, don't run off this way. Talk to me." He was at the door, talking through it. Trying to reach her. "Just tell me what I did and give me a chance to apologize."

Dana pushed her hands through the sleeves of her blouse. With shaking fingers she did up the buttons and managed to mismatch them by one. She didn't have time to redo them. She had to get away from here. Away before she made even more of a fool of herself.

"You made love with me," she accused.

He waited and heard nothing more. "Yes, and...?"

She looked in the mirror. Tears made her look like someone suffering through a bad bout of the flu. Hurriedly, she threw water on her face, trying to make herself presentable. "That's it."

"That's it?" He stared at the door as if, somehow, his

expression, his thoughts, could penetrate the wood. ''Dana, I can't apologize for that, for being made to feel for the first time in so long.'' Frustration, needing an ally, roused anger. ''Besides, you weren't just a passive recipient here. You made love back.'' He thought of the way she'd thrown herself into their lovemaking. ''Hell, you started it.''

The door swung open. She glared at him, breathing fire.

''*I* started it? I'm not the one who nibbled on your lower lip. I'm not the one who kissed your throat, making it impossible for you to breathe.''

A sense of satisfaction rose, ready to quell the argument before it went any further. It felt good, hearing that she'd reacted to him the way he had to her.

''You did later,'' he reminded her.

''Later doesn't count.'' Pushing past him, she located her shoes and scooped them up.

He was right on her heels, growing more confused.

''What the hell is that supposed to mean?'' He passed his hand over his head, a tension headache sprouting just above his eyes. ''And what are we fighting about? I lost the thread.''

She spun on her heel, furious with him, but even more furious with herself. ''We're fighting about lovemaking, we're fighting about trust, we're fighting about—oh, damn it all to hell, you're just confusing me.'' With a strangled cry, she grabbed her purse and ran for the door.

''Dana, at least let me drive you home,'' he called after her.

''No!''

She was gone before he had a chance to put on his shoes. Cursing, he went after her barefoot. The magnitude of the curses grew as he hurried after her. The entrance to his garden apartment was paved with rough stones that bruised the soles of his feet as he ran. The pain made him angrier.

He caught up to her quickly enough. ''Damn it, woman, you are not going out at this time of night to try to hail a cab.''

''I can do whatever I want!'' she retorted, moving away

from him. He was already trying to control her. She'd been right to run when she did.

"The hell you can." He grabbed her arm and pulled her roughly toward the carport and his car.

Angry, afraid, she tried to pull away from him. She might as well have been playing tug-of-war with a grizzly. Her chances of winning were about the same.

Desperate, not sure what he was capable of, Dana tried to brazen him out. "Let go of me or I'll scream."

Working hard at controlling what was going on inside him, Rafe unlocked the car. He yanked open the door on her side.

"I wouldn't advise that." With his hand on her head, Rafe pushed Dana into her seat, policeman-style.

His temper was begging for release, but he knew he would say something that he wouldn't be able to take back, and there was just the slimmest chance that, someday, he might want to. Although right now, he figured they would be ice-skating in hell before that happened.

He kept his silence, knowing he wasn't ready to trust himself yet. Dana stared straight ahead, not uttering a word, cocooning herself in silence.

Though she hated herself for it, for the weakness it symbolized, one rebellious tear overflowed and slid down her left cheek.

Rafe saw it as he turned toward her at the intersection.

Instantly, guilt ate a hole through him.

"Oh, damn it, Dana. I can't stand to see a woman cry." His mother had cried once in helpless frustration because of the way he and Gabe were behaving. It had almost broken his heart. Seeing her that way had generated a turnaround in him. From that day forward, he'd made sure he and Gabe never gave her any more trouble.

It hurt almost as much, seeing Dana cry.

Unable to stop, unwilling to talk, Dana turned her head away.

"I didn't mean that you had to—oh, hell, have it your

way.'' For a second, he swore roundly, then shut his mouth. He left the rest unsaid. But he thought it.

They arrived at her house in what seemed like record time. Still, Rafe had managed to calm down enough to attempt to reason with her again, to find out what it was that had caused her to do such an about-face.

He never had the chance. Dana bolted from the car the instant it came to a stop.

Frustrated all over again, Rafe thought of running after her, of demanding to know what the hell was going on. He decided against it. Her old man would probably have him up on some kind of trespassing charges before he got within two feet of her.

And besides, they could both stand a little time apart to cool off.

It sounded reasonable. Only trouble was, he wasn't feeling very reasonable. He was feeling cheated and abandoned and a great many other things he didn't even know how to begin to describe.

Resigned, Rafe drove away.

Dana let herself into the house as quietly as she could, praying her father was asleep. Or at least out of the way.

For once, her luck held.

She raced up the stairs as silently as she could, her heart pounding with each step she took. She thought her throat was going to burst before she reached her room. Once she did, she threw herself facedown on her bed.

The comforter muffled her sobs.

Like red dye that can never be completely eradicated once it has come in contact with something, Dana remained on Rafe's mind all his waking hours. Sleeping, it was even worse. She slipped into his dreams, and suddenly he was making love with her all over again, experiencing an entire kaleidoscope of feelings, just as he had the first time.

Then he would wake up, more exhausted than when he'd first lain down. And still wanting her.

Angry and confused by the way she'd invaded his mind, he thought of calling her, but to say what? He'd tried to apologize, and that had led to nothing.

And nothing was what he had.

This was absurd, to let a woman, a woman he hardly knew, get to him this way. Especially when there was a good woman waiting for him.

As if to talk himself out of the madness buzzing in his brain, Rafe sought out the one person he thought could neutralize what he was going through. The woman he *should* be having these feelings about.

It was late, and Kate was about to go to bed when she heard the doorbell. Wondering who could be calling at this hour, she made her way to the door and cautiously looked through the peephole.

She had to be wrong.

Kate opened the door and looked at Rafe in stunned but immensely pleased surprise. "Rafe, what are you doing here?"

"Looking for my sanity. Can I come in?"

She realized she was blocking the way. "Of course." She stepped back, letting him enter. "I don't think I understand. What do you mean, you're here looking for your sanity?"

Rafe shook his head. "Never mind, poor joke."

He looked beleaguered, but he was here, and that was all that mattered. Kate thought of quickly changing into her clothes, then decided not to. Maybe he wanted to find her like this, ready for bed. Maybe bed was where he needed her.

She laced her fingers through his and drew him to the bedroom. "You look tense, Rafe. I told you that your hours were too long. Looks like they finally caught up to you."

It wasn't his hours that had caught up to him, Rafe thought. It felt more like his heart had finally found him in.

But he wasn't here to think of Dana. He'd come here looking for Kate, for what he could have with Kate if he only let himself.

"Here, let me help you work out the knots." Kate made him sit on the edge of the bed. She knelt behind him and began kneading his shoulders. "I used to do this for my father at the end of the day. He'd come home tense, frustrated. I'd start kneading his shoulders, and pretty soon he was himself again." As she worked, Kate leaned forward and pressed a kiss to Rafe's neck.

He closed his eyes, wishing he could feel something. Knowing that he was capable of feeling, really feeling, not just reacting like a normal male. But there was nothing, nothing like what he'd experienced with Dana.

Damn Dana, anyway.

He felt sorry for Kate and wished with all his heart that it was different between them. That it was her scent that lingered in his head, instead of Dana's. That it was her voice he heard echoing in his brain, instead of Dana's. "Did you do that for your father, too?"

"No, that's special," she whispered, her voice husky. "Just for you."

Dropping her hands and all pretense of massaging the tension away, Kate moved in front of him. She slipped her robe from her shoulders. Wearing only a thin cotton nightgown, she slid onto his lap, linking her hands around his neck.

The kiss was deep, ardent and soulful. She moaned, pressing herself closer to him, wanting him. Trying her best to make him want her. His heart didn't have to be in it. She could wait for that. As long as she had a part of him, it would be enough for now.

Rafe tried, really tried, to feel something, to let Kate's kiss captivate him the way Dana's had. It would be so simple with Kate. He knew where he stood with her, knew what she wanted of him. He didn't have a clue when it came to Dana. In all honesty, he didn't even know what it was he felt for Dana, only that with her, he *was* capable of feeling.

Unlike with Kate.

Very slowly, he took her hands from his neck. When she

looked at him, dazed, bewildered, he felt like the cruelest man alive. "Kate, I just can't do this. It's wrong. I'm sorry."

Kate sighed, dragging her hand through her hair. The air seemed to shudder from her. Embarrassed, she rose and picked up her robe, then slipped it on. She knew in her heart what he was saying to her, even if she didn't want to hear it.

"So am I, Rafe. So am I." She tied the sash tight, as if that could somehow protect her. "Why did you come here tonight?"

He wouldn't insult her by lying. "I was hoping that I could feel something."

For a moment, temper rose in her eyes. "The way you can with her? The woman who came into the ER with you? You're running some kind of comparison test? What am I, the control case?" she guessed. "Litmus paper?"

"No, you're a wonderful woman, with wonderful qualities." He wanted to hold her, to make her feel better, but he knew it would only accomplish the opposite if he did. "A man would have to be crazy not to want you."

She tried to muster a smile and almost succeeded. "So why don't you?"

He released her hands and rubbed the back of his neck. "Maybe I am crazy. I honestly thought everything that could feel that way about a woman was dead inside me." Gone, along with Debra.

Rafe looked at Kate, trying to make her understand. He hadn't come with the intention of using her, only of seeking her aid. "I thought that if anyone could bring those feelings to life, you could."

Bitterness twisted her lips even as she accepted the inevitable. "But I can't, and she did. To the victor, the spoils." Her expression softened a little as she looked at him. It would be so much easier if she could be angry at him, but she couldn't. It wasn't his fault. It just wasn't meant to be. "So what's her name, this victor?"

They were still friends. There was solace in that. "Dana

Morrow." His expression was rueful. "And I don't know about the victor, Kate. She's a hell of a complicated woman."

Kate took in the information philosophically. "Maybe that was my problem right from the start. I was too damn simple." She looked into his eyes, hoping, she supposed, for a spark of something to work with. She knew before she looked that it wouldn't be there. "My message was there in big block letters." Kate sighed and sat beside him on the bed, a bed she knew they would never share again. "So now what?"

He shrugged, at a loss. "I wish I knew."

"I have a suggestion." When he looked at her, waiting, she told him pleasantly, "Get out of my house." Then she smiled. "And thanks."

He rose to his feet when she did. "I don't understand."

Kate led the way to her front door. "It's very simple. Another man would have tried to use me, to use the situation, before he went on his way. Gotten what he could. But you didn't. It's pretty obvious the way I feel about you." Fondness entered her eyes as she lightly touched his cheek. "Even you couldn't miss it."

He took her hand and lightly pressed his lips to her knuckles, sincerely thankful for her understanding. "I care too much about you to do that to you."

He still didn't see it, did he? Still didn't see what attracted her to him. It wasn't his killer looks, it was his soul.

"It's not me, it's you, Rafe. You're too damn decent." She could have been good for him, Kate thought. Really good. Someone else might not be. "It's going to get you stomped on."

Kate had the wrong idea about Dana. "No, it's not like that. Dana's not interested in stomping. Or even in having a fling."

Opening the door, she could only shake her head. What a waste. "If she's passing up a fling with you, she's an idiot. Sure you want an idiot?"

He wasn't sure what he wanted, only that he wasn't going to string Kate along when there was no hope. There might have been. If Dana hadn't entered his life, he wouldn't have known he was capable of feeling. He would have thought that what he had with Kate was as good as it could be for him. Affection based on mutual respect. But now he knew differently, and it wasn't fair to Kate to give her only half of what she deserved.

"Goodbye, Kate." Lightly, he kissed her lips.

Kate bit back her tears. "Goodbye."

When she closed the door on Rafe, she knew it was for the last time.

The others around her rose, clearing out of the conference room as quickly as possible. They gave the impression of being well-trained rats off to do the piper's bidding. She supposed it was a pretty accurate description.

Dana took her time gathering her files. Friday morning meetings were always long and grueling, and she wasn't feeling that well.

She hadn't felt well since she'd left Rafe's apartment.

"You seem preoccupied these last few days."

She hadn't realized her father had drawn closer to her. Showed how bad off she was, she thought. "Just trying to do a good job, Father." It took an effort to sound aloof, professional, when she felt as if she was falling apart at the seams.

He placed a skeletal hand over the wine-colored leather-bound pad. Looking at it jarred her back into her surroundings and completely out of her mental wanderings.

Having caught her attention, he withdrew his hand. "I know when one of my people is thinking about work. And when they're lying to me."

Dana tried to bluff her way through. "You missed your calling, Father. There's a great deal of money to be made in clairvoyance if you have the right manager." She picked up the pad and began to leave the room.

Things were better between them than they had ever been, but that was a long way from perfect.

He was right behind her. "Don't let this, whatever this is,

get in the way of your performance here.'' He brought the chair around so he blocked her way. ''I won't think twice about firing you.''

Her office, little more than a glorified cubicle though that made no difference to her, was next to the entrance of the conference room. All she wanted was to reach it.

''I never doubted it for a moment.'' Taking a chance, she circumvented his chair. ''If you'll excuse me, I have some work to do on the Johnson case, as you might recall.''

She slipped into her office and sank into her chair. What was the matter with her? Why was she allowing what had happened between her and Rafe to color everything? It had been a week, a whole week since she had run from him, from the trap she'd very nearly walked into. Wasn't that enough time for everything inside her to have settled down?

Apparently not.

She opened a drawer and slipped her pad into it. Contrary to settling down and obligingly shrinking away, her feelings had grown, threatening to become almost unmanageable.

Nothing was unmanageable, she thought, slamming the drawer shut.

Except maybe her waistline.

Today she'd had to struggle with the button on her skirt. Maybe it was her imagination or simple water retention, but it had brought everything home to her that much more vividly.

Hadn't she learned her lesson? Didn't she know that there was no such thing as everlasting love, not for her? Rafe was wonderful now, but Steven had been wonderful once, too. And now look.

Steven.

Dana blew out an impatient breath. She knew what she had to do. She had tried to get in contact with Steven six times. Five more times than she'd thought she would have. Each time she'd gotten his machine. This time—the last time—she was going to leave a message. And if it got erased or was never heard, well, that wasn't her fault. She'd done everything humanly possible to let Steven know he was going to become a father.

As if he wanted to know that.

No one would want to know that, she thought. Not Steven and certainly not her father. Now there was a fun hurdle waiting for her. She didn't look forward to telling her father she was pregnant.

Dana decided to put that off as long as she could, because there was no doubt in her mind as to the outcome. Her father would throw her out, along with Mollie. She wanted to earn a little more money before that happened. She needed to be able to afford a decent apartment when the time came.

She'd originally thought she would eventually have to tell Rafe, as well. But now that wouldn't be necessary. She didn't need the baby to force them apart. They were apart already.

So why the hell couldn't she stop thinking about him? About the way he'd looked when passion had claimed her and they'd made love with such abandon? Every image felt as if it was burned into her brain.

And she didn't like it.

She also didn't like what she had to do now. Dana pulled the telephone over, then tapped out the familiar number on the keyboard.

The phone on the other end rang three times. She braced herself for the message she was about to leave after his recording ended, but instead of a recording, she heard his voice—his nonrecorded voice.

Dana swung her chair around to the window, closed her eyes and tried to pull her thoughts together. *You can get through this.* She took a deep breath and plunged in. ''Steven, this is Dana.''

There was silence, then the voice on the other end mocked her. ''Well, Dana, I wondered when you'd come to your senses and call.''

He rankled her right from the start. ''I came to my senses the day I walked out on you.'' The hell with preambles and niceties. Steven didn't deserve them. "I'm calling to tell you I'm pregnant."

She found the curse he uttered offensive, but she said nothing. The sooner she got off the phone, the better.

"Oh, no, you're not pinning that on me. No way are you suckering me into taking this fall."

A part of her had expected him to deny responsibility, but hearing the words uttered with such rancor hurt more than she'd thought it would. "I'm not trying to pin anything on you, but this baby *is* yours. I was faithful to you."

"I can get three guys to swear you hopped into bed with them." A sliver of panic made his voice gain momentum. "More, if I have to. All of them will testify that you slept around. Are you prepared for that?"

How could she ever have been stupid enough to think she loved him? "I'm not even prepared for *this,* though I thought I was." Anger came to her rescue. The slime ball. The pathetic slime ball! "Listen to me, you poor excuse for a human being. I don't want anything from you. I just thought you'd want to know that you were going to be a father."

"Well, I don't. And I'm not. That bastard you're carrying isn't mine, do you hear me?" He was shouting. "It's not mine!"

Her voice was calm, as steely as his was loud. "I hear you, Steven. Loud and clear."

"Good, and don't bother coming back for anything. I threw all your things out, and the brat's, too."

She'd taken most of Mollie's things with her. As for hers, those things belonged to a person she no longer was. She wouldn't have wanted them even if they were still available, but he'd had no right to throw them out.

Without saying a word, Dana let the receiver drop in the cradle. She would have thrown it and the telephone across the room if it wouldn't have gotten her attention she didn't want.

Boy, could she ever pick them.

Trying to tell herself it didn't hurt, that it certainly didn't matter, Dana turned her chair to face her desk. It was then she realized her door was ajar.

And that her father was sitting in the hall.

Dana swallowed a groan. Things were just getting better and better, weren't they?

Chapter 16

Their eyes locked.

There was no way for Dana to pretend her father wasn't there. That he hadn't heard. Unable to dodge the situation, she plowed straight into the heart of it.

Striding over to the door, Dana pushed it open all the way. Her voice was even, deceptively calm, as she asked, "Is this how you operate, Father? Eavesdropping on your employees?"

He directed his chair into her room and turned to face her before answering. His eyes were steely and unfathomable. "Sometimes that's the only way I get to learn things."

Dana closed the door, wishing she'd been this careful to begin with. She crossed her arms and leaned one hip against her desk, bracing herself for the explosion to come. "Conversation would be another."

Dana knew that expression. He was studying her, and she hadn't a clue what he was thinking.

"Up until very recently," he pointed out, "we haven't had

conversations. What we've had were encounters where you would do as much damage as you could, then flee the scene."

Oh, no, she wasn't about to shoulder the burden of the missteps their relationship had taken. "I wasn't the only one."

"No," he admitted, "you weren't."

The admission stunned her. Her father had always portrayed himself as above reproach. Normally he would have lashed out at her, cutting her to ribbons with his tongue. Or trying to. What was going on? And why was he continuing to look at her like that? As if he was sorting things out in his mind, weighing them. Why didn't he say what he had to say and get it over with? Was it that he'd perfected his game since she'd been away, toying with offenders before summarily drawing and quartering them?

When he finally spoke, it was almost a relief. "So, you're pregnant." There wasn't a trace of emotion in his voice.

The calm before the storm.

Dana raised her chin. "Yes, I am." He continued to look at her. Was he waiting for her to apologize? "I suppose you're going to fire me now."

"Why?" The question was so mildly put that, for a moment, she thought she'd imagined it. "There's nothing in your contract with the firm that forbids you to be pregnant."

When she'd returned, he'd raked her over the coals for coming in late. Now he was shrugging off her pregnancy. What the hell was he up to? Dana pinned him with a look, wishing she could see past his facade. "I don't understand."

"How much more simply do you want me to put it?"

Was she hallucinating?

No, this was real, all right, but it was hardly her father's usual m.o. Dana met his eyes, still waiting for the torrent of vilifying words, the anger, the name calling. None of it was happening.

"What I don't understand, Father, is this display of kindness, this show of—for lack of a better word—support on your part."

Was that a shadow of a smile on his face?

Her father turned his chair and looked out the window. The offices of Paul S. Morrow and Associates occupied the entire top floor of the twelve-story building. From here, when it was clear, like today, he felt he could almost look into the heart of the ocean. The wide, bottomless, endless ocean.

That was the way he'd pictured life once, when he'd begun to make a name for himself. He'd felt there was nothing he couldn't accomplish, nothing he couldn't conquer, if he tried hard enough. But he'd been wrong. He couldn't conquer this. Couldn't conquer what was ahead of him. He could only come to terms with it. And it wasn't easy.

''Perhaps,'' he said slowly, ''when a man comes face to face with his own mortality, it has an effect on everything around him, making it appear different than it once did.''

Dana moved so she was directly in front of him. Maybe she was crazy, flying in the face of this reprieve, but the memory of her mother wouldn't allow her to let the comment slip quietly by.

''And what kind of effect did Mother's mortality have on you?'' There had been no remorse, no hint of acknowledgment of the guilt he bore for that wasted life. If it hadn't been for the showy funeral, Dana would have said he hadn't even noticed her mother had died. Not his wife, but her mother. Jane Morrow had long since stopped being his wife except in name.

Morrow squared shoulders that appeared to be growing ever thinner. ''It made me live faster, play harder, expect even more from you and your sister than I already did.'' His eyes grew distant. Memories intruded on his thoughts, clouding them. ''It made me expect more of myself than I already did. I took higher-risk cases, hell-bent on winning at all costs.'' His mouth curved as his eyes shifted to his daughter. ''Justice be hanged, it's the winning that counts, Dana. The thrill of besting the other side. Your mother's death intensified my need to hold on to life.'' He saw the look entering her eyes and anticipated her. "But your sister's death showed me that no matter what, I couldn't hang on to what was mine."

"If you felt that way, why didn't you come to Megan's funeral?"

"I couldn't. I couldn't face her death. The wounds hadn't healed after your mother's death."

Wounds. Then he *had* felt something, *had* loved them.

"You could have talked to me. We could have been there for each other."

"I didn't know that. I thought you'd only be too pleased to see I had a vulnerable side. Besides, I'd spent all those years building up walls where no one could touch me, hurt me. I didn't know how to dismantle that." He shrugged, helpless to follow any other path than the one he was on. "I'm an old dog, and I don't know any new tricks, so I'll keep doing this one until the circus is finally over for me."

Circus. That was what she'd called their life, *his* life, once. And in truth, at the height of it all, it had seemed that way to her. But not now. Now he and it were respectable and sought-after. There was a great deal of prestige associated with the firm. She supposed he had a right to that. He'd worked hard, sacrificing his family to earn it.

Because the firm's image was tied so closely to his pride, his identity, Dana recanted the irreverent term. "Hardly a circus, Father."

Other memories rose, whispering to him, reminding him of the boy he had been. The boy, at bottom, he would always be. "No, you were right. It is." It was to himself, not to her, that he said, "No matter what I do, I can't leave the con behind."

Dana stared at him, bewildered. Was his mind wandering? Had the disease tainted that, too? "Con?"

Hearing her repeat the word splashed icy water on his thoughts. Regaining himself, he waved his hand, dismissing what he'd said. That belonged to his youth. She needn't know he'd lived by his wits, doing things he wasn't proud of just to put something into his belly.

"Never mind." Before her eyes, he pulled himself together, becoming the man she was accustomed to seeing. Haughty, proud, unyielding. "I'm glad you told that bastard where to get off. You don't need him."

They were in complete agreement on that one. Whatever love she'd felt for Steven was deader than she'd once deemed her father's compassion to be.

"No, I don't." And then a sadness crept in. "But we all need someone."

He looked at his daughter pointedly. "And you have someone."

"You?" she asked uncertainly, unable to believe he was willing to go this far to extend an olive branch to her.

He'd already said more than he should have. She was bright enough to understand. Briskly, he became all business. "I need the notes on the senator's mistress on my desk by three." And then a little of his gruffness receded. "If you're feeling up to it."

"I'm feeling up to it," she answered slowly. It was difficult for her to accept this change in his behavior. She kept waiting to wake up. Or have the trap spring.

But it wasn't a dream, and there was no sign of a trap. Maybe he was on the level.

A bemused smile curved her mouth. "Careful, Father. You act too nice, someone is liable to think you're an impostor."

He laughed shortly. "No chance of that." He opened the door and wheeled himself out. "Remember, no later than three."

"Three," she echoed, closing the door. Dana shook her head in bewilderment. Just when she thought the surprises were over...

"So they still have an annual county fair in Bedford," Dana murmured.

Finishing her toast, she put the A section of the local newspaper on the dining room table. The coming fair, promising to be the best ever—as usual—was the weekly paper's lead story.

It was nice to know there were a few things that hadn't changed. Dana smiled. Some of her favorite memories were centered around going to the fair with Megan. At first, when they were very young, Esther had been in charge of taking them. Although there was one year—one very special year, Dana recalled—when their mother had taken them. That was just before she finally succumbed to her depression. It was as if she'd tried to give her daughters one last memory to treasure.

Later, when they were older, they'd gone to the annual affair with friends. She'd lost her heart and her virginity at the fair late one night behind the fortune-telling tent after everyone else had left the grounds.

This time, her smile was wistful. She'd been so terribly in love. It had lasted all of two months. Two very intense months. It was her first taste of how disappointing love could be.

Still, the fair usually represented the four best days of the year, she remembered. It might be fun to see what it was like now.

Finished with breakfast, Mollie scooted off her chair and rounded the table to Dana's side. Her grandfather had already left for the office. Otherwise, she would never have dared to leave her place without asking.

Mollie peered around Dana's arm at the newspaper. There was a photograph from last year's fair on the front page. "What's a county fair?"

Dana moved her chair back and drew Mollie onto her lap. "A place where we're going to have lots of fun. Are you game for it?"

Excitement colored her cheeks to a faint pink. "Sure. Let's go!"

"Hey, not so fast." Dana laughed, tightening her arms around the wiggling child. "We can't go yet. You have to go to preschool, and I have to go to work," she pointed out.

"Besides, it doesn't start until tomorrow. We'd be standing all alone on the fairgrounds."

"No, we wouldn't," Mollie insisted. "We'd have each other."

Touched, Dana laid her cheek against Mollie's silky hair. "Oh, baby, where would I be without you?"

"Alone?" Mollie guessed. Dana laughed in response. "Aunt Dana?"

"Yes?" Dana continued hugging her, grateful for the precious gift she'd had bestowed on her. Mollie was all that was pure and good in this world. As long as she had Mollie, everything would work itself out.

"You're squishing me."

Dana laughed, releasing her. "Sorry about that. Just getting a little carried away. So, you ready to go to school?"

Mollie was on her feet instantly. "Ready."

The furrows on John Saldana's forehead deepened as he looked at his older son. He'd gotten Rafe to come under the pretext of needing help to load his van with some of the acoustical equipment for the fair tomorrow. Three separate groups from the police department were going to be performing on one of the stages and that required a network of speakers, amplifiers and microphones. It was an excuse to get the son he hardly ever saw over to the house.

His wife worried about Rafe, saying he worked too hard. That he needed to get out more. Most of all, that he needed to get on with his personal life. John was in agreement, but he figured there was no need to verbalize it.

He waited until he had his breath back. Loading the speakers was bad enough. The drums were a bear.

"I'm not taking no for an answer, Rafe. You're coming to the fair, and that's that." John paused, then hit his son with his best shot. "Your mother wants you to. And she could use the company, not to mention the help. You know what she's like. She's so damn generous, she starts giving all those baked goods away."

There was a time when he'd loved the fair. Now it was just another one of the things he didn't have time for. It seemed almost trivial to him. But Rafe knew better than to say that to his father. Especially since his parents were so involved in it.

Rafe blew out a breath, pausing over the kettledrum until his father was ready to begin again. Maybe it was just his mood, he thought. He'd been out of sorts since that night with Dana.

"What about your help?" Rafe pointed out. "You're going to be there."

The look John gave his firstborn said he'd expected better than that from him. He hoisted the kettledrum onto the truck.

"Hey, the Bedford police department is keeping me plenty busy." He climbed on behind the drum and secured it to the side of the van. "Don't forget, the department's one of the major sponsors of this little shindig. All us boys in blue are supposed to be there." He eased himself off the van, deliberately ignoring the hand Rafe offered him. "And that includes your brother, so don't be looking to him to take your place." He went into the garage, Rafe on his heels, to get the last kettledrum. Together he and Rafe moved the instrument to the driveway. "When's the last time we did anything together as a family?"

Rafe angled the drum so the bulk of the weight was with him as they lifted it into the van. "Last month. Mom made Sunday dinner."

Thank God that was the last of them. "Besides eat," John said shortly. Then his expression softened. Rafe was a good kid. It killed him to see his son cutting himself off from the best part of life. A wife, a family. It was all out there waiting for Rafe, but he had to break free of the past and a woman who could no longer be anything more than a memory for him.

John placed his arm around his son's shoulders as best he could, given that Rafe had four inches on him. "C'mon, getting away from the hospital will do you good, and it'll make your mother happy. You can invite Kate.'' There had been no fire there the one time he'd seen the two of them together, but with the right background, who knew?

''Kate and I aren't seeing each other anymore, Dad.''

John looked at him in surprise. Wait until he told Carol. ''Since when?''

''A week ago.'' Rafe didn't embellish. There was no point in telling his father he had met a woman who had unfrozen his heart, only to slash his pride.

John nodded, taking the news in stride the way he did everything that came his way. Looking for the bright side. ''Then going to the fair will give you a chance to look over what's available.'' He grinned at his son, momentarily chasing away the years that marked him. ''Like I said, I'm not taking no for an answer.''

Rafe sighed. His father was like a junkyard dog when he latched on to something. ''Then I won't bother giving it.''

John laughed, rubbing his hands together in victory. He'd had a bet riding on the outcome, and Carol was going to have to pay up. ''I told your mother I'd win you over.''

All right, so he was enjoying himself, Rafe thought. Even if he'd had to unload, carry and then arrange enough folding chairs to seat half of Bedford. Sometimes doing something physical was enjoyable. He needed the diversion of working up a sweat.

He'd arrived at the fairgrounds before seven and immediately been put to work. His mother had claimed him before his father had a chance to. Both belonged to committees that were responsible for putting on the fair.

Carol and John Saldana believed in being a part of whatever was happening in their neighborhood, in their schools, in their community. Good neighborhoods, his father insisted, began with being good neighbors. With his father on the police force and his mother teaching elementary school, they were always in the thick of things. And naturally he and Gabe had always been dragged along in their wake.

They'd had a hell of a good upbringing, he thought.

Rafe glanced toward where his brother was helping harness a horse to a wagon for the hayride. He supposed there were worse ways to spend a Saturday than surrounded by family and friends. The trickle of fairgoers that had begun early this morning was turning into a steady stream of people. A lot of his patients and their families were here. After a while, it was almost a challenge to spot a face he didn't know, at least in passing.

And then there was one he did know but hadn't expected to see. He almost let the pie he was putting out drop on the table.

"Rafe, be careful," Carol admonished. A fondness that was never far away when it came to her sons entered her voice. "I certainly hope you don't hold newborns that way."

"No," he quipped, setting the pie tray down, "I dangle them upside down by their ankles."

From the moment they arrived, Mollie looked as if she'd fallen headfirst into Wonderland. Pulling Dana one way, then another, Mollie couldn't make up her mind where to go. And then her eyes widened with pleasure.

"There's Dr. Rafe!" she exclaimed excitedly, pointing. "Let's go say hi!" Without waiting for Dana's answer, Mollie took off across the grounds.

The last thing Dana wanted was to say hi to Rafe. "No, Mollie, wait." But Mollie was off and running. "Oh, God."

Dana had no choice but to go after her. There were so many people milling around, she was afraid that if she looked away for as much as a second, Mollie would be completely swallowed up.

Like a missile, Mollie hurled herself right into Rafe, throwing her arms around him as he caught her. "Hi, Dr. Rafe! Are you here, too?"

He laughed at the rhetorical question and the enthusiasm with which she'd uttered it. "Looks that way, kiddo." He set her down. "I was just helping my mother set up."

"Your mother?" There was wonder on the small face. "You have a mother?"

As if on cue, his mother came up to join them. No doubt drawn, he thought, by the sight of Mollie. His mother had a weakness for anyone under four feet. It was from her that he'd inherited his love of children. "Yes, Mollie, even doctors have mothers."

Carol smiled at the little girl. "Hello, Mollie." Very formally, she extended her hand. Mollie shook it solemnly. "I'm very pleased to meet you." And then Carol fell back on what she deemed to be her biggest asset, her culinary talents. She pushed forward one of the pieces of pie she'd just sliced. "Would you like some custard pie? I seem to have too many pieces here. I wouldn't want to see them go to waste."

As she stared at the pie, Mollie's mouth watered. She looked over her shoulder, confident her aunt was there. Dana was just coming up behind her. "Can I, Aunt Dana? Can I have a piece of pie?"

Dana couldn't have cared less about a piece of pie. She'd sailed after Mollie, terrified of losing her. She dropped down on one knee, grabbing the little girl by the arms. "Don't you ever, ever do that to me again, Mollie. You know better than to run off in a crowd."

Seeing Dana's worried expression, Mollie's face clouded. "I'm sorry. But I wasn't running off. I was running *to*."

Dana sighed, releasing her. She rose, painfully aware that she was much too close to Rafe. "You sound like a lawyer already." She couldn't stay angry, not with Mollie, even if her nerves did feel as if they were walking the plank because she'd been forced to all but run into Rafe. "Just don't do it again."

One arm around her shoulders, Dana pressed Mollie to her. Her heart began to settle down. Ready to face the next challenge. Rafe.

"And yes, you can have a piece of pie." She looked at Rafe's mother. "I'm sorry, we haven't been introduced."

Dana offered her hand, deliberately avoiding looking in Rafe's direction. "I'm Dana Morrow, Mollie's aunt."

Twenty-five years of teaching had taught Carol Saldana how to read people quickly, and silent looks even faster. There was tension vibrating alongside the polite nods her son and this woman exchanged. Dana Morrow might have been a stranger to her, but definitely not to her son.

Carol smiled warmly, placing her hand in Dana's. "Nice to meet you, Dana. Would you like something to eat?" Not waiting for an answer, Carol began slicing another piece of pie.

Mollie had made herself comfortable at Rafe's feet, sitting cross-legged and savoring her pie. He couldn't have moved if he'd wanted to. "Ma, you keep giving it away, you're not going to raise any money."

Carol nodded. "Good point." She handed the paper plate to Dana. "All right, Rafe, pay for the lady." She placed the knife on the table and put her hand out. "And while you're at it, you can pay for Mollie, too."

He sighed and dug several bills out of his pocket, shaking his head as he gave them to his mother. "That'll teach me to open my mouth around you."

"Yes, it will." Carol smiled, pleased with herself and with the situation she saw. "I won't be needing you any longer, Rafe. You're officially free. Why don't you show Dana and Mollie around?"

Could his mother have been any more obvious? He doubted it. "I was going to see if Dad—"

Carol killed the half-baked excuse. "Dad has the whole police force to work with, not to mention your brother. You were mine for the morning, and I'm setting you free." He'd learned a long time ago there was no arguing with that tone. "Now take advantage of it before I think of something else I need you to do."

Mollie looked at him. "Can you show us around, Dr. Rafe?" she asked prettily. "This is my very first fair ever."

There was no way he could refuse that face. "I guess I can

do that.'' He indicated the last row of folding chairs he'd arranged. ''Why don't we sit down over here until you finish that?''

''Okay.'' Eager to please, Mollie nodded so hard, she almost let what was left of her pie slide off her plate. Rafe righted it, preventing a collision between dessert and grass.

He stepped out of the way to let Dana pass first. Sitting with Mollie between them, Rafe couldn't have felt more awkward than if he'd just been asked to dance *Swan Lake* as the female lead. They still hadn't exchanged so much as one word.

He was determined to be civilized about it, even though he didn't feel very civilized. ''So, how have you been, Dana?''

The sound of his voice, a voice that echoed in her brain at the most inopportune times, had her struggling to maintain her composure. ''Busy. My father really has me hopping.''

Mollie looked at her puzzled, loaded fork in midair. ''I didn't see you hop, Aunt Dana.''

Trust Mollie to ease the tension. Dana leaned over and kissed her head. ''Just an expression, sweetie. Dr. Rafe knows what I mean.''

His eyes met hers over the curly head. ''In this instance, yes.'' And then he looked at Mollie's plate. It was empty. ''You're finished already?''

She grinned, nodding. ''I was hungry.''

He took the plate from her and threw it in one of the trash cans he'd put out. ''Don't they feed you where you live?''

''Sure,'' Mollie answered, ''but not pie like this.''

Rafe laughed. He loved the honesty that existed in children. He glanced at Dana. The honesty that fell by the wayside once children became adults.

''My mother will be very happy to hear your endorsement.'' He offered Mollie his hand. ''Want to go on the Ferris wheel?''

''Yes!'' And then she paused before asking, ''What's a Ferris wheel?''

"Come on, I'll show you." He was already leading the way.

Mollie hesitated for only a fraction of a second. "Can Aunt Dana come along?"

"Only if she wants to." He looked over his shoulder at her. Dana had finished her pie, as well. "I wouldn't want her doing anything she doesn't want to do."

She took the direct hit and recovered immediately. "Don't worry," she assured him, keeping pace. She dumped the plate as she passed the trash can without breaking stride. "She won't."

Rafe stopped, and before she could draw her head back, lightly passed his thumb over the corner of her mouth. Her heart lunged against her chest.

"You had some custard right there." Still looking at her, he licked the custard off his thumb and then hurried off with Mollie.

So much for congratulating herself that the situation was under control, Dana thought.

Why did he have to be so damn charming? They'd gone from the Ferris wheel—which they had ridden twice—to the pony ride—three rides—to the carousel, which was so packed, they only rode once. During all that time, Rafe was completely attentive to Mollie.

He was making it so difficult for her to remain detached. For the past two hours, traipsing from one ride to another, answering Mollie's endless questions and chasing her through the fun house, Rafe had displayed the kind of infinite patience Dana thought was only allotted to mothers, and only to a limited few, at that.

Dana wasn't accustomed to a man showing such warm affection for a child. It certainly wasn't anything she'd grown up with.

With all her heart, she wished she'd never left home. Then maybe, somehow, fate would have led their paths to cross before now.

Dana laughed at herself. She had too much of her father in her to believe that. Besides, there was no use wishing for things that weren't. She was having enough trouble coping with things that were. Like her pregnancy.

With Mollie flagging just a little, Rafe brought her to the rows of folding chairs that were still by and large empty, and would remain so until that evening, when the entertainers began their acts.

"This is fun, Aunt Dana," Mollie announced, as if it was news. "I'm glad we came."

"So am I," Dana agreed. At least for Mollie's sake. Tired, she eased herself into a chair beside her niece.

"Hey, who is this little doll?"

Dana turned to see a man coming up behind them. As she looked closer, it occurred to her that he looked like an older, shorter version of Rafe.

Mollie looked at John Saldana solemnly. "I don't talk to strangers, sir."

Impressed, John nodded. "That's a very good habit, but it's all right to talk to me. I'm a policeman."

The solemn expression vanished, chased away by her smile. "Okay. I'm Mollie Aliprantis." Twisting in her chair, she did the honors. "This is my aunt Dana, and this is my doctor."

John had trouble keeping his expression properly sober. When it came to kids, he was used to Carol exaggerating, but she was right this time. This one was adorable. "Do you always bring your doctor along?"

Mollie shook her head. "No, we met him here."

Rafe laughed as he leaned over to whisper to Mollie, "He's just pulling your leg, honey. This is my father."

Mollie looked down at her leg, which seemed to be right where she expected it to be, unpulled. "A mother *and* a father?"

"And a brother, too," John told her. He beckoned his other son over. Gabe looked reluctant to leave the company of the blonde he was talking to, but he did. It was the uniform that attracted them, John thought. That and the killer Saldana smile. ''Gabe, come on over here. There's someone I'd like you to meet.''

Joining them, Gabe paused to give Dana a quick but very thorough once-over. He definitely liked what he saw. He also noted the proprietary look in his brother's eye.

Well, well, well, that should certainly make their mother happy.

Mollie was staring at Gabe, clearly smitten all over again. He was as good-looking as Rafe, with a certain boyishness to him that Rafe had clearly outgrown. ''I *like* your family, Dr. Rafe.''

Rafe saw his mother, busy selling her homemade pies, pausing to look their way. He could see her antennae going up. *Don't get your hopes up, Mom.* ''They like you, too, Mollie.''

John and Gabe were flanking Mollie. Nothing he liked better than a well-mannered kid, John thought. ''Ever ride in a police car?'' he asked.

''No,'' she breathed, a hopeful expression wreathing her face.

Gabe laid claim to her before his father could, picking Mollie up. ''Well, then, let me give you the grand tour.'' He glanced at Dana, then looked at his older brother. *Nice taste, bro.* ''Why don't you two get some punch or something? This might take a while.''

Mollie was eating this up, Rafe thought, but he pretended not to notice. ''Okay with you, Mollie?''

She looked at Gabe. ''Are you going to be there with me?''

''Stuck to you like glue,'' he promised.

Her face would have been in danger of cracking if she grinned any harder. ''Okay.''

Dana shook her head as she watched the two policemen disappear with her niece. ''She has the makings of an A-one flirt.''

''A flirtatious lawyer.'' Rafe made the association from her earlier comment. He looked at Dana. "Must run in the family."

Dana opened her mouth to retort, then let it go. "I guess I had that coming to me." She pressed her lips together. Apologizing didn't come any easier to her than it did to her father, but she owed it to Rafe, if for no other reason than for the way he'd treated Mollie today. "I'm sorry about what happened."

His hand at the small of her back, he guided her past a cluster of people. "Which part are you sorry for?"

She looked at him. Did he have to ask? "What do you think?"

He took out two dollars and paid the woman at the concession stand for two glasses of punch. He handed one to Dana. "I'm not sure what to think."

If he could be honest, so could she. Dana took a sip before turning toward him. "Rafe, I'm coming from a very rocky place in my life. Trust isn't something I can just give, even if I want to."

"And do you? Want to?" he prodded when she didn't answer.

She was probably going to regret this. "Yes."

He smiled. "Good enough. We'll take it from there. Slow." He glanced toward the police car that had been driven onto the grounds for the day. He could see his father talking Mollie's ears off. "But right now, I think we should rescue Mollie from my father."

"I have a hunch it might be the other way around." She fell into step beside him as he walked toward the police car. And when he took her hand, she left it there, content, for the space of the afternoon, to pretend that everything was all right.

Chapter 17

The evening air was soft and filled with music as it swirled gently around them. On the stage a group was doing justice to the songs that had made them popular more than a quarter of a century ago. The audience, who spanned ages from preschoolers to people in their eighties, swayed and clapped in time, keeping the beat alive.

When he looked behind him, Rafe saw his parents sitting several rows back. They were holding hands instead of clapping. His father was whispering something into his mother's ear. She laughed and swatted at him in that playful way she had when he made her feel like a young girl again.

That was what he wanted, Rafe thought, turning. To have a life like that. To have a love like that in his life. Again.

He glanced at Dana's profile. She seemed completely absorbed in the music, in the moment. Moonlight was as kind to her as sunlight, caressing her skin, accentuating a sensuality that needed little help to stir him.

He felt a pull so strong, so overwhelming, that he thought

it would wrench out his very gut. When he sucked in his breath to steady himself, she looked at him quizzically.

He thought fast. "I think we're losing someone." Grinning, he indicated Mollie, whose head kept nodding as she fought valiantly to remain awake.

Dana felt guilty. She should have taken Mollie home hours ago. It was just that today had been so perfect, she didn't want to see it end. After Mollie had satisfied her desire to ride every ride, they'd run into some of Rafe's patients and their parents making a day of it. Dana recognized several of the women immediately and lost no time telling Nicole Lincoln how happy Mollie was at the preschool.

One of the others, Nicole's older sister, Marlene, had suggested they all take a breather for lunch and Dana had found herself assimilated into a circle comprised of young parents and their children. A group that welcomed her. A group, Marlene confided, that Sheila had once dubbed her baby-of-the-month club, since their due dates had all been a month apart. Nicole added that Sheila had rounded out the club with the birth of Rebecca. As she listened, Dana's secret weighed heavily on her conscience and on her heart.

Mollie had had a ball with the other children, and Dana had felt as if she belonged. With Rafe sitting on the grass beside her, it had had the feel of an impromptu picnic. The years and the sorrow that had brought her had temporarily disappeared.

After lunch, the group had broken up, but not before promises of getting together soon were exchanged. The contented glow that get-together and all the rest of the day had generated was still with her. Maybe it was selfish, Dana thought, but she'd wanted to hang on to it just a little longer.

To remain here with Rafe a little longer.

Yes, it was selfish. Dana put her arm around Mollie, gathering the little girl against her. "It's way past her bedtime."

Pavlov's dog reacting to the dinner bell couldn't have responded faster than Mollie. Her eyes popped open, a protest coming from her rosebud mouth. "Not yet, Aunt Dana. Please, I don't want to go to bed yet."

If there had only been herself to consider, Dana would have remained until the last person left the fairgrounds. But with Mollie added in, the equation changed. Mollie needed her rest. Even Cinderella knew she had to withdraw before midnight struck.

Careful not to jar her, Dana began buttoning the sweater she'd coaxed Mollie into putting on once the sun had gone down. Actually, Rafe had had more to do with getting her into it than she had. All he'd had to do was back up Dana's request, and suddenly Mollie was pushing her arms through the sleeves with zest. Dana smiled. Mollie was crazy about Rafe, there was no doubt about it.

As for her, well, there were a lot of doubts about that. And a lot of rampaging feelings, as well. All she knew right now was that she would have given anything if this night could have gone on forever.

"Oh, I think you've had enough for one day, sugar plum." She glanced at her watch, angling it into the light so she could read the face. It was after ten o'clock. "We've been here almost eleven hours." She took the whimper to be a protest. Poor baby, she thought. "And we can always come back tomorrow."

"Tomorrow," Mollie murmured. The battle with her eyelids was almost completely lost. They were barely fluttering open, each time they sank down.

Rising, Rafe picked Mollie up in his arms. "Up you go, kiddo." With Mollie's head tucked against his shoulder, he looked at Dana. "I'll walk you to your car."

She didn't want him going to any extra trouble. He'd already done so much for Mollie. Dana reached for her niece, ready to take her from him. "I'm parked way over to the side. It's a long walk."

Mollie was staying right where she was. Her last act before surrendering to sleep had been to wrap her small arms around his neck. He laughed softly, holding her to him.

"I don't mind. I'm young, I can handle it. Just lead the way." He nodded toward the exit, then looked at Dana, a smile in his eyes. "Better yet, walk alongside me."

She did as he asked, happy at the way things were turning out. But she felt obligated to warn him.

"You'll be sorry." She wasn't kidding about how far away she was parked. When they'd arrived, the lots were already jammed. She'd had to look for a parking space way out on the perimeter.

It was a great night for a stroll, he thought. Funny, until Dana had come into his life, he'd stopped doing things like that, stopped taking walks, stopped enjoying the simple things around him. Without intending to, she'd awakened him to things he'd let slip by since he'd lost his wife.

It felt good to be alive. To be here with her and Mollie.

"I'm sorry for a lot of things, Dana, and I'll probably do things in the future I'll regret. But carrying a little girl to her car won't be among them."

Dana couldn't help herself. The question came out before she could think to stop it. "What *are* you sorry about?"

Amusement crossed his face. She'd once accused him of prying when he'd asked her personal questions. "Now who's prying?"

Dana bit her lower lip, looking away. She was letting the borders between them blur again, but that was because the day had been so magical. But the day was over. "Sorry."

He'd only meant to tease her, not make her back away. "No, I'm the one who's sorry." He flashed a grin at her. "See, I told you I'd be sorry in the future." He took a breath before he began. "You want to know what I'm sorry about?" He looked at her, their eyes momentarily holding. "I'm sorry I didn't call you the day after I dropped you off at your house."

He'd shifted the emphasis onto himself when she'd been the one who'd run away. She was beginning to believe that was in his nature. To be kind, to spare others' feelings.

"Why?" she asked. She'd wanted him to call, hoped he

would call even as she prayed that he wouldn't. A few times she'd thought of calling him, but then she'd talked herself out of it. There was no point in seeing him. It couldn't lead anywhere.

They'd passed the first lot and were walking through the second one. The lights were fewer out here, spaced farther apart. He was glad he'd insisted on coming with her. For the most part, Bedford was a safe city, but even paradise had its serpent.

"Because," he told her truthfully, "maybe we could have cleared things up sooner."

Nothing concrete had been said. Just feelings piled onto a day that had gone well from the start. "I wasn't aware that we *had* cleared things up."

He stopped walking because he wanted to see her face, all of it, when he asked her, "You had a good time today, didn't you?"

She had. She couldn't remember laughing so much in years. Or feeling so good. "Yes."

Then they were moving forward, which meant things were all right again. Words would come later. For now, it was enough that they were enjoying each other's company again. "Then things are clearing up."

But they weren't, she thought. It wasn't that simple. She was still afraid of being hurt, still afraid of risking her feelings, although she was beginning to feel as if the choice was being taken away from her, slipping through her fingers a little more each time she was around him.

And there was still the secret she was keeping from him. One that would put a whole different slant on their relationship, if not terminate it altogether.

With a pang so strong it startled her, Dana realized that she didn't want to terminate their relationship. Not yet.

She decided it was safest to drop the subject and move on. "What else do you regret?"

He liked the way her hair brushed against his arm as they

walked. Softly, silkily, just the way she'd felt in his arms that night.

"That the evening is over." Mollie began to slip to the side. Gently, he shifted her into place. "I'd like to take you home, Dana," he said quietly, "but I promised to help with the cleanup."

Home. Hers? Or did he mean his? Was he saying that he wanted to make love with her again? She felt her breasts tingling at the very thought of it.

Or was he talking about sex? It would have been easier on her if it was the latter, because then she could dismiss him as being like all the rest.

But she was beginning to think that he wasn't like all the rest. Not at all.

You've been wrong before, she told herself. Look at Steven. He wrote you poetry and swore with tears in his eyes that he loved you.

"I brought my own car," Dana pointed out. "That would make it difficult for you to take me anywhere."

"I'd still like to." His voice was low. If she concentrated, she could almost feel it skimming along her bare skin. Along her face, her arms, her legs. She struggled to shut out its effects. "I'd like to take you places, Dana. Places you've never been."

She'd always been good at game playing, doing it to survive in a world she didn't like. But she didn't want to play games with Rafe. She felt she owed him the truth.

"You already did." Dana looked at him. "What happened between us was very special to me. No one's ever treated me like that before, as if I what I felt mattered more than..." She was saying too much, giving too much of herself away. And allowing him to have too much power into the bargain. That wasn't supposed to happen. Dana shrugged, playing down the emotion behind her words. "Well, no one's ever done that, that's all."

He promised himself never to ask. The past wasn't supposed to have any effect on whatever was happening between them. But maybe it did. Maybe the last man in her life really had scarred her. Scarred her so she couldn't give herself completely.

He needed to know. "You said you were coming from a rocky place in your life—"

"I am. I was." Dana stopped, searching for the right words. Shadows bathed her face as she walked beside Rafe, hiding her expression from him. She tiptoed around the subject carefully, not wanting to say too much, afraid of driving him away too soon. "I was involved with someone. Someone I thought I would be with for the rest of my life."

Someone she'd loved, he thought, maybe even the way he'd loved Debra. It gave them common ground. "What happened?" he prodded gently.

She took a breath. When she spoke again, her voice was devoid of all feeling. She'd learned from the master, she thought.

"He didn't turn out to be the person I thought he was. We began as soul mates and wound up as cell mates." To buy herself some time, Dana smoothed Mollie's hair, though there was no need to. "The last straw came when he was cruel to Mollie. I took her in after my sister and her husband were killed. Steven resented the attention I was giving her."

The name sprang at him. Steven. The man who had made love with her, who had hurt her, was named Steven. He'd never liked that name.

"He gave me an ultimatum. It was either Mollie or him." She shivered. Whether from the breeze or the memory, she didn't know. "I picked Mollie." Her smile was enigmatic. "It wasn't really a contest."

The bitter taste in his mouth surprised him. How could she have stayed with someone like that? "Sounds like a real winner."

She gave Steven his due, knowing he would never have returned the favor, given a chance. She had no doubt that he had run her down in front of all his friends. "Oh, he had his good points." She shrugged, feeling suddenly very cold.

''Unfortunately, they weren't the lasting kind.'' Without meaning to, she stepped up her pace. ''I'd really rather not talk about him.''

Rafe noted her increased speed but didn't mention it. ''Sorry, wasn't my business to ask. I was just curious about the kind of man you allowed into your life.''

She balked at what she took to be criticism. ''It's not a matter of allowing or not allowing, it's...''

''Closing the barn door after the horse is gone?'' he suggested helpfully.

She thought of the pony ride he'd taken Mollie on. And the hayride they'd all gone on. Remembering nudged some of her bad humor to the side. ''You're letting the fair get to you.''

''Yeah, that and other things.'' He didn't want to leave her thinking he had pumped her. ''Since we're exchanging personal information, for the record, I loved my wife very much. Her dying much too soon, cheating me of growing old with her, is one of the things I regret the most.'' He glanced at her. ''I really didn't think I was ever going to feel anything for anyone again.''

He left the sentence dangling. Dana looked at him. ''But?''

''But,'' he repeated, nodding, as if the one word said it all. Because she clearly didn't understand, he explained, as much as he was able. ''That's what I need to explore. That disturbing little word, *but.*'' And to explore it, he needed to be with her. ''Listen, there's this policemen's ball coming up—''

She knew where this was going and needed a minute to gather her thoughts. To make sense of her ricocheting feelings. Dana played for time. ''You're not a policeman.''

He wished she wouldn't keep interrupting. He still wasn't any good at this sort of thing. ''No, but my father and brother are, and they're trying to stick me with all these tickets.''

A smile played along her lips as she asked innocently, ''Are you trying to sell me some?''

''No,'' he said in exasperation, ''I'm trying to *use* some.

Two, to be exact.'' And then he saw the grin. She was putting him on. ''Come with me?''

Senator Johnson's trial date was coming up soon. Her father was insisting that everyone devote all their time to it, in and out of the office.

But she needed this, too. ''When?''

''Next Friday.''

Where had she parked, in the next state? he wondered. They were coming to the end of the last parking lot, and she still wasn't giving any indication that they'd reached her car.

Dana thought, trying to put things in order. Friday. A week from Friday the senator's murder trial was scheduled to begin. More than any of her father's cases in the last few years, this one promised to be a real media event. But it was still two weeks away. Her father couldn't expect her to work every evening.

Dana reconsidered. Well, actually, he could, but she wasn't going to. At least, not next Friday.

''Friday will be fine.''

''Great.'' As he said it, he almost felt like a kid again, getting a date to the prom. An odd reaction for a man his age, he thought, savoring it nonetheless.

Dana stopped beside a dusty-looking white sedan. ''We're here.''

He didn't bother hiding his relief. Even forty-five pounds of spun sugar and heaven began to feel heavy after a while. ''I was beginning to think you'd decided to walk home.''

''I warned you.'' Dana unlocked the door.

''Yeah, you did. I'm not very big on listening to warnings.'' Rafe carefully slipped Mollie into the back seat.

She felt her heart flutter the tiniest bit and told herself she was an idiot. ''That gives us something in common.''

Mollie, her eyes shut tight, murmured, ''No bed,'' then curled up in the back seat. Rafe chuckled as he straightened, carefully drawing his large frame out of the car. ''She's your niece, all right. Stubborn to the end.''

Dana began to check the seat belt, then stopped herself.

Rafe was perfectly capable of buckling Mollie up. She had to start trusting someone sometime. With a snap, she shut the rear passenger door.

And turned straight into Rafe, their bodies brushing against each other. Stiffening ever so slightly, Dana pretended not to notice, but the unguarded look in her eyes gave her away.

She felt something, just as he did, Rafe thought. The question still remained—what?

When she began to open the door on her side, he placed his hand on hers. "I said we'd go slow."

She raised her eyes to his face, her breath catching in her dry throat. "Yes?"

"What I want to know is, is asking to kiss you good-night going too fast?"

She felt the smile coming from the soles of her feet. "I believe Goldilocks said it best, 'No, it's just right.'"

He couldn't think of anything he wanted more than to kiss her. "Always been one of my favorite fairy tales."

Touching her face with the tips of his fingers, trailing them slowly along her jawline to the point of her chin, he allowed himself a moment to savor the feel of her skin before finally pressing his lips to hers.

It felt as if everything within her had been holding its breath, waiting for this moment to happen. When it did, every fiber of her body came alive, leaning into the kiss, into the sensation it created within her.

As it deepened, as it took her away from everything she knew to everything that was wondrous and good, Dana could feel her head spinning again. In the distance, a hundred crickets serenaded them as the night spread its cloak around them.

She could feel her body yearning again, yearning for him. Yearning to feel again the way only he had made her feel. Wanted, precious. Beautiful.

He wanted her. Sweet heaven, but he wanted her. Right here, in this field of neglected weeds, with the lights of the fair shining dimly in the distance, he wanted to make love with her.

Rafe felt as if he was no longer the man he'd been only a little more than a month ago. He wasn't quite sane anymore.

What he was was alive.

Exercising whatever control she had left, Dana placed her hands against Rafe's chest and drew her head back. It took her a second to focus, to struggle out of the swirling haze surrounding her. "I'd better get Mollie home."

Dana was only grateful that she managed not to gasp the words.

Rafe nodded. For a moment he'd forgotten about Mollie. Forgotten about everything except this crying need within him. Denied and locked away for so long, it was ravenous.

He stepped back and held the door open for her. "I'll see you Friday." He closed the door as she buckled her seat belt.

"Friday," she echoed.

He watched her pull out and remained standing there until he could no longer make out her car. Then he walked to the fairgrounds to join cleanup detail. Whistling.

The days between Sunday and Friday were filled with work and second thoughts for Rafe. A great many second thoughts, despite the ragging he'd gotten from his father and Gabe on Sunday when he turned up to help set up again. He'd withstood it all good-naturedly and even suffered his mother's questions, though there were only a tactful few. But underneath, he still wasn't sure what it was he felt when he was around Dana. Whether it was purely physical attraction taken to the extreme, or if there was more to it than that.

There was no denying that their lovemaking had been incredible. Maybe what was bothering him was that he couldn't get a handle on things. On her. Feisty, independent, yet there was obviously something going on under the surface, an inner hurt he saw in her eyes at unguarded moments. He could relate to that.

More than that, he could relate to her. That scared him even as it reeled him in. He wasn't sure if he was ready for that kind of connection to someone again. Could he handle it?

Logically, he knew he should be able to. But emotionally, it was a different story. One that refused to allow him to sneak a peek at the last page.

A call from the hospital had him leaving the fairgrounds just after setup. And just before he figured she would arrive. When he tried to call her later, Esther told him she wasn't in.

They played phone tag. He called her house several times that week, only to be given the same message. The few times Dana returned his call, she got his answering machine at home or his service at the office, never him.

By Friday night, he was wondering if this had been such a good idea. Maybe there was a message in their inability to make contact. Maybe he should let things slide for a while.

He was still saying maybe when he arrived at her door to pick her up.

And to have his breath taken away.

She was wearing a silver gown, one that came demurely to her throat and then wantonly used up all its available material before it reached her back. The shimmering material, slashed all the way to the middle of her thigh, clung to her with every move. It was the kind of gown that could bring a grown man to his knees.

It nearly did him. Especially when he placed his hand on the small of her back and realized that he was touching skin rather than fabric.

"Aren't you afraid of catching cold?" he asked.

But she merely smiled in return. "I think the look in your eyes will keep me warm enough."

"I don't know about you, but I'm going to stay plenty warm tonight trying to keep every available man from running off with you."

"That's the nicest thing you've ever said to me."

"I get better with practice," he promised, opening the car door for her.

"Mind if I cut in?" Gabe asked his brother even as he took possession of Dana.

He danced away with her before Rafe had a chance to say anything. Most likely no, Gabe thought. It would be just like Rafe to be selfish with Dana. Gabe tucked her hand against his chest, smiling at her. He felt pretty confident that most eyes were on them, the way they'd been on Rafe when he had danced with her.

"You look terrific." The look in his eyes, as sensual as Rafe's, reinforced his words. "Has he told you that yet?"

Dana smiled, remembering. "He might have mentioned something along those lines."

Whatever Rafe had said, Gabe knew it wasn't enough. "He was never any good with words. I'm the one with the gift of gab." Gabe inclined his head. "So, on behalf of the Saldana men, let me tell you that you're the most gorgeous woman here." He grinned. "Although my mother gets honorable mention."

"Thank you." Dana's amusement shone in her eyes. She decided that she liked Rafe's brother a lot. And it was easier, being friendly, even being flirtatious, when it didn't count. "Tell me, does that list include your own date?"

"Rosemary?" He grinned broadly. Rosemary DeAngelo was his lady of the month. He liked her the way he liked all the women he went out with. But there was nothing serious in the offing. Just two people enjoying each other's company. Rafe was the serious one, not him. He intended to enjoy himself until he died. "Rosemary's okay. She doesn't make my eyes shine the way you make Rafe's shine, though."

Dana turned her head, trying to find Rafe in the crowd. He hadn't looked very happy when Gabe cut in. "He doesn't look like his eyes are shining to me."

Not conceited. He liked that in a woman. He gave Rafe more points on his choice. "You should have seen him before." For a fleeting second, he was serious. "Whatever you're doing, thanks."

Wait a second. The waters were getting a bit too deep for her. She didn't want Rafe's family misunderstanding things. "But I'm not—"

Gabe didn't need or want explanations, whatever was going on was between his brother and the lady. He might like annoying Rafe from time to time, but he did have a sense of honor about some things. "Hey, it's none of my business, really."

Rafe was suddenly between them, elbowing his brother out of the way. "You've had her long enough."

Hands spread in surrender, Gabe stepped back. "He always did like to hog things," he told Dana. "Have him tell you about the time he took my bike."

"It was *my* bike," Rafe reminded him as he danced away with Dana. He smiled at her. "Thanks for putting up with him."

There was nothing to put up with. "I like him," she said honestly. "I like your whole family. And your friends," she added, thinking of the other day at the fair. "They say you can tell a lot about a man by the kind of friends he has."

"Oh?"

She nodded. "Yours are all so easy to talk to, so down-to-earth."

He glanced to his right, where Gabe stood with some of other men on the force. Most of the faces were familiar to him. "That's because they all want to crowd around you."

"Another compliment?" she marveled. "Two in one evening?"

He drew back a little to look at her. "Hey, I'm as capable of giving one as the next guy."

She laughed, leaning her cheek against his chest again. "Not according to your brother."

"My brother is too busy drooling over you to think straight." He could feel her breath along his chest, even through his jacket and his shirt. Having his hand against her bare back only made him ache for her. "How did you get into that dress?"

"Why?" She raised her head to look at him. Did he suspect? Afraid, she glanced down to see if she was suddenly showing. "Is it too tight?"

"What was it you said the other night? It's just right?" He grinned at her. "Well, it is. But it does make me wonder, though."

"About?"

"About what you have on underneath." He had his suspicions.

Unable to resist, Dana raised herself on her toes and whispered against his ear, "Skin."

He felt the ripple of desire possess him. His body quickened, reminding him how much he wanted her. Ever since he'd taken her in his arms to dance, all he'd been able to think of was making love with her.

His thoughts were on a collision course with the promise he'd made to her. The promise that said he would go slow.

He meant to keep it, he really did. But it wasn't easy. Especially not when she pressed herself against him like this. And not when she smelled this good, like sin served on a golden platter, all warm and tempting.

He tried to focus on taking a cold shower. It didn't help. "That's what I thought."

She smiled as she felt his heart beating hard against her cheek.

Chapter 18

"Looks like the party's breaking up, Cinderella," Rafe murmured against her hair.

The strains of the last dance, a slow one, were fading. Rafe had noted that the crowd had been steadily thinning for the last half hour or so. There was just so much dancing people could take, he mused. He saw his brother getting ready to leave with a redhead he didn't recognize. Nothing new there. Gabe seemed determined to avail himself of the companionship of every female on the planet between the ages of twenty and forty-seven.

Not him. He only needed one. A very particular one. And he was beginning to think that just maybe lightning had managed to strike him twice.

"Hmm?" Dana looked at him. He'd said something, but she hadn't heard. She'd been too busy enjoying the comforting sensation of his heart beating beneath her cheek.

"I think things are winding up." He pointed to several couples who were milling around the exit. Gabe made eye contact before leaving and gave Rafe the high sign. He waved his brother away. Placing his hand lightly on Dana's shoulder, he began guiding her toward the door. ''Time to go.'' They sidestepped several people still gathered around the bar, swapping stories. But even they appeared to be winding down. ''Do you want to go home?''

''Yes.'' Dana turned her head to look at him. She'd made up her mind. ''Yours.''

If a rush of excitement met her words, he managed to keep it under wraps. ''Are you sure?'' he asked carefully.

Her eyes held his, and then she smiled. ''I'm sure.'' And she was. Sure that she wanted this last time with him. And when it was over, when the delicious sensation of his lovemaking and the feelings it brought to life had settled and faded, she would tell him. Tell him what wouldn't be a secret for very much longer. Oh, she might be able to continue for another month or maybe two. She knew of women who didn't show right up to the date of their delivery, but that was rare. He would have to be told before that.

Before their feelings were permanently entangled.

A smile, self-deprecating and small, played across her lips. It might be too late for that.

But come what may, she had to tell him. It was the only decent thing to do. If he turned from her, well, then he would be like all the others, wouldn't he? Putting his feelings before hers. There would be nothing surprising if that was the way he reacted.

And if he didn't…

If he didn't, then he would be one of those rare men who glowed in the dark and made the demons go away. A man who would love her and make her feel safe. Either way, she would know what she had.

Or didn't have.

On the way out, Rafe guided her toward his parents. He'd slipped his hand to the back of her neck, leaving it there.

''Please don't do that,'' she whispered.

Her voice might be low, but there was no disguising the emotion in it. ''Do what?''

"Lead me around like that, like I'm a puppet. It—it reminds me of someone." Steven used to do that. Keep his hand at the back of her neck, moving her around as if she was a mindless rag doll who couldn't walk on her own. It was all part and parcel of the power trip Steven had been on.

Rafe dropped his hand. "Sorry."

She felt bad immediately. "I know it's silly, but—"

"Hey, I said I was sorry, and I am. I don't want to do anything to remind you of someone who hurt you. Anything else?" She shook her head. "Okay. Mind if I just stop to say goodbye to my folks?"

"Only if you don't let me say goodbye, too. And, Rafe?"

"Yeah?"

"It's okay to put your arm around me. I like that."

He grinned as he slipped his arm around her shoulders. "As long as I know."

The road seemed almost serene this time of night. Traffic was minimal, and it felt as if they were masters of all they saw. Ordinarily, that would have been a very secure feeling.

But tonight Dana wasn't feeling secure. She was feeling damn nervous.

It was strange to feel like this, to have all these pins and needles dancing along her body. She knew exactly what lay ahead, at least for the next hour or so. They would make fabulous love and then hold each other as the feeling mellowed. And for just a tiny space of time, she would feel safe.

Until she told him.

Suddenly she didn't want to tell him, didn't want to face what might happen in the wake of her admission. Didn't want to see him turning from her.

But she had no choice.

It was the telling that made her feel like this. That, and the fear that he might think she had been deceiving him all along for her own purposes. Or, worse, for her own amusement.

Well, wasn't she? Wasn't she leading him on in a way, pretending to be free when, in the purest sense of the word, she wasn't? She wasn't free to do what she wanted with whom she wanted. She had an obligation. An obligation to the child she was carrying.

Leaning over, she turned the radio on. She needed something to fill the spaces in her mind, to chase away her thoughts.

Since she'd turned on the radio, Rafe turned it to a station that played the blues. It seemed to match the mood. When he was a kid, he'd thought the blues were depressing. But as he grew older, as he listened not so much to the words but to the music, he'd become a fan.

''You're awfully pensive,'' he said. ''Are you having second thoughts?''

Dana shook her head, trying to sound upbeat. Maybe she was worrying for no reason. ''No, I'm still working on my first ones.''

''Which are?'' He wanted to know every thought in her head, every feeling in her heart. He knew all about personal space and people's need for privacy, but right now he wanted to know everything there was to know about the woman beside him. He smiled. Maybe there was a little of the cop in him, after all.

She couldn't think of anything to tell him, and she wasn't about to tell him what she was really thinking. Not yet.

Dana shook her head. ''Never mind.''

Maybe she thought he was presuming too much. ''None of my business?'' he guessed.

She didn't want him to feel she was pushing him away. That wasn't it at all. She was afraid of pushing him away. As afraid of that as she was of admitting what it was she was beginning to feel for him. ''I didn't say that.''

He shifted slightly, turning his face in her direction, while one eye remained on the road.

''I know, but maybe that's what you thought.'' He wanted her to understand, at least a little. ''Dana, I know I said I'd go slow—''

He saw her eyes widen slightly. ''Maybe you'd better.''

There was apprehension in her expression. Was she changing her mind? "Then you don't want to come to my place?"

"No, I really meant slow, as in slow down." Dana pointed to the speedometer. "You're doing sixty." Rafe glanced at the dash and immediately eased up on the accelerator. "I figured that maybe not all of Bedford's police force is gathered at the Colony Hotel tonight."

"Damn."

Mentally, he upbraided himself for being so careless. He was usually a very conscientious driver. But being around Dana seemed to rob him of the edge he ordinarily had. Like heady perfume, she clouded his mind.

"Now, what was it you were trying to say?" she coaxed as they continued at an acceptable speed.

Maybe what he had to say was best left unsaid for now. Maybe saying it would only make her back away. Or damage what was between them. If you held on to something too tightly, it broke. He knew that, and he didn't want this to break. He wanted to nurture it until it was strong enough to withstand being handled.

"I don't know." He lifted a shoulder carelessly and let it drop the same way. "Must have lost my train of thought."

He was lying, Dana thought. She was about to prod him, then decided against it. Maybe she wouldn't want to hear what he had to say. Because she knew that if he had questions, real questions, she would have to answer them truthfully. She couldn't bring herself to lie to him. There was more involved than keeping to her own code of ethics. She couldn't lie to him, because to lie would cost her the one thing she could always bargain with. Trust. If she lied to him, he wouldn't trust her, not completely, and possibly not ever. And she might want him to…someday.

Wasn't not telling the same as lying?

God, her head was beginning to hurt. Turning the music up louder, she refused to let herself think about it any more.

Light flooded the room, illuminating the clutter. It looked like a family of bears had run riot here. Dana couldn't help grinning. Her grin widened as Rafe hurriedly began to make a vain attempt at cleaning the place up.

"I guess you weren't expecting to bring me here."

He stuffed newspapers that defied folding into a magazine rack. The rack fell over, spilling its contents. Rafe sighed, frustrated. "It does look pretty awful, doesn't it?"

She turned to face him. "Not as far as hurricanes go. But I didn't come here to critique your housekeeping."

He shoved the overflowing laundry basket behind the recliner. There was no way he could hope to make a decent dent in all this. He gave up trying. "Why *did* you come?"

She moistened her lips, nervousness beginning to rise again. "Because I like your company."

Behind him, the basket, top-heavy, toppled. He didn't care. He crossed to her, took her in his arms and held her against him.

God, but she felt good, smelled good. She made his senses churn. Doing nothing more than standing here, he could feel the excitement all through his body. His breath didn't seem to want to last as long as it should. Damn, but she had him almost panting. Any minute now, he was going to sit up and beg.

"Are you really wearing nothing underneath that?"

The question, softly whispered, made her pulse accelerate. Dana raised her eyes to his. "Why don't you find out for yourself?"

He wanted to. Damn, but he wanted to tear the gown from her beautiful body and make love with her right here in the middle of this chaos he called a living room. But then he would be just like the man in her past. The man who treated her like an object. Someone who had seemed one thing to her at the outset, becoming another all too soon. Rafe didn't want her to feel that way about him. Her wanted her to...

To what?

To care for him. The rest, if there was going to be a rest, would come later. Right now, caring was enough.

Gathering her close to him, he made her another promise. One she didn't hear. A silent promise. To take what she offered so generously and savor it the way it should be savored. Slowly, with reverence. Even if it killed him.

Very lightly, with his hands barely touching her shoulders, he grazed her mouth with his, kissing her once, twice, and then again, each time more deeply than the last, until he finally lost himself completely in the kiss.

He discovered that he liked being lost. Liked feeling as if he'd lost his way, as long as it was with her.

Like a man who suddenly had to rely on his other senses in order to see, Rafe skimmed his palms along her body. Touching her, memorizing every curve, every dip, every tantalizing swell. He passed his hands along her body slowly, knowing he was exciting her. And, in knowing, he excited himself. The rush was incredible.

She could feel the frenzy beginning, beating its wings wildly within her. Was it humanly possible to want someone so much and still live? She wasn't sure. All she knew was that she felt as if she was bursting inside. She wanted to feel him, to touch him the way only lovers touched. And to have him desire her.

Even as he molded her to him, Dana began to unbutton his shirt, eager to feel his skin against hers. When one of the buttons held fast, she tugged, almost ripping it off.

He stopped her hands with his, leaning in to nibble on her lower lip. "Hey, slow down, we have all night."

"All night?" She was going to have to get back to Mollie. And if she came in with the morning, it might initiate an argument with her father. She didn't want to risk that. "But I can't—" Rafe kissed her throat, making the words that were forming melt away. Her hands tightened on his shoulders, not to stop him, but to steady herself as she began to lose feeling in her knees. "I've got to—"

"Call home," he urged as one kiss rained down in the wake of the last. "Tell them you'll be there in the morning." And then he drew his head back to look at her. Her pupils were large, her eyes dazed. She'd never been more beautiful to him. "Stay the night with me, Dana."

Oh, God, she wanted to. With all her heart, she wanted to.

"I can't." Her voice became progressively less forceful. "Mollie. My father—"

"Stay for me." The words were whispered along her skin, seductive, sensual. Erasing the last of her protests.

Dana wound her arms around him tightly. The imprint of his hard body heated hers. She was already losing. "God, but you drive a hard bargain."

"I mean to win."

He took full advantage of having her like this, gently making love to her with his hands until she thought she was going to vibrate out of her skin.

He was searching for a zipper at the base of her spine. Dana felt her loins quickening. "How do you take this thing off?"

"First you unbutton it here." Her eyes on his face, she unfastened the three buttons at the back of her neck. The two sides floated down, coming to rest on the tempting swell of her breasts. "And then you tug."

"Like this?" Carefully, as if afraid of hurting her, he drew the material away from her. As it dropped to her waist, he cupped her breasts with his hands, his thumbs gently rubbing against her nipples. Dana moaned, pressing against his palms, reveling in the sensations he was arousing within her. She could feel herself growing damp. Could feel her emptiness crying out for him to fill her.

"Exactly like that," she murmured.

His breath catching in his lungs, Rafe tugged at the gown, easing it over the swell of her hips. The effort was minimal. In a heartbeat the gown sank to the floor.

Venus rising from a silver seashell, he thought. Without a word, Rafe picked her up in his arms and carried her to his bedroom.

Even as a rush came over her, she couldn't help noticing

the state of the bed. In direct contrast to everything else in the apartment, it was neat. She began to laugh.

"What?" Whatever it was, even at his expense, he wanted to share the joke with her. Wanted to share everything with her. Always.

"You made your bed."

The grin was lopsided and sheepish. "That's ingrained. My mother always nagged me about it. Now I make my bed first thing after I get up, usually when I'm still three-quarters asleep."

Gently, he placed her on the blue and beige comforter, then lay down next to her.

"Does nagging work?" She peeled his shirt from him and threw it on the floor.

"Only about making the bed." Though it took an effort to remain still, to keep his hands off her, Rafe let her unbuckle his belt. Anticipation drummed through him as she undressed him, lightly skimming her cool fingers along his upper thighs, knowingly driving him crazy.

Unable to take it anymore, he flipped her onto her back after his slacks and underwear were discarded. For the next part of eternity, he fascinated himself and pleasured her by exploring her body like a man who had never made love to a woman before. He feasted on her with his eyes, with his hands, with his lips and tongue, until there was nothing left of her but a throbbing mass of needs and desires.

When he made her come the first time, she had to bite on her lower lip to keep from crying out, the explosion within her was so violent. So wondrous.

She squirmed against him, feeling his breath hot on her thighs, on that most sensitive part of her. As she began to protest that it was too one-sided, he began again, teasing her, slowly working his way in with his tongue. She grabbed the comforter beneath her and would have torn tufts of it out if she'd had the strength as another explosion rocked her.

Summoning her last bit of strength, she rolled onto him, reversing their positions. Using the same techniques he'd employed on her, she teased, explored and aroused. Growing bolder and more wanton, testing her newfound power, she took her turn at making him want, at making him twist with mounting desire.

She branded him with lips that were by turns cool, passionate, then fiery. With eyes that flashed with delight, she teased him just the way he had teased her, pulling back just before he reached his climax.

Had there been other men who'd felt like this with her? Other men she'd done this with? As quickly as the questions came, they died. He didn't want to know about the men who had come before him.

The only thing he wanted was to make her forget them tonight and all the nights afterward.

His body glistening with sweat, primed, aching, he linked his fingers through hers, pinning her with his weight. Then, holding her a willing prisoner, he kissed her over and over again. Lightly, then passionately, then lightly again, alternating until she was writhing so hard beneath him that he was afraid she would make him come before he entered her.

Unable to hold back any longer, Rafe parted her legs with his knee. His eyes holding hers, he slowly sheathed himself within her.

Dana felt the pulsating need, the hardness she had created, and felt desperately empowered, desperately excited.

Then they gave themselves up to the rhythm that seized them, moving ever faster toward what they both wanted, both needed. And when it happened, when the climax enveloped them both, they clung to it as if it was the very salvation that neither had ever dreamed they would find.

Rafe slowly rolled to the side, gathering her to him. Breathing in deeply of her scent mingled with the sweat of their lovemaking. Wanting her all over again.

He wanted to keep her with him all night, to make love with her over and over again for as long as was humanly possible. Or until he expired. He didn't care which. All he cared about was having her here.

He rubbed his cheek against her hair. He hadn't thought it was possible to feel this content. "Stay with me, Dana."

The euphoria was already leaving, taking her giddy peace with it. In its wake came the burden of what she had to tell him.

What she didn't want to tell him.

Maybe if she said it now, while his eyes were mellow with lovemaking and his body was still warm from hers, he would find it in his heart not to blame her. Not to hate her. "Rafe, I—"

The rhythmic beep emanating from his pager chased away what courage she had, silencing the words she was about to say.

Relief shivered through her at the reprieve. She pulled the comforter around her, then dragged her hand through her hair, trying to make herself presentable. "Shouldn't you answer that?"

It was too late to wish that he had thought to ask someone to take his calls all night. He'd thought a few hours would be enough, never thinking she would come home with him after the dance. "Yes." He sighed, zeroing in on the pager, still clipped to the pocket of his trousers. "I should."

It was his service. Checking in, he listened to the particulars, then nodded. "Tell them I'm on my way and to meet me in the emergency room. And not to panic."

Hanging up, he turned to look at her. She had already gotten her gown and was slipping into it. "I'm sorry about this."

"Don't be. It's nice to know you care. About kids," she added quickly, in case he thought she was taking something for granted. If he cared about her, he would tell her. Until then, she would assume that what was going on between them was a very torrid affair.

It was probably better if she just went with that assumption.

"Whoever called your service at this hour is probably going out of their mind with worry—the way I was. It's nice to know there's a knight in shining stethoscope we can turn to.''

''That's me,'' he muttered. ''Sir Pediatrician.'' He reached into his closet for a pair of jeans. ''No chance of my talking you into staying here until I get back, is there?'' Rafe knew what her answer would be before she shook her head. ''I didn't think so.''

''There's no telling how long you'll be gone, and I should be getting back.'' She slipped her shoes on. ''Can you drop me off on your way there? Or should I call a cab?''

He pulled a jersey on and shoved his feet into a worn pair of running shoes ''No cab.'' He took her arm, heading for the front door. ''One look at that gown and the cab driver will drive straight to Acapulco with you. I'll take you home.'' Longing and a sense of something missed suddenly hit him with the force of a well-delivered punch to the gut. Turning her around, he kissed her passionately. When she stared at him, speechless, he smiled. ''One for the road.''

Dana swallowed, waiting for her voice to return. He certainly knew how to rock her world. ''Kiss me like that again and I won't let you go on the road.''

He laughed, taking her hand again. ''Promises, promises.''

That was all she had to give, she thought, tugging on his hand to make him stop as she grabbed her clutch purse from where she'd dropped it earlier. Promises. Promises he might not want once he knew everything.

Chapter 19

She was setting herself up for a fall.

Dana frowned at her reflection in the mirror as she opened a drawer. There was no getting away from it. She had to face the fact that a reckoning was coming. It was just a matter of time.

Time, the one thing she needed. The one thing she didn't have.

Dana shoved the drawer closed with her hip. They had been seeing each other whenever they could for the past two weeks, filling in the wide gaps in between with short, impulsive phone calls. She'd never believed she could feel so happy, so alive.

As long as she banked down any thoughts of the inevitable.

Dana tossed the underwear she'd just chosen into the cloth overnight bag that lay open on her bed. A pair of white shorts followed.

Funny how feelings refused to be packed away so neatly. No matter how hard she tried to deny it, to keep the lines clearly drawn between enjoying herself and falling in love, she'd gone and done it. No two ways about it, Dana thought, she was an idiot. Reason and logic, joined with the past, hadn't been enough to stop her. Hadn't been enough to prevent it from happening. Like a headstrong child, she'd plunged headfirst into something she'd sworn she would never do.

She'd fallen in love with Rafe.

Dana sighed, adding a pink and white striped pullover to the bag. Emotions weren't subject to sanctions and controls. You couldn't fall in love with someone just because you gave yourself permission to do it. And you couldn't *not* fall in love with someone just because you knew it was wrong. Just because you were so afraid of being hurt again.

Dana pulled a turquoise bathing suit out of her dresser. It was halfway to the bag before she changed her mind. No sense tempting fate. She still wasn't showing, but she didn't want to risk drawing Rafe's attention to her body any more than necessary. That was why all the tops were loose, all the shorts baggy. Her precautions might seem silly since he would certainly see her naked when they made love, but that was different. Because when she was naked, he wasn't really looking at her, he was in the grip of passion, the same as she was, and passion always blurred things.

Like common sense.

She had to tell him. After this weekend, she would have to tell him. She could almost feel the burden weighing her down. The longer she waited, the worse it would seem. She knew that, and yet something within her kept stopping her from telling him. Something within her kept crying out, "More, just a little more."

Her mouth curved. Just like Oliver Twist, she thought, who'd asked for more.

Dana sank down on the bed beside the overnight bag. The problem with more was that it was endless.

Just like her craving for Rafe.

She knew there was no satiating her where Rafe was concerned. It wasn't a matter of once or twice and then she was satisfied and on her way. Until the day she died, she would go on wanting Rafe, wanting to make love with him. Wanting to lie in his arms when the lights were low and breathing returned to normal, feeling safe. Pretending that what there was between them was love. It wasn't such a stretch.

After all, part of it was already true. She loved him.

Dana drew the overnight bag to her. Well, that was it, she decided, closing the flap. She wasn't going to need very much for this weekend.

Rafe had told her to pack only a toothbrush and a favorite lure, if she had one. Dana smiled at the memory of that conversation. She'd thought he was talking about a sexy nightgown. Turned out Rafe was talking about a real lure, the kind used for fishing. She'd been surprised to discover that he loved to fish. She'd never been near a pole in her life. When he heard that, the agenda for the weekend was set—fishing lessons and lovemaking, not necessarily, he made it clear, in that order.

Dana couldn't wait. She didn't particularly want to go fishing, but for him, she was willing to put up with it, hooks, worms and all. Who knew, it might even be fun. Everything, it seemed to her, was fun as long as it was with him.

Early Saturday morning, they were going to drive up to the cabin his parents owned on Lake Elsinore. It would be just the two of them—and the fishing lures. He'd wanted to do something special with her, because he knew this was the last weekend before the trial got under way, now that jury selection was over. From here on in, her hours would be even more limited than they had been. And he understood that, she marveled. There was no indication that he resented having to share her with her work, and certainly no hint that he didn't like sharing her with Mollie. He was in a class by himself.

Maybe, just maybe…

The doorbell rang. Rafe. She grabbed her bag and flew down the stairs, anticipation fluttering through her.

One last weekend, she thought, her feet hitting the stairs.

Forty-eight hours more, that was all she wanted. And then she would tell him.

Rafe looked at her, trying very hard not to laugh. How could anyone with such a graceful body have such an awkward form while fishing? She looked like a mannequin someone had hastily posed before hurrying away.

That was all right, he mused. She had other virtues. If he concentrated, he could still feel her lips racing along his face, her hands eagerly divesting him of his clothing the moment they'd walked into the cabin.

She was like a tigress, a wild creature just barely tamed. He almost hadn't been able to keep up with her. The thought made him grin. The grin grew as he watched in silence while Dana tried to cast again and failed miserably. The line had skimmed the stream and floated back to her like a misshapen boomerang.

At least it was better than her first two casts, which had gotten tangled in the branches above them. Given enough time and patience, he figured he could make a fisherman out of her yet.

And he meant to give her all the time in the world.

"What are you grinning about?" she demanded, reeling her line in, determined to attempt another cast. Eventually it would have to go where it was supposed to, wouldn't it?

"Nothing," he answered innocently, but his eyes continued smiling as Dana got her line caught in the branches again. God, but it was peaceful here. He loved his work, but it was nice to leave everything behind once in a while. As long as he had someone to share it with.

Rafe glanced toward her. "I know I should have told you to bring Mollie, but I wanted to be alone with you."

Maybe it would work better if she ventured a little farther into the stream, the way he did. Standing on the bank and casting wasn't working. She yanked her line from the lowest branch.

"Just you, me and several hundred fish." Or so he had

said. She had yet to see any evidence of that. ''Very romantic.''

Rafe laughed softly. ''You have to keep your voice low, or they'll hear you.''

The pole slipped in her hands as she tried her umpteenth cast. The lure caught the edge of her cutoffs, barely missing her thigh. She gritted her teeth in frustration, working the lure out of the frayed edges. ''I'm not ashamed of what I'm saying.''

He could only shake his head. Maybe this wasn't such a good idea after all. Fishing relaxed him, but it was obviously doing just the opposite with her. ''It's not that. The noise might scare them away.''

''I knew that.'' She blew out a breath. There was a trick to this, she knew it. Why couldn't she get it? ''What I don't know is how to cast this stupid thing into the water.''

Rafe reeled in his line. He'd offered to help her when they started, but she'd insisted on doing it herself. Maybe she would let him help her now.

''Want my help?''

She looked at him, exasperated. Pride shuffled away, head bowed. ''Yes.''

As he began wading toward her, she decided to meet him halfway. The cool water would be a welcome relief on her legs. But as she began to gingerly pick her way over the rocks, she lost her footing. Her feet flew out from under her, and she came down hard, hitting her tailbone on a rock.

For a second Dana felt light-headed and disoriented, and then the pain descended in full force to claim her. An involuntary groan escaped her lips.

Rafe dropped his rod and ran the last few feet to her. Worried, he fell to his knees beside her. ''Are you all right?''

She couldn't speak. All her faculties were focused on trying to deal with the pain that was firing in all directions through her abdomen. Without realizing it, she clutched at his hand, holding on so tightly her fingers were turning white. The pain wouldn't leave.

"I'm okay," she whispered raggedly. "Just let me catch my breath."

She was definitely *not* okay. She was rocking like someone trying to find a place for themselves amid a fiery pit of pain. He turned her face toward the sun for a better view. Her eyes looked dazed.

"I think that's enough fishing for—Dana, you're bleeding."

She couldn't assimilate what he was saying. Something about bleeding? He was staring at the water beneath her. Confused, she looked down.

The water around her shorts was turning a dirty, dull shade of pink. Or was that red? She couldn't think. The pain wouldn't let her. It refused to subside.

And then, suddenly, she realized what it was. Blood. Her blood.

Her nails dug into his hand. "Oh, my God, the baby." Her breath left her as panic leaped into the center of the circle of pain. "I'm losing the baby." Her eyes widened as she stared at the water again. "Rafe, I'm going to lose the baby."

It was his turn to feel confused. What was she talking about?

"Baby?" He stared at her. She wasn't pregnant. Was she? "What baby?"

Hysteria threatened to break through, to sweep her away. This couldn't be happening, not after she'd come to terms with having this baby. Not after she'd braced herself to sacrifice everything to bring this child into the world.

"*My* baby!" Dana cried.

The first time he'd made love to her was over a month ago. It was possible, just possible, that—

Oh, God.

"Why didn't you tell—damn, never mind." This was no time for recriminations or demands. Words could come later. There would be time enough then to sort everything out. He had to concentrate on the emergency he had on his hands.

His thoughts, so jumbled a moment ago, threw themselves

into a structured whole. There was nothing in the house that would be of any help in this situation. She needed a hell of a lot more than peroxide and Band-Aids, or even what he had available in his medical bag. "I've got to get you to the hospital, baby."

Baby, her baby. Dana clawed at him. He had to help, had to save her child. "Rafe, I can't lose this baby. I just can't."

Fear tied a tourniquet around his heart as it fought for control of the rest of him. He couldn't let her see what he was going through. It would only make it worse for her. Damn it, he was trained for this.

No, he was trained for other people's emergencies, not his own. It was always different when it was yours. What if she…

No!

He wasn't going to go there, wasn't going to think that. Nothing was going to happen to her, *nothing*. He wouldn't allow it.

His voice was calm as he said, "You're not going to lose the baby. Just hang on, everything's going to be all right. Do you hear me, Dana?"

Weakly, she nodded, clutching at his words. Holding him to them.

She swallowed a groan as he picked her up, biting hard on her lower lip and not even feeling it. Every step he took vibrated through her, intensifying the pain.

Rafe moved as quickly as he dared. His heart was pounding by the time he reached the car. As gently as he could manage, he eased her into the back seat. "Lie down, Dana."

There was horror on her face, "You've got blood on your shirt."

He looked down. Her blood was smeared across the bottom of his shirt. He had to stop the bleeding, or at least slow it down. He stripped off his shirt, wadded it up, then pressed it between her legs. He wedged his medical bag under her hips, elevating them as best he could.

He guided her hand to the shirt. "Now hold that there. Press as hard as you can," he ordered. "It's the best I can do to stop the bleeding.'' Because she looked so helpless, he stopped to kiss her. It was a rough kiss, an urgent kiss, meant to make him feel better as well as her. ''I won't let anything happen to you, I swear.''

He prayed in his heart that nothing would make him break his promise.

''Hang on,'' he ordered, jamming the key into the ignition.

He knew he was in a race against time. As long as she didn't lose too much blood, there was hope.

Memories of Debra, of the insane ride to the hospital as he tried to outrace death that last time, haunted him. He hadn't made it then, although what he'd expected the hospital staff to do he didn't know. She'd died before he could reach it.

That wasn't going to happen again. Sweet God, that wasn't going to happen again.

Rafe drove from the cabin and its idyllic setting like a madman. There was no hospital between here and Harris Memorial. Familiar with all the back roads, all the shortcuts, he took them at speeds that would have horrified him if he was paying attention to the speedometer. But he wasn't. All he could think was that he had to get Dana to the hospital. To people who could help her. Nothing else mattered except saving Dana.

Sheila felt drained. Perspiration plastered her scrubs to her body, and she could feel a fresh line of sweat trickling down her back. It had been touch and go there for a few minutes. She didn't want to dwell on how it might have gone had Rafe arrived any later.

This, she reminded herself, was one of the good moments. One of those magical saves she had been trained for. It felt a little surreal when it involved a friend.

Two friends, she amended, coming out of the room. Rafe was in the hallway, standing like a steadfast tin soldier, his back pressed against the wall. No doubt for support. He looked terrible, she thought, her heart going out to him. He looked like a man who thought he was on a deathwatch.

He had called her on his car phone, snapping out details, and she'd never heard him sound like that before. As if he was holding himself together through sheer grit. She'd gone racing to the hospital and met them in the emergency room. The rest was a blur of hands, transfusions and efforts that were superhuman and ingrained.

It had worked. Mother and unborn child were both going to be fine.

Rafe came to attention as soon as he saw Sheila. He refused to try to read her expression. Sheila was always determined to be upbeat about everything, no matter what. He wanted to hear the words.

"How is she?"

Sheila wasted no time before reassuring him. "She's going to be fine, Rafe. You got her here just in time. A little longer and...well, no need to go there." She paused. "I'd like her to stay overnight, just to rest, but there's no need to worry. She'll be able to go home in the morning."

An almost overwhelming relief, bordering on euphoria, washed over him, leaving him weak. She was all right. Dana was going to be all right. "And the baby?"

Sheila nodded, looking at him closely. Trying to read his expression. "The baby's safe. Like I said, you got her here just in time." Sheila paused, not knowing exactly how to proceed. How much did he know? "She told you about the baby?"

"No, not exactly." In the absolute sense, she hadn't told him at all. She'd just blurted it out in her panic. He wasn't even sure if Dana knew what she'd said to him. She'd clearly been in shock.

Being a friend meant placing curiosity by the wayside sometimes. The problem was, she was friends with both of them. The only side she wanted to take was the side that saw them happy.

Sheila nodded toward the door behind her. "You can go in to see her now if you'd like."

His mouth hardened a little as he looked toward the room. "Yeah."

When she placed her hand on his arm, Rafe didn't even seem to notice. "Are you all right, Rafe?"

A baby. Why hadn't she told him? Why did he have to find out this way? He shook off his thoughts when he realized that Sheila had asked him a question. "Shouldn't I be?"

There was a defensiveness in his voice. And something else she couldn't quite make out. Tactfully, she backed away. She knew he wouldn't take kindly to being the target of advice right now.

"No, of course not. I'll see you later."

Rafe barely acknowledged her words. He eased open the door to Dana's room and let himself in quietly, in case she'd fallen asleep. He wanted to see her, to assure himself that she was all right, before he released the other feelings that were beating their fists inside him.

Her eyes darted toward the door the moment he entered. Her fear of losing the baby had been set to rest, but another, equally strong fear had taken its place. She held her breath, watching him walk toward her. She expected anger to crease his face, but it didn't. Instead, there was an expression there she couldn't read.

The fear wouldn't go away.

Still weak, she held her hand out to him. "Rafe, I'm so sorry." The words sounded hopelessly insignificant to her ears.

"It's okay, baby, it's okay." Rafe took her hand, wrapping his around it. Color was beginning to slip into her face. She looked exhausted. He knew he should let her rest, but he had to know, had to understand. "Why didn't you tell me you were pregnant?"

They'd given her something to make her relax. She struggled against its effects. She couldn't think, couldn't find the words to make this sound right. Her brain felt like so much wet cotton.

She shrugged helplessly. "Not enough courage."

What did courage have to do with it? Did she think he would reject her? Didn't she know him well enough to realize he wouldn't do that? "Dana, as the baby's father, I had a right to know."

As the baby's father. He thought it was his.

Dana closed her eyes, fighting tears. He'd given her a way out, handed it to her on a silver tray. It was so easy. So easy. She could…

No, she couldn't. Not ever. Not even to keep him.

The next words that came out of her mouth were the hardest she'd ever had to say. "Rafe, it's not your baby."

"Not my—" What did she mean, it wasn't his? "Then who—" An icy hand passed over his heart. "Steven?" He dropped her hand as he spoke.

She pressed her lips together, feeling the tears gathering in her soul, the sickening taste of fear filling her mouth. But he had to be told.

"Yes."

Numb, he could only stare at her. "How long have you known?"

She felt as if every word she uttered was pushing him away from her. "Since the morning before I met you."

He couldn't believe it. Couldn't make himself believe it. She'd known all along. Making love with him, she'd known. "And you didn't say anything?"

His voice was low, emotionless. Steely. Fear slid down her back like an icicle. Not even facing her father had made her feel like this.

Confused, dazed and backed into a corner, she felt herself irrationally lashing out. "What could I say? 'Hello, I'm Dana Morrow, cure my niece and, oh, yes, by the way, I'm pregnant by a man who hates children'?"

She could have found a way to tell him, he thought. There must have been an opening, some point when she felt they were getting serious, when she could have told him. He deserved that from her.

"Does he know?"

She nodded. "He knows," she said bitterly. "And denies it's his. Says he can get a whole clubhouse full of his friends to swear I was the town slut." Dana looked at him. He had to believe her. "I wasn't. I don't sleep around. I never did. And it matters to me that you believe that. You matter." She reached out to him, but he didn't take her hand.

Temper heated the blood in his veins. He raised his voice. "If I mattered so much, why didn't you tell me?"

She wasn't going to cry. She wasn't going to give him the satisfaction of knowing he was hurting her. Didn't he realize the hell she'd been going through? Was still going through? "Don't yell at me," she snapped.

That only added fuel to the fire. "What do you expect me to do, stand up and cheer? Applaud? Just how long did you think you could keep this from me?" he demanded.

"I don't know." As suddenly as her anger had filled her, it drained away. She told him the truth, even though she knew he wouldn't believe her. And it was her fault. "I was playing for time. Days. Minutes. Every minute you didn't know was a minute longer I had with you."

Frustration tore holes in her. She didn't know how to make him understand. She could argue eloquently before a jury, but where her own case was concerned, she couldn't summon the words with which to plead. She could only pray.

"At first there was no reason to tell you. And then there was every reason *not* to tell you." She threw her last card onto the pile. "I was afraid, all right?"

But he shook his head at her, at the words. "I don't know if it's all right. I don't know anything at all anymore."

He was backing away from her. Leaving. And she couldn't blame him. Not rationally. But emotionally, she felt like hurling things at him for disappointing her this way. For deserting her.

Dana drew herself together, trying to ignore the emptiness that was growing within her. "I'm sorry if I can't live up to some pristine image that you have. I can't be like Debra."

She'd struck a direct hit. "Leave Debra out of this."

It was as if he'd stuck a knife into her heart and then twisted it. She'd been wrong about him all along, about his gentleness, his kindness. Terribly wrong. Wrong again. What a surprise.

"Not even good enough to talk about her, is that it?" She spat the words out. "Fine, I won't. Now you get out of my room, Dr. Saldana."

For a second he hesitated. No matter what she'd done, he didn't want to leave her this way. "Dana, I—"

But she wasn't going to listen, didn't want to look at him anymore. "Just get out. Now!"

She maintained her cold fury just long enough for the door to close behind him. And then she dissolved into tears and cried her heart out.

What was left of it.

Chapter 20

"Dr. Saldana, would you be willing to squeeze in Allison Adray this afternoon?" Knocking as she opened the door, Alice peered into the doctor's office. "Her mother just called. She thinks Allison's coming down with something."

Irritated at being interrupted, Rafe glared in the nurse's direction. Was it too much to ask for five minutes of peace?

"Her mother always thinks she's coming down with something. The woman is trying to make hypochondria a family affair. If we're booked, Alice, tell her so," he snapped.

The look on Alice's face brought him up sharply. He could see exactly what she thought of the mood he was in. The mood he had resided in for the past two and a half weeks.

Silently, Alice turned on her heel and walked away. "As you wish, Doctor."

He sighed, trying to control his temper. Of late, he felt as if he was teetering on the edge of losing it all the time. Everything annoyed him. Misplaced tongue depressors, interruptions, the color yellow. Everything and anything. He had to get hold of himself.

"No, scratch that," he called after Alice. "Tell her to get down here as soon as she can. I'll see what's wrong with Allison this time—besides her mother."

"Fine, I'll tell her."

He wasn't forgiven, Rafe thought as he shut the door. But that was her problem. He had other things to deal with than an overly sensitive nurse who doubled as a receptionist.

When the door opened again almost immediately, Rafe threw down his pen in exasperation. Since when had his office been declared an intersection?

"What is it now? All I asked for was a few minutes of peace to write up some notes."

Instead of Alice or one of the other nurses, it was Gabe who walked into the room. He looked a little surprised at the greeting. "Wow, your bedside manner has really gone to hell, hasn't it?"

Rafe gave up on the report. Maybe he could get to it later. "Sorry, just a little on edge lately." He pushed himself back from the desk and looked at his younger brother. Gabe was in uniform, so he was still on duty. "What are you doing here?"

Gabe made himself comfortable in the chair across from Rafe's desk. He noted the tension in his brother's face. Something was up.

"I was in the neighborhood, and I thought I'd let you take me to lunch, seeing as how you're the successful brother." His lopsided grin appeared. "Unless, of course, you're seeing your lady."

His lady. No, she wasn't his lady, Rafe thought. She wasn't his anything, not anymore. Nearly three weeks had gone by since he'd seen her. Three weeks down and a lifetime to go. He figured it would take that long to get his life on an even keel again. Right now, it was completely upended, and he had all he could do to make it from one end of the day to the other.

Rafe turned his attention to the file on his desk. "No, I'm not seeing her."

Though they didn't see each other much anymore, he and Rafe were close enough for Gabe to pick up the nuances that might have escaped others. He'd only seen his brother like this once before.

"You say that with a lot of conviction." He lowered his face until he could get a better look at Rafe's. "Trouble in paradise?"

It was useless to try to concentrate. Not with Gabe yammering at him, getting in his face. And not with his head so messed up.

"No, we just weren't right together." Rafe's voice was cool, detached. "You know how it is." Why did he have to explain himself to Gabe, of all people? "Hell, you go from one woman to another like a bee goes from flower to flower, pollinating them."

Gabe continued studying Rafe as he spoke. "Yeah, I guess I do. But that's me, not you." His eyes met his brother's. "You don't pollinate, Rafe. You're a one-flower bee." Rafe was hurting, Gabe thought. And too bullheaded to admit it. Like all the Saldana men, he supposed. "And you don't attach yourself to that flower unless you're damn sure. Okay, tell me. What gives?"

Talking about his feelings had never come easily to Rafe. It was no different now. "Nothing."

Gabe rose and went to the door. But instead of leaving, he closed it, then returned to face Rafe. "Behind this smiling exterior is a damn good cop, bro. I'm not leaving until I get the goods." Pulling the extra chair around until it was positioned directly beside Rafe's, Gabe straddled it. "Now, are you going to tell me, or are we going to sit here all day, staring at each other?"

Rafe hated being put on the spot, but he knew Gabe wouldn't back off. He hung on like a damn terrier when he wanted to, just like their father. "You want to know? All right, I'll tell you. She's pregnant."

The information took a minute to sink in. And then Gabe

was reaching for Rafe's hand, slapping him on the back. "Hey, congra—"

Rafe pushed his brother's hand away, rising. "It's not mine." He began pacing the room, impatience bubbling in his veins.

Thrown, Gabe could only stare at him. "Not yours? Then whose..."

Angry, without a target to take it out on, Rafe shoved his hands into his pockets. "The last guy she was with."

Gabe was trying to make sense of the fragments coming his way. "She sleeps around." Even as he said it, it didn't feel right. The woman he'd seen with his brother, the woman he'd danced with, didn't seem to be that type.

Rafe wheeled around, defending a woman he'd blocked out of his life. "No!"

Though his brother banked it down quickly enough, Gabe didn't miss the emotion on his face. No matter what he said to the contrary, Rafe had feelings, strong feelings, for Dana. Gabe was willing to bet his badge on it.

Gabe continued studying Rafe's face, his movements. "She break up with this guy before she met you?"

The shrug was halfhearted and dismissive. "Yeah."

Then why was Rafe so mad? Unless...

"And is she going back to him?" Gabe guessed.

"No, and that's not the point." Rafe glared at Gabe, tired of being grilled.

He was good at untangling things, Gabe thought, but he was going to need a little help here. "What *is* the point?" he asked seriously. "It can't be that you don't want kids, because I've seen you with them. Hell, you're better with kids than most people."

Because they were brothers, and because he knew Gabe cared, Rafe struggled to hang on to his temper. To keep from telling Gabe to take his questions and get the hell out. "The point is she kept it from me. She wouldn't tell me, wouldn't be honest with me. If she hadn't fallen..."

Gabe jumped on the information. "She fell?"

"Stop interrupting, damn it!" Rafe dragged his hand through his hair, trying to collect himself. Everything inside him felt raw. "That weekend we went up to the cabin, she slipped on a rock. She came down hard and started bleeding. That's when she told me." Even talking about it upset him. Made him relive it all. "I drove her to the hospital." He began pacing again. "I don't even remember driving. All I could think of was saving her, saving the baby." His mouth twisted in a mocking smile. "I had this crazy notion the baby was mine."

Gabe watched him steadily. "But she told you it wasn't."

"What does it matter what she told me? It's over."

If that was the case, Rafe wouldn't have looked like something the dog dragged in. "Is it?"

Rafe was in no mood for rhetorical questions. "I just said—"

"Yeah, words. I know you, Rafe. Once you're in, you're in. You're not the type to back away. I think you're using this whole thing as an excuse. A smoke screen to hide what's really going on." He knew his brother better than he knew anyone, probably including himself. Gabe rose to face him. "I think you're afraid."

That was absolutely ridiculous. "Of what?" Rafe demanded.

"Of being hurt again. Of what you went through when Debra died." Gabe put his hand on Rafe's shoulder, only to have it shrugged off. Gabe took no offense. If the tables had been turned, he would probably have taken a swing at Rafe. "Think about it."

Gabe crossed to the door. He'd said as much as he could. He couldn't make Rafe see what he refused to see. That part was up to Rafe.

"I'll see you around, bro. Think about it," he repeated, closing the door behind him.

"Dana, I need you."

Startled, Dana looked up slowly from the briefcase she was

packing. Without realizing it, she tightened her fingers on the notes she'd prepared for her father's cross-examination of one of the prosecution's key witnesses.

She had to be dreaming.

All her life, she'd secretly waited for those words. But there had to be some mistake. Her father had always made a point of not needing anyone. He liked comparing himself to a venerable oak. He stood alone.

She let the notes drop into the open briefcase. "Excuse me?"

Impatient, her father pushed his chair into her room. "Something wrong with your hearing? I said I need you." She was still looking at him blankly, as if she'd lost the ability to understand her native tongue. "At the trial today, I need you to sit at the table."

The table was full. There was her father, then David Headley, the second chair, and Alex McGuire, who rounded out the defense team.

"But David and Alex—"

His impatience grew. He didn't stand protests well. "Alex was in a waterskiing accident yesterday." He dismissed the incident as being beneath his interest. "Trying to impress someone. The fool knew better than to take chances." Morrow hated the unexpected when a case was being tried. "I expect my people to remain sane during a case."

She thought of his partner. Surely Wallace would have something to say about him choosing her, even if her father's name was the first on the door. He didn't like using "untried talent," as he called it. The trial was beginning to turn in their favor, with new evidence that cast doubt on the senator's guilt, but it wasn't like her father to venture out on uncertain ground.

"What about Mr. Wallace?"

Morrow's eyes seemed to glitter. "Wallace has taken an early retirement." There was nothing but contempt in his voice for the man he deemed to be a traitor in his ranks. "The very thing he wanted for me. I thought it only fair to return his thoughtfulness.'' Elbows on the armrests, he brought his fingertips together, watching her face. ''That leaves you.''

He'd forgotten about the others, all of whom had seniority on her. ''And—''

He was through bandying this about. ''I know who else I have working for me. I also know their abilities.'' His eyes narrowed. ''I watched you try a case once. You were good. Not spectacular, and you could stand work, but you were good.''

''When? When did you see me?'' He had never been in any courtroom she'd pleaded in. Dana would have sworn to it.

Morrow didn't brook questioning, either. ''My house, girl. I ask the questions. You're who I want. Will you be up to it?''

She swallowed, suddenly feeling breathless and confused at the same time. ''Yes, of course, it's just that you've taken me by surprise.''

The admission pleased him. He laughed to himself. ''That's what I do best. I take people by surprise.'' Feeling expansive, he shared something with her. ''Ever since I was a skinny, snot-nosed kid, I've taken people by surprise.'' He looked away. ''I probably took my father by surprise. He expected me to die in a gutter somewhere.''

Dana felt like someone on the bomb squad, reaching to touch a wire, hoping not to set off an explosion but to prevent one. And to learn from it. Dana kept her eyes on his face, watching for a warning. She inched a little further into uncharted territory. ''You never told me anything about my grandfather.''

He knew that. He'd never told anyone about the family he was ashamed of, the background he'd buried so successfully. Not even his wife. She'd been given very little information, and what there was of it had been false. ''That's because I've always operated on a need-to-know basis. You didn't need to know.''

"And now?" she asked. Did he think she needed to know now? "I'd like to know now," she added.

He looked at her for a long moment, as if a debate was being waged in his mind. And then, finally, he spoke. "There's not much to tell. He was an abusive drunk. That's what made him the perfect match for my mother." There was no nostalgia in his voice, no wistfulness. Just disgust. "Between the two of them, they must have drunk half of Oklahoma dry."

"Oklahoma?" she repeated, confused. "Why Oklahoma?"

He spoke curtly. "Because that's where I'm from."

That wasn't what her mother had told her. "I thought—"

He knew exactly what she thought, because he'd invented it, down to the last detail. And covered his tracks well. "The official story is San Francisco. Wealthy background, breeding, trust fund, best schools." He rattled it off, knowing it by heart. The heart people claimed he didn't have. "The only part of it that's true is the best schools. And you know why?"

Dana slowly moved her head from side to side, her eyes riveted to her father.

"Because I did anything I had to to get into them. I was on the street by the time I was fourteen." There was no humor in his laugh. "If I hadn't been, my father would eventually have killed me." Even as he said it, the beatings returned to him. A belt buckle, newly sharpened, catching his flesh, tearing it as it came down. "It was just a matter of time. I didn't intend to wait for it. So I left, survived, made something of myself. You get famous by being the best, so I became the best, courting the limelight as if it was half debutante, half whore. But you can't court it if you come from roots you're ashamed of. So I cut my roots and didn't look back. After a while, I began to believe in the image I created. I *became* that man.

"There," he said dismissively, "you have it. The real story." It was a moment before he looked at her. She looked appropriately surprised. Good. If there had been pity in her expression, she would have paid dearly for it. "If I left compassion out, it's because I never really came across it until it was almost too late.'' He'd said this much, he thought, he might as well say the rest of it. ''Your mother was compassionate at first, but it was wasted on me, because I had my eye on a goal, and nothing was going to get in my way. Not even her love.''

Dana didn't understand. After years of keeping her out, why the sudden change? ''Why are you telling me all this?''

He didn't like explaining himself, but he supposed, in this instance, because he was the one who had initiated it, he could cut her somc slack. ''I thought maybe you should know. And there's no one to tell you but me. Who knows how much longer I'll be around?''

She hated this talk of dying. Science was progressing all the time. There had to be something that could be done for her father. ''Don't say that.''

He was careful not to show any emotion. Emotion clouded your brain, made you clumsy. And it made you lose.

''Never be afraid of the truth. If you have it, you can use it as a weapon.'' Time was growing short, and he had yet to talk to his people about Day Thirteen of the trial. ''Ready? The car is waiting.''

She nodded. He turned the chair and began to leave the room. ''Father?''

He waited for her to join him. ''Yes?''

''Thanks for telling me.''

He didn't want her thanks, he wanted her loyalty. ''I did it for me, not for you.''

It had a grain of truth in it, but there was more to it than that. She smiled at him and then walked behind, pushing the chair. ''I know, but thanks just the same.''

The second day into that week's proceedings, her father surprised her again. Handing her the notes she'd prepared for the second chair, he had her take over the cross-examination. Stunned, Dana had less than five minutes to pull herself together. She used her edginess to her advantage, wielding it like a well-honed saber. Thrusting, parrying and leaving wounds the prosecution had to deal with.

She was, to his satisfaction, her father's daughter. As he'd known she would be, given the right direction.

When Dana had no more questions for the witness, the judge called a recess. Dana felt as if her knees were about to give out, but it was a good feeling. Her father trusted her. Maybe she was finally on the right track to getting her life in order.

The courtroom rustled as people left their seats. Dana looked in her father's direction, catching his eye. He nodded, saying nothing. She knew better than to expect praise. He'd given her the praise by trusting her.

Relieved, exhausted, Dana sat at the table and began gathering her things. She had two hours before she had to sit here again. Two hours in which to go somewhere and unwind.

Her father and David Headley, the second chair, left while she was still packing her briefcase. She'd turned down their invitation for lunch. She was much too tense to eat.

Thinking she was alone, she was startled when she sensed someone in the room directly behind her. She turned, expecting to see anyone but who she saw.

"Rafe?"

He crossed to her and pushed open the wooden gate that separated the spectators from the players. The greeting he'd rehearsed in his head a dozen times while watching her today seemed trivial and unnecessary.

"My father called me and said he saw you on the news last night. That you were sitting at the defense table. I thought I'd see for myself." The smile was small but genuine. "Pretty impressive." He didn't add that he'd felt proud of her when she'd held up her end against a top assistant D.A.

"Thank you," she responded stiffly, snapping the locks on her briefcase, then picking it up. "If you'll excuse me, I have to be somewhere."

To her exasperation, he fell into step beside her. "Mind if I come along?"

“Yes, I do mind.” Dana stopped and swung around to face him. She wanted no misunderstandings. “The somewhere I have to be is anywhere that you're not.”

He took the direct hit and tried not to wince. “I guess I had that coming.”

Did he think that made them even? That now he could come waltzing into her life and she would welcome him with open arms?

“No, you have a lot more coming than that, but as a criminal lawyer, I know that justifiable homicide isn't always easy to prove.”

He saw the fury in her eyes. And the hurt. He'd done that to her, he thought. The last thing in the world he'd wanted to do.

“Dana, I'm sorry.”

Oh, no, it wasn't going to go like that. “That's it?” she demanded. How dare he? How *dare* he? “You yank my heart out, walk away from me when I need you most, and you're *sorry?*”

He nodded, unable to put it any better than that. “Yes, I'm sorry. Very sorry.”

She wasn't going to be taken in by this. She wasn't. “Fine. Apology accepted. Most men wouldn't be able to deal with the idea of the woman they were currently involved with carrying some other man's child. I understand.” She was trying very hard not to let her voice break under the stress of hiding her emotions. Knowing that was a clear and present danger, she began to push past him. “Now get out of—”

She had to hear him out. He caught her hands in his to keep her from walking out. “I'm not most men, I don't get currently involved, and it's not your baby I have a problem with. It's you.”

She wasn't buying it. She didn't care how sincere his eyes looked. It was a trick, all a trick. “Nicely put.” Her expression was hard, unyielding. She'd learned well from her father. “You're good at twisting knives once you inflict a wound.”

“I have a problem,” he continued, as if she hadn't just

done everything except tell him to go to hell, raising his voice as she walked away, "because I love you."

Dana stopped walking. But she was afraid to turn around. Afraid to hope.

So he came to her. He would have crawled to her if it would have helped.

"Because when I was driving like a madman to the hospital with you bleeding in the back seat, I was completely scared out of my mind that I'd lose you. That you'd die and leave me." Slowly, he circled her, stopping when he faced her. He had to make her understand. "That it was happening all over again, the way it had with Debra. I went to hell and managed to come back the last time. I didn't think I could do it again."

"So you wanted to leave before anything else happened to make you face that kind of ordeal again. All right, I understand. You want—"

"What I want," he interrupted, his hand on her shoulder to keep her from leaving, "is you. The hell of not having you, knowing I could, is worse than anything I could have imagined. I don't even know myself anymore. My patients are backing away from me, my nurses are on the verge of a mutiny, and Sheila…Sheila is threatening to cut off very important portions of my anatomy if I don't straighten up and fly right. I figure that flight has only one destination in its flight plan." He took her hands in his. "Marry me, Dana. Marry me and make me sane again. You'll gain the undying thanks of an awful lot of people."

He was proposing to her. Actually proposing. "It's not every day a girl gets to be a savior."

"No, it's not. Be mine. And I swear, no one will ever love you the way I do."

She smiled. "I already know that."

She'd misunderstood him. He wanted everything to be perfectly clear. "In and out of bed."

"Oh." And then the smile faded, along with the temporary dream. She was an optimist, but not foolishly so. "And the baby? Will you be able to face the baby, knowing it's not yours?''

She was wrong there. ''But it is,'' he insisted. ''The way I see it, if I hadn't gotten you to the hospital in time, that baby would have died. That means I gave it a second chance. I gave it life. That baby is mine as much as it is yours.''

Dana could only look at him in complete disbelief. She was surprised she could find her tongue. ''You would have made a very good lawyer.''

''I'll leave that up to you. One lawyer per couple is plenty.'' He searched her face, trying to find an answer in her expression. ''So, will you? Will you marry me?''

There was so much happiness inside her, she thought she was going to burst. ''What do you think?''

''I think,'' he murmured, feathering his fingers along her face—God, how had he managed to stay away so long? ''If I don't kiss you soon, I'm going to die.''

''Can't have that happening.'' Her eyes were teasing. ''Who would take your place at the wedding?''

''I don't intend for you to find that out. Ever.''

Dana brought his mouth to hers and kissed him. She saw it as an act of mercy. For both of them.

Epilogue

Dana fell back against Rafe's hands, drained, as another hellish contraction receded. Even her eyelashes were heavy with perspiration. It felt as if she'd been at this for hours.

She looked at Sheila, then blinked to see her clearly. Everything looked out of focus in the delivery room.

"Damn, why didn't you tell me it was going to be this hard?"

Sheila shifted on the stool, her back aching. This wasn't going as quickly as she'd hoped, for Dana's sake, it would. Her friend's labor had been going on for seven hours.

She lifted her head to allow the nurse to dry her forehead before the sweat went into her eyes.

"Trust me, you'll forget all about this the first time you hold little what's-it in your arms." She saw the look on Dana's face. Another contraction was coming. Sheila pulled her stool closer. "Just a little more, Dana, push a little more."

Dana wanted to run from the pain, to hide somewhere, anywhere, but it kept finding her, exhausting her. She felt

Rafe gently pushing against her back, moving her into an upright position.

"I don't have a little more," Dana groaned.

Still supporting her, Rafe brought his face in close to hers. "Sure you do. You're the stubbornest woman I know. The stubbornest human being I know," he corrected himself.

He hated seeing her suffering, but there was no way around it. He tried to give her something to hang on to besides the sides of the gurney. He was betting on her feistiness to get her through this.

"Mollie's been waiting outside for hours to find out whether she has a little brother or a sister. How much longer do you intend to keep her waiting?"

They'd made it official. Too impatient to wait, Rafe had married Dana before Senator Johnson's trial was over. Instead of a honeymoon, they'd immediately gone to court to begin adoption proceedings to make Mollie theirs. And then Dana had gone on to be on the winning team of the trial of the decade as the jury brought in a verdict of not guilty. All in all, it had been a hell of a month.

But it was nothing compared to this moment, being here with Dana, waiting for his child to be born. *His* child and no one else's. The bastard whose seed had gone to create this miracle that was happening right before him had signed away all rights, all claims to the baby, in exchange for a set sum of money. This baby was theirs.

"That's right," Dana said, panting, only half feigning anger, "make me feel guilty."

His laugh had tension laced through it. "Hey, what's a husband for if he can't take care of the little things?"

Dana managed to turn her head to look at him. "You wanna have this baby?"

He could always count on her spirit to pull her through. "I'll have the next one."

He would have to, because she sure as hell wasn't going to. She wasn't all that sure she was going to survive this if it went on much longer. "I'll hold you to that," she gasped.

Sheila spared Rafe a glance. It wouldn't be long now, she thought. She could see the baby's head. "She will, you know. You're going to be sorry you made that rash offer in front of witnesses." Sheila peered at Dana. One or two more good pushes were all it was going to take. "I'm just sitting here with my hands out. Give me something to catch, Dana. Push."

Dana gritted her teeth. "Easy for you to say."

And then, as another contraction came, threatening to rip her in half, Dana summoned what was left of her dwindling supply of strength. Concentrating, straining, she pushed with every fiber of her being until there wasn't a breath left in her.

"Good girl, good girl," Sheila coached. "A head, I have a head," she announced excitedly. Her hands flew as she cleared the baby's mouth and nasal passages. "Now give me some shoulders, Dana."

Dana scrunched the sides of her gown in her hands, desperate to hang on to something. "I'll give you more than that if you don't stop sounding like a third-string auctioneer trying to up the ante." She'd never hurt like this before, and she felt too exhausted to try anymore. She'd been pushing for so long. "Can't you just pull it out?"

Sheila empathized. "Not yet."

Rafe could feel Dana flagging. He'd never been on this side of things before, and he struggled to contain his agitation. "C'mon, baby, you can do this. You came back and reclaimed your life through sheer grit. You made your father into a human being and me into a true believer. This should be a piece of cake for you."

The hell it was, she thought, too drained even to be irritated. "If it was a piece of cake I was trying to pass, I'd be done— *Ow.*" Her eyes flew open as a king-size contraction seized her, showing absolutely no mercy. Only stubborn determination kept her from screaming.

Sheila held her breath. "Good one?"

"There is no such thing as a good contraction." The words were individually strained through clenched teeth. Another one was coming on the heels of the last, not even giving her enough time to draw breath. Her hand darted out, clutching at Rafe wildly. He caught it in his. "Oh, Rafe, hold my hand, hold my hand."

"I am holding your hand." And it felt as if she was breaking the bones of his fingers. He saw the expression on Sheila's face, saw the movement in the overhead mirror. His baby was being born. "Oh, honey, here he comes."

"She," Sheila corrected, easing the rest of the tiny body out. She grinned as she cut the cord. "You have a she."

"We have a she," Rafe repeated in awestruck wonder. He had a daughter. Another daughter. There were tears in his eyes as he pressed a kiss to Dana's damp temple, his heart brimming with love. "I always liked being surrounded by females."

Dana offered up a silent prayer. It was over. She slumped against Rafe's waiting arms.

With quick, competent movements, the attending nurse cleaned the baby and wrapped her in a blanket. Sheila took the minutes-old infant and brought her to her parents.

"Dr. and Mrs. Saldana, may I present your daughter to you?" Very gently, Sheila placed the tiny bit of humanity into Dana's arms. This, she thought, was her very favorite part.

Dana pressed her lips together. She wasn't going to cry like some foolish twit. Tears were for sorrow, not for joy. She felt them forming just the same. Comfortable in this new world she found herself in, their daughter was already falling asleep.

Dana looked at Rafe. "Oh, God, Rafe, she's so tiny."

With all the wonder of a first-time father, he touched the tiny clasped hand resting on top of the blanket. It felt so smooth, so doll-like. "They do start out that way," he murmured.

He'd been in this position countless times, looking at tiny newborns, but it had never filled his heart the way it did now.

Sheila smiled. ''Well, you're all ready for the recovery room.''

Dana certainly felt ready for it. But there was a roomful of people waiting down the hall. She knew what they had to be feeling. She'd waited in a claustrophobia-inspiring room all night for Mollie to be born.

Dana looked at Sheila. ''Can we make one side trip?''

Sheila had expected nothing less from Dana. ''All right, but then I want you to rest.'' She grinned at her friend, affection in her eyes. ''It'll be the last time you get to until this little princess goes off to college.''

Dana shifted, looking at her husband. ''Rafe?''

''On my way.''

As soon as Rafe walked into the waiting area, all but one of the occupants rose. Mollie was the first to reach him. She stifled the urge to jump into his arms.

''Is it here yet?'' she asked eagerly. She peered behind her new daddy, hoping to see a bassinet with a baby in it. ''Is it here?''

He grinned at her. He was still getting used to the idea of having one daughter, and now he had two. It was a good number.

''You have a sister, Mollie. Want to see her?'' Mollie's head bobbed up and down as she took his hand and held it. He looked at the others. His parents and Gabe had insisted on being notified the moment Dana went into labor. ''You might as well come, too. She's in the hall.''

''You left my daughter in the hall?'' Paul Morrow demanded, moving forward as the others stepped to the side to allow him to pass.

Rafe had gotten accustomed to the man's crusty manner. According to Dana, her father had softened up considerably. He would hate to have known the man before his so-called transformation.

''She's en route to the recovery room,'' Rafe answered, ''but she wanted to see you all.'' A smile played over his lips as his family crowded around him. ''Can't see why.''

Mollie moved into the hall first, followed closely by her grandfather. That Paul Morrow had insisted on being here at all had been a surprise to both Dana and Rafe. Who said a leopard couldn't change at least a few of its spots?

Family, Dana thought as they gathered around her, was definitely God's greatest invention. Her life had never felt this full.

Mollie hovered beside Dana's gurney on tiptoe. Her attention was riveted to the baby. "She's so little," Mollie whispered.

"So were you," Dana told her. Mollie looked at her in disbelief. Dana smiled. "I'm going to need a lot of help with her. Think you're up to it?"

"Yes, Aunt Da—I mean Mommy." Mollie liked fitting her mouth around the word. It felt good being able to call someone mommy again. Just as good as calling Dr. Rafe daddy. She looked at the baby, wanting to touch her but afraid of disturbing her new sister. "What's her name?"

"We wanted to call her Megan." Dana looked at her father. "Megan Jane."

Paul Morrow nodded, his mouth a tight, neutral line. But there was emotion in his eyes. "It's a good name. She'll be special right from the start."

Standing beside her, Rafe took Dana's hand and kissed it, looking at his newborn daughter. "We already knew that."

Silhouette Stars

Born this Month

Jerry Hall, Tom Cruise, Tom Stoppard, Nancy Reagan, Ringo Starr, Barbara Cartland, Harrison Ford, Linda Ronstadt.

Star of the Month

Cancer

An excellent year ahead in which progress can be made in all areas of your life. There may be a period of change in the autumn but don't be fearful as the outcome will be better than you could hope and you will see the necessity for change. A lucky break in the second half of the year could have you splashing out.

SILH/HR/0007a

SIL H/HR/0007b

Leo

You could find yourself pushing too hard to achieve what you want especially in your personal life. So try a little tact and diplomacy and the results could be better than you dreamed.

Virgo

Travel and romance are both well aspected and if linked you could look forward to an extra special month. Late in the month a friend needs a helping hand but be sure of their motives before offering too much.

Libra

Energy levels are high and there is little you can't achieve. Holidays are well aspected especially those in groups. Career moves at the end of the month get you excited about the future.

Scorpio

Your ability to communicate constructively may help to bring about an improvement in your financial situation. This, in turn, will help you to build towards the future with renewed vigour.

Sagittarius

Romance is in the air and you will feel in demand both with partners and friends, making this a social, easy going month with very little to trouble you, so enjoy!

Capricorn

A social month in which you may have to make unexpected journeys. Work opportunities will bring an added financial boost and you will realise your talents are being fully appreciated.

SILH/HR/0007c

Aquarius

Your love life receives a boost and should become more meaningful than of late. As the month ends you may find your energy levels are getting low so take a break and pamper yourself back to full strength.

Pisces

You have a decisive quality to you this month giving you the courage to make the changes you have long desired to make. Be bold and you'll be amazed by what you can achieve.

Aries

The lack of financial resource has become an area of conflict in your personal life. You need to sit down together and make an effective budget plan. By working in harmony your relationship will improve dramatically.

Taurus

As your confidence returns you will feel more positive and able to tackle life with enthusiasm. A lucky break mid-month gives you cause for a celebration.

Gemini

Travel is never far from your thoughts especially the more adventurous kind and this month should see you planning another experience. A friend may want to join you but be sure they are as bold as you before you commit.

Sometimes bringing up baby can bring surprises —and showers of love! For the cutest and cuddliest heroes and heroines, choose the Special Edition™ book marked

TMB/RTL1